# Where D. H. Lawrence
# Was Wrong
# about Woman

# Where D. H. Lawrence Was Wrong about Woman

David Holbrook

Lewisburg
Bucknell University Press
London and Toronto: Associated University Presses

Associated University Presses
440 Forsgate Drive
Cranbury, NJ 08512

Associated University Presses
25 Sicilian Avenue
London WC1A 2QH, England

Associated University Presses
P.O. Box 39, Clarkson Pstl. Stn.
Mississauga, Ontario,
L5J 3X9 Canada

The paper used in this publication meets the requirements
of the American National Standard for Permanence of Paper
for Printed Library Materials Z39.48-1984.

**Library of Congress Cataloging-in-Publication Data**

Holbrook, David.
    Where D.H. Lawrence was wrong about woman/David Holbrook,
        p.    cm.
    Includes bibliographical references and index.
    ISBN 0-8387-5207-1 (alk. paper)
    1. Lawrence, D. H. (David Herbert), 1885-1930—Characters—Women.
2. Women in literature.    3. Sex in literature.    I. Title.
PR6023.A93Z6316   1992
823'.912—dc20
                                                                    90-56165
                                                                    CIP

PRINTED IN THE UNITED STATES OF AMERICA

For Margot

hoping I'm right

Woman becoming individual, self-responsible, taking her own initiative
—D. H. Lawrence, on the "germ" of *The Rainbow*

... first, the didactic import given by the author from his own moral consciousness; and then the profound symbolic import which proceeds from his unconscious or subconscious soul, as he works in a state of creation which is something like somnambulism or dreaming.
—D. H. Lawrence on the two meanings of art speech,
in *The Spirit of Place*

# Contents

# Lists of Abbreviations and Editions

| | | |
|---|---|---|
| WP | *The White Peacock*, 1911 | Everyman Edition |
| T | *The Trespasser*, 1912 | Heinemann Edition |
| SL | *Sons and Lovers*, 1913 | Heinemann Edition |
| R | *The Rainbow*, 1915 | Penguin Edition |
| WL | *Women in Love*, 1920 | Penguin Edition |
| LG | *The Lost Girl*, 1920 | Heinemann Edition |
| AR | *Aaron's Rod*, 1922 | Heinemann Edition |
| K | *Kangaroo*, 1923 | Heinemann Edition |
| PS | *The Plumed Serpent*, 1926 | Penguin Edition |
| FLC | *The First Lady Chatterley*, 1972 | Penguin Edition |
| JT | *John Thomas and Lady Jane*, 1972 | Penguin Edition |
| LC | *Lady Chatterley's Lover*, 1928 | Penguin Edition |
| VG | *The Virgin and the Gypsy*, 1930 | Penguin Edition |
| SS | Short Stories, 1934 *Tales* | Heinemann Edition |
| MN | *Mr Noon*, 1984 | Cambridge Edition |
| WRA | *The Woman Who Rode Away and Other Stories*, 1950 | Penguin Edition |
| CP | *The Complete Poems*, 1964 | Heinemann Edition |
| PU | *Psychoanalysis and the Unconsious* 1923 | Heinemann Edition |

# Acknowledgments

This book is the outcome of more years of reading, teaching, and arguing about Lawrence than I care to think about. I would like to express my gratitude to all those students who have enjoyed his work with me. I am most grateful to Geoffrey Strickland for detailed criticisms.

I am also grateful to Downing College and especially to the Leverhulme Trust for an Emeritus Research Fellowship, 1989–90, to make further applications of phenomenology to literary criticism, which enabled me to complete the final stages on this and other works.

# Where D. H. Lawrence
# Was Wrong
# about Woman

# Introduction

I hope the reader will accept that this book was written by one who feels a deep debt of gratitude to D. H. Lawrence as a creative writer. Like so many of my generation, I have found great satisfaction in the vividness and vitality of his novels and his portrayals of the truth of experience. There are great moments in his work: the quarrel in *Women in Love* between Birkin and Ursula in the lane when she throws down the ring; the scene in *The Rainbow* in which Tom Brangwen takes Anna the child into the cowshed to calm her; the grave drama of the short story *Odour of Chrysanthemums*. These moments are superb art, and we have read them and taught them for many decades, with a sense that here we have important illuminations of the contemporary consciousness. Lawrence, as F. R. Leavis correctly declared, often attends with profound authenticity to the truths of being, and so takes his place in a tradition to which Dickens, Blake, and Shakespeare belong. Lawrence offers a source of criteria by which we can judge the nature and failings of our civilization, and contemplate the meaning of life.

It is over these questions, as we shall see, that problems arise. I belong, of course, to a critical tradition that supposes that art, as well as providing entertainment, also nourishes the subjective life through enrichment of symbolism and fantasy. Art, as Lawrence himself believes, affects our sympathies and thus has a profound moral effect: "the essential function of art is moral." (*Selected Essays*, 1950, 268) But if this is so, then we must always be asking whether the novelist is giving us insights into life or offering something else: Is his portrayal of experience authentic or inauthentic? We have been persuaded that if a creative artist follows his "daemon," or, as Lawrence put it, "listens to the blood", he will utter truth. Indeed, some authors, like George Eliot, have spoken of being taken over by a "power" that guided their work and that took over their volition as creators—and Lawrence himself refers to this process when he talked of lying like St Lawrence on his griddle, and letting the fires of God blow through him.

But suppose that when the author follows the promptings of the "blood" or whatever mysterious power he believes impels his work, he tells lies? It is possible for authors to lie, as Lawrence again indicated himself when he said, "Never trust the artist, trust the tale." The novel may be, as Leavis emphasizes, a form of thought—a question he argued extensively over Lawrence, but what if that thought becomes the agent of strong impulses to distort the turth of experience because of unconscious psychic needs to do so?

Again, it is possible for this to happen, as Lawrence himself makes clear in his criticism, when discussing Hardy and Tolstoy. Leavis himself found *Lady Chatterley's Lover* a "hateful" book and declared that when he came to write it, Lawrence had forgotten what marriage meant. On the other hand, Leavis endorsed tales such as *The Captain's Doll* and *The Virgin and the Gypsy* in which there are equally perplexing implications about the relationships between man and woman.

The question that arises is—if we feel that a novelist is coming to wrong conclusions about human relationships, or if he seems to be falsifying sexuality, or has his thumb in the scales in his delineations, where shall we turn to estimate how far he has wandered from the truth? Of course, here there are no final answers, and no ultimate source of truth. But we may now, I believe, at least turn to those who have made serious and dispassionate studies of human nature and the emotional and psychic life. We have the reports of those who have listened to individuals in the grave setting of the psychotherapist's consulting room, where there have developed disciplines by which doctor and patient try to find the truth. I have elsewhere explored the kind of phenomenological disciplines that have emerged from psychoanalysis and other forms of therapeutic work under the general heading of philosophical anthropology. There we may find new modes in the understanding of the meanings of consciousness.

As I went on teaching Lawrence and delighting in his work, there seemed to me to be serious divergences between what Lawrence found to be the truth about human experience, my own experience of marriage and family relationships, and what the therapists were saying about man and woman, and their intersubjectivity. At times Lawrence wrote in such a way as to illuminate, in a "whole" way, the same truths as, for example, over Paul Morel's sad experience of his parent's life in *Sons and Lovers*. But there were other works, some of them enthusiastically endorsed by Leavis (as a major Lawrence critic) that seemed to me utterly wrong—wrong both in the way they rendered experience, and also in their "upshot." The word "upshot" seems to me a useful word, and it comes from Leavis in his discussions with Santayana, over questions of literature and philosophy. (See *Scrutiny*, IV, 365–68, 374–75; XII, 249–60.) We must not make the mistake of taking something like Macbeth's speech "Tomorrow and tomorrow and tomorrow" as indicating the philosophy of life of the author of the play, but it is still legitimate to ask what are the implications, for *being*, of the "upshot" of a work like a novel. This is surely especially necessary when (again as Leavis indicates with Lawrence) a writer with tremendous power of expression at his disposal seeks to tell us how to be men and women, and writes with a clear didactic impulse to offer us a new freedom in a vision of what love and sexuality could be (as Lawrence does).

What I found, I believe, was that not only did Lawrence fall into profound falsities in his later works, such as *The Plumed Serpent*, but the falsifications were there from the beginning—arising from the tendency to deal in a certain way with woman. Lawrence's problem with woman will be at the center of my explorations in this work. What is remarkable is the way Lawrence's power as an artist carries us past some of his most singular statements. As we shall see, this extends even to the connections he makes between the emotional life, industry, and society. At the heart of his dealings with woman (and, in consequence, with sexuality) lies a myth—a highly personal mythology belonging to his deepest inner life; we shall find this mythology surfacing in most remarkable ways. It is a certain imago of the mother, and in this we find an archetypal pattern of a kind I have explored in other authors. The basis of this pattern is the fear of woman, developed from certain kinds of experiences of the mother: she may have suddenly weaned the author; she may have died; she may have confused the artist with a dead sibling; she may have sought in the son satisfactions she did not get from the father; she may have dealt with her baby in ways which "impinged" upon him in a traumatic way. But, essentially, for some reason, she is felt to be a being who has, as well as the power to create, the power to destroy, and is, therefore, very dangerous. These tendencies are but an aspect of the universal fear of woman that affects us all, and leaves us (both men and women) possessed to some degree with the Phantom Woman of the Unconscious. In the mythology of many authors, this spectre must be dealt with, and we shall find in Lawrence's novels various ways in which he deals with this dangerous creature.

One agent of the dealings is the fantasy figure of the author himself and at the heart of my analysis of Lawrence is an image of a Phallic Self, and I believe this arises from being idolized by his mother. What better instrument of control over the Phantom Woman could there be than the Self as Phallus that she worshipped? I will expand on this syndrome below (p. 36). This may seem a strange diagnosis of Lawrence's impulses towards falsification, but the reader must judge how successful I am in looking into his meanings around this drama. Take, for instance, Ursula's thoughts at the end of *The Rainbow:*

> it was not for her to create, but to recognise a man created by God. The man should come from the Infinite and she should hail him . . . . The man would come from Eternity to which she herself belonged. (R, 494)

When we know the Lawrence mythology, we recognize this note and the particular kind of ecstatic elation that goes with it (another example is the reflections of Birkin after sexual intercourse with Ursula). The Woman has a special duty to submit to this "man from Eternity" when he strides into the action.

It is this element in Lawrence that generates the "demented fantasies" to which some critics like Kate Millet have objected in the later works. What is extraordinary has been the way in which so much public endorsement has been given to certain manifestations of the impulse to control woman in Lawrence's works and their "upshot." *Lady Chatterley's Lover* is a main case in point. At the time of the trial of that book some extraordinary things were said by the clergy and academics endorsing the "religious" nature of Lawrence's attitudes to sex in the book. Yet the book is extraordinarily vengeful in some of its manifestations (as in the treatment of Clifford), while Mellors's behavior toward Connie is often domineering and exploitative. The falsity in that novel, as we shall see, lies not so much in the portrayal of how lovers behave, but in Lawrence's endorsement, with his thumb in the scales, of certain practices of Mellors's, that is, the way as lover he treats her roughly, the way in which Connie experiences orgasm because of being so treated, and her enthusiasm about sodomy, from which she concludes "What liars the poets were" and "All one wanted was this rather awful sensuality." Frank Kermode even went so far as to call the sodomy "holy communion," with the phallus as the representation of the Holy Ghost. As we shall see, one of the most disturbing aspects of Lawrence's writing is the way in which some of the darkest manifestations of his mythology are couched in powerful religiose terms—as, indeed, for him they needed to be for him since they belong a matters of life-and-death. From the point of view of psychotherapeutic theory, however, they must surely be seen as false solutions.

Indeed, as we shall see, the worst aspect of Lawrence's philosophy of existence, as communicated in the "upshot" of his works, is a recommendation of "rather awful sensuality" as the solution to many problems of love and meaning, and the relationship between man and woman. It was this theme that I detected first in *Lady Chatterley's Lover*, in my first somewhat confused attempt to write a critique of that novel in *The Quest for Love*. The mere attempt to indulge and intensify sensuality is no solution to the problems of love relationships. Indeed, one might turn the problem around entirely and say that until the problems of intersubjectivity are solved, of mutual respect, of giving one another "freedom" without fear (in, say, the way explored by Chaucer in the *Franklin's Tale*), the deepest satisfactions to be found in sexuality cannot be found. Perhaps this is what Leavis meant by saying that Lawrence had forgotten what marriage meant when he came to write his most explicit novel. Certainly, the more one thinks about it, the less one can really accept that Mellors could be a satisfactory partner for Connie on any level except that of being "my lady's fucker": that Lawrence offers him as a possible partner is itself a serious falsification, and has unfortunate implications about his attitude to human beings. Here we have to examine the influence upon him of Frieda, as a representative of the Munich Schwabing movement, and a conveyor of the disturbed psychopathology of Otto Gross. This aspect of Lawrence's milieu seems to have been much neglected, but it helps a great deal to illuminate the way in which he came increasingly to adopt what I call false solutions. As I shall try to show, there is a sense in which the influence of Gross, through Frieda, "hooked in" to Lawrence's psycho-pathology, and the clue to this is to be found in the recently published novel

*Mr Noon*. In this, I believe, we can see how Lawrence ceased to cultivate his "daemon" as a writer in the tradition of (say) George Eliot and the major English writers (*Sons and Lovers*, for example, seems clearly influenced by *The Mill on the Floss*, as is *The Rainbow*) and tended toward what may be called "continental" modes, which, although in one sense they represented an enlargement of Lawrence's vision, also enabled him to write his passionate falsities such as the history of Kate Leslie in *The Plumed Serpent*, and, indeed, the indulgent fantasies about Connie Chatterley.

The most disturbing aspect of this change of direction, and as I see it, the essential forefeiture of his authenticity of "daemon," is that Lawrence seems to head towards death rather than life—to become increasingly nihilistic, increasingly determined to wish the rest of humanity extinguished (so long as he is all right with his woman), and increasingly inclined to reject society, democracy, and the future. The misogyny becomes misanthropy. It has become common-place, in new editions of his work, to say that he was given to "living," and one can see what this means when so much of his work is full of vitality. It is said that he sought to keep the "spark of life" alive during the terrible years 1910–30. But while his vitality is often a matter of appreciation of the landscape, the wild world, the wild flowers of the Italian mountains, as for Alvina, the Lost Girl, there is an increasing tendency to see mankind as dead, and to reject the human world, in flight from it—as in *St Mawr*, in *The Lost Girl* and *Aaron's Rod*. He sees the industrial world as only fit for rejection because it means "the base forcing of all human energy into a competition of mere acquisition" (Moore 1955, 26). The *Scrutiny* movement virtually made this into a political program, and took it as axiomatic that Lawrence was right in finding the failure of the sexual life in modern man tied to the influence of industry and the "will" that served it. It is true that our kind of civilization has elements that are inimical to "being," and that something is seriously wrong with our concepts of ourselves and of what it is to be human; but is Lawrence's diagnosis the correct one?

Can "industry" be such a threat to civilized being as it appears, for example, in the Chatterley novels in which Mellors sees the glowing lights of the pit looking as though they threaten to throttle the life out of him, while he can feel no way to become reconciled with that world of ordinary people around him? This element in Lawrence is surely psychopathological and this dread of the world "out there" found its way through to Leavis and the *Scrutiny* movement, tending to push Leavis into ultimate despair.

If Lawrence is so much on the side of "life," where in his novels does one find a representation of fulfilled sexual potentialities? Where does one find the embodiment of a relationship in marriage, or indeed, in passion, where there is richness and mutual respect—in a few poems, but not elsewhere. In so many relationships in his work there arise conflicts, as if from nowhere, which bring a bleakness and a threat of death that devastates his lovers' lives (as, for instance, between Will and Anna). At times his world feels as if it were about to be drowned in hate, and often he endorses counteractions that are themselves based on hate, as when he commends certain forms of sexual adventurism, adultery (in *Glad Ghosts*), even murder (in *The Fox*), the predatory exploitation of an inexperienced girl (*The Virgin and the Gypsy*), the control of a woman by leaders capable of murder (*The Plumed Serpent*) involving the denial of woman's capacity for orgasm, and everywhere forms of enthusiastic perversion—the meaning of which, as psychotherapy tells us, lies in the hostility inherent in them.

The hate and nihilism in Lawrence have gone largely unnoticed, not least by Leavis, who erected him into an idealized figure, especially to reject T. S. Eliot as, by contrast, ultimately uncreative. Eliot was a divided man alleges Leavis: in Lawrence there were no divisions. For Leavis even to question the marvelous genius of Lawrence was unforgivable, but his very incantations on the subject of Lawrence seem to belong to a certain blindness, a certain kind of involvement in what must be called Lawrence's propaganda. If one reads large amounts of Lawrence, as I have had to do for this book, one becomes exhausted by the deluges of propaganda directed against the human race and society, but one also comes to see that, in many works, the drama itself, with its "upshot," is propaganda too—very seductive because it tends to enlist us in the fear of woman and the impulse to control her. To unravel this requires a painstaking and cool examination of the meaning of Lawrence's art, and it is this phenomenological study I have attempted here.

*       *       *

Those of us who have been persuaded in the past to accept Lawrence and his work as touchstones for our own lives and our studies of literature and society have come to find a growing sense of something being seriously and increasingly wrong as Lawrence's *oeuvre* developed. (A colleague writes, "I used to use Lawrence as a sex manual myself, which explains my original puzzlement.") One characteristic example is the question of sexual jealousy, which will become a focal question below. Do people suffer when their partners display physical unfaithfulness? Some who have tried to offer us a new morality seek to persuade us that there need be no such problem. In *Mr Noon*, Gilbert, who is an autobiographical character, tells Johanna, who derives as a character from Frieda, that it "doesn't matter" that she has been unfaithful to him. Yet, in other works, such as *Anna Karenina* or *Mansfield Park* unfaithfulness causes deep pain and even destroys lives. Did Lawrence the propagandist take over from Lawrence the novelist in *Mr Noon*? But there are falsities of that kind in many other works, which did not, like *Mr Noon*, get put aside because of uncertainty. How, then, did so many of us come to accept him as a prophet of the life of the soul and the sexual emotions, and especially an illuminator of the nature of woman?

It seems to me that F. R. Leavis seriously misinterprets Lawrence, and champions his views when they are insupportable. Somewhere, for instance, discussing *The Captain's Doll*, Leavis declares that Lawrence is "profoundly and wonderfully right about the long-standing relationship of man and wife." Discussing *Women in Love*, Leavis says, "Only love, real love, can justify marriage, but, there being no such thing as "perfect love," the essential marriage-understanding is that the relationship between the two individual beings shall be permanent, transcending change" (Leavis 1976, 88). But this, as we shall see, quite distorts the discussion, and fails to embrace Lawrence's doubts about love, or to include the sense of Birkin's special status as a "god." It is all very well to insist, as Leavis did, that the novel represents a form of "thought," but I defy anyone to produce any kind of conclusions about the "upshot" of *Women in Love*, or indeed any of Lawrence's work, which could provide a basis for conducting one's life, or even coherent ideas about the nature of love. Leavis says, "I have not been trying to define the thought that is *behind* the novel-long tale (he is talking about *The Captain's Doll* (1976, 121)). . . . The tale itself *is* the thought." And in his exegesis Leavis shows that in his art we must respect the "precision and completeness of the thinking." Leavis reiterates that "art is the truth about the real world" and so we are entitled to examine the truths presented, despite Leavis's enthusiasm about Lawrence, insistently using words like "genius . . . genius . . . marvellous . . . marvellous, marvellous" like an incantation—leading to his final conclusion on Lawrence that "there is in him no basic contradiction."

As Roger Poole (1979, 60) has noted, reading *D. H. Lawrence, Novelist* is rather like being submitted to a prolonged indoctrination. "It is not so much that life is *shown* to be present in Lawrence, as that it is *insisted upon as being there*" As usual, in his examination of the text, Leavis brings out a good deal. I examine the story in detail below and show that many questions arise. These raise the question Lawrence himself discussed over the novelist and his novel in his essay "Morality and the Novel": "If the novelist puts his thumb in the pan . . . then he commits an immoral act." Further, he added

> The novel is not, as a rule, immoral, because the novelist has any dominant *idea* or *purpose*. The immorality lies in the novelist's helpless, unconscious predeliction. (D. H. Lawrence, 1936, 525)

We shall often find Lawrence, the novels coming as he said "unwatched from one's pen" in the grip of distortions that were unconsciously important to him, and criticism has too much ignored these. For example, in discussing *The Rainbow*, Leavis says nothing about Lawrence's preoccupation with "sinister tropical beauty" in sex, or his enthusiasm for "unnatural acts of sensual voluptuousness" (R, 240). Of Lawrence's greatest novel, *Women in Love*, Leavis wrote: "What is symbolised is that normative relation between the man and the woman which Birkin ultimately achieves with Ursula, and in which alone Gerald can escape disaster" (Leavis 1955, 194). Is any of this true?

As a teacher, I have been occasionally been brought up sharp by a comment like this in a student's essay:

> This tentative consciousness is developed suddenly by an encounter with a prostitute. . . .
> This is followed by Tom's meeting with the girl . . . a meeting which consolidates the change worked in him by the prostitute and which brings thousands of new possibilities before him. (A student teacher writing about *The Rainbow*)

If we believe that English is an important humanities subject, and that within that subject the "great novelists" are sources of valuable insight, what shall we say about the effect on students, when they gather from a novel, with our endorsement, that an "excursion," as Lawrence calls it, can enrich a committed relationship? The problem becomes more acute, over Will Brangwen's episode with the girl he takes to the cinema, discussed below. The problem is not that the episode is realistic: married men often become aware of the sexual possibilities of other women, and curious about them. What matters is the attitude of the author to what happens and over Will's yearning to be unfaithful I believe Lawrence again has his thumb in the scales. The episode is full of hostility, but rather than depict this, Lawrence approves of the excursion and shows it to bring enrichment to Will's marriage. Not only that—he makes it a reason for Will and Anna to "break through" into a new kind of perverted sensuality, as if this were the solution to their problems.

There is a good deal of this in Lawrence, as we shall see, and it seems to me to place a large question mark against the kind of literary teaching and criticism that regard a novel by Lawrence almost as a tract on marriage, and the relationship of the sexual life to problems of civilization. In *Thought, Words and Creativity (1976)*, Leavis tries to show that Lawrence is a religious writer who was trying to define in his art a relationship between the individual and the world—meaning the world in the largest possible sense: the universe and the world of created life. Thus, Lawrence is concerned for the survival of civilized humanity, and at the heart of this is his concern "with the vitally essential but terribly difficult relationship between the fully individual man and the fully individual woman". (1976, 63) Moreover, the need is for spontaneity. Leavis uses the word "manhood"; Leavis endorses Lawrence's notion of "manhood," which, he urges, entails the completeness that manifests itself in responsibility—the responsibility that "fits" one to "act spontaneously in one's impulses." Much of this we may concede. As Leavis shows, Lawrence believed that woman was one "bank" of his life, his life being a river flowing between woman and the world, in this quest for ultimate meaning. But it is not true to say that he solved these problems and some of his notions are very questionable. In *The Plumed Serpent*, the concept of "manhood" becomes a very strange one indeed.

The Leavis interpretation is that against the dehumanization of our industrial society Lawrence opposed the quest for fulfillment of potentialities of being ("So that which is perfectly ourselves can take place in us" as Birkin urges in *Women in Love*, 163). He stood for "spirit" against a mechanization and the will that serves it, most tellingly "placed" in Gerald Crich. He stands for the "organic" community and unique being as against the nullifying "social idea" (embodied in Skrebensky).

In man-women relationships Lawrence sought to define union in separateness: perfect balance between man and woman, recognizing each other's freedom. Love must be the core to one's life, and relationships with women are how our primary source of meaning, since God is dead. In a study that invokes ideas from existentialism and psychotherapy, *The Art of the Self in D. H. Lawrence*, a woman critic, Dr. Beede Howe, quotes the revealing exchange between Birkin and Gerald:

> "The old ideals are as dead as nails—nothing there. It seems to me there remains only this perfect union with a woman—a sort of ultimate marriage—and there isn't anything else."
> "And you mean if there isn't the woman there's nothing?" said Gerald.
> "Pretty well that, seeing there's no God"
> "Then we're hard to put to it," said Gerald. (WL, 64)

Obviously the question arises as to whether woman can be made into a substitute for God in this way. What happens if this burden is placed upon her by someone in whom there is a deep fear of the Phantom Woman of the unconscious?

From the exchange between Gerald and Birkin, Marguerite Beede Howe argues that the crucial issue is *certainty about one's being*. She tries to trace Lawrence's quest for unity of the self, for a sense of meaningful existence. She shows that in one sense he failed because he could not feel convinced that he had saved himself. But she also argues that Lawrence was mistaken to believe that he had failed:

> To judge from the bleakness of *Lady Chatterley's Lover* Lawrence's final insight is that the philosophy of existence can provide no salvation in our time. In this respect he was mistaken (Beede Howe 1977, 139)

Beede Howe makes an exploration of the philosophical issues pursued in Lawrence's work, and brings to our notice the whole question of his influence on our lives, in the context of twentieth-century problems of existence.

Lawrence's desire, as she shows, was to persuade man to find his unconsciousness and unite it with the rest of his personality. This was to be achieved through sexuality, but one of the central problems in Lawrence is that sex seemed at times "existentially repugnant to him." Lawrence wanted us to find the dark centers of sexual potentiality, but then he also had a deep schizoid fear of "merging" with another person. Beede Howe quotes Lawrence on himself as Birkin in *Women in Love:* "the merging, the clutching, the mingling of love was madly abhorent to him."

Beede Howe emphasizes rightly that Lawrence can now be seen to belong to a whole modern movement toward unity of being: "modern philosophy (particularly phenomenology) points that our sense of reality, including the reality of ourselves, arises from conscious reflection on what we know intuitively.... To be whole, according to Lawrence, we need to be in touch with our unconscious, and to be in touch with our unconscious, we need— quite literally—sex."

Following this kind of emphasis in Lawrence, Beede Howe sees his path as running parallel to much in contemporary psychology and philosophy: "His main concern—the sense of wholeness and meaningfulness—is now our main concern." She adds,

> Lawrence's one great lesson is the necessity of wholeness, of integrating rational and non-rational experience. In the end he seems to have despaired of it, at least for the mass of mankind ... time has shown Lawrence's pessimism to be premature.... Much of recent psychology is an attempt to integrate, as Lawrence did, rationality and the many areas of unconscious awareness into a meaningful self. (Beede Howe 1977, 180)

These are the concluding sentences of Beede Howe's book, and they indicate how she recognizes Lawrence's quest as an ontological one—a search for the meaning of existence, and the integration of the self and the realization of the potentialities of being. (See also, David Kleinbard, "D. H. Lawrence and Ontological Insecurity," *PMLA* 89 (1974), 155.)

As an artist in his greatest work, Lawrence is truly phenomenological, that is, he gives us the whole experience, depicted in all its ranges of consciousness, in the desire to integrate unconsciousness and rational, explicit awareness, to give "being" a wholeness. He depicts will and intellectualization (and "wordiness" as in Clifford) as enemies to being.

But there is also a damaging intrusion into his art of a continual flow of what I have called propaganda He actually uses the vivid power of his art to *rationalize.* By "rationalize" here I do not mean putting into rational terms so much as making personal distortions seem rational and true when they are in fact full of falsification—the term as used here comes from psychoanalysis. His rationalizations are *defenses*, against recognition of problems within himself, and of the truth, so, even as he explores the truth, he falsifies attitudes to it. Moreover, the decline of his art (which Beede Howe clearly delineates in her chapters on *Kangaroo* and *The Plumed Serpent*) goes with a failure of Lawrence's confidence in the female element, in creativity itself. Something else takes over—itself a kind of will, so that an energy that sought to redeem being ends up in a strange kind of misanthropy, full of paranoia and distrust of humanity:

"Don't trust *anybody* with your real emotions, if you've got any: that is the slogan of today. Trust them with your money, even, but *never* with your feeling. They are bound to trample on them." D. H. Lawrence, *Sex, Literature and Censorship*, 1959, 90.

Beede Howe says "Mellors is heroic, in accepting vulnerability, and tenderness. And he is tragic: he knows he will soon be lost." But Mellors is not positive enough to be tragic. He is too hopeless about the "insentient iron world," and he is not sufficiently "man alive" at all levels, intelligence, "blood," and being, to stand for any meanings that can be upheld, in the *Dasein* sense, against death and nothingness. His main positive is in "the blood": his sexual performances, which in any case have a fairy-tale quality, and in the realism of the future he offers, such as it is. In the end he is a kind of hippie, as Margaret Beede Howe sees: his half-hope, drop-out attitude to life marks "a rather hopeless conclusion to (the) life-long struggle for the self's autonomy."

We can now look back at Lawrence and ask, from the point of view of an interest in philosophical anthropology to help our literary criticism, what went wrong? Beede Howe's book is a brave and startling contribution to that question. Her limitation is that she builds her case too much on the more unsatisfactory Lawrence passages—and not on the best enactments of human experience as much as on his more mystical flows:

> the body of the mysterious night, the night masculine and feminine, never to be seen with the eye, or known with the mind, only as a palpable revelation of living otherness, &c.

This kind of incantatory prose suggests sometimes that Lawrence was flinging himself at mysteries, and failing to grasp them by falling into believing and even worshipping his own propaganda.

By "propaganda" here I mean two things. One is that the writing is often an attempt to vindicate his own defenses and false solutions. The other is that he has picked up the influence of sexual revolutionism, and is seeking to enlist us in transforming civilization on principles learned from the Schwabing movement of Otto Gross.

Besides the record of experience as Lawrence gives it, there is the question of beliefs and what I call "models." Here, the novel published recently is a crux, *Mr Noon*. This work will be examined below, but it should surely have prompted a much deeper crisis in Lawrence studies than it did for it reveals a completely altered perspective in Lawrence's views of personal relationships, through the influence of Frieda, and through her, of the German Munich-Schwabing Bohemian world, to whose view of man, woman, and sexuality Lawrence was attracted, despite himself.

What *Mr Noon* reveals is how the world, which opened up to Lawrence when he encountered Frieda, offered him what seemed to be a means of escape from his old ghosts through the new dimensions of amoralism in sexual behavior that he found in German sexual revolutionism. It would seem that Frieda herself had an inclination to be sexually generous in an extraordinary way. In *Mr Noon* Gilbert has only been with Johanna—who "is" Frieda—for a few minutes when she asks him to come to her room. Johanna is first observed in the novel being carried away by her train far beyond her proper station because a Japanese stranger is feeling her knee in the restaurant car. There seems little doubt that Johanna is a portrait of Frieda and that her sexual generosity verged on nymphomania.

This behavior has behind it the whole philosophy of a German movement, from Schwabing, the Greenwich Village of the Munich of the time. Lawrence actually took on with Frieda a sometime mistress of one of Europe's most outrageous sexual revolutionaries, Otto Gross, and we must dwell for a space on this connection. Gross appears in *Mr Noon* as "Eberhard," and he has been a past lover of "Johanna." Frieda was always in contact with Otto Gross. Gross (1877–1919) was a one-time disciple of Freud who became a proponent of sexual libertarianism and drugs, conducted orgies, and was militantly promiscuous, with two mistresses at once for most of the time. He had affairs with both Frieda and her sister, to whom he gave baby, and he seemed responsible for the deaths of at least two women.

We may pick up the atmosphere of Gross's world, for instance, from the moment enshrined in a postcard referred to by Martin Green in his book on *The von Richthofen Sisters* (1974):

> It has a picture of the Marienplatz on one side, and on the other the name and address of Else Jaffe in Heidelberg, to whom it was sent, bearing salutations and brief messages from Edgar Jaffe, Otto Gross, Frieda Gross, Erich Mühsam, Regina Ullmann, and Frieda Weekley, all of whom were sitting round a table to write it. Regina Ullmann . . . was being analyzed by Otto Gross and was much under his influence: in 1908 she bore him a child. Frieda Weekley for a time thought she was pregnant by Gross, and Else Jaffe's third child, born in 1907, was Gross's son. Frieda Gross was soon to bear a child to Ernst Frick, her husband's disciple. . . . Thus Gross had created round that table a cell, a cell of the new life. . . . (Green, 90)

Such sex revolutionaries leave a trail of misery behind. Besides the women Otto Gross left behind him dead, there were how many miserable children brought up in confusion? How many lives ruined by drug addiction?[1]

Frieda's letters to Gross have nearly all disappeared, but there are one or two, as Martin Green reports.[2] She avows her love for "you—and—your—teaching," but sometimes reproaches Gross for not living up to it, with not being spontaneous enough, and with idealizing her. His mind, as he acknowledged, was remarkably abstract. Of his relationship with Frieda's sister Else and Frieda's correspondence about it, Green says that "it was a very pedagogical and salvationist enterprise, their eroticism. They were going to *save* Else" (62). This salvationism evidently rubbed off on Lawrence. It seems clear, says Green, that Frieda was creating a little Munich-Schwabing of sexual liberation around her in Nottingham. There are intimations of that, Green suggests, in Ursula Brangwen. ("It is neatly symbolic that the patron saint of the Schwabing church was Saint Ursula.)"

At the time Lawrence ran away with Frieda, this man she admired was teaching and practicing anarchism, and was breaking the law in dangerous ways, suffering the retribution of society. He was arrested and confined as insane soon after Lawrence reached Cerici: Karl Jung defended him. Frieda told Lawrence that he was "another Otto" and another Ernest Frick: she wrote this to Frieda Gross. When Frieda and Lawrence arrived in Germany in 1912, Frick was under arrest in Switzerland on charges of anarchist conspiracy. He was discharged and returned home, only to be rearrested because other prisoners testified to his having carried a bomb. Frieda was mixed up with these individuals. She wrote to warn Gross, who was being persecuted by police and doctors, not to cross the Swiss border, and lawsuits were brought against Frieda and Frick by Hanns Gross—all of which, no doubt, she related to Lawrence.

As Martin Green writes, "One of the main postulates of Gross's ethic, of Schwabing's as a whole, was the saving power of sexual freedom. Possessiveness and jealousy, he believed, could be overcome by the moral effort of sexual self-liberation" (91). While Lawrence believed that "this process of death has got to be lived through," and wanted to discard old bad habits of feeling, he was not at ease with decadence, and in his picture of Loerke gives his judgment on it. Yet as *Mr Noon* shows, he was immensely attracted by the new "continental" perspective of sexuality that came to him from Frieda, as we shall see when we get to that novel. In examining that novel, too, we shall see what conflict arose, between the new view and the Anglo-Saxon tradition to which Lawrence belonged as a writer who cherished discipline and productivity, and as a novelist who sought meaning in commitment and integrity, not least between lovers.

It was Gross, of course, who believed that primitive man had made all the great discoveries, and that our civilization was corrupt at the roots. Lawrence's gipsies, grooms and Cipriano-Ramòn figures are heirs to this primitivism. Just as Lawrence tried to vindicate "naked desire" and "touch" as the focus of our needs, Gross believed that pleasure was the only source of value. As Green says, he believed that "only by re-entering into the Paradise Lost of polymorphous perversity can man renew himself" (Green, 1974, 44). When Connie Chatterley makes her way through the spring flowers to be sodomized by Mellors, she is reentering the Paradise or Garden of Eden of polymorphous perversity. Lawrence is trying, as Gross did with his patients, to help her and his readers towards a sexual immoralism. It had been Frieda Richthofen who had "removed the shadow of Freud from his path" in this aim and inspired Lawrence to write the sagas of sexual immoralism. There was no intention of the "democratisation of sexual joy" (as the *New Statesman* called it at the time of the *Lady Chatterley* trial). Gross hated the democratic principle. His was clearly, too, a *sauve qui peut* principle, based on Max Stirner's view that society could benefit best by recognizing itself as a union of egoists.[3] (There was even a group of followers of Stirner, egoistical nihilists, in Germany who deliberately based their lives on crime.)

*Mr Noon* makes it clear how much Lawrence encountered these ideas when he entered into his relationship with Frieda. Of course, outwardly he no doubt found much in the Schwabing atmosphere uncogenial, and he would not have gone so far as to accept Gross's view that "chastity, fidelity, self-sacrifice and self-denial were all moralistic corruptions of moral feeling" (Green 1974, 91). But there are surely echoes of what he learned from the Gross world in Connie Chatterley's reflections on how Mellors was a man who "dared to do it" (that is, perform sodomy), as well as in the various recommendations of sexual adventurism in the moments when women admire men who murder, as in *The Plumed Serpent*, Kangaroo, and *The Fox*, or when women respond to abrupt or contemptuous or dominating sex as never before to normal sex?

Lawrence, after all, was devoted to Frieda who often behaved, as we learn from *Mr Noon*, in ways that defied normal morality, and often seemed inspired by Gross's kind of immoralism. For instance, shortly after Lawrence died, her own daughter became, like Connie Chatterley, physically feverish and enfeebled. Frieda devised a sexual remedy, and sent a young Italian stone mason to make love to Barbara as she lay in bed. As Green says, this is both like and unlike Lawrence's own faith in sex:

> Sending such a man to such a girl's bed is just what Lawrence had done imaginatively, in *The Virgin and the Gipsy*, which was written just before he died and was after all, about Barbara . . . . (Green 1974, 213)

Else was shocked, and Lawrence would have objected, on principle. But the incident is enough to confirm Frieda's *unscrupulousness*, and the degree to which she was a follower of Otto Gross's fanatical sex theory. *Mr Noon*, again, reveals how unscrupulous she was. Lawrence obviously invokes Gross's revolutionism in his stories of protagonists exerting their sexuality against the deadness of society. It should perhaps be noted that Gross was also, from early adulthood, a morphine addict, who, at times, seemed likely to destroy himself. In his influence there was an element of the death-circuit:

> He had a profound influence on people, introduced them to narcotics, broke down their sexual and social inhibitions, freed them from their scruples of conscience and even enabled them to kill themselves. (Green 1974, 63)

In this, too, we may find a clue to some of Lawrence's more negative impulses. As well as Gross's influence on Frieda, we must also be aware of her own rebellion against "spiritual" and "intellectual" life values. Indeed, what

Martin Green calls her "cynicism about life-values" is a cynicism that we find in Lawrence delineated in Winifred Inger, but he often expresses it himself in his misanthropic outbursts.

Lawrence put up a great deal of (puritan) resistance to the influence of Schwabing. As Green points out, Frieda after all married a man who believed in marriage and fidelity, but, whatever Leavis may have said about Lawrence being "normal, central and sane," there was much in his own nature that responded to the unconscious dynamics in Gross's sexual theories that reached him through Frieda, and his own sexual program for the world displays some of the same psychopathological elements.[4]

From his seduction into Frieda's amoralism, I believe Lawrence came to turn against his own true daemon, and the best traditions of the English novel by allowing himself to be, to some extent, "unEnglished." The great tradition of the English novel may be said to be the quest for autheticity in the existentialist sense. For us to become what in ourselves we yearn to become requires that we seek an authentic self. (See the present author's *The Novel and Authenticity*, 1987.)

Authenticity belongs to the realm of meaning, and it is important to note that in reaching this position psychoanalysis has come to reject the Freudian model of human nature, which saw man as primarily concerned with his "instincts" of sex and aggression: the assumption that we are at the mercy of our "wants." Lawrence, under Gross's influence, tended to accept that "wants" model ("I want that pound of peaches, I want that woman") in which our primary needs were to be a "good animal" (see the letter quoted below, p. 72). With such a model, the problem of meaning cannot be solved. It seems clear from the novel *Mr Noon*, and the way he put it aside how much he inwardly suffered. But in trying to solve the problem, I believe, he turned away from his own inclination towards true solutions and into false solutions. He thus betrayed his own creative flame.

I shall try to avoid becoming involved in unravelling Leavis's obsessions with Lawrence, but perhaps one passage where Leavis becomes seriously confused may be examined—the essay on *Anna Karenina*. Leavis is doubtful about Lawrence's endorsement of Anna's passionate entanglement with Vronsky: "no one in the world is anything but delighted when Vronsky gets Anna Karenina." Leavis's reaction is "Oh, come!" (F. R. Leavis, 1967, 20) His response should have been stronger than that. Vronsky's impulses have behind them a good deal of egoism and a delight in conquest, while there is something willful in Anna. And what of the motto of the book, "Vengeance is mine: I will repay"? Leavis thinks that the tragedy has to do with the impossibility of the lovers finding a place in society at any level, but what of the essential inauthenticity of the liaison? Lawrence's attitude, Leavis shows, is quite coarse; "Why, when you look at it, all the tragedy comes from Vronsky's and Anna's fear of society.... They couldn't live in the pride of their sincere passion, and spit in Mother Grundy's eye. And that, that cowardice, was the real 'sin.' The novel makes it obvious, and knocks all old Leo's teeth out." (Lawrence quoted by Leavis, 1967, 20–21)

It is astonishing, declares Leavis that "so marvellously perceptive a critic" could simplify in that way, but that is just how Lawrence does simplify in his own stories from the need to vindicate his own sexual revolutionism. Leavis is aware of the influence of Frieda, and notes that there are elements in the Lawrence-Frieda relationship that make it parallel to the Vronsky-Anna relationship. Then he makes a remarkable confusion: "Anna was not an amoral German aristocrat." (Leavis, 1567, 22) Frieda, says Leavis, "attained a floating indolence of well-being as, placidly undomesticated, she accompanied Lawrence about the world (we always see *him* doing the chores." (Leavis, 1967, 22)[5]

The weakness of Lawrence's work, as an artist, over women, is not that he came to be married to an "amoral German aristocrat," or that she made him do the chores. It is that, in his writing he came to be corrupted, in part by Frieda's sexual adventurism, but more seriously by the egoistic theory of sexuality adopted from the revolutionarism of her sometime lover. It is very revealing that this echoed something in Lawrence, in his defiance of the rules of society, and his opposition to this "repression" on philosophical grounds that were based on a radical misconception as to the primary needs of men and women. Lawrence's approval of the Vronsky-Anna relationship, against "Mrs. Grundy," belongs to the aggressive gesture towards "polymorphous perversity" that made him the author of so many works that celebrate it, and to see this illuminates much in his attempt to assault the public, use the vernacular sex words, and offend taste. At the same time it marks his failure to grasp the tragedy of the woman, like Anna Karenina, who seeks to escape into a new "free" mode of being-in-the-world, and who finds herself in the toils of a destructive egoism in mere sensuality (a problem traced and well understood by Edith Wharton).

*     *     *

I had so thoroughly accepted that Lawrence stood for life and sanity that I remember being deeply shocked when a psychotherapist, whose work I respected, said that he was a "very neurotic man." I think I was equally shaken to read Dr. Beede Howe's attribution to him of schizoid characteristics. Yet, the more one reads of his biographical details, the more disturbed he seems to have been. It is important to make this clear, not least because some of Lawrence's disturbed behavior reveals the meanings behind some of his major preoccupations in his writing. There is, for example, Frieda's letter to Middleton Murry of 18 December 1951:

> Sometimes he went over the edge of sanity. I was many times frightened but never the last bit of me. Once, I remember, he had worked himself up and his hands were

on my throat and he was pressing me against the wall and ground and cried out: "I am the master. I am the master." I said: "Is that all? You can be master as much as you like, I don't care." His hands dropped away, he looked at me in astonishment and was all right.

It would seem from this account that Lawrence was at that moment in the grip of a delusion. He had projected over Frieda some phantom from his unconscious, and felt that he must establish mastery over this dynamic. When the real woman declared her indifference to his desire for mastery, he recovered, but there are many questions raised by such a phenomenon. Why should a man feel that in some way the woman threatened him? How can a man confuse a real woman with a projection from his inner world? How can an individual be so divided that he can turn against the person most dear to him? What was the source of the phantom in the first place?

There are parallel incidents in Lawrence's life. Undoubtedly in a sense he was a wife-beater. We many take Mabel Sterne's reports with a pinch of salt, but she reports that when she and Frieda bathed at Hot Springs, this "big voluptuous woman," standing naked in the dim light, was covered with "great black and blue bruises" on her body.[6] Perhaps the most disturbing story of Lawrence's deranged behavior concerns not a woman but a bitch, the wretched Bibbles, that Mabel had given him. The little animal came on heat, and Lawrence refused to confine her, believing that the creature had been trained by him and would obey him, but she went off with a dog, and Lawrence is reported to have brooded fiercely, his head sunk on his chest in the characteristic posture he adopted during his depressions. He beat the bitch up, and she ran away for several days. Knud Merrild reports that "he was completely out of his mind."[7] He chased Bibbles, kicked her, lifted her up, and threw her down several times.

Such an intense response to a bitch suggests that Lawrence had deep reactions in him, prompted by the creature's sexuality. Her creativity perhaps conveyed to him an uncontrollable element in the female, which unconsciously he feared and hated. She perhaps stood for intense feelings about woman betraying him. The little dog was the woman taken in adultery, and Lawrence exerts his cruelty over her as if she were a dangerous woman.

Such behavior toward a female dog is revealing because of its symbolism, which verges on the insane so we may suspect that Lawrence was always striving against deep unconscious preoccupations, over woman and sexuality. Many commentators have remarked on the horror that often emerges, in his attitudes to sexuality, a horror against which he strove, not least through his writing. H. A. Mason makes some interesting observations in an article titled "Wounded Surgeons" in *The Cambridge Quarterly* Vol 11 No1, 1982, p189. He quotes Lawrence on the hero of *Women in Love*, the autobiographical character Birkin, "The incapacity to love, the incapacity to desire any woman, positively, with body and soul, this was a real torture." "He despised himself, essentially, in his attempts at sensuality." Mason also quotes Jessie Chambers, "I could not help feeling that the whole question of sex had for him the fascination of horror." Mason reports on some revelations of George Neville's, Lawrence's close friend, including one scene in which Lawrence revealed he had no knowledge of female nudity. Neville pencilled in the pubic hair on a naked woman Lawrence had drawn, whereupon Lawrence leapt out of his chair and pummelled Neville, crying "You dirty little devil. It's not true. It's *not* true, I tell you." Neville later also chides Lawrence for seeking sexual experience as mere experience, declaring this to be an insult to the woman.

Beneath these problems we may detect a deep reluctance in Lawrence to embrace the reality of female sexuality, his approach to woman being formed by the strong hold on him exerted by his mother so that "woman" for him is the ideal, while his own character was affected by his mother's idolization of him—a question we shall examine further. If we gather the many perceptions of Lawrence's attitudes to woman and sex, we must surely admit that there was something very abnormal about them?

It will help us in examining both Lawrence's treatment of men and women and his social and political views, if we understand the psychoanalytical concept of "projection." As Ann Ulanov (1981) says, in *Receiving Woman:*

> In the case of wife-beating we see projection working in its most primitive form. There the husband projects on to the wife fearful images in himself that he violently repudiates. He then punishes her for having them while indulging those impulses in himself in the beating process. (58)

The process originates in our problem over ambivalence: we are a mixture of love and hate, good and bad, but by projection we can avoid accepting this.

> To some degree we treat the other person as a blank screen on to which we can cast various aspects of our personalities that we somehow cannot consciously acknowledge. (Ulanov 1981, 57)

Exporting our less palatable aspects may have serious consequences. In marriage and close relationships we often see the following process depicted in Lawrence:

> by seeing our partners as the cause of tension, we can persuade ourselves that if only he or she would change, harmony would be returned. We thereby project our own self-image as good, free of negative reactions and troublesome attitudes. We do so by projecting the bad on to someone else. (Ulanov 1981, 58)

Some of the liveliest and most convincing moments in Lawrence's novels come when a woman like Ursula, taking on a refreshing realism, resist such projections, as with Birkin we hear the echoes of Frieda's rejections. Often, too, Lawrence rationalizes his projections, and turns the hostility into a philosophy of personal relationships.

Other incidents reported by various biographers bring us closer to the novels. There was an occasion when Catherine Carswell took her bad temper out on Donald: "You ought to hit her!" said Lawrence furiously. "Hit her hard. Don't let her scold and nag. You mustn't allow it, *whatever* it is you have done!" Returning a book by Jung to Katherine Mansfield, he wrote in an accompanying letter, "I do think a woman must yield some sort of precedence to a man, and he must take this precedence. I do think men must go ahead absolutely in front of their women, without turning round to ask for permission or approval from their women. Consequently the women must follow as it were unquestioningly. I can't help it, I believe this. Frieda doesn't. Hence our fight."[8] The amazing thing is the degree to which Frieda submitted. Cecily Lambert experienced an incident at Grimesbury Farm in which Lawrence forced Frieda to scrub the floor. "She burst into tears and got down to work, though not meekly, fetching a pail of water and sloshing around with a floor cloth in a bending position (although he had told her to kneel), bitterly resentful at having to do such a menial task quite beneath the daughter of a baron, at the same time hurling every insult she could conjure up at D.H., calling him an uncouth lout &c."[9] It seemed to Cecily that Lawrence wanted to humiliate Frieda.

As we shall see, this impulse to humiliate woman is the most disquieting aspect of Lawrence's writing.

Katherine Mansfield, who was the model for Gundrun, reacted violently against *The Lost Girl* because of this kind of tendency in Lawrence's novel: Lawrence, she said,

> denies his humanity. He denies the powers of the Imagination. He denies Life—I mean *human* life. His hero and heroine are non-human. They are animals on the prowl. . . .
>
> He says his heroine is extraordinary, and rails against the ordinary. Isn't that significant? . . . Take the scene where the hero throws her in the kitchen, possesses her, and she returns singing to the washing-up. It's a *disgrace*. Take the rotten rubbishy scene of the woman in labour asking the Italian into her bedroom. All false. All a pack of lies! . . .
>
> The whole is false—*ashes*. . . . Oh, don't forget where Alvina feels "*a trill in her bowels*" and discovers herself with child. A TRILL—what does that mean? And why is it so peculiarly offensive from a man?[10]

The last phrase indicates that Katherine Mansfield perceived that one of Lawrence's motives in seeking to reduce and humiliate woman is his jealously of her creativity, and that the most disturbing aspect of his books is his propaganda that makes it seem that woman *likes* being dominated.

At the same time he was aware of the humiliation to himself in his hostility to woman: "You have no idea, Brett, how humiliating it is to beat a woman; afterwards one feels simply humiliated" (Brett 1974, 271).

These biographical glimpses hardly enable us to "psychoanalyze" Lawrence, but they do help us to pick up one or two main dynamics in his work insofar as his work attempts to develop a philosophy of being. He said: "My great religion is a belief in the blood, the flesh, as being wiser than the intellect. We can go wrong in our minds. But what our blood feels and believes and says is always true" ( Letter to Ernest Collings, Moore 1962, 179).

When we "hear" the "blood," how do we know that this is the voice of authentic being, and how do we know it is not the voice of false promptings? Katherine Mansfield spoke of a "black devil" in Lawrence (Moore, 1955, 368): supposing, when we listen to the "blood," what we hear is the voice of that devil? If, as Lawrence said, "a real neurotic is half a devil", how does he know which half to listen to? If he says, "Your solar plexus is where you are you .... It is your first and greatest and deepest center of consciousness", suppose the "solar plexus" prompts us to act in ways of lust and domination directed *against* our better nature?

As we shall see, serious difficulties arise over such beliefs. If the blood speaks truth to us, do we then follow our "wants" as hunger or lust dictate? If the solar plexus is "me", my first and deepest center of consciousness, then what if a spasm of rage in my solar plexus urges me to be cruel to woman or a dog?

Such questions cannot be answered without examining our *model* of human nature, and our philosophy of human nature.

How is our identity formed? It seems clear from the work of Winnicott and others that we become ourselves through a complex relationship between our mothers and ourselves, and in the first few months of life, our relationship between ourselves and our mothers is crucial. The mother is capable of "creative reflection"; the infant, as it were, looks into her mind to see kind of idea of him she has. He looks into her eyes, to see himself emerging. At first the baby experiences only disconnected sensations. Only by degrees does he bring these together so as to become one single unified individual, and at the same time find his mother as one continuous person—thereby completing the discovery of the I–Thou, and also finding a real world to which to relate. These primary experiences condition the adult's capacity to find himself, the world, and "the other". Through such processes we discover the capacity to relate to others, especially to woman, and to "Mother Earth." Our feelings about the whole world are conditioned by the experiences we have of the mother in these formative months and years.

What concerns us here is what is likely to happen if these processes go wrong. The incidents referred to above suggest that Lawrence was capable at times of seriously losing his reality-sense and he also had especially deep disturbances of his capacity to relate to woman. From various moments in his works, which we shall examine, it seems clear that these may be traced to the special kind of relationship he had with his mother in infancy. Here, of course, there is no biographical evidence of the earliest stages, nor can there be. The only evidence is from the works themselves, which we may examine just as a psychotherapist examines the dreams and fantasies of his patient, to try to

recreate his infant life. For instance, there are Somers's dreams of a woman
ghost in his psyche in *Kangaroo*, the ghost of the dead mother in *Sons and
Lovers*, and some of the poems in *Look! We Have Come Through!*

Here we shall need to attend closely to Lawrence's vivid symbolism, and use
our phenomenological disciplines of interpretation. A recurrent important
symbol is the moon, and I see the moon in his work as a symbol of the
mother's face, the mother's scrutiny. That mother he had taken into himself
was projected over the moon, and whenever his characters approach a moment
of *the need of confirmation*—that is, at the moment the *need for reflection*
appears, the moon rises. This moon often seems to be menacing and a rival
to the developing sexual relationship. (Examples are discussed below—when
the moon rises as Paul Morel is about to kiss Miriam, and of course the scenes
between Ursula and Skrebensky and Ursula and Birkin involving the moon,
in which it is associated with reflections in water. The moon and moonlight are
also significant in *The Trespasser*.)

The moon is a symbol of woman because it has a monthly cycle and is
changeable; it is associated with Diana and chastity, being cool white light at
night as against the strong hot light of day that tends to be male in myth. There
is also the magical quality of moonlight associated with night and love, and
so it is a symbol of the *mysterium tremendum*. As I see it, the moon is a
powerful symbol of the power of the mother's redeeming love in *The Ancient
Mariner* (the moon is called "she"), and in *Frost at Midnight* the moon's light
is associated with apperception—that is, seeing reality with all one's feelings
engaged in a meaningful way. This kind of symbolism is illuminated a great
deal by Winnicott's insights into the mother's "mirror role" and how in the
infant's response he finds reflection a source of confirmation and meaning,
while his creative perception is also inevitably associated with love and hate.[11]
Lawrence seems to have had special feelings about being seen in the face of
another person, as often in the poems "being seen" is an important experience
for the infant in psychic parturition. It is a special capacity of the woman, in
her role as reflecting mother, to enable a child to make use to her capacity for
*being for*, by looking in her eyes. When Birkin looks into the face of the dead
Gerald, "he remembered also the beautiful face of one he loved, and who had
died still having the faith to yield to the mystery" (WL, 540)—who seems
clearly *Lawrence's* mother.

What is seen in the mother's face is the self, and so *identity* is closely related
to *gender*. To know oneself in this way belongs to the female way of knowing,
and this, Winnicott insists, comes first—being comes before doing, and in our
experience of the female mode lies the basis of all our powers as separate
autonomous beings. Lawrence was very much aware of the needs of human
beings for the experience of "being" in this feminine mode, and he had an
astonishing capacity to identify with women. He was also a very feminine man
himself, and there are many places where he seems to see men as woman sees
them. He often seems, through his protagonists, to yearn for a man, as for

George in *The White Peacock*—thus raising questions of his possible homosexual component, as many have suggested.

All these features of Lawrence suggest that he had problems consequent upon difficulties with his mother as an infant. It is possible that there may have been a number of reasons for this. One of his central short stories is *Odour of Chrysanthemums* in which the woman protagonist seems clearly based on his mother. In that story the woman becomes aware that in the realm of sexual love she never "found" her husband. She also feels that she has failed him, by her denial of his bodily being. In *Sons and Lovers*, too, Lawrence shows that he sensed that his father and mother did not have a satisfactory sexual relationship, and that this explains their estrangement and hostility. It is generally assumed that since she did not have a rich sexual relationship, Mrs. Lawrence turned to her son, and with him established a close and intense relationship with a sexual component. We may then perhaps see her as a "Jocasta" mother, as Matthew Besdine calls it,[12] who, in the absence of a fulfilling love life of her own, focuses her emotional life on the child. In the resulting fused symbiosis, there is no effective father to ensure the child's separation, self-differentiation, and growth towards autonomy and identity. Such an adult may experience love and intimacy as a contaminated, incestuous, guilty bondage, and may have his human relationships forever undermined by these feelings. According to Besdine, such problems are often found in the genius and extraordinary achievers, who also display a fear of love, strong paranoid trends, a distrust of authority, and a homosexual component.

There are other dynamics that may affect the formative relationship between mother and infant; a mother may wish strongly that her infant was of another sex. Winnicott, for instance, reports a case in which a man was handled by his mother as if he were a girl—with the consequence that he had a "split-off" girl self within his own personality. A mother may handle her child as if he were the reembodiment of a child who has died (and we know that Lawrence's mother was grieving deeply for another child, Ernest, who had died before Lawrence was born). There is also the possibility that the sexual libido, which a mother suppresses in herself where her husband is concerned, may be directed to the infant, whom she thus turns by her handling, if he is a boy, into an "idolized phallic object," a kind of hallowed embodiment of male potency.

This concept comes from a psychoanalytic student of gender, Robert S. Stoller, from his *Perversion—the Erotic Form of Hatred*. Stoller's relevant chapter here is on "Symbiosis Anxiety." As a student of gender, Stoller was puzzled by the fact that more men become sexually perverted than women. He postulates that men have a more difficult path to find their gender while a woman can identify with her mother from the beginning. The amazing thing is that a boy baby can come out of a woman's body, and has to make his path away from her toward male identity.

In the beginning there is a sense of primordial oneness with the mother, but in a sense this primordial at-oneness with a female must be counteracted. For a woman to support this, she must be wishing for and enjoying a masculine son. If she has this underlying motivation, she will encourage the development of behavior she considers masculine, a process that goes on endlessly day and night.

If she cannot enjoy the idea of her son's becoming masculine, she will communicate to him a disapproval of behavior she considers masculine.

Psychological studies of transsexual children have found that there can be boy children of three or four who are already confused with girls, regardless of what clothes they wore.

> When playing, these boys wish to do as if they were girls; they take only girls' roles and are accepted almost immediately by girls when playing girls' games from which other boys are excluded. (Stoller 1976, 139)

We know that at school Lawrence was mocked by the call "Dicky, Dicky Denches, plays with the wenches," and was thought to be effeminate (Moore 1955, 44),

The kind of mother who is likely to cause this problem in her child, says Stoller, has little sense of worth for her femaleness and femininity.

> Her own mother treated this girl as a neuter; her father, more admiring, encouraged her to identify with his masculine interests. (Stoller, 1976, 141)

The kind of man she marries tends to be passive and distant. "He is expected to support his family and then simply offer himself up to his wife as an object of derision." (Stolle, 141) It is impossible to say whether there was such a problem behind Lawrence's birth (though we may take clues from *Odour of Chrysanthemums* and *Sons and Lovers*). What we can say is that he was very much preoccupied with these themes of passivity and distance in the male, and the impulse in the woman to feel derision—the tendency in woman to hate and humiliate the maleness in a man.

Whatever the circumstances, the effect is that the "primaeval symbolic goodness both mother and infant experience may not only support but also threaten psychic development ... that symbiosis, if too intense and too prolonged, can damage developing masculinity" (Stoller 1976, 136).

The infant male that is born is perceived by the mother as beautiful and graceful, he is the best thing that ever happened to his mother.

> Finally, after years of quiet hopelessness, without a sense of worth about her sex or gender identity, filled with hatred and envy of males ... she has created a piece of herself ... the best of herself, her own ideal—the *perfect phallus*. (Stoller 1976, 141; my italics)

The word that has haunted me in writing about Lawrence has been the word "idolization." I believe here we have a clue to its source—*the mother's idealization of a phallic boy born from herself that has none of the qualities she envies and hates in the male.* A symbiosis is established from both, and is maintained fiercely by such a mother, "for she has enfolded within her now the cure for her lifelong hopeless sadness." (Stoller, 1976, 142) Joy is the energy that forces her to maintain excessively close body and psychic contact for too many hours and too many years. She binds her son unto herself, and uses this to "undo her own traumatic infancy."

Stoller relates this to homosexuality, possibly the latent homosexuality one often finds in Lawrence—like Birkin's yearning for "something else," some cosmic union with a man—has its origins in symbiotic anxiety. Stoller refers to discussion of Schreber in Freud's cases, which finds in homosexuality *"the desire to merge again with the mother."* It is really a "transexual tendency" and we may relate it to Lawrence's uncanny ability to identify with woman.

There are two other features of symbiosis anxiety that Stoller refers to:

> the mother, in her representation as an evil, hated creature may also lend herself to the task of permitting the symbiosis-mother to be repressed: one would hardly wish to merge with a witch (Stoller, 1976, 150)

Other links between Lawrence's fantasies are suggested by other observations by Stoller. For instance: "One can wonder if at its most primitive level, perversion is that ultimate in separations, mother-murder." (Stoller, 1976, 150) Perhaps here we have clues to Lawrence's idolization of polymorphous perversion and his strange dealings with murder.

According to Stoller's theory, masculinity starts as a movement away from the blissful and dangerous, forever-remembered and forever-yearned for, mother-infant symbiosis. In his efforts to remove himself from her, the boy will find great pleasure in a *sense of mastery* (cf. Lawrence's "I am the master").

One further aspect may be mentioned, to do with homosexuality: *penetrating a woman's body would be too risky.* This may perhaps help explain the combination of yearning and dread Lawrence experiences about entering a woman's body. It may help us understand Birkin's yearning for some "other" kind of love. It may help us understand Lawrence's preoccupation for sex without preliminaries, in "the sudden haste of his possession," sex like a "dagger thrust," and, of course, his obsessions with explicitness, with perversions and sodomy, the cultivation of the "indifferent" man, and the need for *risk*. To be caught *in flagrante* confirms the masculinity that is sought. (Lawrence and Frieda were arrested in Metz for making love in public, and there are passages in the work, notably *Sons and Lovers*, in which lovers make love deliberately in places where they will be seen.)

Although Lawrence is offered to the world as the "High Priest of Love" who is going to teach us to be men and women, there are also passages in which he seems to lack experience, or even not to understand what sexual activity means. There is, for example, the astonishing remark of Johanna's in *Mr Noon* about making love three times in a quarter of an hour. There are episodes like Gerald's mastering of the horse in *Women in Love*, the famous wrestling scene, and, of course, his whole preoccupation with sexual explicitness and the penis. I suggest this may indicate a traumatic experience of the Primal Scene in Lawrence's infancy, leading to the fetischistic element in his work. This becomes a manifestation of the idolized phallus, as in The Chatterley books and *The Plumed Serpent*. Parkin even becomes "a fountain filled with blood," and the subject takes on a religiose quality, linked with the belief that Lawrence and his heroes were "Sons of God" and not human at all. In the light of Stoller's analysis, I believe we have to say that this tendency manifests against the true work of a novelist, since it tends to make the writer deal with sexual objects rather than persons. It belongs to *splitting*: "Splitting, dehumanization, fetishization, and idealization result from failure of empathy and diminished or inhibited capacity to identify with others." (Stoller, 1976, 134) This tendency thus works in the opposite direction from the interests of a genuine novelist. It becomes ridiculous, of course, when Connie adulates Parkin's penis and declares it more beautiful than all the people of the neighborhood, or declares that it connects the lovers with the stars. It belongs, in Lawrence's progression, to the phenomenon by which he declares his separation from the rest of humanity, and "ordinary people" in favor of some lofty destiny, from which he consigns human beings to perdition. This is why it is such a relief when the genuine novelist temporarily reasserts himself, as when Parkin has a row with Connie, or Hilda declares ironically that then penis tends to wither like the grass, or Ursula tells the god-like Birkin that he is perverse. But with Kate, removed into the mysterious interior of Mexico, the element of realism comes to be lost. There is a tendency in Lawrence to pursue a separation of phallic sex, in a fetishistic way, from the life of whole persons and their love, and this has had, by example, a seriously damaging effect of the modern novel in which we now have a novel actually entitled *Sexual Intercourse*, while a coarse language of sex is now obligatory, in all creative writing.

Stoller links the elements of *hostility*, *risk*, and *revenge* in perversion: "we can expect ... to find fantasies of revenge against the traumatizer, primarily mother, sometimes father "(Stoller 1976, 119).

In Stoller's view, perversions are an attempt to overcome the primary psychic damage done to the pervert, *in revenge*. We may find this motive both in Gross and Lawrence, in their recommendation of "polymorphous perversion." Here, indeed, we may detect the dangers of listening to the "dark gods." As Stoller says, "*Perversion is hatred, eroticized hatred*" (122; my italics).

In these insights we may find the possible connections between sex, love, hate, and death. There are many ways of looking at the origins of our unconscious fears of annihilation associated with woman and emotional need. The Jungians speak of the various facets of woman: we find our origins in her body, then she becomes our partner, and finally we go down into the body of Mother Earth. Woman is thus for us, archetypally, both the source of our origins and also our goal in death. Object-relations psychology would perhaps tend to see woman as the creature upon whom we totally depend in our infancy. Because we are so wholly dependent upon her, we glimpse the possibility that she is as likely to have the power to destroy us as well as create us. It is the dependence that is terrible. Thus, the figure of the witch always complements the figure of the Virgin Mary or Primavera as the source of life.

Because of this, various writers in psychoanalysis trace the source of the widespread fear of woman in all societies to our experiences in infancy. Karl Stern, for instance, in *The Flight from Woman*, begins his exploration from his experience of men who expressed a "maternal conflict and a rejection of the feminine." In these individuals he found a *terror of dependence:*

> The very possibility of being in the least dependent or protected, or even being in love, amounts to nothing less than a phantasy of mutilation or destruction. (Stern 1970, 5)

Lawrence speaks clearly of this kind of fear in poems such as *Song of a Man Who Is Not Loved*. In these insights we may find the source of his dread of mutilation and destruction coming from close intimate contact ("horrible merging"). Stern links these psychological problems with philosophical issues over Lawrence and his century that concern us very much. Lawrence, of course, sees the difference between what we may call "male" and "female" modes of knowing.

Lawrence understood this, and is himself concerned with the capacity to know by sympathy, by "feeling with," as through union with the knowable, and by intuition.

Behind this philosophical question of apparently academic interest, says Stern, lurks a profound sense of dread, and this dread, as I have suggested, attaches itself to "the problem of woman." Woman stands for, symbolizes, *is* the focus for our awareness that we need to be *in touch with being*, and able to find a meaning in life in a world that is menaced by the lack of meaning and the elimination of *being*.

Among other things, Karl Stern is concerned to trace the development of a certain modern form of nihilism from René Descartes, through Schopenhauer, to Sartre. These forms of nihilism represent a serious alienation from Mother Earth, because "male" analytical and materialist philosophies of existence, based on alienation from Nature, have triumphed, and this alienation he tries to trace to psychic roots, as in Descartes, of the fear of woman. Later philosophers, whose own infant lives were deeply disturbed, have added to the dark tradition—including Schopenhauer and Sartre. (It is interesting to note that Harry T. Moore says "much of the vitality in Lawrence looks like Schopenhaurian will." Moore, 1955, 105)

The philosophical problems are bound up with problems of society and politics, and no one was aware of these more than Lawrence himself. (See, for instance, his *Study of Thomas Hardy:* "the works of superogation of our male assiduity help us towards a better salvation," *Phoenix,* p. 488.)

There are some further relevant papers by D. W. Winnicott that need to be borne in mind in examining such questions. The political implications of the unconscious fear of woman are discussed by him in "Some Thoughts on the Meaning of the Word Democracy" in *The Family and Individual Development* (1965).

In psychoanalytical and allied work, he says, it is found that all individuals have in reserve a certain fear of woman. In a footnote he relates this to the fear of the parents of very early childhood, the fear of a combined figure ("a woman with male potency included in her powers [witch]") and "fear of the mother who has absolute power at the beginning of the infant's existence to provide, or to fail to provide, the essentials for the early establishment of the self as an individual" (1965, 164).

Some individuals have this fear more than others, but it can be said to be universal. This unconscious fear of woman, suggests Winnicott, lies behind much unfairness to women in social and political life, and is responsible for the immense amount of cruelty to woman, "which can be found in customs that are accepted by almost all civilisations." (p164)

The root of this fear, declares Winnicott, is known. Its origin is in dependence—in infancy the mother's devotion is absolutely essential for the individual's healthy development. The fear is an acknowledgement of this debt which is too awful to acknowledge openly: it exists in the form of a fantasy woman in the unconscious, who *has no limits to her existence or power*, and who is feared for the possibility of her domination. Individuals will even put themselves under authoritarian domination in order to avoid domination by this fantasy woman.

The question of domination is discussed in the postscript to *The Child and the Family* (1964), where Winnicott makes the point that "the fear of domination does not lend groups of people to avoid being dominated: on the contrary it draws them towards a specific or chosen domination" (p143). Winnicott was evidently pondering the phenomenon of Nazi Germany (his radio talks to mothers were given in the period 1940–50), but we may take his observations here and apply them to D. H. Lawrence. Throughout his work me may find a profound fear of woman—and much of his work is devoted to the attempt to overcome that fear. In the end it led him to an obsession with domination, so that in some works he identifies with the dominator, who subdues woman. To this the remarks made by Winnicott on the psychology of the dictator are relevant, made in the Introduction to the Penguin edition of *The Child, the Family and the Outside World:*

> he is trying to control the woman whose domination unconsciously he fears, trying to control her by accommodating her, acting for her, and in turn demanding total subjection and "love." (1964, 10)

We shall find this unconscious dynamic powerful in *Kangaroo* despite Lawrence's occasional doubts, and we may find in it a clue to Lawrence's distaste for democracy. From Otto Gross through Frieda he picked up a view, to which he was already inclined, that most human beings were contemptible and in need of "proper ruling" by a few capable individuals. In his history textbook (for Oxford University Press) he writes at the end of how the salvation of Europe will depend upon "one great chosen figure" who will be "supreme over the will of the people" (Moore 1955, 306).

These aspects of Lawrence's psychology will prove to be relevant when we are examining his political conclusions. His unconscious fear of woman inclined him toward political impulses that seemed to require more and more control. He tended to reject democracy, while an energetic misanthropy grew in him that had a powerful misogynist component: all these tendencies are paramount in *The Plumed Serpent*, and appear in *Kangaroo*.

But the political elements in Lawrence also require our attention to focus on the problem already discussed—"projection," in relation to these complexities of gender. As we have seen, in some of the incidents of his life, Lawrence seemed to be projecting fantasies, as over Frieda and Bibbles. Lawrence also tended to project his own inner "badness" on to "society." We can perhaps see what is happening when Birkin hates Ursula as the Great Mother or when Gerald tries to kill Gundrun, but less obvious is the way he projects inward fears and darkness over woman and society at large.

This kind of projection in Lawrence goes with an increasing paranoia, and increasing tirades against *them*, as in *Women in Love*. There seems clearly an element of "schizoid superiority" in his ferocious disdain for those over whom Lawrence has projected weaknesses and elements he fears in himself, confirming Margaret Beede Howe's diagnosis of the schizoid problem in Lawrence. As his rage against "society" develops, along with it seems to grow an increasing sense of isolation: these was nowhere that Lawrence could settle, and he seemed to grow increasingly isolated from all possible communities.

The schizoid element noted by Beede Howe is relevant in our examination of Lawrence's attitude to the world. His characters experience unusual feelings of insecurity of identity, of emptiness of being, of feelings of loneliness and isolation, and of futility and despair, and of nihilism, for which "bad thinking" and hate may be necessary compensations. These kinds of feelings in schizoid individuals are examined by Guntrip, including the absolute sense of aloneness accompanied by horror often experienced by Lawrence's characters such as Mellors. We may recall the line in *Song of a Man Who Is Not Loved*, "I see myself isolated in the universe." As W. R. D. Fairbairn has also pointed out, the schizoid person often becomes an artist, because he seeks to live in his art, rather than in the real world. We get a glimpse of this process in Lawrence, of his feeling that he is dealing with unreal realities, in his writing, in a letter to Bertrand Russell (?15 March 1915):

> ... I am struggling in the dark—very deep in the dark—and cut off from everybody and everything. Sometimes I seem to stumble into the light, for a day, of even two days—then I plunge in again, God knows where and into what darkness of chaos ... It becomes a madness at last, to know one is all the time walking in a pale assembly of an unreal world—this house, this furniture, the sky and the earth—whilst oneself is all the while a piece of darkness ... (Moore, 1962, 330)

Later, he adds:

> I feel there is something to go through ... It may be only in my own soul—but it seems to grow more and more looming, and this day time reality becomes more and more unreal, as if one wrote from a grave or womb ... (Moore, 1962, 230)

It is as if he is seeking to become reborn, through his own creative effort, and we may apply this insight to his works, in which he often seems to be acting out his own drama, narcissistically, to overcome the schizoid feeling of darkness and emptiness in himself, which he could not otherwise deal with. A schizoid element also lies, I believe, behind Lawrence's sympathy with the theories of Gross, leaning towards moral inversion and the solutions of hate, out of a fear of love.

In trying to relate Lawrence's personal problems to his art, I am not trying to show that he was a "sick" man, though there are those who believe his tuberculosis had a profound effect on his psyche. I am rather trying to displace the insistence some have placed on his *normality*, and to suggest that where he goes in for false solutions, the clues to these may be in the phenomenology of his psychopathology.

It needs to be said, of course, that if Lawrence had not had the psychological problems I am attending to, he might not have been such a great artist. The emotional difficulties, problems of gender and identity, in turn, generated those existential problems in dealing with which he was a characteristic twentieth-century figure. His writings were in a sense an attempt to engage with these problems. He spoke himself of "shedding one's sickness in books." Alas, one of the things that psychoanalysis has established is that it is sentimental to believe that one can so cure oneself by writing. John Bowlby has written of the intractability of the "psychic tissue", and we know from psychotherapy how difficult it is to overcome psychic problems.

This is not to say that our difficulties are beyond hope. Lawrence was also right to believe that "it is the way our sympathies flow and recoil that really determines our lives"—and here such cultural experiences as the novel can help. But here again there is a problem, because, as his works demonstrate, a novel can be a powerful influence persuading us towards false solutions. It is this that makes criticism necessary.

In my criticism I employ the phenomenological analysis of symbols. Is this a valid approach? Lawrence was well aware of the dimension: "The novels came unwatched from one's pen." In a letter to D. W. Lederhandler on 12 September 1926, Lawrence says:

Yes, the paralysis of Sir Clifford is symbolic—all art is *au fond* symbolic, conscious or unconscious. When I began *Lady C.* of course I did not deliberately work symbolically. But by the time the book was finished I realised what the unconscious symbolism was. And I wrote the book three times—I have three complete MSS— pretty different, yet the same. The wood is of course unconscious symbolism— perhaps even the mines—even Mrs. Bolton. (Moore 1962, Vol.II, 1194)

Did Lawrence realise what the unconscious symbolism was? He may have seen that the wood represented the deeper layers of being with which (he felt) we must be in touch. But what he was almost certainly inhibited from realizing was the degree to which much of his work, even the great autobiographical novel *Sons and Lovers*, represented in some of its aspects a *defense* against insight, despite his courage in exploring his own tormented experience. Some of his work becomes in some of its aspects part of a propaganda and a mythology that are prompted—by way of defenses—to obscure the truth of his deeper self to himself, and to involve us in his falsifications.

# 1

# Difficulties over Woman in
## *The White Peacock* and *Sons and Lovers*

Many of the Lawrence ingredients are present in *The White Peacock*—the tenderly poetic sense of life in the natural world of flowers and creatures, the fascination with what women wear, the insights into the dynamics between human beings, the awareness of the deeper passions beneath daily life, especially young adolescents and young adults, whether it is a question of flirtations or killing animals. Some of the scenes of domestic life are superb—for example, the chapter in which Cyril Beardsall and his mother visit the house where the dead Father is lying ("The Father," chap. 4).

Many of the episodes of passion and personal development are convincing, especially the scenes of George's gradual decline into alcoholism, and his violence with his family.

Here, however, I want to concentrate on an underlying current in the book that relates to the problem over woman in all of Lawrence's work.

The problem is there in the title: woman is the white peacock that is beautiful and exceptional, but also vain, and destructive—liable to spoil a man's life. So, while the novel may not be directed by a thesis, it is, in one sense, a piece of personal propaganda for Lawrence's view of sexual relationships. In this, it contains two interwoven strands. One is the particular view of sexual relationships that clearly has behind it the mother's influence; the other is the son's view of woman that derived from this. Even this novel, as I shall try to show, contains a surprising amount of hostility toward woman. But there was (in Lawrence's view) a "cure" for woman: she must be subjected to a certain kind of passionate "treatment."

Here emerges the theme, so powerful in the last book, that woman is powerfully attracted by a man's sheer sensual power. Lettie, for example, calls George her "taureau," and George is associated with a certain stance toward his cows. But in stretching out towards deep sensuality and then retreating, there is a price to pay—and the price that the *man* may pay can be his own destruction. By contrast, the "normal" straightforward relationship of ordinary courtship is seen as full of foreboding, and in the end also brings a kind of forfeiture. Normal love seems lesser than other forms of sexuality.

Interesting answers begin to emerge, I believe, if we ask, what is the central theme of *The White Peacock?* What is the central thematic *relationship*?

The answer is very much bound up with the *homosexual* relationship between the "I" of the novel, Cyril, and George. In a sense George goes to pieces because he is lured away from this and is tempted first into yearning for Nettie, and then into marrying the easy-going Meg—into *family life*. There is an undercurrent, or "subplot," related to this, which is the relationship of both George and Cyril to the gamekeeper Annable. Later, despite the fight they have with the man, Cyril finds him attractive, and makes him a companion. It is Annable who produces the symbol of the book's title, the White Peacock: a woman has ruined Annable's life, and this woman is the White Peacock. In *The White Peacock* the impulse of man to man seems especially powerful:

> George was sitting by the fire, reading. He looked up as I entered, and I loved him when he looked up at me, and as he lingered on his quiet "Hallo!" His eyes were beautifully eloquent—*as eloquent as a kiss*. (WP, 97; my italics)

The important thing to note about this homosexuality is that it is unself-conscious, and is like the ("normal") homosexuality of adolescence. It has none of the mawkish self-awareness of E. M. Forster's *Maurice*, but it conveys a sense, which is evidently that of the young Lawrence, that there is a kind of untroubled and profound tenderness of meaning between men that does not have the disturbing and trying elements such as are depicted in all the relationships with woman.

It often seems at times as if Lawrence is seeking, as it were, to "present" man to woman. Here there are eulogies of George's beautiful physique, which (the "I" of the story feels) Nettie should admire. There seems to be in this a feeling that Nettie should fuel the kind of glow of love such as Cyril feels about him, as in the above passage. It is as if Lawrence is saying virtually, "If only women could feel the kind of love we men feel." In chapter 5, George is mowing. "That's a fine movement!" exclaims Leslie (Leslie is the "mentalizing" looker-on at this body-life).

> We moved across to the standing corn. The sun being mild, George had thrown off his hat, and his black hair was moist and twisted into confused half-curls. Firmly planted, he swung with a beautiful rhythm from the waist. On the hip of his belted breeches hung the scythe-stone; his shirt, faded almost white, was torn just above the belt, and showed the muscles of his back playing like lights upon the white sand of a brook. There was something exceedingly attractive in the rhythmic body. (WP, 54)

As often in this book, Cyril tries, as it were, to transfer this mannish eroticism to Nettie's sensibility: "I spoke to him, and he turned round. He looked straight at Nettie with a flashing, betraying smile. He was remarkably handsome" (WP, 54). The physical effort of the man's body is itself made erotic: Lawrence offsets George's bodily life against Leslie's neater kind of existence. Leslie does not have "the invincible sweep" of George's scything, and in discussing this and Lettie's attempts to tie up sheaves, Lawrence shows that he knows that while there is explicit, mental knowledge, there is also body-knowledge that cannot be made explicit.

This kind of body life and knowing are embodied in George's arms:

> "Do you know," she said suddenly, "your arms tempt me to touch them. They are such a fine warm colour, and they look so hard."
> He held out one arm to her. She hesitated, then she swiftly put her finger-tips on the smooth brown muscle, and drew them along. Quickly she had her hand into the folds of her skirt, blushing.
> He laughed a low, quiet laugh, at once pleasant and startling to hear. (WP, 55)

Later, she looks fully at his physical beauty, "as if he were some great firm bird of life."

We cannot help believing that feeling George's arm is something he would have liked his *mother* to do, and there are many passages in this first novel that may be interpreted as images of how the boy-son Lawrence would have liked his mother and father to enjoy one another bodily.

We need to remember the opprobrium on sexuality Lawrence must have encountered at home. He takes it for granted, for instance, that Cyril's mother would be coldly disapproving about his visits to Strelley Mill to see Emily:

> "Where have you been Cyril, that you weren't in to dinner?"
> "Only down to Strelley Mill," said I.
> "Of course," said mother coldly.
> "Why of course?" I asked. (WP 10)

In that cold "of course" we hear the voice of the mother (Mrs. Morel/ Lawrence) who is jealous of her son's relationship with a rival woman (Miriam/Jessie–E.T.), and her "puritan" antipathy to sexuality.

Lettie has caught some of this cold denial of the body from her mother. Over the rabbit-chasing episode she says, "Men are all brutes" (58). And in a long discussion of some pictures (by painters it must be said one has never heard of—presumably these were painters discussed from books by E. T. and Lawrence)[1] she says to George:

> "As for me, the flower is born in me, but it wants bringing forth. Things don't flower if they're overfed. You have to suffer before you blossom in this life. When death is just touching a plant, it forces it into a passion of flowering. You wonder how I have touched death. You don't know. There's always a sense of death in this home. *I believe my mother hated my father before I was born. That was death in her veins for me before I was born. It makes a difference—*"
> As he sat listening, his eyes grew wide and his lips were parted, like a child who feels the tale but does not understand the words. (WP, 33; my italics)

In the undercurrent of the book it is Lawrence who is talking as much as Lettie. The passage explains his need to redeem love and meaningful existence from a home where these had gone dead. What Lawrence sees through Cyril's eyes is "the parents" entering their doomed relationship. As nearly always in Lawrence, the development of a courtship brings on doom:

> In the wood the wind rumbled and roared hoarsely overhead, but not a breath stirred among the soddened bracken. . . .
> Armies of cloud marched in rank against the sky. . . . The wind was cold and disheartening. The ground sobbed at every step. (WP, 97)

There follows the moment when George's eyes, to Cyril, are as "eloquent as a kiss." Again, by contrast with the doomed courtship of the parents, homosexual love seems to offer a purity and safety that cannot be guaranteed when woman is involved. By a strange turn, Lawrence wants to give back that love to woman, through George: George is milking and speaks with hostility of woman. Julia the cow has hit him with her horns and he knocks her hip bone with the stool. Of Lettie he says:

> "I should like to squeeze her till she screamed."
> "You should have gripped her before, and kept her," said I.
> "She's—she's like a woman, like a cat—running to comforts—she strikes a bargain. Women are all tradesmen."
> "Don't generalize, it's no good."
> "She's like a prostitute—"
> "It's banal! I believe she loves him."
> He started and looked at me queerly. He looked quite childish in his doubt and perplexity.
> "She, what—?"
> "Loves him—honestly."
> "She'd 'a loved me better," he muttered . . . . (WP, 100–11)

Lettie has "led him on," but there is in Lawrence a feeling behind the exchange that it would have been "better" for Lettie to have had a "real" man like George, with his kind of physique (though George has been described earlier [73] as a "bit of a waster").

So, from this early novel, we become aware that behind the enactments of the art, there is a developing sexual attitude that has an intensely moral purpose. There is a certain kind of fulfillment that involves certain ranges of being—an authenticity—while those who settle for something less are morally inferior.

Lawrence, at this stage, of course, cannot be explicit, but he feels he must try to deal with the realities of sexual adventure of his time.[2] Lettie, at one point in *The White Peacock*, is shown to have a physical aversion to love-play of a masturbatory kind. We recall how, after feeling George's muscles, she hides her hand in her skirt. Later, at a moment when Leslie stays the night, she does not appear at breakfast, and seems ashamed of her hands. It is an extraordinary passage:

> In another minute she came downstairs. She was dressed in dark, severe stuff, and she was somewhat pale. She did not look at any of us, but turned her eyes aside. . . . He turned sharply with a motion of keen disappointment.

He drives off, but comes back. They walk down the path.

> "You—are you—are you angry with me? he faltered. Tears suddenly came to her eyes. . . .
> "I don't see why—why it should make trouble between us, Lettie," he faltered. She made a swift gesture of repulsion, whereupon, catching sight of her hand, she hid it swiftly against her skirt again.
> "You make my hands—my very hands disclaim me," she struggled to say.
> He looked at her clutched fist pressed against the folds of her dress.
> "But—" he began, much troubled.
> "I tell you, I can't bear the sight of my own hands," she said, in low, passionate tones.
> "But surely, Lettie, there's no need—if you love me—"
> She seemed to wince. He waited, puzzled and miserable.
> "And we're going to be married, aren't we?" he resumed. . . . (WP, 196)

She refuses to kiss him. The episode points to one of the problems behind sexual relationships in Lawrence's day: an engaged couple of this lower middle class could not risk sexual intercourse, and so, perhaps selfishly, Leslie involves her in masturbating him before she is ready for full sexual relationship leaving her frustrated and ashamed. The strength of Lettie's reaction also seems to indicate a degree of body-shame that we can relate to her earlier remarks to George about her mother hating her father, and to Cyril's feelings of doom about their engagement.

Homosexual love, by contrast, does not have these dangers. In *The White Peacock* it is important to note that Cyril (whose closeness to Lawrence is clear) declares that his body-contact with George outshines any other such closeness in his life:

> We stood and looked at each other as we rubbed ourselves dry. He was well-proportioned, and naturally a handsome physique, heavily limbed. He laughed at me, telling me I was like one of Aubrey Beardsley's long, lean, ugly fellows. I referred him to many classic examples of slenderness, declaring myself more exquisite than his grossness, which amused him . . . he knew how I admired the noble, white fruitfulness of his form. As I watched him, he stood in white relief against the mass of green . . . I remembered the story of Annable. (WP, 248)

This takes us back to the strong homosexual element in the passage of the gamekeeper, and to the "white peacock" outburst.

He saw I had forgotten to continue my rubbing, and laughing he took hold of me and began to rub me briskly, as if I was a child, or rather, a *woman he loved and did not fear*. (WP, 248; my italics)

In that latter phrase Lawrence gives us a clue to his homosexual inclinations. Love between men has a purity that avoids the dangers encountered with women:

I left myself, quite limply in his hands, and, to get a better grip of me, he put his arm round me and pressed me against him, and the sweetness of the touch of our naked bodies one against the other was superb. It satisfied in some measure the vague, indecipherable yearning of my soul; and it was the same with him. When he had rubbed me all warm, he let me go, and we looked at each other with eyes of still laughter, and our love was pure for a moment, *more perfect than any love I have known since*, either for man or woman. (WP, 248; my italics)

There follows, in richly poetic prose, a description of George's work with the horses among the wild flowers. We may compare this with the very different picture of a heterosexual relationship, given in the story of Annable, which Cyril remembers at that idyllic moment:

I should meet her in the garden early in the morning when I came in from a swim in the river . . . and she'd blush and make me walk with her. I can remember I used to stand and dry myself on the bank full where she might see me—I was mad on her—and she was madder on me . . . I let her do as she liked with me. . . . Then gradually she got tired—it took her three years to be really glutted with me. I had a physique then. (WP, 166–67)

He, too, has hard arms in his sleeve, like George. He continues:

"She wouldn't have children—no, she wouldn't—said she daren't. . . . But she cooled down, and if you don't know the pride of my body you'd never know my humiliation. . . . She began to get souly . . . I was her animal—*son animal—son boeuf*." (WP, 167)

He runs away; she marries someone else, and then dies.

"So she's dead—your poor peacock" I murmured. . . .
"I suppose," he said, "it wasn't all her fault."
"A white peacock, we will say," I suggested. (WP, 168).

Earlier we have seen the peacock to which Cyril obliquely refers.

The peacock flapped beyond me, on to the neck of an old bowed angel, rough and dark, an angel which had long ceased sorrowing for the lost Lucy, and had died also. The bird bent its voluptuous neck and peered about. Then it lifted up its head and yelled. The sound tore the dark sanctuary of twilight. The old grey grass seemed to stir, and I could fancy the smothered primroses and violets beneath it taking and gasping for fear. (WP, 169)

The keeper says "Hark at that damned thing!"

> "The poor fool!—look at it! Perched on an angel, too, as if it were a pedestal for
> vanity. That's the soul of a woman—or—it's the devil . . . ."
>     "Just look!" he said, "the miserable brute has dirtied that angel. A woman to the
> end, I tell you, all variety and screech and defilement." (WP, 165)

Not long afterward, "the moon looks like a woman with child. I wonder
what Time's got in her belly." In fact, Time has his (Annable's) death in her
belly.

Whenever he find the moon in Lawrence, we may find her a symbol of the
mother. Beneath this strange episode of Annable, which is clearly central to
the book with the title *The White Peacock*, we may detect a seething sense of
doom, emerging from the woman's belly. She is a white screeching vain bird,
who defiles the idealistic image (of an angel) on which she perches, and brings
death to man. This, by implication, is what Lettie does, too, in her way. She
is the devil who ruins man's life. It seems hardly surprising that it seems
blissfully safer to enjoy love between man and man instead though that, too,
ends (with Annable) with death and (with George) in decadence. Both events
are, in one way or another, attributed to the effects of the behavior of the
white peacock woman, who, though she appears beautiful, is really vain and
egoistic and exudes a destructive hate. It is also important to note that the
white peacock defecates on the angel. Woman is capable of *defilement*. So,
even in this early work, we find Lawrence symbolizing the fear of woman as
a creature capable of blighting a man's life. Behind the idyllic portrayal of
country life and of adolescent awkwardness, we find an undercurrent of bitter
hatred of woman, and even of the potentialities of her body.

These potentialities include giving birth, and so we need to examine
carefully how Lawrence portrays infants. This, in turn, raises questions about
his attitude to sexuality and its outcome. What was it, beyond sexual
experience with a woman, that Lawrence hungered for? There are moments
when we have a powerful glimpse of yet another kind of love, of which Cyril
(the "I" protagonist) is deeply envious. This is the mother's love for her baby.
The most powerful of these passages are in chapter 4, "Domestic Life at the
'Ram.'" Lawrence's impulse is to show George embroiled in domestic life with
all its cares, all bustle and flurry, with Meg in "a most uncomfortable state."

But, as with the scene with the baby in E. M. Forster's *Where Angels Fear
to Tread*, the beauty and nobility, the "life" of the baby, takes over. Emily
is holding one; and Cyril is jealous:

> She persisted in talking to the baby, and in talking to me about the baby, till I wished
> the child in Jericho. This made her laugh, and she continued to tantalize me. The
> hollyhock flowers of the second whorl were flushing to the top of the spires. The bees,
> covered with pale crumbs of pollen, were swaying a moment outside the wide gates
> of the florets, then they swung in with excited hum, and clung madly to the furry
> white capitals, and worked riotously round the waxy bases. Emily held out the baby

to watch, talking all the time in low, fond tones. The child stretched towards the bright flowers. The sun glistened on his smooth hair as on bronze dust and the wondering blue eyes of the baby followed the bees. Then he made small sounds and suddenly waved his hands, like crumpled pink hollyhock buds.
"Look!" said Emily, "look at the little bees! Ah, but you mustn't touch them, they bite." (WP, 303)

It is a beautiful moment, redolent with symbolism of sexuality—of real sexuality, full of danger, too, as the child tries to touch the bees, and the danger is in Emily's relationship to Cyril:

Thus she teased me by flinging me all kinds of bright gazes of love while she kept me aloof because of the child. (WP, 304)

Later, they watch Meg feeding and bathing one of the babies "humbly." Because she is so Madonna-like, it is a "wonder."

She handled the bonny, naked child with beauty of gentleness. She kneeled over him nobly. Her arms and her bosom and her throat had a nobility of roundness and softness. She drooped her head with the grace of a Madonna, and her movements were lovely, accurate and exquisite, like an old song perfectly sung. Her voice, playing and soothing round the curved limbs of the baby, was like water, soft as wine in the sun, running with delight. (WP, 308)

Emily baths the other baby, her fingers trembling with pleasure as she loosens the little tapes.

"Ha!—Ha-a-a!" she said with a deep-throated vowel, as she put her face against the child's small breasts, so round, almost like a girl's, silken and warm, and wonderful. She kissed him, and touched him, and hovered over him, drinking in his baby sweetness, the sweetness of the laughing little mouth's wide, wet kisses, of the round waving limbs, of the little shoulders so winsomely curving to the arms and the breasts, of the tiny neck hidden very warm beneath the chin, tasting deliciously with her lips and her cheeks and the exquisite softness, silkiness, warmth, and tender life of the baby's body. (WP, 309)

It is a rapturous passage, like the description of an act of love, but sensual rather than sexual. It seems to suggest that Lawrence is exploring here an experience he would deeply wish to have had, but felt he had not had. We may see, I believe, much of his own preoccupation with bodily sexuality as being an attempt to make good that deficiency, the desire to experience richly sensual "truth" between "mother and infant."
Strangely, at once, in the next paragraph, he makes the generalization:

A woman is so ready to disclaim the body of a man's love; she yields him her own soft body with so much gentle patience and regret: she clings to his neck, to his head and his cheeks, fondling them for the soul's meaning that is there, and shrinking from his passionate limbs and his body. It was with some perplexity, some anger and bitterness that I watched Emily moved almost to ecstasy by the baby's small innocuous person.

"Meg never found any pleasure in me as she does in the kids," said George bitterly, for himself (WP, 309)

In the next paragraph there is more radiant description of Meg with her baby: "She brought his fine hair into one silken upspringing of ruddy gold like an aureole."

The tragedy of George seems to be that he cannot fulfill with Nettie the promise of glowing body life, and the magnetism between their eyes; nor does Meg find body-pleasure in him as she does in her child, while Cyril never fulfills himself with Emily. The radiant promise of meaningful, of virtually religious, love that Meg and Emily display with their infants, like Madonnas, contrasts sadly with their inability to enjoy, with equal ecstasy, the lower bodies, the passionate limbs, of the men. They maintain instead with them a "spiritual" enjoyment of what Lawrence calls" the upper self."

We have been inclined to take this distinction as true, but from our reading of autobiographical accounts by "E. T." and Helen Corke, as well as biographical facts, it seems likely that this was a rationalization of problems within Lawrence himself. Lawrence seems to have kept one woman as "morphia" (sexual experience) while enjoying ideal experiences with others, while "E. T." declares that hesitation about sexual giving was his, not hers. So perhaps the bitter envy the Cyril-Lawrence character feels is a question not of the *women*'s capacities to enjoy the men's bodies, but a question of *the man's guilt* over sexuality. (In *The Trespasser* there is a strange discussion that seems to be about impotence, as if it were not the woman Helena's desire that the relationship is platonic, but the *man's* reluctance [T, 62 and 163].) From the juxtaposition here of the babies enjoyed like Christ-children, and the men's bitterness, we may suspect that at the root of the envy is Lawrence's own feeling that he could not bring the ecstasy of ideal love together with the rich sensuality of the body.[3]

There is an extraordinary tension in *The White Peacock* between the impulse towards "life," and the record of frustration and the failure of fulfillment. We have seen above the richly poetic passage, where Emily is holding one of Meg's babies as they watch the bees working in the hollyhocks. Throughout the book the descriptions of natural phenomena, flowers and birds especially, are full of promise, as they are in the wood idyll of *Lady Chatterley's Lover*. At the same time there are a few deeply disturbing passages in which, in their dealings with animals, human beings seem destructive—as with the marauding dogs, and when the mother lets a sickly chick she is warming step into the fire. Right at the beginning of the book George is shown teasing some field bees, while Cyril protests: "When he had finished he flung the clustered eggs into the water and rose." (WP, 4).

Throughout the book there is a reiteration of the point of view, no doubt implanted in young Lawrence's mind by his mother, that "men are brutes." After the account in the chapter "The Scent of Blood" some of the protagonists talk about this:

> "The sport's exciting while it lasts," said Leslie.
> "It does you more harm than the rabbits do us good," said Mrs. Saxton.
> "Oh I don't know, mother," drawled her son, "It's a couple of shillings."
> "And a couple of days off your life."
> "What be that!" he replied, taking a piece of bread and butter and biting a large piece from it.
> "Pour us a drop of tea," he said to Emily.
> "I don't know that I shall wait on such brutes," she replied, relenting, and flourishing the teapot.
> "Oh," he said taking another piece of bread and butter. "I'm not all alone in my savageness this time."
> "Men are all brutes," said Lettice hotly, without looking up from her book.
> "You can tame us," said Leslie, in might good humour.
> She did not reply. George began, in that deliberate voice that so annoyed Emily:
> "It does make you mad, though, to touch the fur, and not be able to grab him"—he laughed quietly.
> Emily moved off in disgust. Lettie opened her mouth sharply to speak but remained silent.
> "I don't know," said Leslie. "When it comes to killing it goes against the stomach."
> "If you can run," said George, "you should be able to run to death. When your blood's up, you don't hang half-way."
> "I think a man is horrible," said Lettie, "who can tear the head off a little mite of a thing like a rabbit, after running it in torture over a field."
> "When he is nothing but a barbarian to begin with—" said Emily.
> "If you begin to run yourself—you'd be the same," said George.
> "Why, women are cruel enough," said Leslie with a glance at Lettie. "Yes," he continued, "they're cruel enough in their way"—another look, and a comical little smile.
> "Well," said George, "What's the good finicking! If you feel like doing a thing—you'd better do it."
> "Unless you haven't courage," said Emily, bitingly.
> He looked up at her with dark eyes, suddenly full of anger.
> "But," said Lettie—she could not hold herself from asking,
> "Don't you think it's brutal now—now that you *do* think—isn't it degrading and mean to run the poor little things down?"
> "Perhaps it is," he replied, "but it wasn't an hour ago."
> "You have no feeling," she said bitterly. (WP, 58–59)

The passage is central to the theme of the book and, indeed, to Lawrence's preoccupations. The problem of the blood lust men feel when running down rabbits is obviously related to the experience of sexual relations as in the poem *Love on the Farm* (*CP*, 42): Leslie's glances at Lettie indicate this, as do Emily's remarks about courage.

What does Leslie mean by his reference to cruelty? Probably he refers to

Lettie's capacity to tease, that is, to arouse men passionately, leaving them painfully frustrated. Later, she coaxes George to kiss her passionately, but then goes away immediately, so that he, also distressed by his disloyalty to Meg, is violently sick, and Cyril "thinks" a Latin tag about physical repulsion. George is also one who, though he delights in his physique and passionate impulse, does not exhibit courage in his personal relationships. He has a strange sense of futility: "And what is there that's worth anything?—what's worth having in my life?" As we have seen, he is even described as "a bit of a waster." Has the decline of agriculture and the closure of the skill something to do with George's decline? In what we would nowadays call "Lawrentian" terms, George should have been the liberating force in Lettie's life, yet she can only play the "forbidden game" with him, while he fails continuously to make a forceful and decisive claim for her although quite early in the book he is seemingly in love with her.

> George did not return to her till she called him to help her. Her colour was high in her cheeks. "How do you know you did not?" she said, nervously, unable to resist the temptation to play this forbidden game.
> He laughed, and for a moment could not find any reply.
> "I do!" he said. "You knew you could have me any day, so you didn't care."
> "Then we're behaving in quite the traditional fashion," she answered with irony.
> "But you know," she said, "you began it. You played with me, and showed me heaps of things—and those mornings—when I was binding corn, and when I was gathering the apples, and when I was finishing the straw-stack—you come then—I never forget those mornings—things will never be the same. You have awakened my life—I imagine things that I couldn't have done."
> "Ah!—I am very sorry, I am so sorry."
> "Don't be!—don't say so, But what of me?"
> "What?" she asked rather startled. He smiled again he felt the situation, and was a trifle dramatic, though deadly in earnest.
> "Well," said he, "You start me off—then leave me at a loose end. What am I going to do?
> "You are a man," she replied. (WP, 129–30)

They talk to one another in a trance-like way: "You can go on—which way you like" . . . "Never mind—never mind" . . . "I am so sorry." We have a developing sense that Lettie has exerted a destructive influence on his life by being fascinated by his robustness and his physical beauty, while preferring the respectable and more submissive, polite, and courteous Leslie. (There is, of course, a class element in all this.) At one point she tried to withdraw from her engagement with Leslie, but he is ill, and uses his weakness to make her feel obliged to come back to him.

Her cruelty to George is not a conscious enjoyment of cruelty, but she is a flirt and (in our coarse terms) a "prick teaser." Yet at the same time (as we see in the incident about masturbation) she suffers from a certain sense of repulsion over sexual experimentation just as she comes of age. Lawrence's portrayal of women's use of power over men while shrinking from full sensual exchange with them in early adulthood is superb: the theme is pursued in *The Trespasser*.

George is also too blame for allowing himself to be drawn, for exerting his physical charm at Lettie, and yet for not being a "man" in the terms in which she urges him to be. There are often moments when Lettie seems deeply disappointed that George is not bolder. In the words of the folk song, he "lost pretty Nancy by courting too slow." On his part there are fears of sensuality, too, as is made clear when he and Lettie are discussing some pictures.

> "Wouldn't it be fine?" he exclaimed, looking at her with flowing eyes, his teeth showing white in a smile that was not amusement.
> "What?" she asked, dropping her head in confusion.
> "That—a girl like that—half afraid—and passion!" he lit up curiously.
> "She may well be half afraid, when the barbarian comes out in his glory, skins and all."
> "But don't you like it?" he asked.
> She shrugged her shoulders, saying:
> "Make love to the next girl you meet, and by the time the poppies redden in the field, she'll hang in you arms. She'll have need to be more than half afraid, won't she?"
> She played with the leaves of the book and did not look at him.
> "But," she faltered, his eyes glowing "it would be—rather—"
> "Don't, sweet lad, don't!" she cried laughing.
> "But I shouldn't—" he insisted, "I don't know whether I should like any girl I know to—"
> "Precious Sir Galahad!" she said in a mock-caressing voice, and stroking his cheek with her finger. "You ought to have been a monk—a martyr, a Carthusian."
> He laughed, taking no notice. He was breathlessly quivering under a new sensation of heavy, unappeased fire in his breast, and in the muscles of his arms. He glanced at her bosom and shivered. (WP, 34)

This is a characteristic passage in which Lettie, not yet herself awakened to sexual passion, and inexperienced in arousing men, evokes in George the first stirrings of the awareness of possibly having sexual relations with a woman. But what is interesting in his fear—the way he looks at her bosom and shivers, and by his pauses shows that he is deeply guilty and conventionally shocked at the possibility, "it would be—rather— . . . I don't know whether I should like any girl I know to. . . ."

Lettie has just made a long speech about how, "As for me, the flower is born in me, but it wants bringing forth. . . . You have to suffer before you blossom in life"—and there follows the strange remark about her father hating her mother before she was born.

We may suppose that Lawrence had an acute sense of the element of oral impulse behind sexual feelings.

This has a schizoid element (the fear of love as too dangerous) and also represents an infant's fear of love and of sexual intercourse as a kind of eating liable to consume. (I am here drawing on insights of Winnicott and Melanie

Klein.) Lawrence seemed to have retained in his inner life such an infant dread of sexuality, and in this book, I believe, the fear of woman, the dread of body-relations with ber, and the hostility that is a defense against this, all surface from time to time, as in the central image of the white peacock.

These problems give a clue to George's terrible decline—for in fact, despite all the "life" in it, and the snatches of joy, *The White Peacock* is a *terrible* book. We glimpse, in the descriptions of George's rich bodily life, and in Lettie's beauty and intelligence, possibilities of fulfillment. We see the harvest of sexuality in the babies that they bear—when Cyril sees them asleep together he thinks of the lark chicks he has seen hatched on the surface of the ground in a field. Yet neither for Lettie nor George is there fulfillment, while Leslie simply seems diminished rather than enrichened by his marriage, while even Cyril does not marry Emily to whom he has been progressively attracted. The end of the novel is disturbingly bleak.

George declares that he hates Lettie, and feels insulted by her. He turns philistine and considers her singing of Debussy and Strauss an "idiocy" at a time when down-and-outs are sleeping under the arches of the Thames bridges:

"fooling about wasting herself . . . and the poor devils rotting on the Embankment."
(WP, 318)

George realizes that if he had married Lettie "we should have been like a cat and a dog; I'd rather be with Meg a thousand times—now!" But of one remark of George's, Cyril says: "I know he meant her shirking, her shuffling of her life" (WP, 318).

Lettie sings but she doesn't write poetry. She claims that her real productivity is in being a mother. But Lawrence offers her married life as a failure:

There was a touch of ironic brutality in her now. She was, at bottom, quite sincere. Having reached that point in a woman's career when most, perhaps all, of the things in life seem worthless and insipid, she had determined to put up with it, to ignore her own self, to empty her own potentialities into the vessel of another or others, and to live her life at second hand. This peculiar abnegation of self is the resource of a woman for escaping the responsibilities of her own development. Like a nun, she puts over her living face a veil, a sign that the woman no longer exists for herself; she is a servant of God, of some man, of her children, or may be of some cause. As a servant, she is no longer responsible for herself, which would make her terrified and lonely. Service is light and easy. To be responsible for the good progress of one's life is terrifying. It is the most insufferable form of loneliness, and the heaviest of responsibilities. So Lettie indulged her husband, but did not yield her independence to him; rather it was she who took much of the responsibility of him into her hands, and therefore he was so devoted to her. She had, however, now determined to abandon the charge of herself to serve her children. When the children grew up, either they would unconsciously fling her away, back upon herself in bitterness or loneliness, or they would tenderly cherish her, chafing at her love-bonds occasionally.
(WP, 316–17)

*The White Peacock* was published when Lawrence was only twenty-six. He can't have been much older than Lettie when he wrote this passage. It is a weary and cynical passage for a young man: does such a young woman reach an age, in her mid-twenties, when "all the things in life seem worthless and insipid"?

Reading the passage carefully, it makes sense if we take it that it is about Mrs. Lawrence, his mother, but we may extend this insight by looking at *Sons and Lovers*. We have seen the exchanges about cruelty, and about the brutality of men and women. "Ironic brutality" is a strong phrase, and it is possible that such a woman who teased George so cruelly in her early twenties might well become hard in her marriage. In the background I feel there is the young Lawrence's dismay at the harsh attitude of rejection in his mother—his dismay at her attitude to his father. Why couldn't they have a rich, happy sexual life so that he could identify with them, and find his own way to fulfillment? Instead there was her ironic rejection, on the lines of "men are brutes."

Lettie "empties her potentialities into the vessel of another of others" and so "lives her life at second hand." But here, surely, Lawrence is thinking of his mother's complaints, that her life has been directed from its possible fulfillment by having to care for a miner's son and his family?

> This peculiar abnegation of self is the resource of a woman for escaping the responsibilities of her own development. (WP, 316)

While Lettie (in Lawrence's opinion) thus shuffles and shirks by "compromising" with ordinary life, George goes to pieces in his marriage like Annable. Life comes to seem to him "an aimless, idiotic business," and he exhibits his own brand of "sardonic brutality." He becomes a nihilist:

> "I am like this sometimes, when there's nothing I want to do, and nobody I want to be near. Then you feel so rottenly lonely, Cyril. You feel awful, like a vacuum with a pressure on you, a sort of pressure of darkness, and you yourself—just nothing, a vacuum that's what it's like—a little vacuum that's not dark, all loose in the middle of a space of darkness, that's pressing on you." (WP, 321)

Lettie has failed to become a poet, George feels he should have made something of himself, become "poet or something, like Burns." George feels he has grown up too soon like corn in a wet harvest: "I s'll rot." He wanted something that would have made him grow fierce, and that's why he wanted Lettie. Again, we have an egoistic emphasis: George wants Lettie not for himself, not because he loves her, but to give *him* strength. There seems no doubt that there is something of Lawrence in George—certainly something of Lawrence's father.

Both forms of decline are terrible. Lettie speaks of the misery of this "torpor" ("she would write to me in terms of passionate dissatisfaction: she had nothing at all in her life, it was a barren futility," WP, 323). She seems full of passion and energy, but it "all fizzles out in day to day domestics." She writes "screeching" letters (we remember the peacock), and she feels a "trifle demented."

George becomes an alcoholic, who sometimes comes home mad drunk. He is redeemed a little by a girl child. He takes up socialism, but then drops out of it. He is "selfish to the backbone," and comes to care neither for his wife or his children, "only for himself": an egoist.

In a sense (in the chapter *Pisgah*) in which George and Lettie are alone together again on Lettie's thirty-first birthday, he condemns marriage. Once he felt that "things had a deep religious meaning, somewhere hidden, and you reverenced them." Now, "What is there left for me to believe in, if not in myself?" (WP, 335)

Lettie urges him to consider himself necessary as a father and husband. He declares that "marriage is more of a duel than a duet. One party wins and takes the other capture, slave, servant—what you like." (WP 335) Here are the beginnings of Lawrence's feeling that men and women are natural enemies.

Lettie does not protest, and George goes on, "I can't give her any of the real part of me, the vital part that she wants. . . . I feel that I'm losing—and dont care." (WP, 335)

Lettie sings to him, and plays with his hair, parting it—back to her old ways of teasing. The effect is to make him proclaim his loneliness, and to say "we can't go on . . . it must be one way or the other." But Lettie cannot relinquish her children—and, indeed, has no intention of committing herself to George. The chapter in some way does not ring true: for one thing, it seems again that Cyril is present, yet the ways in which Lettie and George speak and act have an intimacy that could only come if they were alone, especially since their mild flirtation is adulterous.

Toward the end of the book, we feel that Lawrence has his thumb in the scale because of his own views of existence and his own dread of marriage, that is, he is saying that he cannot accept marriage as a fulfillment because it would be just like Mummy and Daddy again:

> I was weary of babies. My friends had all grown up and married and inflicted them on me. There were storms of babies. I longed for a place where they would be obsolete, and young, arrogant, impervious mothers might be a forgotten tradition. (WP 350)

This is an astonishing paragraph—expressing a deep hostility to women's creativity, about which earlier there has been so much envy.

Alice had made a bad marriage. She relates another anecdote of George's mad alcoholic cruelty; now he has the D. T.s, and hardening of the liver. He looks at Cyril "with dull eyes of shame." He cannot eat, and can no longer work. He is in the prime of life, but is thin bellied, and was "bowed and unsightly." There is nothing left for him but death:

He turned to me, his dark eyes alive with horror and despair. "I shall soon—be out of everybody's way!" he said. His moment of fear and despair was cruel. I cursed myself for having raised him from his stupor. . . .
He sat apart and obscure among us, like a condemned man. (WP, 360–61)

The whole novel thus turns out to be terrible spectacle of a man destroyed by a white peacock of woman. It is full of hostility to woman, envious of her creativity, and dwells often on the alternative of homosexuality.

\*     \*     \*

*Sons and Lovers* is perhaps Lawrence's most successful work and a great tragic novel. At the same time it seems it takes many liberties with the truth. What is the truth about that early life at Eastwood? *Sons and Lovers* is "a work of fiction on a frame of actual experience" as Lawrence himself says somewhere in *The Letters*, but those who read E. T.'s *Memoir* and Helen Corke's *In Our Infancy* will know that there is a considerable difference between other participants' views of the events and the novel. Of course, there is always a problem of judging between a number of personal accounts of the same events, but both E. T. and Helen Corke accuse Lawrence of distorting "life" and raise problems of integrity:

He had sometimes argued—in an effort to convince himself—that morality and art have nothing to do with one another. However that might be, I could not help feeling that integrity and art have a great deal.to do with one another. (E. T. [Jessie Chambers] 1935, 204)

The whole problem, clearly, centers on Lawrence's devotion to his mother, and her domination of him:

*Inexorable love!* The fiercely possessive little woman feared and hated the artist-soul in Jessie Chambers, and the intuitive power that stimulated and supported the artisan-soul of David Lawrence. The self of her son which was remote, incomprehensible to her, she denied and rejected. His spirit must be bound within the circle of *her* world, where she might dominate and control it. Jessie, of her very nature, opposed the maternal tyranny. The Lawrence family, revolving unconsciously round the matter, its power-centre, was inimical to Jessie's decentralising influence . . . .
David . . . saw her pitiful and tragic. . . . His utter reaction towards his mother implied revulsion from Jessie Chambers. His mother should remain his eternal love. His wife, since sex must be appeased, should be a girl of simple type, who would never challenge the maternal claim.
"It doesn't matter who one marries," David had insisted to Muriel [Muriel is another name for E. T. or Jessie]. (Corke 1975, 197–98)

At the moment his mother was dying, Lawrence met Louie Burrows and became engaged to her. No doubt she is part of Clara in *Sons and Lovers*, but from all accounts she represented the libidinal partner who would not rival the mother's claim. And, as we now learn, Lawrence's attention was divided among four women. The central question was, which woman rivalled the mother? The problem arises that the woman who was most important to him prompted a sense of doom, because she comes into conflict with the internalized mother. E.T. says, for example, that her sister's final verdict on Lawrence was "He sees the light and chooses the dark." She says, of meeting him at railway station:

> The misery I saw depicted in his face was beyond anything I had ever imagined. Utterly lonely, he looked as if his life had turned to complete negation. His expression at that moment was the direct development of the face that he used to turn towards the dark fields when he would declare, in agony of frustration: *"Nothing matters."* ("E.T." [Jessie Chambers] 1935, 213)

Earlier she records how "below the surface was a hopelessness hardly to be distinguished from despair. He seemed like a man with with a broken mainspring. With all his gifts, he was somehow cut off, unable to attain that complete participation in life that he craved for" ("E.T." [Jessie Chambers] 1935, 199).

Helen Corke records a parallel torment with Lawrence,

> With David I never rest; we are always wondering, exploring, beating out tracks in a spiritual wilderness. Who is the leader, he or I? We urge one another on, we tire each other out, we get mutually weary—he sometimes angry. Out of a dark mood we may dig a sharp crystal of truth, out of a tortuous argument a clear psychological deprivation. He is still *wunderkind* to me. But his tenderness, his rare penetrative sympathy come out to me no more. Always he is asking of me something not mine to give, asking, and knowing at the same time that he is crying for the moon or perhaps only the moon's reflection in water. (Corke 1975. 207)

As we shall see, these latter words are strangely significant.

What was the drive beyond Lawrence's torment, with its destructive impulses at times, recorded so well by these young women who knew him? In *Psychoanalysis and the Unconscious* he utters that *cri de coeur*, "a man finds it impossible to realize himself in marriage. He recognizes the fact that his emotional , even passional, regard for his mother is deeper than it could ever be for a wife" (PU 206) He also wrote, "Nobody can have the soul of me. My mother has it, and nobody can have it again" (Moore, 1962, 70)

In the light of psychoanalytical insights, we must surely find that there was something deeply disturbed in Lawrence's experience of the maternal psychic matrix. One important aspect of this is the problem represented in *Sons and Lovers* by the death of William (transmuted from the death of Ernest in real life.) The pivot of his (Paul's) life was his mother: "William was dead—she would fight to keep Paul" (SL, 230). So one aspect of Paul—Lawrence's life—was being (unconsciously) pressed into the ghostly place left by the dead sibling. Lawrence may have been confused by his mother with his dead brother

Ernest. Certainly there seems no doubt that his mother's overpossessiveness was deepened by the loss of this precious child for whose ghostly nonexistence D.H. felt he had to try to make up. In all this lay the roots of serious existential difficulties, not least about *women* because the formative experience of being mothered was complicated by an urgent need to replace a lost sibling's life, to lift the mother's depression in bereavement, and to recompense for her failure in married love. A number of possibly traumatic experiences seemed to have come together. Mrs. Lawrence, after Ernest's death, lost her gaiety and sat and grieved. Lawrence himself developed a serious pneumonia that permanently damaged his health. Harry T. Moore refers to Lawrence's experience of his mother's bitterness at Ernest's bereaved woman's over-protestations, and also his deep revulsion at an attack on him, just at this time, by a gang of girls in the factory where he worked, who tried to expose him. All these experiences could have deepened a proclivity to associate love and sex with dread, and beneath them, as I believe, is a deeper problem of his mother's idolization of her son.

Certainly "making up a life that has been lost" is, as we shall see, a significant theme in *Sons and Lovers*. Of the mother, the novel say, "The prospect of her life made her feel as if she were being buried alive" (SL, 11) and Paul says in a significant passage,

"Never mind, little, so long as you don't feel life's a paltry and miserly business, the rest doesn't matter, happiness or unhappiness." (SL, 276)

Mrs Morel replies that he should say rather that he wants her "to live," while on his part he prays that *he might not be wasted*. In this we reach to the center of Lawrence's concern that his mother's *life should not be a meaningless waste*. If it were left to be so, his life would be blighted in its turn, a phenomenon of which he speaks clearly (through Somers) in *Kangaroo*.

To try to overcome the problem of the mother's total possessiveness that had so crippled him Lawrence wrote *Sons and Lovers*. Here we have to bear in mind that there was both a conscious purpose to depict the tragedy of his mother's life and to save it from meaninglessness, *and* that there were unconscious elements—to give the mother a fulfilling experience such as she had never had from the father. This, of course, would mean some conflict with the father, though, as we shall see, the Oedipus role is somewhat complicated.

The synopsis from which he wrote *Sons and Lovers* is given clearly in a letter (to Edward Garnett, 14 November 1912, Moore 1962, Vol. 1, 160).

I tell you it has got form—*form:* haven't I made it patiently, out of sweat as well as blood. It follows this idea: a woman of character and refinement goes into the lower class, and has no satisfaction in her own life. She has had a passion for her husband, so the children are born of passion, and have heaps of vitality. But as her sons grow up she selects them as lovers—first the eldest, then the second. These sons are *urged* into life by their reciprocal love of their mother—urged on and on. But when they come to manhood, they can't love, because their mother is the strongest power in their lives, and holds them. It's rather like Goethe and his mother and Frau von Stein and Christiana. As soon as the young men come into contact with women, there's a split. William gives his sex to a fribble, and his mother holds his soul. But the split kills him, because he doesn't know where he is. The next son gets a woman who fights for his soul—fights his mother. The son loves the mother—all the sons hate and are jealous of the father. The battle goes on between the mother and the girl, with the son as object. The mother gradually proves stronger, because of the tie of blood. The son decides to leave his soul in his mother's hands, and, like his elder brother go for passion. He gets passion. Then the split begins to tell again. But, almost unconsciously, the mother realises what is the matter, and begins to die. The son casts off his mistress, attends to his mother dying. He is left in the end naked of everything, with the drift towards death.

It is a great tragedy, and I tell you I have written a great book. It's the tragedy of thousands of young men in Englnad—it may even be Bunny's tragedy. I think it was Ruskin's, and men like him—Now tell me if I haven't worked out my theme, like life, but always my theme. Read my novel. It's good novel. If you can't see the development—which is slow, like growth—I can.

This is the synopsis of the *novel*. In an earlier letter he relates his love-story (to Rachel Annand Taylor, 3 December 1910, Moore 1962, Vol 1, 69):

My mother was a clever, ironical delicately moulded woman of good, old burgher descent. She married below her. My father was dark, ruddy, with a fine laugh. He was a coal miner. He was one of the sanguine temperament, warm and hearty, but unstable: he lacked principle, as my mother would have said. He deceived her and lied to her. She despised him—he drank.

Their married life has been one carnal, bloody fight. I was born hating my father: as early as ever I can remember, I shivered with horror when he touched me. He was very bad before I was born.

This has been a kind of bond between me and my mother. We have loved each other, almost with a husband and wife love, as well as filial and maternal. We knew each other by instinct. She said to my aunt—about me:

"But it has been different with him. He has seemed to be part of me."—And that is the real case. We have been like one, so sensitive to each other that we never needed words. It has been rather terrible and has made me, in some respects, abnormal.

I think this peculiar fusion of soul (don't think me highfalutin) never comes twice in a life-time—it doesn't seem natural. When it comes it seems to distribute one's consciousness far abroad from oneself, and one understands! I think no one has got " understanding" except through love. Now my mother is nearly dead, and I don't quite know how I am.

Perhaps Lawrence meant to write "who I am," but "how I am" can also mean "how I came into being" or "how I am going to maintain a sense that I AM." It would have been useful to have D. W. Winnicott's comments on this amazing passage. There is indeed no path to "understanding" without love—that special kind of love called by Winnicott "primary maternal preoccupation," a schizoid state of extension of the mother's identity—to allow "fusion of soul." The mother does experience the infant as "part of me," while telepathy, speechless communication, is an essential part of this intersubjectivity. How does the mother "know" what her baby wants, since he cannot talk, and crying is no more than a general command for attention? She *knows*—though Lawrence is right, this particular kind of knowing, this particular kind of at-one-ness *does* only come "once in a life-time." Only once in a lifetime is one's consciousness distributed "far abroad from oneself." The mother may experience this several times in a number of confinements, but she experiences it as an adult woman "being for" her infant, and later regaining her "self-interest." If the baby dies, she may experience a schizoid illness, but the baby only experiences the at-one-ness, the other as subjective object, once in a life-time. After that, just as the skull begins to harden immediately after birth, psychologically there is no going back ("Oh I am too big to go backwards," Sylvia Plath, *Poem for a Birthday*).

Because of this, it is serious for a youth and adult to go on yearning for this kind of primary merging long after infancy. Such an individual has never been properly "disillusioned" (to use Winnicott's word) to discover the other as objective object and the self as independent. Here we have indicated a deeper problem than that simply of a dominant mother in love with her son: the problem of symbiosis anxiety, which I have examined above.

Lawrence was partially aware of this disability. To E.T. he said: "I've always loved mother ... I've loved her, like a lover. That's why I could never love you."

There is one very puzzling but also illuminating reference to his similarity to J. M. Barrie in this respect. He wrote to E.T.:

Do read Barrie's *Sentimental Tommy* and *Tommy and Grizel*. I've just had them out of the library here. They'll help you understand how it is with me. I'm in exactly the same predicament. ("E.T." [Jessie Chambers] 1935, 182)

I find *Sentimental Tommy* quite unreadable, but there is a passage in *Tommy and Grizel* that might well at Lawrence addressing "E.T."

Was he a knave? He wanted honestly to know. He had not tried to make her love him. Had he known in time he would even have warned her against it. He would never have said he loved her had she not first, as she thought, found it out; to tell her the truth then would have been brutal; he had made-believe in order that she might remain happy. Was it even make-believe? Assuredly he did love her in his own way. She was far more to him than any other person except Elspeth; he delighted in her and would have fought till he dropped rather than let any human being injure her. He was prepared to marry her, but if she had not made that mistake, oh, what a delight it would have been to him never to marry any one. He felt keenly miserable. He was like a boy who has been told that he must never play again.

"Grizel, I seem to be different from all other men; there seems to be some curse upon me. I want to love you, dear one, you are the only woman I ever wanted to love, but apparently I can't. I have decided to go on with this thing because it seems best for you, but is it? I would tell you all and leave the decision to you were it not that I fear you would think I wanted you to let me off."

... he saw himself a splendidly haggard creature with burning eyes standing aside while all the world rolled by in pursuit of the one thing needful; it was a river and he must stand parched on the bank for ever and ever. (Barrie 1900, 178–80)

Lawrence must have identified with Tommy in this mood—not least with the feeling that "he was like a boy who has been told that he must never play again." His problem was (as we have seen he admits over Birkin) that he was actually unable to love.

Play, as we have seen, is an important component of the developmental process between mother and child: it is the origin of culture and symbolism. In the relationship between man and woman, play develops into the kind of civilized interests shared between Miriam and Paul on the one hand and into love play (as between Beatrice and Paul, or Paul and Clara) on the other. In *Sons and Lovers* Lawrence shows how play "belongs" to the mother, so that for Paul these forms of play are inhibited. (The play with the girls in the famous bread-burning scene leads inevitably to an offense to Mater.)

The mother, in her loving play, is a creative mirror, making "creative reflection" possible. It is also possible for the world to be stripped of its meaning by the failure of creative reflection in these positive dynamics, so that "Nothing matters!"

There is an important moment in *Sons and Lovers* where the moon appears:

An enormous orange moon was staring at them from the rim of the sandhills. He stood still, looking at it.

"Ah!" cried Miriam, when she saw it.

He remained perfectly still, staring at the immense and ruddy moon, the only thing in the far-reaching darkness of the level. His heart beat heavily, the muscles of his arms contracted.

"What is it?" murmured Miriam, waiting for him.

He turned and looked at her. She stood beside him, for ever in shadow. Her face, covered with the darkness of her hat, was watching him unseen. But she was brooding. She was slightly afraid—deeply moved and religious. That was her best state. He was impotent against it. His blood was concentrated like a flame in his chest. But he could not get across to her. There were flashes in his blood. But somehow she ignored them. She was expecting some religious state in him. Still yearning, she was half aware of his passion and gazed at him, troubled.

"What is it?" she murmured again.

"It's the moon," he answered, frowning.

"Yes," she asserted, "Isn't it wonderful."

She was curious about him. The crisis was past. (SL, 193)

The moment is one in which one might expect the man to kiss the woman, but "The fact that he might want her as a man wants a woman had in him been suppressed into a shame." The moon here, I believe, symbolizes the mother's face of bereaved depression, but also of the despair of ever becoming fulfilled and meaningful if the son "betrays" her: the face of destructive envy. The moon mother, suddenly appearing like this, has a paralyzing effect on

Paul Morel. Significantly, the girl's face is blank, too ("Her face, covered with the darkness of her hat, was watching him unseen"). She is in her "best state" of a passionate mysterious awe, yet he "cannot get across to her." Often in Lawrence the light of the moon is not benign love but a powerful sterility, menacing.

This moon symbolizes Lawrence's deepest fears that the malignant aspects of the internalized mother, her denial of his creative relationship with the world by her possessive destructiveness, will annihilate him. Significantly, the moon is also powerfully there in the earlier scene when Mrs. Morel is locked out. The world of the flowers in the moonlight seems another world than that of her marital domesticity, and it is this world her son wants to give her, the world of mysterious beauty, as in the sexuality of the lilies *yet with this aspiration he is involved in his doom.* "She is in me," and until he has redeemed her, he cannot begin to live in a fulfilled way because he is still "part of her."

Lawrence has, as I have said above, an amazing awareness of his own doom. He delineates it in *Sons and Lovers.* Helen Corke echoes his "inexorable love." She observed that what Mrs. Lawrence was mainly concerned to do was to maintain her possession of the *artistic* influence over Lawrence. Mrs. Lawrence envied the female element creativity both in Jessie Chambers and in Lawrence himself. She quotes:

Ever at my side,
Frail and sad, with grey, bowed head,
The beggar woman, the yearning-eyed,
Inexorable love goes lagging. (CP, 62)

Yet Lawrence is able to depict this inexorable love, with its double bind:

"No mother—I really *don't* love her. I talk to her, but I want to come home to you."

He had taken off his collar and tie, and rose, bare-throated, to go to bed. As he stooped to kiss this mother, she threw her arms round his neck, hid her face on his shoulder, and cried, in a whimpering voice, so unlike her own that he writhed in agony:

"I can't bear it. I could let another woman—but not her. She'd leave me no room, not a bit of room—"

And immediately he hated Miriam bitterly.

"And I've never—you know, Paul—I've never had a husband—not really—"

He stroked his mother's hair, and his mouth was on her throat. (SL, 229)

Then, a few moments later, she says, "Perhaps I'm selfish. If you want her, take her, by boy." Since she had destroyed his affection for Miriam by emotional blackmail, this clinches the double bind.

Lawrence's fantasy impulse, which he turned into his art, was to give his mother a good husband, a good sensual experience, and this lies at the heart of his sexual programe. But what we might call the "true self" in him and in

Paul Morel deeply resents the inauthenticity of his role. He is angry at the difference in ages. In the quarrel over Miriam, Paul bursts out,

> "You're old, mother, and we're young." He only meant that the interests of *her* age were not the interests of his. But he realized the moment he had spoken that he had said the wrong thing. (SL, 228)

Lawrence can even be lightly ironic here. Paul says comically in his portentous adolescent way, "You don't care about Herbert Spencer." Later the resentment in Paul Morel breaks out in a way that is both more poignant and psychopathological. We hear the anguish of the man who is still relating to his mother as an infant, and wants to keep her (as an infant does) "his," without any recognition of the difference in-generations:

> "Why can't a man have a *young* mother?' What is she old for?..."
> "What are you old for?" he said, mad with impotence. "*Why* can't you walk, Why don't you come with me to places?"

When she cannot walk up a hill, "he wanted to cry, he wanted to smash things in fury."

Such insistent feelings ("all the time" he was "wanting to rage and smash things and cry") surely belong to a failure to become properly "disillusioned," to find and accept reality?

All through *Sons and Lovers* Mrs. Morel plays with her son like a lover, Lawrence says, but in fact more like a mother with her infant. At first, she is in love with her baby:

> She had dreaded this baby like a catastrophe, because of her feelings for her husband. And now she felt strangely towards the infant... she had not wanted this child to come, and there it lay in her arms and pulled at her heart. She felt as if the navel string that had connected its frail little body with hers and not been broken... with all her force, with all her soul she would make up to it for having brought it into the world unloved. (SL, 44–45)

Holding up the child to the sunset,

> She saw him lift his little fist. Then she put him to her bosom again, ashamed almost of her impulse to give him back again whence he came. (SL, 45)

So, this child, whom she calls Paul, came from heaven and has a special messianic purpose for her: he is a god.

When she takes him to his first job, "She was gay, like a sweetheart" (SL 103). She has for him "a rare intimate smile, beautiful with brightness and love" (SL, 104). She teaches her son, by *play and charm*, to see the world with a creative glow, as in the charming passages about the black grapes and the fuchias, on one of their expeditions. His mother here is shown teaching her son to see the world. She reflected his creative powers:

> Mrs. Morel clung to Paul. He was quiet and not now brilliant. But until he stuck to his painting, and still he stuck to his mother. *Everything he did was for her.* She waited for his coming home in the evening and then she unburdened herself of all she had pondered, and of all that had occurred to her in the day. He sat and listened with his earnestness. The two shared lives. (SL, 127; my italics)

He responds to the way she dresses like a sweetheart.

> Suddenly she appeared in the inner doorway rather shyly. She got a new cotton blouse on. Paul jumped up and went forward.
> "Oh, my stars?" he exclaimed. "What a bobby-dazzler?"
> She sniffed in a little haughty way, and put her head up.
> "It's not a bobby-dazzler at all!" she replied. "It's very quiet...."
> "...do you like it?"
> "Awfully! you *are* a fine little woman to go jaunting out with...."
> "Too young for me, though, I'm afraid," she said.
> "Too young for you!" he exclaimed in disgust. "Why don't you buy some false white hair and stick it on your head." (SL 135)

These exchanges might seem sickly and morbid were is not that we, too, are charmed by this boy and girl play between son and mother. And there are the positive aspects of the tenderness between them: "I've never had a glory of the snow in my garden in my life...she was full of excitement and elation... The garden was an endless joy to her." (SL, 179)

We are made aware by Lawrence, however, of the consequences of this closeness between them. First, there is the inevitable denial of sex. In one sense "his mouth was on her throat," and in another "he took ease of her." The tenderness between mother and son takes bodily form appropriate to infant-mother relationship. It is perhaps better called sensual, it is not sexual, but it could preempt sexuality. I am not quite sure what "he took ease of her" means. Some believe it refers to a form of masturbation. But there is an element in it, certainly, of a sexual relationship between the mother and the idolized image that she has made of him—a phenomenon which I discussed above (p. 36). Mrs. Morel speaks of sexual love as "disgusting ... bits of lads and girls courting," and her jealousy of Paul's adolescent sexual yearnings is evident.

Any other woman as the object of love must not be libidinal: that would be an offense to mother. She must not usurp the mother's role of play. Attention to lovely things in nature was something his mother taught him, and this is her exclusive purlieu. Miriam has the impulse to go into ecstasies over a wild rose or other flowers, but in this the usurps the mother's function, and so must be criticized. "Why do you always gloat on things so?" she is asked. ("He hated her as she posed over things" [SL, 313].) Miriam also intrudes on the inspirational role. "I can do my best things when you sit there in your rocking chair, mother," says Paul. "From his mother he drew out the strength to produce: Miriam urged this warmth into intensity." The mother's response to this is "she will suck a man's soul out." So, Paul tells Miriam, "It's so damned spiritual with you" (SL, 203). The role of ideal object has been appropriated exclusively by the mother.

"The pivot of his life was his mother," and at the deepest level this was a central issue of meaning in life.

The problem is discussed between mother and son in the chapter "Clara" (SL, 275–76). In this, Lawrence rejects the goal of happiness. It is for happiness that people strive in our hedonistic society, and this is not enough:

> "My boy," said his mother to him, "all your cleverness, your breaking away from old things, and taking life in your own hands, doesn't seem to bring you much happiness."
> "What is happiness," he cried. "It's nothing to me! How *am* I to be happy?" (SL, 275)

The mother goes on, "But you could meet some good woman who would *make* you happy." But the mother has shown herself resistant both to his relationship with the "artistic" Miriam and the libidinal women like Clara. He says "His mother caught him on the raw of his wound of Miriam." He rejects her goal of "mass of soul and physical comfort" and says he despises it: "Damn your happiness."

But his mother protests that he *ought* to be happy: "One *ought* to be happy, one *ought*." One may see in this her unconscious guilt that her son's anguish is in some measure due to her exploitation of him by making him into the lover her husband never was. Lawrence, however, sees this as the mother struggling to claim the son for "life":

> By this time Mrs. Morel was trembling violently. Struggles of this kind often took place between her and her son, *when she seemed to fight for his very life against his own will to die.* He took her in his arms. She was ill and pitiful. (SL, 276; my italics)

Leavis commends Lawrence for his courage in this book at expressing the overpossessiveness of the mother, but here Lawrence shows himself unable to escape from the double bind that makes it seem that the mother's possessiveness, which (as is clear even from the novel) denied Paul's independent life seriously, and is really life-promoting, as she disguises it. Paul Morel falls into her demand to redeem her life.

> "Never mind little," he murmured. "So long as you don't feel life's paltry and a miserable business, the rest doesn't matter, happiness or unhappiness."
> She pressed him to her.
> "But I want you to be happy," she said pathetically.
> "Oh, my dear—say rather you want me to live." (SL, 276)

In this scene we can see how much Lawrence accepted his mother's view of the reality. The difficulties and torment Paul suffers are clearly caused by his entanglement with his mother, but not only is Mrs. Morel seen to be clearly attributing them to Miriam, Lawrence himself blames her!

> Mrs. Morel felt as if her heart would break for him. At this rate she knew he would not live. He had that poignant carelessness about himself, his own suffering his own life, which is a form of slow suicide. It almost broke her heart. With all the passion of her strong nature, she hated Miriam for having in her subtle way undermined his joy. It did not matter to her that Miriam could not help it. Miriam did it, and she hated her.
>     She wished so much he would fall in love with a girl equal to be his mate—educated and strong.... He seemed to like Mrs. Dawes. At any rate that feeling was wholesome. His mother played and prayed for him, *that he might not be wasted.* (SL, 276; my italics)

Lawrence is only partially able to "place" Mrs. Morel's attitudes. In the *Letters*, as we have seen, he attributes her overpossessiveness to her loss of William: "She could not bear it when he was with Miriam. William was dead. She would fight to keep Paul" (239).

It is also clear that there is an egocentric element in Mrs. Morel's dominance that is a perversion of love. She uses the primacy of the mother's love to enslave her son. The next paragraph begins:

> And he came back to her. And in his soul was a feeling of the satisfaction of self-sacrifice because he was faithful to her. She loved him first; he loved her first. And yet it was not enough. His new young life, so strong and imperious, was urged towards something else. It made him mad with restlessness. She saw this, and wished bitterly that Miriam had been a woman who could take this new life of his, and leave her the roots. He fought against his mother almost as he fought against Miriam. (SL, 239)

Mrs. Morel demands the impossible: that she be left with her infant son (the "roots") while the woman has the adult son. Interpreted, this means she is unwilling to allow the man to have his adult freedom at all—his authenticity. This authenticity, denied, not only leaves Paul with a feeling "urged towards something else," but has a consequent effect on Lawrence's other main characters—like Birkin at the end of *Women in Love* with whom he identifies. It is *Lawrence* who is "urged towards something else," and this "something else" is a meaningful existence that is not undermined by the crippling polarity of his soul toward possession by the mother of its primary life. This yearning makes the most of his protagonists still unsatisfied at the ends of his novels.

The mother tried to get from her son her "rights" to a fulfilled life, as is made clear in "The Young Life of Paul," and she does this out of bitterness and despair. Paul watches his mother ironing:

> Her still face, with the mouth closed tight from suffering and disillusion and self-denial, and her nose the smallest bit on one side, and her blue eyes so young, quick and warm, made his heart contract with love. When she was quiet, so, she looked brave and rich with life, but *as if she had been done out of her rights*. It hurt the

boy keenly, this feeling about her that *she had never had her life's fulfillment:* and his own incapability to make up to her hurt him with a sense of impotence, yet made him patiently dogged inside. *It was his childish aim.* (SL, 76; my italics)

The child's ambition to make his mother's life good is appropriate. It belongs to the oedipal pattern whereby the son learns to relate to woman on his way to adult potentiality—dislodging the father in fantasy, and taking his place. Later, normally, the son finds he can take his father's place, but with another woman, who, because she is free and young, can really relate to him, in the way he seeks as the mother cannot. In Lawrence's *Sons and Lovers*, there is a strange inappropriateness in the physical gestures ("his mouth was on her throat") since they are not normal huggings. They seem body-gestures more appropriate to breast-feeding in infancy; but neither are they adult sexuality ("he took ease of her"). It is a confusion of all three: "Her breast was there, warm for him...she pressed him to her breast, rocked him, soothed him like a child." (SL, 400). This confusion in the area of body-intimacy drove Lawrence to explore such intimacy so compulsively in his writing.

In fantasy, Lawrence sought to give his mother the kind of rich sensual experience she complained of never having had (Mrs. Morel, "I've never had a husband not really"). Then, when writing about the courtship of this parents, he writes:

the dusky-golden softness of this man's sensuous flame of life, that flowed off his flesh like the flame from a candle, now baffled and gripped into incandescence by thought and spirit as her life was, seemed to her something wonderful, beyond her. (SL, 16)

The image of the candle is important. In the poem *All Souls* he writes a memorial poem to the dead mother, and the candles burnt on All Souls Day bring him to declare that he will burn a candle to her memory:

Those villages isolated at the grave
Where the candles burn in the daylight...

The naked candles burn on every grave
On your grave, in England, the weeds grow.

But I am your naked candle burning,
And that is not your grave, in England,
The world is your grave.

And my naked body standing on your grave
Upright towards heaven is burning off to you
Its flame of life, now and always, till end

       *     *     *

I am a naked candle burning on your grave. (CP, 233)

This is surely an extraordinary poem for a man to write on his honeymoon, for it conveys the impression that he feels his own phallic potency is an attempt to give the dead woman meaning to her life. His "burning" is

a flame that goes up
To the other world, where you are now.

So, we may see Lawrence's whole emphasis on "body knowledge" as a tribute to his mother, related to his ambition to give her life meaning by giving her the libidinal experience she lacked. As with his extrapolation from his own sexual experience into a political program in *Manifesto*, this became a program. Note, "I conceive a man's body as a kind of flame, like a candle flame, forever upright and yet flaming." Here we need to quote the whole passage, part of which has been quoted above:

My great religion is a belief in the blood, the flesh, as being wiser than the intellect. We can go wrong in our minds. But what our blood feels and believes and says, is always true. The intellect is only a bit and a bridle. What do I care about knowledge. All I want is the answer to my blood, direct without fribbling intervention of mind, or moral, or what-not. I conceive a man's body as a kind of flame, like a candle flame, forever upright and yet flowing: and the intellect is just the light that is shed on to the things around. But I am not so much concerned with the things around— which is really mind,—but with the mystery of the flame forever flowing, coming God knows how from out of practically nowhere, and being itself, whatever there is around it, that it lights up. We have got so ridiculously mindful, that we never know that we ourselves are anything—we think there are only the objects we shine upon. And there the poor flame goes on burning ignored, to produce this light. And instead of chasing the mystery in the fugitive, half-lighted things outside me, we ought to look at ourselves, and say "My God, I am myself!" That is why I like to live in Italy. The people are so unconscious. They only feel and want: they don't know. We know too much. No, we only *think* we know such a lot. A flame isn't a flame because it lights up two, or twenty objects on a table. It's a flame because it is itself. And we have forgotten ourselves. We are Hamlet without the Prince of Denmark. We cannot be. "To be or not to be"—it is the question with us now, by love. And nearly every Englishman says "Not to be." So he goes in for Humanitarianism and suchlike forms of not-being. The real way of living is to answer to one's wants. Not "I want to light up with my intelligence as many things as possible" but "For the living of my full flame—I want that liberty, I want that woman, I want that pound of peaches, I want to go to sleep, I want to go to the pub and have a good time, I want to look a beastly swell today, I want to kiss that girl, I want to insult that man." Instead of that, all these wants, which are there whether-or-not, are utterly ignored, and we talk about some sort of ideas. I'm like Carlyle, who, they say, wrote 50 volumes of the value of silence. *Letters*, ed Huxley, 1932, 94–95. (17 Jan. 1913—the year in which *Sons and Lovers* appeared).

This is a highly revealing passage in full. Ostensibly it is on the value of not being explicit and not trying to live merely at the level of intellectual knowing. It is true that we need to cultivate "being" and the deeper levels of awareness and wisdom, but is the intellect such an enemy? And what about intelligence and the true self with its need for meaning?

If we ask these questions, we may begin to see where Lawrence went wrong. Lawrence says Mrs. Morel was a puritan, in whom the sensual life was "baffled and gripped into incandescence by thought or spirit." The urge to give the mother a sensual richness she never knew, as by that "candle flame" of a "man's body" is set against the intellect and will he felt to be inimical. I believe his opposition to these has behind it his experience as an infant of her "impingement," her intrusive way of dealing with him, and the polarity she directed at him to compensate for the failure of her sexual life, as well as the loss of a sibling and her idolization of him.

This resistance may be linked with the philosophical "model" he adopts here. If "the real way of living is to answer to one's wants" then this suggests that our primary needs are instinctual, as Freud saw them. It is as well to be aware of one's sensual and other hungers, but what later psychoanalysis seems to have discovered is that the satisfaction of "wants" does not bring satisfaction. Rather it demands a sense of meaning. By this light "to light up with my intelligence as many things as possible" *is* a more primary need than "living the full flame" in the kind of terms Lawrence uses. Of course, Lawrence himself did illuminate many things with his intelligence, but he has the urge he displays here to throw off "puritanism" because he associated it with his mother's coldness—that coldness the widow reflects upon at the end of *Odour of Chrysanthemums*, which had blighted her sexual fulfillment. The impulse also led Lawrence to embrace the cult of sensuality in the attitudes of the German sexual revolution to our needs. As we shall see, it hooked into his psychopathology.

Later we shall have to look at what Lawrence meant by "touch" and "manhood." Throughout his work Lawrence displays an urgent feeling that woman needed a certain kind of assertive male, and in this we find out a great deal about Lawrence's positive feelings about his father despite his declaration that he was born hating him. His love for his father surfaces, and Lawrence often reveals a gratitude for the male presence as, in *Lady Chatterley*, or Mrs. Bolton's talk of the "touch of a man," and in *Sons and Lovers*, when Mrs. Radford says,

"A house of women is as dead as a house wi' no fire, to my thinkin' . . . I like a man about, if only he's something to snap at." (SL, 278)

What is significant is that Lawrence associated a certain way of talking with male sexual attention, for when Paul is successful in libidinal sexuality, he *talks like his father*.[4] Morel talks to his wife in that vernacular, joking, teasingly tender manner Lawrence associates (in *Lady Chatterley*) with *male play:*

"Oh, tha' mucky little 'ussy, who's drunk I sh'd like ter know? . . . Shouldn't ter like it?" he asked tenderly, "Appen not, it 'ud dirty thee . . . ."
She had never been "thee'd" and "thou'd" before (SL, 17)

This is how Paul talks to Clara, after making love to her by the river.

> "But thea shouldna worrit!" he said softly pleading.
> "...And now I'll clean my boots and make thee fit for respectable folk." (SL, 332–33)

The use of the father's vernacular is a further indication that in his creative fiction Lawrence seeks symbolically to give his mother meaningful fulfillment by entering into the image of the father, and making love to the mother. His purpose is to make good the mother, and in this there is a powerful impulse to *mold* the mother, that is, in the spirit of his remarks above, to *form* the woman. The young Paul Morel bursts out with fury, belaboring the mother because she is not as he would have her to be, young, and able to relate to him, so, this controlling element remained as a powerful element in Lawrence's attitudes to women. To want a "soul union" as Miriam does threatens possessiveness like the mother's in this sphere, where she exerts her "inexorable love" against the man's creativity. Thus, Paul declared of Miriam, "I want a woman to keep me but not in her pocket." From this derives the stern imposition of control on woman, as in *The Captain's Doll* and *The Plumed Serpent*.

If the woman becomes too libidinal on the other hand, this becomes too much of a threat because it seems to be a betrayal of the mother, who never had that experience. Lawrence is well aware of the effect of death on sex. As his mother is dying Paul goes to Clara for soothing sexual relief.

> "Take me!" he said simply. Occasionally she would. But she was afraid. When he had her then, there was something in it that made her shrink away from him—something unnatural....
> She was afraid of the man who was not there with her, whom she could feel behind this make-believe lover; somebody sinister, that filled her with horror.... He wanted her—he had her—and it made her feel as if death itself had her in its grip. She lay in horror. (SL, 411)

Paul wants from her the comfort, appropriate to a child, he can no longer get from the mother, so Clara takes a ghost, the infant Paul, while the adult man is away, polarized in his grief toward the problem of nothingness.

In both kinds of love, Lawrence therefore discriminates against the woman The woman must be formed and taught how she is to relate to him, how to find him. Lawrence wanted to believe that "love...is the high-water mark of living." He wanted to overcome the old traditional view put forward by Clara's mother: "There is one thing in marriage that is always dreadful but you have to bear it"—and in many respects he did, but the problems are more intractable than he allowed. Therefore, Lawrence is bedeviled by the conscious cry, "I don't want another mother," while being compelled to see all his human relationships as being in competition with the mother, and the sexuality of her son with her death—with the implication that if she dies because of his disloyalty he will be sorry and that will spoil his relationships. When Paul squares up to his father, she becomes more seriously ill, and this draws him even closer into the oedipal net. Paul, like Hamlet, actually asks her not to go to bed with her husband.

Play with Miriam is more serious: it takes the form of the admiration of the wild rose in the dark. But this is too much like Mrs. Morel's worship of the lilies in the mysterious moonlit world when the father shuts her out in the backyard. When it comes to sex, therefore, Miriam is (according to Lawrence) passive, a sacrificial victim, and "clenched." Sex is a death:

> she lay to be sacrificed for him . . . why the dull pain in his soul . . . why did the thought of death, the afterlife, seems so sweet and consoling. (SL, 310)

E.T. gives a different version of the real events. It was she who was ready and willing for a "full relationship." It is possible, I believe, to see how distorted Lawrence's account is by reading *Sons and Lovers* closely. Paul gives Miriam little or no consideration for the difficulties of the initial stages of a sexual relationship, and for the effect of the anxieties of not being married. (By contrast in his letters, Lawrence is often deeply anxious about what people think of his affair with Frieda.) Clearly, Paul's girl would have been anxious to a degree that would inhibit sexual relationships. Miriam protests that "it would come alright if we were married." But it is not, and she is "clenched." Paul concludes, "It had always been a failure between them" and "it would never be a success between them." (SL, 312)

One wonders what Lawrence meant by his hints about the sexual experience here. Is it simply that the woman could not relax at all or that she suffered from a form of vaginismus? Some say the episode is a classical study of female frigidity.

From poems like *Manifesto* and from *Lady Chatterley*, however, one suspects that Paul–Lawrence was so busy discriminating against the woman (trying to make sure *she* responded properly to *him*) that he exerted an aura over the sexual act in which relaxation was impossible. Since his sexual acts have a therapeutic purpose directed at redeeming the mother, he seems unable ever to really concern himself with the arousing, satisfying, and fulfilling of the woman's needs. He is more interested in power of a kind, rather than making love, and yet his attitude to relationships remain infantile.

Miriam says, "It has failed because you want something else," and Lawrence says, "He was a baby" (SL, 319).

Paul discriminates against Clara in a different way. For him, "sex is the culmination of everything." He idolizes it:

> "All our intimacy culminates there.
> "Not for me," she said.
> He was silent. A flash of hate for her came up. (SL, 386)

She goes on to say she hasn't *got* all of him, and "is it *me* you want, or is it *It?*"

> "If I start to make love to you," he said, "I just go like a leaf on the wind."
> "And leave me out of count," she said.
> "And then is it nothing to you?" he asked, almost rigid with chagrin.
> "It's something, and sometimes you have carried me away—right away—I know—and—I reverence you for it—but—" "Don't 'but' me," he said. (SL, 387)

Once they had experienced great heights of togetherness ("when the peewits had called"), Paul experiences feelings as if he and Clara "were licked up in an immense tongue of flame." The passage of self-revelation indicates a one-sidedness, and this, in turn, reveals the reason for Lawrence's treadmill of obsession with sexual performance.

> Gradually, some mechanical effort spoilt their loving, or, when they had splendid moments, they had them separately, and not so satisfactorily. So often he seemed merely to be running on alone. . . . Their loving grew more mechanical. . . . Gradually they began to introduce novelties. (SL, 387)

They loved near the river bank where people would pass. "And afterwards each of them was rather ashamed." What Lawrence is indicating, whether he realized it or not, was a movement into forms of perverted sex, to seek to overcome feelings of inadequacy, the inner dread associated with sexual love. As we shall see, he went further along this path, and one of the elements in his tendency towards perversion is that, as here, of *risk* (see also the end of *John Thomas and Lady Jane*.) Significantly, after this tormented failure, the next scene is Paul's dreadful fight with Dawes, which leads, ultimately, to a strange sense of blood-bond between them: even such conflict with its homosexual undercurrents is "safer."

The failure with Clara is surely related to two common Lawrentian demands: one, that the woman must provide some cosmic satisfaction and confirmation, and then extend this to demand a cosmic or religious satisfaction from the woman who now must take the place of God. Clara and Paul make love "to know their own nothingness." "It was almost their belief in life." They become "blind agents of a great force" (SL, 377), but then he discovers that it doesn't mean as much to her as to him—indeed, hardly anything, because he has not learned to love her, to find her, and to enrich *her* life.

Clara, according to E.T., is a clever adaptation of three people (1935, 202): "the compensation is unreal and illusory." Anyone knowing Lawrence's work can detect how it is well on the way to *Lady Chatterley* and how much it is falsified.

We need to preserve, in the face of Lawrence's falsification, the recognition that man's primary needs are for love ("meeting") and meaning. We feel authenticity when we read: "They preferred themselves to suffer the misery of celibacy, rather than risk the other person'' (SL 297). He is at his best in giving us the phenomenological record of the experience of life—as in the great scenes of *Sons and Lovers*—Mrs. Morel shut out; the baking of the bread; making love to Clara by the river; Mrs. Morel's death.

But the bewilderment over woman and sex in this novel is profound, and Lawrence is not able to find any way out, only inadequate alternatives. Perhaps in this respect it has a tragic quality, like *Odour of Chrysanthemums*, even in Paul Morel's dark confusion at the end?

# 2

# True and False Solutions in the Short Stories

In the stories we find both some of Lawrence greatest art and some of his worst falsifications.

## Odour of Chrysanthemums

Lawrence's *Odour of Chrysanthemums* must surely be the masterpiece among his short stories? All the best qualities of his art are to be found in it, and all are brought to bear on a tragic question of the meaning of life, raised by the invocation of death.

At the same time, the story takes us into the deepest of Lawrence's preoccupations—the meaninglessness of the parents' sexual lives, and the problem of what woman may do to man.

The story opens with sharply realized detail: there is a symbolic counterpoint all the way through, between *engines* and *life*. "The small locomotive engine, Number 4, came clanking, stumbling down from Selston with seven full wagons." (SS, 184) The machine world is mechanical and arithmetical (Number 4, seven wagons). By contrast, the living things are mysterious—the gorse flickers indistinctly, the colt is startled. The story is richly poetic, and this opening paragraph strikes the contrast between the rhythms and modes of natural life and man-made mechanisms, culminating in

> The two wheels were spinning fast up against the sky, and the winding-engine rapped out its little spasms. The miners were being turned up. (SS, 184)

This winding engine sounds all the way through the story, as it must have done all through Lawrence's life in Eastwood. Its noises are heard even inside the houses, and they are signs. The colliery families listen to these sounds, which not only tell them the time of day, shift-times and so on, but also whether there is an emergency or an accident. The noises of mining run like an ostinato bass throughout the story.

The contrast evoked by the opening is parallel to that in the opening pages of *The Rainbow:* between the life of the rural countryside, and the industrial modes imposed upon it. The pit and railway are male spheres; the animals, the trees and shrubs, the flowers, and the child in the woman's womb, all belong to the female.

In the pit world there is a menace, as to the living flesh:

> The pit-bank loomed up beyond the pond, flames like red sores licking its ashy sides, in the afternoon's stagnant lights. (SS, 184)

At the same time, there is a menace in the natural world, and so a tension grows beneath the surface of the scene:

> A large bony vine clutched at the house, *as if to claw down the tiled roof* . . . the child showed himself before the raspberry canes that rose *like whips.* (SS, 184–85; my italics)

These are only touches, but they introduce a note of pain, while there are other signs of life being blighted:

> Round the bricked yard grew a few wintry primroses. . . . Beside the path hung dishevelled pink chrysanthemums, like pink cloths hung on bushes . . . he tore at the ragged wisps of chrysanthemums and dropped the handfuls along the path. (SS, 185)

We may recall the moment in *Sons and Lovers* when Mrs. Morel is locked out by her husband, and touches the white flowers in the moonlight. There they symbolize a fulfillment of being which she is denied: a beauty, a mystery, a potentiality, for which she yearns, and her touch is a touch on the phallic, in that sense. In *Odour of Chrysanthemums*, the woman's creativity (we gradually learn she is pregnant) is seen in the context of a flowering nature that has become wintry, ragged, and even sinister, by the sooty hand of industry.

It is this contrast that gives the setting to the conversation between Elizabeth Bates and her father. He is getting married again, for comfort. Both reflect on Elizabeth's husband's alcoholic "bouts": "it's a nice thing, when a man can do nothing with his money but make a beast of himself." In the exchange are implicit values of decency, and it is clear that Walter's offenses are grave. "It's a settler, it is—." From the exchange and the scene, we begin to feel that something is seriously wrong, that the characters cannot understand. The consequences are visible in the odd look of the child's clothes:

> He was dressed in trousers and waistcoat of cloth that was too thick and hard for the size of the garment. They were evidently cut down from a man's clothes. (SS, 185)

The pit is the center of the community, and outside the red sores of the spoil fires dominate the scene, along with the spinning headstock. Indoors, the fire dominates, burning the coal the miner hews:

All the life of the room seemed in the white, warm hearth and the steel fender reflecting the red fire. The cloth was laid for tea; cups glinted in the shadows. (SS, 187)

In the domestic scene, the child shows his mother's qualities in his "silence and pertinacity" as he whittles a piece of wood. In his "indifference to all but himself," his mother sees the father. She "seemed to be occupied by her husband." There is a tense contrast between the warm and glowing domestic scene, with the potatoes cooking and then being drained into a drain in the yard, and the failure of the man to come home, among the "sombre groups" in the street.

The little girl enters with "a mass of curls, just ripening from gold to brown." The tender presentation of the children above whose heads the drama is enacted is deeply moving. The figures are so clearly seen. The mother is "a tall woman of imperious mien, handsome, with definite black eyebrows. Her smooth black hair was parted exactly." (SS, 185), But, "Her face was calm and set, her mouth was closed with disillusionment." (SS, 185) In the disillusionment there is the antipathy to joy that seems so much the habit of the people of the industrial Midlands:

The girl crouched against the fender slowly moving a thick piece of bread before the fire. The lad, his face a dusky mark on the shadow, sat watching her who was transfigured in the red glow.
"I do think it's beautiful to look in the fire," said the child.
"Do you?" said her mother. "Why?"
"It's so red, and full of little caves—and it feels so nice, and you can fair smell it."
"It'll want mending directly," replied her mother, "and then if your father comes he'll carry on and say there never is a fire when a man comes home sweating from the pit. A public-house is always warm enough." (SS, 188)

When the man is brought home dead, he is still warm from the heat underground, yet we learn from the mother's somewhat bitter remarks that he has taken to drink because he finds a comfort and warmth in the pub that she has failed to provide at home. This is the child's sense of beauty and comfort: the woman deprived of her own fulfillment is incapable of poetry. Darkness falls on the room, and as the mother reaches up at last to light the lamp, we see her just "rounding with maternity":

"You've got a flower in your apron?" said the child, in a little rapture at this unusual event.
"Goodness me!" exclaimed the woman, relieved. "One would think the house was afire." (SS, 189)

The darkness and the lamplight evoke their tension: "The light revealed their suspense so that the woman felt it almost unbearable." Something has gone wrong, and it is either the father likely to be brought home dead drunk or something worse. The fire, the light, and the flower suggest subtly the human life that has promise, but which is limited and cramped by this life of poverty and danger, and of privations of the emotions and spirit. The child puts the pale chrysanthemums to her lips and murmurs."Don't they smell beautiful!" The mother gives a short laugh and says,

"No . . . not to me. It was chrysanthemums when I married him, and chrysanthemums when you were born, and the first time they ever brought him home drunk, he'd got brown chrysanthemums in his button-hole." (SS, 189)

She is telling them that the marriage is meaningless, and they sit "wondering." We may assume that the story is written by a man who, as a child, heard often from his mother that her sexual life was meaningless, and by such hints so, too, was his birth. The chrysanthemums become a symbol of symbols gone meaningless, too.

Bitterly ironical is Elizabeth Bates's next outburst

"Eh, he'll not come now till they bring him. There he'll stick! But he needn't come rolling in here in his pit-dirt, for *I* won't wash him. He can lie on the floor . . . (SS, 190)

It is *death* that is to oblige her to wash him, and the decent rituals of the mining community. Even as she condemns her man, she makes him a "singlet" of flannel that "gave a dull wounded sound as she tore off the grey edge." (SS, 196)

What she listens for now is *footsteps* and *voices*. And "her anger was tinged with fear." She goes over to Mrs. Ryley's, where she observes the mess in the kitchen with disapproval. On the floor are twelve shoes: six children! "No wonder!" Mrs. Bates sighs to herself. Ryley has left Walter "finishing a stint":

He stood perplexed, as if answering a charge of deserting his mate. Elizabeth Bates, now certain of disaster, hastened to reassure him. (SS, p193)

Now, it begins to seem a *relief* if Bates were to be found in the pub, dead drunk or not. She hears Mrs. Ryley run across the yard and open her neighbour's door: "suddenly all the blood in her body seemed to switch away from her heart." From now on, we follow closely the pangs in the woman's heart and body, as she responds to the sounds, of voices, of feet, of the pit-engine, and at last the sight of her dead husband.

She was startled by the rapid chuff of the winding-engine at the pit, and the sharp whirr of the brakes on the rope as it descended. Again she felt the painful sweep of her blood, and she put her hand to her side, saying aloud, "Good gracious!—it's only the nine o'clock deputy going down," rebuking herself. (SS, 193)

In this story, one is powerfully reminded that Lawrence was a coal-miner's son; his life is soaked in the pit lore and its modes of consciousness.

With marvelous subtlety (a subtlety that has learnt much from Dickens), the dire news of Walter's accident is brought by the silly old mother, who merely says, "Eh, Lizzie, whatever shall we do, whatever shall we do!" (SS, 194). The old woman is presented with great dignity and poignancy. She dare not say the truth, but wails at it obliquely. The wife has to utter it, with superb courage:

> "Is he dead?" she asked, and at the words her heart swung violently, though she felt a slight flush of shame at the ultimate extravagance of the question. Her words sufficiently frightened the old lady, almost brought her to herself. (SS, 194)

Ryley has sent her to prepare Elizabeth.

At once, the woman thinks of her future: "If he was killed—would she be able to manage on the little pension and what she could earn?—she counted up rapidly" (SS, 194–95). If he was hurt—how tiresome he would be to nurse, but perhaps it would keep him from the drink. "But what sentimental luxury was this she was beginning?" The story is written with a stark and unflinching realism.

The old woman is already maudlin about the lad she brought up: "He was a jolly enough lad wi' me." She has a sense of guilt about how he has gone wrong: "I don't know how it is." The impending news of his death is like a judgment that gets the next-of-kin reconsidering their relationship to the man, and estimating his life. Behind these ruminations they hear the pit engine with a new and strange sound. And the news of the death comes with blunt suddenness:

> "The doctor says 'e'd been dead hours. . . ."

The man has not been broken: the rock fall "'niver touched 'im,"

> "'E wor smothered!"

Lawrence manages here to use the vernacular with serious dramatic power. It is not exaggerated to call his language Shakespearean because it is used with the same respect for humanness, the same dignity and sense of pity, with no touch of the impulse to patronize or guy. One would say, on the strength of this story, that Lawrence *loved* his colliery people. How did it happen, in his later work, that he came to find them "carrion bodied"?

The widow contemplates the room where the body will be laid. There are two vases holding chrysanthemums: "There was a cold, deathly smell of chrysanthemums in the room." She fetches an old tablecloth and another cloth, to save her bit of carpet, and then she fetches a clean shirt, and *puts it to the fire to air*. This last is perhaps the most touching point in the whole story. Lawrence's careful description of the simple steps Elizabeth Bates takes, toward the last provision for her husband, evokes a whole working class tradition of decent attention to the dead in a community all too used to sudden death and injury. Again, she hears the noise of feet, as the men, stumbling, bring the body. The first she sees of her dead husband is his "nailed pit-boots."

The scene is described with painful exactness: the men knock over a flower-vase and the wife has to mop the water up. The pit manager retells what happened, so that the "horror of the thing bristled upon them all." The children wake and have to be firmly suppressed; the most disruptive noise is the foolish old mother moaning and wailing. The men tiptoe away, and do not speak until they are out of earshot of the wakeful children—who are, of course, supposing their father is dead drunk. Every detail is given with dreadful exactness in a level prose of great economy.

The wife has to work hard to get the man's heavy boots off, and she gets the old woman to help her. The awful truth is not spoken—that they must lay out the corpse before *rigor mortis* sets in. And they must wash him. This, of course, is a significant and deeply symbolic task for the woman in a pit community has the role of washing her man when he comes home especially his back, where he cannot wash himself. Whatever a miner and his wife shared or did not share, this intimacy must be performed. We are told that when Mrs. Lawrence found she had to perform this task, she was appalled. It is seeing Mellors (Parkin) washing his own white body that first arouses Connie Chatterley's desire for the "touch of a man."

This last intimacy with the dead miner's body reveals the failure of the Bates's marriage. They had never known one another at the level of being-to-being:

> When they arose, saw him lying in the naive dignity of death, the women stood arrested in fear and respect . . . Elizabeth felt countermanded. She saw him, how utterly inviolable he lay in himself. She had nothing to do with him. She could not accept it. Stooping, she laid her hand on him, in claim. He was still warm, for the mine was hot where he had died . . .
>
> Elizabeth embraced the body of her husband, with cheek and lips. She seemed to be listening, inquiring, trying to get some connection. But she could not. She was driven away. He was impregnable. (SS, 199)

The impregnability is the impregnability of death. It is also that in the dead body is crystallized the alienation of the one being from another. They had never found one another in such a way—the way of being, the essential I–Thou—which can transcend death.

To the old woman he is again the child she bathed.

> They never forget it was death, and the touch of the man's dead body gave them strange emotions, different in each of the women; a great dread possessed them both,

the mother felt the lie was given to her womb, she was denied; the wife felt the utter isolation of the human soul, the child within her was a weight apart from her. (SS, 199)

Lawrence brings out the mystery. Each is a living creature, obeying the dynamics of life on earth. The children are conceived and grow apart. The man and woman live and die as creatures. Yet there are bonds and these can transcend: in the end of the foolish old mother seems closer to the man; the wife cannot pass some barrier:

Elizabeth sank down again to the floor, and put her face against his neck, and trembled and shuddered. But she had to draw away again. He was dead, and her living flesh had no place against his. (SS, 200)

To the mother he is a "lamb": "white as milk he is, clear as a twelve-month baby, bless him, the darling!" To the wife,

Life with its smoky burning gone from him had left him apart and utterly alien to her. And she knew what a stranger he was to her. (SS, 200)

This utter, "intact separatedness" had been obscured by the "heat of living." This fact is "too deadly" for her.

There had been nothing between them, and yet they had come together, exchanging their nakedness repeatedly. Each time he had taken her, they had been two isolated beings, far apart as now. He was no more responsible than she. The child was like ice in her womb. For as she looked at the dead man, her mind, cold and detached, said clearly, "Who am I? What have I been doing? I have been fighting a husband who did not exist. *He* existed all the time. What wrong have I done? what was that I have been living with? There lies the reality, that man." And her soul died in her for fear: she knew she had never seen him, he had never seen her, they had met in the dark and fought in the dark, not knowing whom they met nor whom they fought. . . . For she had been wrong. She had said he was something he was not; she had felt familiar with him, whereas he was apart all the while, living as she never lived, feeling as she never felt. (SS, 200)

The moment of death not only brings the recognition that she has never truly known him. She also sees him as he really is, or was—not her idea of him, or her projection over him. And her sense of "wrongness" (as a student points out) is that she has *denied* his body, denied him in his "living as she had never lived":

She looked at his naked body and was ashamed, as if she had denied it . . . she had denied him what he was—she saw it now. She had refused him as himself. And this had been her life, and his life. She was grateful to death, which had restored the truth. (SS, 201)

The implication is that it is her own impulse to deny the male life in him, his fulfillment, for which she feels compunction. While she is aware of the agony the man has suffered in dying, she seems to reflect on an agony he has suffered at the hands of her denial of his body's life:

> What had he suffered? What stretch of horror for this helpless man! ... She had not been able to help him. He had been cruelly injured, this naked man, this other being, and she could make no reparation. (SS, 201)

She and the man had been channels through which life flowed to issue in the children, but their life together had not fulfilled itself in their beings, so she feels helpless and to blame.

> She felt that in the next world he would be a stranger to her ... they would both be ashamed of what had been before. (SS, 201)

The children had come, "for some mysterious reason," but "The children did not unite them."

> They had denied each other in life ... it had become hopeless between them long before he died. (SS, 201)

Now, "it was finished then." Pressed to the limit by death, the life before her seems to be meaningless at the depth of being and she holds herself to blame, for denying him at this level: the level of bodily, sexual, existence and of love.

> A terrible dread gripped her all the while: that he could be so heavy and utterly inert, unresponsive, apart. The horror of the distance between them was almost too much for her—it was so infinite a gap she must look across. (SS, 201)

The old woman and the widow clothe the corpse, and the woman goes back tidy the kitchen:

> She knew she submitted to life, which was her immediate master. But from death, her ultimate master, she winced with fear and shame. (SS, 202)

The reason is that she has no Dasein, no sense of "being there" in a meaningful way, derived from her closest relationship in marriage. She only has a sense of the utter gulf between beings. But this is something for which she is herself to blame because of her denial of her husband's being and because of the failure of love, under her "imperious disillusionment."

In this tragic story, Lawrence asserts that nothing could be more terrible, than that life should come to an end, and reveal that a marriage—the closest and most intimate relationship—is meaningless.

# True and False Solutions

He subtly attributes this to the woman's denial of the man's body and being: if we relate it to his view of the mother, it is here deeply sympathetic to the father and critical of the mother.

In this story we have a penetrating realism, and a compassionate awareness of the tragic plight of all human beings, who need to find a meaning in their lives, through love, in the face of death.

## The Fox

By contrast, *The Fox* is one of the most false of Lawrence's stories, and it is most astonishing that F. R. Leavis approves of it. He declares that it is "a study of human mating," and as so often when he discusses Lawrence, he uses the word "marvellous." It is a study, he says, "of the attractions between a man and a woman that expresses the profound needs of each and has its meaning in a permanent union" (Leavis 1955, 260). Later he says, "It is an idea of *marriage* that presents itself":

> marriage as the whole fulfilling of life of which, is his unanalytical and unintrospective manner, he has so strong a sense.... It is a study of youthful *love*, done, in its firsthandedness, its unconventional truth, with an exquisite delicacy that is wholly Lawrence. (Leavis, 1955, 262)

What is good about the story, it is true, is that at moments Lawrence can convey the way in which, intuitively, a deep emotion can take hold of "ordinary" people. Some scenes are superb, as for instance the moments when Henry and March sit together in the shed, moving as if inexorably, by hesitant verbal exchanges, into closeness—even as he cannot get an understanding out of her, or when she first puts on a woman's frock, and he is afraid of her body.

However, the crux of the story is the murder, accidentally, for the purpose, by the hero of his woman's partner, Banford, so that he can have March for himself. The killing is fully endorsed by the author, and profound satisfaction is felt when the unconscious will to destroy Banford is enacted: the "upshot" of the tale can only be that if someone stands in the way of our fulfillment, it is acceptable to destroy them. What kind of marriage would follow such an acting out of unconscious motives? Had Leavis considered that question? Leavis says that "all Henry's conviction and grasp of his purpose are needed to rescue March—for that is what it amounts to...." He goes on "Henry cannot but *will* Banford's death."

> The accident by which he kills her *is* willed, and it comes as a wholly significant *dénouement*. On the point of striking the final blow with the axe, he tells her that she had better stand further away, but tells her in such a tone that, the relations of hostility between them being what they are, she will certainly defy him: "the tone

of his voice seemed to imply that he was being falsely solicitous, and trying to make her move because it was his will to move her." (Leavis 1955, 263–4)

One might accept that an individual could be exculpated from killing someone from an unconscious motive, but the problem is never perhaps quite so clear-cut. Henry says things to himself in such a way that it is clear, as we shall see, that he was not acting from unconscious motives but acting out motives in such an aware way that he was culpable. (What would we say to a murderer who declared, "I had to do it"?) Yet Leavis clearly endorses the killing:

> The willed accident is the external event that completes the significance of the essential Lawrentian drama—Henry *had* to will Banford's death; and March, who wept in her dream over the dead Banford—the dream that betrayed her own profound desire to marry Henry, can, now that Banford *is* dead, say to herself that it is better so. (Leavis 1955, 264)

Leavis may well conclude his analysis of *The Fox* by declaring that "the psychological truth of *The Fox* is compelling," but it leaves us with considerable problems. Leavis talks about the "normative conclusions that preoccupy Lawrence elsewhere," but as if sensing objections based on a close examination of the implications, says that "the tale can hardly seem involved in any questionable generality of intentions," because of "the concrete specificity of the situation presented."

Does this mean that if we are presented with a piece of "life" that seems psychologically convincing, we need not invoke the problems of the "message," or "upshot" of what is offered?

There are, as we shall see, excellent moments in *The Fox:* moments when Lawrence is able to achieve, in the heat of his stirred imagination, that exactness of realization that makes us feel, "yes—it is like that!" But there are also moments when the writing is not convincing. One of these significantly is the killing itself:

> There was a moment of pure, motionless suspense, when the world seemed to stand still. Then suddenly his form seemed to flash up enormously tall and fearful. (SS, 474)

The unreality of the fantasy is indirectly indicated by Lawrence's repetition of the phrase "No-one saw." Why should no one else see? The father is there, and March, but they do not see because what is being acted out is a dream:

> No one saw what was happening except himself. No one heard the strange little cry which the Banford gave as the dark end of the bough swooped down, down on her. No one saw her crouch a little and receive the blow on the back of the neck. No one

saw her flung outwards and laid, a little twitching heap, at the foot of the fence. No one except the boy. And he watched with intense bright eyes, as he would watch a wild goose that he had shot. Was it winged, or dead? Dead! (SS, 474)

Henry turns the body over, which is "quivering with little convulsions" like the fox before in its death agonies. "The back of the neck and head was a mass of blood, of horror." Henry thinks:

> The inner necessity of his life was fulfilling itself; it was he who was to live. The thorn was drawn out of his bowels. (SS, 474)

Before he strikes, "in his heart he had decided her death." He thinks to himself consciously,

> "If the tree falls in just such a way, and spins just so much as it falls, then the branch there will strike her exactly as she stands on top of that bank." (SS, 473)

And afterwards, feeling no guilt or remorse, he merely exalts: "the inner necessity of his life was fulfilling itself. . . . The thorn was drawn out of his bowels."

The last phrase quoted, I believe, gives us a clue to the unconscious impulse behind the dream. Banford is a thorn in the flesh of the protagonist—or rather in his "bowels": Lawrence and others often use the bowels to mean the inner psychic life (as does the Psalmist). The elation Lawrence feels in his fantasy is that of having killed the aspect of woman that haunts him in his psychic life—his internalization of the mother. The dead phallic tree is employed to immobilize the castrating mother. Now Henry is free to hold March in submission, under control, now that the menacing phantom woman of the unconscious has been destroyed.

Leavis has a good deal to say about the dreams, but he fails to see that the whole story is a dream—a wish-fulfilling dream of a most dangerous kind. The "whole fox motive" he says "in all its development is remarkable for its inevitability of truth and the economy and precision of its art." But it that so? What is this fox? Says Leavis,

> He is a male creature, of a fascinating strangeness and vitality; a marauder out of the unknown, a kind of incalculable enemy, to be guarded against (and we see how subtly vigilance becomes positive seeking). (Leavis 1955, 258)

The fox may symbolize the mystery of wildness, but is it "vitality" to maraud and destroy chickens? And what about this:

> Suddenly he bit her wrist, and at the same instant, as she drew back, the fox, turning to bound away, whisked his brush across her face, and it seemed his brush was on fire, for it seared and burned her mouth with a great pain. She awoke with the pain of it, and lay trembling as if she were really scared. (SS, 430)

What is symbolized by the biting and the fire? In one sense, her fears of the sexual life, but in another, there is such satisfaction in the infliction of pain, in the outrageousness, and the phallic (hunting) energy of the fox that, I believe, we may find in it a particular idolization in Lawrence's fantasies, as here and elsewhere, of the phallic self, in its brutal hunger, a hunger for power.

When the fox has been shot, March dreams of burying Banford in the fox skin in the horrible wood box (that Leavis tells us symbolizes the dead tree that is to kill her). "It seemed to make a whole, ruddy, fiery coverlet." This, says Leavis, gives the drama its "emotional depth and dignity" and "conveys with astonishing vividness and subtlety the emotional dilemma, the complication of her feelings, caused by her solicitude and fears for Banford, for whom she has been the man." (Leavis, 1955, 259) But what does it mean? Leavis doesn't try to say. Perhaps what we can say is that March's dream belongs to the same mode as Henry's hate. Banford is to be dead and buried and given in death at least the care and devotion of glamorized hate: the fox-like manifestation of contempt and will that Lawrence celebrated in himself, as against the "carrion bodied" and those who stood in his path.

Even in death the fox embodies this phallic assertiveness, which is a beauty to March. By shooting the fox Henry has, as it were, possessed this and has taken over from the fox.

> March said nothing ... her face was pale and her eyes big and black, watching the dead animal that was suspended upside down—white and soft as snow his belly: white and soft as snow. She passed her hand softly down it. And his wonderful black-glinted brush was full and frictional, wonderful. (SS, 451)

One wonders what "frictional" means exactly, except to give the tail a more phallic connotation? The fox is the ithyphallic god.

> She passed her hand down this also, and quivered. Time after time, she took the full fur of that thick tail between her fingers, and passed her hand slowly downwards. Wonderful, sharp, thick, splendour of a tail. (SS, 451)

Here we have the sons-of-God-and-the-daughters-of-men theme, of which we shall see much later, as over Connie with Mellors's private parts. As always, the woman has to learn to respect and admire—submit to—the mysterious preponderance of the foxy male, the phallic, the *phallos*.[1]

It is revealing that there is a certain carelessness about what exactly the fox does represent. To March at first it seems to represent the mystery of wildness, of animal drive, then the animal sexuality in herself. It then becomes Henry's will and mating drive, and then in her dream the pain of recognizing sexuality. But then, in the second dream, it seems to be the murderous hostility of sexual impulse to anything that stands in its way. Why then does *Banford* die in twitches like the fox since she isn't the fox? The fox symbol, actually, is rather vague as though the author couldn't bother to make his mind up.

*The Fox* as a story is a piece of sheer propaganda. Two women try to live alone, representing the two aspects of women, mother and not-mother. Into their not very successful seclusion of effort to make a go of the farm walks the Lawrence-like protagonist, who tells them they need a man about the place in characteristic Morel-like tones. Then, of course, the one who is not chosen is jealous, and speaks in a cold, nagging, destructive way, in a characteristic Mrs. Morel-like manner, so she has to be killed, because she is the Mrs.-Morel-thorn-in-the-bowels. And she is killed, hooray! This is really all there is to it.

The relationship between Banford and March is clearly not a lesbian one, but one of those platonic relationships women strike up for expedient purposes, though later Lawrence writes about it as if it were a kind of "love" devoted to an absurd dream of happiness (which it isn't at all at the beginning.) March, at the outset, "would be the man about the place," and she wears puttees and breeches, so that she looks "almost like some graceful, loose-balanced young man." Yet "her face was not a man's face, ever," and (as Leavis says) she is very much a woman. However, I believe, because she is such an unawakened virgin who looks in some ways like a man, we have in her, as she becomes the object of Henry's attentions, something of that yearning for a relationship with a male, that homosexual yearning we note in *The White Peacock* and in *Women in Love*. March is also a bit like Lawrence, "a creature of odd whims and unsatisfied tendencies" who wants to "paint curvilinear swans on porcelain, with green background, or else make a marvellous fire-screen by processes of elaborate cabinet work." (SS, 419–420) So, we may see the story in narcissitic terms, as the dramatisation of inner dynamics.

The fox (SS, 420) was "as difficult as a serpent to see," and they find it hard to track him. He is the snake in Eden. March has the habit of musing, and it is in one of these muses that she sees him.

> She was always lapsing into this odd, rapt state, her mouth rather screwed up. It was a question whether she was there, actually conscious present, or not. (SS, 421)

It is in this mood that she sees the fox

> What was she thinking about, Heaven knows. Her consciousness was, as it were, held back.
> She lowered her eyes, and suddenly saw the fox. (SS, 421)

The fox is "he" and so seems the embodiment of the male principle, and "he looked into her eyes, and her soul failed her. He knew her, he was not daunted" (SS, 421).

This gives her "wide, vivid dark eyes, and a faint flush in her cheeks." Lawrence was fascinated by the way in which a (predatory) male could look at a woman and gain control over her, as we shall see, in *The Virgin and the*

*Gypsy*. It is important to note here that this has to do with power, the power of one person over another, and especially with male power over woman.

> Now, the fox seems to have entered her brain: she did not so much think of him: she was possessed by him. She saw his dark shrewd, unabashed eye looking into her, knowing her. She felt him invisibly master her spirit. (SS, 422)

But then, why is the effect of this appearance—the fox being so indifferent to her—to exact "possession" and to "master her spirit"?

Now, after the fox's "impudence," March's mind is unconsciously absorbed by him. The fox has "dominated her unconsciousness, possessed the blank half of her musing." The influence of the fox comes over the like a spell—and she even smells his odor at such moments. He had become a "settled effect in her spirit." We could say, I suppose, that the fox now symbolizes her need for a man, a mate, who, in Lawrence's terms, can subdue her.

Henry is clearly another version of the fox when he appears. March takes up a gun when he is heard approaching without warning.

He is described as exerting a parallel influence on her:

> He had a ruddy, roundish face, with fairish hair ... his eyes were blue, and very bright and sharp. On his cheeks, on the fresh ruddy skin were fine, fair hairs, like a down, but sharper. It gave him a slightly glistening look. (SS, 424)

> to March he was the fox. Whether it was the thrusting forward of his head, or the glisten of fine whitish hairs on the ruddy cheek-bones, or the bright, keen eyes ... but the boy was to her the fox. (SS, 425)

Leavis is right to applaud the exactness with which Lawrence does the scenes of the man's intrusion: the way they give him tea, the way he gradually insinuates himself. His portrayal of this class of English people, too, is done without condescension or contempt. Indeed, since he gives the "inwardness," he dignifies their humanity.

> The manner of speaking, in much of the dialogue, is good, too: "Oh, we'll see. We shall hold on a bit longer yet," said March, with a plangent, half-sad, half-ironical indifference. "There wants a man about the place," said the youth softly. (SS, 428)

When asked about his life, "He continued to answer with courteous simplicity, grave and charming." There is no reduction of the characters. Indeed, Henry Grenfel has a good deal of Lawrence in him.

The weakness comes with the idealization of the fox-Lawrence figure who puts a spell on the woman to awaken her:

> he was here in full presence. She need not go after him any more. There in the

shadow of her corner she gave herself up to a warm, relaxed peace, almost like sleep, accepting the spell that was on her. . . .
    She need not any more be divided in herself, trying to keep up two planes of consciousness. She could at last lapse into the odour of the fox. (SS, 429)

March has been seeking the fox because he gave her his funny contemptuous look. She wants to kill him, but the fox is a symbol, and so we may see that she was looking for something in herself because she wanted to confront it. Now this need fixes itself in the young man opposite, and "she was still and soft in her corner like a passive creature in a cave."

It is at this point that March has her first dream of the fox with the fiery tail. Since this tail later becomes a phallus, it seems obvious that Lawrence intends the dream to represent March being seared with the power of her own sexual needs. Characteristically to Lawrence these are conceived in painful and sadistic forms, as if sexuality were something fearful.

The way the man makes himself at home is very convincingly done: and then it strikes him "why not marry March": "his mind waited in amazement . . . why not?" And the paragraph ends with the sentence, "He was master of her." If there is an idea of marriage, must it be in terms of "he was master of her"? When George Eliot says of Rosamond, vis-à-vis her husband, "she had mastered him" in *Middlemarch*, we are invited to see Lydgate's submission as a humiliation and tragedy: Why should March's subjection be such a triumph, in Lawrence's idea of love and marriage? Here, the whole pursuit of a mate is presented in terms of hunt and conquest.

Mating in *The Fox* is presented as if it were like hunting. Henry "would have to catch her as you catch a deer or woodcock when you go out shooting." Why is marriage conceived so much, in this story, in terms of *death*?

It's no good walking out into the forest and saying to the deer, "Please fall to my gun." No, it is a slow, subtle battle. . . . You have to be subtle and cunning and absolutely fatally ready. It becomes like a fate . . . it is a battle never finished till your bullet goes home. . . . It is your own *will* which carries the bullet into the heart of your quarry. . . . It happens like a supreme wish, a supreme act of volition, not as a dodge of cleverness. (SS, 434)

Later, "he wanted to *bring down March as his quarry*, to make her his wife" (my italics). The man's voice is "softly insistent," and "she seemed to be in his power." Henry has a "penetrating" and "too hot" bodily presence (like the fox) and "a queer instinct for the night." To March the fox seems to be "singing wildly and sweetly lie a madness" round the house "so tenderly."

After a sharp involuntary exclamation about his presence, March confesses to Henry that for her he is the fox. "Perhaps you think I've come to steal your chickens or something, "he says, and then uses his suggestive voice to disavow that he is the fox and kisses he. "It seemed to burn through her every fibre" So, the kiss is like the blow from the fox's brush in her dream.

Henry, in response to the women's quarrel over him, goes out and shoots the fox. As I have suggested, in doing so he takes the fox into himself, replaces the for, "acts for" the fox. But in doing so he draws out of March a strange impulse towards a sadistic response to the mating theme:

> the marvellous white teeth beneath! It was to thrust forward and bite with, deep, deep, into the living prey, to bite and bite the blood. (SS, 451)

Insofar as the fox is a disembodied phallus, he belongs somewhat to the oral stage by which I mean March is compulsively attracted to Henry's sexual hunger, and her own. This, to Lawrence, is the basis of marriage in this tale. He on his part (SS, 453) has even decided she is going to Canada with him, *without her being consulted*—and Leavis approves! In the discussions of this aspect of the problem there is far too little of the traditional and warm-hearted humanistic good sense of "ordinary" people. Although Henry says: "I don't want to press you to do anything you don't wish to do," he clearly doesn't mean it:

> He had set his mind on her. And he was convulsed with a youth's fury at being thwarted. To be thwarted, to be thwarted! It made him so furious inside that he didn't know what to do with himself. (SS, 454)

What I suppose Leavis admires in the tale is the way Lawrence makes it a "destiny" that the man is attracted to this particular woman. He has even decided that she is to come to Canada with him, although he has not even told her, as it appears in the conversation they have about this (SS, 453). Reflecting on his influence with her, he thinks, "She might come over to him. Of course she might. *It was her business to do so*" (SS, 545; my italics).

It is revealing to study the terms in which Henry is made to be so antipathetic to Banford. If one knows one's Lawrence, she comes to bear singular resemblance to the Mrs. Morel of *Sons and Lovers*, and the protagonist of the short story *Odour of Crysanthemums*. Watching the women climb to the house, he sees Banford, "frail thing that she was, but with that devilish little certainty which he so detested in her. . . . And if looks could have affected her, she would have felt a log of iron on each of her ankles as she made her way forward." (SS, 454). He then breaks out into hostile thoughts that have a special intensity:

> "You're a nasty little thing, you are," he was saying softly across the distance.
> "You're a nasty little thing. I hope you'll be paid back for all the harm you've done me for nothing. I hope you will—you nasty little thing. I hope you'll have to pay for it. You will, if wishes are anything. You nasty little creature that you are." (SS 455)

She keeps slipping backward, but if she had been slipping towards the Bottomless Pit, he would not have gone to help her. He sees March go down to help her, and take all the parcels, while Banford is left holding a bunch of yellow crysanthemums.

> "I'd make you eat them for your tea, if you hug them so tight. And I'd give them you for breakfast again, I would. I'd give you flowers. Nothing but flowers." (SS, 455)

Is it too fanciful, to suggest that this woman is the ghost mother who appears in *Kangaroo*, threatening to blight the life to Somers? That it is the flower-loving mother, who haunted Lawrence?

And when the women quarrel about him, Banford begins to talk like Mrs. Morel:

> "Letting a boy like that come so cheeky and impudent and make a mug of you. . . . How much respect do you think he's going to have for you afterwards?"
> ". . . We ought never to have lowered ourselves. And I've had such a fight with all the people here, not to be pulled down to their level . . . ."
> "I shall never know moment's peace again while I live, nor a moment's happiness." (SS, 447)

Of course, Banford is trying to exert a double bind on March, and thus Lawrence would naturally draw on his mother's modes of establishing a clinch for such dialogue. But the words seem to belong more to the modes used by parents hostile to a son's developing interest in other women, with the unconscious urge to spoil the new relationship, than those that might seem more appropriate for the jealousy of a woman partner. Banford, for instance, talks like Mrs. Morel of being left with nothing if March and he married and they lived together:

> "No, I simply couldn't stand it. I should be dead in a month, which is what he would be driving at, of course. That would be his game, to see me in the churchyard." (SS, 446)

It all seems reminiscent of Mrs. Morel's response to Miriam.

When Henry announces their engagement, Banford looks at March like "a bird that has been shot." (SS, 444) The youth is bright and gloating. Not one word is said to Banford about how this is to affect her life.

Of course, behind this mythical tale of killing the ghostly mother to find one's way to an adult sexual relationship, there is an undercurrent of finding out about male and female. There is much play with gender, symbolized by the way the women dress in men's clothes—an echo, no doubt, of the tremendous changes brought by the Great War, when women broke away from their traditional patterns, and wore men's clothes as land girls. Henry thinks of the female body beneath the male clothes;

> The Banford would have little iron breasts, he said to himself. . . . But March, under

her crude, fast, workman's tunic, would have soft, white breasts, white and unseen. So he told himself, and his blood burned. (SS, 457)

This theme, actually, generates one scene that belongs very much to the best of Lawrence, as novelist. It develops when Henry goes to tea, and March is dressed for once in a woman's frock. This brings out Henry's respect for her femininity, and his awe at it, and his own responsibilities, as her lover: "He felt a man, quiet, with a little of the heaviness of male destiny come upon him" (SS, 458). What is "real" is the response of one character to another:

> "Well, I never knew anything make such a difference!" he murmured, across his mouthfuls.
> "Oh goodness!" cried March, blushing still more. "I might be a pink monkey!" (SS, 458)

"No, she was another being"—and we recall we have ourselves seen women change so, when some intuitive dynamic within them transforms them, through love, into "receiving woman," or when, quite simply, they wear feminine clothes. Lawrence is aware, too, of the heavy sense of responsibility this brings to a man: "He felt a man, with all a man's grave weight of responsibility."

Also exact to the experience of life are the moments in the shed between Henry and March, where he seeks to persuade her to marry him:

> He took her to a dark corner of the shed, where there was a toolbox with a lid, long and low.
> "We'll sit here a minute," he said. And obediently she sat down by his side.
> "Give me your hand," he said. (SS, 462)

These scenes are done with delicacy, and they are convincing. As Leavis says, *The Fox* is "compelling" and even the close "belongs to the concrete specificity of the situation presented."

But what of the upshot? Leavis is positive. "What we have," he has told us is "much more fully and unequivocally a study of love . . . of the attraction between a man and a woman that expresses the profound needs of each and has its meaning in a permanent union" (Leavis 1955, 260) That sounds like a normative conclusion, but can we take the relationship between Henry and March as propitious for that "permanent union"?

> She would have to leave her destiny to the boy . . . . He wanted no more than that. He wanted her to give herself defences, to sink and become submerged in him . . . . He wanted to veil her woman's spirit as orientals veil the woman's face. He wanted her to commit herself to him, and put her independent spirit to sleep . . . . He wanted to take away her consciousness, and make her just his woman. Just his woman.
>     . . . even the responsibility for her own soul she would have to commit to him. He knew it was so, and obstinately held out against her, waiting for the surrender. (SS, 478)

So the story ends as a fantasy of domination, of having woman finally under control, like a fox has a chicken, and the fantasy is clearly one in which Lawrence identifies himself:

> He believed that as they crossed the seas, as they left England which he so hated, because in some way it seemed to have stung him with poison, she would . . . give in to him. (SS, 479)

What is there in the story to suggest that *Henry* is poisoned by "England"? Or indeed that he hates it? It was Lawrence who hated England, and hoped that when he was in Europe with Frieda things would be different—and his ghosts would be exorcised.

*The Fox* is yet another attempt to exorcise the ghosts, and the clues are to be found in the honeymoon poems.[2] In *The Fox* Lawrence uses all the power of his art to serve his own propaganda purposes. The woman has a secret yearning for the foxy wild passions of sexual love: a desire even that they be fiery. Along comes a man who will give it to her—not only sex—but death, the death of her own independent self and especially the death of that element in woman that is dangerously reminiscent of a dominant mother. Then there is another complication—the maleness of woman, as in March. Henry becomes excited by the idea that beneath March's male-like clothes there is a woman's body, but then this exciting woman-man must have her will broken, and be turned into a woman, fully under control.

> Then he would have all his own life as a young man and a male, and she would have all her own life as a woman and a female. There would be no more of this awful straining. She would not be a man any more, an independent woman with a man's responsibility, (SS, 479)

To Lawrence, an independent woman, allowed to be free, is too much like a man: a woman must submit, and even lose her consciousness. At the end, he wants her to "submit" and "lose her consciousness" to become "just his woman."

As the story proceeds, Lawrence seems to hate Banford more and more. At the beginning, we sympathize with her, but often Lawrence discriminates against his own character, as she comes to embody the barriers on Henry's "fulfillment." At first it is "In her thin, frail hair were already many threads of grey."

But she becomes by degrees "fretful," and increasingly jealous—like a possessive mother, then "nervy" and "a frail little thing," with "blank, reddened eyes," and a "plaintive, fretful voice" that has a "thread of hot anger and despair." Now she becomes "superstitious" and "sulky," and we get the feeling that Lawrence has turned against her.

Now, "he disliked the Banford with an acid dislike," while March dreams of Banford dead in a coffin with the fox skin symbolizing that their sexuality has killed her. Banford bursts out into jealous sobs:

> suddenly burst into a long wail and a spasm of sobs. She covered her face with her poor, thin hands, and her thin shoulders shook in an agony of weeping. (SS, 460)

Henry is contemptuous—"let her cry." He utters his "terrible signalling" to March, and she can't think of Jill any more. When they came in again, Banford looks "frightening, unnatural. . . . Evil he thought her look was." (SS, 464)

We could, in a sense, suppose that the relationship between March and Banford was a normal working friendship; it is the intense fox-cunning exercise of power by Henry over March that is abnormal. So, when March is left to sort things out with Banford, her subsequent letter seems good sense:

> When you aren't there I see what a fool I am. When you are there you seem to blind me to things as they actually are. You make me see things all unreal, and I don't know what. (SS, 466)

Isn't that the effect of the fox? Of herself and Banford she says, "we have a life together." Henry the Fox, when he reads her letter of dismissal, goes "pale, almost yellow" around the eyes with fury "like a fox." He makes off to the farm, and we turn at once to March's dealings with the tree: to the drama of the unconsciously for-the-purpose manslaughter scene.

Banford is now marked out as the victim: "'Oh!' cried Banford, *as if afraid*. 'Why it's Henry!'" With March, "It is all over with her." Henry looks up at the tree and says to himself, "If the tree falls in just such a way . . . the branch there will strike her exactly as the stands on top of that bank."

> In his heart he had decided her death. A terrible still force seemed in him, and a power that was just his. (SS, 473)

It must be noted that his murderous impulse is not unconscious: "he thought to himself" and the thought is verbalized, followed by a *decision* in the heart.

And his heart held perfectly still, in the terrible pure will that she should not move. When he advises Banford where to stand, he does it (foxily) in such a way that he knows she will disobey him:

> The tone of his voice seemed to her to imply that he was only being falsely solicitous and trying to make her move because it was his will to mover her . . . . He held himself, icy still, lest he should lose his power. (SS, 473)

Surely, nothing could be more dangerous than condoning the acting out of dream motives—even unconscious motives? The question in *The Fox*, of course, is the degree to which the impulse to murder could be claimed to be "unconscious." And then there is a more subtle problem for the author is more guilty than his character. Banford's murder may come with what Leavis calls "perfect dramatic rightness," but the rightness may be the fulfillment of a particularly false fantasy, which is all the more dangerous, because its underlying true intent may be hidden. In this case, I believe Banford's murder represents the acting out of the *author*'s unconscious hatred of one aspect of the internalized mother—a tendency that could be especially full of dangers if acted out in real life.

There are further questions to do with deeper aspects of symbolism and meaning here: if the fox symbolizes maleness or male sexuality to March— her unconscious desire to "mate"—what is the meaning of Henry's act of shooting it? What is the basis of Henry's impulse to take "responsibility" and decide that March "had to be passive, to acquiesce"?

Lawrence himself said, "The great relationship, for humanity, will always be the relation between man and woman" (Inglis, *A selection from Phoenix*, p. 180) If this is so, what is the message of *The Fox*?

The murder achieves a number of ends at once. For one thing, it brings to Henry a sense of release and fulfillment totally endorsed by the author's radiant presentation of it:

> He watched with intense, bright eyes, as he would watch a wild goose he had shot. Was it winged, or dead? Dead!
> Immediately he gave a loud cry....
> He knew it, that it was so. He knew it in his soul and in his blood. The inner necessity of his life was fulfilling itself, it was he who was to live. The thorn was drawn out of his bowels. (SS, 474)

At the same time the murder renders March into submission to the Fox: here is "mastery":

> She began to grizzle, to cry in a shivery little fashion of a child that doesn't want to cry, but which is beaten from within, and gives that little first shudder of sobbing which is not yet weeping, dry and fearful.
> *He had won.* She stood there absolutely helpless.... (SS, 475; my italics)

Henry has no compassion for these female victims:

> Among all the torture of the scene the torture of his own heart and bowels, he has glad, he had won.... She would never leave him again. He had won her. And he knew it and was glad, because he wanted her for his life. His life must have her. And now he had won her. It was what his life must have. (SS, 475)

Now we have one of Lawrence's tirades against "love":

She felt the weary need of our day to *exert* herself in love. But she knew that in fact she must to more exert herself in love. He would not have the love which exerted itself towards him. It made his brow go black. No, he wouldn't let her exert her love towards him. No, she had to be passive, to acquiesce, and to be submerged under the surface of love. She had to be like the seaweeds she saw as she peered down from the boat. (SS, 476)

Lawrence types away, in his fantasy, and now seems imaginatively far from the farm, Banford, and March. (What seaweed? What boat?) Is Lawrence now writing about some woman in his own life, or some phantom in his own unconscious?

Never looking forth from the water until they died, only then washing, corpses, upon the surface. But while they loved, always submerged, always beneath the wave. Beneath the wave they might have powerful roots, stronger than iron; they might be tenacious and dangerous in their soft waving beneath the flood. (SS, 476)

What is it all about? In some half-mystical way, it is about some deep dread of woman that Lawrence feels, and how she must be kept down.

Then he tries to justify his endorsement of Banford's murder and the subjugation of March by a long diatribe against March's impulse to be "responsible" for "Jill's health and happiness and well-being"—indeed, for "the well-being of the world." We have a long and irrelevant sermon of "the awful mistake of happiness" the search for happiness always ends in "bottomless nothingness."

Always beyond her, vaguely, unrealizably beyond her, and she was left with nothingness at last. The life she reached for, the happiness she reached for, the well-being she reached for, all slipped back.... She wanted some goal, some finality— and there was none. Always this ghastly reaching, reading, striving for something that might be just beyond. Even to make Jill happy. She was glad Jill was dead. (SS, 477)

If Jill married a man, it would have been the same—striving to make the man happy, and always achieving failure. "Little foolish successes in money or in ambition." You can love yourself to ribbons, and strive to make another happy, and it will always come to catastrophic failure:

The awful mistake of happiness ... everything was only a horrible abyss of happiness ... the more you reached after the fatal flower of happiness. ... The flower itself—its calyx is a horrible gulf, it is the bottomless pit. (SS, 477)

At the beginning of the tale there is no sense that March is devoted to finding happiness for Jill, so what is this sermon directed at?

That is the whole history of the search for happiness ... it ends ... in the ghastly

sense of the bottomless nothingness into which you will inevitably fall if you strain
any further. (SS, 477)

It is as if Lawrence wants us to believe that it is better for Jill to be killed,
because she was only being urged towards nothingness by March's impulse to
please her. Women, in any case, are very limited beings in this respect:

And women? What goal can any woman conceive, except happiness? Just happiness,
for herself and the whole world. That and nothing else. And so, she assumes the
responsibility, and sets off towards her goal. She can see it there, at the foot of the
rainbow. Or she can see it a little way beyond, in the blue distance. Not far not far.
    But the end of the rainbow is a bottomless gulf ... a void pit which can swallow
you ... the illusion of attainable happiness! (SS, 478)

March's aspirations had become "An agony, an insanity at last." *Henry's
murder has now saved March from insanity*! A stroke of health indeed!

She was glad it was over .... She would never strain for love and happiness any
more. And Jill was safely dead. Poor Jill, poor Jill. It must be sweet to be dead.
(SS, 478)

We leave Henry and March, he wanting her to submit, she wanting to see what
was ahead:

Sometimes he thought bitterly that he ought to have left her. He ought never to have
killed Banford. He should have left Banford and March to kill one another. (SS, 479)

But that was only impatience, and he knew it. It is clear from this that he
is culpable, but his only guilt is a manifestation of impatience. All he has to
do, really, is to wait for her to "close her eyes at last, and give in to him,"
so that he may reap his murder's reward. He is "waiting for the surrender"
and she is "like a child struggling against sleep."
    How can we escape the implication that, rather than waste oneself in
devotion in love or seeking to find happiness for another, the man should, in
a spirit of egoistical nihilism, annihilate and subdue when people stand in the
way of his will?
    *The Fox* is an extraordinarily Nietzschean, if not fascistic, story, deeply
immoral. In it, Lawrence used all his imaginative powers of realization for
propaganda purposes, for deeply corrupt ends. It suggests strange things
about Leavis's attitude to marriage that he should offer this endorsement of
murderous power as a definition of love!

## The Captain's Doll

*The Fox* in no isolated case of falsification of the problems of relationships in Lawrence's work. The story already referred to, another that Leavis also powerfully endorses, *The Captain's Doll*, is worse. It contains many imaginative felicities like the comic conversation between the captain's wife and Hennele, when the former doesn't know it is she who is his mistress. If we examine it closely, we shall find the "upshot" of the piece is propaganda for Lawrence's unconscious mythology.

One of the most striking parts of the story is when the captain takes Hannele out for a climb on a glacier. Lawrence skips over the problem of how a woman, who has been the mistress of a man and has been brusquely treated by him, would agree to go on a glacier walk with him and of how a woman engaged to another rather bourgeois "intended" would feel able to do so. It is clear that Lawrence has some "glacier-climbing material" he wants to make use of, and what we have, in fact, as the climax of the story is a Lawrence–Frieda quarrel during an outing on a glacier.

The glacier has its symbolic significance: the captain looks down into its crevasses and sees deep colors in the ice. The glacier is savage, and stands for "life"—the deep natural life to which we must be responsible. The exchange between the ex-lovers lacks conviction; we know that in the end they will become lovers again. There is something at a deep tacit level that is impelling them together, yet the story is something of a confidence trick. Lawrence wants to tell us that *he* had decided that in man-woman relationships it is necessary for the woman to know and obey the man. Love will not do: it is threatening—it threatens the man with "horrible merging," with becoming a *husband*. Lawrence cannot bear the thought of becoming a husband, and he uses the word with some contempt. There are many places in his work where the concept of husband is despised and assaulted, as in *Lady Chatterley's Lover*. Also, a *marriage for love* would threaten him with being made into a doll, so he must postulate some other kind of relationship.

The story, thus, is sheer propaganda for Lawrence's brand of discrimination against woman. Despite the vividness of the art, the symbolism of the doll, the glacier, the man's cold and rather schizoid behavior toward his object, the conclusion doesn't emerge inevitably from the art.

The excellence of the story—its "life"—is in the record we have in it of a row between Frieda and Lawrence, while walking up to see a glacier. That comes from "life," indeed. Yes, of course, there is great creative power in the dialogues, but it will not do to discriminate as Leavis does, against the "female ego." Leavis says that the doll, which his mistress Hannele makes of the captain, and the "demand for love on equal terms" from her are expressions of the *female ego*, while the captain's strange attractiveness represents the "profound vital maleness." His movement closer to Hannele represents the "non-ego promptings of his individuality." The whole clue to emotional life, again, it seems, is to escape the "ego" and "self-hood," and find one's identity at a deeper level. All this is a rationalization of Lawrence's fear of woman; it does not belong to "life" as the Frieda-quarrel does.

A clue to the propaganda manipulation is the author's unfairness to his own character in Mrs. Hepburn. The captain (of course) is a mystery; the woman is contemptible:

> in a funny little cape of odd striped skins, and a little dark-green skirt and a rather fuzzy sort of hat ... perhaps in a chic little boudoir cap of punto di Milano, and this slip of frail flowered silk ... oh, merciful heaven, save us from other people's indiscretion. (SS, 508)

The man, made into a puppet by Hannele, is made ridiculous on his honeymoon by his wife: "Him on his knees, with his heels up!" And every now and then, the hatred of the author for his character shows through, as with the italicization here: "Her face looked yellow, and *very* wrinkled."

Mrs. Hepburn dies in a most convenient sudden way, and Lawrence adopts a "good job!" attitude to her quittance. She falls out of a third floor window while putting a camisole out to dry.

Captain Hepburn at once asks Hannele, "Won't you come over for a chat?"
She finds him smoking "with a faint smile."

> "But now," he said, "I feel very strangely happy about it. I feel happy about it. I feel happy for her sake, if you can understand that. I feel she has got out of some great tension. I feel she's free now for the first time in her life." (SS, 514)

Again we have the fantasy of "freedom" when someone who is a barrier to fulfillment dies. It is quite unbelievable that anyone could talk so. Remember that this man was supposed to see his wife's body immediately after the fall, so he presumably attended to the funeral arrangements. Only someone seriously deficient in affect could talk as Captain Hepburn talks about a woman with whom he had shared the flesh exchanges of married life, and by whom he has had children, only a day or so after her awful death. One only has to turn to the profound tragic realism of *Odour of Chrysanthemums* to see that *The Captain's Doll* is simply unrealized.

Again, the impulse to make another "happy" is satirized: "For my life, I didn't know what to do, except try to make her happy." (SS, 517) But he, on his part, looked out at the moon (being a mystery): "I look right out—into freedom—into freedom." (SS, 517) The captain feels an axe go through his relationships to everyone, and though he goes to see his children, he wishes them "everything except any emotional connection with himself."

> He was deeply, profoundly thankful that his wife was dead ... poor thing, she had escaped and gone her own way into the void, like a flown bird. (SS, 518)

Both the essential indifference to the children and this good-riddance attitude to the wife seem to belong to wish-fulfillment rather than realism.

Once more Lawrence develops a further diatribe against love: "Love. . . . That tiresome word Love . . . he shuddered at the thought of having to go through such love again" (SS, 519). But he is drawn back again to Hannele, who is about to make a conventional marriage. They go out for the walk on the glacier, and here the exchange, at times, has that good ironic quality of Lawrence's own rows with women put into books

"For what purpose does a man usually ask a woman to marry him?"
"For what *purpose*!" she repeated, rather haughtily.
"For what reason, then!" he corrected. (SS, 548)

It moves towards propaganda over the question of the woman making the man into a puppet. They are clearly intensely drawn toward one another, but they openly declare otherwise: "I *know* there's no love between you and me." This is good, but the captain is shown to have his mysterious mastery. He lets her go to try to get away in the omnibus, but then they get in together, and (with marvelous comedy) shout their intimacies above the noise. He declares, "I don't want a marriage on the basis of love." What he seems to mean is that the kind of love he has experienced so far is too possessive, like that symbolized by the doll, and the image of him on his knees on his wedding night.

But what he *says* is,

"I want marriage. I want a woman to honour and obey me."
"If you are quite reasonable and *very* sparing with your commands," said Hannele. "And very careful how you give your orders."
"In fact, I want a sort of patient Griselda. I want to be honoured and obeyed. I don't want love." (SS, 552)

Hannele reacts by talking of Griselda's attitude to "a bullying fool of a husband."

"Honour, and obedience: and the proper physical feelings," he said. "To me that is marriage. Nothing else." (SS, 553)

"The theme and creative impulse," Leavis coos, "are as I have said, essentially normative." He resists angrily the implications of some that Lawrence preached "what he itched, it is alleged, to practise—a bullying male dominance."

In defining the norm with which he is preoccupied . . . it is with significant propriety that he makes Alexander Hepburn invoke the traditional formulation. A man is a man and not a woman, and a woman is a woman and not a man. . . . Hepburn uses "honour and obey" to point to the positive aspect of the profound conviction to which experience has brought him, the conviction that he has "always made a mistake, undertaking to love." (Leavis 1955, 220)

Yes, it might be better not to undertake to love, but it could also be said that perhaps he shows too little respect for the "otherness"—the independent free existence of woman and her needs. His wife is a cipher to him, and Hannele a mistress less interesting than the moon, and a possible wife to be obliged to submit! Perhaps he is simply afraid of love because love (as to Lawrence) is full of threats of domination and "horrible merging."

Interestingly, the doll, he says, "sticks in me like a thorn." We may recall in *The Fox* the way the murder of Banford draws the thorn out of the protagonist's bowels.

> If a woman loves you, she'll make a doll out of you.... And when she's got your doll, that's all she wants. And that's what love means. (SS, 554)

Thinking psychoanalytically, we have to see the doll as the phallus, and so Lawrence's fear again is that of the Castrating Mother, or the dominating woman who may turn you into her phallic object. The man has to resort to machismo to resist that fear: "I'm going to East Africa to join a man." Like Henry, he fails to ask if she'd like to join him. The woman, as so often in Lawrence, has to trot behind with the basket on her head as the man rides ahead on the camel.

> "She'll come along with me, and we'll set ourselves up there."
> "And she'll do all the honouring and obeying and housekeeping incidentally while you ride about in the day and stare at the moon in the night...."
> "... she'll be my wife, and I shall treat her as such. If the marriage service says love and cherish—well, in that sense I shall do so." (SS, 554)

This, says Leavis, "expresses Lawrence's profoundest insights into relations between man and woman, and his accompanying convictions about the nature of a valid marriage." (1955, 203) If we don't accept this, we are accused of "a refusal, or an inability, to attend to them for what they are." (1955, 203) Well, we do attend to them, and in light of everything we know from our own experience and the experience of others, as well as in the light of the wisdom of psychoanalysis and other forms of philosophical anthropology, we know them to be rubbish. Alexander's defensive, pseudo-masculinist posture is as far from a formula for valid marriage as anyone could get.

Perhaps there is hope in Hannele's sarcasm: "Ghastly fate for any miserable woman," and "Don't be a solemn ass." That she succumbs perhaps is indicated by her, "I won't say it *before* the marriage service. I needn't need I?"—and perhaps we note that, as we do often, woman, who is really much more mysterious than man, will stand up to him. She has some power over him: "And come tomorrow will you?" she said. "Yes, in the morning" (SS 555). Most of the exchange is again devoted to Lawrence's propagandist wish-fulfillment. Yes, as Leavis says, she realizes that his stance makes him supremely important to her. She is, in a sense, giving him "a run for his money," but there is more than "accord" between them. Lawrence fantasies surrender, and seeks to persuade us that there is a definition of marriage in the sense that there will be between them a fight to the death.

*   *   *

Our response to *The Captain's Doll* is altered radically by reading *Mr Noon*. The insistence on "honour and obey" seems clearly related to Lawrence's anguish over Frieda's promiscuity, and this explains its minatory nature in his attempts to control woman.

There are also, of course, elements in the story that redeem it: the way, for instance, in which Hannele, in the spirit of Frieda at best, laughs at the captain, humors him, tells him he is a fool. We can take it as comedy, as we take Lawrence and Frieda themselves, often in an ironic spirit: whatever nonsense they talk, they can't do without one another, and their quarrels show them more truly married then any of the Captain's pronouncements about matrimony, or their guarded agreements. There is thus a tension in the story between what Lawrence wants to believe about "manhood" and marriage, and the way in which, in spite of himself, the novelist in him portrays the life of his characters.

In a sense one is reacting against Leavis's solemn interpretation of the "upshot" of the story. If one accepts his view then the work falls very far short of being as definitive in a positive way as Leavis takes it. In an essay by Rosemary Gordon, a psychoanalytical commentator, she says that the solutions in the story are male chauvinist, while the view of relationship expressed is infantile, and more appropriate to a relationship with the mother. Lawrence's attempt to exert control over woman is based on an extraordinary view of woman's capacity to control the man:

> *any* woman today, no matter *how* much she loves her man—she could start any minute and make a doll of him .... If a woman loves you, she'll make a doll of you .... And when she's got your doll, that's all she wants. And that's what love means. And so I won't be loved. And I won't love .... I'll be honoured or obeyed; or nothing. (SS, 554)

What command over life and death, says Dr. Gordon the captain imputes to a woman! And what a murderous force he espies in her love.

> This cold, cynical, imperious and dominant stance that he claims as his right to impose on her, how sad, and how laughable it appears. No wonder Hannele manages to accept this formal condition. Did she know how empty, how toothless a condition it was? Clearly, his was not a relationship to a person, to a particular woman, to the Countess Hannele. It was a relationship to an abstraction, to a phantasy figure inside him, to a part of his inner psychic world. And it had really more of the qualities of the infant's relationship to his mother, than to the experience of an actual girl or woman in later life. (Gordon 1978, 265)

This, from the training analyst of the Society of Analytical Psychology, is worth having. Yet it is this view of relationship, expressed by Lawrence speaking through the lips of his autobiographical character, that gained such approval from Leavis.[3] Lawrence, trying to throw off the woman who made him into a phallic object, comes full circle and embodies in Captain Hepburn the impulse to go back to the infant's relationship to the mother—but he is not really developing an awareness of what a relationship to a real woman might be at all.

## The Virgin and the Gypsy

One of the themes in *The Virgin and the Gypsy* is the need for the youngest daughter Yvette to fulfill her sexual desire. It is important to note that the story ironically depicts Ernest Weekley's background in the family that Lawrence scathingly caricatures. The virgin is in a state of adolescent revolt from her family, while the gypsy is seeking to seduce her partly as a gesture of definace and challenge to established society:

> his race was very old, in its peculiar battle with established society, and had no conception of winning. *Only now and then could it score.* (SS, 1071; my italics)

There is more than a touch of Otto Gross about this story, for if we look closely, we can see that the gypsy offers his desire in *contempt*. His eyes continually offer "the naked insinuation of desire" that, for Lawrence, is all that matters. He, of course, is the usual "aloof" creature of the phallic consciousness:

> his manner was subdued, very quiet: and at the same time proud, with a touch of condescension and aloofness. (SS, 1057)

Moreover, "he managed to insinuate such a subtle suggestion of submission into the male bearing" (SS, 1057). It is this that overwhelms Yvette's will, and she looks at him with "childlike eyes, that were as capable of double meanings as his own."

They are talking about a candlestick. He looks back into her eyes with "that naked suggestion of desire which acted on her like a spell and robbed her of her will."

We have the Sleeping Beauty theme, and it is not long before we realize that the gypsy is that ithyphallic idolized self-figure that stalks the pages of the Lawrence mythology:

> "That gipsy was the best man we had, with horses. Nearly died of pneumonia. I thought he was dead. He's a resurrected man to me. I'm a resurrected man myself, as far as that goes." (SS, 1078)

In the deeper mythology "Joe Boswell" is the Lawrence who has been resurrected, in this life, into a new body, and who has the magical (godlike) power to bring the dead mother to life. When the gypsy embraces Yvette, we have yet another fantasy of divine resurrection.

Lawrence's seductions are not really portrayals of adult sexuality as much as wish-fulfillment fantasies of the revival of the mother. The men who do this seem to belong to another race; they are magic. Since it is a matter of life and death and nothing must be allowed to stand in its way, the problem is *beyond morality*: it is essentially a problem of being. This explains the hostility of Lawrence to morality, a stance he took in from Frieda's Grossian unscrupulousness.

When Yvette's father exerts his traditional and punitive morality, it is important to note that the meaning of Yvette's existence is threatened. He forbids her to associate with the Eastwoods because they are immoral ("a man who goes off with an older woman for the sake of her money"). Lawrence obviously has a certain bitter feeling about this kind of morality since he encountered some of it when he took Frieda from Weekley, but his portrayal of the clergyman, Yvette's father, is something of a caricature:

> "Say no more!" he said, in a low, hissing voice.
> "But I will kill you before you shall go the way of your mother."
> She looked at him .... *For her too, the meaning had gone out of everything.* (SS, 1081; my italics)

To Lawrence the conventional morality of the Saywell's is not only a repression of sexual urges, but destroys meaning, and as we have seen, Lawrence's whole oeuvre is directed at giving meaning to the phantom woman.

Yvette's mother, "she-who-was Cynthia," has gone off herself with "a young and penniless man." She, too, has sought sexual fulfillment: "While some of the women kept silent, they knew" (SS, 1025). Yvette is to follow in her mother's footsteps. The gypsy woman tells her,

> There is a dark man who never lived in a house. He loves you. The other people are treading on your heart. They will tread on your heart till you think it is dead. But the dark man will blow the one spark up into fire again. Good fire. You will see what good fire. (SS, 1050)

Thus, we have the need of a woman, like Connie Chatterley, to have her "haystack set on fire." Yvette feels there is a duplicity somewhere, and we might be excused the suspicion that the gypsy woman is in a malicious conspiracy with the man, to seduce young middle-class women out of malice. But Lawrence doesn't see it like that. Yvette's *true needs of being* are to be evoked by the dark man:

> She wanted, now, to be held against the slender, fine-shaped breast of the gipsy. She

wanted him to hold her in his arms, if only for once, for once, and comfort and confirm her. She wanted to be confirmed by him, against her father, who had only a repulsive fear of her. (SS, 1082)

We need not doubt that a young virgin, harassed by moralizing parents, might fantasy like this, but the question is whether to act out this desire would be to fulfill her true needs. To Lawrence it would. When Yvette discusses sex with her sister and says "Perhaps we haven't really *got* any sex, to connect us with men," Lawrence goes on:

> She felt rather like Peter when the cock crew, as she denied him. Or rather, she did not deny the gipsy; she didn't care about his part in the show, anyhow. It was some hidden part of herself that she denied: that part which mysteriously and unconfessedly responded to him. And it was a strange, lustrous black cock that crew in mockery of her. (SS, 1074)

The cock is the mocking phallus of blood that the resurrected man offers. "His shadow was on her" (SS, 1066). The cock is the ultimate blood to which we must listen.

There are two passages where the reality of the attraction breaks into the story. One is a discussion of "common sensuality"; the other is of the possible relationship between Yvette and the gipsy.

In the first, the gipsy returns to Yvette's consciousness "with painful force":

> "What is it. Lucille," she asked, "that brings people together? People like the Eastwoods, for instance? And Daddy and Mamma, so frightfully unsuitable? And that gipsy woman who told my fortune, like a great horse, and the gipsy man, so fine and delicately cut? What is it?"
> "I suppose it's sex, whatever that is," said Lucille.
> "Yes, what is it? It's not really anything *common*, like common sensuality, you know, Lucille. It really isn't" (SS, 1073–74)

Of course not—it is not merely lust. It is rather the mystery of attractiveness of being between men and woman for which there is no accounting. Yvette goes on:

> "Because, you see, the *common* fellows, who make a girl feel *low:* nobody cares much about them . . . . Yet they're supposed to be the sexual sort."
> "I suppose," said Lucille, "there's the low sort of sex, and there's the other sort that isn't low." (SS, 1073–74)

They agree that perhaps they "haven't sex," and Lucille declares that it was a pity it was ever invented. Yvette goes on:

> "Yes! Sex is an awful bore, you know, Lucille. When you havn't got it, you feel you

*ought* to have it somehow. And when you've got it—or *if* you have it—"she lifted her head and wrinkled her nose disdainfully—"you hate it." (SS, 1074)

This young lady, obviously is due to be taught a lesson, which the gypsy-dynamic of Lawrence is going to give her.

But is the gypsy the "real thing"? Lawrence portrays his characters expressing his doubts:

> The little jewess gazed at Yvette with eyes of stupor.
> "You're not in love with that *gipsy*!" she said.
> "Well," said Yvette. "I don't know. He's the only one that makes me feel—different. He really is!"
> "But how? How? Has he ever *said* anything to you?" (SS, 1077)

He has just looked at her, with that naked desire, "as if he really, but *really*, desired me," says Yvette, "her meditative face looking like the bud of a flower." The Jewess thinks the man has a cheek to look at Yvette like that, but the major declares "desire is the most wonderful thing in life. Anybody who can really feel it, is a king, and I envy nobody else!" (SS, 1078)

Desire is not merely appetite for Lawrence, but the problem is how we know. Don't we, the readers, know that the gypsy's desire for Yvette has a strange component of cocking a snook at "established society"? And what would happen if (like Frieda) we always answered the call of "the blood" whenever it came along?

> "*How* could it be the real thing" (exclaims the Jewess). "As if she could possibly marry him and go round in a caravan!"
> "I didn't say marry him" said Charles
> "Or a love affair! Why, it's monstrous! What would she think of herself! That's not love! That's prostitution!" (SS, 1078)

Charles's reply is so "Lawrentian" as to be ludicrous: "That gipsy was the best man we had, with horses." Charles is made to stand for some "liberated" wisdom about sex, but what he offers is Lawrence propaganda. The gypsy turns out, as we have seen, to be "resurrected man": he is destiny! He is *Lawrence*—come to awaken Yvette as yet another manifestation of resurrecting the dead mother.

The dead Mother apppears in another form in the story, of course, as Mater: "one of those physically vulgar, clever old bodies." There is a great deal of satire and comedy around this Mater, and the aunt, but it suffers from too much hostility ("toad-like," "prognathous," "her coffin-like mouth"). This betrays in Lawrence a need to hate. There *is* one moment when Yvette herself gives herself over to the joys of hatred.

> It was Granny whom she came to detest with all her soul . . . her Yvette really hated,

with that pure, sheer hatred which is almost a joy. Her hate was so clear, that while she was feeling strong, she enjoyed it. (SS, 1083)

We are, again, beyond morality. Yvette also hates the rectory: "Hate kindled her heart, and she lay with numbed limbs." Contemplating the swarthy gypsy woman, Yvette

"liked the danger and the covert fearlessness of her. She liked her covert, unyielding sex, *that was immoral*, but with a hard defiant pride of its own." (SS, 1050; my italics)

It is impossible to avoid the sense that behind this lies the fervent moral inversion of the Grossian influence.

What is the connection between the catastrophe at the end, and the ironic, bitter portrayal of the heavily moralistic life of the rectory? To get his dénouement, Lawrence has to burst a reservoir. Of course Leavis saw this as symbolic of the deeper forces of being breaking their bounds. We might agree that it represents the dark forces in life with which we need to come to terms, but the story is not tragic, and in the end, despite its thrilling immediacy, the flood appears as a piece of *Deus ex machina*. As this, it achieves two results: it enables the awful old Mater to be swept away, with a "glint of a wedding ring" (again, the old dead parental marriage is annihilated), and it enables the gypsy to go to bed with Yvette, and yet to become a hero.

Lawrence portrays the conventional family as a source of death of the spirit. Here, in this family, we have the awful "coupling" of the parents, whose sexual life has gone dead. The wife has departed (despite her husband's passionate love for her); the aunt's sex is maimed; the Mater is a powerful and dominating force for blighting and falsification.

But how can the answer to this be a gypsy who lusts after one of the daughters, but who then, by coincidence, comes to save her life by warming her in a bed in the unsafe ruins of the rectory, damaged by a flood? The flood creates the situation necessary to the Lawrence daydream—that of life-or-death. The heroic, god-like self now revives the dead mother-woman.

"Warm me!" she moaned, with chattering teeth.
"Warm me! I shall die of shivering." A terrible convulsion went through her curled-up white body, enough indeed to rupture her and cause her to die. (SS, 1094)

It is difficult to tell whether Lawrence meant them to have sexual intercourse. It seems likely that he did, since we have the customary electricity:

And though his body, wrapped round her strange and lithe and powerful, like tentacles, rippled with shuddering as an electric current, still the rigid tension of the muscles that held her clenched steadied them both, and gradually the sickening violence of the shuddering, caused by shock, abated, in his body first, then in hers, and the warmth revived between them. And as it roused, their tortured, semi-conscious minds became unconscious, they passed away into sleep. (SS, 1094)

Realistically, we may say that in such a shock, it would he very unlikely that sexual love would be possible. Since Yvette is a virgin, it could be painful and difficult, and a distressing experience. As Lawrence shows in *Sons and Lovers*, potency is the first victim of shock and distress.

But that is to bring the fantasy into too real a focus. The kind of life-restoring coition Lawrence fantasies, it should be noted, is often virtually *unconscious*, as at the end of *Glad Ghosts*. It is like an erotic dream. It is moreover important for there to be darkness and unconsciousness—perhaps it is important that the true motive should not be seen. It is, in fact, incestuous coition with the mother that is desired, to bring her back to life, and so to restore meaning to the world. (In *The Princess*, the revival of the Sleeping Beauty brings willful domination from the man, and death—one can never know how it is going to turn out.) It is for similar reasons that it must take place in huts or other remote areas, or in wild spots, ranches in the mountains, and so on.

Also, it is often only a single occasion, as here. Of course, if one is bringing the woman out of death, or kissing her to life like Sleeping Beauty, it need only be done once, but this means that there can be no question of *love* in terms of the ongoing of a mutual commitment. All one has (if one is to be realistic) is an animal act.

Yvette wakes up wondering "where was her gipsy of this world's end tonight?", but what has come to an end is merely her sojourn in the world of death. "He was gone!" She is numb and disappointed. The gypsies have struck camp.

And Yvette, lying in bed, moaned in her heart: "Oh, I love him! I love him! I love him!"...

Yet practically, she too was acquiescent in the fact of his disappearance. *Her young soul knew the wisdom of it.* (SS, 1097 my italics)

Though Lawrence himself was no seducer, his work often reads like propaganda for a seducer. The young virgin Yvette is only grateful for the naked desire the gypsy has directed at her, and the opportunity for him to gratify it. She is then grateful and understands why he must disappear—any love affair with him, or marriage, is impossible. It was just that one-night-stand awakening she wanted—that was the inner voice, about which the colorful cock crew.

Although Yvette cries out using the word "love" at the end, there is nothing about love in this story. One cannot call a gypsy's insolent naked desire, with its contemptuous subversiveness, love, nor can Yvette's immature infatuation with the gypsy be called love.

Leavis seems completely mesmerized by this story. He says that "The Tale is a tenderly reverend study of virginal young life. As such it seems to me unsurpassable . . . . The freshness, the inexperience, the painfully conscious ignorance, the confidence and the need to believe in life are touchingly evoked" (Leavis 1955, 291). Despite the evidence in the story that the gypsy is plotting his seductive promiscuity with Yvette, Leavis is prepared to swallow him whole. "The difficulty," he says, "is not a matter of anything strange or abnormal about the relation"—an extraordinary statement for someone who objected to Will Ladislaw as an appropriate partner for Dorothea Casaubon.

> It is that the indispensably unambiguous precision is so hard to achieve: the terms to hand (a significant fact, bearing pregnantly on the essential difficulty of the achievement and its importance) are of so little use; the necessary definition required Lawrence's genius and the resources of his art. (Leavis 1955, 292)

Leavis avoids the issue completely, by murmuring "genius" and making it seem that art of such quality must not be questioned. But can one accept this?

> One can say that, for Yvette, the gipsy represents the antithesis of the rectory, with its baseless self-love, its fear of life, its stagnation and its nullity . . . the essential theme of the tale has nothing to do with Wraggle-taggle-gipsyism. The one word one has to use is "desire." It is a necessary word. (Leavis 1955, 292)

Desire may be "real," and, of course, it is set against the rectory and its nullity. But the way in which the gypsy evokes the desire in Yvette is full of duplicity and the impulses of power and exploitation. The gypsy is married, and evidently not a possible partner who can offer anything by way of stability of relationship or shared interests to Yvette. Leavis may tell is that the story is done with delicacy, sensitiveness, and tact. The bursting of the dam may have a symbolic effect in Lawrence's impulse to sweep away "stagnation," and in the way the gypsy warms Yvette into "life." But one would have liked to have pressed Leavis further on his admission:

> At the close is the cool recognition that the affair (if it can be called an "affair") with the gipsy is no more than what it is—or rather, has been (or *could* have been).
>
> And Yvette, lying in bed, moaned in her heart: "Oh, I love him! I love him!" . . . Yet practically she was acquiescent in the fact of his disappearance, Her young soul knew the wisdom of it.

The bursting of the dam belongs as much to the flood in *The Mill on the Floss* as to a wish-fulfillment fantasy—an indulgence in fantasy to overcome the evident truth that the gypsy represents nothing that could be a real and proper partner for the girl, in any sense whatever. In the world of the reality of perception of (say) a Jane Austen or a George Eliot or a Henry James, all that this seducer of vicious duplicity could generate in her life, by this brief "affair," would be serious and lasting damage to her emotional life. Lawrence is acting out in fantasy something he wanted to do for his own emotional purposes, that is, to express his contempt for the "stagnation" of the Weekley family (which quite possibly did not deserve it; some observers have much respect for Weekley) and to indulge in the triumph over a "tender young virgin," while once more performing his phallic resurrection of woman, to restore her to life.

We might, I suppose, look at the tale in yet another way, as if it were a symbolic dream. It could be argued, on Freudian lines, that the tale enacts the need for a young virgin to learn to embrace her libidinal self, like Beauty and the Beast. The stern and emotionally dead family could represent the Superego, the internalized bans and prohibitions of the family in a repressive society. The gypsy represents the libido, the sexual urge, and all the dark forces with which we need to come to terms. The libidinous sexual drive knows no morals; it is indeed "naked desire." The gypsy's look penetrates to Yvette on another plane—and, indeed, Lawrence often explores that kind of strange message that reaches across from man to woman, beyond their intellectual awareness and will. Old Granny could represent the danger of femininity remaining forever unfulfilled in this way, going dead and malevolent so it is satisfactory that she is swept away by the flood.

However, suppose a patient had such a dream, what would a therapist say? Would he not warn against acting it out? If Frankl and Rollo May are right, Freudian analysis based on "release" theory may prompt a patient to become sexually active, but still fail to solve the essential problem, which is the need for a meaningful relationship, for love. Only if that yearning is fulfilled can we, at the deepest level of being, find that sense of uniqueness in ourselves, through meeting with the unique other, in love. The gypsy simply does not offer any such solution, and, indeed, he threatens the dangers of a "thoroughly decadent sensualism": at the end, he "lives in hopes," coarsely.

Behind this again is the question of "models." Of course, we have sexual desire, but it is not true that the sexual instinct is so primary and powerful that it threatens to tear us to pieces if it is not fulfilled. There is a deeper problem— that of the meaning of our being. It is that which certainly can tear us to pieces since this is a question of the *Dasein*, of what meaning to set against death.

This tragic perspective puts a big question mark against a story like *The Virgin and the Gypsy*. What can it profit a wayward young virgin, in the perspective of the *Dasein*, to lie with a gypsy in the fortuitous circumstances of a flood rescue, when she had been secretly lusting for him? What meaning could that possibly give to her life, except that of a dangerous and reckless adventure with no future, except perhaps a miserable one? Is this even the clue to the emotional flowering of that "bud"? It would be interesting to try to write a sequel in which—in the mode of (say) George Eliot or Edith

Wharton—the effects of the idolization of the equestrian gipsy on any future positive relationship in Yvette's life were portrayed. In that there could be tragedy indeed.[4]

## St. Mawr

For a long time I accepted Leavis's high valuation of this story. Now it seems to be full of paranoia and to offer, ultimately, in its "upshot," only escapism. It contains, of course, the essential Lawrentian themes—Rico is a fraud both in art and life; Lou Witt is an unawakened woman, only gradually emerging to the awareness of the emptiness of her life. Her marriage (as so often with marriages in Lawrence) becomes sexless. Her mother is all American will and represents mature feminine experience, but she has never really been touched by love and the deeper vibrations of being. (Because she is older and can be seen with detachment Mrs. Witt is a triumph, seen with sympathy and wit: hence perhaps her name—she *is* the ironic intelligence and sees that life can only be sometimes and partially satisfactory.)

Who is to offer the great and deeper realms of being? First, a stallion whose name is close to Lawrence's, St. Mawr. He stands for uncompromising dignity of being, the nobleness of animal existence and potency, but as we shall see, his meaning is ambivalent. Significantly, he is also not an effective mating animal. There is then the groom Lewis, whose name is also like Lawrence, he is the natural man, bearded, *noli-me-tangere* visionary, and one who declares that *after he has been with women he does not feel himself*, that is, he feels a dread of loss of self in sexual giving. Mrs. Witt falls in love with him, and we see the source of her success as a character. She has much of Frieda's scathing intelligence and is not afraid to speak out (as Ursula speaks out).

And then there is Lou herself, who increasingly "becomes" Lawrence, flying from the world of men into the wilds.

Leavis sees *St. Mawr* as a perfect masterpiece, and it is true that its language is rich, it is vivid, and the portrayal of characters like Mrs. Witt and Lewis is superb. But what about its "upshot"—for it undoubtedly is offered as a message, a fable?

The word "quick" occurs in the preceding pages: "I want the wonder back again," cries Lou Witt. In St. Mawr, with his great body glowing with power, and with "the vivid heat of his life," she finds that quickness of life. In the horse we are to see the mystery of being in man made manifest. The men she has met have not been animals in the best sense of the word, and again we have a lecture on Pan.

But then St. Mawr rears and falls over backwards on Rico, or is pulled by Rico on top of himself (SS, 610). Presumably the point is that Rico does not have that deep tacit power over the animal that Phoenix and Lewis have—intuitive gifts to be in harmony with nature. This potency, as least in Phoenix, is admired for its taciturnity, and for its cruelty—he is cruelly teasing to the maids, for instance.

What of the use of a horse to symbolize qualities not found in man? St. Mawr rears because he sees the skin of an adder shining in the sun—an adder that has been killed by stones. Rico is badly hurt, and Young Edwards is kicked in the teeth. St. Mawr "seemed to be seeing legions of ghosts, down the dark avenues of the centuries that have lapsed since the horse became subject to man" (SS, 611). In one sense, the trouble is that Rico has not properly managed St. Mawr's horse-hood, because he is inadequate in his own manhood. Yet what about the snake? And what is the meaning of St. Mawr's intractability?

By degrees, Lou and Mrs. Witt come around to the view St. Mawr is to be protected. Rico and Flora Manby are in league to shoot him or castrate him. A great deal of comedy is made of the impulse of the Church of England dean and his wife to have the horse shot or castrated because of that "brute male strength." Lawrence satirizes the English middle-class society that hates "life" and all its power, danger, and beauty.

There is another unconscious element: the vicious rearing is also the enactment of a wish-fulfillment. Lawrence wanted to exert his revenge on Rico, who is so impotent as a man and an artist, and so superficial, quickless, and mechanical. The snake, as in the poem *Snake*, and another symbolism that belongs to Lawrence's own deeper mythology.

> If there is a serpent of secret and shameful desire in my soul, let me not beat it out of my consciousness with sticks. Let me bring it to the fire to see what it is. For a serpent is a thing created. Even my horror is a tribute to its reality. And I must admit the genuineness of my horror, accept it, and not exclude it from my understanding.... Come then, brindled abhorrent one, you have your own being and your own righteousness, yes, and your own desirable beauty. ("The Reality of Peace," quoted by Harry T. Moore, 1955, 332)

Lawrence, like Blake, tried to see that "everything that lives is holy." Then what about vicious horses, snakes, the impulse to smash snakes, and the *impulse to hate men* like Rico? What about *evil*?

The episode in St. Mawr is a manifestation of the evil he recognizes there to be in himself and the world, even in the "quick" animal.

> And she had a vision, a vision of evil . . . she became aware of evil, evil, evil, rolling in great waves over the earth. (SS, 612)

This is a strange thought for Lou because of an unfortunate accident with her husband on a horse. Of course, in Lou we are seeing the characteristic Sleeping Beauty awakening, but she is (like Ursula) also Lawrence himself:

> Always she had thought there was no such thing—only a mere negation of good.

> Now, like an ocean to whose surface she had risen. She saw the dark-grey waves of evil rearing in a great tide. (SS, 612)

Such a paranoid feeling *might* arise in anyone who was in a state of shock after such a violent incident, but Lawrence often shoots off into what is clearly a rumination of his own:

> And it had swept mankind away without mankind's knowing. It had caught up the nations as the rising ocean might lift the fishes, and was sweeping them on in a great tide of evil. They did not know. The people did not know. They did not even wish it. They wanted to be good and to have everything joyful and enjoyable. Everything joyful and enjoyable, for everybody. This was what they wanted, if you asked them. (SS, 612)

Whatever has this got to do with it? It is very difficult to follow Lawrence's thought here. What has St. Mawr's fury and the injury of Rico to do, even at the symbolic level, with the "tide of evil" that apparently has led people to want "enjoyment"?

It is difficult to see the socialities of Lou Witt's acquaintance, or even Mrs. Witt's kind of American-willed consciousness as "evil."

> at the same time, they had fallen under the spell of evil. It was a soft, subtle thing, soft as water, and its motion was soft and imperceptible, as the running of a tide is invisible to one who is out of the ocean. And they were all out in the ocean, being borne along in the current of the mysterious evil, creatures of the evil principle, as fishes are creatures of the sea.
>
> There was no relief. The whole world was enveloped in one of great flood. All the nations, the white, the brown, the black, the yellow, all were immersed. (SS, 612)

Everyone wanted a good time all round, and yet some strange thing had happened, "and that vast mysterious force of positive evil was let loose."

It is this that she sees in St. Mawr, working his hooves in the air: "Reversed, and purely evil." But how can the antics of a frightened and rather awkward horse symbolize a tide of evil that was overwhelming the world? What can be the message for us, since one is clearly intended?

> What did it mean? Evil, evil, and a rapid return to the sordid chaos! Which was wrong, the horse or the rider? or both? (SS, 613)

Lawrence is confused. He puts his trust in pure animal quickness, and it shows itself vicious and hateful. What then? Lou thinks of Rico's face:

> His fear, his impotence as a master, as a rider, his presumption. And she thought with horror of those other people, so glib, so glibly evil. (SS, 613)

At the heart of the rage is Lawrence's misogyny:

> What did they want to do, those Manby girls? Undermine, undermine, undermine. They wanted to undermine Rico, just as the fair young man would have liked to undermine her. Believe in nothing, care about nothing: but keep the surface easy, and have a good time. *Let us undermine one another. There is nothing believe in, so let us undermine everything. But look out! No scenes, no spoiling the game.* (SS, 613)

It is perhaps true that St. Mawr's outburst reminds us that in dealing with "life" we are dealing with something dangerous, and it is this such superficiality denies. Is it not an exaggeration to call such ordinary superficiality "evil"?

> The evil! The mysterious potency of evil. She could see it all the time, in individuals, society, in the press. There it was in socialism and bolshevism: the same evil. (SS, 613)

Surely this is paranoia run riot?

> Fascism would keep the surface of life intact, and carry on the undermining business all the better. All the better sport. Never draw blood. Keep the haemorrhage internal, invisible. (SS, 613)

The only thing that unites the themes here is Lawrence's paranoid fears and dislikes, and these pages are nonsensical mumbo-jumbo:

> Mankind, like a horse, ridden by a stranger, smooth-faced, evil rider. Evil himself, smooth-faced and pseudo-handsome, riding mankind past the dead snake, to the last break. (SS, 613)

How can the story *St. Mawr* be seen as "perfect" and as an example of Lawrence's "thought" as a creative writer when he is so intemperate?

> People performing outward acts of loyalty, piety, self-sacrifice. But inwardly bent on undermining, betraying. Directing all their subtle evil will against any positive living thing. Masquerading as the ideal, in order to poison the real. (SS, 613)

The note struck is clearly a response to the Great War, and perhaps his response to the reviews in the press of Lawrence's erotic novels. What we have, as in many of his later works, is a nihilistic turning against "humanity":

> Creation destroys as it goes, throws down one tree for the rise of another. But mankind would abolish death, multiply itself million upon million, rear up city upon

city, save every parasite alive, until the accumulation of mere existence is swollen to a horror. But go on saving life, the ghastly salvation army of ideal mankind. (SS, 614)

Lawrence has the bit between his teeth and gallops away beyond misogyny into hostile misanthropy:

> At the same time secretly, viciously, potently undermine the natural creation, betray it with kiss after kiss, destroy it from the inside, till you have the swollen rottenness of our teeming existences.... Production must be heaped upon production.... Judas is the last God and, by heaven, the most potent. (SS, 614)

We might suppose Lawrence is concerned with ecological problems like today's green parties, but he goes on:

> Man must destroy as he goes, as trees fall for trees to rise. The accumulation of life and things means rottenness. Life must destroy life, in the unfolding of creation. (SS, 614)

How does this relate in any possible sense to the story of St. Mawr and Rico and the rest? Lawrence, like Leavis, ultimately, had no hope:

> What's to be done? Generally speaking, nothing. The dead will have to bury their dead, while the earth stinks of corpses. *The individual can but depart from the mass, and try to cleanse himself.* Try to hold fast to the living thing, which destroys as it goes, but remains sweet. (SS, 614; my italics)

So, it is *sauve qui peut*—and especially save myself. Lou, like Lawrence, is off to the desert. But what is this "living thing *which destroys as it goes*"? What is it that the St. Mawr–Lawrence "quick" life has the authority to destroy? The pages of mumbo-jumbo end in a paroxysm of paranoia:

> And in his soul [Lawrence had clearly and wildly forgotten he is supposed to be portraying a *woman's* thoughts] fight, fight, fight to preserve that which is life in him from the ghastly kisses and poison—bites of the myriad evil ones. Retreat to the desert, and fight. But in his soul adhere to that which is life itself, creatively destroying as it goes: destroying the stiff old thing to let the new bud come through. The one passionate principle of creative being, which recognizes the natural good, and has a sword for the swarms of evil. Fights, fights, fights to protect itself. But with itself, is strong and at peace. (SS, 614)

Not only does the self-saving impulse, couched in such terms, not emerge out of the logic of the story, but in what way does Lou destroy anything, except supposedly by putting her marriage in jeopardy? There is not even any firm break there. Toward the end Mrs. Witt suggests that Rico will come to find her at the ranch, and Lou does not reject this. It could be creative to quit a marriage at such a point, but that is not Lawrence's point. What he seeks to justify is pure, devoted misanthropy, to quit the world of civilized man totally, and take refuge in escapism and hate.

The rejection of consciousness, intelligence, and community—of the future and hope—is disguised by the idolization of the "quick" animal

> The wild animal is at every moment intensely self-disciplined, poised in the tension of self-defence, self-preservation, and self-assertion. (SS, 615–16)

This is nonsense, and the parallel, which Lawrence examines to Rico's disadvantage, is false.

Of course, we need to embrace our animal nature, our deeper intuition, and our qualities that belong to the universal life-pulses, but our problems belong to intelligence and civilization, to a specifically human consciousness. In this, paranoid retreat is useless; it is merely a self-preserving escape from the problem.

There is a problem—of the meaning of life, of love and work and belief. We do urgently need a new kind of consciousness, open and expanded, and directed toward a new sense of man's place in the world. To this, indeed, Lawrence, even by his descriptions of the beauty of the natural world, has contributed.

But in that he idolized retreat and escape, and the abandoning of civilization in hatred of man and in disgust and hostility, he failed seriously to lead us toward true solutions.

## *The Woman Who Rode Away*

*The Woman Who Rode Away* is Lawrence's *She*, but Lawrence's "she" is by no means a *mysterium tremendum* here. There *is* a mystery about her ("she was some mystic object to them, some vehicle of passions too remote for them to grasp," [SS, 69]), and she is nameless. She is also an exercise in the totally controlled, subjugated, and annihiliated woman as the exorcism of the dreaded woman, so that male mastery may be upheld. Lawrence seems at times to "place" this, but the appeal of it triumphs as power. Lawrence has imagination enough to be aware of how terrible it would be for someone to be caught in the toils of the fantasies of others endowed with a religious meaning, and he can identify sufficiently with the woman to portray her awareness of her predicament with some sympathy. However, the sympathy is not fully realized, but is rather subdued under the awe and excitement with which Lawrence indulges in the fantasy of what he would unconsiously like to do to woman. The upshot is "She gets what she deserves"; it is "inevitable that what is done to her must be done, in order that the world should be put right," or "that my soul should be put right."

In the Introduction Richard Aldington tells us that Lawrence was "at once horror-stricken and fascinated by the old Mexican belief that power could be acquired by cutting out the heart from a living victim to hold up, still palpitating to the blood-red sun'' (SS, 8). But what kind of power are we dealing with? The story, which Aldington believes "gives us Lawrence at one of his most inspired moments," was suggested by Lawrence's wanderings through remote parts of Mexico. Mabel Luhan believed that the cave is one near Taos, and the story was suggested to Lawrence by her account of her psychic experiences. He certainly seems to have intended her as the woman.

If this is so, then the story may be in response to a woman with whom Lawrence had great difficulty: she seems to have been a very possessive American matron. She said "the womb in me roused to reach out and take him" (Luhan 1932, 37). There was considerable conflict between Frieda and Mabel, not least over a proposal that Mabel and Lawrence should write a book together. Frieda wrote,

> And there was a fight between us, Mabel and myself: I think it was a fair fight. One day Mabel came over and told me she didn't think I was the right woman for Lawrence. (Frieda Lawrence 1934, 136)

Lawrence is reported by Frieda to have said,

> "All women are alike . . . bossy, without any decency; it's your business to see that other women don't come too close to me." (Quoted by Luhan 1932, 244)

This is the voice we hear distinctly behind *The Woman who Rode Away*. Mabel Luhan reported that Lawrence declared to her, in a dangerously intimate moment, that there as "something more important than love— Fidelity!" (Luhan 1932, 69). She said,

> I wanted to seduce his spirit so that I could make him carry out certain things. I did not want him for myself in the usual way of men with women . . . . But I actually awakened in myself, artifically, I suppose, a wish, a wilful wish to feel him . . . .
> I did this because I knew instinctively that the strongest, surest way to the soul is through the flesh. (Luhan 1932, 69–70)

This is the woman Lawrence sends packing in fantasy in this story. There must have been some fascination in Lawrence for this woman, the same kind of fascination that impelled him towards Lady Ottoline because in their strong-willed attempt to dominate, such women were like his mother. In the end Lawrence wrote of Mabel that he was

> Tired of her, the bully, with that bullying, evil, destructive, dominating will of hers.—Oh, these awful cultured Americans, how they lack natural aristocracy.—She doesn't let one alone, we have no privacy, and wherever we go, she has to drag that fat Indian along, that fat Indian chauffeur of hers.[5] (Merrild 1939, 28)

Elsewhere he wrote:

> [Mabel] is a little famous in New York and little loved, very intelligent as a woman, another "culture-carrier," likes to play the patroness, hates the white world and loves the Indians out of hate, is very "generous," wants to be "good" and is very wicked, has a terrible will to power, you know—she wants to be a witch and at the same time a Mary of Bethany at Jesus's feet—a big, white crow, a cooing raven of ill-omen, a little buffalo ... we are still "friends" with Mabel. But do not take this snake to our bosom. You know, these people have only money, nothing else but money. (Frieda Lawrence 1934, 158–59)

I invoke these biographical details only in order to suggest that there was some provocation behind Lawrence's story—that he wrote it in revenge for Mabel Luhan's possessiveness, as he wrote his portrait of Lady Otteline in Hermione to do the same to her. Mabel Luhan herself reports that when a Taos gossip told her that Lawrence had said she tried to make him fall in love with her and tried to take him up on the roof to force him to make love to her, that she had an "evil, destructive, dominating will," and "that it would be the end of her," she fainted away for twenty-four hours. When Lawrence heard of this, he said her will had been defeated for the first time and that she couldn't stand it.

Perhaps we may see the story as an attempt to show how a woman's will could "be the end of her."

*The Woman Who Rode Away* is a powerful contribution to the fantasies of false solution. Because it is so powerfully written (the descriptions of the countryside are marvelous), because of the kind of satisfactions it offers, and because of its strong unconscious elements, such a story—although a "fiction"—must surely contribute a great deal that is false to the consciousness of readers, not least in urging them to accept that "mastery" is necessity.

The critical passage is perhaps this, where Lawrence makes explicit his intentions:

> Her kind of womanhood, intensely personal and individual, was to be obliterated again, and the great primaeval symbols were to tower once more over the fallen independence of woman. The sharpness and the quivering nervous consciousness of the highly-bred white woman was to be destroyed again, womanhood was to be cast once more into the great stream of impersonal sex and impersonal passion. Strangely, as if clairvoyant, she saw the immense sacrifice prepared. (WRA, 71)

Here we may recall the remark from the *Letters* quoted below a propos of *The Rainbow:* "It's no use ... the woman looking to sensuous satisfaction for their fulfillment" (Huxley 1932, 316) Lawrence had theories about what should happen to woman, and often we find it stressed in his work that women must submit to something "inhuman." Here the instructional symbolism of the story, its *propaganda* purpose, is made clear—"the great primaeval symbols were to tower once more over the fallen individual independence of woman.'' (WRA, p70) It is not only in this *one* woman that Lawrence wishes to show happening ''the sharpness and the quivering nervous consciousness of the highly-bred white woman was to be destroyed again.'' (WRA, T1) He wants it, by example, to happen to woman all over. Why ''once more'' and ''again''? I suppose he means ''as I have shown before in my work.'' The biblical reference is, of course, to Daniel 6.

''She'' at the beginning of the story is married to a *miner*, albeit a silver miner. She has two children, but, like Frieda, turns her back on them, and they play very little part in the story. (The way she just leaves them is how Lawrence wished Frieda could have left hers.) The husband is totally devoted to industrial effort and ''marriage was the last and most intimate bit of his own works.'' She is the girl from Berkeley, California.

> Her conscious development had stopped mysteriously with her marriage, completely arrested. Her husband had never become real to her. (WRA, 46)

The husband is an active rancher, and an idealist who ''really hated the physical side of marriage.'' Thus, the beginning is a parallel to *Women in Love*, in which the Criches are supposed to symbolize the death of being, under effectiveness and ''go'': ''She must get out.''

Then a young man says to her, ''I wonder what there is behind those great blank hills.'' His peculiar vague enthusiasm for unknown Indians found a full echo in the woman's heart.

> She was overcome by a foolish romanticism more unreal than a girl's. She felt it was her destiny to wonder into the secret haunts of these timeless, mysterious, marvellous Indians of the mountains.
> She kept her secret. (WRA, 49)

Lawrence is critical of her romantic impulse, of course, as he was critical of Mabel Luhan's ''love'' of the Indians. He is going to show us that the Indians were really terrible, and not to be romanticized. But his Indians are romanticized in a different way, not the husband's ''low-down and dirty, insanitary, with a few cunning tricks'' Indians, but the Indians of Lawrence's Nietzschean imagination, Dionysiac Indians: ''the old priests still kept up the ancient religions, and offered human sacrifices—so it was said'' (WRA, 49).

The woman makes her crazy plans. The woman rides off. We are invited to approve of this quest for authenticity: '' 'Am I *never* to be let alone? Not one moment of my life?' she cried, with a sudden explosion of energy.'' (WRA, 50). She is not afraid, despite the frightening country. She is curiously not lonely. ''And a strange elation sustained her from within . . . She was buoyed up always by the curious, bubbling elation within her'' (WRA, 51).

She has the ''feeling like a woman who has died and passed beyond.''

She was not sure that she had not heard, during the night, a great crash at the centre of herself, which was the crash of her own death. Or else it was a crash at the centre of the earth, and meant something big and mysterious. (WRA, 52)

This note recurs and recurs. And we may say, I believe, that this makes "she" the dead mother, or the woman taking the path of the dead mother, or the mother-like Mabel being consigned to that path. *Woman* was being consigned to that path, symbolically, in order to complete certain psychic processes— even to *lay her to rest*, to lay the "bad" mother in the female element of the self to rest. The story is really part of a *mourning* process, and Lawrence's propaganda against woman emerges from a mourning process too.

She gradually reaches a state, in that beautiful countryside, in which she has no will of her own. Attitude and the weariness bring this about, but we may note that she moves into an ever-increasing state of forfeiture of will under the spell of Lawrence's own fantasy-spinning need to subdue her.

She meets at last the wild Indians whom she has come to see with long black hair over their shoulders. The interesting word that Lawrence soon uses is "inhuman." The Indian spokesman notes in her "her own female power" with its "childish, half-arrogant confidence." It is that that must be broken, and he also notes in her eyes "a curious look of trance." The spell is beginning to work.

Consciously, Lawrence isn't altogether lost in his fantasy. He says comically of one of the Indians, "he did not look as if he had washed lately." But the spell grows on him as it grows on the reader: his very imagination, following its intuitive part, develops as a wish-fantasy, enacting what he (Lawrence) would like to do to the fantasy woman.

"What do *you* want to do?" the Indian asks her. To their consternation she says she wants to visit the Chilchui Indians—"to see their houses and to know their gods."

The Indians begin to establish their mastery. One of them beats her horse to urge it forward. When the woman cries, "Don't do that!" she meets the inscrutable response:

She met his black, large, bright eyes, and for the first time her spirit really quailed. The man's eyes were not human to her, and they did not see her as a beautiful white woman. He looked at her with a black, bright, inhuman look, and saw no woman in her at all. As if she were some strange, unaccountable *thing*, incomprehensible to him, but inimical. (WRA, 55)

Here I believe we may speak of tactics. Lawrence is full of rage against the white, "independent," self-conscious woman. He wants to strip her of her power and the way to do it is to enter into a supposed primitive consciousness, by which *she is not a woman at all*. If we go back to the primitive sense that woman is only "the space between the stars," then indeed we have conquered her. Thus, the Indians see this woman, who has put herself in their hands, not sexually but as "a piece of venison" (WRA, 57) or even "some giant female white ant." In this we have the *depersonalization of the object*, and so "the woman was powerless." It is the mother's animus he is seeking, in fantasy, to subdue.

At the same time "there came a slight thrill of exultation. *She knew she was dead*" (WRA, 55).

Why should a woman feel exultation, at the onset of her death, and at the denial of her human reality? Sexually, they deny her, too, by taking no interest in her whatever at night; she doesn't have that card to play. (Incidentally, Lawrence is making a useful point, that with the Indians, their sexuality belongs to a pattern of meaning and is not mere sensuality. It is surely very unlikely that a woman in this state would *not* have been sexually approached.)

In the Indians' eyes now she sees only a "remote, inhuman glitter." There is not even "derision in their eyes."

> They were inaccessible. They could not see her as a woman at all. As if she *were* not a woman. (WRA, 57)

"She could see it was hopeless to expect any human communication" with the old Indian who greets them. When she tells them she does not want to bring the white man's God, and is weary with Him, but wants to look for theirs, a "thrill of triumph and exultance" passes through them—nothin "sensual or sexual" in their look at her, but a "terrible glittering purity."

> She was afraid, she would have been paralysed with fear, had not something died within her. (WRA, 61)

She seems now to have been driven from the beginning by a death-wish.

The description of the terrain and the Indian places is superb, deeply convincing, and realized. This makes it all the more shocking when suddenly, "with great power," she is stripped. Her boots are slit with keen knives, and her clothing is slit so that it "came away from her." The old man touches her breasts and her back, "as if Death itself were touching her." Yet she totally fails to respond to this in outrage. She feels neither ashamed nor tempted, only "sad and lost." The episode has a dream-like quality like the fantasies of George MacDonald in *Phantastes* and *Lilith*. This is because there are now no *real* responses. Actually no woman would behave under such humiliation, so without distress. But "she" does because "she" is a fantasy woman under control—under the control of Lawrence's daydream.

The men regard her, as such creatures do in dreams, each with a "strange look of ecstasy on his face," or with "a curious look of triumph and ecstasy" or with "curious solicitude." They give her an emetic drug that sedates her, while one old man exhibits an "almost fatherly solicitude." All this "care" is part of the control. Underneath the cure is "something terrible." A special Indian who sits with her is "darkly and powerfully male" yet he doesn't ever make her "self-conscious or sex-conscious" (WRA, 68).

> She was not in her own power, she was under the spell of some other control. (WRA, 69)

Never has Lawrence written so much like Ian Fleming for Fleming's sex fantasies have this undercurrent of the ominous, and the curious gloating note of control. (See the present writer's *The Masks of Hate*, 1972.) It is intensely sadistic.

Indians now dance, wearing fox skins between their legs, the phallic symbolism of which is obvious from *The Fox*, and there is an "inhuman male singing." It is at this point that we have the paragraph discussed above about women's consciousness. The women to them, one Indian explains, are merely the spaces that keep the stars apart (and a "touch of derision came into his eyes"). The woman is now in a "trance of agony" as she listens to the drums, and men singing:

> like wild creatures, howling to the invisible gods of the moon and the vanished sun. Something of the chuckling, sobbing cry of the coyote, something of the exultant bark of the fox, the far-off wild melancholy exultance of the howling wolf, the torment of the puma's scream, and the insistence of the ancient fierce human male, with his lapses of tenderness and his abiding ferocity. (WRA, 71)

It is impossible not to feel that with the repetition of the word "exultant" that Lawrence is not enjoying the "insistence of the ancient fierce human male." Now, through the voices of a "young Indians", he invents a mythology: "'White people,' he said, 'they know nothing . . . we know the sun, and we know the moon'" (WRA, 72). When a white woman sacrifices herself to their gods, then the gods will begin to make the world again. It seems like a paradigm of the Lawrentian view of the separateness of man and woman: "The sun he is alive at one end of the sky . . . and the moon lives at the other end" (WRA, 72). The white man, according to the Indian, stole the sun, but doesn't know how to keep him. The white women, accordingly, don't know what to do with the moon: "The moon she got angry with white women . . . the moon, she bites white women—here inside" (WRA, 72-3). The Indian women get the moon back, and the woman asks the young Indian about the hatred:

> "No, we don't hate," he said softly, looking with a curious glitter into her face. (WRA, 73)

Lawrence is denying that in that inhuman glittering look can be anything called hate, yet the symbolism of his mythology here belongs to hate and hate has its roots deep in the irreconcilability of father and mother, male and female, sun and moon. Here the "white woman" who contains the "moon" that "bites her," that is, who cannot accept her feminity, is to be transformed, redeemed into a fulfilled woman by death. What can it all mean? Since the moon is invoked, we must surely, as so often in Lawrence, find the Mother or female principle. With the sun and the moon some problem of the relationship between the parents is here being represented. What did Lawrence *suppose* he meant by the moon here? Some form of primal being? The fully meaningful life he wished for his mother?

> She herself would call to the unseen moon to cease to be angry, to make peace again with the unseen sun like a woman who ceases to be angry in her house. (WRA, 74)

"She" promises the young Indian they will get the sun back, and he goes away in exultance.

> She felt she was drifting on (to) some consummation, which she had no will to avoid, yet which seemed heavy and finally terrible to her. (WRA, 74)

The Indians make her succumb to their vision, but the vision is Lawrence's: the incantatory prose depicting her consciousness becomes that vision of Lawrence's own self resurrected. Here is the ecstatic prose of Lawrence's narcissism:

> it seemed to her there were two great influences in the upper air, one golden towards the sun, and one invisible silver; the first travelling like rain ascending to the gold presence sunwards, the second like rain silverily descending the ladders of space towards the hovering, lurking clouds over the snowy mountain top. Then between them, another presence, waiting to shake himself free of moisture, of heavy white snow that had mysteriously collected about him. And in summer, like a scorched eagle, he would wait to shake himself clear of the weight of heavy sunbeams. And he was coloured like fire. And he was always shaking himself clear, of snow or of heavy heat, like an eagle nestling. (WRA, 75)

This phoenix-creature is clearly the Lawrence self that needs some profound (parental) crisis to bring him into being, to be a son of God to the daughters of men. Here is another version of the Sleeping Beauty myth, only this time the sun is the Son, who is to plunge with the great icicle into the woman in a death-consummation with the dead mother. The sun-icicle-"she" conjunction is a form of primal scene.

The woman wears blue now because she is the wind, the unseen ghost of the dead mother:

> "It is the colour of what goes away and is never coming back, but which is always here, waiting like death among us .... It is the colour of the dead ... you are the

messengers from the far-away. you cannot stay, and now it is time for you to go back." (WRA, 76)

Now the Indian must give the moon to the sun. "The sun, he is shut out behind the white man, and the moon, she is shut out behind the white woman." So—everything in the world gets angrier. The sun is to leap over the white man and come to the Indian again. "She must die!"
The Indian accuses her along with all other white women:

"You shut the gate, and then laugh, think you have it all your own way . . . ."
"Have I got to die and be given to the sun?" she asked.
"Some time," he said, laughing evasively. "Sometime we all die" (WRA, 77)

The obstructive mother-imago or the obstructing attachment to a mother-woman's will must be put to death but in terms of being given to the Son (sun) so that he (Lawrence) may arise. The female independence Lawrence hates so much seems to him to be a dynamic that "shuts the gate" and thinks she has it all her own way. She must, in fantasy, be put to death. No wonder "she" is surrounded by fierce men displaying the exultance of those that are going to triumph.
The woman "gladly" takes her sedation, and the Indian priests who strip her again now rub her body with sweet-scented oil, and "massage all her limbs, and her back and her sides with a long, strange, hypnotic massage." (Actually, this seems like some strange masturbation fantasy.)

Their dark hands were incredibly powerful . . . the hands worked upon the soft white body of the woman . . . absorbed in something that was beyond her. They never saw her as a personal woman: she could tell that. She was some mystic object to them. (WRA, 79)

Lawrence writes about this is a strange incantatory way, as he does about sexual acts elsewhere. He makes it clear that, like the sodomy in *The Rainbow* and *Lady Chatterley's Lover*, it is done in hate and hostility:

the grimness of ultimate decision, the fixity of revenge, and the nascent exultance of those that are going to triumph. (WRA, 79)

Yet, like the other woman, she *wants* this:[6]

She knew she was a victim; that all this elaborate work upon her was the work of victimising her. But she did not mind. She wanted it. (WRA, 79)

I believe that those who really respond to Lawrence without discrimination want to believe this, and wish to share his unconscious belief that woman wants to be controlled and killed:

she thought, "I am dead already. What difference does it make, the transition from the dead I am to the dead I shall be, very soon! (WRA, 81)

She is led to an amphitheater in a cave. Down the front of a wall hangs "a great, dripping, fang-like spoke of ice," the death phallus. It is the shortest day, and the last day of her life. She is made to stand, stripped, in her strange pallor, "facing the iridescent column of ice, which fell down marvellously arrested." Naked priests surround her, and one fumigates her. Perhaps Lawrence had in mind rituals of purification performed in Ancient Greece; to the western mind, it is significant, these were performed to purify those who had committed murder.

What murder has "she" committed? She has failed to create whole being in the son, by a failure to reflect.

> those that held her down were bent and twisted round, their black eyes watching the sun with *a glittering eagerness*, and awe, and craving. The black eyes of the aged caique were fixed like *black mirrors* on the sun, as if sightless, yet containing some terrible answer to the reddening winter planet. And all the eyes of the priests were fixed and *glittering* on the sinking orb. (WRA, 83)

The reference to glittering objects reveals that behind the symbolism is the problem of the mother's eyes. At last creative reflection is coming but as antireflection with triumphant murder: "Their ferocity was ready to leap out into a mystic exultance, of triumph" (WRA, 83). When the sun should strike the ice phallus, "Then the old man would strike, and strike home, accomplish the sacrifice and achieve the power" (WRA, 83).

The story ends: "The mastery that man must hold, and that passes from race to race" (WRA, 83). It does pass from father to son for the same black, empty concentration of hostility in the old man's face is the same as the black hostility in the drunken Morel who shuts his wife out in the garden. Only here it is not seen with dismay as a degraded way for a human being to behave. Here it is idolized as a necessary, religious act, devoted in all solemnity as a way of restoring the world, while for the woman it represents a kind of fulfillment by the utter and passive extinction of herself. At least (the exaltation suggests) she has lived and tasted of that inhuman state of being a kind of god, in touch with some god-like phantom male, and the sun's rays gleaming on the phallus, as the possibilities of a new life are imminent through murder.

Surely there is something in Kate Millet's opinion that Lawrence's later works are "demented fantasies"? The story has a corrupt and degraded beauty. It seems, plausibly, to be a picture of an awful possibility, but it is not like *Heart of Darkness*, a placing of primitive evil as a threat to intelligence and values. Primitive evil is portrayed with mounting excitement as a new source of being and fulfillment, and as embodying what we all (really) want to do in the road to mastery over the phantom woman. Whatever it might do at the conscious level, at the unconscious level the story could only work as a subtle encouragement to the bad old hostilities that have dogged us since the world began.

## *Smile*

There are a number of other short stories I would like to discuss in detail, but space is limited. Another "demented fantasy" is the short story *Smile* that follows immediately after *The Woman Who Rode Away* in the volume under discussion. This, one gathers, was written in some spirit of vengeance against Middleton Murry. *Smile* is about the secret glee and delight a character feels when his wife dies that, willy-nilly, appears on his face at the obsequies. Matthew, the protagonist, is clearly a Lawrentian *alter ego*. When the nuns (of whose "volumes of silky black skirts" Matthew is aware) lift the veil from his wife's face to reveal the dead, beautiful composure:

> instantly, something leaped like laughter in the depths of him, he gave a little grunt, and an extraordinary smile came over his face. (WRA, 86)

In response, the startled nuns smile, too:

> the dark Ligurian face of the watching sister, a mature, level-browed woman, curled with a pagan smile, slow, infinitely subtle in its archaic humour. It was the Etruscan smile, subtle and unabashed, and unanswerable. (WRA, 86)

Obviously, Lawrence is reading into this story his response to the Etruscan tombs. The Etruscan people never forgot

> The mystery of the journey out of life, and into death; the death journey and the sojourn in the after-life ... throes of wonder and vivid feeling throbbing over death. Man moves naked and glowing through the universe. Then comes death: he dives into the sea, he departs into the underworld. (*Etruscan Places*, 84)

The sea represents the source of all things and the place into which all things are devoured back: the sea the people knew. The dolphin plunges back.

> He is so much alive, he is like the phallus carrying the fiery spark of procreation down into the wet darkness of the womb ... and the sea will give up her dead like dolphins that leap out and have the rainbow within them. (*Etruscan Places*, 84)

Lawrence writes of death and resurrection in an ecstatic tone, and invokes Christ in a strange Lawrentian way, yet while he makes it clear that he does not share the Christian belief in resurrection, he has a queer personal belief in some kind of resurrection, which is part of his personal mythology.

The "Etruscan" smile on the man's face, which she catches from Matthew, is thus the mysterious smile of the primitive belief that the dead woman has entered a new state of being.

Even the Mother Superior has a smile grow over her face, and even as she comforts a weeping young man, "the chuckle was still there."

Matthew turns in fear to see if his dead wife has observed him. The woman, as so often in Lawrence, is presented with patronizing contempt (like the wife in *The Captain's Doll*): very different from the way the dead miner is presented in *Odour of Chrysanthemums* or the dead mother in *Sons and Lovers:*

> Ophelia lay so pretty and so touching, with her peaked, dead little nose sticking up, and her face of an obstinate child fixed in its final obstinacy. (WRA, 86)

Matthew thinks, ironically, "I knew this martyrdom was in store for me."

> She was so pretty . . . so worn—and so dead. Ophelia had always wanted her own will. (WRA, 87)

The prose takes on that "good job" tone that Lawrence so often adopts over the dead woman—over Diana Crich, over the wife in *The Captain's Doll*, and *The Woman Who Rode Away*. The dead wife seems to nudge Matthew, who smiles, then cries, "*Mea Culpa! Mea Culpa!*"—and yet he is inwardly wishing he could hold the creamy-dusk hands of the sister "voluptuously." Everytime he dwells upon his own faults, and thinks *Mea Culpa!* However, something nudges him in the ribs and urges him *Smile!*

The sisters believe the dead woman has seen her husband: "For the first time they saw the faint ironical curl at the corners of Ophelia's mouth" (WRA, 88). Then they murmur a prayer for the anima: the same word Lawrence uses in writing about the Etruscan afterlife.

Matthew is now a forlorn figure: he has lost his hat, and he is utterly smileless. It would seem that he is in confusion.

The reader's confusion arises from the fact that, although conventional obsequies and illusions about death are penetrated, what is revealed is a "reality" highly colored by Lawrence's propaganda. Even in the beyond-death, the woman seems ironically triumphant, and even in his bereavement the man seems glad she is dead. The business-like mien of the nuns is superbly and ironically done, but no one can read the story without finding himself touched by the repugnant vibrations beneath the surface about woman.

## Glad Ghosts

The strange topography of Lawrence's underworld is also present in the uncanny story *Glad Ghosts*. The protagonist speaks in the first person, and has clear affinities with Lawrence. He makes an affirmation of the Lawrence faith:

> I did care about some passionate vision which, I could feel, lay embodied in the half-dead body of this life. The quick body within the dead, I could *feel* it. And I wanted to get at it, if only for myself. (SS, 862)

Again, we have unawakened woman, over who Lawrence and his characters are fascinated. Morier looks reflectively at the colonel's wife, who has no sexual relations with her husband:

> I looked back at her, and being clairvoyant in this house, was conscious of the curves of her erect body, the sparse black hairs there would be on her strong-skinned dusky thighs. (SS, 881)

There are two seriously unawakened women, and there is a powerful maternal presence, the mother of Carlotta as well as two powerful ghostly presences—the house ghost, and the ghost of the Colonel's Lucy. She wants to live in his body, so while the story is a kind of ghost story, it has beneath the surface a number of elements that belong to Lawrence's underworld. In Morier he displays once more his impulse to look at every woman in terms of her sexual potentialities, and her capacity for being awakened.

Two women needing awakening! There is not the slightest recognition that both women have husbands. Lord Cathkill actually polarizes himself towards Mrs. Hale "in a throb of crude brutality," because he felt it "would not work with the dark young woman." He handed Carlotta over to Morier because with him she would be "safe from the doom of his bad luck," while he "with the other woman would be safe from it too" because she "was outside the circle."

As they dance, a kind of frost intrudes, and Lady Cathkill asks if Lucy is there, the ghost of the Colonel's first wife. Morier feels as if he were resisting a cold current. There are heavy thuds and crashes and movements of drapery. Some believe it is hysteria overtaking them. The house feels hollow and gruesome.

There is a Lawrentian note in Morier's musings:

> I was looking back over my life, and thinking how the cold weight of an unliving spirit was slowly crushing all warmth and vitality out of everything. (SS, 885)

At the level of the underlying topography, the story records, behind the urgent erotic impulse to awaken the "dead" woman, the ghostly presence of the dead mother who both impels it, and also threatens the awakening out of jealousy.

He feels his life-flow sinking in his body. He urges Carlotta to "side-step" out of this "tangle."

> "A little while ago, you were warm and unfolded and good. Now you are shut up and prickly, in the cold. You needn't be. Why not stay warm?" (SS, 885)

The voice is the voice of Paul Morel talking to his mother, asking her not to be old—asking her *not to be dead*. Yet what else can "side-stepping" mean in the context except adulterous sex? She is locked in some tangle with her mother-in-law:

> In such a battle, while one has any life left, one can only lose it. There is nothing positively to be done, but to withdraw out of the hateful tension. (SS, 886)

Lawrence's remedies are often either flight (to withdraw) or *sexual side-stepping*. The whole "dead" house here is under the deadening influence of female ghosts, and it is in resistance to this, as always, that Lawrence seeks his desperate remedies. The story is a wish-fulfillment fantasy in which the protagonist is accorded a potency that can even overcome the ghost of the dead mother (as Lawrence could not).

> "fancy having a loving face, and arms, and thighs. Oh, my God, I'm glad I've realised in time." (SS, 888)

And now Lord Cathkill's conversion takes on a religious dimension as he expresses the Lawrentian version of Christian myth:

> "Oh, but if one had died without realizing it!" he cried. "Think how ghastly for Jesus, when he was risen and wasn't touchable! How very awful, to have to say *Noli me tangere*! Ah, touch me, touch me, *alive*!" (SS, 888)

Lawrence had his own attitude to Christ's resurrection. He couldn't accept the idea of resurrection of the body after death—he wanted it this side of death. Why does Cathkill wish Carlotta to have her body-life, even if he can't give it her? Behind this is surely Lawrence's mythology of the need to give to the dead mother a fulfillment she never had!

Besides the man, woman must be redeemed:

> It was as if a slow, restful dawn were rising in her body, while she slept. So slack, so broken she sat, it occurred to me that in this crucifixion business the crucified does not put himself alone on the cross. The woman is nailed even more inexorably up, and crucified in the body even more cruelly. (SS, 889)

What does this mean? Cathkill has stopped making love to his wife out of grief because of the deaths in their lives, which exposed the unawakened nature of their sexuality. But Morier goes on,

> Oh, Jesus, didn't you know that you couldn't be crucified alone?—that the two thieves crucified along with you were the two women, your wife and your mother! You called them two thieves. But what would they call you, who had their women's bodies on the cross? The abominable trinity of Calvary! (SS, 889)

How does this relate to the story? Carlotta may be said to have been "crucified" in that her sexual potentialities have been killed, but in what way is "the mother" involved? Cathkill's mother is a sad woman, but it is difficult to see her as crucified, or to see that she makes up an "abominable" trinity.

The invoked myth serves to justify Morier's adulterous inclinations, which now become a religious mission:

> I felt an infinite tenderness for my dear Carlotta. She could not yet be touched. But my soul streamed to her like warm blood. (SS, 889)

The story is very complex, but it illuminates a good deal of the Lawrence unconscious mythology in its concern to exorcise ghosts and the mother-influence. Its solutions are not only unreal, but immoral.

Lord Cathkill makes love to the wife of Colonel Dale, who is drawn off to have a fantasy coition with his dead wife, while Carlotta (Lady Cathkill), in the disguise of the family ghost, turns Mark Mariot's limbs to silk. Out of these dream liaisons come two children: Gabriel and Gabrielle. The embarrassing religiosity in the piece indicates the kind of fantasy it is, and we have the uncomfortable sense that the author is entering into both liaisons like Zeus. When Cathkill becomes "Luke," he talks like Lawrence and enthuses about the body like Lawrence—and so enables Lawrence to have the woman whose thighs and dark pubic hair he fantasies early in the story. In the person of the protagonist, Mark Morier, he is able to have, as a spiritual dream experience, an adulterous liaison with Carlotta. Out of these ghostly coitions are born two "angels." We might say that while Lawrence may be ambivalent about procreation, it is possible to bypass the dangers and dreads by having a strictly ghostly coition that produces angels rather than "ordinary" babies such as any normal "couple" of detested mundanity might have. Only by such very special conditions can the *doom of the house* be avoided. But the sexual doom which dogged Lawrence could not be evaded by such magical, fantasy means, and insofar as the story belongs to wish-fulfillment, it has little or nothing to add to our understanding of our humanness.

The prevalence of ghosts in the story perhaps puts us on our guard against Lawrence's earnestness. How serious is he? It seems unlikely that those who might be supposed to have come back from the dead would be concerned to promote adulteries or to feel that the most significant meaning was that of sexual body-life, or, indeed, that "life" means that kind of liveliness.

One final thing may be noted: Morier's coition with the Carlotta ghost was of one night, deeply beyond consciousness. The child born of this may have had Cathkill and the mother to look after it, but Morier carefully has no part in its future. The dream stays as far away from responsibility to the future of sexual reality as it is possible to get. To invoke such a thing is, in any case, irrelevant to get another myth of that mythical resurrection by which "as deep answers deep, man glistens and surpasses himself":

new-awakened God calling within the deep of man, and new God calling answer from the other deep. And sometimes the other deep is a woman. (SS, 896)

Once more we have a narcissistic, masturbatory fantasy of "the Sons of God with the daughters of men."

## The Man Who Died

*The Man Who Died* is another encapsulation of the inner Lawrence topography or myth-pattern. To take it as Lawrence's critical restatement of the history of Christ is, of course, proper since this is how he meant it. This may also be seen as the "offered" surface. The story may be seen as Lawrence's myth of himself, as a schizoid individual identifying with Christ.

The original title was "the escaped cock," and we any interpret this as meaning the escape of the libidinal and sexual capacities from bondage and from the psychic wounds of the past. In his body Lawrence was inhibited by tuberculosis and in his psychosomatic sexual life.

Jesus, to him, stands too much for the renunciation of sexual fulfillment and for the demand to be served by his followers with the "corpse of their love." To Lawrence love must be a matter of giving oneself to a world "glowing with desire," like the cock, who, in coition is "The wave-tip of life overlapping for a minute another, in the tide of the swaying ocean of life." (SS, 1106)

The trouble with Jesus is that he strove too much; he has left his striving self in the tomb. It was fear, the ultimate fear of death that made him mad, and drew others into his religion out of "the egoistic fear of their own nothingness." (SS, 1116) Now it is Jesus's time to be alone, and he chooses the "phenomenal world." He seeks to live the rest of his alloted time in "the greater life of the body," recognizing that "virginity is a form of greed" (SS, 1110) and then even the Madeleine "wanted to take without giving." "Reborn, he was in the other life, the greater day of the human consciousness." (SS, 1129) He "seeks to set the little life in the context of the greater life." (SS, 1129).

This expansion of consciousness, however, is only to be achieved, obviously, by a limited number of persons. Jesus's mistake was to teach the peasants to be lifted up. Clods are to be turned over for refreshment, but it is wrong to lift them up. Throughout the story there is the refrain of a disgust with humanity, and the development of the capacity for sexual love in Jesus is done in the midst of evil among the slaves, and hostility from the mother (of the priestess of Isis): the key boy slave in the story beats and rapes the slave girl. There is nothing to be hoped for from common humanity. There, Jesus has made a fundamental mistake: "They murdered me and I lent myself to murder."

The salvation of the escaped cock or released Jesus is only for the "sons of God." Jesus has coition with the priestess of Isis, as Osiris, and she believes he is Osiris. It is not a relationship based on love or any kind of mutual sharing—it is a one-night stand, and although a child will be born of it, Jesus accepts no real responsibility, but escapes again (from the hostility of the common people) saying to himself, "Tomorrow is another day," but "rare women wait for the re-born man," and again Lawrence's fantasy is of god-like potency in single god-to-goddess coition. In that tenderness, all the pain of the crucifixion is reexperienced: the experience of the tenderness of the woman's body is "more terrible and lovely than the death I died." Somehow, all tolerant Pan is worked in, along with Christ and Osiris, in the usual Pantheon of religiosity.

The story is beautifully written, but bankrupt. By this I mean that it offers no profound existentialist criticism of Christianity, or any source of new modes of being. The tragic problem is simply not encountered. Suppose one gives oneself to the "phenomenal" world and copulates ecstatically like a cock, what then of the Dasein? What of being-unto-death? There is nothing "egotistical" about this kind of contemplation. It may be thought to be egotistical to want to be "saved." Perhaps that is what Lawrence meant. Merely to choose to have "one's day" is not enough for most beings who need a meaning in their lives. And since it would seem Christ here chooses *love*, love with a woman, there would need to be more substance to love. Here, the concentration is too much on the penis-ecstasy, whether we take the cock's momentary flutterings, or the slave-boy's rape, or Christ's agony in the bed of the priestess of Isis. That is, if we relinquish the "striving self," and go in for the ecstasy of desire, even as part of the throbbing of the "greater life," this is liable merely to exacerbate the problem of meaning in existence, rather than solve it.

The theme is paralleled in the story *Sun* as it is in the novels: more and more Lawrence advocates *escape*. To overcome the "incapacity to feel anything real," we must "mate with the sun" like the woman in *Sun*. A certain contempt for all other human beings must drive us into eccentric modes of exposing us to the sun, which will warm us right through. Other people are "graveyard worms." In *Sun* the woman's grey-faced husband is rejected with contempt. The woman *really* wants the peasant at the foot of the garden (and Lawrence reluctantly avoids giving her to him). "I want, I want" becomes his whole motto, and in the end the message of *Sun* is no more than what the travel brochures offer. Jesus, in *The Man Who Died*, rejects humanity, those who love him, and his loyal followers, to find satisfaction with a woman he essentially deceives. Yet his doom still pursues him—not least from the mother-figure and the "common people." He becomes, like Mellors, Aaron, and the other Lawrentian heroes, a false god and a drifter.

## The Daughters of the Vicar

We may return with relief to a story that belongs to "true solutions." In *The Daughters of the Vicar* we have another very fine story in which one daughter, May, marries a cold, reserved, automaton of a man and is obviously condemned to a loveless and meaningless sexual life (the sources are George Eliot and perhaps Elizabeth Gaskell). But Louisa fixes a love on a miner, Alfred, who is devastated emotionally by his mother's death, and she arouses him from his grief and bereavement, into passion for her, and ultimately love. Again the need is seen as the need for love in the widest sense—"object-seeking," and as a way to find, in the uniqueness of the loved person, a sense of meaning. This determined love has to be upheld against opposition and envious hatred, but this determination is shown to gladly embrace responsibilities and the future.

*Daughters of the Vicar* contrasts significantly with *The Virgin and the Gipsy*—and to our reading of the latter we can bring much from our readings of Lawrence's other work. While Yvette's life is threatened with meaninglessness by the heavy and destructive morality of her rectory life, her yearning is not directed at an object. Her yearning is in response to "naked desire," and the cock that crows for her is that of the libidinal. The same is true of the Christ who rises again to sexuality in *The Man Who Died:* the cock that crows is the animal libido, and the implicit model is not one in which the libido is object-seeking.

In *Daughters of the Vicar*, the love relationship for which the characters strive, so that their lives can have meaning in the face of death and dead morality, obviously leads out towards the community, toward redemption of the family, toward work, toward a future, with children and responsibilities, toward "for richer or poorer" and "in sickness and in health." It leads towards *marriage*, and its portrayal of human sexuality and emotional need is real and powerful.

# 3

# *The Rainbow*—once *The Wedding Ring*

There is a great deal in *The Rainbow* that we recognize, gladly, as belonging to truth. The scenes with Anna, for example, as when Tom Brangwen comforts her as her mother is in labor, are masterly. So are his portrayals of this child (see, for instance, her encounter with the geese, [R, 69]), and Tilly, who is done with a quality learned from Dickens and George Eliot, but is also superbly Lawrentian. Tom's own puzzled anguish is done (we have to say) with love. The byre scene is intensely imagined, and the most telling touches come from the intensity of the vision: "filling a pan with chopped hay and brewer's grains and a little meal," "the silky fringe of the shawl swayed softly, grains and hay trickled to the floor," "There was a noise of chains running, as the cows lifted or dropped their heads sharply." Then:

> The beast fed, he dropped the pan and sat down on a box, to arrange the child.
> "Will the cows go to sleep now?" she said, catching her breath as she spoke.
> "Yes."
> "Will they eat all their stuff up first?"
> "Yes. Hark at them."
> And the two sat still listening to the snuffing and breathing of cows feeding. (R, 79)

The child's sobs punctuate the passage, as does the man's tormented concern for his wife, and his urge to distract the child from her anxious need for her mother. As in *Odour of Chrysanthemums*, the presence of the ultimate birth in this case is given us, while the rain and darkness represent "the infinite world, eternal, unchanging" that is there "as well as the world of life." With amazing economy, the episode conveys to us a total authenticity, not the least the powerful sense conveyed of another deeper level of being in us.

So does the account of the death of Tom, and much about Ursula's experience of college and her teaching—one of the most important pieces of writing about education in our century. These are all episodes about the meaning of existence and in them Lawrence demonstrates a remarkable, if often disturbing, courage.

It is not long before we become aware that some of the deepest turbulence in *The Rainbow* feels extraneous and seems not, in some way, inevitable to the novel. This centers around the problem of woman.

Lawrence was writing *The Rainbow* when he married (its alternative title was *The Wedding Ring*). It is first mentioned in a letter to Pinker on 5 December 1914, and Lawrence was married on 13 July 1914. He was putting his marriage experience into the novel (and into his study of Thomas Hardy: see the letter of 15 July 1914, written two days after his wedding, Moore 1962, 287). What I propose to concentrate on here is the fact that the least satisfactory elements in *The Rainbow* seem to be the consequence of Lawrence importing into the novel elements from his own marital troubles,[1] and, alas, importing Frieda's influence and the rationalizations that compromise with her generated.

The first marriage episode (of Tom Brangwen) is largely about the experience of commitment, and about Tom's experience of someone else's child. It is superb and completely "realized."

It is when we come to Anna's marriage to Will that something strange begins to happen. We find ourselves bewildered by long episodes in which characters battle one another, unable to find solutions. Moreover, Anna startles us by being quite unlike what we suppose Anna really would be as a grown woman. After the wedding she seems much less convincing. Will, like so many of Lawrence's characters, is, to a great extent, Lawrence himself (as Lawrence indicates by his choice of the Phoenix as a sign on the butter-stamper he makes for Anna). Can we explain the conflict that arises between Will and Anna (despite their promising beginnings) as an import from Lawrence's own experience that has no justification in the novel? The couple are "seething with hostility" (R, 160); their relationship is "stained with blood" (R, 170). Will seeks "confidence in the abidingness of love" but cannot find it.

The conflict develops into a *murderousness*—and it is in this, I believe, that we find imported into the Will-Anna relationship the anxieties of the Frieda–Lawrence marriage especially when Will says "I'll let you know who's master." We recall the autobiographical note in which we find Lawrence trying to throttle Frieda, yelling "I'm the master." The fact that Anna becomes "Anna Victrix" is highly significant, yet it doesn't seem to naturally to emerge from her background.

Also revealing is Anna's rejection of Will's cultural and religious interests: "She did no service to his work as a lace designer"; "She jeered at his soul." Is the account Lawrence's vengeance for Frieda's irony, directed at his religiosity, his idealism, and the threat that she seemed to him at time? On Will's part there is a dread of dependence that seems very much like Lawrence's: "the shame of his need of her" ("And, God, that she is necessary!").

The dread of happiness that suddenly emerges in the novel is surely something from Lawrence's own tormented response to experience.

And in all the happiness a black shadow, shy, wild, a beast of prey, roamed and vanished from sight, and, like strands of gossamer blown across her eyes, there was a dread for her. (R, 180)

The question that arises is—surely there is nothing in Anna's background to generate such seething dread and hate? She just would not have turned out to be the creature who has an unconscious impulse to make her husband miserable:

> She was rather surprised to find that she did *not* intend her husband to be hopping for joy like a fish in a pond. (R, 176)

This may be what Lawrence secretly felt about Frieda, but it is not really Anna.

Lawrence does attribute to Anna characteristics that nothing in her background accounts for, such as having "a curious contempt for ordinary people." Lawrence calls this a "benevolent superiority." Again I believe we may see this as an import from Lawrence's own life: Anna mistrusts intimacy, she shrinks from commonplace people, she is close to Baron Skrebensky. In these pages surely we have hints that these are elements of Frieda von Richthofen rather than Anna.

Why should the sexual life of Will and Anna be so crippled? Neither has suffered from the ugliness or oppression of industrial society; neither has the kind of "Will" Lawrence supposes to be the mark of the devotee of industry and the machine. Yet the word "cripple" is used of Will: "Was he impotent, or a cripple or a defective, or a fragment." (R, 187).

To most readers, I suspect, the turbulent and seething relationship between Will and Anna comes as a surprise. The couple begin their marriage in the most propitious circumstances. There is a natural conflict over her step-father Tom, but in the end they are put to bed with all the beneficent blessings of the old "organic" community. Yet when Anna makes Will go and sleep in the spare bed, for instance, he feels so rejected he can hardly bear it:

> He could not bear the empty space against his breast, where she used to be. He could not bear it. He felt as if he were suspended in space, held there by the grip of his will. If he relaxed his will he would fall, fall through endless space, into the bottomless pit, always falling, will-less, helpless, non-existent, just dropping to extinction, falling till the fire of friction had burnt out, like a falling star, then nothing, nothing, complete nothing. (R, 188)

This is surely a recognizable prose version of the poem *Song of a Man Who Is Not Loved* in which Lawrence records his own feeling of going out of existence because love is withdrawn:

> I am too little to count in the wind that drifts me through .... (CP, 223)

In *The Rainbow*

> In his soul he was desolate as a child, he was so helpless. Like a child on its mother, he depended on her for his living. (R, 190)

He becomes "a crawling nursling," and he has to find an "absolute self" instead of a "relative self." The "relative self" is that that is ever-dependent on the relationship. ("he must have a woman. And having a woman, he must be free of her. For he could not be free of her" [R, 187]). The absolute self is that mature self that is capable of being alone.

What are the sources (the etiology) of such turbulence and dread, and especially the sense of predatory tigers and other animals lurking in the atmosphere. Can we believe that the murderous and "corrosive" quality of the love can be natural to these characters? "He was cruel to her," "He felt as if he was being buried alive," there was "something dark and beastly in his will," and so on.

When Anna is dancing naked and exulting in her pregnancy, it seems unconvincingly perverse of Will to respond in such a wounding way, rather then be glad for her:

> The vision of her tormented him all the days of his life, as she had been then a strange exalted thing having no relation to himself. (R, 185)

The process recorded is that Lawrence traces in *Manifesto* and other poems—the painful process of discovering that the "other" is a separate being (and being so, if she died, or rejected him, or left him, he could die, too, which is the fear at the heart of all dependence).

What Lawrence was not aware of, was how exceptional—one has to say, *how pathological*, his own case was. Like Lawrence as in the poem (and in Paul's treatment of Miriam), his protagonist tries to project his own problems over the women ("It's something in yourself," he replied, "something wrong in you.")

Will wants "the abidingness of love," but he doesn't get it. *He isn't satisfied*. When Lawrence uses this term, he does not mean sexual satisfaction in the usual sense. She is satisfied, both by sexual love and her pregnancy, but

> To him it also was agony. He saw the glistening, flower-like love in her face, and his heart was black because he did not want it. Not this—not this. He did not want flowery innocence. He was unsatisfied. The rage and storm of unsatisfaction tormented him ceaselessly. Why had she not satisfied him? He had satisfied her. She was satisfied, at peace, innocent round the doors of her own paradise. (R, 182)

The tigers and leopards surely are symbols of this oral intensity arising from the fear of love, and a dread that the (schizoid) oral impulse is so intense it will eat up the other and the world. While everyone has a modicum of such fears, they do not have them with Lawrence's kind of intensity. We often encounter characters in Lawrence's novels who suffer from deep and unquenchable *dissatisfaction* despite forms of fulfillment that would satisfy normal people.

Then, out of this dissatisfaction, a strange inverted logic appears—because of the fear of love, and the feeling that it can never be enjoyed, there is a compensatory impulse to give oneself up to the joys of hatred in such people:

> Let her not come with flowery handfuls of innocent love. He would throw these aside and trample the flowers to nothing. He would destroy her flowery, innocent bliss. Was he not entitled to satisfaction from her, and was not his heart all raging desire, his such a black torment of fulfillment. Let it be fulfilled in him, then, as it was fulfilled in her. He had given her fulfillment. Let her rise up and do her part.
>
> He was cruel to her. But all the time he was ashamed. And being ashamed, he was more cruel.... He was shackled and in darkness of torment. (R, 182)

Here we may recall the strange incidents related above from biographical sources and the conflict over "mastery," and here he makes Anna's resistance to Will's overdependence look like a struggle over mastery. It is inconceivable that Anna (after her benign experience of maleness in her step-father Tom) should be so cruel as to cry, as she does, "Anna Victrix!" immediately after the birth of her baby.

In a sense Lawrence is bringing himself, with terrifying honesty of a kind, to recognize that however creative a man can be, the woman always conquers in the end because she can create a new human being. He deeply resents this, and so he makes Anna crow over Will, rather than feel the triumph to be one in which they can both share.

Here we have to touch on a very unhappy problem. The very symbol, the rainbow, is of promise, and the child stands under the arch of the heavens, which stands for the parents' love. We have this image at the end of this chapter: "her doors opened under the arch of the rainbow." (R, 196) Lawrence himself had no children, and more often than not in his work reveals a tendency to reject the child, or to regard it as a "side-issue." Though *The Rainbow* has this powerful symbolism, Lawrence wants sex to be seen as a power in our lives that need not lead to procreation. He wants to vindicate sex as positive in itself, but here again he becomes inflenced by his own unconscious feelings about children and procreation, including that strange hostility to the woman's procreativity we noted in *The White Peacock*.

Parallel to this is the obsessional and even suffocating preoccupation with sex that develops in Lawrence's work. Will's and Anna's honeymoon period is a portent of this treadmill—perhaps with its roots in Lawrence's own honeymoon. His couples tramp around and around, with endogenous disruptions emerging to thwart them, and they get nowhere except deeper into an intensifying sense of isolation and self-enclosure. Perhaps *The Trespasser* here is a portent in which the torrid but nonsexual union between Siegmund and Helena is stifling in its obsessional quality: their love simply does not release them to the world, and ends in death. Lady Otteline Morrel had some comments to make that seem illuminating on this subject. Of Lawrence's portrayal of female psychology in *The Rainbow*, she said, "It is always his wife." Otteline often displayed a great deal of insight and common sense over

D. H. Lawrence. For instance, her reaction to *Goats and Compasses*, Lawrence's 1915 statement of his philosophy, is most penetrating:

> It seems to me deplorable tosh, a volume of words, reiteration, perverted and self-contradictory. A gospel of hate and violent individualism. He attacks the will, love and sympathy. Indeed, the only thing that he doesn't revile and condemn is love between men and women. But after all what does sexual love lead to, if there is nothing outside to grow out to? For two people, simply to grow in, and in, into each other, does not satisfy a man for long; perhaps a woman might be content, for women are more possessive. I feel very depressed that he has filled himself with these "evening" ideas. They are, I am sure, the outcome of Frieda . . . .
>
> How Lawrence, as I knew him, who seemed so kind and understanding and essentially so full of tenderness, could turn round and preach this doctrine of hate is difficult to understand . . . . I suppose having accepted Frieda as his wife and finding in her some instinctive satisfaction, he has to suppress his human pity, his gentle and tender qualities, to enable him to fight her and this makes him raw and bitter inside. (Gawthorne-Hardy 1974, 93)

Like the suppressed prologue to *Woman in Love*, this bombastic, pseudo-mystical, psychophilosophical treatise dealt largely with homosexuality. (Cecil Gray said of it, "a subject, by the way, in which Lawrence displayed a suspiciously lively interest at this time" (Nehls 1957–59, 582).)

The puzzle is how Lawrence connected the destruction of the "old world," that is, of course, the theme of *Women in Love*, with the homosexuality—the discussion of the physical attraction that Gerald had for Birkin in the suppressed Prologue. At the time he began *Women in Love*, Lawrence was yearning for Middleton Murry who had gone away.

To unravel this kind of problem, we must examine the writings as dramatizations of the inner world. Lady Otteline, in her comments above, shows that she recognized that Lawrence's problems, as expressed in his manifesto, were those of an obsession with the sexual because, in some way, he failed to find perspectives beyond to "grow out to."

Anna does see a horizon, away ahead:

> From her Pisgah mount, which she had attained, what could she see? A faint, gleaming horizon, a long way off, and a rainbow like an archway, a shadow-door with faintly coloured coping about it. Must she be moving thither? (R, 195)

She sees "It is beyond." She has her own deep satisfaction in her children, but her husband feels he "must put out his own light."

Like the men characters in *The White Peacock*, Will is intensely jealous of the woman's procreative capacity.

> A pang of dread, almost guilt, as of insufficiency, would go over him as he heard her talking to the baby . . . a denial was upon him, as if he could not deny himself. He must, he must be himself. (R. 194)

The problem is how this impulse to "be oneself" is to be fulfilled.

What happens, then, as the woman reveals herself as a being apart, happy in her own creative fulfillment? She is not the man's mother, she will not accept his overdependence, she is not him (a narcissistic projection), yet he cannot exist without her.

> She was indeed Anna Victrix. He could not combat her any more. He was out in the wilderness, alone with her. (R, 193)

We may, I believe, begin to unravel Lawrence's social policy, the grounds of his social sexual theory:

> for his own part, for his private being, Brangwen felt that the whole of man's world was exterior and extraneous to his own real life with Anna. (R. 193)

> the great mass of activity in which mankind was engaged meant nothing to him. (R, 193)

Lawrence is confronted with the essential questions: What does one live for? What is the relation of the creative couple to the world? Here it is a question of giving the world a bad name and hanging it. Will reflects on "what more would be necessary":

> What did he live for then? ... Anna only, and his children...? Was there no more! He was attended by a sense of something more, something further, which gave him absolute being. It was now as if he existed in Eternity, let Time be what it might. What was there outside? The fabricated world, that he did not believe in? What should he bring to her, from outside? Nothing? Was it enough, as it was? He was troubled in his acquiescence. She was not with him. Yet he scarcely believed in himself, apart from her, though the whole Infinite was with him. Let the whole world slide down and over the edge of oblivion, he would stand alone. But he was unsure of her. And he existed also in her. So he was unsure. (R. 193–94)

Will is Lawrence here, who has thrown himself at the woman ("there must be a woman") to find ultimate confirmation of his being, yet the woman moves apart, into her own creative existence, and won't accept the role of sustaining him as a mother sustains a baby. (Anna makes Will sleep in the spare bed implying he must stand on his own feet, physically.)

However, he is not going to engage with the rest of the world to find a sense of identity. If he (by "he" I mean Lawrence) had found fulfillment of being in love, he could have returned to the world with strength. But he isn't going to return to it *from weakness*; he is going to reject it utterly. Thus, Will thinks of how London was created by "savages":

> The ponderous, massive, ugly superstructure of a world of man upon a world of nature! It frightened and awed him. Man was terrible, awful in his works. The works of man were more terrible than man himself, almost monstrous. (R, 193)

Lawrence's social-sexual policy is one that emerges from weakness—from a sense of being impotent and crippled. Because of his essential dissatisfaction, and because his search for ultimate meaning and confirmation from woman has failed, he is prepared to reject and destroy the rest of the world:

> sweep away the whole monstrous superstructure of the world of today, cities and industries and civilisation, leave only the bare earth with plants growing and waters running, and he would not mind, so long as he were whole, had Anna and the child and the new, strange certainty in his soul. (R, 193)

This increasingly becomes Lawrence's policy of rejection and flight as long as the sexual quest can continue in its remote huts and lonely ranches, deep wilds of Mexico, and the mountains. The policy is self-defeating because it marks the same *regression* that makes Will (like Lawrence) a "crawling nursling" seeking to be reborn. All "masculine" or "doing" activities are to be renounced, so the energy of men in industry, cities, and even civilization are to be renounced in favor of a life that reverts entirely to the sexual. Everyone is to be seen in terms of their sexual potential.

Will's devotion to religion, his idealism, his search for Beauty and the Absolute are related to Lawrence's creativity. At the same time, in Will, he traces a man's awakening (or rebirth) predominantly in terms of sexual potentialities. At the beginning of chapter 7, when the Brangwens are introduced to the Skrebenskys, one gets a sense that everyone is looking at everyone else in terms of their sexual potentialities. (And some of Lawrence's comments are rather sloppy—for instance on pp. 198–99 the new baroness is described variously as a "kitten," a "weasel," a "ferret," and a "stoat"!)

There is more than a touch of Frieda in Anna, as when she undermines Will's Absolute by pointing out the humanistic irony in the sculptures in Lincoln cathedral:

> He was disillusioned. That which had been his absolute, containing all heaven and earth, was become to him as to her, a shapely heap of dead matter—but dead, dead.
>
> His mouth was full of ash, his soul was furious. He hated her for having destroyed another of his vital illusions. Soon he would be stark, stark, without one place wherein to stand, without one belief in which to rest. (R, 205)

It is quite out of character for Anna to do such a thing to her husband; she doesn't have that kind of attitude to life. But it was exactly what Frieda did to Lawrence, and in it there is a touch of Grossian anarchism. Like Will, Lawrence has been persuaded that his idealism is a failure: "He was also slightly ashamed, like a man who has failed, who lapses back for his fulfillment" (R, 207). He has been persuaded that this can be related to his sexual limitations:

> If only there were not some limit to him, some darkness across his eyes.... He must submit to his own inadequacy, the limitation of his being. He even had to know

of his own black violent temper, and to reckon with it. But as she was more gentle with him, it became quieter. (R, 210)

The essential difference between Will's relationship with Anna and Lawrence's with Frieda is in the relationship with the children. Lawrence portrays marvelously both Anna's devotion to her baby, and the essential flexibility of young parents in their growth toward full parental care and tenderness. (Incidentally, to anyone who turns back from *Women in Love* to *The Rainbow*, it is shocking to contemplate the way Lawrence endorses the view of the adult Ursula and Gudrun in their parents' empty bedroom—that the parental marriage has been dead. By that time, of course, we are in a different world and a different book, and the parents are more like Mr. and Mrs. Morel, or Mr. and Mrs. Lawrence.)

In his relationship with his daughter Will displays strange and reckless proclivities: "he had a curious craving to frighten her, to see what she would do with him" (R, 225). There was a "curious, taunting intimacy" between them, and there is something clearly deeply wrong with Will in his relationship to Ursula, some strange identification with her by his own infant self. "He was at this time, when he was about twenty-eight years old, strange and violent in his being, sensual" (R, 226). The fundamental problem, as we have seen, is that Will cannot establish a satisfactory relationship between his love for Anna and the world.

It is perhaps over Will and Anna that Lawrence takes the first step toward false solutions. Here I believe the episode when Will picks up a girl in the cinema is one of the most significant (chapter 8, *The Child*).

I am not saying that Lawrence is failing to be realistic. People do behave like this, and many of Will's impulses are portrayed with insight. In a way Lawrence is right in showing that if a man finds his marital relationship bafflingly tormented, he may well turn to other women. But how he handles the incident is most revealing.

Because of the hostility between himself and Anna, Will feels

another self seemed to arrest its being within him . . . gradually he became indifferent of responsibility. He would do what pleased him and no more. (R, 227)

He waits, like a hunter, and he picks up a girl in a cinema. It is important, when later he finds in her Absolute Beauty, to note that "she was rather small, *common*." Throughout there is a note of contempt for this libidinal object, who does not command respect (as Anna does):

A gleam lit up in him: should he begin with her? Should he begin to live the other, the unadmitted life of his desire? Why not? He had always been so good. (R, 227)

The perceptive reader will note that the anguish that afflicts them would seem to be an anguish that arises from the very intensity of the passion and the associated dread of dependence. What is this "unadmitted life of his desire"? And what of that, "He had always been so good"? In Lawrence's ambivalence here we may, I believe, detect elements from Frieda's Grossian persuasions, as revealed in *Mr Noon*.

> Save for his wife, he was virgin. And why, when all women were different? Why, when he would only live once? He wanted the other life. His own life was barren, not enough. (R, 227)

No doubt there is some irony in Lawrence making Will reflect that *his* life was barren? Will reflects on the vulnerability of his victim; the oral (hate) impulse is to be indulged:

> Her open mouth...appealed to him.... It was open and ready. It was so vulnerable. Why should he not go in and enjoy what was there?... She would be small, almost like a child.... Her childishness whetted him keenly. She would be helpless between his hands. (R, 228)

And Will's impulse is one of *power:*

> His soul was keen and watchful, glittering with a kind of amusement.... He was himself, the absolute, the rest of the world was the object that should contribute to his being. (R, 228)

Is Lawrence being diagnostic, aware fundamentally that Will is perversely drawn to exert his power over this wretched girl? Is Lawrence aware that there is no "fulfillment" here? Or does he write this episode under the same ambivalence that we find in *Mr Noon*, where he shows that he has had to compromise over Frieda's infidelities? After all, in 1915, in "The Reality of Peace" and other philosophical essays, Lawrence had argued that the repression of any desire is harmful: "those who have come to terms with their darkest desires are the true illuminati" (Roberts and Moore, 1968, p669, 4). He also agreed with Ottoline that "one should go to different persons to get companionship for the different sides of one's nature" (Lacy, 1971, 785). It is not at all clear that Lawrence sees the *hostility* behind such a yearning toward promiscuity.

Will's handling of the flirtation is skillful with the undercurrent of an intense and, we have to say, *perverted* skill. It is a real *seduction*, the exercise of power by one over another.

> It was a pleasure to him to make this conversation, an activity pleasant as a fine game of chance and skill.... His senses were alert and wilful. He would press his advantages.

The (libidinal) object is reduced to an object: "he was quite unaware that she was anybody. *She was just the sensual object of his attention*" (R, 229).

The devotion to the seduction requires a dissociation from the rest of the world, such as responsibilities and obligations:

> He had a free sensation of walking in his own darkness, *not in anyone else's world at all. He was purely a world to himself, he had nothing to do with any general consciousness.* (R, 230; my italics)

The deed requires a deep dissociation, "just his own senses were supreme".

> All the rest was external, insignificant, leaving him alone with this girl whom he wanted to absorb, *whose properties he wanted to absorb into his own senses.* (R, 230; my italics)

He has reduced her to a breast, totally under his oral appetite. She does not count as a person:

> He did not care about her, except that he wanted to overcome her resistance, to have her in his power, fully and *exhaustively* to enjoy her. (R, 230; my italics)

It is clear that Lawrence, the novelist, sees the degree of dehumanization and dissociation involved. It is also to Lawrence, the sexual revolutionary, that this indulgence in egoistical nihilism is *necessary*, and all his enthusiasms are devoted to endorse the thrills of power. She fits so well into Will's side:

> It seemed like a new creation to him, a reality an absolute, an existing tangible beauty of the absolute. It was like a star. Everything in him was absorbed in the sensual delight of this (R, 230)

He reflects dimly on his infidelity, but dismisses it:

> His fingers had often touched Anna on the face and neck like that. What matter! It was one man who touched Anna, another who now touched this girl. He liked best his new self. He was given over altogether to the sensuous knowledge of this woman, and every moment he seemed to be touching absolute beauty, something beyond knowledge. (R, 231)

Lawrence has insight into the split. Perhaps he took a clue from Hardy (*The Well-Beloved, Tess*—in which Angel declares Tess a totally different being after she confesses her previous love affair to him). There is no doubt a placing in the fact that we have been told she is really a common little girl, and yet Will is finding "something beyond knowledge" in caressing her. There is also a sense in which Lawrence is enjoying, and leading the reader to enjoy, this indulgence in an act of sensuality totally split off from any considerations— either of the person of Anna and responsibilities to her, or of the girl who is the victim of Will's power.

Very close, marvelling and exceedingly joyful in their discoveries, his hands pressed upon her, so subtly, so seekingly, so finely and desirously searching her out. (R, 231)

His detailed description of the attempted seduction is lyrical with the indulgence of deceit, cunning, and power: what is lyricized (and idealized) is a really brutal exploitation (with a fantasy behind it of emptying the breast):

he was patiently working for her relaxation, patiently, his whole being fixed in the smile of latent gratification, his whole body electric with a subtle, powerful, reducing force upon her . . . . He let the whole face of his will sink upon her to sweep her away. (R, 231)

Marvelous, we respond. How powerful! But then perhaps we recapture our *savoir faire*, and wonder rather whether we are not really enjoying something cruel. The girl gives a horrible cry, but Will speaks "as if calmly," and

Her cry had given him gratification . . . there had broken a flaw into his perfect will. He wanted to persist, to begin again, to lead up to the point where he had let himself go on her, and then manage more carefully, successfully. So far she had won. And the battle was not over yet. (R, 232)

What is the essential difference between Gerald's exercise of will, as over the horse in *Women in Love*, and this? Yet this episode is not intended to demonstrate anything negative or destructive in Will. *It is the means to his fulfillment:* "another voice woke in him and prompted him to let her go—*let her go in contempt*" (R, 232).

When Will's "veins fused with extreme voluptuousness," it was with sadistic satisfaction. What happens in this episode is not done with any tender consideration for what is happening in the consciousness or internal life of the girl but in contempt for her as a person. It is a mere exercise in *power*.

The zest leaves. He realizes he is not going to take her, but he remains coldly "immoral." When she accuses him of wanting "it," he replies: "*I* know what I want," he said, "What's the odds?" (R, 232) He is coldly indifferent that she should know he is a married man, and about the strange power he has over her. He is "quite indifferent," he goes home.

Even so far, we may reflect that if we examine the scene realistically, there would have been something desperate about it: that in Will there would have been more guilt and shame; that it would have been more cold and sordid. It is Lawrence who has idealized the marvelousness of the adventure, the electricity, the power, the voluptuousness, the intoxication, and the sadistic satisfactions, even in his contempt, splitting, and dissociation (Will didn't even know her name).

What follows is even more disturbing. Anna notices (as a wife would) the "latent, almost sinister smile, as if he were absolved from his 'good' ties"— the very way the word "good" is put in inverted commas seems to me to hint at the presence in the background of a Grossian amoralism. Lawrence repeats: "As for his humble, good self, he was absolved from it." (R, 234) *Mr Noon* reveals that here we have a record of Lawrence himself being persuaded to drop his attachment to puritan morality. Anna is not shown as jealous, or deeply hurt, or alarmed, or threatened even though she detects the possibility of infidelity, which would, of course, destroy her world. She doesn't even care that he is lying. *She likes it better.*

> Here was a new turn of affairs! *He was rather attractive, nevertheless.* She liked him better than the ordinary mute, half-effaced, half-subdued man she usually knew him to be. So, he was blossoming out into his real self! (R, 234, my italics)

The man who prides himself over common girls he picks up in the cinema, whom he reduces to screaming dread by his "subtle" seduction, may consider himself "blossoming out" at last into his "real self"! *He* is not "mute, half-effaced, half-subdued!" How does Anna respond when she divines him? "It piqued her . . . . Yet not without a pang of rage . . . which would insist on their old, beloved love, their old accustomed intimacy, and her old established supremacy." (R, 234)

If you are tired of your "old . . . accustomed intimacy," why not try this method of triumphing over the woman you fear—that is Lawrence's sinister message. The way for Will to break the triumph of "Anna Victrix" is to go in for sensual, depersonalized adventures: the episode cannot be read in any other way. It marks a significant break from the emphasis on authenticity in the great tradition of the English novel.

> She was ready for the game. *Something was liberated in her.* She liked him. She liked this strange man come home to her . . . . *She has been bored by the old husband . . . .* She challenged him back with a sort of radiance, very bright and free. (R, 235; my italics)

It may be that couples can come to terms with one another's infidelities and that there are worse things in marriage, but here the suggestion is that, because of this inclination to infidelity on Will's part, there comes a new development in the marriage. The marriage began in the most propitious circumstances and was rich and passionate, but then things went wrong. What is the answer? The intention is to suggest that a new dimension opens after Will exerts his domination on another woman, and thus learns how to treat a woman "properly". Here we find in *The Rainbow* that corrupt distortion of perspectives that we have become more aware of since the publication of *Mr Noon*.

He becomes a new kind of husband—no longer the old boring one. Anna is now in a kind of radiance:

> She too could throw everything overboard, love, intimacy, responsibility. What

were her four children to her now? What did it matter that this man was the father of her four children.

He was the sensual male seeking his pleasure; she was the female ready to take hers: but in her own way. A man could turn into a free lance: so then could a woman. *She adhered little as he to the moral world.* (R, 235; my italics)

Lawrence wants to insist that sex apart from procreation can be rich and valid in itself. However, it is a false note to suggest that a woman can feel that it doesn't matter that her husband, who is the father of her four children, might be promiscuous: she would recognize the hostility in it.

The "excursion" now proves to be beneficial in a different way. It leads to an abandonment of the moral position, so that perversions may be indulged. "The little creature in Nottingham had but been leading up to this." (R, 235) Incidentally, what about her? She is simply one of the common people presumably to be contemptuously exploited for the benefit of the protagonists. Disturbed and hurt, she is simply dismissed.

Now the abandonment of the "moral" position in relationships permits a parallel abandonment in their sexual life: "They *abandoned in one motion the moral position*, each was seeking gratification pure and simple" (R, 235 my italics). Will can now be fulfilled by imparting into his sexuality the same "marauding" quality he exercised with the girl in the cinema: "She waited for his touch as if he were a marauder who had come in, infinitely unknown and desirable to her" (R, 235). The "upshot" is that the answer to the torments in a relationship is a degree of *depersonalization* of the other: "He had an inkling of the vastness of the unknown sensual store of delights she was" (R, 236). Though Lawrence raptures about the "several beauties of her body," it is an approach that now reduces the women to a mere breast, to be taken from:

There was no tenderness, or love between them any more, only the maddening, sensuous lust for discovery and the *insatiable*, exorbitant gratification. (R, 236)

There is more to follow about the "undiscovered . . . and ecstatic places of delight in her body" that drove him "slightly insane."
He was obsessed, and they exert

a sensuality violent and extreme as death . . . . It was all the lust and the infinite, maddening intoxication of the senses, a passion of death. (R, 237)

What Will is shown to "learn" from his adventure is an abandonment of the "moral position" so he can give himself up not only to lustful impulses, but hostile forms of sexuality from which all the elements of mutual respect are dissociated.

What Lawrence (betrayingly) does not see is that the episode has been an experiment in *triumphing* over a woman—Will's "escapade" is an exercise in *power:*

alone with this girl whom he wanted to absorb into his own senses. He did not care about her, except that he wanted to overcome her resistance, to have her in his power, fully and exhaustively to enjoy her. (R, 230)

In this, as so often in Lawrence when a man behaves *cruelly* and dominates a woman, he is "blossoming out into his real self," while the woman loves it. *Anna*, the wife, loves *the cruelty:* "to his *latent cruel smile* she replied with brilliant challenge" (R, 235; my italics).

Here, there is a significant note, and we can see the influence of Frieda's Otto-Gross immoralism: "he expected her to keep the moral fortress."

> She too could throw everything overboard, love, intimacy, responsibility . . . . He was the sensual male seeking his pleasure, she was the female ready to take hers. (R, 235)

So—the model that takes "naked passion" is the true one: they "abandoned in one motion the moral position, each was seeking gratification pure and simple." He is "infinitely unknown and desirable to her. And he began to discover her."

Lawrence cannot yet be specific, but there is no doubt he means that by the impulse to infidelity and the abandoning of the moral position Will and Anna are introduced to the joys of perversion:

> He had an inkling of the vastness of the unknown sensual store of delights she was. With a passion of voluptuousness that made him dwell on each tiny beauty, in a kind of frenzy of enjoyment, he lit upon her: the beauty, the beauties, the separate, several beauties of her body. (R, 236)

One might suppose that Will and Anna had discovered one another satisfactorily on their wedding night, and in the days after, during which, with the door shut and all sense of time suspended, they make love:

> As they lay close together, complete and beyond the touch of time or change, it was as if they were at the very centre of all the slow wheeling of space and the rapid agitation of life, deep, deep inside them all, at the centre where there is utter radiance, and eternal being. (R, 145)

What more could one ask for? Lawrence, however, needed something "beyond." Will's higher potentialities seem to be concerned with every little detail of his wife's body: "He would say during the daytime: 'Tonight I shall know the little hollow under her ankle, where the blue vein crosses.'" (R, 236). But this obsession with physical details has an oddly perverted air, and it gradually becomes clear that there is one particular physical entity with which Will (and Lawrence) are preoccupied. The clue is given in that word "separate," and in references to the "undiscovered" and "hidden places of delight"—the thought of which "sent him slightly insane."

He was obsessed.

And there follows a very strange remark: "If he did not discover and make known to himself these delights, *they might be lost for ever*" (R, 236, my italics) There follow further sentences with strange, compulsive energy. He wished he had a hundred men's energies. He wished her were a cat, to lick her with a "rough, grating, lascivious tongue," and "he wanted to wallow in her."

Some of the impulses belong to normal sexuality. Perhaps here, for instance, we have a reference to the discovery of oral sex, but the word "wallow" seems to suggest that the paen here is to sensual indulgence such as a baby seeks, or perhaps a man who feels he has lacked certain oral, wallowing gratifications in infancy. The emphasis now falls on *secrecy* and the *sinister*, and

> a sensuality violent and as extreme as death . . . . It was all the lust, and the inifinite, maddening intoxication of the senses, a passion of death. (R, 237)

This, I believe, brings us to the essentially perverted in Lawrence.

> He had always, all his life, had a secret dread of Absolute Beauty . . . . It was immoral and against mankind. (R, 237)

Now, in reaction, Will gives himself to the "immoral":

> Now he had given way, and with infinite sensual violence gave himself to the realization of this supreme, *immoral*, Absolute Beauty, in the body of woman. (R, 237; my italics)

Here, as we shall see, we have an enthusiasm about perversion that has its roots in the relationship between the mother and the infant, and leads to a need to hunt out the secret "shames" of the body:

> All the shameful natural and unnatural acts of sensual voluptuousness which he and the woman partook of together, they had their heavy beauty and their delight. Shame, what was it? *It was part of extreme delight*. It was that part of delight of which man is usually afraid. Why afraid? The secret, shameful things are most terribly beautiful. (R, 238; my italics)

This is not Will "thinking"—it is Lawrence telling us. The most revealing thing is that he uses the word *shameful* not *shameless*. If men and women perform cunnilinctus or fellatio or sodomy in a shameless abandon, that may be their joy. Lawrence's excitement lies in the fact that the acts were *secret* and *shameful* and that both enjoy them *because of this*. The shame is part of the perverse delight, and so, by implication, are the triumph and cruelty in the background. These perversions are beautiful—espcially "heavy, fundamental gratification," a phrase that cannot but mean sodomy.

We shall look at other eulogies of sodomy in Lawrence, but it is important to note that it always belongs to "the impulse to dominate." The end of this important chapter in *The Rainbow* is

> She seemed to run in the shadow of some dark, potent secret of which she would not, or whose existence even she dared not become conscious, it cast such a spell over her, and so *darkened her mind*. (R, 239; my italics).

What really excites Lawrence is the secret of triumphing over woman, controlling her and exorcising her, not least by anal intercourse, which has a symbolic value in avoiding the phantom mother in the matrix, as we shall see.

Here we may for a moment look forward to the sequel. The same kind of development occurs in *Women in Love*. This time it is Birkin who becomes "lascivious.' He, too, becomes "strange."

> The strangeness of his hands, which came quick and cunning, inevitably to the vital place beneath her breasts ... carried her through the air as if without strength, through black magic, made her swoon with fear ... it was horrible. (WL, 463)

"She felt the strange licentiousness of him hovering upon her"—she is "in dread." "What would he do to her?"

Again, the woman is fascinated by the "repulsive" licentiousness and "mocking brutishness."

> She gave way, he might do as he would. His licentiousness was repulsively attractive. (WL, 464)

And then, again, the perversions become acceptable:

> How could anything that gave one satisfaction be excluded? What was degrading? Who cares? Degrading things were real, with a different reality ... why not be bestial, and go the whole round of experience? She exulted in it. She was bestial. How good it was to be really shameful. There would be no shameful thing she had not experienced ... no dark shameful things were denied her. (WL, 464)

Again, it must be noted, the word is *shameful* and not *shameless*—and what the enthusiastic propaganda disguises is the fact that behind the enthusiasm to be "bestial" is the impulse to subdue and dominate that is really irreconcilable with a free and mutual living relationship. What Lawrence is mainly interested in, in his enthusiasm for perversion, is *power over woman*.

This new sensual, perverted, and depersonalized sexuality is, in *The Rainbow*, the clue to the solution of one's ultimate relationship to reality.

> And gradually Brangwen began to find himself free to attend to the outside life as well. His intimate life was so violently active, that it set another man in him free ... he wanted to be unanimous with the whole of purposive mankind. (R, 238)

\* \* \*

In *The Rainbow* we find a social and political theory developed from this concern for sexual fulfillment between man and woman on the basis of the abandonment of the moral position. There are many clues to the origins of Lawrence's sexual-social theories in chapter 7 of *The Rainbow*, "Shame." In many ways Ursula is Lawrence in his adolescence. Much about Ursula's developing adolescence is superbly done. For instance, her sense, after the end of her first encounter with Skrebensky, that some young self has died in her:

> She knew the corpse of her young, loving self, she knew its grave. And the young loving self she mourned for had scarcely existed, it was a creature of her imagination. (R, 357)

Chapter 7 contains, compressed into a compact space, a number of central Lawrentian themes: the question of Christianity and Christian love; sexuality and homosexuality; the effect of the attachment to industry and coal-mining; the nature of the modern man and woman.

It is important that Ursula's crush on her lesbian teacher is seen as immediately following her reflections on religion. Winifred has had a scientific education, and the effects of scientific materialism are important in her young life, as they were in Lawrence's. Winifred humanizes religion for her: "Gradually it dawned upon Ursula that all the religion she knew was but a particular clothing to a human aspiration" (R, 341). Christianity accepted crucifixion to escape from fear, but that which was feared was not necessarily all evil. In philosophy, "*she was brought to the conclusion that the human desire is the criterion of all truth and all good.*" This is put in the month of a young woman Lawrence later calls "perverted," yet it seems very much like his own fundamental philosophy, at the center of which is "naked desire."

> Ursula, under these blandishments, dreamt of Moloch. Her god was not mild and gentle, neither Lamb nor Dove . . . . She was weary to death of mild, passive lambs and monstrous doves. (R, 342)

Ursula is also shown to have a predeliction for "giving oneself over to the joys of hating":

> Raging, destructive lovers, seeking the moment when fear is greatest, and triumph the greatest, the fear not greater then the triumph, the triumph not greater than the fear, these were no loves nor doves. She stretched her own limbs like a lion or a wild horse, her heart was relentless in its desires. It would suffer a thousand deaths, but it would still be a lion's heart when it rose from death, a fiercer lion she could be, a surer, knowing herself different from and separate from the great, conflicting universe that was not herself. (R, 342–43)

To this, Miss Unger's militant feminism adds fuel, and while she may be expressing the propaganda of the women's liberation movement of her time, she also sounds very much like Lawrence:

The men will do no more—they have lost the capacity for doing . . . . Love is a dead idea to them. They don't come to one and love one, they come to an idea, and they say "You are my idea," so they embrace themselves. (R, 343)

She will not be a man's idea

"As if I exist because a man has an idea of me! As if I will be betrayed by him, lend him by body as an instrument for his idea, to be a mere apparatus of his dead theory." (R, 343)

Men are "impotent" and they "can't *take* a woman."

All the women and men Ursula meets in Winifred Unger's circle are "inwardly raging and mad." Ursula sinks into a "black disintegration," and by degrees she begins to sense the deadness of the "heavy cleaning of moist clay" in the lesbian woman: her sterility. Winifred cuts her losses, however, as she has obviously experienced this kind of thing before.

Ursula decides to marry Winifred Unger to her Uncle Tom. The episode is not very convincing; it does not seem real. It does, however, have considerable symbolic value: "The fine, unquenchable flame of the younger girl would consent no more to mingle with the perverted life of the elder woman" (R, 344). The proper partner for her is Tom, who "no longer cared about anything on earth, neither man nor woman, nor god nor humanity. He had come to a stability of nullification. He did not care any more, neither about his body nor about his soul" (R, 345).

He lives from moment to moment, a life of survival. "He believed neither in good nor evil. Each moment was like a separate little island, isolated from time and blank, unconditioned by time." One might suppose him a proper partner for a woman who sees existence in humanistic scientific terms, but it seems strange that this independent modern woman should be led into marrying a man who, one might think, represents the acme of industrial, bourgeois manhood.

Tom is a pit manager, totally devoted to a new mining community, newly created, ugly, and totally utilitarian. Here we have the "carrion-bodied colliers" of Lawrence's exile years:

Colliers hanging about in gangs and groups seemed not like living people, but like spectres. The rigidity of the blank streets, the homogenous amorphous sterility of the whole suggested death rather than life. There was no meeting place, no centre, no artery, no organic formation. (R, 345)

Lawrence often expresses his horror at the way the British towns were spreading "like a skin-disease" and of the inorganic lack in them of form and meaning. In this, his resistance to the ugliness and formlessness of modern physical living, he had a point, and the essence of the culture and environment movement that he inspired is that this all indicates a serious boss of *meaning:* "the meaningless squalor of ash-pits and closets and irregular rows of the

backs of houses" each with its small activity made sordid by barren cohesion
with the rest of its small activities. Farther off was the great colliery that went
night and day."

The whole place was just unreal, just unreal. (R, 346). Tom Brangwen does
not even really believe in it: "It was like some gruesome dream, some ugly,
dead, amorphous mood become concrete" (R, 346).

The colliery landscapes, then, to Lawrence, looked like the projection into
the world of some subjective element, some ugly, dead "mood." Ursula and
Winifred see the men in this scene thus:

> Like creatures with no more hope, but which still live and have passionate being, with
> some utterly unliving shell, they passed meaninglessly along, with strange, isolated
> dignity. It was as if a hard, horny shell enclosed them all. (R, 346)

This note is struck elsewhere in *The Rainbow*, especially at the end.

The problem is thus one of what the industrial-colliery environment has
*done to men*, as women see it. Ursula is a young woman full of hope; Winifred
Unger is an older woman whose perversion is associated with her feeling that
men have become "impotent" and unable to "take on" women. They are
shocked and starked by the life led under the shadow of the "great,
mathematical colliery."

But why, then, should Winifred Unger, whom Ursula loves, be attracted to
a representative of this world? "She was afraid of him, repelled by him, and
yet attracted."

We may, I believe, detect in the background the first disturbing experience
of Mrs. Lawrence when she found she had to wash her miner husband's back.
That is, Lawrence is again confronting the problem of giving his mother a
meaningful sexual life by proxy.

> The fine beauty of his skin and his complexion, some almost waxen quality, had the
> strange, repellant grossness of him, the slight sense of putrescence, the commonness
> which revealed itself in his rather fat thighs and loins. (R, 347)

Then Lawrence confronts what the pit did to his father: "The pits are very
deep, and hot, and in some places wet. The men die of consumption fairly
often. But they earn good wages" (R, 348). Now we approach the essential
problem of the relationship between the colliery and the married (sexual) life,
that is, the dead husband of the woman who serves Tom's team was a loader
like Lawrence's father:

> "John Smith, loader. We reckoned him as a loader, he represented himself as a
> loader, and so she knew he represented his job. *Marriage and home is a little
> sideshow.... The pit matters.* Round the pit there will always be the side-shows,
> plenty of 'em." (R, 348-94, my italics)

This was what Lawrence could not bear: that a man's identity was bound up entirely with *male doing*, and the industrial enterprise. To him, *living* was what matters, and especially marriage and sexual love (not, especially, "home"). He felt that in that industrial society a man was reduced to being simply a "loader," and only the pit mattered—his relationship with his woman was reduced to a sideshow.

> "Every man his own little side-show, his home, but the pit owns every man. The women have what is left. What's left of this man, or what is left of that—it doesn't matter altogether. The pit takes all that really matters." (R, 349)

Lawrence's whole life, in a sense, was devoted to rejecting this as an impossible state of affairs for human beings.

Winifred agrees:

> "It is the office, or the shop, or the business that gets the man, the woman gets the bit the shop can't digest. *What is he at home, a man? He is a meaningless lump—a standing machine, a machine out of work.*" (R, 349; my italics)

Ursula looks out and sees the "proud, demon-like" colliery: "How terrible it was! There *was* a horrible fascination in it."

> Human bodies and lives subjected in slavery to that symmetric monster of the colliery. (R, 349–50)

Lawrence makes a wider assertion:

> No more would she subscribe, to the great machine *which has taken us all captive* .... It had only to be forsaken to be inane, meaningless. And she knew it was meaningless. But it needed a great, passionate effort of will on her part, seeing the colliery, still to maintain her knowledge that it was meaningless. (R, 350; my italics)

Industry, the machine, technology and science are not meaningless insofar as we may put them to proper uses. What we may say of them is that in themselves they cannot solve the problem of meaning, and they threaten meaning only insofar as they take over the whole of man's life. The primary of being, of meaning, of the *Dasein* in the face of death must come first. This is a valuable existential emphasis.

Why, then, does Ursula want her mistress married to Tom?

> Her Uncle Tom and her mistress remained there among the horde, cynically reviling the monstrous state and yet adhering to it, like a man who reviles his mistress, yet who is in love with her. (R, 350)

He "only wanted the great machine":

> She knew moreover that in spite of his criticisms and his condemnation, his only moments of pure freedom were when he was serving the machine. (R, 350)

When *"he was free from hatred of himself,"* it is as if Lawrence felt that service to the machine could only be an escape from self-loathing, while for Winifred *her* attachment to the machine is but a manifestation of her scientific materialism:

> She too, Winifred, worshipped the impure abstraction, the mechanisms of matter. There, there, in the macine, in service of the machine, was she free from the clog and degradation of human feeling. There, in the monstrous mechanism that held all matter, living or dead, in its service, did she achieve her consummation and her perfect union, her immortality. (R, 350)

The machine and service to the machine suits those *who cannot bear themselves as human,* who cannot bear the "mire and blood." He sees it as a false solution, linked with Tom's "corruption" and "putrescence," and Winifred's perversion, and her intellectual scepticism and scientific materialism.

Ursula (Ursula–Lawrence) reacts extravagantly to this false solution, into another: "Hatred sprang up in Ursula's heart. If she could she would smash the machine. Her soul's activity would be the smashing of the great machine" (R, 350). She wants to smash the colliery and the Moloch of the great machine (yet not long ago she had found Moloch attractive). Yet she wants Winifred to marry Uncle Tom, even though the mistress seems like a great prehistoric lizard, and her lover a decaying marsh monster of "succulent moistness and turgidity."

She is glad:

> Their marshy, bitter-sweet corruption came sick and unwholesome to her nostrils. Anything, to get out of the foetid air. She would leave them both for ever, leave for ever their strange, soft, half-corrupt element. Anything to get away. (R, 351)

Behind it is perhaps a strange unconscious fantasy of the Primal Scene.

But does the "upshot" of the episode make the kind of social-political sense so many Lawrence commentators seem to think? One might reject the attachment of certain people to the machine; their thinking based on it; the excessive claims they allow, for the machine to dominate their lives. This surely does not justify an impulse to smash the machines, nor would smashing the machines solve the problem, since the problem is one of consciousness, and the need to recognize the needs of being. Brangwen, in fact, marries Winifred because he wants children: "He would let the machine carry him; husband, father, pit-manager, warm clay lifted through the recurrent action of day after day by the great machine from which it derived its motion" (R, 352). In a sense, Lawrence has found his father, and has explored why he hated him:

"He had the instinct of a growing inertia, of a thing that chooses its place of rest in which to lapse into apathy, complete, profound indifference" (R, 352). That was the threat to Lawrence, in finding and embracing the male element. He is attached to woman, not only because he was in love with his mother, is mourning for her, and wants to redeem her. The male element, in its possession by "the pit" and the machine, offered no lively basis for meaning in existence, only apathy and indifference. It was this subjective problem that he turned into a sexual-social theory, in which the machine is the enemy to sexual life with the woman, by which meaning in being is to be found.

*     *     *

It is this theory, rooted in his subjective problems, that makes his sex obsessional. Sometimes Lawrence is a caricature of himself. His propensity to seek the sexual potentialities in everything—dogs, figs, buds, tortoises—becomes grotesque and limiting. The Sleeping Beauty myth often prompts a ridiculous intensity of symbolism that needed restraint under the scrutiny of a self-critical irony. An example is the moment when Anthony Schofield, Maggie's brother, shows Ursula the rhubarb. He is like a "faun," with a "curious light in his face."

> Like the light in the eyes of the goat that was tethered by the farmyard gate. (R, 413)

Later, his eyes have in them "some of that steady, hard fire of moonlight which had nothing to do with the day." (Ah, we feel, here comes you-know-who!)
And so he takes her into the darkness where

> the little yellow knobs of rhubarb were coming. He held the lantern down to the dark earth. She saw the shiny knob-end of the rhubarb thrusting upwards upon the thick red stem, thrusting itself like a knob of flame through the soft soil. This face was turned up to her, the light glittering on his eyes and his teeth as he laughed, with a faint, musical neigh. (R, 414)

If you can do that with rhubarb you can do it with anything. Once again Lawrence is on the seduction trail. Anthony's eyes "were luminous with a cold, steady, arrogant-laughing glare."

> There seemed a little prance of triumph in his movement. She could not rid herself of a movement of acquiescence, a touch of acceptance. Yet he was so humble, his voice so caressing. (R, 414)

We may note in the words the excitement about power—the power of the faun-like man over the woman, and the capacity of his *voice* to induce "acceptance."
One cannot read *The Rainbow* without becoming conscious of Lawrence's

intense *oral* power; it takes on, at times, an incantatory quality. Its original title reveals that it was written out of the anxieties of getting married, or early marriage. In this commitment there was a deep fear of love because of its intense oral dangers, like Ursula's tigers. The oral intensity itself is an exercise of a certain kind of defense against these dangers.

Lawrence often gives himself away, that is, he describes the intensity of a character's passion, and you realize that he is really telling us what it is like for him. Tom Brangwen, for example, becomes angry with Lydia because she chatters on about her life in Poland. Instead of being glad *for her*, he feels she is annulling him: "And gradually he grew into a raging fury against her" (R, 62). He makes no retaliation on her, but is "solid with hostility." This, in turn, makes her aware of him, and "it irritated her to be made aware of him as a separate power" (R, 62). She lapses into a "sort of sombre exclusion" while he is "stiff with a will to destroy her as she was." It is never long in Lawrence before the characters, in intimacy, want to destroy one another.

Then, suddenly, there was connection between them again. A passionate flood breaks, and he feels he could "snap the trees off as he passed." He waits for her, however.

> She was sure to come to him at last, and touch him. Then he burst into flame for her, and lost himself. They looked at each other, a deep laugh in the bottom of his eyes, and he went to take of her again, *wholesale*, mad to *revel in the inexhaustible wealth of her, to bury himself* in the depths of her in an *inexhaustible exploration*, she all the while revelling in that he revelled in her, *tossed all her secrets aside and plunged to that which was secret to her as well*, whilst she quivered with fear and the last anguish of delight. (R, 62–63; my italics)

It is useful to look at the language here, and to ponder its meaning since this kind of language develops from *The Rainbow* on. A similar kind of language is used before even Tom and Lydia have sexual intercourse; it actually has something of the quality of Bunyan's language (and Lawrence often becomes biblical in style when he is describing sex):

> He waited till the spell was between them again, till they were together within one rushing, hastening flame. And then again he was bewildered, *he was tied up as with cords*, and could not move to her. (R, 56; my italics)

Yet all she does is to put her hand inside his shirt. Though Lawrence says "he bungled in taking her," he does not mean sexual taking. He means in receiving her being into his presence, but we may note the strange phrase italicized, which has the power of Bunyan's "That sentence lay like a millpost at my back." The state of reflective expectation in love, in Lawrence, exerts an intense physical power in his novels, and it is created and exerted by oral power itself, by words.

To go back to the earlier paragraph, I believe we may say that the intense expectations that Lawrence verbalizes between lovers have an oral quality that belongs more to the *expectation of the breast* in an infant than to adult life, and has in the background an expectation-fantasy of Kleinian proportions, that is, it is an urgent oral fantasy of getting the goodness out of the breast. There are, of course, elements of infant hunger in all sexuality, and sex has a regressive element in it. It belongs rather to an infant hunger for the *breast* to speak of revelling in the "inexhaustible wealth of her" and of an *inexhaustible exploration*. Moreover, it belongs more to intense infant fantasy to speak thus of plunging to *that that was secret to her as well*. All those strange impulses in Lawrence to dig satisfaction out of every corner of a woman's body arise from this intense oral-schizoid infant quality. Hence, too, of course, the endless *dissatisfaction*, for in Winnicott we have a number of indications that suggest that for some infants who spin unbridled fantasies of consuming the inner riches of the mother, no feed is adequate by comparison with the fantasied feed, which remains to torment them (as they go on crying after a satisfactory feed). Others for whom actual satisfaction removes a manic hunger, which has spun fantasies that convince them they are richly alive—once fed, the bright fantasy is dispelled, and they feel threatened with doom and death, so with much human sex.

Both responses are found again and again between Lawrence's lovers, and no doubt this was how he himself experienced sexual expectation and satisfaction.[2] This we may connect with his denial of woman's satisfaction, for if sexual peace is dreaded as bringing the threat of inanition, the woman's satisfaction would be the most threatening thing in the world: the "terrible painful unknown" that lurks in the background of all sexual acts for Lawrence.

It is this that explains such episodes as between Ursula and Skrebensky, toward the end of the book:

> She was still fiercely jealous of his body. In passionate anger she upbraided him because, not being man enough to satisfy one woman, he hung around others.
> "Don't I satisfy you?" he asked of her, again going white to the throat.
> "No," she said. "You've never satisfied me since the first week in London. You never satisfy me now. What does it mean to me, your having me—"
> She lifted her shoulders and turned aside her face in a motion of cold, indifferent worthlessness. He felt he would kill her . . . .
> At such moments, when he was mad with her destroying him, when all his complacency was destroyed, all his everyday self was broken, and only the stripped rudimentary, primal man remained, demented with torture, her passion to love him became love, she took him again, they came together in an overwhelming passion, in which he knew he satisfied her.
> But it all contained a developing germ of death . . . . After each contact his mad dependence on her was deepened, his hope of standing strong and taking her in his own strength was weakened. He felt himself a mere attribute of her. (R, 463)

Did he satisfy her or not? On what does it depend? As always with Lawrence, it sounds like a fight to the death. Though Lawrence is so explicit about sex, it is often impossible to know what he means. What, for instance, does "taking her in his own strength" mean? One suggests that Lawrence had certain rules for sexual love, and that one of the rules had to do with any gesture on the woman's part that seemed, in any way, to make the man an "attribute" of her. But behind the endless vague reflections on the modes of passion there lies always the deeper problem of that expectant vision of exhausting the last secret hiding places of a woman's body, which no mere human act could satisfy. This in turn explains why sex in Lawrence often has to be "inhuman" or super-human, and why it has to be all angels and stars with a residue of yearning for some ultimate "other" kind of yearning.

After many readings, I still find it hard to see what goes wrong between Skrebensky and Ursula. Of course, for F. R. Leavis it is easy: Skrebensky represents "the social idea," but how can we accept that there is a connection between sexual fulfillment and ideas or devotion to "society"? On pages 476–77 Skrebensky and Ursula seem to have as satisfactory a conjunction as any lovers could have. She, admittedly, "does not feel beautiful," and seems cold, though he "seemed almost savagely satisfied."

The next episode is deathly only with that perversity that Lawrence can organize. The reason becomes clear in the symbolism of the moon: he has injected into their life the blighting presence of his own internalized hostile mother imago. Of course, sexual fulfillment is not to be separated from the nature of what people are, or from how lovers see one another. Skrebensky's utilitarianism could become so repulsive to a sensitive woman like Ursula that she might come to feel unsatisfied, despite orgasm. Such torment as that of these lovers is not to be explained in terms of "ideas" about "society"; it would have an endogenous origin, in infantile traumata in the inner life. Lawrence's "sexual program" fails to take this into account.

*    *    *

As I have hinted above, while the sexuality in Lawrence is obsessional, it has a mythological quality for him that relates the question to the meaninglessness that threatens the imago of the Dead Mother unless he can in some way resurrect her. With Ursula, the third woman in the generations, there is a special destiny, and she may be taken to represent woman with the new educated and independent consciousness. She does indeed seek higher things, and in this is like Lawrence himself in youth. But why, as she contemplates "What in herself she really is" is that "real" self so wild and primitive?

> That which she was, positively, was dark and unrevealed, it could not come forth. It was like a seed buried in dry ash. (R, 437)

The world of her education is a lamplit world "lit by man's completest consciousness."

> Yet all the time, within the darkness she had been aware of points of light, like

the eyes of wild beasts, gleaming, penetrating, vanishing. And her soul had acknowledged in a great heave of terror only the outer darkness. (R, 437)

In the outer darkness, "She saw the eyes of the wild beast gleaming from the darkness." Others say there is no darkness, but she sees

grey shadow-shapes of wild beasts, and also . . . dark shadow-shapes of the angels, whom the light fenced out, as it fenced out the more familiar beasts of darkness. And some, having for a moment seen the darkness, saw it bristling with the tufts of the hyena and wolf . . . .
    The angels in the darkness were lordly and terrible and not to be denied, like the flash of fangs. (R, 438)

Here, I believe, we must approach the unconscious mythology. The intention was to show progress: Lydia enters the world of the farm in the organic community, and she and her husband lead an unself-conscious life of blood relationship. With Will and Anna there is more consciousness, and the woman sinks to a breeding creature, satisfied with that (perhaps one could call Anna Tolstoyean?). Ursula is a quite different kettle of fish, totally self-aware, educated, choosing independence, going out into the world, going to the Strand Palace Hotel with her lover. She is the girl of the post-Great War emancipation of woman, and the lesbian, feminist Winifred Unger is an ancillary to this—only in her the perversion is shown to be a form of mechanistic materialism in the approach to the sensual life that finds its complement in the servant of industry (thought it doesn't all quite tie up). Ursula turns down a perfectly straightforward offer of marriage, from Alexander Schofield of the erotic rhubarb, for something higher.

However, what is lacking in each generation is any benign, substantial fulfillment. Despite the original title, *The Wedding Ring*, and the symbolism of the rainbow (which seems to shift), *none of the women achieve fulfillment.* Lydia is a cipher, and when she sees Tom Brangwen dead, her situation seems like that of the woman in *Odour of Chrysanthemums*.

Anna, the child who loves life and has such a rich relationship with her mother and stepfather, after her ecstatic love-relationship, and all the endorsement of her marriage, comes to be a destructive woman who sneers at Will's ideals, and threatens to destroy his soul. She becomes a breeding woman, totally happy in her continual pregnancies, and beyond her husband. He becomes a cipher, and ends up as a craft instructor for Nottingham. In the next novel, unbelievably, the Brangwen parents become symbolic emblems of parental death and sexual sterility.

Ursula, who is such a marvelous being, has her excitement at being alive, at natural life, at being—as when she studies the amoeba. She has a higher destiny, intelligence, a wide view of civilization, a cosmic perspective.

Yet after the first exquisite moments with Skrebensky, *in both episodes*, something *deathly* springs up between them. In the first she destroys him, either with some strange kind of sterile kiss, or by masturbating him. In the second, the "death" seems to come out of some aspect of her inward life. Lawrence (commended by Leavis) tries to show this deadness comes from his "social idea," his devotion to duty, his utilitarianism. In any realistic terms, however, surely we must say it could only come from within: it is *endogenous*.

The clue to its unconscious origins lies in the symbolism. As so often in Lawrence, the doom often comes after the *moon* rises. Thus, *The Rainbow* turns out to be another novel about the unconscious fear of woman. With Ursula, Lawrence is seeking further solutions to this dread. The Ursula–Skrebensky episode that concludes *The Rainbow* is obviously a most important one in the Lawrence canon, yet examined closely it is extremely confused.

Leavis, of course, simplifies it to fit his thesis: Skrebensky is a Bethamite (R, 328–29) and so belongs to "mechanism" and "will" to functional man so he is sexually inadequate. Skrebensky thinks in the utilitarian way:

> The good of the greatest number was all that mattered. That which was the greatest good for them all, collectively, was the greatest good for the individual. (R, 328)

One may agree that Skrebensky is wrong, that Bethamite reductionism is vicious, and no doubt his social ideas affected Skrebensky's social behavior. But it is difficult to believe that a Benthamite cannot love or make love adequately, or to see in what way whatever it is that goes wrong between Ursula and Skrebensky is affected or dominated by such social beliefs. Leavis's interpretation cannot be sustained. For instance, on page 449 Skrebensky sees all the "normal" people as mechanical puppets, while he "has a sense of voluptuous richness in himself." It is not true that Ursula and Skrebensky are not in love, or that "will" has supplanted love in them. She loves him virtually to the end; he is with her "in a rich, pulsing world." Without her, he is "ash, machine and decomposition." Her absence destroys his being. "She loved Skrebensky—of that she was resolved."

Why, then, do things go wrong? Here, I believe there are a number of answers, some of which are not reconcilable. In the end, just before the event with the horses, and when she is pregnant, Ursula decides to be like her mother—a "dutiful" pregnant wife: "her mother was right" ... was it not right for her as it had been for her mother?" (R, 484). She rejects her "illusory fulfillment."

> She knew that Skrebensky had never become finally real. (R, 494)

He belongs to the past, and she looks to the future, but then the encounter with the wild horses suggests she is reserved for some higher destiny. What that "destiny" is is most revealing.

The episode with Skrebensky could have been a very great passage. It is clear that, *whatever the problem*, their marriage is not "meant." It could have taken on the tragic quality of an episode in which fate, the way things turn out, does not lead to fulfillment. When Skrebensky cries in the taxi, it approaches this stature: it is a painful and beautiful recognition of the "not-meant" quality of some relational encounters. It could have been as tragic as certain events in Tolstoy.

What mars it is a certain willfulness on the author's part, reminiscent of Hardy's. For some reason, one becomes aware Lawrence is not going to let his "independent" heroine *have* her independent path, despite references to how the "kernel" is the "only reality," that is, the true self of being. As the drama unfolds, the author's psychopathology interferes, as it does with Hardy, and Lawrence has his thumb in the scale.

It is not true that Skrebensky's "social idea" undermines the relationship. The "death" is an *endogenous* dynamic, that is, it springs from within, and *it comes from her*. Each time there is a sudden decline and turnabout in the passion, it is *Ursula's* destructive dynamic that brings it about, and she more or less admits this in her letter and her last admissions to herself.

There are two aspects to this yearning. For one thing Ursula speaks of how there are probably lots of men in the world she could love (R, 475), and in talking to Rosemary she talks in such a way that the other woman realizes "then you don't love him." She has not yet found the uniqueness of the other in love.

At a deeper level, and a level at which Lawrence is not aware of what this means, she is affected by the *moon*. That is, *she* is disturbed as a version of Lawrence, by *Lawrence*'s own inner dread of the dead mother. And here there is not only the moon, but also the Thalassal sea:

> The trouble began at evening. Then a yearning for something unknown came over her, a passion for something she knew not what. She would walk the forshore [*sic*] alone after dusk, expecting, expecting something, as if she had gone to a rendezvous. The salt, bitter passion of the sea, its indifference to the earth, its swinging, definite motion, its strength, its attack, and its salt burning, seemed to provoke her to a pitch of madness, tantalizing her with vast suggestions of fulfillment. (R, 478)

By contrast, Skrebensky does not have a soul that could "contain her in its waves of strength, nor his breast compel her in burning, salty passion." The polarity in Lawrence is toward the whole earth as toward the mother. As he identifies with Ursula, Skrebensky cannot live up to that ideal polarization, anymore than Miriam could for Paul; the Thalassal witch annihilates Skrebensky, because she has supplanted him in Ursula's heart.

The parallel with the passage in *Sons and Lovers* is close. The moon suddenly appearing transforms the relationship:

> Suddenly, cresting the heavy, sandy pass, Ursula lifted her head, and shrank back, momentarily frightened. There was a great whiteness confronting her, the moon was

incandescent as round furnace door, out of which came the high blast of moonlight, over the seaward half of the world, a dazzling, terrifying glare white light. They shrank back for a moment into shadow, uttering a cry. He felt his chest laid bare, where the secret was heavily hidden. He felt himself fusing down to nothingness, like a bead that rapidly disappears in an incandescent flame. (R, 479)

She gives her breast to the moon; he stands behind encompassed, "a shadow ever dissolving."

She kisses him, with "a beaked harpy's kiss." He feels the ordeal of proof is him for life or death. She refuses to make love in a hollow, but insists on remaining in the moonlight, where she lies with "wide-open eyes looking up at the moon." There, "He came direct to her, without preliminaries." Reading the descriptions of sexual acts in Lawrence, it seems normal tender foreplay felt dangerous to Lawrence; he has an evident proclivity for rather sudden and even brutal acts. Sexual acts also seem to him to be like crucifixion and death: "She held him pinned down at the chest, awful. The fight, the struggle for consummation was terrible" (R, 480). When he looks at her, her eyes look rigid, and a tear falls, glittering in the moonlight. He feels as if a knife were being thrusted into an already dead body.

He plunges away from the "horrible" figure; she trails her "dead body" back to her house, all within her cold, dead, and inert. They are like two dead people. Ursula's letter to him is strange:

> It was given to me to love you, and to know your love for me. But instead of thankfully, on my knees, taking what God had given, I must have the moon in my keeping, I must insist on having the moon for my own. Because I could not have it, everything else must go. (R, 485)

Who was she to be wanting some fantastic fulfillment in her life?

All this gives us many clues, to the dissatisfaction Lawrence inflicts upon his characters for here Ursula is Lawrence, and it is again the mother-domination that spoils the love. She, like Lawrence, cannot accept the promise of a love, because "she must have the moon in my keeping," must take the Mother (not Ursula's but Lawrence's) into her keeping and seek a fulfillment of the kind insisted upon by the maternal power (which, of course, for many mother-dominated individuals means no other relationship). Toward the end we have a hint that Ursula (who is here so much Lawrence) is being kept for a better fate, and this fate belongs to his powerful unconscious mythology. I have pointed out that in Lawrence's novels, whenever the moon appears, we have the face of the dead mother, and she casts a shadow on adult sexual love ("a shadow always dissolving"). When the moon rises on Ursula with Skrebensky, she "is" D. H. Lawrence experiencing the inhibiting power of the Dead Mother in the unconscious. The moon's other face in this is that of the Ideal Object, the supreme Ideal Object that is the perfect mother of the Union of Being. In this respect, Ursula yearns for an "illusory fulfillment." "I must have the moon in my keeping" means, in the private mythology, "I must save myself for the Union with a Son of God who can resurrect the Mother."

At the conscious level, Ursula is meant to represent the "modern woman" in Lawrence's scheme of things, and she is shown as one who seeks *clitoral satisfaction,* as if this were wrong.

What is the great final test of Skrebensky at the end of the book? It is highly significant that *The Rainbow*, originally entitled *The Wedding Ring*, should end with this test. The words repeated in it give significant clues: the "beaked harpy." Lawrence later spoke out against the "beaked" clitoris. Skrebensky comes to her "without any preparation"—does this mean without foreplay? The act is a failure. Ursula insists it is done on a heap of shingle, *in the moonlight*. Whatever Lawrence intended, the episode conveys the impression that woman, yearning for something unknown, can put a man to the test, insisting that he satisfy her "beaked" clitoris, and virtually destroy him. All he can say is, "Have you done with me?" And she will reply, "You couldn't . . ." meaning "You couldn't satisfy me." Yet, of course, there have been earlier occasions when he has clearly "satisfied" her, earlier their sexual passion has seemed perfect.

How does the episode look if we take it that Ursula "is" Lawrence himself? We may then deduce that at times *he* would insist on a "trial" *against the moon*. It is the malignant moonlight shining from the Dead Mother that destroyed his sexuality at times and made him feel that everything was "dead." He didn't know whether to attribute this to female emancipation, the menacing destructiveness lurking in human, or to fate. He had various sexual theories, and various social-sexual theories, but these remained of the nature of what the analysts call "offered causes"—really, disguises of the real problem. We expect there to be a development and growth between Ursula and Skrebensky, but it doesn't come. I believe Lawrence expected more fulfillment and change in himself when he married—when he was to be "reborn" out of his woman, but I believe it didn't happen. He declared that "one sheds one's sicknesses in books," but this didn't bring about the change he wanted.

Two things seem to happen: first, Ursula yearns for a new destiny—some man come from Infinity who will lead her completely out of her "condition" (in Sartre's sense), and second, because she is always liable to arouse this ghost of one's dark inheritance, woman becomes the danger that must be controlled.

Ursula is drawn to want a new destiny in *The Rainbow* when she watches the train on the downs above Arundel Castle. She cries over the train, which seems to be a symbol of the true self (Interesting that the machine-smashing Ursula–Lawrence should take a machine as such a symbol!):

its courage carried it from end to end of the earth, till there was no place where it did not go. Yet the downs, in magnificent indifference, bearing limbs and body of the sun, drinking sunshine and sea-wind and sea-wet cloud in its golden skin, with superb stillness and calm of being, was not the downs still more wonderful? The blind, pathetic, energetic courage of the train as it steamed tinily away through the patterned level to the sea's dimness, so fast and so energetic, made her weep. Where was it going? It was going nowhere, it was just going. So blind, without goal or aim, yet so hasty! (R, 464)

It is an existentialist passage, symbolic of the progress of the soul through life. By contrast with the train, Ursula wants to belong to a "cosmic" life: "intercourse with the everlasting skies." She takes her clothes off and renounces making love in *houses*, and especially she hates *beds*. She makes her lover take all his clothes off, and they run about naked on the downs. They make love thus, but

her eyes were open looking at the stars, it was as if the stars were lying with her and entering the unfathomable darkness of her womb, fathoming her at last. *It was not him.* (R, 465; my italics)

Ursula (Ursula–Lawrence) yearns for a cosmic union (such as one experiences with the mother as an infant). She used this (which she later rejects as an "illusory, conceited fulfillment which she imagined she could not have with Skrebensky") to be critical of, and then destroy her love with Skrebensky. While clearly he could "physically" satisfy her, he could never satisfy this ultimate longing to be at one with the sun, the stars, the moon, the downs, and the whole earth.

The last chapter seems something of a large attempt to tie up the loose ends, but it also has a *deus ex machina* quality. The horses that frighten Ursula may symbolize the dark unknown forces of one's own destiny, or one's deeper self (the shadow as Jung called it) though they also seem something of a device to get rid of her baby. Her part in the self-defeat of herself over Skrebensky is hardly solved by the stirring recommendation "to be continued in our next" (i.e., in *Woman in Love*):

The man should come from the Infinite and she should hail him. She was glad she could not create her man . . . the man should come out of Eternity to which she herself belonged. (R, 499)

What are the implications of this? Not, I believe, commendable, as Leavis thinks, as a manifestation of a deep religious awe, and a surrender to the *Ahnung*, a sense that they "one does not being to oneself."

I believe rather that Lawrence is reserving this character for himself, so that he can use her as a medium to enact the two desires that now compel him: to lift his sexual experience totally out of the "reality" of the world (increasingly rejected by Ursula as dead, mechanical, a husk, prison, etc.) and to put woman under (magic) control, because she it too dangerous to be free. Out of this develops an extraordinary wish-fulfillment theme. Indeed, I would go further and say that the solution is a magic fantasy that verges on the insane.

The mystical belief is set forth at the end of the chapter "The Widening Circle." Lawrence compares the Resurrection of Christ with his kind; Christ's is no good, of course, because it is a useless after-death, wan and bodiless.

> But why? Why shall I not rise with my body whole and perfect, shining with strong life? Why, when Mary says: Rabboni, shall I not take her in my arms and kiss her and hold her to my breast? Why is the risen body deadly, and abhorrent with wounds?
>
> The Resurrection is to life, not to death. Shall I not see those who have risen again walk here among men perfect in body. (R. 281)

What can Lawrence possibly have meant? The clue appears in the next paragraph:

> assured at last in wholeness, perfect without scar or blemish, healthy without fear of ill-health? Is this not the period of manhood and of job and fulfillment, after the Resurrection? (R, 281)

We have taken all this Pickwickianly, I suppose, to mean that Lawrence is yearning for a new freedom from darkness for Ursula in this life, and then he seems to be speaking of himself and all of us, as if a resurrection were possible death:

> Can I not, then, walk this earth in gladness, being risen from sorrow? Can I not eat with my brother happily, and with joy kiss my beloved . . . . Is heaven so impatient with me, and better against this earth, that I should hurry off, or that I should linger pale and untouched? (R, 282)

As he goes on, I believe, we hear the cry of a man who wishes to escape from his own doom as a victim of tuberculosis, and as a man with a schizoid yearning for rebirth, who fantasies a kind of resurrection—in the case of his mythology, to be achieved through the Resurrection of the Dead Mother, who in turn would redeem him:

> Is the flesh which was crucified become as poison to the crowds in the streets, or is it as a strong gladness and hope to the, or the first flower blossoming out of the earth's humus? (R, 282)

Lawrence is struggling against the death-obsessed, life-denying element in Christianity, but it is not at all clear what he really believes except for that general note of a yearning to be reborn into a more vital form of being. To Ursula, at the beginning of the next chapter, religion becomes "a tale, a myth, an illusion" that "one knew was not true—at least, *for this present-day life of ours.*" So what is true? Lawrence can't tell us, except for his vague sense of "something working entirely apart from the purpose of the human world" (R, 436). When it comes to religion, Lawrence's view, like Ursula's, is that it is "an enemy to those who believed in the humanity of Christ" (R, 274).

To her, as to Lawrence, Christ merges into the Mother image that embodies the mystery of life:

> To her, Jesus was beautifully remote, shining in the distance like a white moon at sunset, a crescent moon beckoning as it follows the sun, out of our ken. (R, 275)

It is at this moment that Lawrence embarks upon the daughters of men theme for Ursula, as for Lawrence, sexual love, on certain conditions, becomes the focus of religion and meaning. The passage obviously has great significance for Lawrence since she hears the voice in church:

> "The Sons of God saw the daughters of men that they were fair: and they took of them wives of all which they chose. "And the Lord said, My spirit shall not always strive with man, for that he also is flesh. (R, 276)

Lawrence would have responded to the promise that "my spirit shall not always strive with man"—with its suggestion that there could be an end to the torment of love. The passage also reveals his impulse to seek a state larger than life:

> "There were giants in the earth in those days; and also after that, when the Sons of God came in unto the daughters of men which were of old, men of renown."
> Over this Ursula was stirred as by a call from afar off. In those days, would not the Sons of God found her fair, would she not have been taken to wife by one of the Sons of God? It was a dream that frightened her, for she could not understand it. (R, 276)

Some passages of the rumination are excellent, as the portrait of the mind of an intelligent adolescent girl reflecting upon her religion, but there is a sense in which Lawrence was recording his *own* religious thoughts in adolescence and in which he is redeeming his mother through Ursula, in his private mythologies.

> These came on free feet to the daughters of men, and saw they were fair, and took them of wife, so that *the women conceived and brought forth men of renown.* This was a genuine fate. She moved about in the essential days, when the Sons of God came in unto the daughters of men. (R, 276; my italics)

As we shall see, Lawrence becomes increasingly preoccupied with the phallic god-hero—himself in disguise—who is "unaccountable":

> Jove had become a bull, or a man, in order to love a mortal woman. He had begotten in her a giant, a hero.
> Very good, so he had, in Greece. For herself, she was no Grecian woman. Not Jove nor Pan nor any of there gods, not even Bacchus nor Apollo, could come to her. But the Sons of God who took to wife the daughters of men, these were such as should take her to wife.

She clung to the secret hope, the aspiration .... So utterly did she desire the Sons of God should come to the daughters of men .... The fact that a man was a man, did not state his descent from Adam, did not exclude that he was also one of the unhistoried, unaccountable Sons of God. (R, 276–77)

When Birkin comes to Ursula, it is the Sons of God with the daughters of men, and the same phrase is used when Mellors comes to Connie Chatterley. Skrebensky is no god, so he has no chance:

Who was she to have a man according to her desire? It was not for her to create, *but to recognise a man created by God. The man should come from the Infinite and she should hail him* .... *The man would come out of Eternity to which she herself belonged.* (R, 494; my italics)

The collier, as we saw above, is claimed by the pit, only a mechanical lump of him left for the woman. Skrebensky, settling for the "social idea," comes to be classed with this "functional man," and with the dead father.

The parental sexuality as between father and mother—so angrily rejected in *The Rainbow* and *Women in Love*—was too "real" or "ordinary"; there must be some reaching after a higher plane. The position is really almost Nietzschean: "Truth is ugly. We have *art* lest we *perish of the truth*" (*Will to Power*, 822). It is the artist–God–Birkin–Lawrence figure who is to redeem all:

In everything she saw she grasped and groped to find the creation of the living God, instead of the old, hard barren form of bygone living. Sometimes great terror possessed her. Sometimes she lost lost touch, she lost her feeling, she could only know the old horror of the husk which bound in her and all mankind. They were all in prison, they were all going mad.

She saw the stiffened bodies of the colliers, which seemed already enclosed in a coffin, she saw their unchanging eyes, the eyes of those who are buried alive. (R, 495)

This note is one we recognize as belonging to Lawrence's later work. The old dead life is that of his home, of Nottingham, of family connections, and his mother's death and her existential failure. It is also the failure of his own existential being in his inner schizoid sense of emptiness and meaninglessness. This "old horror of the husk" is what he projects over society and mankind, and it impels him to wish all mankind away so long as he could solve his problems: "it will never be springtime in the world for us."

Of course, one can see that there were aspects of the catastrophe of 1914–18 that might make anyone feel like that, but, in fact, Lawrence did not get married until a week or so before the war broke out, while *The Rainbow* came out in September 1915, and *Women in Love* was finished in November 1916. ("The book frightens me: it is so end of the world. But it is, and must be, the beginning of a new world, too," [Huxley, 1932, 396].) The books were written before the disasters of 1914–18 really overwhelmed, so what is this dead old world?

You ask me about the message of *The Rainbow*. I don't know myself what it is:
except that the older world is done for, toppling on top of us: and that it's no use
the men looking to the woman for salvation, *nor the women looking to sensuous
satisfaction for their fulfillment. There must be a new world.*[3] (Huxley, 1932, 316;
my italics; 7 February 1916, to Lady Cynthia Asquith)

The bad old world was an inner condition of Lawrence himself. In the same
letter he reports how stress on his nerves has "set up a deferred, inflammation
in all the internal linings." "I have felt very bad, so nearly disintegrated into
nothingness." He speaks of "all that fever and inflammation and madness":
"I feel very queer after it—sort of hardly know myself." It was his own
psychological condition and his physical sickness that made him feel that "this
world of ours has got to collapse now, in violence and injustice and
destruction, nothing will stop it."

The only thing now to be done is either to go down with the ship, sink with the ship,
or, as much as one can, *leave* the ship, and like a castaway live a life apart . . . . I
will not live any more in this time. I reject it. (Huxley 1932, 317; 7 February 1916,
to Lady Otteline Morrell)

"I will save myself," he says, but even so, woman must not try to find her
fulfillment, even though behind his creative impulse is the fantasy-attempt to
redeem the meaninglessness of his mother's life by sending the Sons of God
to the daughters of men.

From biographical evidence, Lawrence seems to have suffered a severe
crisis, between the writing of *The Rainbow* and *Woman in Love*. He had been
working "frightfully hard" on *The Rainbow* in the months before Spring
1915, at which time he suffered a deep depression. He and Frieda had both
suffered from influenza before his fatal visit to Cambridge, and he was ill in
other ways, some of which suggest that his tuberculosis, which lay at the root
of his problems, was troubling him. The visit to Cambridge left him "very
black and down," and a very deep crisis followed that seems to have been a
complex process involving many aspects of his life. By 1917 he was writing to
E. M. Forster, "I am so weary of mankind."

The failure to solve his problems in marriage by all his effort in writing was
one factor in Lawrence's increasing despair and bitterness, and this he
projected over outer reality in various ways. It obviously bore on his
philosophy of life.

At the same time, he was appalled by the Great War, and the atmosphere
of death and destruction it brought to Europe and the world. For a sensitive
man like Lawrence, the effects of the war must have been traumatic at a deep
level.

Paul Delaney quotes some revealing passages from the *Letters:*

I am afraid of the ghosts of the dead. They seem to come marching home in legions

over the white, silent sea, breaking in on us with a roar and white iciness . . . . The
touch of death is very cold and horrible on us all . . . . It is the whiteness of the ghost
legions that is so awful. (Huxley 1932, 222; March, 1915, to Lady Otteline Morrell.)

The "whiteness" is to be noted. We remember that when Mellors looks out
at the mining villages from the hut in the woods, it is the whiteness of the lights
that seem to menace him and his woman, the "white hands in the air" that
seem to threaten to throttle him. Lawrence went to Bognor for the day once,
and saw on the pier a young soldier whose leg had been amputated: "strangely
self-conscious and slightly ostentatious: but confused. As yet, he does not
realise anything, he is still in shock." "Lawrence," says Delaney, "seemed to
see in him an image of his own condition, reduced almost to a shade by his
nervous crisis and gazing out, still dazed, at the sea . . . 'a white, vague,
powerful sea . . . . I cannot tell out why, but I am afraid.'" (Delaney, 1979,
108).

We may, I believe, from a phenomenological analysis, see that for
Lawrence the war, and the machine in war, was to be blamed for his own
illness and his sexual troubles. The war castrated Clifford Chatterley, and
other Lawrence characters have been so damaged by the war. There seems to
have been a connection in his mind between the war, which demonstrated the
horror of the machine, and the machine that claimed his miner father and
allowed him only a minimal life in the home for his wife, that is, the death
of his parents' marriage he felt to be attributable to the way in which industrial
life and the machine had claimed his father. Now the machine was spreading
death all over the world, and especially menacing that search for "being"
through sexuality.

The unconscious factors mingled with this sense of doom are very complex.
Paul Delaney suggests that the poem *Meeting Among Mountains* (p, 224) can
be interpreted as showing that Lawrence was subconsciouly accepting
impotence and tuberculosis as condign punishment for ousting Weekley from
Frieda, with all the consequential oedipal guilt. Certainly Lawrence was
tormented by guilt and by hatred of Frieda's yearning for her children, but we
also have to ponder the strange symbolism of Lawrence's identification with
Christ. (Delaney suggests he grew a beard to look like Christ and his father
who was bearded; for him this seems to be the first step in the movement
towards the masculine mystique.) The unconscious appeal of Christ to
Lawrence was that he symbolized the possibilities of schizoid suicide—that
ultimate regression that was to be a rebirth, of which the Phoenix was his
symbol. Lawrence yearned to become reborn out of his psychic predicament
of being unable to love, and his sexual perplexities, through regression into
death, followed by a new resurrection even as a "son of god." We have seen
this symbolism, of course, in *The Man Who Died*, and it is uttered in many
poems.

In the poem *Eloi, Eloi, Lama Sabachthani?*, as Paul Delaney points out,

Lawrence identifies with the war dead, in terms of his own rebirth and resurrection. (However, we should note that the terrible cry, which is the title of the poem, is Christ's outburst to the Father, asking whether He had forsaken Him.) For Lawrence, the death of the world in war had to some extent the appeal of a new kind of suicidal cleansing, and this we find expressed in the poem. It ends, "I walk the earth intact hereafterwards."
This death is an expiation of guilt:

> The crime full-expiate, the Erinnyes sunk
> Like blood in the earth again; we walk the earth
> Unchallenged, intact, unabridged, henceforth a host
> Cleansed and in concord from the bed of death. (CP, 1964, 743)

It is useful to follow this poem through. It begins

> How I hate myself, this body which is me;
> How it dogs me, what a galling shadow

This is surely intensely schizoid, as is his reference to "But then, that shadow's shadow of me, / The enemy!" The "jeopardy" of war seems to make for the possibility of killing off the old self:

> Nay, now at last thank God for the jeopardy,
> For the shells, that the question is now no more before me (CP, 1964, 743)

The loud cry of the shells, in some way, gives him peace; the psychoanalyst would say the war externalizes his inner conflict. He fantasies the death of "my man":

> This death, his death, my death—
> It is the same, this death.

At this point, we find a strange connection between the urge towards schizoid and Lawrence's suppressed homosexuality. Homosexuality has an element in it of narcissism, and here we find clearly a symbolism of Lawrence *bayoneting himself*, with a sexual connotation. (We may surmise that in trying to solve his heterosexual problems by anal sex, Lawrence was unconsciously avoiding the discovery of a different sexual organ than his own, and by turning woman into a kind of *encul* man, preserving his narcissism even in the act that most offers an escape from it.)

> . . . And I knew he wanted it.
> Like a bride he took my bayonet, wanting it,
> Like a virgin the blade of my bayonet, wanting it,
> And it sank to rest from me in him,

And I, the lover, am consummate,
And he is the bride, I have sown him with the seed
And planted and fertilized him (CP, 742)

Again, looked at phenomenologically, this helps us to understand why, from time to time, Lawrence was fascinated by murder: it offered the possibility of *sowing* a new self in the corpse of the old. There follows a confused expression of hatred of woman for interfering in this act of murderous self-replacement:

But what are you, woman peering, through the rents
In the purple veil...
...
Is there no reconciliation?
Is marriage only with death? (CP, 742)

The distant suffering and death of the war, with which Lawrence identifies, in a fantasy of schizoid suicide, becomes mingled with the strife between himself and Frieda, and the disillusionment of love which has failed:

I had dreamed of love oh love, I had dreamed of love,...
My body glad as the bell of a flower
And hers a flowerbell swinging...
Why should we hate, then, with this hate incarnate?
Why am I a bridegroom of War, war's paramour?
What is the crime, that my seed is turned to blood,
My kiss to wounds?
Who is it will have it so, who did the crime?
And why do women follows us satisfied,
Feed on our wounds like bread, receive our blood
Like glittering seed upon them for fulfillment? (CP, 742)

This is a terrible poem, and the question cried out is the same question that lies behind *The Rainbow:* where do the terrible rages and destructiveness come from between lovers? Lawrence wants to expiate the destructiveness and endogenous fury within him that has spoiled his hopes for love, and that makes him feel that "women" are feeding upon his wounded body like that of Christ until he can, by identifying with the slaughtered, find a new self.

There are two extremes behind this yearning of Lawrence's for solutions to his problems. One is his belief that in giving oneself to a woman, one was embarking on an ontological adventure: "the great living experience for every man in his adventure into the woman... he embraces in the woman all that is not himself" (Moore 1962, 324). "I go to a woman to know myself... to explore into the unknown" (Moore 1962, 318.) But then, as *The Rainbow* makes clear, the torment of destructiveness was not exorcised by the adventure of love. The radical confrontation, as Paul Delaney puts it, between one's own subjectivity and that of the alien other was for him the crucial mode of self-realization, yet this had only left him feeling still doomed and full of dread.

As Paul Delaney says, Lawrence came to pursue an "ultimate heterosexual experience that would bring together the angel and the animal, the genital and the anal" (Delaney 1979, 64) Under Frieda's enthusiasm, Lawrence came to be drawn into perversions: perhaps behaving like Paul Morel and Clara in *Sons and Lovers*, Lawrence and Frieda were arrested in Metz for making love in public (see David Garnett, "Frieda and Lawrence" in Stephen Spender, ed., *D. H. Lawrence, Novelist, Poet, Prophet*, 1973, 38).

What, then, about homosexuality? Here, at the explicit level, Lawrence recoiled, yet he did so with such fury that one suspects his disturbed fascination. This has a good deal to do with the crisis that struck him between 1915 and 1917. On the one hand, he was writing poems like *New Heaven and New Earth*, about finding the excitements of anal sex with woman. On the other hand, he was describing a characteristically schizoid feeling about life:

> I am struggling in the dark—very deep in the dark—and cut off from everybody and everything . . . sometimes I am afraid of the terrible things that are real, in the darkness, and of the entire unreality of these things I see. It becomes like a madness at last, to know one is all the time walking in a pale assembly of an unreal world . . . whilst oneself is all the while a piece of darkness pulsating in shocks . . . . The whole universe of darkness and dark passions . . . the subterranean black universe of the things which have not yet had being—has conquered me for now, and I can't escape. (Moore 1962, 329)

It is not that Lawrence revolted so strongly against the corruption at Cambridge (as he saw it) that he became disillusioned. Instead, he found the "principle of evil" in these people, and turned both misanthropic and obsessed himself with murder as a means to schizoid regeneration through death and rebirth. These impulses were not temporary, either; they persisted into his later work, such as *The Plumed Serpent*, as we shall see.

Lawrence projected dynamics of his inner world onto others, and projected them onto Bertrand Russell: so fiercely did he do this on one occasion that Russell actually contemplated suicide. He called Russell "the super war-spirit" who wanted to "jab and strike like the soldier with the bayonet." But, as we have seen from the poem *Eloi . . .*, it was Lawrence who wanted to strike, in a strangely homosexual way. In the short story *England My England*, war is seen as a destructive rival to man's great adventure, his relation to woman. Perhaps Lawrence associated a number of evils altogether, the war slaughter, the black beetles of Cambridge, homosexuality, and even Russell's pacifism, as projections of his own inner destructiveness, that "mortification" in his inner life, which seemed to threaten his life. Somehow, this mortification must be cut away.

He seemed to see "evil" out there in the world, in Keynes and Cambridge: "I am sick with the knowledge of the prevalence of evil, as if it were some insidious disease." Then the temptation arose in him, to "give himself over to the joys of hatred and get what, satisfaction he could out of that":

> I have had a great struggle with the Powers of Darkness lately. I think I have just got the better of them again. Don't tell me there is no Devil, there is a Prince of Darkness. Sometimes I wish I could let go and be really wicked—kill and murder—but kill chiefly. I do not want to kill. But I want to select whom I shall kill. Then I shall enjoy it. The war is no good. It is this black desire I have become conscious of.... This is the very worst wickedness, that we refuse to acknowledge the passionate evil that is in us. This makes us secret and rotten. (Huxley 1932, 237)

The trouble for Lawrence, with his "wants" model, of course, is that in that philosophy of being there is no indication where one draws the line.

Out of this crisis Lawrence began to write a philosophy called *Morgenrot*, the title borrowed from Nietzsche ("red dawn"). In *The Study of Thomas Hardy* he had argued for a benevolent principle of growth and freedom in nature. Now he emphasized the "principle of evil" and proclaimed that life was a struggle between two equal forces: "Shelley believed in the principle of evil, coeval with the principle of good. That is right."

Murder thus took on for Lawrence a therapeutic role, and we can see how might have arrived at this, from his feelings about the war, in relation to his own impulse to renew himself by murdering his (bad) "other." He even argued to Lady Otteline that, whatever she said about love being all, much rottenness would have to be destroyed before love could prevail (the subjective element here is evident):

> Surgery is pure hate of the defect in the loved thing. And it is surgery we want, Cambridge wants, England wants, I want.... There is in us what the common people call "proud flesh"—i.e. mortified flesh; which must be cut out; it cannot be kissed out, nor hoped out, nor removed by faith. It must be removed by surgery... I thought the war would surgeon us. Still it may. But England at home is as yet entirely unaffected (Huxley 1932, 234)

So he must save the world from sexual death, but that this was an attempt to save himself becomes clear the more he cries that he would let the world be destroyed so long as he and his woman were saved. What stuck after this crisis was his misanthropy ("You must not believe in the people") and his anti-democratic stance, that is, his hatred of "ordinary" people—those he had been so sympathetic to, in his earlier work, and whose life was the springs of his art as well as the attractions of resurrection—his continual need to fantasy the magical resurrection of Woman—and murder, "I would like to kill a million Germans—two million."

This misanthropic crisis that Lawrence suffered meant that the end of *The Rainbow* is still essentially bleak.

At the beginning of the novel, the pulse of life beats through the men of the organic community; at the end, all Ursula sees is squalor—the hard, cutting edges of the new houses spread over the hills in "insentient triumph." The colliers are buried alive. All is "the expression of corruption triumphant and unopposed, corruption so pure that it is hard and brittle" (R, 495). It is true, Ursula sees the rainbow, and the rainbow is a sign that the world will not be destroyed. Even the "ordinary people" who are so despised in *The Rainbow* and *Woman in Love* will perhaps be transformed:

> And the rainbow stood on the earth. She knew that the sordid people who crept hard-scaled and separate on the face of the world's corruption were living still, that the rainbow was arched in their blood and would quiver to life in their spirit, that they would cast off their horny covering of disintegration, that new, clean, naked bodies would issue to a new germination, to a new growth, rising to the light and the wind and the clear rain of heaven. She saw in the rainbow the earth's new architecture, the old, brittle corruption of houses and factories swept away, the world built up in a living fabric of Truth, fitting to the overarched heaven. (R, 496)

*The Rainbow* offers to portray the relationship between man and woman in sexual love and society, seen in a historical perspective. Lawrence felt there was a hostile power in modern civilization that was inimical to sexual love. He also felt that certain men (like Skrebensky, Gerald Crich, and Clifford Chatterley), who gave themselves to industry, the "social idea," and the machine are sexually inadequate in consequence.

When he forgets his theory and records human reality honestly, Lawrence gives the lie to his own sociology, by showing human beings as disordered in the "organic" community, as much as in the machine world. Thus, the sexual problems between men and women were just as difficult in that traditional community before the triumph of the machine. At the beginning of *The Rainbow*, for example, Tom's brother Alfred, who marries a chemist's daughter, is unfaithful to her, and goes with strange women ("and became a silent, unsuitable follower of forbidden pleasure," R, 14)—obviously a sexual disaster. Frank, the other brother, marries "a little factory girl" who "insinuated herself into him and made a fool of him." Tom's own sexual life is tormented until he meets the Polish lady. He then has lustful and gross encounters, one with a woman who is using him in an episode with her "real" man. He considers this "the most glorious adventure," and he was mad with desire for the girl.

> Afterwards he glowed with pleasure. By Jove, but that we something like! He stayed the afternoon with the girl, and wanted to stay the night. She, however, told him this was impossible: her own man would be back by dark, and she must be with him. He, Brangwen, must not let on that there had been anything between them. (R, 23)

We may reflect miserably that this encounter is not unlike some enthusiastically recorded in Lawrence's late stories, and even *Lady Chatterley:* "By Jove, that was something like!" even sounds like Mellors. We get a glimpse in it of something coarse in the days of the idealized past before the "machine" took over in 1914–18.

And when it comes to marriage, what can be more tormented than Tom Brangwen's deep dread and hate:

The time of his trial and his admittance, His Gethsemane and his triumphal entry in one, had come new . . . when he approached her, he came to such a terrible painful unknown . . . there was severance between them, and rage and misery and bereavement for her, and deposition and toiling at the mill with slaves for him. (R, 58–63)

As we read these pages, we come to realize that again there is a good deal of Lawrence's own experience in this, and of his marriage ("bereavement" being a reference to Frieda's misery at being parted from her children). It was *he*, Lawrence, who felt that going to a woman was like Christ being crucified—the word "deposition"gives this away.

But if man and woman seem to have as many difficulties in the old organic community as in the machine society, what of Lawrence's more liberated and independent people of the new era? For Tom Brangwen he would be a *nothing* without the Polish lady: "Unless she would come to him, he must remain as a nothingness . . . . He was nothing. but with her, he would be real" (R, 41). There is no such feeling in Yvette about her gypsy where her longings are confined to "naked desire." It is not Lou Witt's yearning, in *St. Mawr:* her goal is not meaning in love, but a fugitive desire to get away from it all. The fantasy in *Glad Ghosts* is of unions impelled by "naked desire" rather than any existential meaning. We cannot imagine Connie Chatterley saying about Mellors "with him, she would be real," that is, love that makes the other unique being indispensable is not a primary reality in Lawrence's later sexual world, as it is in the early works and in *Look! We Have Come Through!*

Tom Brangwen sees his destiny with the Polish lady as belonging to some "larger purpose." It is this that Leavis approves, with his inclination to approve of anything that was "religious" though not Christian:

he knew he did not belong to himself. He must admit that he was only fragmentary, something incomplete and subject. There was the stars in the dark heaven travelling, the whole host passing by on some eternal voyage. So he sat small and submissive to the greater ordering. (R, 40)

This was a key passage for Leavis, in his insistence on Lawrence's religious qualities. In this marvelous episode we have a deep sense expressed that a man's destiny can overtake him, in which *the libido is object-seeking*, and the need for love belongs to the *Dasein*, that is, it is in the sense of the uniqueness of the other, and the mystery of the I–Thou is bound up with the question of meaning in existence. This meaning is *rooted*, as Brangwen is rooted in his farm, but also seems to belong to the greater perspectives of the cosmos and world history. Whether or not Lawrence really believed there was a "greater ordering," it is difficult to say. He seems, as we shall see, to have believed that life had a dynamic of its own, and that human life was not necessarily the acme of its purpose.

The religious note at the end of *The Rainbow* seems less a submission to the mystery of life than a movement on Ursula's part to be fulfilled by that "man from Eternity."

> So utterly did the desire the Sons of God should come to the daughters of men, and she believed more in her desire and its fulfillment than in the obvious facts of life. (R, 277)

This is bound up with a yearning for a divine union with a race of men who are not fallen sons of Adam:

> Who were the Sons of God? . . . these men were not begotten by Adam . . . perhaps these children, these Sons of God, had known no expulsion, no ignominy of the fall. (R, 276)

By contrast there are "the *sordid* people who *crept hard-scaled* and *separate* on the face of the *world's corruption*" (R, 495; my italics).

She who is set aside and above this rut common humanity is destined to submit to a man who (as the language indicates) is identified with Christ.

Like so many tuberculosis sufferers (and schizoid individuals) Lawrence often indentified with Christ and aspired to a certain kind of special relationship with other (fictitious) gods. As Paul Delaney points out, the Phoenix was also a symbol of Christ (Lawrence was struck by this in Mrs Heather Jenner's *Christian Symbolism* which he read in December 1914: Moore, *Letters*, 1962, 304: See Delaney, 1979, 31 and fn. 304.) There is a disturbing sense that Lawrence actually believed this special quality of himself, in an almost literal way: he was a son of god, and not a member of the fallen race of Adam at all.

Once Ursula has received the telegram telling her Skrebensky is married, she reflects on the Second Coming:

> Who was she to have a man according to her own desire? . . .
> It was not for her to create, but to recognise a man created by God. The man should come from the Infinite and she should hail him . . . .
> The man should come out of Eternity to which she herself belonged. (R, 454)

The rest of the world seems somewhat inferior; the people she watches are enclosed in a "husk." In the colliers (who have "stiffened bodies") she sees "a sort of suspense," and "the same in the false hard confidence of the women" (R, 494). She sees the possibilities of "the creation of the living God" instead of "the old, hard, barren form of bygone living." But, "she could only know the horror of the husk which bound in her and all mankind. They were all in prison, they were all going mad" (R, 495). What is this that binds us all in? In what way are we all going mad as Lawrence so often tells us we are?

She saw the hard, cutting edges of the new houses, which seemed to spread over the hillside in their insensient triumph, a triumph of horrible amorphous angles and straight lines, the expression of corruption triumphant and unopposed; corruption so pure that it is hard and brittle. (R, 495)

There is no doubt that a new ugliness in the industrial Midlands overwhelmed the old and that the church became "obsolete." But in what way do these "brittle," "corrupt" housing estates threaten Ursula so much, that it needs the image of the rainbow to transcend them?

She knew that the sordid people who crept hard-scaled and separate . . . on the face of the world's corruption (R, 495)

This is a key moment in *The Rainbow*. And what is the force of that odd and "separate"? Why are these people of the Midlands "sordid" and "buried alive" with their "horny covering of disintegration"?

She saw in the rainbow the earth's new architecture, the old, brittle corruption of houses and factories swept away, the world built up in a living fabric of truth, fitting to the over-arching heaven. (R, 496)

But is the man from Eternity coming for all of us? Did Lawrence suppose that the salvation of Europe would depend on "one great chosen figure" who will "be supreme over the will of the people," which is how he talks in his History? What political and social policy is implied in Lawrence's vision?

I believe one phrase gives us the clue: "horrible coupling." Ordinary life represented the dreaded life of the parents: it is this that must be broken away from for a new life.

Paul Delaney, in *D. H. Lawrence's Nightmare*, points out in an insightful way the inconsistency in *The Rainbow* in terms of the philosophy of being. Ursula's discovery of an existentialist position, as in her conflict with her biology teachers, culminates in the feeling that "to be oneself was a supreme, gleaming triumph of infinity." This is juxtaposed against Skrebensky's aspiration to be "just a brick in the whole social fabric."

Ursula's vision of a *social* transformation at the very end of the book is inconsistent with what has preceded it—"one might say that she has been converted to her author's way of thinking" (Delaney, 1979, 76). Lawrence himself at the time declared, "we are no longer satisfied to be individual and lyrical." By the time he had begun writing *Women in Love*, his social attitude had again reversed itself, says Delaney, "from the vision of a regenerated community to the savage misanthropy proclaimed by Birkin, and from the historicism of the first novel to the eschatology of the second . . . . Lawrence bitterly rejects in his sequel to *The Rainbow* what had previously nourished his imagination." (Delaney, 1979, 76–7) In this fatal development, there is, of course, much that is deeply subjective, not least Lawrence's "great struggle with the Powers of Darkness."

Leavis's work on Lawrence implies a moral position that if one has sexual difficulties, one is virtually a fallen being, having failed to achieve that "mutual acceptance of otherness and separateness" and the (religious) dimension of accepting that "one does not belong to oneself." Once one discovers the underlying Resurrection myth, and takes in the flavor of the misanthropy, the "upshot" is very different.

In *The Rainbow* there are many assumptions that, because of these subjective roots, need careful examination. For instance, Lawrence seems to believe implicitly in instinct ("With all the cunning instinct of a breeding animal" [R, 354], "her instinct fixed on him" [R, 55].) Lawrence has a certain conception of the relationship between one generation and the next, which is embodied in *The Rainbow*, but the way he portrays the interactions of generations seems to have none of the realism we have since taken in from psychotherapeutic insights about parents and children. As I have said, Anna would not have turned out as she did—impelled by envy and the impulse to reduce another being (cf. "She was surprised that she did *not* intend her husband to be hopping for joy like a fish in a pond" [R, 176]; "You don't let me *live*" [R, 186]). She would be unlikely to be as destructive as she becomes though it is true that characters never turn out in life quite as they might be expected to.

But what *does* Lawrence say in this novel about "mutuality" in marriage? ("Another woman would be woman . . . the case would be the same" [R, 187].) I believe that Lawrence never solves this problem in his art, so his characters often go through long torments. (cf. Anna and Will, R, 157–76, and the long distress between Ursula and Skrebensky) when Lawrence seems to be seeking insight but fails to gain it. The episodes often offer us little or nothing by way of increased sympathy with, or understanding of, the problems of men and women. There is no end or no answer to the fierce hunger of the man. There is a deepening lack of confidence in the "abidingness of love," (R, 167) and there is often the sense that there "was something he wanted, some form of *mastery*" (R, 174; my italics): see Lawrence on the "old position of master of the home" (R, 173–4)

Then, because the problem is insoluble, he becomes nihilistic. Insights fail; the sicknesses are not "shed"; the doom seems intractable, and even enthusiastic perversions do not work. Thus his bitterness about such anguish comes to be turned in a social programe, imbued with misanthropy:

Sweep away the whole monstrous superstructure of the world today, cities and industries and civilisation, leave only the bare earth with plants growing and water running, and *he would not mind so long as he were whole.* (R, 193; my italics)

There is a great deal about "maximum self" in *The Rainbow*, and there is much about "potent darkness." However, whatever Leavis may say, the emphasis of *The Rainbow* is *not* on mutality in marriage, nor on an immanence in created life, or in human beings, that transcends love and sex. The main burden of much of the propaganda is an attempt to vindicate a ruthless male need to satisfy an insatiable, "disordered" sexual appetite, which even rejects the need to find mutuality at times, and this is vindicated by the man's divine status. Much of *The Rainbow* reads, for a great deal of the time, as if it were written by someone who had never himself discovered the capacity in sex to find the "significant other," to really find respect for the reality of the woman partner. As in *Lady Chatterley's Lover*, there is much that leads in a quite false direction in the attempt to satisfy the existential hunger, and "deepest need," by "rather awful sensuality"—and this could endorse false solutions that involve a cruel domination of one partner by the other, done in the name of a god-man and resurrection. Leavis said that by the time he came to write *Lady Chatterley's Lover*, Lawrence had forgotten what marriage meant, but the same essential deficiency is present in *The Rainbow*.

# 4

# *Women in Love—*
# and the Man from the Infinite

*Woman in Love* is perhaps Lawrence's most important novel. It is about the relationship between man and woman in relation to questions of being, our fundamental needs, the meaning of existence, and the nature of the cosmos. The best art in this novel comes where he shows the man and the woman being forced to accept their deepest needs in surrender to the love that is growing between them (e.g., as in the chapters entitled "Excurse" and Moony").

However, there seems to be many things about the novel that are not true—which do not ring true in the same way. Here again, I doubt the implicit sociology of "will" and sex, despite Leavis's endorsement when he sees Gerald's psychopathology as representing the psychopathology of our civilization. How insightful is Lawrence's sexual theory, as embodied in the "upshot" of this novel?

*Women in Love*, again, was written out of Lawrence's perplexities over marriage, and over the way destructiveness can emerge out of the heart of love. Indeed, by now, he is doubtful about love altogether. The love Birkin feels for Ursula is full of death, as is evident from the moment when the dreadful drowning accident in Willey Water happens. This drowning itself has its own symbolism. It stands itself for the deathly effects of "horrible merging": "Diana had her arms tight round the neck of the young man, choking him." ("'She killed him,' said Gerald.") (WL, 212) The symbolism in this disturbing chapter, "Water-Party," conveys Lawrence's deepest fears of commitment in love, and expresses a dark undercurrent of fear associated with sexual joy that is central to the novel.

It is highly significant that the Brangwen parents appear on their way to the party, since the chapter is about what marriage is like. The way the sisters tease their parents and the way they respond is superbly done—and is rather like the way people behave at a wedding, which is a lighthearted occasion, but also has strong undercurrents. The father is "stiff with rage," the girls are "weak with laughter." There is a tension between the ordinary people (*"un peu trop de monde,"* said Ursula . . . "), and the "special" Brangwens and Birkin. Gudrun hates to hear some girls say of Hermione "Doesn't she look *weird*!"

Gradually the romantic tension of the event deepens: the girls (improbably) bathe naked, and Gudrun does her strange dance to the Highland Cattle, "her breasts lifted and shaken towards the cattle, her throat exposed as in some voluptuous ecstasy towards them." The atmosphere becomes Dionysiac, and Ursula declares, when the men come up, "I think we've all gone mad." Birkin suddenly kisses her, in his "slack-waggling dance."

"No, don't!" she cried really afraid.
"Cordelia after all," he said satirically. She was stung, as if this were an insult. She knew he intended it as such, and it bewildered her. (WL, 189)

And it might since Cordelia was a daughter resisting a dominating and cruel demand from her father. On her part, Gudrun is driving the cattle mad. To show she is not afraid of Gerald (who tells her he owns the cattle), she gives a light stinging blow on the face with her hand:

she felt in her soul an unconquerable desire for deep violence against him . . . .
"You have struck the first blow," he said . . . . (WL, 191)

"Don't be angry with me," she says, and he replies, "I'm not angry with you. I'm in love with you." (Later we learn "He had killed his brother, when a boy, and was set apart, like Cain.")
    Out of this tense family background, the young people emerge, full of dangerous potentialities for sexual love, as symbolized by the dancing, the cattle, the slightly aggressive kisses, the blow in the face, and the water. Death and destructiveness emerge out of the very rhythm of life. Of the marsh Birkin says

"It seethes and seethes, a river of darkness," he said, "putting forth lilies and snakes, and the *ignis fatuus*, and rolling all the time onwards. . . ."
    "What does?"
    "The other river, the black river . . . the dark river of dissolution." (WL, 192)

This river of death or dissolution is also a river of corruption. Birkin says, "our flowers are of this—our sea-born Aphrodite, all our white phosphorous flowers of sensuous perfection, all our reality, nowadays" (WL, 193). Ursula asks whether Aphrodite is really deathly.

"I mean she is the flowering mystery of the death process . . . when the stream of synthetic creation lapses, we find ourselves part of the inverse process, the blood of destructive creation . . . then the snakes and swans and lotus-marsh-flowers—and Gudrun and Gerald—born in the process of destructive creation."
    "And you and me—?" she asked.
    "Probably." (WL, 193)

Ursula protests that she doesn't feel they are flowers of dissolution (*fleurs du mal*). She talks about roses of happiness, but Birkin reverts to talk about death:

"You are a devil, you know, really" she said. "You want to destroy, our hope. You *want* us to be deathly."

"No," he said, "I only want us to *know* what we are." (WL, 194)

The marsh (like the fertile silt of Shakespeare's Nile) may bring both lilies, but it may also bring forth snakes, corruption, and death. Above it shines the moon as the symbol of the mother: "As the golden swim of light overhead died out, the moon gained brightness, and seemed to begin to smile forth her ascendency" (WL, 194). The incipient lovers light lanterns, which are lesser lights to the moon, with great excitement. Ursula and Birkin's lamp has "the heavens above and the waters under the earth"; that of Gerald and Gudrun displays a "great white cuttle-fish . . . a face that stared straight from the heart of the light, very fixed and coldly intent." They swap lanterns. Actually, at this point, it is very difficult to know who is talking, and the couples merge in the darkness. Gudrun has Gerald to herself, and their progress seems blissful: "her breast was keen with passion for him, he was so beautiful in his male stillness and mystery." (WL, 199)

They even say things to one another such as we might expect Birkin and Ursula to say:

"There is a space between us," he said . . . .
"But I'm very near," she said . . . .
"Yet distant, distant," he said. (WL, 198)

However, this degree of commitment evokes that fear of death that always lurks behind Lawrence's dealings with love. Birkin allows himself to regress, to lapse:

Now he had let go, imperceptibly he was melting into oneness with the whole. It was like pure, perfect sleep, his first great sleep of life. He had been so insistent, so guarded, all his life. But here was sleep, and peace, and perfect lapsing out. (WL, 199).

Gerald also allows himself to lapse, and at once the night is broken by the horrified response to Diana's drowning.

Where Gerald is concerned, it is as if the active man, the man of will, is caught out the moment he "lapses."

But, of course, Lawrence wishes to present Gerald (based on Middleton Murry) as a fore-doomedly tragic figure: "It was as if he belonged naturally to dread and catastrophe, as if he were himself again" (WL, 200). The dreadful experience is done superbly, but one is puzzled, all the same, by Lawrence's tragic intentions:

Oh, and the beauty of the subjection of his loins, white and dimly luminous as he climbed over the side of the boat, made her want to die, to die. The beauty of his

dim and luminous loins, as he climbed into the boat, his back rounded and soft—ah, this was too much for her, too final a vision. She knew it, and it was fatal. The terrible hopelessness of fate, and of beauty, such beauty!
     He was not like a man to her, he was an incarnation, a great phase of life. (WL, 203)

Perhaps here Lawrence picks up a note from Hardy. Gerald declares, "There's one thing about our family, you know . . . . Once anything goes wrong, it can never be put right again—not with us" (WL, 206). It seems to me more likely that in Gerald Lawrence embodies the possibility that *he* himself is a fatal, death-belonging character, and that in trying to characterize the Middleton-Murry–Katherine Mansfield relationship as such, he was trying to escape his doom by exporting it into them, his feelings of doom being involved with his incipient tuberculosis.
     In the symbolism of the chapter, Gerald is a kind of Orpheus who goes down into the realm of death to fetch up Diana as the moon shines above, "with almost impertinent brightness." The mother, that is, is presiding and watching, while, as the new generation became involved in their emerging sexuality, death threatens them. In a strange way, the drowned Diana symbolizes the dead mother—Lawrence's mother, with whom her name links her, by way of the moon. She is the mother discussed in the darker areas of the soul (represented by the marsh) that threatens to kill at the heart of sexuality. If we realized this, we may understand better the odd exchange between Birkin and Ursula about the death:

"Do you mind very much?" she asked him.
"I don't mind about the dead," he said, "once they are dead. The worst of it is, they cling on to the living, and won't let go." (WL, 207)

This surely points to the drowned Diana being a symbol of the dead Mrs. Lawrence, who so threatens Lawrence's sexual life. As we shall see, this fear intensifies in the chapter "Moony." Everything, in Birkin's dealings with others and the world, is conditioned not by Birkin's mother's death, but *Lawrence's* mother's ghost. Therefore, one more death doesn't matter:

"Yes," she said. "The *fact* of death doesn't really seem to matter much, does it?"
"No," he said. "What does it matter if Diana Crich is alive or dead?"
"Doesn't it?" she said, shocked.
"No, why should it? Better she were dead—she'll be much more real. She'll be positive in death. In life she was a fretting, negated thing." (WL, 208)

Ursula proclaims him horrible, and surely he is for this, at such a moment, is a despicably callous remark. How can one say of anyone, "No! I'd rather Diana Crich was dead. Her living was all wrong" (WL, 208). Here, I believe, we catch a glimpse of that strange psychopathological element in Lawrence, to which his admirers are so strangely indifferent. We found it in *The Fox*, and in *The Smile*, and will see it again—a certain gladness about the death of people he rejected or detested.

Lawrence can be understood better here if we see that he is talking about death in the symbolism of his mythology: it is that death that is a *beginning* for which he yearns:

> "Yet you don't want to die," she challenged him.
> He was silent for a time. Then he said, in a voice that was frightening to her in its change:
> "I should like to be through with it—I should like to be through with the death process." (WL, 208)

Whatever can this mean? It now appears not only that Gerald belongs to death and must visit death in this chapter, but that Birkin, who finds himself in love with Ursula, is also seeking to pass through death. I believe there are in this a number of symbolic strands—an unconscious yearning for ultimate regression and rebirth: the urge to go the world of death where the mother is, to find further psychic rebirth; and the impulse to lapse out in a woman's lap, to find renewed being.

> "There is life which belongs to death, and there is life which isn't death. One is tired of the life that leads to death—our kind of life. But whether it is finished, God knows. I want love that is like sleep, like being born again, vulnerable as a baby that just comes into the world." (WL, 208)

Besides seeing it as an exploration of the meaning of love and marriage, we can also see *Women in Love* as an attempt to complete the process of mourning. "Our kind of life" does not mean (as Leavis would take it) "industrial society" but the state of having a mourning consciousness, an inner life blighted by grief. Lawrence, like Birkin, yearns for this to be "finished," and he wants love as part of the process of being reborn out of his devastated world, from which all meaning has been driven by the mother's death. We hear nothing of Birkin's mother's death, except at the end. When she appears, she is clearly *Lawrence's* mother: "He remembered also the beautiful face of one whom he had loved, and who had died still having the faith to yield to the mystery" (WL, 540). Ursula asks,

> "Why should love be like sleep?" she asked sadly. ". . . so that it like death—I *do* want to die from this life—and yet it is more than life itself. One is delivered over like a naked infant from the womb, all the old defences, and the old body gone, and new air around one, that has never been breathed before." (WL, 208)

This is clearly a fantasy of death as (schizoid) rebirth, since it can only make sense in some such light, as Ursula reflects:

> She knew, as well as he knew, that words themselves do not convey meaning, that they are but a gesture we make, a dumb show like any other. (WL, 209)

There is another meaning beyond those words of Birkin's, ar
is revealed only by the schizoid diagnosis. But, she persists, "
say you wanted something that was *not* love—something b
(WL, 209).

Birkin reflects that "to know . . . was to break a way throug_ ..._ wans or
the prison as the infant in labour strives through the walls of the womb . . . in
the struggle to get out."

The moment develops into a good piece of drama in the novel, where they
declare their love, and kiss tenderly. The moment is all the more moving
because it is "inappropriate," yet it is, of course, because of the death,
intensely *appropriate*, too. The symbolism here becomes very revealing
because it makes it clear the "something" beyond love that Birkin seeks is to
be born into a new state of being.

When Ursula kisses Birkin back, he becomes a "perfect hard flame of
passionate desire for her?"

> Yet in the small core of the flame was an unyielding anguish of another thing.
> (WL, 210)

What can this possibly mean? Lawrence gives us no clue. Does he mean
Birkin's yearning for Gerald? Or for the dead mother?

> But all this was lost; he only wanted her, with an extreme desire that seemed
> inevitable as death, beyond question. (WL, 210)

Birkin lapses into passion, but

> Far away, far away, there seemed to be a small lament in the darkness. (WL, 210)

What lament? Birkin reflects,

> "I was becoming quite dead-alive, nothing but a word-bag" he said in triumph,
> scorning his other self. Yet somewhere far off and small the other hovered. (WL,
> 210)

Lawrence gives us in Birkin an account of his own struggle, between two
selves—the nihilistic, despairing, sneering self, and the other that dares to
love, and to burn off into a new life, exorcising the mother. Yet from time to
time she laments, and so the move towards love is deeply bound up with
death—only it is Lawrence's mother's death, not Birkin's mother's.

The chapter ends with an exchange between Birkin and Gerald. Birkin urges
Gerald not to pursue the bodies: "But you, you spoil your own chance of
life—you waste your best self" (WL, 211). What, in the context, does this
mean? "You give yourself into horrors, and put a mill-stone of beastly
memories round your neck" (WL, 211). It makes no sense at all for Birkin to
tell Gerald not to "waste himself" seeking the body of his drowned sister. It

only makes sense if it is one dramatized self of Lawrence telling another not to seek the dead Diana-mother-figure in her state of death. Again we have a clue to the strange yearning in Birkin, which is for a relationship with this dissociated pure male self. Gerald says, "'You mean a lot to me, Rupert, more than you know,'" and later, "'We're all right, you know, you and me.'" (WL, 211–212)

The strange and haunting chapter, Water-Party, is a drama, virtually, between Lawrence's endo-psychic components as he contemplates the question "What is love?" What love brings is the confrontation with ultimate meaning, and so it is like death. It offers possibilities of a new beginning, so it is like ultimate regression and rebirth. To Gerald, it means thoughtful analysis and duty; to Gudrun a part to act; to Ursula longing (but she is "capable of nothing"); to Birkin a division between the self that wants to give itself to a new state of being, and the self that is nihilistic in grief, hearing a lament for the dead mother.

As he reaches the culmination of his portrayal of the destructive relationship between Gerald and Gudrun, Lawrence says,

> But between two particular people, any two people on earth, the range of pure sensational experience is limited. The climax of sensual reaction, once reached in any direction, is reached finally, there is no going on. There is only repetition possible, or the going apart of the two protagonists, or the subjugating of the one will to the other, or death. (WL, 508)

This would only be true where there is a voracious appetite that remains unsatisfied as it seems to have done in Lawrence. Lovers who find fulfillment are not obsessed like this with the "range" of "pure sensational experience" like Paul and Clara, or Gerald or Gudrun. Gerald and Gudrun share many tender and intimate moments. They meet in many ways; and though they seem at times to be unable to love, it is difficult to see where exactly the failure lies. But a strange ambivalence is also to be found in the progress of the relationship between Birkin and Ursula.

\*       \*       \*

At best, there are passages that show the *novelist* at work, until he spoils it. One of the most marvelous passages in Lawrence occurs in the chapter "Excurse" (23) in *Women in Love*, and it is marvelous because Ursula here is given to us as a real woman. For once Lawrence happily embraces a woman's needs, her reality, and her "separate, separate" existence. The dialogue breaks, in its realization, away from the Lawrentian mouthings. The complex sexual and fertility symbolism of the girl's unconscious plucking at berries is a lovely touch, and a means by which Lawrence keeps the scene authentic:

And in the stress of her violent emotion, she got down from the car and went to the hedgerow, picking unconsciously some flesh-pink spindleberries, some of which were burst, showing their orange seed.

"Ah, you are a fool," he cried, bitterly, with some contempt.

"Yes, I am. I *am* a fool. And thank God for it. I'm too big a fool to swallow your cleverness" (WL, 345)

Note how "flesh-pink" makes the caress by poetic symbolism erotic, yet inexplicit, while conveying beauty, creativity, awe, and even fear (cf. "burst"). Lawrence realizes the woman's *nous* that rumbles his attempts to cloak his special pleading with weighted arguments:

"Go to your spiritual brides—but don't come to me as well, because I'm not having any, thank you. You're not satisfied, are you? Your spiritual brides can't give you what you want, they aren't common and fleshy enough for you, are they? . . . You will marry me for daily use . . . I know your dirty little game." (WL, 345)

It is wonderful to hear the rhythms of a real woman's anger and pride, with their roots in real bodily jealousy, from a Lawrence who feared that womanly reality so!

He stood in silence. A wonderful tenderness burned in him, at the sight of her quivering, so sensitive fingers: and at the same time he was full of rage and callousness. (WL, 346)

The experience is done with great accuracy—the reality of this woman obliging Birkin to respect her and thus to love her more deeply because she has exerted her right to challenge him:

"This is a degrading exhibition," he said coolly.

"Yes, degrading indeed," she said. "But more degrading to you . . . ."

"*You*", she cried. "You! You truth-lover! You purity-monger! It *stinks*, your truth and your purity . . . . You, and love! You may well say you don't want love. No, you want *yourself*, and dirt and death—that's what you want. You are so *perverse*, so death-eating. And then—"

There's a bicycle coming," he said, writhing under her loud denunciation.

She glanced down the road.

"I don't care," she said.

Nevertheless, she was silent. The cyclist, having heard the voices raised in altercation, glanced curiously at the man, and the woman, and at the standing motorcar as he passed.

"—Afternoon," he said, cheerfully. (WL, 347)

This is a wonderful comic touch that has the effect of deflating the lover's portentousness, and exposing what they share with common humanity. Ursula walks away from Birkin after flinging down the rings: "He felt tired and weak. Yet he also was relieved . . . . No doubt Ursula was right" (WL, 348). This

marks a great spiritual moment in Lawrence. Here is no fear of female
domination that must be "broken," but a recognition of the woman's right
to express truths with her intelligence, and that one should be prepared to
accept her estimation of experiences in life. Here we follow the development
of a relationship that is deeply sexual, but the growth of love is in the whole
complex of being, not least the intelligence.

> He knew that his spirituality was a concomitant of a process of depravity, a sort of
> pleasure in self-destruction . . . . But . . . was not Ursula's way of emotional intimacy,
> emotional and physical, was it not just as dangerous, as Hermione's abstract spiritual
> intimacy? Fusion, fusion, this horrible fusion of two beings. (WL, 348)

But here, instead of special pleading in the sloganizing, we have repulsion and
fear *placed* as being in Birkins's mind, as Ursula leaves him stunned by the
energy of that rage that goes with love. How we possess the scene as the
delineation of what really happens between a woman and a man! The lie is
given to Birkin's recoil from "horrible merging" by his immediately bending
down to pick up the ring though he does it from a sense that it is a pity they
should lie there, rather than as an acceptance of her love. Yet,

> He could not bear to see the rings lying in the pale mud of the road. He picked them
> up, and wiped them unconsciously on his hands. They were the little tokens of the
> reality of beauty, the reality of happiness in warm creation. But he had made his
> hands all dirty and gritty. (WL, 348)

The phrase "happiness in warm creation" is significant. The rings make
Birkin's hands dirty—this symbolizes the down-to-earth quality of the real
marriage, and the "messiness" of the bodily reality that Birkin fears about
love. In picking the rings up he comes to take up the reality of beauty and of
bonds so much more powerfully real than his fear. He is overcome:

> There was a darkness over his mind . . . there was a point of anxiety in his heart now.
> He wanted her to come back. . . . He breathed lightly and regularly like an infant,
> that breathes innocently, beyond the touch of responsibility. (WL, 349)

His anxiety is that she will not come back, he accepts now that he cannot live
without her. He recaptures in this moment the innocence of the infant whose
joy is that of being beyond the acceptance of the "responsibility" of
disillusion. He wants now to take up Ursula as an adult woman. The pain is
the pain of accepting reality. The moment is grave and tender:

> She was coming back. He saw her drifting desultorily under the high hedge,
> advancing towards him slowly. He did not move, he did not look again. He was as
> if asleep, slumbering and utterly relaxed.
>     She came up before him, hanging her head.

"See what a flower I found you," she said, wistfully a piece of purple bell-heather under his face...
Everything had become simple again.... It was peace. (WL, 349)

Yes, we cry! It is like that! The mutual recognition is deeply moving. "He stood up and looked into her face. It was new and oh, so delicate in its luminous wonder and fear." The most moving thing about this passage of very great writing is that Lawrence is able to see that the woman is afraid, too, and in both the anxieties and disturbances aroused by love are tenderly met, side by side, in simplicity of mutual regard.

The chapter achieves a profound seriousness over the way the lovers accept their fate: "She went very still, as if under a fate which had taken her." (WL, 350). Lawrence conveys beautifully the strange sense one has, that perhaps the best moments of love are a dream.

Was it all real? But his eyes were beautiful and soft and commune from stress or excitement, beautiful and smiling lightly to her, smiling with her. (WL, 350)

By simple gestures the acceptance of one by the other is conveyed:

"Did you find the rings?"
"Yes."
"Where are they?"
"In my pocket."
She put her hand into his pocket and took them out. (WL, 350)

Then they leave behind them "this memorable battlefield."

But now, by degrees, Lawrence spoils it. It is illuminating to examine how he does this. From time to time Ursula takes on a really independent, living presence: "Your spiritual brides can't give you what you want, they aren't common and fleshy enough for you, are they?" (WL, 345). We feel perhaps that at last Birkin's monstrous narcissism, his nihilism, what she calls his Sunday-school impulse to preach, are broken through. We are seeing Birkin's "death-eating" placed.

However, the rest of the chapter takes a strange tack. Birkin has been thoroughly challenged in his yearnings for "spirituality" by Hermione (with whom, according to Ursula, he has all the same a "foul" sex life). At last the pretensions seems dismantled, but now Lawrence begins to reestablish them and to falsify. Just as we have breathed a freer air, to be given a real independent woman, Lawrence puts her under control again:

She saw a strange creature from another world in him. It was as if she were enchanted, and everything were metamorphosed. She recalled again the old magic of the Book of Genesis, where the Sons of God saw the daughters of men, that they were fair. And he was one of these, one of these strange creatures from the beyond, *looking down on her*, and seeing she was fair. (WL, 352; my italics)

Lawrence, that is, turns the man into a god. He "smiles faintly," his eyes have that "faintly ironical contraction." She puts her arm around his loins, her face against his thighs, with a sense of a "heavenful of riches," and then, for page after page, we have that religious note that is to establish that Birkin is "not a man" but "something more"—a note that indicates that Lawrence has left behind the reality of real human lovers and is making a claim for his god status:

Unconsciously, with her sensitive finger-tips, she was tracing the back of his thighs, following some mysterious life-flow there. She had discovered something, something more than wonderful, more wonderful than life itself. It was the strange mystery of his life-motion, there at the back of the thighs, down the flanks. It was the strange reality of his being, there in the straight downflow of his thighs. *It was here that she discovered him one of the Sons of God such as were in the beginning of the world, not a man, something other, something more.* (WL, 353; my italics)

Without in the least doubting the mystery of being, we must place this kind of fantasy in Lawrence as something close to religious fanaticism:

It was the daughters of men coming back to the Sons of God, the strange *inhuman* Sons of God who are in the beginning. (WL, 353; my italics)

He has found "one of the first most luminous daughters of men," but she clearly does not have his status. Lawrence persists with his tedious overinsistence on "electricity":

a living fire ran through her . . . a dark flood of electric passion . . . a rich new circuit, a new current of passional electric energy . . . released from the darkest poles of the body . . . a dark fire of electricity that rushed from him to her. (WL, 353)

Not only is this obsessiveness boring; it exerts an oppressive purpose of triumph over woman:

She seemed to faint beneath . . . . It was a perfect passing away . . . sweeping away everything and leaving her an essential new being, she was free in complete ease, her complete self. (WL, 354)

He stands before her "glimmering,"

There were strange fantasies of his body, more mysterious and potent than any she had imagined or known . . . . And now, behold, from the smitten rock of the man's body, from the strange marvellous flanks and thighs, deeper, further in mystery than the phallic source, came the floods of ineffable darkness and ineffable riches. (WL, 354)

The beautiful moment of mutual giving seems to have evoked in Lawrence deep fears of what might follows; and so he must cast a spell in which the man in celebrated as superhuman, magical, ineffable, and invulnerable, even against woman:

> The sense of the awfulness of riches that could never be impaired flooded her mind like a swoon, a death in most marvellous possession, mystic-sure. (WL, 356)

It is at this moment that they write their resignations: cut themselves away from the world, into that fatal absorption in their own special world that is such a false step in Lawrence, leading lovers into their self-enclosed treadmills of obsession:

> She knew there was no leaving him, the darkness held them both and contained them, it was not to be surpassed. Besides, she had a full mystic knowledge of his suave loins of darkness, dark-clad and suave, and in this knowledge there was some of the inevitability and the beauty of fate, fate which one asks for, which one accepts in full. He sat still like an Egyptian Pharaoh, driving the car. He felt as if he were seated in immemorial potency, like the great carven statues of real Egypt, as real and fulfilled with subtle strength as these are, with a vague inscrutable smile on their lips. He knew what it was to have the strange and magical current of force in his back and loins, and down his legs, so perfect that it stayed him immobile, and left his face subtly mindlessly smiling. He knew what it was to be awake and potent in that other basic mind, the deepest physical control, magical, mystical, a force in darkness, like electricity. (WL, 358)

The most interesting word here is "control." It is by becoming nonhuman, a god, separated off in "immemorial potency" that Birkin, as an auto-biographical protagonist, hopes to escape the dangers of woman and love. Birkin virtually becomes a sculpture:

> His arms and his breast and his head were rounded and living like those of the Greek, he had not the unawakened straight arms of the Egyptian, nor the sealed, slumbering head. A lambent intelligence played secondarily above his pure Egyptian concentration in darkness. (WL, 359)

Lawrence writes of how "They would give each other this star-equilibrium which alone is freedom," but it is the god-like man who is written up into immemorial potency, while the woman is reduced to an admiring sycophant. Again, their coition is like that of a human woman with a god:

> Quenched, *inhuman*, his fingers upon her unrevealed nudity were the fingers of silence upon silence, the body of mysterious night upon the body of mysterious night, the night masculine and feminine, never to be seen with the eye, or known with the mind, only known as a palpable revelation of living otherness. (WL, 361)

She "received the maximum of unspeakable communication in touch, dark, subtle, positively silent, a magnificent gift." The jargon becomes so turgid that one wonders exactly what is going on, but the tone of the whole is evident. She is being given a great gift from the gods, and she, in "perfect acceptance and yielding" is the ideal woman of human submission to something so much larger than human. The darkness and unspeakableness is emphasized to cast a spell against the dangers, and yet, by contrast with the scene where Ursula speaks for herself, she seems, by the end of the chapter, extinguished, drowned in this pharoah's narcissism.

If one reflects on experience, the second half of this chapter just does not ring true. Lawrence tries to peg it to reality, as they pour the tea, and he buys some chocolate. From time to time we have "real" conversation:

"Everything is ours," she said to him.
"Everything," he answered.
She gave a queer little craving sound of triumph.
"I'm so glad!" she cried, with unspeakable relief. (WL, 355)

Superb! But then, as so often, the authenticity is drowned under a deluge of propaganda. For instance, there is a continual stream of denunciation of ordinary life—especially "ordinary couples":

One cannot contemplate the ordinary life. (WL, 422).

there's no meaning in it.... If I thought my life was to be like it, I'd run ... with the ordinary man, ... marriage is just impossible. (WL, 422)

The old way of love seemed a dreadful bondage ... the horrible privacy of domestic and connubial satisfaction was repulsive ... meaningless entities of married couples. (WL, 223)

Lawrence seems in this to be impelled again by unconscious factors. The ghost of the dead mother haunts him and tells him, as she tells Somers in *Kangaroo*, that his own life must be meaningless if he cannot revive in her some sense of a meaningful existence, but he knows well enough that her married life was meaningless, and a matter of mechanical performance ("Tic tac"), and so deathly, in any existential sense. Thus, any movement of his lovers toward a normal married relationship threatens death, and *Women in Love* is full of conversations about love and death, emerging from their sense of horror at such commitment.

The novel, indeed, becomes largely a dialogue on these questions, and as G. D. Klingopulos said reviewing F. R. Leavis's book on the novelist in *Universities Quarterly*, (February, 1956, Vol 10, No 2, 189) it tends to become a vehicle for ideas, rather than a novel in which the ideas are clearly acted out. We cannot find out adequately the difference between the relationship between Birkin and Ursula and that between the relationship between Birkin and Ursula and that between Gudrun and Gerald. For instance, "One can deduce it but it is not presented."

The enormous exaggeration Lawrence makes of his character's states of mind becomes clear if we look at the beginning of chapter 15, "Sunday Evening." For example, "Her passion seemed to bleed to death": ⌐

> the life-blood seemed to ebb away from Ursula, and within the emptiness a heavy despair gathered. Her passion seemed to bleed too death, and there was nothing. She sat suspended in a state of complete nullity, harder to bear than death. . . . "I shall die. I am at the end of my line of life." She sat crushed and obliterated in a darkness ⌐ that was the border of death. (WL, 214)

Ursula has to take a leap like Sappho.

> The knowledge of the imminence of death was like a drug . . . she knew that she was near to death . . . fulfilled in a kind of bitter ripeness, there remained only to fall from the tree into death. (WL, 214)

The last thing she experienced with Birkin was an exchange of passionate and tender kisses. Yet here she is, thinking, "Death is a great consummation, a consummating experience. It is a development from life" (WL, 214). Later, "She could feel, within the darkness, the terrible assertion of her body, the unutterable anguish of dissolution" (WL, 215). Lawrence goes on: "better die than live mechanically a life that is a repetition of repetitions." Now it seems that death is invoked at this moment because it presses upon her the ultimate existential realities. In the face of death, one could "wash off all the lies and ignominy and dirt."

The mood Ursula is in belongs to being, as against the mechanical routine ⌐ of work.

> Tomorrow was Monday. Monday, the beginning of another school-week! Another shameful, barren school-weak, mere routine and mechanical activity. Was not the adventure of death infinitely preferable? . . . A life of barren routine, without inner meaning, without any real significance. How sordid life was . . . . How much cleaner and more dignified to be dead. (WL, 216)

Her position seems to be a *Culture and Environment* one:

> No flowers grow upon busy machinery, there is no sky to a routine, there is no space to a rotary motion. And all life was a rotary motion. And all life was a rotary motion, mechanized, cut off from reality. (WL, 216)

No doubt we all feel like this at times, but the yearning is not for a new dimension of being. It is a yearning for a death that will spite *humanity*. Leavis did not look closely enough at Lawrence in this (strange) vein:

> What a gladness to think that whatever humanity did, it could not seize hold of the kingdom of death, to nullify that. The sea they turned into a murderous alley and a soiled road of commerce. . . . Everything was gone, walled in, with spikes on the

top of the walls, and one must ignominously creep between the spiky walls through a labyrinth of life.

But the great, dark illimitable kingdom of death, there humanity was put to scorn. (WL, 217)

This compensates for the "sordidness" of our humanity. "In death we shall not be known, and we shall not know." We must look forward to this.

I do not question that people, when they fall in love, have dark and desperate struggles with their own souls, and feel a sombre quality about the gravity of their commitment, but I believe few people experience the profound dread and nihilism Lawrence attributes to Ursula, or feel that love brings such a threat of death.

Without denying the forces behind our sexuality ("He would be able to destroy her utterly in the strength of his discharge," WL, 71) it surely cannot be true that human beings, so much of the time, struggle so bitterly to destroy others or prevent them from destroying themselves? Most people do not find sex so destructive or dangerous, nor is there so much fiendishness in daily life: "The strong, indomitable thighs of the blond man clenching the palpitating body," etc, etc.

Toward humanity at large meanwhile there is a deeper bitterness that cannot be accounted for by the Great War, or by the troubles Lawrence and Frieda had in the early years of their relationship, or by Lawrence's guilt about leaving England to marry a German aristocrat. It is more than a revulsion from the English Midlands, as Gudrun expresses it when she returns ("she regretted she had ever come back" [WL, 14]). It is such a deep loathing of ordinary men and women, of humanity, that it expresses a wish from time to time that man should be exterminated leaving a world purified of man, and so clean and primal again.

\*          \*          \*

In this examination of *Woman in Love* I am trying to indicate the powerful negative elements in it, the sense of doom and death, leading to misanthropy. I am also trying to reject the oversimplification Leavis has imposed on the novel, making it into his kind of moral fable. As in so many works of Lawrence, there is the mark of the artist realizing life in his novel, often confused with the imprint of the propagandist—propagandist for his (Grossian) sexual theories and his secret fanatical belief in his role as a god. In the background is the menacing ghost of the mother, threatening not only love but the very meaning of life.

These elements may be traced vividly in the remarkable chapter "Moony" (WL, chap. 15, 276ff). Ursula, feeling bereft of Birkin who has gone abroad,, yearns for "pure love." She goes out in a despairing mood and makes toward Willey Water. As we have seen, water has a powerful symbolism in *Women in Love*. It is the great natural force in us, and the urges that rise within us.

Beneath it lies the death that overtook Diana Crich. Ursula suddenly sees the moon:

> it seemed so mysterious, with its white and deathly smile. And there was no avoiding it. Night and day, one could not escape the sinister face, triumphant and radiant like the moon, with a high smile. (WL, 276)

Significantly, Lawrence speaks of "face . . . like this moon," and anyone who has savored the powerful symbolism of the moon's face in the poetry of Sylvia Plath ("the moon is my mother") will recognize here the ghost of the mother's face—Lawrence's mother, since it cannot be Ursula's or Birkin's. This face is sinister, triumphant, and disdainful for it is she who stands between Ursula (who "is" Lawrence) and Birkin (who is also his alter-ego).

"She suffered from being exposed to it." Often characters in Lawrence suffer from the moon—Paul as he is about to kiss Miriam; Ursula making love to Skrebensky under the moon. When she sees the moon reflected in the water, "for some reason she disliked it. *It did not give her anything* . . . she wanted another night, not this moon-brilliant hardness. She could feel her soul crying out in her, lamenting desolatedly" (WL, 277, my italics). Ursula sees in the moon no help or consolation, only a reflection (as in *Lawrence's mother's face*) of her own misery, in defeat in seeking love and reflection.

Birkin is there; he must have come back. He does not know she is there, and is talking to himself. He throws dead husks in the water and says aloud: "Cybele—curse her! The second *Syria Dei*! Does one begrudge it her! What else is there—?" (WL, 278). Cybele was known to the Romans as the Great Mother or the Mother of the Gods. Her orgiastic worship was directed by eunuch priests known as Corybantes, and in Greece she was identified with Rhea, the mother of the Olympian gods. In one gnomic outburst by Birkin, Lawrence identifies the moon here as a symbol of the Mother, of the Mother of Gods, and as the focus of orgiastic sexuality—that orgiastic sexuality that for Lawrence was the focus of his attempts to exorcise the ghost of the mother.

Birkin throws stones into the reflection of the moon, and what Ursula sees is a menacing and mysterious image: "It seems to shoot out arms of fire like a cuttle-fish, like a luminous polyp, palpitating strongly before her". (WL, 278). A moment later, "the moon had exploded on the water, and was flying asunder in flakes of white and dangerous fire." There follows an intense passage in which this menacing image is developed. I will only select fragments, and these are enough to show that a certain kind of threatening white fire "out there" is felt by Lawrence to be especially menacing to the possibilities of love (lights such as Mellors in the Chatterley novels feels to be threatening him and his love):

> like white birds, the fires all broken rose across the pond . . . battling with the flock of dark waves that were forcing their way in . . . at the centre, the heart of all, was

still a vivid, incandescent quivering of *a white moon not quite destroyed*, a white body of fire writhing and striving and not even now broken open, not yet violated. It seemed to be drawing itself together with strange, violent pangs, in blind effort (WL, 278–79; my italics)

The moon is later "regathering itself insidiously," "the heart of the rose . . . in an effort to return." Everything Birkin does to get rid of the image of the menacing Cybele mother fails: "And he was not satisfied. Like a madness, he must go on." Every time the moon draws itself together, he attempts to shatter and dispel it. Ursula swoons, no doubt feeling the mad desperation of this attempt to exorcise a threatening ghost and perceiving in it the *hostility to dangerous woman*. She asks, speaking at last:

"Why should you hate the moon? It hasn't done you any harm, has it?"
"Was it hate?" he said. (WL, 280)

The exchange illuminates much in Lawrence (for instance, the "I am the Master").

He wants a different light from Ursula: "There is a golden light in you, which I wish you would give me." She says she thinks he only wants "physical things"; she wants him to "serve my spirit." He wants "that golden light which is you" (we may remember Gross's reference to Frieda's "sunniness"). But Birkin wants more, he needs "to press for the thing he wanted from her, the surrender of her spirit." So, they begin to wrangle, and "the paradisal disappeared from him." "I wouldn't give a straw for your female ego—it's a rag doll." (EL, 282) The exchange has in part the refreshing realism of the novelist ("*you—you* are the Sunday school teacher," she exclaims), but Lawrence has his thumb firmly in the scales—Birkin is *right*, whatever she says.He kisses her, but at once this kindles "the old destructive fires," and she puts on her hat and goes home.

Birkin doesn't want just "a further sensual experience." He dwells on an African fetish he has seen at Hallidays, the main charactheristic of which its "long protuberant buttocks, so weighty and unexpected below her slim long loins," suggesting "purely sensual understanding, knowlege in the mystery of dissolution," This is expressed in a strange way:

There is a long way we can travel, after the deathbreak: after that point when the soul in intense suffering breaks, breaks away from its organic hold like a leaf that falls. (WL, 286)

Birkin yearns for Gerald, "one of these strange wonderful demons from the north, fulfilled in the destructive frost mystery," an omen of "universal dissolution" frightend by these symbols of dissolution. Birkin is frightened, and contemplates a retreat into "pure, single being," "a lovely state of free pround singleness,'' but then decides to go to Ursula to ask her to marry him.

The exchange with Brangwen is superbly done, as is Ursula's startled response. At this level, the words used cannot be brought to engage with the inner turmoil and fight to the death. Comically, Ursula turns on both men accusing them of bullying her. Her father calls her "an idiot" and "a self-opinionated fool," and they are all, in great comedy, at sixes and sevens. She goes to Gudrun for female sympathy, and they discuss Birkin:

> "He couldn't bear it if you called your soul your own . . . ."
> "Yes," said Ursula, "You must have *his* soul." (WL, 297)

The proposal is a fiasco. Ursula is left wondering what she wants.

> She knew what kind of love, what kind of surrender he wanted . . . . She wanted unspeakable intimacies . . . . He did not believe in final self-abandonment. He said it openly . . . . She was prepared to fight him for it. (WL, 299)

The words and phrases "drink him down," "complete self-abandon," and "quaffed to the dregs" reveal the underlying schizoid fear that close relationship will be a mutual eating, and that love is extremely dangerous.

The chapter had superb moments, which we recognize as rendering the underlying turmoil beneath relationship—yes, it is like that. We might, for example, see Birkin's fears as being like those of Levin in *Anna Karenina*, but on the other side of the coin, there is distortion: the dread of the destructive mother is intensely powerful both in Birkin and Ursula. The remedy for this is adhered to by Lawrence the propagandist. Eventually Ursula's will must be broken, and to make it possible to accept the dangers of love, she must surrender her will totally to the god-man, that is Lawrence's definition of "equilibrium." This God-man has a powerful inclination toward fetishistic perversion, the demon of homosexuality, and "ultimate dissilution" in death—more, certainly, that would seem to make it possible for him to achieve "balance" like the stars.

\* \* \*

Lawrence's philosophy of existence is persistently stated in *Women in Love*, both in the action and the embodiment in character's thoughts and words of the Lawrentian message. Birkin is thinking:

> "God cannot do with man." It was a saying of some great French religious teacher. But surely this is false. God can do without man. God could do without the ichthyosauri and the mastodon. These monsters failed creatively to develop, so God, the creative mystery, dispensed with them. In the same way the mystery could dispense with man, should he too fail creatively to change and develop. The eternal creative mystery could dispose of man, and replace him with a fine created being. Just as the horse has taken the place of the mastodon. (WL, 538)

Birkin is reflecting on the dead body of Gerald. He ponders that Gerald might have found a way out of the ice, taking "the great Imperial road leading south to Italy." But "what then? Was it any good going south, to Italy? Down the old, old Imperial road?" It we take into account the way in which the geography here relates to Lawrence's own wanderings, we can interpret it as meaning, "How could Gerald have escaped his doom? Would it have saved him, to go down to the warmer and more relaxed countries of the Mediterranean, or would he simply have found himself following the old Imperial road, Napoleonic or Roman, for, after all, there have been men of will in the southern lands too." And then we can add the thought, "Would *power* have solved his life-problem?"

So Gerald is almost a type, a species:

> Whatever the mystery which has brought forth man and the universe, it is a non-human mystery, it has its own ends, man is not the criterion. Best leave it all to the vast, creative, non-human mystery. Best strive with oneself only, not with the universe. (WL, 538)

Lawrence seems to be saying, at the end of *Women in Love*, that one can "strive with oneself," but "not with the universe." One should not try, as Gerald did, to exert one's will as "matter," and one's "condition" (in Sartre's sense). But what does this mean? Birkin's reflections could lead to a situation in which we might console ourselves with the thought that even if we did destroy ourselves, that wouldn't be the end of it:

> If humanity ran into a cul-de-sac, and expended itself, the timeless creative mystery would bring forth some other being, finer, more wonderful, some new, more lovely race, to carry on the embodiment of creation. The game was never up. The mystery of creation was fathomless, infallible, inexhaustible, for ever. Races came and went, species passed away, but ever new species arose, more lovely, or equally lovely, always surpassing wonder. The foundation-head was incorruptible and unsearchable. It had no limits. It could bring forth miracles, create utterly new races and species in its own hour, new forms of consciousness, new forms of body, new units of being. To be man was as nothing compared to the possibilities of the creative mystery. To have one's pulse beating direct from the mystery, this was perfection, unutterable satisfaction. Human or inhuman mattered nothing. The perfect pulse throbbed with indescribable being, miraculous newborn species. (WL, 538)

While to defer to the great creative mystery seems a useful check to hubris, this rejection of human uniqueness, consciousness, and the responsibility of knowing seems the ultimate irresponsibility. To be fully human surely we need to accept the awful fact that (as Polanyi has argued) we are the only *knowers*. Without human consciousness, the universe would be that much more meaningless. It may be we should not (like Gerald) exert our conscious will on life. But is Birkin's position really an acceptance of life? So often he becomes a vehicle for wishing humanity and life destroyed as if he (as Lawrence's alter-ego) could still survive *as a god*.

How does Gerald represent the failure of humanity in any biological sense? Surely it is Birkin who reports himself as a manifestation of humanity's failure? We have noted the background to the writing of this novel—1914–18—which may explain this feeling but it is also a manifestation of Lawrence's sickness, his recognition of his own destructive and incapacitated side so Gerald and Birkin both represent aspects of Lawrence, split-off dynamics of himself, as do Gudrun and Ursula. From the sense of his own inward badness, Birkin–Lawrence develops a universal misanthropy in chapter 11, "An Island." If *Women in Love* is a dramatization of inner conflict, we have to say that Lawrence fills his characters with his own dreads and failures and projects over their world his own sense of dread and doom.

This hatred of humanity reverberates throughout *Women in Love*. Birkin watches the countryside from a train and is

> filled with a sort of hopelessness. He always felt this, on approaching London. *His dislike of mankind, of the mass of mankind, amounted almost to an illness.* (WL, 66; my italics)

Lawrence even recognizes in his autobiographical hero the psycho-pathological nature of his own hate. He is also aware that others do not share it:

> "People give me a bad feeling—very bad."
> "Don't you feel like one of the damned?" asked Birkin ... as they watched the hideous great street.
> "No," laughed Gerald.
> "It is real death," said Birkin. (WL, 67)

A genuine philosophical point emerges out of Lawrence's program: one cannot find one's identity in the "social idea." Insofar as he develops an existential view out of this, he celebrates being, the unique individual experience in an existentialist way. When Birkin speaks of the "centre and core" of his life being "the love between you and a woman," Gerald is made to say that his life "doesn't centre at all": "it is artificially held *together* by the social mechanism" (WL, 64). We may note that this comes just before the revealing passage about woman taking the place of God. But are these really the alternatives—*either* belonging (through the "social idea") to dead letter humanity, *or* finding meaning through love of a woman since God is dead, and putting the burden of significance on her?

> Birkin, watching like a hermit crab from its hole, had seen the brilliant frustration and helplessness of Ursula. She was rich, full of dangerous power. She was like a strange unconscious bird of powerful womanhood. He was unconsciously drawn to her. *She was his future.* (WL, 102; my italics)

We can see the veracity of Gerald's remark, "Then we're hard to put to it".

(Should this not be "Then we're hard put to it"?) Birkin, in his hard (schizoid) shell of regression, is hoping that Ursula will bring him to life.

Lawrence's objection to the "social idea" is thus a rejection of all other human beings, humanity, because he finds there in them the intractable humanness he grapples with in himself. Superior to this mass humanity is the intensely idealized super-self of "immemorial potency," the depersonalized phallic god self.

Again, we have Birkin as mouthpiece (and if anyone protests that Birkin is a character, remember what a considerable emphasis Leavis put on such passages):

> "We are all different and unequal in spirit—it is only the *social* differences that are based on accidental material conditions. We are all abstractly and mathematically equal, if you like. Every man has hunger and thirst, two eyes, one nose and two legs. We're all the same in point of number. But spiritually there is pure difference and neither equality nor inequality counts. It is upon those two bits of knowledge that you must found a state. Your democracy is an absolute lie—your brotherhood of man is a pure falsity, if you apply it further than the mathematical abstraction. We all drank milk first, we all eat bread and meat, we all want to ride in motor-cars—therein lies the beginning and the end of the brotherhood of man. But no equality.
>
> But I, myself, who am myself, what have I to do with equality with any other man or woman? In the spirit, I am as separate as one star is from another, as different in quality and quantity. Establish a state on *that*. One man isn't any better than another, not because they are equal, but because they are intrinsically *other*, that there is no term of comparison." (WL, 115–16)

Yes, but no one defending democracy would claim that the state must be founded on the basis of a belief that human beings are equal or comparable in all respects, or indeed any other than the limited few to which Lawrence points. Democracy concerns itself with equal *rights*, and equal opportunities, at the political level. This need not be a threat to "disquality" and indeed may make individual fulfillment possible. But, as so often, both with Leavis and Lawrence, the reject of democracy goes with a schizoid superiority that shows it cannot trust human nature and can display only contempt for it:

> "I want every man to have his share of the world's goods, so that I am rid of his importunity, so that I can tell him: 'Now you've got what you want—you've got your fair share of the world's gear. Now, you one-mouthed fool, mind yourself and don't obstruct me.'" (WL, 116)

What, one wonders, did Birkin mean by "you *one-mouthed* fool"? These Socratic dialogues are part of "the message" of the book:

> "And why is it," she asked at length, "that there is no flowering, no dignity of human life now?"
>
> "The whole idea is dead. Humanity itself is dry-rotten, really. There are myriads of human beings hanging on the bush—and they look very nice and rosy, your

healthy young men and women. But they are apples of Sodom, as a matter of fact, Dead Sea Fruit, gall-apples. It isn't true that they have any significance—their insides are full of bitter, corrupt ash.'' (WL, 140)

Ursula is made to resist this view. She protests there *are* good people, but Birkin persists: "Mankind is a dead tree, covered with fine brilliant galls of people.''

"They won't fall off the tree when they're ripe. They hang on to their old positions when the position is over-past, till they become infested with little worms and dry-rot.'' (WL, 140)

Birkin goes on to admit that he hates himself:

"I detest what I am, outwardly. I loathe myself as a human being. Humanity is a huge aggregate lie: and a huge lie is less than a small truth.'' (WL, 141)

From this he proceeds to a rejection of love:

"they say that love is the greatest thing; they persist in *saying* this, the foul liars . . . It's a lie to say love is the greatest. You *might* as well say that hate is the greatest, since the opposite of everything balances. What people want is hate—hate and nothing but hate.'' (WL, 141)

There could be some excuse for this at the time of the 1914–18 War and its mass perversions of emotion, but Birkin goes further:

"I abhor humanity, I wish it was swept away. It could go, and there would be no *absolute* loss, if every human being perished tomorrow. The reality could be untouched. Nay, it would be better. The real tree of life would then be rid of the most ghastly, heavy crop of Dead Sea Fruit, the intolerable burden of myriad, simulacra of people, an infinite weight of mortal lies.''
"So you'd like everybody in the world destroyed?'' said Ursula.
"I should indeed.''
"And the world empty of people.''
"Yes truly. You yourself, don't you find it a beautiful thought, a world empty of people, just uninterrupted grass and a hare sitting up.'' (WL, 144–42)

Creation doesn't depend upon man: "Man is a mistake, he must go.''

"If only man was swept off the face of the earth, creation would go on marvellously, with a new start, non-human. Man is one of the mistakes of creation—like the ichthyosauri. If only he were gone again, think what lovely things would come out of the liberated days;—things straight out of the fire.'' (WL, 142)

Of course, in a sense, Birkin's rantings are placed ("a certain impatient fury in him'') but he is still talking like this at the end, as we have seen. And Lawrence himself talks like it, too.

It is, again we have to say, schizoid talk: the hunger for a new thing to come "out of the fire" is a symbol of schizoid rebirth. The elder-flowers and blue-bells are "pure creation" and so is the butterfly.

"But humanity never gets beyond the caterpillar stage—it rots in the chrysalis, it never will have wings. It is anti-creation, like monkeys and baboons." (WL, 143)

It is his hatred of his own unfulfilled humanity that Birkin–Lawrence is projecting over "humanity" and is prepared, dangerously, to wish humanity extinguished, if he could be all right—a note in Lawrence we have noted elsewhere, and have found in others—the Timon note.

There is some irony directed against the view. We have a refreshing moment in which Ursula is persistently not schizoid:

"And if you don't believe in love, what *do* you believe in?" she asked, mocking. "Simply in the end of the world, and grass?"
He was beginning to feel a fool.
"I believe in the unseen hosts," he said. (WL, 144)

Birkin retreats into "a certain insufferable aloof superiority": schizoid superiority. Yet in the description of Ursula's response it is clear that Lawrence feels, and wants us to feel, that Birkin is a very special soul for whom Ursula's awe is called out: "Ursula disliked him. But also she felt she had lost something" (WL, 144). She sees a certain "Sunday-school stiffness" in him, but also

the moulding of him was so quick and attractive, it gave such a great sense of freedom: the moulding of his brow, his chin, his whole physique, something so alive, somewhere, in spite of the look of sickness. (WL, 147)

Only a man who thinks he is a god can talk like this: "The whole idea is dead. Humanity itself is dry-rotten ... abhor humanity, wish it was swept away" (WL, 141) Of course, this is Birkin speaking, and Birkin is only a character in a novel. But Birkin is so close to Lawrence that the 'upshot' of the novel must be seen in the light of his misanthropic theme.

We find this note often elsewhere—and it is not always convincing that the destructive thoughts belong to the "stream of consciousness" in the character. For instance, in *The Rainbow* we have Will's impulses:

And yet, for his own part, for his private being, Brangwen felt that the whole of the man's world was exterior and extraneous to his own real life with Anna. Sweep away the whole monstrous superstructure of the world of today, cities and industries and civilisation, leave only the bare earth with plants growing and waters moving, and he would not mind, so long as he were whole, had Anna and the child and the new, strange certainty in his soul. Then, if he were naked, he would find clothing. Somewhere, he would make a shelter and bring food to his wife. (R. 193)

It is a great relief when the novelist capable of comic irony takes over from the propagandist. There is, for instance, the conversation at the beginning between Ursula and Gudrun

> "What do you think of Rupert Birkin?" she asked, a little reluctantly, of Gudrun. She didn't want to discuss him.
> "What do I think of Rupert Birkin?" repeated Gudrun. "I think he's attractive—decidedly attractive...."
> "But he's a wonderful chap, in other respects—a marvellous personality." (WL, 22)

So the presentation of Birkin–Lawrence is not without all criticism, and Lawrence takes himself off. For instance, the Birkin letter that Halliday reads out is a pastiche of himself by Lawrence:

> "Isn't that the letter about uniting the dark and the light—and the Flux of Corruption?"
> "When the desire for destruction overcomes every other desire." (WL, 432)

> "And in the great retrogression, the reducing back of the created body, of life, we get knowledge, and beyond knowledge, the phosphorescent ecstasy of acute sensation." Oh, I do think these phrases are too absurdly wonderful. Oh, but don't you think they are—they're nearly as good as Jesus. (WL, 433)

Minette declares it is "awful cheek to write like that" and the Russian declares "He is a megalomaniac, of course, it's a form of religious mania. He thinks he's the Saviour of man."

While Lawrence satirizes his own more schizoid proclivities, to sermonize and save the world, identifying with Christ, he also has Gudrun snatching the letter away, crying "Why is Rupert such a *fool* as to write such letters to them? Why does he give himself away to such *canaille* ?" (WL, 435). It is not that Lawrence is really ridiculous, but that the Halliday set are too much of a low mob to understand his genius. Birkin is introduced at the beginning as a very special character: "a wonderful chap." One characteristic of this marvelous personality, however, is his hatred for and disdain of the rest of humanity, and we can't get out of this by simply accepting that this is some characteristic of an unredeemed Birkin. Lawrence speaks to us through Birkin, and nowhere does he place Birkin's misanthropy:

> "People don't really matter.... They jingle and giggle. It would be much better if they were just wiped out. Essentially, they don't exist, they aren't there." (WL, 27)

After a discussion of love in relationship to the meaning of life, to which we shall return, Birkin realizes that Gerald "wanted to be fond of him without taking him seriously." Then there follows a typical Birkin reflection, and we must say a typical Lawrentian reflection:

"Well, if mankind is destroyed, if our race is destroyed like Sodom, and there is this beautiful evening with the luminous land and trees, I am satisfied. That which informs it all is there, and can never be lost. After all, what is mankind but just one expression of the incomprehensible. And if mankind passes away, it will only mean that this particular expression is completed and done. That which is expressed, and that which is to be expressed, cannot be diminished. There it is, in the shining evening. Let mankind pass away—time it did. The creative utterances will not cease, they will only be here. Humanity doesn't embody the utterance of the incomprehensible any more. Humanity is a dead letter. There will be a new embodiment, in a new way. Let humanity disappear as quickly as possible." (WL, 65)

The sense of being special and apart from the general run of humanity, the distaste for ordinary life and coupling, and, indeed, distaste for life itself are pretty well evenly distributed among the four main characters. If we listen carefully, we can hear the nihilism in the soul of Paul Morel at the end of *Sons and Lovers* coming from the mouths of each of the four, and their dialogue often seems like Lawrence in dialogue with himself. For instance, discussing Winifred with Gerald, Birkin says (WL, 233):

"She'll never get on with the ordinary life. You find it difficult enough yourself, and she is several skins thinner than you are. It is awful to think what her life will be like unless she does find a means of expression, some way of fulfillment, You can see what mere leaving it to fate brings. You can see how much marriage is to be trusted to—look at your own mother.

There is a special kind of attitude that focuses on Birkin. (Paul Delaney says, "in describing the final harmony of Birkin and Ursula he was presenting a wishful fantasy rather than the actual state of his marriage in 1916" 1979, 226.) Leavis takes Lawrence to mean, in his dealings with Birkin as with Brangwen, that we "do not belong to ourselves," we must serve life in the cosmos, but I believe that Lawrence's mysticism is more doubtfully explained than that. In a fantasy of wish-fulfillment, he seeks to overcome his misery and impotence by a fairy tale assertion of his own divinity.

Seeing Birkin going into the Post Office, Ursula asys to herself,

Strange, he was. Even as he went into the lighted, public place he remained dark and magic, the living silence seemed the body of reality in him, subtle, potent, indiscoverable, There he was! In a strange uplift of elation she saw him, the being never to be revealed, awful in its potency, mystic and real. This dark, subtle reality of him, never to be translated, liberated her into perfection, her own perfect being. She too was dark and fulfilled in silence. (WL, 359)

Note for one thing that the words potent and potency are repeated in each passage. Another word that is reiterated is *real* to insist upon the *reality* of his *potency*, about which in life he was deeply anxious.

Another important word and concept behind the passages is control: in the first, Birkin is compared to statues that have a power to awe and control, and in the second passage the power of this "magical" "inscrutable" control is exerted over Ursula. Her apprehension of his potency, never to be revealed, never to be translated, gives her liberation.

There is an insistent emphasis on the unseeable, unknowable mystery for the being awake and the potency exists in "that other basic mind, the deepest physical mind." Here Lawrence speaks of the life of the body, which feels real pain and joy, and where he speaks of this deeper realm of being, we must applaud his insights for this is a valuable emphasis that the body has its own modes of wisdom. We all know that certain troubling information may only penetrate our intellect superficially, only later does its import reach the deeper centers. It is an important emphasis, too, when he declares that we should not try to impose the intellectual mind in the analysis of "the physical mind" but there is also a strange corollary of this emphasis, which is the insistence on darkness and hiddenness: a version of the myth of Psyche, but with a particular Lawrentian quality. Lawrence sometimes displays a deep fear of being intruded upon, a paranoid guilt, and at other times a need to be overlooked in intimacy. When Birkin and Ursula go off into the wood at the end of "Excurse," Birkin extinguishes the lamps, "and it was pure night": "The world was under a strange ban, a new mystery had supervened." (WL, 360). It is always important to Lawrence that the physical encounter between man and woman should be in the dark. He seems to have found making love in the light "stifling" (not for man and man, because Birkin and Gerald wrestle naked in the light, fully aware):

> Quenched, inhuman, his fingers upon her unrevealed nudity were the fingers of silence upon silence, the body of mysterious night upon the body of mysterious night, the night masculine and feminine, never to be known with the eye, or known with the mind, only known as a palpable revelation of living otherness. (WL, 361)

On her part she knows communication by touch, "a mystery, the reality of that which can never be known, vital, sensual reality that can never be transmuted into mind content." There can be such an unknown and mysterious beauty about sexual meeting at this deep "mindless" level, but there is an aspect of Lawrence's overinsistence (what, for instance, can "Quenched, inhuman . . ." mean?) that speaks of a certain dread in which there is a need to put the world "under a strange ban."

The "ban" I believe is evoked to prevent sexual meeting being like Mother and Father, and behind that fear is a deeper dread of the intrusion of the Mother. Everything in Lawrence comes back to that, and his search for "the night masculine and feminine," to be "pure" and unintruded upon, belongs to this quest. This also, oddly enough, is a quest to be "inhuman" above or beyond the limitations of being merely human. There is a schizoid element in Lawrence's yearning for special conditions for sexual meeting and a desire again to be in another dimension than that of the human.

\*　　　\*　　　\*

One dreaded possibility is that marriage may be like that dead relationship between the parents:

> "You can see how much marriage is to be trusted to—look at your own mother."
> "Do you think mother is abnormal?"
> "No! I think she only wanted something more, or other than the common run of life. And not getting it, she has gone wrong perhaps."
> "After producing a brood of wrong children," said Gerald gloomily.
> "No more wrong than any of the rest of us," Birkin replied. "The most normal people have the worst subterranean selves, take them one by one."
> "Sometimes I think it is a curse to be alive," said Gerald, with sudden impotent anger.
> "Well," said Birkin, "why not! Let it be a curse some-times to be alive—at other times it is anything but a curse. You've got plenty of zest in it really."
> "Less than you'd think," said Gerald, revealing a strange poverty in his look at the other man. (WL, 234)

He is exploring the problem of one's psychic inheritance—the durability of the psychic tissue, the "curse" of the inheritance of the mother's frustration in one's own sexual life. Here Birkin offers a kind of resignation.

Yet earlier in the same chapter, "Man to Man," Birkin, lying ill, seems to feel it would be better to die than "accept a life one did not want."

> But best of all to persist and persist, and persist for ever, till one were satisfied with life. (WL, 223)

In this persistence, against all one's schizoid problems, however, love remains the great bafflement:

> The old way of love seemed a dreadful bondage, a sort of conscription. What it was in him he did not know, but the thought of love, marriage and children, and a life lived together, in the horrible privacy of domestic and connubial satisfaction, was repulsive. He wanted something clearer, more open, cooler, as it were. *The hot narrow intimacy between man and wife was abhorrent.* The way they shut their doors, these married people, and shut themselves into their own exclusive alliance with each other, even in love, disgusted him. It was a whole community of mistrustful couples insulated in private houses or private rooms, always in couples, and no further life, no further immediate, no disinterested relationship admitted: a kaleidoscope of couples, disjoined, separatist, meaningless entities of married couples. True, he hated promiscuity even worse than marriage, and a liaison was only another kind of coupling, reactionary from the legal marriage. Reaction was a greater bore than action.
>
> On the whole, *he hated sex*, it was such a limitation. It was sex that turned a man into a broken half of a couple, the woman into the other broken half. And he wanted to be single in himself, the woman single in herself. He wanted sex to revert to the level of the other appetites, to be regarded as a functional process, not as a fulfilment. (WL, 233; my italics)

This latter note emerges again, as we have seen, in *The Captain's Doll*. If we examine carefully both the dialogue in *The Captain's Doll* and Birkin's sick ruminations, I believe we can say that Lawrence is exploring the possibility of dehumanizing sex to separate sexual "function" from love because love is so dangerous, not least because of the inheritance it ties one to. Here Lawrence is expressing through Birkin a disgust at ordinary sexual love, horror at the "hot, narrow intimacy" between man and wife. Lawrence sees sex as a form of crippling. To escape the horrors of "connubial satisfaction" Birkin wants something "clearer, more open, cooler"—that is, a functional sex from which emotion is divorced. Strangely enough, despite himself, Lawrence is here virtually reproducing the working class view that there is one thing that spoils marriage—sexual passion. "He believed in sex marriage," but

> beyond this, he wanted a further conjunction, where man had being and woman had being, two pure beings, each constituting the freedom of the other, balancing each other like two poles of one force, like two angels, or two demons.
>
> He wanted so much to be free, not under the compulsion of any need for unification, or tortured by unsatisfied desire... the merging, the clutching, the mingling of love was become madly abhorrent to him. (WL, 224)

The words in the last sentence reveal the underlying (schizoid) horror, of the oral intensity of love, that is, the dread that to give oneself in love inevitably means the loss of self and being. Lawrence's misanthropy developed out of his desperation, like Birkin's, to over-come such dread of love, knowing what duplicity there was in his own life.

With Frieda, as many accounts make clear, his life was a lie. (Middleton Murry wrote, "The effects of this ghastly lie he lives through Frieda have become permanent—I don't believe there's the slightest chance of his getting rid of them now." Bertrand Russell Archives, JMM to OM, 14 May 1915.)

The Murrys, of course, blamed everything they hated in *The Rainbow* on Frieda, and felt deeply critical of her after sharing a house with the Lawrences. In return, Lawrence based the relationship between Gerald and Gudrun on Murry's relationship with Katherine Mansfield, but here again, he also grafted onto that relationship a great deal from his own struggles with Frieda. There can be no doubt that in his writing Lawrence was working out distressing problems in his inner world in an attempt to come to terms with a profoundly falsified life. He wrote, "At present my real world is the world of my inner soul, which reflects on the novel I write. The outer world is there to be endured" (Moore 1962, 435).

What he had to endure becomes clear from Katherine Mansfield's description of a Lawrence quarrel: Lawrence, she said, was completely lost, like a gold ring in that immense German Christmas pudding that is Frieda. She went to tea, and there was an exchange about Shelley.

> And straightway I felt like Alice between the cook and the duchess. Saucepans and frying pans hurtled through the air. They ordered each other out of the house—and

the atmosphere of HATE between them was so dreadful that I could not stand it;
I had to run home. (Mansfield, letter, 1915)

Lawrence went to dinner with the Murrys that evening, but Frieda would not
come.

He sat down and said, "I'll cut her throat if she comes near this table." After dinner
she walked up and down outside the house in the dusk and suddenly, *dreadfully*, L.
rushed at her and began to beat her. They ran up and down out on the road,
scuffling. Frieda screamed for Murry and for me—but Lawrence never said a word.
He kept his eyes on her and *beat* her. (Mansfield, letter, 1915)

Later, Lawrence and Frieda made it up, but Katherine Mansfield says, "its
horribly tragic, for they have degraded each other and brutalised each other
beyond words.... I hate them for falsity. Lawrence has definitely chosen to
sin against himself and Frieda is triumphant." (Katherine Mansfield to
Ottoline Morel, Humanities Research Centre Texas, ?17 May 1915).

It is this essential falsity underlying Lawrence's life and work that we have
to confront. He offered to teach us how to be men and how to be women, but
his own life was this degradation and brutality. Yet Lawrence projected it
away from himself. As Katherine Mansfield herself said, in their house,
"whatever your disagreement is about he says it is because you have gone
wrong in your sex." The deep disabilities that made him attack Frieda are
projected over the world, which must be destroyed, to eradicate them. His
world becomes colored by a paranoid-schizoid fantasy. He has a hallucinatory
image of his relationships with people ("the swine are rats, they bite one's
hand.... I think it would be good to die, because death would be a clean land
with no people in it; not even the people of myself"—the latter a very revealing
remark; Lacy, 1971, 1142, 6 November 1916):

I must say I hate mankind—talking of hatred, I have got a perfect androphobia.
["Androphobia" is a slip for "anthropophobia."—Author] When I see people in the
distance, walking along the paths through the fields to Zennor, I want to crouch in
the bushes and shoot them silently with invisible arrows of death. I think truly the
only righteousness is the destruction of mankind, as in Sodom. Fire and brimstone
should fall down.
     But I don't want even to hate them. I only want to be in another world than
they ... Oh, if only one could have a great box of insect powder, and shake it over
them, in the heavens, and exterminate them. (Zytaruk 1972, 91–92)

One cannot certainly separate the "upshot" of Lawrence's explorations of
sexuality from these problems nor from his politics. He believed that "there
must be an aristocracy of people who have wisdom, and there must be a Ruler:
a Kaiser: no Presidents or democracies" (Moore 1962, 352), and since woman
is at the root of the matter, then woman must be put under strict control:

Woman must have their own political structure . . . there must be a rising rank of woman governors . . . culminating in a woman Dictator, of equal authority with the Supreme Man. (Moore 1962, 355)

Winnicott's insights into the internalized phantom woman are relevant here and we may see how Lawrence developed his attitudes to woman in society in his later work. Naturally, female emancipation, which had developed considerably throughout the war, filled him with distaste, and in response to woman's desire for sexual satisfaction, he developed a demand that she should yield in total submission to masculine domination.

Though the recognition of the effect of one generation's sexual life on the next is not consistent in *The Rainbow* or *Women in Love*, Lawrence has a sense that parental influence is important, and this generates one of the more revealing moments in *Women in Love*. A clue to the dread of being made meaningless by one's mere human origins is revealed in the chapter entitled "Flitting." Ursula has left her family to Birkin; she has not seen her parents since her marriage. The parents have moved, and the sisters visit their parents' house. "A stark, void entrance-hall struck a chill to the hearts of the girls":

The sense of walls, dry, thin, flimsy seeming walls, and a flimsy floor, pale with its artificial black edges, was neutralizing to the mind. Everything was null to the senses, there was enclosure without substance, for the walls were dry and papery. Where were they standing, on earth, or suspended in some cardboard box? (WL, 420)

The key words are "void," "neutral," and "null." The papery enclosure is also significant.

"Imagine that we passed our days here!" said Ursula.
"I know," cried Gudrun. "It is too appalling. What must we be like, if we are the contents of *this*!" (WL, 421)

Elsewhere, they find the "sense of intolerable papery imprisonment in nothingness," and the place resounds with "a noise of hollow, empty futility."

They went indoors again, and upstairs to their parents' front bedroom. . . .
It was void, with a meaninglessness that was almost dreadful. "Really," said Ursula, "this room *couldn't* be sacred, could it." (WL, 421)

Behind this scene we can surely hear Mrs. Morel, "I never had a husband—not really," and his insistence, "so long as you don't feel life's paltry and a miserable business." To a man to whom "the pivot of his life was his mother," the definition of love must be one that makes certain love is not like that marriage—which was void, neutral, and null.

The scene in which Gudrun and Ursula look at their parents' empty bedroom is convincing, yet as the conversation develops, it clearly belongs to Lawrence's propaganda:

> "It all seems so *nothing*—their two lives—there's no meaning in it. Really, if they had *not* met, and *not* married, and not lived together—it wouldn't have mattered, would it?"
> "...if I thought my life was going to be like it...I should run." (WL, 422)

The last line is almost Lawrence speaking to us. At first, fresh from reading *The Rainbow*, I wanted to protest that surely the life of Will and Anna was no nullity, but then I realized that the family in *Women in Love* is quite different. The parents of Ursula and Gudrun are quite different from the parents of *The Rainbow*—both more like the Morels. They cannot be believed to be the passionate, if tormented, Will and Anna, and display none of their creativity, secret mystical power, or even their intense destructiveness. When Gudrun speaks, she speaks with all Lawrence's contempt for "ordinary" English married life: "one cannot contemplate the ordinary life—one cannot contemplate it." Birkin, of course, by contrast is a "special case":

> "But with the ordinary man, who has his life fixed in one place, marriage is just impossible." (WL, 422)

What Gudrun wants is a *Glücksritter*, and we note that the word came from Frieda, who had left Professor Weekley for a roaming unstable writer. His thumb comes heavily into the scale, against being "ordinary" for to be ordinary is to be like "home," and

> "I know," said Ursula, "we've had one home—that's enough for me."
> "Quite enough," said Gudrun.
> "The little grey home in the west...."
> "Doesn't it sound grey, too." (WL, 422)

Birkin arrives, and at once "she became suddenly so free from the problems of grey homes in the west." "He was frightened of the place too." The episode is very revealing once we have glimpsed the clue to Lawrence's whole purpose in the novel, that is, to exorcise the inheritance in "marriage" and his own psychic life vis-à-vis woman, his own sexual ghosts:

> "This is a ghostly situation," he said.
> "These houses don't have ghosts—they've never had any personality, and only a place with a personality can have a ghost," said Gudrun.
> "I suppose so, Are you both weeping over the past?"
> "We are," said Gudrun grimly. Ursula laughed.
> "Not weeping that it's gone, but weeping that it ever *was*," she said. (WL, 423)

Birkin's presence, "lambent and alive," made even the impertinent structure of the dull house disappear. Thus, Birkin–Lawrence is the great exorciser. Gudrun cannot bear the idea of being put in a house (by Gerald).

> "Why *does* every woman think her aim in life is to have a hubby and a little grey home in the west? Why is this the goal of life? Why should it be?" said Ursula. (WL, 423)

Birkin answers in French, "*Il faut avoir le respect de ses bêtises*"—one must have respect for the stupidity of others—*du papa* and *de la maman*, as it turns out in the subsequent exchanges.

Midway Birkin's ruminations appear to be moving in the direction of the recognition of mutual respect and freedom, the progress goes false. His ruminations end in hostility:

> But it seemed to him, woman was always so horrible and clutching, she had such a lust for possession, a greed of self-importance in love. She wanted to have, to own, to control, to be dominant. Everything must be referred back to her, to woman, the Great Mother of everything, out of whom proceeded everything and to whom everything must finally be rendered up. (WL, 224)

Quite clearly, on pages 224–25, in these opening pages of the chapter "Man to Man," we have more than a record of Birkin's "stream of consciousness." Lawrence takes over to put forward his own ruminations and his own hostility to woman. Birkin never gives up his yearning for something "beyond" the relationship with woman, and urges that woman must "submit"—a principle over which there is much more propaganda in Lawrence's later works. Moreover, we also know from external evidence that the depiction of Hermione is a spiteful caricature of Lady Ottoline Morrell and expresses Lawrence's powerful feelings of compulsion-rejection where she was concerned:

> It filled him with almost insane fury, this calm assumption of the Magna Mater, that all was hers, because she had borne it. Man was hers because she had borne him. A Mater Dolorosa, she had borne him, a Magna Mater, she now claimed him again, soul and body, sex, meaning, and all. He had a horror of the Magna Mater, she was detestable. (WL, 224)

Behind Birkin's tirade here, of course, is Lawrence's dominating mother. It is true that all human beings *are* created by woman, and all begin life within a woman's consciousness. Yet only those with whom something has gone traumatically wrong with psychic parturition are repelled by this truth. Not all mothers claim their sons "soul and body"—and we have no indication anywhere that *Birkin* had an overdominant mother.

Birkin rails against Ursula: "she too was the awful arrogant queen of life, as if she were a queen bee on whom all the rest depended.'' (WL, 224) Perhaps the redeeming feature of the presentation of Birkin in *Women in Love* is that Lawrence clearly *loves* his character, and identifies so strongly with him, that at best we enter into a sympathetic compassion for him, an impulse to *understand* him. We "allow," as it were, this element of "play" in Lawrence, as we recognize what he is doing.

Then the search for understanding flips over into propaganda, as here, for in delineating Birkin's hatred and fear of Ursula (because it is a case of "And God! That she is necessary!''), he comes to discriminate against her: "He saw the yellow flare in her eyes, he knew the unthinkable overweening assumption of primacy in her" (WL, 224–25). That "unthinkable" is a give-away word, that conveys dread assertings that if she were allowed domination (as the castrating Mother) it would destroy him.

> She was unconscious of it herself. She was only too ready to knock her head on the ground before a man. But this was only when she was so certain of her man, that she could worship him *as a woman worships her own infant, with a worship of perfect possession.* (WL, 225; my italics)

What Birkin fears is the kind of impingement Lawrence suffered as an infant, and that he fears when it comes to marriage. Again, what he wants is a nonhuman purity:

> that which is manly being taken into the being of the man, that which is womanly passing to the woman, till the two are clear and whole as angels, the admixture of sex in the highest sense surpassed, leaving two single beings constellated together like two stars. (WL, 225)

In its examination of the marriage problem, *Women in Love* tackles again and again the inescapable truth that man is born of woman, and that in each human makeup there are the tissues in the psyche, of gender taken in from the father and from the mother.This cannot be escaped, as psychotherapy knows all too well: in every sexual act there are four psychic participants, the father and mother of each partner. Lawrence wanted it to be otherwise because the psychic tissue was too dangerous: better be angels or stars, with sex reduced to a function. ("On the whole he hated sex.")

In his next paragraph, which is clearly not Birkin but Lawrence lecturing at us, we have offered a new cosmology of sex:

> In the old age, before sex was, we were mixed, each one a mixture. The process of singling into individuality resulted in the great polarity of sex. The womanly drew to one side, the manly to the other. But the separation was imperfect even then. And so our world-cycle passes. There is now to come the new day, when we are beings each of us, fulfilled in difference. The man is pure man, the woman pure woman, they are perfectly polarized. *But there is no longer any of the horrible merging, mingling self-abnegation of love.* There is only the pure duality of polarization, each

one free from any *contamination* of the other. In each, the individual is primal, sex is subordinate, but perfectly polarized. Each has a single, separate being, with its own laws. The man has his pure freedom, the woman hers. Each acknowledges the perfection of the polarized sex circuit. Each admits the different nature in the other. (WL, 225; my italics)

One might say, I suppose, that some of the stages in this argument represent positive insights into Lawrence's application of his intelligence to the problem, as he embodies it in Birkin. Its existential emphasis on authenticity of gender, at the end, is valuable. The clue to freedom in sexual meeting does lie in recognition of the "different nature of the other" and that each has a "single, separate being, with its own laws." But the error is in seeking "perfect" polarization, since we have the (inescapable) problem of the male element in woman and the female element in man. The idealization to which Lawrence yearns becomes a stick to beat the human, and much of the language does not bear scrutiny. What does he mean by "our world-cycle passes"? And where is this "new day"? It *looks* as if Lawrence is seeking, through Birkin, a new mode of consciousness between man and woman. but he becomes obsessed with dread of "merging." The word "contamination" is revealing here.

It could well be that many of Lawrence's problems, as well as his amazing insights (as into how women are feeling), could have arisen from a split-off female element. The very structure of *Women in Love*, with its opposed (polarized) couples, could itself be a dramatization of the split-off female element problem of gender in Lawrence's inner world. Perhaps these ruminations of Birkin are around this question:

And why? Why should we consider ourselves, men and women, as broken fragments of one whole. . . .
    Always a man must be considered as the broken-off fragment of a woman, and the sex was the still aching scar of the laceration. Man must be added on to a woman, before he had any real place or wholeness. (WL, 225)

Perhaps Lawrence's very obsession with sex was an attempt to heal the fragmentation, seeking a solution on the symbolic lines of Plato's *Symposium*?

For instance, in the chapter "Death and Love," Gerald crushes Gudrun to his breast:

It was like a madness. Yet it was what she wanted, it was what she wanted . . . she knew that under this dark and lonely bridge the young colliers stood in the darkness with their sweethearts, in rainy weather. And so she wanted to stand under the bridge with *her* sweetheart, and be kissed under the bridge in the invisible darkness. . . .
    Ah, it was terrible, and perfect. Under this bridge, the colliers pressed their lovers to their breast. And now, under the bridge, the master of them all pressed her to himself! And how much more powerful and terrible was his embrace than theirs . . . .
    So the colliers' lovers would stand with their backs to the walls, holding their sweethearts and kissing them as she was being kissed . . . . (WL, 372–73)

Gerald is a kind of master-of-the-colliers, and so an embodiment of the male elements of Lawrence's coal-miner father. Such are the dangers in giving oneself up to such passion, however, that Gudrun's sexual life culminates in death; she embodies that part of Lawrence that was fascinated with but feared the masculinity of his father.

In an earlier chapter we learn how Gudrun is half-aware of the coarse regard of the work people of Beldover. As the sisters pass, a man says "in a prurient manner" to the younger one: "'What price that, eh? She'll do, won't she?' 'I . . . I'd give my week's wages just for five minutes.'" To Gudrun they are "sinister creatures, standing watching after her, by the heap of pale grey slag." "'It has a foul kind of beauty, this place,' said Gudrun." There is a miner washing, a thumb-nail sketch done with the tenderness such as Lawrence uses to describe the life of the colliers.

> It seemed to envelop Gudrun in a labourer's caress, there was in the whole atmosphere, a resonance of physical men, a glamorous thickness of labour and maleness, surcharged in the air. . . .
> To Gudrun . . . it was potent and half-repulsive . . . she realised that this was the world of powerful, underground men who spent most of their time in the darkness. In their voices she could hear the voluptuous resonance of darkness, the strong, dangerous underworld, mindless, inhuman. (WL, 128)

The "disruptive force" of the men, who sound like "strange machines," awakens in her a "fatal desire" and a "fatal callousness"; it is all "sickeningly mindless."

Gudrun's tragedy, then, is Mrs. Lawrence's—to be bewitched by the dark mindlessness of the colliers, especially the supercollier, Gerald. She is the female proclivity of the mother to be bewitched into "a strange, nostalgic ache of desire, something almost demoniacal, never to be fulfilled . . . like any other common girl of the district."

> Sometimes she sat among louts in the cinema: rakish-looking unattractive louts they were. (WL, 130)

But, like Lawrence, and the other protagonists, she is threatened by this degradation:

> All had a secret sense of power, and of inexpressible destructiveness, and of fatal half-heartedness, a sort of rottenness in the will.
> . . . she felt she was sinking into one mass with the rest. . . . It was horrible. (WL, 131)

Later she develops an "apprehensive horror of people in the mass" (WL, 176).

So much for Gudrun's brand of schizoid superiority. With Ursula the emphasis is a little different—at the beginning of the chapter "Moony" she has lost hope in the world:

One was a tiny little rock with the tide of nothingness rising higher and higher. She herself was real, and only herself ... the rest was all nothingness. She was hard and indifferent, isolated in herself. (WL, 275)

Ursula, too, is schizoid and contemptuous of the world:

There was nothing for it now, but contemptuous, resistant indifference. All the world was lapsing into a grey wish-wash of nothingness, she had no contact and connection anywhere. She despised and detested the whole show. (WL, 275)

It is surprising how little notice has been taken of this continual note in Lawrence of regarding adult humanity with contempt and despisal:

From the bottom of her heart, from the bottom of her soul, she despised and detested people, adult people. She loved only children and animals.

She loves animals because "each was single and to itself, magical."

It was not referred away to some detestable social principle. It was incapable of soulfulness and tragedy, which she detested so profoundly.
... she had a profound grudge against the human being. *That which the word "human" stood for was despicable and repugnant to her.* (WL, 275; my italics)

No doubt everyone has moments like this, but in Lawrence it is a persistent and recurring state—the main target of the contempt seems to be human consciousness itself.

With such a misanthropy in the art, how can Lawrence offer us an endorsement of marriage? If Gudrun yearns for kisses in the dark and Ursula yearns for love, obviously marriage is in view. Birkin and Gerald discuss it in the chapter, "Marriage or Not": "'One does have the feeling that marriage is a *pis aller*,' he admitted." To Birkin, it is repulsive.

"Marriage in the old sense seems to me repulsive. *Egoisme à deux* is nothing to it. It's a sort of tacit hunting in couples: the world all couples, each couple in its own little house, watching its own little interests and stewing in its own little privacy—it's the most repulsive thing on earth." (WL, 397)

Gerald agrees that "there's something inferior about it." It's a habit of cowardliness, avers Birkin (we may pick up in the background, I feel, a touch of Lawrence's despisal of the Weekley marriages that he had disrupted).

"You've got to take down the love-and-marriage ideal from its pedestal. We want something broader. I believe in the *additional* perfect relationship between man and man—additional to marriage."
"I can never see how it can be the same."
"Not the same—but equally important, equally creative, equally sacred, if you like." (WL, 397–98)

Gerald can't see it, because he is already "doomed" ("Marriage was like a doom, to him"). Significantly, Lawrence puts this in terms of the colliery: "to become like a convict condemned to the mines of the underworld, living no life in the sun, but having a dreadful subterranean activity" (WL, 398). He wants to commit himself to Gudrun and cannot accept Rupert's offer of a bond of "pure trust and love." What Birkin offers is this pure bond that was to be entered into "and then subsequently with the woman."

It is a strange yearning, and has about it the air of an impulse to survive. As we have seen, all the main characters have a dread of sinking into the ordinary, especially ordinary coupling. This ordinary coupling is like that between the collier father and the mother, and this threatens meaning; it is a sinking into that nothingness and nullity of the "underground" life of marital "merging"—the horrible merging that threatens death. There is a deeper drive behind Lawrence's contempt for ordinary coupling. Take the chapter, "A Chair,"—it is excellent in portraying the altercations between Birkin and Ursula over the chair, which is the symbol of the domestic. Yet even here the sexuality of the couple they observe in the shop is presented in the way of despisal—of fear of the ordinary. Rupert, as usual, is away into Rodin and Michaelangelo. He doesn't want a home (as Lawrence never wanted a home):

> "And we are never to have a complete place of our own—never a home?" she said.
> "Pray God, in this world, no," he answered.
> "But there's only this world," she objected. (WL, 402)

A home, of course, is what Mummy and Daddy have, and we have seen the sister's reaction to the meaninglessness of their parents' empty home. But now Birkin and Ursula see a couple who want a home: the woman is pregnant, and the man looks "like one of the damned." They are buying an "abominable article"—an iron washstand.

The man is presented with extraordinary animus: he "curiously obliterated himself, as if he could make himself invisible as a rat can." "He was a still, mindless creature, hardly a man at all ... he had some of the fineness and stillness and silkiness of a dark-eyed silent rat." The couple are presented in the terms "almost insolent," "hostile," "suggestive mocking secrecy," "jeering warmth," "blousy," a "gutter presence." Again, the groom is described as "a quick, vital rat."

And this is marriage:

> "Oh don't break you neck to get there," said the young woman. "'*Slike when you're dead— you're long time married.*'" The young man turned aside as if this hit him. (WL, 405–6; my italics)

Ursula and Birkin have an extraordinary snobbish conversation about them, and about inheritance and marriage, and Birkin returns to his theme of an "ultimate" relationship with Gerald, as if this (essentially Bloomsbury) idea would save him from the common touch.

Where is the meaning of life to be found? Gudrun does not find it with Gerald. Living awake she thinks ironically,

> at the same instant came the ironical question: "What for?" She thought of the colliers' wives, with their linoleum and their lace curtains and their little girls in high-laced boots. (WL, 470)

All she seems to have is "perfect moments," yet a terrible cynicism overwhelms her.

I find it very difficult to say what is wrong between Gerald and Gudrun. We know that they are based on John Middleton Murry and Katherine Mansfield:

> Lawrence believed, or tried to believe, that the relation between Katherine and me was false and deadly; and that the relation between Frieda and himself was real and life-giving: but that his relation with Frieda needed to be completed by a new relation between himself and me, which I evaded. . . . The foundation of it all is the relation between Lawrence and Frieda. That is, as it were, the ultimate reality. That foundation secure, Lawrence needs or desires a further relation with me, in which Katherine is temporarily but totally ignored. By virtue of this "mystical" relation with Lawrence, I participate in this pre-mental reality, the "dark sources" of my being come alive. From this changed personality, I, in turn, enter a new relation with Katherine. (Murry, 1935, 413)

Katherine was tired of Lawrence's obsession with sex and suggested sarcastically that he change the name of his cottage to "The Phallus." She wrote to Kot:

> I don't know which disgusts me more: when they are loving and playing with each other or when they are roaring at each other and he is pulling out Frieda's hair and saying "I'll cut your bloody throat, you bitch." (Quoted in Hahn, 1975, 177)

Leavis endorses Lawrence's moralistic discrimination against Gerald and Gudrun, and sees them as representing will in the service of industry, as ice and death.

It appealed to Leavis to see the failure of Gudrun and Gerald as a manifestation of the utilitarian ethos and the "social idea": hence the equation of industrial will and bad sex, or inability to love. But this "culture and environment" interpretation doesn't really satisfy. Gerald is limited, but not that limited. What he and Gudrun do embody are Lawrence's own schizoid proclivities; their England seems a projection of his own problems:

> "Oh God, the wheels within wheels of people, it makes one's head tick like a clock, with a very madness of dead mechanical monotony and meaningfulness. How I *hate* life, how I hate it. How I hate the Geralds, that they can offer nothing else." (WL, 522)

This is Gudrun, but she speaks as a dynamic component of Lawrence.

> The thought of the mechanical succession of day following day, day following day, *ad infinitum*, was one of the things that made her heart palpitate with a real approach of madness. The terrible bondage of this tick-tack of time, this twitching of the hands of the clock, this eternal repetition of hours and days—oh God it was too awful to contemplate. . . .
> All life, all life resolved itself into this: tick-tack, tick-tack, tick-tack. (WL, 522)

Gerald was the same ticking. "Gerald, with a million wheels and cogs and axles."

> Let them become instruments, pure machines, pure wills, that work like clockwork, in perpetual repetition. (WL, 524)

The deadness is a schizoid deadness, a feeling of meaningful and mechanical existence, with no rich emotional center or meaning. The connection with the industrial world is essentially symbolic, the link being the nothingness and meaninglessness to which Mrs. Lawrence's life with a collier husband had led.

It is the schizoid dynamics in Gerald that kill him, and it is then that Birkin more or less sees enacted his own impulse to have the world destroyed so that a new world can emerge. "The mystery of creation was fathomless" (WL, 538). We have examined this episode above, but it reveals Gerald's death as a fantasy of schizoid suicide from which the new Birkin birth is to emerge. Yet in the end he clings to the "need" for Gerald.

> "To make it complete, really happy, I wanted eternal union with a man too; another kind of love."
> "I don't believe it," she said. "It's an obstinacy, a theory, a perversity."
> "Well—" he said.
> "You can't have two kinds of love. Why should you!"
> "It seems as if I can't," he said. "Yet I wanted it."
> "You can't have it, because it's false, impossible," she said.
> "I don't believe that," he answered. (WL, 541)

Despite the fulfillment of the love between Birkin and Ursula, Birkin is still yearning at the end for "something else"—a relationship with Gerald. How can we interpret this?

I have suggested that one problem of the novel is its narcissism. I believe there is also a problem of envy: envy of woman, but *also of the healthy man.* Harry T. Moore makes this point, and it seems valid Gerald is the focus of Lawrence's envy of the healthy, potent, normally effective male human being, who is not tormented as he is by the dread of woman, sex, death, and humanity. This envy impels him to make a distorted travesty of Gerald out of

Middleton Murry, and to falsify him into a deathly and destructive man of will and the industrial urge.

But what, then, about the homosexuality.

The startling thing is the energy of the urge between them:

> There was a pause of strange enmity between the two men, that was very near to love. It was always the same between them; always their talk brought them into a deadly nearness of contact, a strange, perilous intimacy which was either hate or love, or both ... *the heart of each burned for the other.* They burned with each other, inwardly. This they would never admit. (WL, 37; my italics)

Neither will admit the urge: "They had not the faintest belief in deep relationship between men and men, and their disbelief prevented any development of their powerful but suppressed friendliness."

Envy here merges with the unconscious myth. Possibly the relationship between Middleton Murry and Katherine Mansfield was normal, and it was this that made Lawrence envious—worse, it exposed his own sexuality as full of death. Thus, he identifies in a strange way with Murry, and gives this the strange gloss of wanting, in some way, by a homosexual relation with Murry, to redeem Katherine. In any case, it is as if in Lawrence's dreams of Rananim, everyone is being drawn into the toils of his own narcissism. In the novel, Birkin, Ursula, Gerald, and Gudrun are all dynamics of his own inner world, and the problem of what is "deathly" or not is by no means as moralistically simple as Leavis makes out.

Birkin says to himself, "Am I my brother's keeper?" and then remembers it was Cain's cry. "And Gerald was Cain, if anybody. Not that he was Cain, either, although he had slain his brother." (WL, 28). Birkin reflects on this in relation to general existential problems:

> Is every man's life subject to pure accident, is it only the race, the genus, the species, that has a universal reference.... Has *everything* that happens a universal significance? (WL, 28)

"Why seek to draw a brand and a curse across the life that had caused the accident?" I just hear in this paragraph an undercurrent of anguish that makes me feel that in Gerald we have a touch of the experience of the death of William Ernest Lawrence, and the ghost that haunted the Lawrence household as David Herbert took his place in his mother's heart, after a long illness. With no more evidence than a sense of a vibration parallel here to Mahler's grief for his sibling Ernst, I believe that the yearning Birkin has for Gerald has its roots in *the death of Lawrence's brother.*

Lawrence, who had displaced his brother in his mother's affections, then found her possessively in love with him. The ghost of the brother is bound up for him with the problem of woman. He would be bound, too, to be guilty. Gudrun is made to say

> "to think of such a thing happening to one when one was a child, and having to carry the responsibility of it all through one's life. Imagine it, two boys playing together—then this comes upon them, for no reason whatever—out of the air. . . . Murder, that is thinkable, because there's a will behind it. But a thing like that to *happen* to one—"
> "Perhaps there *was* an unconscious will behind it," said Ursula. (WL, 53)

"Where does his go go to?" Gudrun has asked. Leavis sees Gerald's will as a servant of industrialism and as belonging to utilitarian mechanism, life-denying, but perhaps Gerald's will has its origins in quite another problem—that of guilt over a sibling's death.

Birkin, talking to Gerald, pours scorn on all devotion to the needs of others. The miner, he says, lives for the "Brocken Spectre":

> He sees himself reflected in the neighbouring opinion, like a Brocken mist, several feet taller on the strength of the pianoforte, and he is satisfied. He lives for the sake of that Brocken spectre; the reflection of himself in the human opinion. You do the same. If you are of high importance to humanity you are of high importance to yourself. (WL, 61)

Birkin challenges Gerald, "What do you live for?" and dismisses service to humanity: what about if we had all the coal and pianos? "First person singular is enough for me", he declares, "I live because I am living." All Gerald can fall back on is the "plausible ethics of productivity."

It is true that we must insist on the needs of being, which are not satisfied by mere attention to industrial go, or the opinion of neighbours, or by the kind of aspiration colliers had for pianos. On the other hand, to seek the meaning of one's existence merely in terms of the "first person singular" can lead to a kind of narcissistic self-enclosure that defects its own existential object. Birkin finds himself poles apart from Gerald.

> "Gerald," he said, "I rather hate you."
> "I know you do," said Gerald, "Why do you?"
> Birkin mused inscrutably for some minutes. . . .
> ". . . There are odd moments when I hate you starrily," (WL, 62)

The latter word is strange, and one wonders what it means. To meet as "stars" is one of Birkin's ambitions with a woman, but the odd combination of mysticism and childishness makes me feel Birkin is talking to a sibling. The important discussions that follow are like conversations between two brothers—or, one might say, like a conversation between a brother and sibling's ghost.

"I want the finality of love."

"The old ideals are dead as nails—nothing there. It seems to me there remains only this perfect union with a woman—sort of ultimate marriage—and there isn't anything else." (WL, 64)

It is at this point that there follows the exchange about God.

"And you mean if there isn't the woman, there's nothing?" said Gerald.

"Pretty well that—seeing there's no God."

"Then we're hard to put to it." (WL, 64)

Birkin cannot help seeing how "beautiful and soldierly" Gerald's face is:

There was something very congenial to him in Birkin. But yet, beyond this, he did not take much notice. He felt that he, Gerald, had harder and more durable truths than any the other man knew. He felt himself older, more knowing. (WL, 64)

There follows a tirade by Birkin about letting "mankind pass away—time it did."

Gerald conducts a mundane affair for a couple of days with Julius Halliday's mistress, Minette.

"I liked her all right, for a couple of days," said Gerald.

"But a week of her would have turned me over. There's a certain smell, about the skin of those women, that in the end is sickening beyond words—even if you like it at first." (WL, 106)

The intimacy between Birkin and Gerald, not least when they are looking at the world of women, is very much like that between brothers:

He was looking at the white legs of Gerald, as the latter sat on the side of the bed in his shirt. They were white-skinned, full, muscular legs, handsome and decided. Yet they moved Birkin with a sort of pathos, tenderness, as if they were childish. (WL, 107)

The relationship between Gerald and Birkin is one of the chief puzzles of *Women in Love*, and from some of his remarks on homosexuality, it would seem that Lawrence was as puzzled as anyone. There is something somewhat ghostly about the relationship, and so one looks for unconscious elements in it (as well as the revelation, discussed below, that Compton Mackenzie declared that Lawrence told him his greatest sexual satisfaction came from a homosexual relationship in his youth, p. 358).

It seems possible that the relationship is intensely fraternal: that Lawrence, having been confused by his mother with the ghost of her previous son who had died, gave him a kind of alter ego, so Gerald becomes William to Birkin's

Bert, and they have shared the same woman, Mrs. Lawrence. There are those occasional Latin tags that Lawrence inserts here: *Integer vitae scelerisque purus* ("The man of upright life and pure from guilt"—from Horace) and *salvator feminis* (WL, 109). He says, "They always wanted to be free each of the other," but "there was a curious heart-straining towards each other."

What is noticeable is that two of the most intense episodes involving Gerald follow significant encounters with woman. Gerald's violent suppression of his horse follows immediately after the scene in which Birkin is biffed by the Castrating Mother figure, Hermione, in the subsequent chapter.

Hermione strike Birkin on the head (an experience Lawrence himself suffered enough from Frieda) and he retreats ("He did not want a woman—not in the least") into a wood. Probably suffering from concussion, he strips, and sits down naked among the primroses. He finds the fir trees and other plants "more delicate and more beautiful than the touch of any woman":

> What a dread he had of mankind, of other people! It amounted almost to horror, to a sort of dream terror. . . . If he were on an island, like Alexander Selkirk, with only the creatures and the trees, he would be free and glad. (WL, 121)

The problem of woman is thus the problem of enduring her impulse to murder you, and your own to murder woman.

The other episode with Gerald, which involves the question of how to deal with woman, is the wrestling match, and this follows the moment when Birkin proposes to Ursula. Both this, and the episode with the horse, are dream-like and intensely physical in nature, enacting the question of how to deal with woman—although the second is, of course, a scene of wrestling with a man. Perhaps we could say that in the first the man is dealing with the female element, and in the second with the male element. Both are symbolic acts of sexual engagement, and seem to raise the whole question of Lawrence's feelings about sexual intercourse. Why was he so impelled to delineate this experience, to force it into words, to describe it in the basic Anglo-Saxon language, and to be so preoccupied with sexual explicitness?

The answer, I suggest, is that at a certain level Lawrence remained puzzled as to the nature of sexual experience, at a deep traumatic level, emerging from infant experience of the Primal Scene. Perhaps we can take into account here lines from the poem *Discord in Childhood:*

> Within the house two voices arose, a slender lash.
> Whistling she-delirious with rage, and the dreadful sound.
> Of a male thong booming and bruising, until it had drowned
> That other voice in a silence of blood. (CP, 36)

Mine here is the kind of conjecture for which one cannot find evidence, but from time to time there is the strange preoccupation with mechanical and meaningless activity, as in the passages about "tic tac." In the small house in

Eastwood, perhaps the child Lawrence became aware of the sounds of what must seem to him meaningless sexual activity, which, because of his fantasy involvement and its appetitive intensity, seemed terribly threatening but meaningless. This could explain many of his preoccupations, his particular dread of horrible merging, and other horrors, while his intense need to delineate sex would then seem to be an attempt to overcome the consequent traumata.

This, of course, would put a different light on the relationship between "will," the industrial world, and personal relationships. Gerald mastering the horse in the chapter entitled "Coal-Dust" represents the father gaining control over the mother. It is preoccupied with the way in which mastery must be exerted over the female element and over being. I am sure the scene obtains its disturbing force by being a fantasy of sexual intercourse between father and mother. There is no mistaking the sexual undertones:

> a glistening, half-smiling look came into Gerald's face. He brought her back again, inevitably. . . .
> It seemed as if he sank into her, magnetically, and could thrust her back against herself. (WL, 122)

Such violence is how sexual intercourse between parents would seem to a child.

> she convulsed herself utterly away from the horror . . . but he leaned forward, his face shining with fixed amusement, and at last he brought her down, sank her down, and was bearing her back to the mark.
> . . . It made Gudrun faint with poignant dizziness, which seemed to penetrate her to the heart. (WL, 123)

Gerald is, in one sense, showing the girls how to make a female submit (as Lawrence shows us in *Lady Chatterley*) how a "real man" gets across "a lady": note here, "a sword pressing into her":

> He bit himself down on the mare like a keen edge biting home, and forced her round. She roared as she breathed, her nostrils were two wide, hot, holes, her mouth was apart, her eyes frenzied. It was a repulsive sight. But he held on her unrelaxed, with an almost mechanical relentlessness, keen as a sword pressing into her. (WL, 123-24)

There are many phrases here that associate with the descriptions of sexual intercourse of a slightly sadistic kind ("dagger thrusts") in *Lady Chatterley*. Lawrence is here, I think, impelled to recreate in this act of cruel domination a phantasy memory of parental sexual intercourse: "the man closed round her, and brought her down, almost as if she were part of his own physique."— which is just as a child would see the physical one-ness of man and woman. Here we have the roots of Lawrence's fear of "horrible merging,"in a fantasy of the "combined parents."

The scene is superbly "realised," to use Leavis's word, but the meaning of it is more complex than Leavis allows.

"And she's bleeding! she's bleeding!" cried Ursula, frantic with opposition and hatred of Gerald. She alone understood him, in pure opposition. (WL, 124)

Gudrun turns white then seems to faint: "The world reeled and passed into nothingness for Gudrun, she could not know any more." She turns "cold and indifferent."

Gudrun calls out like a witch, "I should think you're proud." But the gatekeeper is half-admiring: "A masterful young jockey, that'll have his own road, if ever anybody would" (WL, 125). Ursula protests that the mare is probably much more sensitive than the man, but Gudrun is as impressed as Ursula is later to be impressed by Birkin's god-like qualities, in much the same language:

Gudrun was as if numbed in her mind by the sense of indomitable soft weight of the man, bearing down into the living body of the horse: the strong indomitable thighs of the blond man clenching the palpitating body of the mare in pure control; a sort of soft white magnetic domination from the loins and thighs and calves, enclosing and encompassing the mare heavily into unutterable subordination, soft blood subordination, terrible. (WL, 126)

The sight brings out a powerful blood urge in Gudrun to encounter the passion of men in the coal district, in subsequent pages. So, however much Gerald's domination and will are seen to lead to his death, his domination over the mare is also admired, and evokes in Gudrun an impulse to be dominated.

A parallel scene, the wrestling, symbolises engagement with the male element. When Birkin's proposal to Ursula fails, he goes to Gerald, whose face lights up "in a sudden, wonderful smile." There develops a strange under-current between the men, who are restless and bored. Why doesn't he hit something, Birkin asks?—and they begin to discuss fighting. Gerald looks down at Birkin:

and his eyes flashed with a sort of terror *like the eyes of a stallion*, that are bloodshot and overwrought, turned glancing backwards in a stiff terror.
"I feel that if I don't watch myself, I shall find myself doing something silly."
"Why not do it?" said Birkin coldly. (WL, 302; my italics)

The homosexual element is clear as they discuss Birkin's exercises in ju-jitsu with a Japanese: "He was very quick and slippery and full of electric fire." Gerald's eyes light up. They begin to wrestle:

He impinged invisibly upon the other man . . . and then suddenly piercing in a tense fine grip that seemed to penetrate to the very quick of Gerald's being. . . . He seemed to penetrate into Gerald's more solid, more diffuse bulk, to interfuse his body through the body of the other, as if to bring it subtly into subjection, always seizing with some necromantic foreknowledge every motion of the other flesh. (WL, 304–5)

Here, too, we have the impulse towards magical control—this time over a man. Birkin slides quite unconscious over Gerald: "The world was sliding, everything was sliding off into the darkness. And he was sliding, endlessly, endlessly away" (WL, 305). To ease himself up, Birkin puts his hand down, and it touches the Gerald's hand:

> And Gerald's hand closed warm and sudden over Birkin's, they remained exhausted and breathless, the one hand clasped closely over the other. It was Birkin whose hand, in swift response, had closed in a strong, warm clasp over the hand of the other. (WL, 307)

"The wrestling had some deep meaning to them—an unfinished meaning." Birkin says, "We are mentally, spiritually intimate, therefore we should be more or less physically intimate too—it is more whole." " 'It is rather wonderful to me' replies Gerald."

Birkin thinks how different Gerald's body is from his: "as far, perhaps, apart as man from woman, yet in another direction." But it was really Ursula, it was the woman who was gaining ascendence over Birkin's being at this moment. "His mind had reverted to Ursula." He tells Gerald that he has proposed to her. It is thus clear that the wrestling episode represents a necessary test, to do with Birkin's fear of commitment to a woman.

One of the problems is how to make sexual love meaningful, with the ghost of the mother in the background expressing a sense of meaninglessness. After their discussion of love, after the wrestling, Gerald says to Birkin: "I don't care how it is with me—I don't care how it is—so long as I don't feel. . . . So long as I feel I've *lived*" (WL, 311). The words clearly echo those of Paul Morel to his mother, and her reply, "Eh, my dear—say rather you want me to live" (SL, 276).

I believe we may see both episodes involving Gerald represent the attempt to find meaning in physical encounter, of a sexual kind, in someone who had been puzzled by the Primal Scene experienced as a child.

Thus, Lawrence finds physical love with woman so likely to be meaningless, that he must always be hankering after "something else." The quasi-homosexual experience of Gerald remains in Birkin's mind.

Toward the end of the chapter entitled "A Chair" he says to Ursula:

> "One has a hankering after a sort of further fellowship." "But why?" she insisted. "Why should you hanker after other people? Why should you need them?"
> This hit him right on the quick. His brows knitted.
> "Does it end with just our two selves?" (WL, 409)

As we have seen, when they commit themselves to one another, Birkin and Ursula at once give up their jobs. He is endlessly dismissing the rest of humanity, but yet he yearns for "others": "Must one just go on as if one were alone in the world—the only creature in the world?" (WL, 409)—that is, actually, how Lawrence often did go on.

> "You've got me," she said. "Why, should you *need* others. . . ." "I *know* I want a perfect and complete relationship with you: and we've nearly got it—we really have. But beyond that. *Do* I want a real, ultimate relationship with Gerald? Do I want a final, almost extra-human relationship with him—a relationship with him—a relationship in the ultimate of me and him—or don't I?" (WL, 410)

As we have seen, at the end, Birkin is still hankering for this "ultimate" relationship with Gerald.

Toward the end, as the relationship between Gerald and Gudrun becomes deathly, Ursula asks Birkin to take her away. Behind the subsequent discussion between the sisters is an obvious reference to Lawrence's own movement abroad, away from England. Gudrun says, "But don't you think you'll *want* the old connexion with the world—father and the rest of us, and all that it means, England and the world of thought" (WL, 492). Rupert Birkin is right, says Ursula, to want "a new space to be in." This is the impulse behind *Women in Love*—to get rid of all the old human background, and to enter a new dimension, but what lures in an *inhuman* dimension. Gudrun declares that you can't suddenly fly off to a new planet. Ursula replies, "One has a sort of other self, that belongs to a new planet, not to this" (WL, 493). Gudrun says she believes that love is the supreme thing, in space as well as earth. "'no,' said Ursula, 'it isn't. *Love is too human and little*'" (WL, 493).

It is strange to have this from Ursula, but then she goes on, in characteristic Birkin-propaganda terms.

> "'I believe in something inhuman, of which love is only a little part. I believe what we must fulfill comes out of the unknown to us, and it is something infinitely more than love. It isn't so merely *human*.'" (WL, 493)

Gudrun says something patronizing about "Rupert's Blessed Isles," but clearly Ursula is uttering a Lawrentian faith.

The new "space" must be like god or pharoahs, at least for the man. It must take on the ultimate qualities of a relationship with a man that has none of the dangers of a relationship with a woman. Above all it must be *inhuman*, beyond or above the human; it must belong to some "unknown" impulse in the cosmos.

He returns to the theme when Birkin looks at the corpse of the dead Gerald: in his body he sees the nonhuman mystery at work. Birkin remembers most the moment when Gerald's hand closed on his:

> Birkin remembered how once Gerald had clutched his hand with a warm momentaneous grip of final love. For one second—then let it go again, let go for ever. If he had kept true to that clasp, death would not have mattered.

What can this possibly mean? Birkin goes on

Those who die, and dying still can love, still believe, do not die. They live still in the beloved. Gerald might still have been living in the spirit with Birkin, even after death. He might have lived with his friend, a further life. (WL, 540)

It is difficult to know what this means. Does it mean that Gerald would have been saved from death by some "ultimate" homosexual relationship with Birkin? Birkin goes on here to remember" the beautiful face of one whom he had loved, and who had died still having the faith to yield to the mystery." Lawrence is still casting about around the anguish of his mother's death and the problem of belief in anything. As with the discussion between Gudrun and Ursula, he continues to pursue the problem of "What can we possibly believe in, in order to find life has a meaning of any kind? Love? Beyond love?"

At least, now he and Ursula love, they have transcended death,

"You've got me," she said.
He smiled and kissed her.
"If I die," he said, "you'll know I haven't left you."
"And me?" she cried.
"And you won't have left me," he said. "We shan't have any need to despair, in death."
She took hold of his hand.
"But need you despair over Gerald?" she said.
"Yes," he answered. (WL, 540–41)

The novel ends, enigmatically, even after over five hundred pages of discussion of the nature of love:

"Did you need Gerald?" she asked one evening.
"Yes," he said.
"Aren't I enough for you?" she asked.
"No," he said. "you are enough for me, as far as woman is concerned. You are all women to me. But I wanted a man friend, as eternal as you and I are eternal."
"Why aren't I enough?" she said. "You are enough for me. I don't want anybody else but you. Why isn't it the same with you?"
"Having you, I can live all my life without anybody else, any other sheer intimacy. But to make it complete, really happy, I wanted eternal union with a man too: another kind of love," he said.
"I don't believe it," she said. "It's an obstinacy, a theory, a perversity."
"Well—" he said.
"You can't have two kinds of love. Why should you!"
"It seems as if I can't," he said. "Yet I wanted it "You can't have it, because it's false, impossible," she said.
"I don't believe that," he answered. (WL, 541)

What are we to make of this? Birkin is persistent, and Lawrence's last line is to reject accusations that it is an impossibility? I think that we need to take into account Lawrence's strange preoccupation with death. For example, in what sense shall they not have "any need to despair, over death." In what sense will he not "leave her"?

Here I believe we need to go back to the wrestling episode:

> He seemed to penetrate into Gerald's more solid, more diffuse bulk, to interfuse his body through the body of the other, as if to bring it subtly into subjection, always seizing with some necromantic foreknowledge every motion of the other flesh. . . . It was as if Birkin's whole physical intelligence interpenetrated into Gerald's body, as if his fine, sublimated energy entered into the flesh of the fuller man, like some potency, casting a fine net, a prison, through the muscles into the very depths of Gerald's physical being. (WL, 305)

It is a fantasy of Lawrence, with this physical weakness, entering the body of a healthy man. This is why one has such a feeling about narcissism in this chapter "Gladiatorial," which title itself is significant ("moraturi te salutant!"). Lawrence wanted to die and be resurrected into a healthy self.

This resurrection theme is expounded at great length, as we have seen, in Ursula's thoughts in chapter 10 of *The Rainbow*, "The Widening Circle," where we first encounter the reference to the Sons of God with the daughters of men. Ursula is a young woman, and Lawrence is portraying the kind of deep preoccupation an adolescent may have. At the same time, clearly, he is presenting his own ruminations, and they tie in with other writings. He is also recalling his own adolescent ruminations.

Ursula finds the humanity of Jesus distasteful. It is the vulgar mind (WL, 274) that will "allow nothing extra-human, nothing beyond itself to exist." Ursula's mother will not allow the ultra-human to exist; Ursula is with her father in his mysticism. Anna has become immersed in quotidian realities, Will had a dark, subject hankering to worship an unseen God." Ursula was "all for the ultimate." Jesus, to her, was beautifully remote, like "a white moon at sunset."

We may perhaps turn this all around, autobiographically, and say that it was Lawrence's mother who gazed out at the life of the spirit, and it has she who idolized him into the ithyphallic column of blood.

But on page 276 of *The Rainbow* we come to an interesting development. Ursula reflects that the Lord said "My spirit shall not always strive with Man, for that he also is flesh."

> "There were giants in those days; and also after that, when the Sons of God came unto the daughters of men, and they bare children unto them, the same became mighty men, which were of old, men of renown." (R, 276)

She is reflecting on *Genesis*, VI:4. "It was a dream that frightened her."

> Who were the Sons of God?
> . . . *Yet there were men not begotten by Adam*
> Who were these, and whence did they come? They too must derive from God. (R, 276)

Perhaps, she thinks, "these children, these sons of God, had known no expulsion, no ignominy of the fall." Then comes that strange phrase, "she moved about in the essential days, when the Sons of God came in unto the daughters of man." These, the Sons of God, were such as should take her to wife.

> She clung to the secret hope, the aspiration. She lived a dual life, one where the facts of life encompassed everything, being legion, and the other wherein the daily facts of daily life were superseded by the eternal truth . . . she believed more in her desire and its fulfillment than in the obvious facts of life. The fact that a man was a man, did not state his descent from Adam, did not exclude that he was also one of the unhistoried, unaccountable Sons of God. (R, 276–7)

I believe that here Lawrence is recording something profound about his own experience. *He was, secretly, a religious fanatic.* He dealt in one self with penetrating intelligence with ordinary reality and existence, but in a secret part of him he believed that he belonged to a special kind of "giant" or "mighty man of renown" who *was not a son of Adam*, who had not experienced the humiliation of the fall. He was *unhistoried* and *unaccountable*, too. This kind of man need not look to another world to be resurrected but *could be resurrected in this.* It was a fantasy by which he could escape his mortality as a tubercular and schizoid individual.

I think we may here invoke also a number of deep psychological problems in Lawrence. First, his dread of tuberculosis and his secret horror that he might be doomed. Second, his schizoid problems of the dread of inner emptiness and his fear of love. (Adam, after all, was cast out of Eden because he came to be aware of his nakedness and sexuality, and his love-needs, and this kind of self-consciousness was a focus of dread for Lawrence.) Third, there was his childlessness, about which he must have brooded a great deal (for "they bore children unto them," the daughters of men). Fourth, because of this, if for no other reason, Lawrence must have been deeply jealous of woman, and this explains much of his hostility to her (such jealousy is common in creative men, as we know from individuals like Mahler; their own creativity being in some way woman-like, they resent the woman being culturally creative as well as sexually creative, as if the sexual creativity were enough for them). Finally, he identified with Christ-Phoenix. Resurrection had in some way to be turned into a process that happened in *this* life.

When Ursula comes to reflect on Easter in *The Rainbow*, this becomes clear. She sees in the Easter myth a "rhythm of eternity in a ragged, inconsequential life." But the Resurrection had become shadowy and overcome by the shadow of death. The Ascension was scarcely noticed, a mere confirmation of death. "What was the hope and fulfillment? Nay, was it all only a useless after-death, a wan, bodiless, after-death?" (R, 281) This Ursula cannot bear, and Lawrence cannot bear: "from the grave . . . the body rose torn and dull and colourless." (R, 281). Ursula studies the gospel story to try to see a way out of this.

Alas, for the wavering, glimmering appearance of the risen Christ.
Alas, that so soon the drama is over: that life is ended at thirty-three, (R, 281).

Who can doubt that Lawrence was reflecting on his own fate? "Alas, that a risen Christ has no place with us!" (R, 281) Lawrence is striving to relate the Christ-myth to his many problems, especially that of a need for rebirth of being, so he offers a revised Christology:

But why? Why shall I not rise with my body whole and perfect, shining with strong life? Why, when Mary says: Rabboni, shall I not take her in my arms and kiss her and hold her to my breast. Why is the risen body deadly, and abhorrent with wounds? (R, 281)

Mary was the Mother of Jesus, so here the Ursula–Lawrence fantasy relates the problem of Resurrection to the dead mother, and the impulse is strangely erotic towards her. The problem of finding a new birth into wholeness clearly associates in Lawrence's mind with being born again now by finding the mother through the tomb and perhaps *her* resurrection:

The Resurrection is to life, not to death. Shall I not see those who have risen again walk here among men perfect in body and spirit, whole and glad in the flesh, living in the flesh, loving in the flesh, begetting children in the flesh, arrived at last to wholeness, perfect without scar or blemish, healthy without fear of ill-health. Is this not the period of manhood and of joy and fulfillment, after the Resurrection? Who shall fear the mystic, perfect flesh which belongs to heaven?
    Can I not, then, walk this earth in gladness, being risen from sorrow? Can I not eat with my brother happily, and with joy kiss my beloved, after my resurrection, celebrate my marriage in the flesh with feastings, go about my business eagerly. (R, 281–82)

Clearly, by now Lawrence has forgotten all about Ursula—for it is a *man* speaking and clearly it is himself and his marriage he is writing of as well as of his dead mother and dead brother. For himself he seeks a new state of "the mystic, perfect flesh which belongs to heaven"—that is, to become a God or Son of God.

Is heaven impatient for me, and bitter against this earth, that I should hurry off, or that I should linger pale and untouched? (R, 282)

Ursula Brangwen had no such problems. Lawrence did, and in these passages we can see how this impulse to become a god, and his occasional belief that he had become one, developed. This entering into a super-state came about through sex, and through sex that involved a certain kind of discrimination against woman, a denial of her equal participation, a reduction of her to slave: in His will is her peace.

This is what is wrong with the end of the chapter entitled "Excurse in *Women in Love*." Birkin becomes a god, becomes self-deified.

She saw a strange creature from another world in him. It is as if she were enchanted, and everything were metamorphosed. She recalled again the old magic of the Book of Genesis, where the sons of God saw the daughters of men, that they were fair. And he was one of these, one of these strange creatures from the beyond, looking down on her, and seeing she was fair. (WL, 352)

Stroking his thighs, she discovers him "one of the sons of God such as were in the beginning of the world, *not a man, something other, something more*" (WL, 353; my italics).

This was release at last. She had had lovers, she had known passion. But this was neither love nor passion. It was the daughters of one coming back to the Sons of God, the strange inhuman sons of God who are in the beginning. (WL, 353; my italics)

We read this as an allegory, or as hyperbole; "at this moment of ecstasy in love" we think "Ursula finds her man as a good." *But is is not meant like that at all.* Birkin has seemed human enough, in the marvelous first half of the chapter, but now *Lawrence means literally* that he is a god. Birkin is the *Salvator Femininis*:

She was . . . a paradisal flower . . . beyond womanhood. . . . It was all achieved for her. She had found one of the Sons of God from the Beginning, and he had found one of the first most luminous daughters of men. (WL, 353)

As we see in an earlier quotation, the concept of "manhood" that Leavis picks up means for Lawrence a special category of existence, which belongs to godliness. Rather than a new and humble recognition of the *Ahnung*, however, I believe it is rather demented mumbo-jumbo. The "source" is deeper than the "phallic source": "from the smitten rock of the man's body . . . came the floods of ineffable darkness and ineffable richness" (WL, 354). I have often felt, when reading Lawrence in this vein, that he was simply overdoing it. Though we can have feelings of high ecstasy in sexual love, it must puzzle many who read of such long-sustained ecstasies. Lawrence was, I conjectured, rather faking it, but now I see that we are dealing with something much more like a religious tract, or a life of a saint, or some divine revelation. *It bears no relationship at all to normal sexuality or ordinary human existence*: it is an attempt to portray the experience of a man who has *become* God. It is thus no use complaining that, psychologically, or existentially, it was wrong for Birkin and Ursula to write their job resignations! Gods like Zeus don't go on with their teaching jobs! Once one attains this status, "with his strange, non-human singleness," all earthly considerations become irrelevant. Thus, "he sat still like an Egyptian Pharoah . . . in immemoral potency." (WL, 358) Birkin has become a deity, Greek or Egyptian, mystic and real, evoking in the woman a "perfect being" by mystic potency.

When I examined such passages as attempts to portray sexual reality and the human experience of being, I thought they were nonsense. Now that I find them to be attempts to portray the experience of gods, I do not find them less nonsense—indeed, they now seem to me awful and fanatical nonsense. In a sense they also evade criticism, as much as the ghastliness of the Greek gods as depicted in Greek tragedy must evade criticism, since they belong to myth. But the problem with a novel—even a novel as dramatic poem—is that is offers to deal with the real, and we do not have god's advantages. We are only human and our solutions must be human.

If we look at the relationship between Gerald and Gudrun in this light, perhaps the problem is that the metamorphosis doesn't come off, and Gerald doesn't become a god.

> There was about him a curious and almost godlike air of simplicity and naive directness. He reminded her of an apparition, the young Hermes. (WL, 388)

Gerald plunges into her, and he is a man again. "Mother and substance of all life she was." He clings to her like an infant and "he was infinitely grateful, as to God, or as an infant is at its mother's breast." Between this couple there is only the *normal* dependency, the normal love-needs, the normal regression to infantile states (all beautifully described on pages 388–90), but it does not work as it did not work for Lawrence. This is *profane* love. Only when the man is a *god* will it work (because then the woman must submit to a superior power). Where the woman is in the god-role, there is bound to be death. Gerald may be "inevitable as a supernatural being" (WL, 386) in Gudrun's bedroom, but he is not a god so it is no good. So much for Leavis's attempt to draw a moral about the "willed" relationship between Gerald and Gudrun. It is rather a caricature of *normal* relationships, with which the fake god-like ones are contrasted. It is not a question even of idolization, but a question of a fanatical and demented religious delusion being preferred to normal existence. Lawrence secretly believed he is one of the elect, and his unconscious persists in a dogged literalness here.

Of course, in passing, we may note the sodomy and other "shameful" acts perpetrated by Birkin and Mellors—as with Zeus, a god can do no wrong. Without the godliness, there is only, in relationship, as Gudrun sees it,

> the inner, individual darkness, sensation within the ego, the obscene religious, mystery of ultimate reduction, the mystical frictional activities of diabolic reducing down, disintegrating the vital organic body of life. (WL, 508)

God could do without man (WL, 538). What was now needed was "some other being, finer, more wonderful, some new, more lovely race, to carry on the embodiment of creation." To be man was as nothing compared with the possibilities of the creative mystery (WL, 538):

To have one's pulse beating direct from the mystery, this was perfection, unutterable satisfaction. Human or inhuman mattered nothing. Ther perfect pulse throbbed with indescribable being, miraculous unborn species. (WL, 538–39)

Birkin believes he has achieved this; so did Lawrence. It is one thing to defer to the great mystery of existence, but it is surely another to believe that, in a state superior to all other humanity, one has given oneself to the creative pulse and *is* "it."

Perhaps, in the last few pages of *Women in Love*, Lawrence is saying that if only Gerald (the "denier") had *worshipped* Christ–Lawrence–Birkin and become a true disciple, he would have been saved for life!

A clue to the power of this unconscious material is given in *The Horse Dealer's Daughter*: "The life she followed here in the world was far less real than the world of death she inherited from her mother" (p. 355). When we read Lawrence, we need to remind ourselves that the world of death in which he is pursuing the possibilities of bringing the mother back to life is far more real to him than the real world. It is because of this that Lawrence at times really seems to believe he is a god, like the count in *The Ladybird*: "He was something seated in flame, in flame unconscious, seated erect, like an Egyptian King-god in the statues." (SS, 412).

There are occasional phrases that presumably most readers pass by without giving them much attention. Some of these phrases seem not to refer to anything within the story itself; they refer to a continuing universal mythology in Lawrence's mind, as for instance, when Ursula in *The Rainbow* muses on, "The man would come out of Eternity to which she herself belonged" (R, 494, see above p. 000). The reader alert to Lawrence's modes will respond inwardly "Guess who?"

Lawrence assiduously endorses, through his characters, his idolization of himself. When Ursula's lover does come, he is a very special human being:

"I think he's attractive, decidedly attractive. What I can't stand about him is his way with other people—his way of treating any little fool as if she were his greatest consideration. One feels so awfully sold, oneself. . . ."
    One *must* discriminate," repeated Gudrun. "But he's a wonderful chap, in other respects—a marvellous personality." (WL, 23)

The special consideration to which Gudrun refers is given to women. We have traced through *The Rainbow* and *Women in Love* the continual declarations that "Humanity is a dead letter," while ordinary men are later seen from *Lady Chatterley* to *The Plumed Serpent* as "carrion bodied" to "mongrels." While Birkin thinks "man is a mistake and must go," he believes in the "unseen hosts" (WL, 144) and displays a "certain insufferable aloof superiority." While Ursula objects to this, and sometimes denounces it refreshingly, Lawrence's view of his Birkin-self is ambivalent. he continues to think of himself as "wonderful":

> There was this wonderful, desirable life-rapidity, the rare quality of an utterly
> desirable man, and there was at the same time this ridiculous, mean effacement
> into a Salvator Mundi type and a Sunday-school teacher, a prig of the stiffest type.
> (WL, 144)

The Salvator Mundi, however, gradually triumphs, despite this self-criticism, as in the solemn incantations later of *The Plumed Serpent*, in which the Lawrence self is split into two, Ramón and Cipriano. I cannot help feeling that the self-deification of Lawrence has something to do with this homosexual dynamic. Perhaps here one might explore the narcissistic element psycho-analysis has diagnosed in homosexuality (the desire to find on one's partner only one's own kind of organ of gender). In Lawrence this dynamic seems to move away from the human and human solutions altogether.

Perhaps we can say about *Women in Love* that it assails courageously the problem of what love and marriage are, and how they relate to the problem of life—the problem of the meaning of existence, but the novel was written out of a tormented condition of persisting grief for the mother, whose funereal presence persisted in his unconscious. Because of her the female element is full of dangers, and so Lawrence seeks in various ways to symbolize the necessary subjugation of the woman. This is vindicated by a yearning toward the beyond-human, the inhuman, where the old human horrors are transcended: stars and angels. But one realm of this beyond-the-dangers-of-woman-love lies the possibility of "ultimate" pure man-love. This has both a narcissistic quality, and a ghostly quality.

The last few pages reveal Lawrence's characteristic twentieth-century predicament. God is dead. Woman is the source of meaning in being, in love-relationship. But what if that kind of relationship is itself full of dread and death unless control can be exerted by raising it to the god-like state, with the human daughter in submission? Maybe a more ultimate love can be found in some ultimate relationship with a man? Yet men can have a death-impulse, too.

The clue to creative fulfillment is not found because the central fulfilling couple are not related to any real community, to any life-tasks, and they do not contemplate children—and so a future. Nothing draws them out of themselves, to serve the world and find meaning and continuity.

None of the characters are able to love: what fulfillment means Lawrence seems unable to find, since Birkin remains in the end unsatisfied. There does seem to be a clue that even Birkin and Ursula fail to achieve mutual orgasm:

> She knew he loved her: she was sure of him. Yet she could not let go a certain hold
> over herself, she could not bear him to question her. She gave herself up in delight
> to being loved by him. She knew that, in spite of his joy when she abandoned herself,
> he was a little bit saddened too. She could give herself up to this activity. But she
> could not be herself. She *dared* not come forth quite naked to his nakedness,
> abandoning all adjustment, lapsing in pure faith with him. She abandoned herself

to him, or she took hold of him and gathered her joy of him. And she enjoyed him fully. But they were never *quite* together, at the same moment, one was always a little left out. Nevertheless she was glad in hope, glorious and free, full of life and liberty. And he was still and soft and patient, for the time, (WL, 490)

What does Lawrence mean? Did he know what he meant? Behind his confusion lies his own tormented feelings about the failure to achieve sexual harmony, combined with the distress caused by Frieda's love affairs, Gudrun's affair with the decadent Loerke's being a portrayal of the kind of thing Lawrence had to endure. In this anguish Lawrence could not but reject "the horrible privacy of domestic and connubial satisfaction," and turned increasingly toward the impulse to declare "man is a mistake" and "I hate humanity. I wish it was swept away." While Loerke embodies much that Lawrence hated in his attitudes to sexuality and art, he also embodies much that was growing in the compromising Lawrence himself:

"Pah—*l'amour*. I detest it. *L'amour, l'amore, die liebe*—I detest it in every language. Women and love, there is no greater tedium," he cried.
    She was slightly offended. And yet this was her own basic feeling. Men and love—there was no greater tedium. (WL, 516)

The whole of *Women in Love* vibrates with this theme of dissatisfaction with love—even from one who, like Birkin, is seeking a new religion through sexual meeting. It is a manifestation of desperation.

*    *    *

As one reads through Lawrence, one finds an archetypal story emerging. It belongs, as I have suggested, to the unconscious topography in Lawrence's psyche, which I am trying to understand in terms of bereavement and his earliest experience of the mother who is dead.

We see in *Sons and Lovers* how Miriam proved to be impossible as a partner because she threatened to usurp the mother's place. In life Frieda seems to have transcended this problem, but one aspect of it remained, in that by making a relationship with her Lawrence was performing an oedipal act of supplanting Professor Weekley, the father of Frieda's children. At the same time, as we can see in the poems, his mother's ghost haunts his honeymoon and the novels he wrote just after, and as I have suggested, his quest for meaning in love is an attempt to give meaning to his mother's life, and even to give her a rich sexual experience.

The archetypal Lawrence story therefore contains the following elements:

1. A woman is unawakened.
2. She may be involved in a dead marriage.
3. Along comes a figure who is often a dynamic of Lawrence himself in disguise.
4. This figure *brings back the woman from the dead.*

5. He is a god, or has magical powers; the yearning is towards the nonhuman or transhuman.

6. The consummation takes place in the outdoors or in a hut, often associated with hunters and wild animals, away from the human world of ordinary coupling and in defiance of it. (The house is too much like home and the parental bed is death.)

7. The woman revived from the dead is very dangerous and must be brought, by a lordly kind of treatment, to submit, and by aggressive handling to adore. She must *worship* the man.

8. Or she may turn malignant and turn on the protagonist (as in *The Princess*). Because of this the most successful men protagonists are capable of murder (Cipriano, Jack in *Kangaroo*, the Fox), and murder is necessary to maintain *power* over her.

The nature of the male protagonist is of great interest since this illuminates Lawrence's philosophical anthropology. He is "different," and his exceptional powers are those of an uncanny *animal quality*, or animal-handling quality. He is usually good with horses, (and these horses may be seen as symbols of "the shadow": in Jung's terms the hero male must be particularly skilled in dealing with the mother's Animus). The preeminent Lawrentian hero isn't an educated, civilized intelligence: he tends to be a loner or outcast. Morever, additional aspects are:

9. It is the "machine," "out there," that is the "enemy," and this is often declared with great intensity, verging on the paranoid. It manifests itself in white lights (and we may associate this with the Moon-mother's face).

10. The awakening (as in *The Virgin and the Gypsy*) often turns out to be a single event. It is no guarantee of an ongoing love relationship. (It is a one-off Resurrection.)

11. Apart from this god-like resurrection, all other relationships, belonging to ordinary coupling, are of no importance: one must rise above them.

12. So long as the central self and his woman are saved, all humanity is rejected, together with the future of human kind.

# 5

# Authenticity and Inauthenticity: *Mr Noon*, *The Lost Girl*, and *Aaron's Rod*

Our whole perspective on Lawrence's work must surely be altered by reading the full text of *Mr Noon*, which was published complete by Cambridge University Press in 1984.[1] Even though this work was never published in its day, its effect as an autobiographical novel shifts completely the grounds of our understanding of all Lawrence's works, not least where sexuality is concerned.

*Mr Noon* raises important questions of the relationship between Lawrence's own life and his art. The editor of this volume, Lindeth Vasey, tells us that "it is an obvious trap...to make over-simple correspondences between Lawrence's art and his life," but perhaps no other work is so closely a fictionalized autobiography, and the important biographical episodes are hidden in the notes. Our attention is drawn to the history of the actual writing of the novel, but the quite staggering revelations in it, confirmed by evidence from biographical sources, are tucked away in the notes. How commonly known is it, for example, that Frieda was unfaithful to her new husband on their honeymoon?[2] And that both she and her sister had love affairs with the German sex revolutionary Gross whose letters she kept all her life?

*Mr Noon*, of course, was never published in any final form approved by Lawrence, and so our criticism of it can never be just, but we must be concerned with its final "upshot." What *Mr Noon* reveals is that Lawrence was seriously compromised by the circumstances of his own marriage, and by the influence of German sexual revolutionism. As we shall see, there were two developments pulling in different directions. On the one hand, Frieda's "free" approach to sexuality helped Lawrence over his problems of bringing together in woman the ideal and the libidinal (so clear, for instance, in the abandoned Prologue to *Women in Love*), and undoubtedly he loved her. On the other hand, there was a deep resentment in him, and an unconscious fear of woman, which impelled him to seek very strange solutions to the sexual problem.

Lawrence began *Mr Noon* in May 1920, but despite several attempts never finished it. Part I was published in *A Modern Lover* in 1934 (this was later collected in *Phoenix II* in 1969). Part II was only published for the first time in 1984. The historical sequence is discussed at length in the Introduction. The publication of *Kangaroo* in 1923 may have affected Lawrence's feelings about the unpublished work; it precluded the use again of the war material. *Aaron's Rod*, finished in 1921, asserted a different view of the relationship between man and woman from that in the earlier works, and this novel makes clearer the new direction. Marriage after 1921 is seen as unsatisfactory because women are too concerned with pleasing themselves sexually—the way forward is proper submission to the man. Lindeth Vasey sees Part II of *Mr Noon* as an "elegaic backward glance to Lawrence's old belief in the primacy of the loving relationship between man and woman." But is it? A closer examination seems to reveal that Lawrence records in it an unsolved perplexity of not being able to resolve two opposing views of man-woman relationships. If I am right, there is a serious dissociation between what he wants explicitly to do in the novel, and what lies beneath the surface.

We suppose that Lawrence was striving towards Jung's kind of individuation. His protagonists talk like this:

> "What I want is a strange conjunction with you—not meeting and mingling—but an equilibrium, a pure balance of two single beings—as the stars balance each other." (WL, 164)

This is Lawrence's yearning at best. And at best he sought integration, and a recognition that

> Through the mode of dynamic objective apprehension, which is our day we have gradually come to call imagination, a man may in his time add on to himself the whole of the universe, by increasing pristine realization of the universal. This in mysticism is called the progress to infinity ... *Psychoanalysis and the Unconscious*, 1960 Viking ed, 40. See also Gordon, 1978 on Lawrence and individuation.

This is all very fine, and seems to indicate that "religious" aspect of Lawrence's quest. However, when we read *Mr Noon* we find a curious light is thrown on a number of Lawrence's proclivities.

Gerald Noon, in the first part of the novel, "is" George Neville, Lawrence's youthful friend with whom he used to have the kind of adolescent discussions of woman and sex one has at that time. The essence of the first part is that Gilbert has a "spoony" sexual adventure with a meaningless girl for whom the author has only spiteful contempt. Her father catches them *in flagrante* and fights with the man. Later he finds out his identity from his name in a book on *Conic Sections* (Gilbert read maths at Trinity and is a maths teacher) and writes to the Education Authorities. Gilbert is sacked—as Neville was, in reality, for a similar offense. Neville did actually make a girl pregnant, and married her, disastrously. Lawrence said of this, as Mason points out, "Thank God ... I've been saved from that ... so far." (ET, 1935, 126) This predicament of Neville's was, says H. A. Mason,[3] "one of the greatest sex-shocks Lawrence ever felt," and it was the consequence of what Lawrence's mother

called "only five-minutes self-forgetfulness." Jessie Chambers reported all
this:

> He told me these things in a voice that sounded sick with misery, and I felt very
> concerned, wondering why he should take it so to heart. Then he startled me, by
> bursting out vehemently: "Thank God ... I've been saved from that ... so far."
> ("ET", 1935, 126)

In Part II, Gilbert becomes D. H. Lawrence, and the novel becomes a record
of his early days with Frieda. The tone and manner are quite different, and
there are those lovely descriptions of places and people in Germany—prose
parallels to the honeymoon poems in *Look! We Have Come Through!* The
beautiful and awe-inspiring countryside has a profound effect on Gilbert's
soul, but our trouble as readers is that we do not feel very convinced that the
Mr Noon of the first section has a soul like that of the Mr Noon of Part II,
while Gilbert of Part II is not the Paul Morel figure, with poetic depth of
feeling, of *Sons and Lovers*. He is never endowed with Lawrence's zest,
intelligence, fervour, passion, or creativity; he is a cipher, a ninny, who is
simply steered about, occasionally thinking to himself "By Jove, this is a real
love affair." When Johanna barks at him like a dog, the implicit criticism is
all too near the bone.

By contrast with Lawrence, Gilbert is totally uninteresting, and on one
occasion, when a waiter walks away from him muttering "Imbecile!" we can
only concur, as we do when the Baron calls him a *Gewöhnlicher Lump*.
Although Lawrence tells us that this couple live on a superior plane in "the
love of two splendid opposites" in which she is "a she cat who would give him
claw for claw," Gilbert is never the forceful Lawrence who stands up to his
woman standing up to him. On her part, she is more of a trollop than a tiger.
Lawrence tells us they are "beautiful brinded creatures," but Johanna remains
an unscrupulous baggage and Gilbert an unattractive nonentity. And while
Lawrence strives to turn the story into comedy, all that comes over is an
unpleasant facetiousness, often directed against the reader, whom he seems to
identify with some hostile Sunday newspaper critic who had offended him.

The failure of tone is inevitable, because of the falsity of his moral and
existential position. Indicatively, what goes seriously wrong is the sexual
"wisdom." Gilbert, for instance, is commended by Johanna for having made
love three times in a quarter of an hour—"So well, too." It is impossible
to know what to say about such a report: one doesn't want to labor its
ludicrousness and impossibility. What can Lawrence have meant? (Why did
Frieda never correct it?)

There are moments all the same that ring true and beautiful:

> As she rolled over in the pallid, pure, bluey-effervescent stream, and he saw her
> magnificent broad white shoulders, and her knot of hair, envy, and an almost hostile
> desire filled him. She came from the water full-blown like a water-flower, naked and

delighted with her element. And she lay spread in the sun on the clear shingle. And he sat in his lean, unyielding nudity upon a geat pinkish boulder, and he looked at her, still with the dark eyes of a half-hostile desire and envy. Strange enemies they were, as a white seagull and a gold land-hawk are enemies. And he brooded, looking at her as her strong bosom rose and fell, and the full breasts lay sideways. And with a sort of inward rage he wished he could see her without any darkness of desire disturbing his soul. (MN, 211)

This is perhaps evidently a first draft (there are too many "ands"), but it is the true Lawrence, in which the deeper sexual polarity and the "difference" is *done*.

There are moments when what I call the true Lawrence surfaces, but what surely emerges in *Mr Noon* is a radical division between this Lawrence who belongs to the great English tradition of authenticity in the novel and a Lawrence who is confused by the casuistry of sexual revolutionism.

At the beginning of *Mr Noon* the protagonist, Gilbert, is released from his English moral ideas by a view of the Alps; his English standards suddenly seem to him too "tight." Soon, he meets Johanna and within a few minutes she is asking him up to her room. The attitudes to sexual relationships of the English Midlands, one might say, come into contact with those of Bohemian Schwabing. As we find, in Johanna are embodied the principles of the revolutionism of Otto Gross: *pleasure is the only source of value.*

What *Mr Noon* reveals is the powerful influence of Otto Gross on Frieda, such as is examined by Martin Green in his book *The Van Richthofen Sisters: The Triumphant and the Magic Modes of Love* (1974), all of which illuminates a great deal in Lawrence's later work. We must look for a while at Gross. Gross was disappointed with Freud, and needed ideas that would release him more completely from paternal authority. He found these in Nietzsche and in anarchism, both of which influences were powerful in Schwabing, in the Cosmic Circle, and the Aktion Gruppe. Also influential in this atmosphere were Kropotkin and the sinister figure of Max Stirner, the egotistical nihilist.

For many years Gross exerted a profound influence on women and men in Germany's anarcho-nihilistic Bohemia. He may be surely placed among those fanatical moral inversionists whom Michael Polanyi discusses in *Knowing and Being*. Like de Sade, he sought to declare (as de Sade does through one of his characters), "I have destroyed everything in my heart that might interfere with my pleasures." Gross's ruthlessness stopped at nothing. Gross had a particular preoccupation with Cain and seems to have had a responsibility for the deaths of a number of women. He gave his mistress Sophie Benz poison with which she killed herself; he knew she was in a suicidal mental condition but refused to commit her to an institution. This was not the first such event. In 1906 Otto had given poison to Fraulein Lotte Chatemmer in Ascona, and she too killed herself (this was after she had refused to come to him for psychiatric treatment). He would have been prosecuted for this, had not his father, Hanns Gross, forced him to undergo psychiatric treatment. Stekel diagnosed Gross as severely neurotic, and Jung diagnosed him later as schizophrenic.

The suicides of Sophie Benz and Lotte Chatemmer could be seen as forms of euthanasia, but they could also be seen as manifestations of an insane hatred of woman. In 1913 Gross was arrested on the orders of Hanns Gross, his father, by the Berlin police, as a dangerous psychopath. C. G. Jung issued a certificate to that effect, and Gross was taken to Austria to be confined in an asylum. Hanns Gross, the father, certainly seems to have shown paternal tyranny. He sought a legal suit to deprive Gross's wife Frieda of her legal rights as mother and wife. (She was also a disciple of sexual freedom and was living with Ernst Frick the anarchist.) Hanns Gross wanted the child Peter to live with him and the other children to be denied the name of Gross.

So Otto Gross became a martyr with the Bohemian public, to the Father and Son struggle, and there was much discussion in the press. Jung edited a symposium in defense of Otto, and the Akademische Verband für Literatur und Musik in Vienna printed ten thousand handbills saying "Free Otto Gross." He was released on the condition he went into analysis with Stekel.

Gross now wrote a new Ethic, and through this and other publications, he and Jung provided the inspiration for the German Dadaist movement. It was Gross's view, as expressed in his *Aktion* essays, that the psychology of the unconscious is the philosophy of revolution. (We can see how anarchistic contemporary writers like R. D. Laing are the heirs of Gross.)

The poet Werfel was one of the writers figuring in this milieu. Alma Mahler seems to have been engaged, no doubt inspired by Mahler's evocation of love, to battle for Werfel's mind against Gross. She records with disgust the dirt, disorder, and vice of the Gross circles in which she found Werfel. And Green points out that both Frieda and Alma took their lovers away from the major theorist of the sexual revolution, but the powerful ideas lived on.

Martin Green, after noting Gross's death, goes on to discuss the ideas of the "Cosmic Circle." The *Kosmische Runde* stood for life-values, for eroticism, for the value of myth and primitive cultures, for the superiority of instinct and intuition to the values of science, for the primacy of the female mode of being. There is also an existential component:

> One must trust to the life process itself, to Life. Reason and the culture of Reason hypostatizes life by weighing, counting, measuring everything. But life is a flowing, a process immeasurable. (Green, 1974, summarizing Klages, p. 79)

There is a great deal in the philosophies of the Cosmic Circle that finds its way into the more mystical and didactic parts of Lawrence's work, and there are dark areas of belief in "blood" that suggest an undeniable affinity with Nazi ideology. (Max Weber was repelled by the *Kosmische Runde*.) The danger was that the sensualization of existence urged by these sexual revolutionaries tended to go with the dissolution of political organization and the decline of political life. Their common theme was the way "society" has confined man's potentialities, and in this the mind is the soul's enemy: we may find traces of this anti-intellectualism in Lawrence. Despite his moderation, Lawrence's "blood-knowledge" belongs to the Germanic revolutionary myths as Green shows, not least in his worst "Almanacking." Green compares Lawrence's foreword to *Sons and Lovers* 1913 edition with Bachofen's remarks in *Urreligion*. The chapter in Green is very disturbing (1974, 32–100). Lawrence, as Green says, was not at ease with decadence, but he took on a woman who had been the mistress of a man who declared, "You know my belief that a new *harmony* in life can be generated only by *decadence*—and that the wonderful era we live in is destined, *as the age of decadence*, to be the womb of the great future." Lawrence reiterated that "the whole of our era will have to go": "This process of death has got to be lived through."

These revolutionaries exalted the feminine principle ("Everywhere the material, feminine, natural principle has the advantage"), and (according to Green) they attached considerable importance to the dominant woman, a role assumed by Frieda Weekley. Green declares.

> In this crucible were fused those ideas of the Meaning of Life, of the Earth, of Woman, which inspired Otto Gross to his mission in life, which gave Frieda Weekley her glorious identity, which gave D. H. Lawrence the informing ideas of his art. (Green 1974, 85)

One of these informing ideas is the principle expressed in Lawrence's foreword to *Woman in Love*: "Nothing that comes from the deep, passional self is bad, or can be bad"—a seriously mistaken assumption, surely?

In *Mr Noon* Johanna was only with Eberhard, she says, for two weeks. It seems sexual revolutionaries are not the kind who can sustain a relationship.[4] He was "a marvellous lover," of course, if only for a fortnight.

> "But I knew it was no good. He never let one sleep. He talked and talked. Oh he was so marvellous. I once went with him to a zoo place. And you know he could work up the animals, by merely looking at them, till they nearly went mad."
>
> "A psychiatrist."
>
> "Perhaps! Perhaps! He took drugs. And he never slept. He just never slept. And he wouldn't let you sleep either. And he talked to you while he was loving you. He was wonderful, but he was awful—He would have sent me mad. Perhaps I am a bit mad now. . . . He was so beautiful, like a white Dionysus . . . . You couldn't try to keep a man like that . . . . The only thing I couldn't quite stand, was that he would have two women, or more, going at the same time." (MN, 126–27)

This was the genius at love: "spiritual"—"he may have been demoniacal, but he was spiritual."

As Johanna speaks, we hear Lawrence talking in the same voice:

> "He made me believe in love—in the sacredness of love. He made me see that marriage and all those things are based on fear. How can love be wrong? . . . then there can't be love without sex . . . . Love *is* sex. But you can have your sex all in your head, like the saints did. But that I call a sort or perversion. Don't you? Sex is sex, and ought to find its expression in the proper way—don't you think?" (MN, 127)

The Lawrence antipathy to "sex in the head" and Clifford's kind of verbalizing impulse perhaps came from Gross via Frieda. Sex in the head may be a "perversion," but so, too, may be sex divorced from love and meaning, as writers like Rollo May and Victor Frankl have reported. It can lead to a "decadent sensualism" that has become detached from love as *sub specie aeternitatis*. Here Johanna looks into Gilbert's eyes and says, "you wouldn't like to come to me?"—and this opens the floodgates of continental amoralism.

*Mr Noon* failed as a work of art because Lawrence could not get the tone right, and this is not merely a question of style. The unfinished, unpublished novel shows him in a deep moral conflict, which is also an existential conflict. The best part of the book is the middle section that is the prose parallel to the honeymoon poems. In the descriptions of the Tyrol and the valley of the Isar, these pages are beautiful, and they reveal the sense of a widening horizon that his marriage to Frieda brought to Lawrence.

There is a lovely description of the Alps:

> The great Isar valley lay beneath them in the spring morning, the pale icy green river winding its way from the far Alps, coming as it were down the long stairs of the far foot-hills, between shoals of pinkish sand. (MN, 107)

This scenery is said to have had a profound effect on Gilbert:

> The sense of space was an intoxication for him. He felt he could walk without stopping on to the far north-eastern magic of Russia, or south to Italy. All the big spreading glamour of mediaeval Europe seemed to envelop him.... The bigness: that was what he loved so much. The bigness, and the sense of an infinite multiplicity of connections. There seemed to run gleams and shadows from the vast spaces of Russia, a yellow light seemed to struggle through the great Alp-knot from Italy. (MN, 107)

These "seemed to break his soul like a chrysalis into a new life."

In these passages we find clues to the enormous changes that come over Lawrence, when after falling in love with Frieda, he was introduced to her aristocratic German background, to Europe, and to this larger perspective. It was not simply a geographical change. It implied a new rejection of his roots—the roots not only of the Midlands community (such as is embodied in *The Rainbow*) but also in his absorption of religion and its cultural modes, and of English literary culture itself:

> For the first time he saw England from the outside: tiny she seemed, and tight, and so partial, Such a little bit among all the vast rest. Whereas till now she had seemed all-in-all in herself. Now he knew it was not so. Her all-in-allness was a delusion of her natives. Her marvellous truths and standards and ideals were just local, not universal. They were just a piece of local pattern, in what was really a vast, complicated, far-reaching design. (MN, 107)

There seems to be no doubt that these paragraphs are a record of an experience that happened to Lawrence.

And he became unEnglished. His tight and exclusive nationality seemed to break down in his heart. He loved the world in its multiplicity, not in its horrible oneness, uniformity, homogeneity ... it was so nice to be one among many, to feel the horrible imprisoning oneness and insularity collapsed, a real delusion broken, and to know that the universal ideals and morals were after all only local and temporal. (MN, 108)

The unEnglishing of Lawrence may have widened his perspectives as a novelist. On the other hand, his best work surely remains well within the English tradition. In *Mr Noon* there are passages by the great novelist, not least the moments of supreme comedy. There are moments captured from the early love affair—as when the lovers are surprised by a caller in their cheap hotel; or by the woman's mother, the Baroness, whom they see coming up the road when they are only hastily clothed after an act of love; or when they try to cope with a huge feather bed; or enjoy the simple food and village life of remote and lovely places; or when they sleep and make love in an uncomfortable and icy hay hut; or when Johanna mocks him by pretending to be a dog on all fours. The world is seen in these scenes with all the intensity and meaning that love yields, and as so often in Lawrence, it is when he can bring to life a real woman to challenge him, he achieves real art. His *daemon* can really speak.

The fly in the ointment of Lawrence's attitudes to marriage is Frieda herself, portrayed here as Johanna. It seems possible that a strong reason for not completing and publishing *Mr Noon* was that it was too revealing a portrait of her. And it certainly makes clear to us the degree to which Frieda had experienced, has been influenced by, and *admired*, the Otto Gross whose position was one of contempt for all normal human bonds. The truth, revealed in Johanna, is that such a woman is morally repulsive. Johanna and Lotte are shown in this book—willy-nilly—to be unscrupulous and deceitful. They have learnt from Gross not only to be compulsively promiscuous ("In nice men I understand such a lot that I feel *forced* to have them"—Johanna), but also to erect into moral principles and political programes their own immoralist and duplicitous behavior. It was surely Gross who taught Johanna to say, "I think the noblest thing is to overcome jealousy" (MN, 165) and to turn her nymphomania into a belief that "I believe one should love as much as one can"—which really means "give sex as much as one can." We are on the road to the Chatterley maxim that "warm-hearted fucking" will redeem the world.

Johanna is clearly a nymphomaniac, whatever Grossian rationalizations she might have put forward for her promiscuity. The strange thing is Lawrence's failure to *place* this. Unashamedly reporting her erotic encounter on a train with the Japanese she declares that after meeting another Japanese,

"I always knew after that that I wanted a brown baby. Yet there I've got an honest English husband and two sweet boys, and I'm adored for being a white snowflower. Don't you think it strange?" (MN, 125)

She jibes at Gilbert's Englishness, because she believes he, too, wants the "snowflower." This is a jibe at the cold English belief that fidelity matters and that deceit and betrayal are reprehensible. So what are we to make of it? She boldly reveals that her affair with Eberhart (Gross) was quite recent, long after she was married, and after having Gilbert she immediately entertains Captain Daumling, who is estranged from his wife. Other lovers are mentioned, without even being filled in as people.

The most revealingly significant episode in *Mr Noon* comes towards the end of the novel, when the protagonist Gilbert and his woman Johanna are walking in the Alps. The episode is clearly autobiographical and based on Lawrence's honeymoon.

> "I want to tell you something." He stood on the stony-rocky little path on the slope-face, with the black mass of the valley-head curving round, and the gulf of the darkening valley away below....
> "I want to tell you. Stanley had me the night before last."
> Everything went vague around them.
> "Where?"
> "The evening we slept at the Gemserjoch hut." The vagueness deepened. Night, loneliness, danger, all merged.
> "But when?..."
> "...He had me in the hay-hut—he told me he wanted me so badly...."
> ...it was such a surprise to him, that he did not know what to feel, or if he felt anything at all. It was such a complete and unexpected statement that it had not really any meaning for him. (MN, 276)

The difficulty Lawrence had writing this scene reveals the pain that lay under the surface, and the way in which he seeks to compromise: the conflict shows in the style. It is this devastating record of Frieda's infidelity on honeymoon that is central to *Mr Noon*, to its ambivalence, and Lawrence's inability to finish it. (Of course, Gilbert and Johanna are not on honeymoon, though to the English mind she would be considered to be committed to him. The autobiographical episodes, however, quite clearly come from Lawrence's own experience.)

How confused the response is may be seen from the contradiction in atmosphere. At one level, a deep sense of shock sets in. Everything goes vague around them: "Night, loneliness, danger, all merged." Significantly there is no great response realized in Gilbert, and the matter is dealt with in limpid tones that remind one of the school-girlish prose of the present-day fashionable woman novelist:

> it was such a surprise to him; that he did not know what to feel, or if he felt anything at all. It had not any meaning for him.

Absurdly (and it is surely sheer sentimentality and falsity?), Gilbert *throws his arms round her*! "Never mind, my love,' he said. 'Never mind. Never mind. We do things we don't know we're doing.'"

"He rose above the new thrust on wings of death": this lame phrase is as much as Lawrence can do here by way of registering the shock in its menace to loyalty and integrity—to *meaning*. It is impossible to believe that the author of *Look! We Have Come Through!* ("And, God, that she is necessary!"), or the poem *Fidelity* could write like this about a moment of betrayal.

The prose registers Lawrence's deep sense of shock, as with the ominous description of the landscape, the "vagueness," and the sense of "loneliness, danger," and he then summons up a completely false irony, to alter the perspective:

> Johanna did not at all care for the conclusion "that it did no matter." Those marvellous pearls of spiritual love. "I love you—and so what did it matter!" fell on completely stony ground. (MN, 277)

Gilbert has said that "things we don't know we are doing . . . they don't signify. They don't signify really, do they? They don't really mean anything, do they? I love you—and so what does it matter" (MN, 276)—yet Lawrence must ridicule this response. Gilbert tries to kiss Johanna passionately, but she is mute and unresponsive, quite unyielding. What exactly is happening? Why does she tell him?

> "Didn't you *know*? Didn't you suspect anything?" said Johanna, rather gloomy.
> "No," he answered, with his clear face of innocence.
> "No—never. It wouldn't have occurred to me." (MN, 227)

She feels "rather put out" by his passionate spiritual forgiveness; "put in a false position than ever before." It is (under the confusions of Grossian philosophy) even as if *she* is the victim of humiliation, rather than him: "forgiveness is a humiliating thing to the one forgiven." But wasn't the humiliation his when she is unfaithful to him? And doesn't she suggest she *wanted* him to suspect—so, what were her motives? Were they not full of hostility?

Lawrence's misery is evident in the undercurrents of those last pages. He is, of course, writing of the events same time afterwards, and knows as he writes what is going to happen. In the previous chapter, Gilbert is afraid of the mountains:

> Gilbert was really rather frightened. There was something terrific about this upper world. Things which looked small and near were rather far, and when one reached them, they were big, great masses where one expected stones, jagged valley where one saw just a hollow groove. (MN, 263)

The topography is imbued with the record of Lawrence's world being totally unheaved, and his perception damaged.

Such terrible, such raw, such stupendous masses of the rock-element heaved and confused. Such terrible order in it all . . . he felt all the suspended mass of unutterably fierce rocks round him, he knew it was not human, not life-size. It was all bigger than life-size, much bigger, and fearful, (MN, 263)

There is a menace in the air, and in the mountains that frighten him Gilbert sees "the eternal and everlasting loneliness."
Time and time again references to the Christ figures and their symbolic form becomes clear:

a last little crucifix—the small wooden Christ all silvery-naked, a bit of old oak, under his hood. And neither Stanley nor Gilbert made any jokes. He was so old and rudimentary. (MN, 265)

But He is also an image of humiliation and betrayal. In his anguish over woman, Gilbert finds his mother ideal in the mountains:

a great peak, a magnificent wedge of iron thrust into the upper air, and slashed with snow-slashes as if it were dazzlingly alive . . . it was one of the perfect things of all life, that single great sky-living blade of rock. . . .
    He had to go to a brow to look clear *at his queen*. She was beyond this valley—and beyond other valleys. Other, blunter peaks rose about her. Yet she lifted her marvellous dark slopes clear. . . . And he was satisfied—one of the eternal satisfactions that man can find on his life-way. He felt a pure, immortal satisfaction—a perfected aloneness. (MN, 266–67; my italics)

The infidelity has already happened by this time, and it drives Lawrence–Gilbert back to a terrible aloneness with the Dead Mother as a peak of Mother Earth. When they descend, they see another Christ:

At the back sat a ghastly life-size Christ, streaked livid with blood, and with an awful, dying, almost murderous-looking face. He was so powerful too—*and like a man in the flush of life who realises he has just been murdered.* (MN, 268; my italics)

The notes tell us this is in a chapel near St. Jacob at Larch (see "Christ in the Tyrol," *Phoenix* 85 and "The Crucifix Across the Mountains," *Twilight in Italy*), but it does not tell us that this is how Lawrence, from his true daemon, saw himself after Frieda has murdered *him*, even in the flush of life. The letters INRI over Christ's head are jeered at by the man who has betrayed Gilbert as spelling "Inry":

"There's Inry selling joints," said Stanley sardonically.
But Gilbert was startled, shocked, and he could not forget. Why?
*Why this awful thing in a fine, big new shrine?*
*Why this.* (MN, 268; my italics)

How could this ugly death be delivered to him, in the heart of his new sacredness of marriage?—The meaning is clear, and Gilbert is in a frenzy to get out of his situation. "He realised that his fever, his frenzy was something unnatural." Gilbert felt afraid: "A distinct sense of fear possessed him." (The evidence of this all being autobiographical is (say the notes) in David Garnett's *Golden Echo* 247-8 and *Letters* i.444.) All this ominousness is leading to the anguished discovery of Frieda–Johanna's betrayal.

The next chapter is headed "A Setback": that, according to his propaganda position, is all it is to Lawrence, at the level of rationalization. From this time on, his position is totally falsified because he must try to exculpate Frieda—or at least try to establish an immoralist atmosphere in which questions of damage, harm, murder, and the destruction of meaning do not matter. The daemon knows better: "Gilbert felt rather in an alas-and-alas mood. His spirits had all gone flat." (MN, 272)

The profound corruptness of Lawrence's compromise with Frieda's promiscuity is indicated by his falsification here:

> The words fell into the deep geysers of his soul, leaving it apparently untroubled. But in the end the irritable waters would boil up over this same business. (MN, 278)

Is that all? The onus is thrown on the "irritable waters"; it is as though they will be annoyingly disturbed, when he would prefer them not to be. Yet there is a sneaking recognition that he is only "apparently untroubled," and the real catastrophe is hidden by his attempt at compromise. So he must try to write of a sympathetic character in such a moment, but without passion or feeling. Under the influence of Grossian revolutionism, he must make Gilbert think, "'he believed people must do what they want to do'" (MN, 273). This comes not from an imaginative realization of the episode, but from the propaganda for sexual liberation that Lawrence wanted to believe.

*Why not*? This question suddenly emerges in Lawrence's reflection, over another earlier sudden sexual adventure by "Johanna." All Lawrence can say is that Gilbert's soul has a nasty tendency to to "all acid and hard" over the infidelity—as if this was just some Antediluvian English response to the new Alpine perspectives of European sex.

As for Johanna, she just believes in love all round. When any man who needs it comes along, she must give it to him, whatever happens to bonds:

> He knew that Johanna believed in much love, à la Magdalen. "For she hath loved much." And he himself, Gilbert, he could stand aside for a moment. (MN, 277)

However, she declares, "It wasn't much, anyhow. It meant nothing to me. I believe he was impotent." But wouldn't she have known? This is the most extraordinary aspect of *Mr Noon*—some of the references to sexual matters seem to have no real experience behind them.

Beneath the unsatisfactory surface on *Mr Noon* there is a record of a humiliation. When they see a crucifix, Stanley sings the music hall song about Henry VIII, a notoriously fickle husband, the symbolism of the comparison between a supposedly sexual promiscuous king and the king of the Jews is obvious. As we also know, Lawrence identified closely with Christ—and the end of the book is full of those images of crucified figures of Christ, some broken and dilapidated. When depressed, Lawrence used to sit with his head bowed, and we can see in these broken hanging figures a picture of his inner soul. Frieda's infidelity, he is telling us, crucified him.

When Emily Kahn, in *Lorenzo*, says that

> Lawrence was always jealous and had already accused Frieda of betraying him with a woodcutter with whom she spent several hours on an island on the Isar—and he might well have been right. (Hahn, 1975, 127)

I used to find this difficult to believe, but *Mr Noon* confirms it as true. Looking back at the poems, one may find, I believe, the same dismay now revealed in them, as in the poem *Misery*:

> Out of this oubliette pot between the mountains...
> Why don't I go?
> Why do I crawl about this pot, this oubliette, stupidly?
> Why don't I go?
> But where? (CP, 224)

The next poem is about one of the crucifixes:

> at the foot of the sunken Christ
> I stand in a chill of anguish, trying to say
> The joy I bought was not too highly priced. (CP, 225)

What does this mean? I believe it may mean that he wishes he could get right out of a situation in which the woman he loves is compulsively unfaithful, but he cannot, because he wouldn't now know where to go. This is the price of his joy. And at the same time he wrote *Song of a Man Who Is Not Loved*:

> I see myself isolated in the universe, and wonder
> What effect I can have....
>
> I hold myself up, and feel a big wind blowing
> Me like a gadfly into the dusk, without my knowing
> Whither or why or even how I am going. (CP, 222)

The experience obviously brought out Lawrence's deepest fears of woman—the Earth-Woman-as-Death now menaces him (this is after a row between Johanna and Gilbert about a postcard he was writing to a previous girlfriend):

The sudden dark, hairy ravines in which he was trapped: all made him feel he was caught, shut in down below there. He felt tiny, like a dwarf among the great thighs and ravines of the mountains. There is a Baudelaire poem which tells of Nature, like a vast woman lying spread, and man, a tiny insect, creeping between her knees and under her thighs, fascinated. Gilbert felt powerful revulsion against the great slopes and particularly against the tree-dark, hairy ravines in which he was caught. (MN, 251)

We have looked at Lawrence's fears, and if we think about them, they all focus in the female genital. It is there that one ploughs and sows. It is there that one moves mergingly toward the womb or matrix and so from that darkness may emerge the Castrating Mother. In the fantasy of the unconscious, the woman's genital is the gate to the other (grave) world and also the gate by which the witch woman can come into this. As Rosemary Gordon points out from a Jungian perspective, woman is at first the origin of one's being, from the womb; next, the focus of one's search for the union of being; and last, as "Mother Earth," the grave to which one returns. This symbolism of the female image lurks in a man's phenomenology, and with someone like Lawrence, in writing an episode like this, he would inevitably connect the feeling of doom in Gilbert with a female landscape in which his life seems menaced.

The vagina is thus the grave, and when the mother is dead, it is again the place where she lurks. One's impulse to merge with the All-in-All in sexual union draws one into the grave, so the predicament of Gilbert is the doom Lawrence unconsciously expected. It wasn't until I heard a passage from *Mr Noon* read on the radio that I finally understood the symbolic meaning of that last section in the Alps. It is in the intense feeling of loneliness:

The eternal and everlasting loneliness. And the beauty of it, and the richness of it. The everlasting isolation in loneliness, while the sun comes and goes, and night falls and rises. The heart in its magnificent isolation like a peak in heaven, forever. The beauty, the beauty of face, which decrees that in our supremacy we are single and alone, like peaks that finish off in their perfect isolation in the ether. The ultimate perfection of being quite alone. (MN, 264)

It is just at this moment in Gilbert's meditation that Johanna comes back with Stanley.

On the next day they find themselves in a landscape that has a symbolic relevance:

At length they came to a last strange and desolate hollow, a sort of pot with precipice walls on the right. Over the ridge they came, and down the long, slanting track between huge boulders and masses of rock, down into the shallow prison. How was one to get out? They scanned and scanned ahead: but only precipices, and impassable rock-masses, and a thin water-fall. The water fell into the wide, shallow summit-valley. How did it get out again. They could not see. . . . It seemed impossible there was a way out. (MN, 265–66)

This is just before Gilbert comes across his "queen" peak, and feels in its contemplation his "pure, immortal satisfaction—a perfected aloneness."

We may contrast the profound sentiments directed toward Mother Earth here with those depicted, between Johanna and Gilbert, over her infidelity: it doesn't signify, it doesn't matter, it meant nothing. Clearly Lawrence shrinks from the reality of his predicament, toward solace in his thrilling response to the mountains. But, of course, all this is recollected in retrospect, and this makes it all the more terrible: how could one find a way out?

There is a menacing privy: "It consisted simply of a long shaft which descended into unknown and unknowable depths . . . our friends never forgot it" (MN, 273).

The last phrase indicates the autobiographical nature of the story, and the symbol is that of the connection of the natural functions *with the grave*. The tone, however, goes wrong again:

> Do not grumble, gentle reader, at this description. Don't talk to me about bad taste. You will only reveal your own. Strange are the ways of men. And since these are the ways we have to follow, why make any pretence. (MN, 273)

This is a totally false voice, and it suggests that Lawrence knew it was he who was involved in a pretense for he pretends to be telling us "the ways of men," the truth. Yet he is falsifying by denying that this incident was a serious defeat of his whole world.

They pass through desolate villages, with melancholy cow-bells sounding, to a desolate, end-of-the-world-valley-head: "The world was a desert, a cold desert of rock." (MN, 275) Johanna loses her composure, and becomes like a child. It is at this moment, which is like a crisis moment in Bunyan's *Pilgrim's Progress*, that she says "I want to tell you something." (MN, 276) As we have seen, he finds her confession such a shock he denies it, declares it has no meaning: Yet "he slung to her passionately in a sudden passion of *self-annihilation*." (MN, 276, my italics). Johanna declares the infidelity meant nothing to her. "I believe he was impotent"—one of those unbelievable remarks in Lawrence one cannot fathom, for it is hardly a question of belief. "It meant nothing to me,' she said gloomily." But there is another of those crucifixes:

> a little, wind-weathered crucifix. And one leg of the old grey wood had broken at the knee, and hung swinging in the wind from its nail. Funny the Christ looked, like a one-legged soldier; but pitiful, forlorn, the ancient, snow-harried little crucifix, all falling to bits. (MN, 278)

Obviously, a symbol of the deeper self terribly wounded. Hardly surprising that

> a certain heaviness, darkness came over Gilbert. As a heaviness and an inert darkness

follow most exaltations. *He felt he could not see the world. His soul was rather dreary and hard. And he wished he could get back his own real, genuine self.* (MN, 278; my italics)

What "exaltations"? We have seen Gilbert seeking annihilation of the self for the self has become threatened. Can he ever get back his own "real, genuine self"?

When they lose their way, the daemon speaks:

There was some part of his life lost to him. There was some part of his life lost to him. He felt it with hateful fatality. Because he had taken the wrong road. He had made a mistake. He hated now, with deep, acid hatred, to think of the scene on the pass of the pass-head: Johanna's confession and his passionate getting over it. He hated to think of it. His soul was all gone acid and hard. (MN, 279)

Earlier (after quoting Gorky on "the tragedy of the bedroom" and attributing it to Tolstoy whom he calls a "quite comical fool"), Lawrence had written:

Only those who know one another in the intricate dark ways of physical custom can pass through the seven dark hells and the seven bright heavens of sensual fulfilment. And this is why marriage is sacred. And this is perhaps the secret of the English greatness. The English have gone far into the depths of marriage, far down the sensual avenues of the marriage bed, and they have not so easily, like the French or Germans or other nations, given up and turned to prostitution or chastity or some other *pis aller.* (MN, 191)

Of course, Lawrence has to correct himself and say it is all at an end: "*cul de sac* and white-livered fawning." For once he has revealed his true (English) sense of sexual authenticity with those values and standards such as Gilbert is made to dismiss as "tight," are regard as changed once he has became "unEnglished".

The falsity of Lawrence's tone in *Mr Noon* is utterly alien to everything that we admire in the achievement of the great novelist. If there is one thing that we love in Lawrence, it is the sense of total integrity between lovers—Paul to Miriam, Tom to Lydia, Will to Anna, Birkin to Ursula. Even in the couple in *Odour of Chrysanthemums* there is a deep loyalty in marriage, despite the couple's terrible estrangement: a loyalty of the destiny of souls. Suppose any of these had had sexual love with another partner, in a spirit of "why not?" It would be as if the skies had fallen.

As will be seen, the whole problem with *Mr Noon* is that Lawrence cannot help showing in it that to Johanna–Frieda open sex with anyone who turned up, who seemed to want it, had a positive moral purpose, yet in the perspective of his earlier moral approach, his *English* approach we might say, such behavior must surely threaten to make sex meaningless. For if love is sub specie aeternitatis, then mere "naked desire" can have no such reference.

In the Prologue to *Women in Love* Lawrence shows that for him perhaps one escape from inhibition was a compensatory impulse to "be sensual," to go for a woman "the very scent of whose skin soon disgusted him." Frieda's very immoralist sensuality had that kind of appeal, and, it would seem, gave Lawrence a new dimension in what I believe we must call "hate" sex. We may recall, Otto Gross emphanized "polymorphous perversity" as the way to reform society.

Later, the comparison becomes even more complex when in chapter 16, ("Detsch") of *Mr Noon* Lawrence aggressively defends Johanna's sexual activity with Rudolph then ridicules the latter for becoming emotionally involved and hurt, while turning vituperatively upon the reader in defense of his own tone of facetious libertinism. Here *Mr Noon* reveals in a deeply disturbing way that streak of coarse immoralism, and a corruption, that affects much of Lawrence's later work. In this incident alone *Mr Noon* reveals the catastrophe that overtook Lawrence under the influence of Frieda.

Detsch was much warmer than Munich, so Johanna "sunned herself" (it was Otto Gross who called her "sunny" and declared that her sunniness transformed his life), and flirted with her old friend Rudolf von Daumling.

Daumling is based on Udo von Henning, whom Frieda had an affair with in May 1912, two months after she had met Lawrence. He wrote to her "you are using Henning as a dose of morphia" (Lawrence himself had had a woman in his adolescence whom he called Morphia because he had her only for sex). In the novel he presents it in an uncertain manner:

> Johanna, of course, who took her sex as a religion, felt herself bound to administer the cup of consolation him.
> "... You might give any woman a good time, why do you sit moping?" (MN, 139)

She urges him on,

> "But you don't love me, Johanna," he said.
> "Yes, I do, why not?"
> Which is one way of putting it. Why not? (MN, 139)

Despite the public gaze and the lynx-eyed wife, and despite the fact that she has only just awakened Gilbert to his first "cyclone of actual desire," Johanna and Daumling embark on a momentary furtive adulterous affair under the "why not?" posture. The purpose is merely to demonstrate to Daumling that he is still potent:

> She found occasion to draw her old Rudolf to her breast, and even further.
> "Ja *Du*!" she said to him, teasing. "*Du*! *You*! You, to say you can't love any more."
> And he laughed, and blushed, and was restored in his manliness. For in spite of Tolstoi and Chastity, he had found his own impotent purity unmanly, and a sense of humiliation ate into him like a canker. Now that Johanna had demonstrated his

almost splendid capabilities, he felt he had been rather a fool. And he was rather pleased with himself.

But—! But—! He wanted love. And Johanna only loved him because—why not? Well, and why not?

It *ought* to be sufficient reason. (MN, 140)

The tone is disturbingly false. There is on the one hand the attempt to vindicate Johanna's "sexual generosity," yet Gerald speaks of "the tangle and nastiness of it all"—indicating the inevitable inauthenticity and duplicity, which seems close to Lawrence's own experience, and to truth. But where can such a "placing" note come from, if "everything goes"?

Because the tone becomes wrong, a false note creeps in—a tone that is coy in the sickly way of the pornographer, the *Playboy* writer, so familiar to us today. This tone works by salacious understatement, and thrusts upon us a manic vindication of lust: "She found occasion to draw her old Rudolf to her breast, *and even further*" (MN, 140, my italics). The word breast suddenly turns from being a metaphor of compassion, to a pornographic image. Johanna's taunting is that of the courtesan; the reference to his blushes a mark of the seductress' triumph. The phrase "splendid capabilities," again, is the language of the world of liberated sex—a reference to a good, lasting erection. This often seems the language of pornography, the jovial tone that of the lascivious writer.

Lawrence tries to vindicate this corrupt language by his reference to Tolstoi and purity, and endorses Johanna's *curative* posture to her nymphomania. He is here, Pandarus-like, giving his full endorsement to her "why not?" while jeering at the captain's desire for love: for—we have to say—the *meaningful sex* that could help him.

Now elsewhere, of course, we have had a good deal of rejection of love by Lawrence. His "fighting" sensuality is superior to "lovey-dovey," and he (as with the captain in *The Captain's Doll*) does not want love in marriage. Here the captain's desire for love, quite natural when he has been seduced by such a generous fount of sunshine, is denounced, and there is worse to come.

But then, Gilbert reflects on "the tangle and nastiness of it all." Later,

he felt wretched, and not his own skin. He felt thoroughly humiliated, and now knew he was embarking on a new little sea of ignominy. (MN, 150)

Then in talking about the Baroness, Lawrence writes: "And having all her life to enjoy an unfaithful, gambling husband." The question must arise if, as with Joanna, it doesn't matter if one is unfaithful, on what grounds is one to make these judging insights that belong to interpersonal reality?

A facetious tone is employed to disguise the falsification of the reality:

In whizzed the train for Paris, out stepped Mr Noon, in a new suit and with a Gladstone bag.

"I was awfully afraid you wouldn't come," said Johanna.
"Here I am," said Gilbert. After which Johanna felt a perhaps even purer compassion for her poor Rudolph. And he, to his credit, found compassion even more humiliating than impotence.
Whereupon he wrote quite long poems, in which Gilbert all-unwittingly fluttered in a dark *Unglücksrabe*, raven of woe. (MN, 140)

The tone is hopelessly wrong. Infidelity doesn't matter; the poor chap could at least compensate by writing ridiculous verses. But beneath the surface, too, is a maliciousness: "he, to his credit, found compassion even more humiliating than impotence." The tone is "serve him right," and the phrase "to his credit" adds a sadistic little twist to the pleasure in another's pain and discomfort.

There follows a passage that attempts to justify Johanna's sexual attentions to Rudolf, in between cataclysmic sexual episodes with Gilbert, leading to Rudolf's humiliation and Gilbert's being double-dealt with. The reader who might object is told that such compassionate sex therapy on Johanna's part is really noble, and when Rudolf came to want her to love him, that represented an idealism which is the equivalent of wanting a baby's dummy. Moreover, any male reader who has doubts may himself be suspected of suffering from the same kind of infantilism: he is told that he needn't read the nasty book any more for it is a story of a woman who is not going to show one spark of nobility, but will follow her sensual desire wherever it leads her. Lawrence has obviously been rattled by being told by a critic his heroines are "not noble," but what his splenetic tone and fury attempts to conceal is the reality of his heroine's really ignoble unscrupulousness

I ask you, especially you, *gentle* reader, whether it is not a noble deed to give to a poor self-mistrustful Rudolf substantial proof of his own virility. We say substantial advisedly. Nothing ideal in the air. Substantial proof of his own abundant adequate virility. Would it have been more noble, under the circumstances, to give him the baby's dummy-teat of ideal sympathy and a kind breast? Should she have said: "Dear Rudolf, our two spirits, divested of this earthly dross of physicality, shall fly untrammelled. . . ." Should she have proceeded . . . to whoosh with him in unison of pure love through the blue empyrean, as poor Paolo and Francesca were forced to whoosh on the black winds of hell. (MN, 140–41)

The answer to Lawrence here is—do sexual acts have a meaning, or not? Does *love* have any meaning at all? Only two pages before Johanna shuts her door, and we have the religious language of sexual meaning:

The sultriness and lethargy of his soul had broken in a storm of desire for her, a storm which shook and swept him at varying intervals all his life long. (MN, 136)

That act of passion had a meaning that is to last all Gilbert's life. But only a few lines later, Rudolf, who was "not happy with his wife" and does not "know what he lived for," is given the "cup of consolation" by Johanna:

"Johanna, of course, who took her sex as a religion, felt herself bound to administer the cup of consolation to him" (MN, 139). We have seen that Johanna felt she must give her sexual favors as a form of understanding, but we cannot surely but feel that in her Grossian enthusiasm, turning from healing Gilbert to healing Rudolf, she has reduced the meaning of the sexual act to a panacea, a mere cure. Lawrence's reference to Paolo and Francesca is enough, surely, to remind us that love can be as strong as death, that is, as a source of meaning. It is his uncertainty over this dilemma that prompts some of the most distasteful paragraphs in the whole of Lawrence:

> Is the baby's dummy-teat really the patent of true female spirituality and nobility, or is it a fourpence-halfpenny fraud? Gentle reader, I know *your* answer. But unfortunately my critics are *usually* of the sterner sex, which sex by now is so used to the dummy that its gentle lips flutter if the india rubber gag of female *spiritual* nobility is taken away for one moment. (MN, 141)

The sarcastic tone disguises the real problem. It is not that Johanna is not a spiritual woman. It is rather that she seems driven by an (immoralist) *idea* or by a self-regarding will, and that she is *not* pursuing a deep sense of authenticity to herself like an Ursula or Alvina Houghton. And while we are prepared to stomach Lawrence's sermonizing when he is offering us greater fulfilment, in terms of throwing off dead old concepts of spiritual love, we are not prepared to swallow his enconiums for nymphomania.

We do not object to Johanna because she is a Magdalen-whore: we would be prepared to accept her as such. But the novel offers her as Gilbert's destiny, for his lifelong cataclysm, and in that light, we are uneasy when she takes any man she fancies, over any page she likes. What Lawrence's propaganda paragraphs here also disguise is the pain that she caused: her sexual intervention in Rudolf's marital affairs and his impotence, like sex therapy, may reassure him of his organic potency, but it fails to help him in the least to solve the question of *what he lived for*. We know that; we know from cases in psychotherapy that Johanna's kind of intervention could only do harm, compound his predicament, and yield more pain and woe. The corruption Lawrence shows, his essential fraudulence here, is in the fact that he, too, might know this, but falsifies it, in the same campaigning voice with which he seeks to tell us how to be man and how to be woman. The corruptness explains why the tone is so wrong and offensive:

> He was crying for a dummy, and to have his not particularly beautiful feet washed with spikenard and long hair. Poor Johanna—how we know that little adjective of condolence from side to side: poor Johanna had gone to the wrong shop with her wares. The above-mentioned substantial proof only proved a larger thorn in the flesh of the poetic captain, a thorn which had ceased to rankle, and now rankled again. Therefore his poetry, like pus, flowed from the wound. We are sorry to be distasteful, but so it strikes us. (MN, 141)

The passage is the more disturbing because Lawrence goes on writing as if he were writing about the actual man, Udo von Henning, with whom Frieda had had an affair. While he defends Frieda as a Magdalen, he also displays his hate and jealousy by the undercurrent of distaste:

> Fortunately the war came in time, and allowed him to fling his dross of flesh disdainfully down the winds of death, so that now he probably flies in all kinds of comforted glory. I hope really he's not flying in our common air, for I shouldn't like to breathe him. That is really my greatest trouble with disembodied spirits. I am so afraid of breathing them in, mixed up with air, and getting bronchitis from them. (MN, 141)

Lawrence's personal animus shows through unpleasantly not least because of its spitefulness.

Johanna, if he can help it, will never show a spark of nobility. We are infantile to demand any such thing:

> Therefore, oh sterner sex, bend your agitated brows away from this page, and such your dummy of sympathy in peace. Far be it from me to disturb you. I am only too thankful if you'll keep the indiarubber gap between your quivering innocent lips. So, darling, don't *look* at the nasty book any more: don't you then; there, there don't cry, my pretty. (MN, 141–42)

But, we must protest, it is not *our* position that is the infantile one. It is the position of the captain at the end of *The Captain's Doll* that is infantile, as Dr. Rosemary Gordon argues, writing on Lawrence in a Jungian journal, (Gordon, 1978) and it is Frieda–Johanna's in her intense oral posture to the world, and Lawrence's in his admiration of her untrammelled appetite.

In chapter 23, in Riva, Gilbert, like Will and Birkin, finds a new thrill in sodomy. The reference is not quite explicit, but when one knows the parallel episodes in *Women in Love* and *Lady Chatterley's Lover*, it is not difficult to decipher:

> Something seemed to come loose in Gilbert's soul, quite suddenly. Quite suddenly, in the night one night he touched Johanna as she lay asleep with her back to him, touching him, and something broke alive in his soul that had been dead before. A sudden shock of new experience. Ach, sweetness, the intolerable sensual sweetness, the silken, fruitlike sweetness of her loins that touched him, as she lay with her back to him—his soul broke like a dry rock that breaks and gushes into life. Ach richness—unspeakable and untellable richness. Ach bliss—deep, sensual, silken bliss! It was as if the old sky cracked, curled and peeled away, leaving a great new sky, a great new pellucid empyrean that had never been breathed before. (MN, 290)

I suppose one could see this simply as the prose parallel to the poems that Lawrence wrote about suddenly "finding" his wife as another person:

It was the flank of his wife
I touched with my hand, I clutched with my hand...
I was carried by the current in death
Over to the new world, and was climbing out on the shore. (CP, 256ff)

These poems seemed to me, until I read *Mr Noon*, marvelous records of the proper discovery of the "otherness" of the loved one. After reading *Mr Noon*, however, one sees in them a new and sinister meaning. The hints of some revolutionary sensual development are clear: Gilbert could never have achieved this new life with the girl he flirted with at home in England—Emmie. What was needed for his resurrection was something *not nice*:

If he had married some *really* nice woman ... then he would never have broken out of the dry integument that enclosed him ... the act of birth, dear reader, really is not and cannot be a really nice business. It is a bloody and horrid and gruesome affair. And that is what we must face. (MN, 291)

The hints are subdued, about what kind of a "fight" Lawrence is writing about: the Lady Chatterley novels fill it in. The clue to the new world is that Johanna has he *back* to him. As he puts it in *New Heaven and Earth*:

I am here
risen and setting my feet in another world risen,
accomplishing a resurrection ... living where life was never yet dreamed of ...
I am the discoverer!
I have found the other world! (CP, 259)

The other world is not the woman's separate being but a way of enjoying sensuality with her that both avoids the dangers of her creativity as a mother, and denies her femininity.

What is noticeable both in *New Heaven and New Earth* and *Mr Noon* is the elated sense of relief expressed over this experience: "Behold a new Gilbert!" It is an escape from prison, and so it becomes a political program of a Grossian kind: "It needs a fight with the matrix of the old era." The word *matrix* is important: the womb, which one is in contact with through the vagina, is seen both as that which belongs to the mother and that which must be broken or burst away from. It is also the old social and political habits—"womb ideas"—that we must overthrow. It is not quite clear from *Mr Noon* exactly how Lawrence thought the kind of sensuality Gilbert finds may be adopted by us to make the world anew, but after the sodomy,

Behold a new Gilbert. Once the old skies have shrivelled, useless to try and retain their ancient, withered significance. Useless to try and have the old values. They have gone. (MN, 290)

Sodomy can do more than provide a new life for a man: it can lead us all into a new world.

So it is with man, gentle reader. There are worlds within worlds within worlds of unknown life and joy inside him. But every time, it needs a sort of cataclysm to get out of the old world into the now. It needs a very painful shedding of an old skin. It needs a fight with the matrix of the old era. (MN, 290)

The word matrix as I have said is significant, for it is the old mater that Lawrence fights to escape the doom from the phantom mother within. The shadow of the internalized inhibiting mother lurks within woman's body in the vagina. It is against that that we must struggle, and this becomes politicized: "a bitter struggle to the death with the old, warm, well-known mother of our days" (MN. 290).

It is really astonishing how Lawrence gives himself away: that "warm" for instance reveals how his excitement over sodomy has to do with fear of the cradling mother, who threatens "horrible merging."

Fight the old, enclosing mother of our days—fight her to the death—and defeat her—and then we shall burst out into a new heaven and a new earth, delicious. But it won't come out of lovey doveyness. (MN, 290)

Love is feared because it belongs to the mother: hostility, a fight, contempt, and hate are better circumstances for sexual union, opposed to the world at large "out there," where ordinary couples are horribly repeating the sexual meaninglessness of the parents. The "new earth" won't come from the "lovey-dovey" feelings such as Lawrence sneers at throughout his later works in ordinary people. The new era demands anything but a normal human love; It demands (as with Gross) polymorphous perversity, whose symbolic meaning lies in hate.

New life will come from those who can be *real men* and dare to act in this way. "He had dared to do it" thinks Connie, when she is sodomized in hostility by Mellors, who is angry with Hilda. In *Mr Noon* the perverted act is done in hostile revenge for the infidelity with Stanley. Thus, our new world is to come from revenge directed against the fears of the mother lurking in the vagina, and of the womb as a grave. As we have seen, in the closing pages of *Mr Noon*, the Alps themselves look like a woman's body that threatens to trap Gilbert in the grave, in his distress.

Besides sodomy, the other guarantee against the threats of love (which, as the schizoid individual fears, is "horrible merging") is the dog-and-cat kind of relationship: one that is in continual conflict. "The fight, thank god, is for ever" (MN, p174); "The fight, gentle reader, the fight! Up boys and at 'em!— 'em, of course, meaning the women." (MN, 186); if one seeks a new heaven and a new earth, "It will come out of the sheer, pure, consumated fight." (MN, 290)—once (as here) he has thrown off the "old values" and gone in for sodomy. Earlier Gilbert had reflected that Johanna was "more like a blunderbuss than a lily," and "what was the good of love that wasn't a fight" (MN, 173). When Johanna–Frieda was unfaithful, however, what did one do about that? The answer seems to be that she must be possessed anally in revenge so that in this there is a new "bursting" into a new dimension:

> Where the soul fights blindly for air, for life, a new space.

And out of this strong symbolic solution develops the Lawrentian political program:

> The matrix of the old mother-days and mother-idea is hell beyond hell at last, that which nourished us and our race becomes the intolerable dry prison of our death. Which is the history of man. (MN, 290)

So, we have the clue to the growing tendency in the late Lawrence to wish the world destroyed as long as he was all right with his women. As in some of the honeymoon poems, the more the world is destroyed, the better he will like it.

> And once it has become an intolerable prison, it is no use presùming what is outside. We don't know what is outside, we can never know till we get out. We have therefore got to fight and fight and fight ourselves sick, to get out. Hence the Germans really made a right move when they made the war. Death to the old enshrouding body politic, the old womb-idea of our era! (MN, 290-91)

In these passage from *Mr Noon*, we must surely feel very doubtful about the way in which he turned his feelings about woman and sexuality into a political program. Take, for instance, the famous passage about the ugliness of Teyershall, in *Lady Chatterley's Lover*, on which a great deal of the "Culture and Environment" movement was based, perhaps the roots of his rejection of England lie in Lawrence's psychopathology? Is this really the way out? We may remember that he wrote:

> "If I knew how to, I'd really join myself to the revolutionary socialists now. I think the time has come for a real struggle. That's the only thing I care about: the death struggle. I don't care for politics. But I know there *must* and *should* be a deadly revolution very soon, and I would take part in it if I knew how." (Moore, 1962, 649, 20 January 1921)

Nothing surely could be more dangerous than projecting one's own death wish thus on to the political scene? The true self that sees what is primary in man-woman relationships is confused and compromised by Frieda, her views and her behavior. The pain was there in Lawrence, but he must try to deny it, and even reject his forgiveness as a "spirituality" to be thrown off. The sadness emerges again when Lawrence describes the bundle of clothes Lotte has sent to Frieda:

> an enormous black hat of chiffon velvet and black plumes, huge: a smaller hat of silky woven straw, very soft: a complicated Paquin dress of frail, dark-blue, stone-blue silky velvet. (MN, 292)

Somehow these garments are terribly, terribly sad. In the background of our minds are Mrs. Lawrence's (Mrs. Morel's) excitements and her clothes as well as Lawrence's own fascination with women's clothes, and those of the woman he loved. Here they came out of the hat box with poignant emptiness and menace, and so the manuscript ends.

*Mr Noon* reveals the confusion of perspectives on sexuality that Lawrence suffered, after he ran off with Frieda Weekley. Lawrence seems earlier, through Gilbert, tormented by a spectacle of his woman dancing with a peasant. It is as if he is witnessing the Primal Scene:

> He caught her beneath the breasts with his big hands and threw her into the air, at the moment of dance crisis, and stamped his great shod feet like a bull. And Johanna gave a cry of unconsciousness, such as a woman gives in her crisis of embrace. And the peasant flashed his big blue eyes on her, and caught her again. (MN, 250)

The peasant embodies what Lawrence calls "naked desire":

> the peasant desired her, with his powerful mountain loins and broad shoulders. And Gilbert symbolised with him. But also he was unhappy. He also saw that legitimately Johanna was the bride of the mountaineer that night. (MN, 250).

This response is very puzzling. What man feels that his own woman could legitimately become the bride of another? How could he sympathize with a peasant who wanted his own bride?

Gilbert, however, is unhappy because he sees that "she would never submit."

> She would not have love without some sort of spiritual recognition. Given some spiritual recognition, she was a queen, more a queen the more men loved her. (MN, 250)

It seems odd that even Gilbert should, as it were, want his woman to be a woman who wasn't interested in "spiritual recognition," or at least something more than mere desire. It is very difficult to follow Lawrence in this novel, for whenever any kind of conscience or sense of value and meaning is attached to love, he rails against it as spirituality. Yet when (as we have seen) he contemplates that mountain peak that is his "queen," it is the spirituality that he appreciates. It is as if he wants to split ideal queen woman totally from the libidinal woman, such as might have had sexual congress with the peasant:

> But the peasant's was the other kind of desire: the male desire for possession of the female, not the spiritual man offering himself up sexually. She would get no worship from the mountaineer: only lusty mating and possession. And she would never capitulate her female castle of pre-eminence. She would go down before no male. The male must go down before her. "On your knees, oh man!" was her command in love. Useless to command this all-muscular peasant. So she withdrew. She said *Danke-schön*, and withdrew. (MN, 250)

Lawrence rails against spirituality because he is contemptuous of the way Weekley had worshipped Frieda. But in this novel, in which Gilbert is him, where exactly does he stand, as Gilbert more or less identifies with this peasant? Gilbert sees the "animal chagrin" in the other man, but one would suppose he'd be pleased—after all, it would have been uncomfortable to say the least if Johanna had disappeared upstairs with the peasant.

However, he slips strangely in Gilbert's ruminations, from thinking about the peasant's frustration, to thinking about how Johanna will frustrate him! "The lady had let him (the peasant) down. *The lady would let him down as long as time lasted*" (MN, 250, my italics). This cannot mean the peasant, so it must mean Gilbert (= Lawrence): but how?

> He would have to forfeit his male lustihood, she would yield only to worship, not to the male overweening possession.
> Gilbert was in a bad mood. He knew that at bottom Johanna *hated* the peasant. How she would hate him if she were given into his possession! And yet how excited she was. And he, Gilbert, must be the instrument to satisfy her roused excitement. It by no means flattered or pleased him. He sympathised with the peasant. Johanna was a fraud. (MN, 250)

What man would be pleased to be swept by his woman into a sexual excitement generated by another man—and a man she hates into the bargain? But that isn't the point here: what Gilbert seems to resent is that Joanna *didn't* give herself to the peasant's desire, thus showing she, too, wanted spirituality.

One's response to *Mr Noon* is thus confusion on confusion, and this seems clearly due to Lawrence's predicament. One only has to return to the honeymoon poems to see what kind of blow must have been struck him by the incidents related in *Mr Noon*, in which Frieda was unfaithful. This explains the undercurrent in the last passages, of desert, waste, bleak sterility: the lovers walk on over the Alps—yet at one point come by mistake into a circle, a huis clos. This upsets Gilbert, Lawrence tells us, more than the infidelity. Yet it has its own underlying symbolism—despite their commitment, are they to return to Johanna's earlier state (as with Daumling and the others) of continual liaisons? Is there to be no progress towards the star-like state of meaningful relationship? In the end Gilbert finds a new world in sodomy. At the end, too, Lotte sends a bundle of new fashionable clothes, and this perhaps suggests a menace of the domination of his life by the powerful and unscrupulous Richthofen sisters. Then, too, the comic thing is that these sisters, so emancipated, so amoral, so sunny, and free, are *terrified* of their father! When Gilbert approaches them at the fair, they have to hustle him away:

> Johanna said fiercely, in a half whispering voice:
> "Go away! Go away, Papa is just behind! Go away, he is not to see you! Go away, you don't know us."

Gilbert went pale and looked at Johanna.

"Allez! Allez donc!" said Lotte, in her deep sardonic voice.

"Et au revoir. Mauvaise occasion." And she nodded her head, and made eyes at him. (MN, 158)

Comically enough, one is reminded of Emmie on the greenhouse floor, with her father bursting in, and all that Richthofen sisters sexual revolutionism, their "liberated" behavior, is revealed as an adolescent revolt against a German father. ("In Germany, when the father comes home, even the walls seem to pull themselves closer together.") Gilbert, in this encounter, shows himself to be the ninny he is throughout: "Fumbling with his hat, he stepped back" (MN, 159). Gilbert, however, in a Lawrentian moment, is right: "The tangle and nastiness of it all." And as Lawrence admits, he *is* being humiliated and is embarking on a sea of ignominy. This remark, it should be noted, comes just before Johanna goes back to the captain again, to put a candle in the cathedral with him, as a memory to their love, which has lasted only a day or two, until Gilbert reappeared. If all this is not "nastiness," it is mad, and from time to time Gilbert does try to grope around for some of those English morals and standards. Johanna declares, "I am a bit mad." Gilbert urges her to run away with him. At least Eberhard (Otto Gross) did not do that:

"it's four years since Eberhard. He showed me one could be free. But he didn't take one away. . . . And then I really believed one shouldn't wait for one man. *That* is the mistake. I believe he is right there. One should love all men: all men are loveable somewhere."

"But why love all men? You are only one person. You aren't a universal. You're just a specific unit." (MN, 164)

For once we hear Lawrence speaking: Johanna declares she *understands* something in each man she meets:

"Oh Good God!" he said. "Do you love for what you can understand? . . ."

"You might as well call yourself Panacea—," he said sarcastically.

". . . A damned patent medicine poisons more than it cures."

"Don't you believe in love!" she cried. . . .

"Not in general love."

"What in then?"

"In particular love I may believe." (MN, 164)

Of course, we may suppose the experience of Johanna's availability was overwhelming for Gilbert (though we don't care much about him as he is such a booby). What is disastrous is the glimpse we get that it doesn't mean very much *to Lawrence*:

She lifted her eyelids with a strange flare of invitation, like a bird lifting its wings.

> And for the first time the passion broke like lightning out of Gilbert's blood. The sultriness and lethargy of his soul had broken into a storm of desire for her, a storm which shook and swept him *at intervals all his life long*. (MN, 136; my italics)

We might have supposed this was the beginning of a Lawrentian love affair, a marriage sacredness, which commands total commitment, and the onset of a life–long meaning in sex—that is the pattern with Birkin and even with Connie. But now we detect a note of mocking, by which Lawrence is jeering at his own earnestness about sexual authenticity: "Oh wonderful desire, violent genuine desire! Oh magnificence of stormy, elemental desire. . . . Oh cataclysm of fulminous desire in the soul." And just over the page, the same woman is giving Daumling sex therapy. How seriously are we to take this? Here the tone becomes uncertain and disastrously flippant: "This is a trick of resurrection worth two." Are we to be serious? Perhaps we should never have been serious? Is all that about "fulminous desire" always perhaps a come-on in Lawrence? Yet it is Lawrence who is so solemnly religious about sex. Here, he seems to be laughing at himself as a victim of this trollopy German, but neither he nor we know how to respond—hence the failure.

Lawrence realizes that his essential reader may—certainly on second reading—have doubts, so, here he turns on him.

> Not, dear moralist, to break him against the buttresses of some Christian cathedral which rose in his path. Not at all. If flung him smack through the cathedrals like a long-shotted shell. Heaven knows where it did fling him. . . .
> But for the moment, I insist on apostrophising desire, intense individual desire, in order to give my hero time. Oh thunder-god, who sends the white passion of pure, sensual desire upon us, breaking through the sultry rottenness of our old blood like jagged lightning, and switching us into a new dynamic reaction, hail! (MN, 137)

We may not that Lawrence here rejects Christianity and its morals, and now he assumes (taking as evidence the newspaper critic who has upset him) that the reader will be both curious and condemnatory (and his petulant response illuminates his impulse towards explicitness):

> No, gentle reader, please don't interrupt, I am *not* going to open the door of Johanna's room, not until Mr Noon opens it himself. I've been caught that way before. I have opened the door for you, and the moment you gave your first squeal in rushed the private detective you had kept in the background. Thank you, gentle reader, you can open your own doors. I am busy apostrophising Jupiter Tonans, Zeus of the thunder-bolt, the almighty Father of passion and sheer desire. I'm not talking about *your* little messy feelings and licentiousness, either. I'm talking about desire. (MN, 137)

"Naked desire," of course, is the central value in *The Virgin and the Gypsy*, and it is the touchstone in the Lady Chatterley books. But in his obsession with it, in Lawrence's *Mr Noon*, the reality of complex between couple and world is never found, while his attitude to his readers suffers disastrously.

Where, in *Mr Noon*, does one find any iota of the valid truth expressed in
the poem *Fidelity* (CP, 476)

And when, throughout all the wild orgasms of love
slowly a germ forms, in the ancient, once-more-molten rocks
of two human hearts, two ancient rocks, a man's
                    heart and a woman's,
that is the crystal of peace, the slow hard jewel of trust,
the sapphire of fidelity.
The gem of mutual peace emerging from the wild chaos of love.

It was surely Lawrence's treachery to this perception in *Mr Noon* that made
it impossible for him to complete and publish that novel.

*     *     *

## The Lost Girl

By contrast, we may look at a successful novel on the theme of sexual
relationships.

*The Lost Girl* seems to me almost perfect, as a novel on the Lawrentian
theme, of the deepest authenticity of "being." Alvina Houghton, growing to
be past her prime in a small North Country town, Woodhouse, holds out
against various lovers whom she detects are more concerned with their own
egos and male prowess than loving her for herself, eventually meets an Italian
young man, Cicio, whose real name is Marasca Francesco, a laborer from
Pescocalascio; Pancrazio, which is Picinisco in the wild mountains behind
Caserta. He is working in a troupe of entertainers and dancers, called the
Natcha-Kee-Tawara led by a remarkable Madame Rochard. Alvina, who plays
the piano for silent films is her father's *palais*, called Houghton's Endeavour,
falls in love with Cicio, and, when her father dies and she is left with almost
nothing, marries him and goes to live with him in terribly primitive conditions
in a peasant house in the mountains. She becomes pregnant, and Cicio goes
off to join the Italian forces—Italy has just declared war on Germany in the
1914–18 war—and it is doubtful whether he will ever come back. She is lost
to English provincial society and its values, and to all intents and purposes to
the world, but we have a feeling she could not have done anything else. When
he says he expects his call-up, this exchange follows:

"Are you sorry you came here with me, Allaye?" he asked. There was malice in the
very question.
    She put down the spoon and looked up from the fire. He stood shadowy, his head
ducked forward, the firelight faint on his enigmatic, timeless, half-smiling face.
    "I'm not sorry," she answered slowly, using all her courage, "Because I love
you—" (LG, 368)

Later, she says: " 'I love you, even if it kills me,' she said" (LG, 369)—and the determination of her love makes him agree to make up his mind to come back: " 'We have our fate in our hands,' she said" (LG, 370). Since this was rewritten in 1920, it was surely very unlikely that either Lawrence or his readers would have believed that. (The manuscript of the first draft, apparently, and significantly, was with Frieda's relations in Germany from 1914 to 1919.) We finish the book with a sad uncertainty as to whether Alvina will die in childbirth, or whether she will use her remaining £60 to try to get back to England, or wait in the miserable mountain village until Cicio returns from the war, perhaps crippled, to lead a life of penury, ugliness, and hardship. Yet we cannot feel that she has done anything wrong or false.

The novelist does not sentimentalize the nature of the man with whom Alvina takes up. Alvina is warned in absolutely plain terms what kind of man he is: "He is a man of the people, a boatman, a labourer, an artist's model. He sticks to nothing" (LG, 199). Later Madame adds,

"I know something of these Italian men, who are labourers in every country, just labourers and under-men always, always down, down, down—... And so, when they have a chance to come up ... they are very conceited, and they take their chance. He will want to rise, by you, and you will go down, with him." (LG, 199)

While Alvina is not much more than a member of the class of lower employers, she will raise him in his eyes, because she is English, but Madame warns her that the Italians do not have *homes* like the British. The men, as we see later, belong to the market square, they have ungovernable tempers, and beat their wives. The portrait of Cicio is as honest as E. M. Forster's is of Gino in *Where Angels Fear to Tread*, and Lawrence's Neapolitan is a far primitive and even less promising character than that son of an Italian dentist.

Yet Alvina finds what we can only call fulfillment. As it is with Forster, Italy is magical in its natural seasons:

In February, as the days opened, the first almond trees flowered among the grey olives, in warm, level corners between the hills. But it was March before the real flowering began. And then she had continual bowl-fuls of white and blue violets. She had sprays of almond blossom, silver-warm and lustrous, then sprays of peach and apricot, pink and fluttering.... She came upon a bankside all wide with lavender crocuses ... She felt like going down in an oriental submission, they were so lovely, so supreme. She came to them in the morning, when the skies were grey, and they were closed, sharp clubs, wonderfully fragile on their stems of sap, among leaves and old grass and wild periwinkle. They had wonderful dark stripes running up their cheeks, the crocuses, like the clear proud stripes on a badger's face, or on some proud cat. She took a handful of the sappy, shut, striped flames. In her room they opened into a grand bowl of lilac fire. (LG, 363)

Cicio works in the fields, plowing with two white oxen, or weaving baskets, a Neapolitan craft. Meanwhile Alvina would sew for her coming child or spin wool.

She was happy in the quietness with Cicio, now they had their own pleasant room. She loved his presence. She loved the quality of his silence, so rich and physical. She felt he was never very far away . . . he clung to her presence as she to his. (LG, 362)

What we feel she has achieved is a real, existential state of being, in touch with the natural world, and with her husband, who is both richly intimate and yet at times distant with that inscrutable, reserved distance of the rather primitive man, which Lawrence admired so much. Cicio is no god; he is no member of the "Sons of God" elite of Lawrence's imagination, and he does not enforce divine submission on Alvina to serve Lawrence's propaganda purposes.

The propaganda purposes seem to be diverted in this novel, in an unusual way. While Lawrence identifies superbly with Alvina, she does not really become a dynamic of Lawrence's self, an alter ego, to enact the drama of his *thèse*. Like Ursula at best, she becomes a very real person for us. But she is like Lawrence in her restless urge to get out of England, and at times we see this urge through Lawrence's eyes. There is, for instance, no great need for Alvina to see England as such a hateful and dead place as Lawrence saw it after his wartime experiences, but when Alvina looks back at the White Cliffs of Dover, we see them through Lawrence's eyes:

England, beyond the water, rising with ash-grey, corpse-grey cliffs, and streaks of snow on the downs above. England, like a long, ash-grey coffin slowly submerging. She watched it, fascinated and terrified. It seemed to repudiate the sunshine, to remain unilluminated, long and ash-grey and dead, with streaks of snow like cerements—that was England! Her thoughts flow to Woodhouse, the grey centre of it all. Home! (LG, 321)

We may draw a parallel between Alvina's path and Lawrence's. Indeed, we may remind ourselves, so many of his book are about people quitting. This has a symbolic significance, which we need to examine phenomenologically, as a feature of Lawrence's consciousness. Of course, it has connections with certain life-realities. Lawrence's movements were often attempts for one thing to deal with his health problems of pulmonary complaints and tuberculosis. Then, since he had married a German woman whose family was connected with well-known figures like the air ace Baron von Richthofen, he had had unpleasant experiences with British security and the suspicious people of Cornwall. The English authorities and the police had also taken action against some of his more outspoken books, and were to arrest his pictures.

The real alienation, I believe, had deeper psychological roots. It was again the feeling that "home" was the source of his psychic and emotional ghosts. Just as, throughout *Women in Love*, he expresses a dread and horror of "ordinary coupling," so he sought to escape the ghosts of his past by moving continually about the world, and by expressing the *Wanderlust* in his writings. But the geographical quest could not really solve the psychic problem: the ghosts that blighted Lawrence's life were in his "psychic tissue," not in the

White Cliffs of Dover on the backstreets of "Woodhouse," over which he projected them. His reaching out into the wild places of the world, whether in Mexico, or the mountains behind Caserta, felt like a *sacrifice*.

These new gods, the new countries, the new modes of living, as he found, and as Alvina found in the icy-mountainous region of Pancrazio, were harsh tyrants, even in the existential moment of fulfillment. It is this experience that generated in Lawrence a kind of addition to the very sacrifice itself, and even a masochistic kind of process of immolating himself (as in Mexico) in disaster. He reflects in this novel on Alvina's "sacrifice":

> How unspeakable lovely it was, no one could ever tell, the grand, pagan twilight of the valleys, savage, cold, with a sense of ancient gods who knew the right for human sacrifice. It stole away the soul of Alvina. She felt transfigured in it, clairvoyant in another mystery of life. A savage hardness came into her heart. *The gods who had demanded human sacrifice were quite right, immutably right. The fierce, savage gods who dipped their lips in blood, these were the true gods.* (LG, 344; my italics)

In this perhaps we can see the germ of the nonsense that is to culminate in *The Plumed Serpent*. There is an odd slip in the poetic logic, which runs, I believe, like this. Alvina, like Lawrence, is made to escape to Italy because she finds "ordinary," conventional England insufferable, because it offers no way out. She either has to marry some man she is indifferent to, or to take on spinsterhood, and a life of lowly, dull service with limited horizons. Through her, Lawrence again eulogizes the rejection of *ordinary humanity*. In him, as I try to show throughout this book, there was a schizoid rejection of humanness that verges at times on the psychopathological. He is happier with flowers and animals, or wild landscapes, whereas, whenever we encounter any human beings, they are "mongrels" (like the Mexicans in *The Plumed Serpent*) or here "like a gang of grey baboons." The dismal truth we have to come to terms with is that Lawrence *hated* ordinary people—at least after *Sons and Lovers* and *Odour of Chrysanthemums*.

By a slip of poetic logic, Lawrence moves from his hatred of ordinary humanity (who have threatened his soul, with bringing it into the same dead meaninglessness as Mother and Father's relationship) into an idolization of *human sacrifice* where he could feel that he was in touch with a force of creation, or a wild dynamic, or another dimension as of the gods, which menaced humanity, then he could feel he was close to a new source of meaning and being.

In *The Lost Girl* there are only one or two pages touching this psychopathological idolization of brutality. It is important that we notice them.

Alvina, as Lawrence makes clear, is an exceptional being:

> So far, the story of Alvina is commonplace enough. It is more or less the story of thousands of girls . . . if we were dealing with an ordinary girl we should have to carry

on mildly and dully down the long years of employment; or, at the best, marriage with some dull school-teacher or office-clerk.

But we protest that Alvina is not ordinary. Ordinary people, ordinary fates. But extraordinary people, extraordinary fates. Or else no fate at all. The all-to-one pattern modern system is too much for most extraordinary individuals. It kills them off or throws them disused aside. (LG, 95–96)

So far the paragraphs seem to be written out of love for Alvina and concern for her fulfillment, but now a note of bitterness creeps in:

We detest ordinary people. We are in peril of our lives from them and in peril of our souls too, for they would down us one and all to the ordinary. (LG, 96)

And Lawrence talks of the "regular machine-friction of our average and mechanical days."

Far from being written from a concern to redeem humanity, much of Lawrence in this vein was written in hatred of humanity ("Awful things men were, savage, cruel, underneath their civilisation" [LG, 152]) and in a strange *sauve qui peut* spirit: "if only *I* could be saved, with my women, the rest of the world may as well be destroyed." Far from generating a deep sense of the mystery of life and our necessary deference to the something other than ourselves, this is much more likely to encourage indifference, egocentricity, and a preoccupation with the false solutions of a strength rooted in hate as in the view that "the gods who demanded human sacrifice were quite right, immutably right." In our admiration for the novel there is another serious stumbling block, and that is Cicio's primitive indifference, his sexual primitiveness, and his capacity for violence. One sympathizes with Gino in Forster's *Where Angels Fear to Tread*, even when he tortures Philip by attacking his broken arm. The man, after all, has had the baby he adored killed by these hostile English people. But suppose Forster's heroine in *Room with a View* had run off with the Italian who stabs another in the square?

Cicio displays nothing less than murderousness in his quarrel with Max: "From under the edge of his waistcoat, on the shoulder, the blood was already staining the shirt" (LG, 168). In the end, I suppose, we shrug and declare that there is no accounting for tastes—if a girl falls in love with a primitive Italian capable of murderous rage, then that is the way things go. Only there is a slight tendency for Lawrence to present the girl as not only forgiving Cicio, but being actually drawn to his violent proclivity, as Kate is drawn to the murderousness of Cipriano ("It was marvellous . . .").

When Alvina is engaged to an elderly surgeon, Dr. Mitchell, and at a moment when she rebuffs him, he turns violent, we can see that this is the very moment that she must see, from her authenticity, that it will never do to marry him. He has revealed the kind of underlying rage that would make him a cruel tyrant in marriage.

> With a barely perceptible shake of the head, she refused, staring at him all the time. His ungovernable temper got the better of him. He saw red, and without knowing, seized her by the shoulder, swing her back, and thrust her, pressed her against the wall as if he would push her through it. His face was blind with anger, like a hot, red sun. (LG, 293)

Immediately, we feel he has forfeited his claim as a suitor, despite the way he now grovels to her feet in desperate apology. "'Forgive me!' he said. 'Don't remember! Forgive me! Love me!'" But what about Cicio? What, indeed, about the very moment when he first possesses her?

While we may understand Alvina's fascination with Cicio despite all his primitive qualities, and while we may recognize that courting must be a matter of giving way to passion, we may have doubts about Alvina's response to her first act of love with Cicio, which seems little better than a rape:

> She gasped.And as she gasped, he quite gently put her inside her room, and closed the door, keeping one arm round her all the time. She felt his heavy, muscular predominance. So he took her in both arms, powerful, mysterious, horrible in the pitch dark. Yet the sense of the unknown beauty of him weighed her down like some force. If for one moment she could have escaped from that black spell of that beauty, she would have been free. If she could, for one second, have seen him ugly, he would not have killed her and made her his slave, as he did. But the spell was on her, of his darkness and unfathomed handsomeness. And he killed her. He simply took her and assassinated her. How she suffered no one can tell. Yet all the time, his lustrous dark beauty, unbearable. (LG, 223)

She cries, and he smiles, his smile deepening to a heavy laughter.

> He intended her to be his slave, she knew. And he seemed to throw her down and suffocate her like a wave. (LG, 223)

Next day, he looks at her "from under his long dark lashes, a long, steady, cruel, faintly-smiling look from his tawny eyes, searching her as if to see whether she were still alive. And she looked back at him, heavy-eyed and half subjected. . . . And she turned her face to the wall, feeling beaten. Yet not quite beaten to death. . . . He wanted to make her his slave."(LG, 223).

This first enslaving, deathly encounter is perhaps the only moment at which *The Lost Girl* comes near the every-woman-adores-a-fascist mode, such as prevails in *The Plumed Serpent*. On another occasion, when Cicio overwhelms Alvina and determines to make sexual love to her in the empty Houghton house (LG, 256), the account seems quite normal, as a depiction of passion:

> There comes a moment when fate sweeps us away. Now Alvina felt herself swept. . . . It was what she wanted. . . .
> Noises went on, in the street, overheard in the workroom. But theirs was a complete silence. At last he rose and looked at her."Love is a fine thing, Allaye," he said. (LG, 256)

At such a moment, we say, "Yes! It is like that!" We do not say that about the previous passage, as we do not find giving in sexual love a death or an enslavement, nor a kind of rape.

Having said as much about our doubts and reservations, and allowing Cicio to be taken in terms of Lawrence's mythology, we may pay tribute to *The Lost Girl* as an enjoyable novel that takes the serious and significant path of following this exceptional girl's pursuit of authenticity.

The whole Houghton's endeavor episode perhaps comes from *Hard Times*, but yet becomes something eminently Lawrentian, too. Mr. May is a triumph and, interestingly enough, a kind of caricature of Lawrence himself, sexually:

> Nothing *horrified* him more than a woman who was coming-on towards him. It made him hate the whole tribe of woman: horrific two-legged cats without whiskers. . . . He liked the *angel*, and particularly the angel-mother in woman. (LG, 117)

Houghton himself, Miss Pinnegar, and Madame are superbly memorable characters, and embody widely different forms of wisdom, or nonwisdom, success, and failure. They convey with richness the strange culture and moeurs of the time.

But the greatest triumph, of course, is Alvina. Whatever we may feel about Cicio and Lawrence's view of him, with his serpent-like indifference, we are throughout convinced that, yes, Alvina Houghton *would* behave like that. She has a sense of her own authentic needs that we admire as we admire that of Elizabeth Bennet; and if we think about it, the existential theme is much the same as Jane Austen's—given all the trying circumstances, with old maidenhood encroaching, what is it a woman ultimately wants? And here the answer is not falsified, nor sentimentalised, nor idolized: she will love Cicio and go with him, even if he kills her.

Because of this theme, the book is a very benign one, and while there are in it recognitions of the terrible things in the world, it is also a book that conveys a love of the world. On her great trip across Europe in the war, Alvina

> watched spell-bound: spell-bound by the magic of the world itself. And she though to herself, "Whatever life may be, and whatever horror men have made of it, the world is a lovely place, a magic place, something to marvel over. The world is an amazing place." (LG, 326)

Because she embodies Lawrence's more positive impulses of love and awe, and his fascination with people and their modes of survival, we follow her with admiration, and have our sympathies enlarged by her tormented and rapturous experiences. She is one of the most sympathetic of all Lawrence's women and is by no means anybody's slave, sexual or otherwise. And perhaps in her endeavors with Cicio we have a better picture of marriage, too, than anywhere else in Lawrence.

One of our final conclusions about Lawrence's "message" or "upshot" must surely be that Lawrence's solutions are too fugitive. He himself was always fleeing. Lawrence himself saw this:

> We make a mistake in forsaking England and moving out into the periphery of life. After all, Taormina, Ceylon, Africa, America—as far as *we* go, they are only the negation of what we ourselves stand for and are: we're rather like Jonahs running away from the place where we belong. (Moore 1955, 360)

The woman rides away; Lou Witt rides away; so do Kate, Aaron, and the Lost Girl. Connie runs away to the hut, in a woodland idyll, and then is going away—somewhere (but where!). What do they find? In every case, there is, it seems to me, a deep sense of loss—the woman is sacrificed. The Lost Girl finishes up pregnant in primitive conditions with her husband probably doomed and herself probably going to die in childbirth. In none of these instances does any protagonist find anything except a certain "freedom" that must surely be a delusion. What kind of future has Alvina's child? And there is no peace in the soul, either, for the lost girl has profound misgivings in the end.

* * *

## Aaron's Rod

The gradual shift toward false solutions, however, becomes clear again, in *Aaron's Rod*, where the failure may be studied in the "upshot." *Aaron's Rod* must be the most tedious of Lawrence's novels. There are some marvelous moments—the family scene with the Christmas tree at the beginning, for instance, and a splendid row on a train, over Aaron's seat. But for the most part the book is dead—the characters largely without interest, while Aaron himself is more of a boor than Mellors. Usually, when Lawrence depicts the female breaking away to find existential fulfillment, there are interesting developments even if they are false. With Aaron, nothing happens of any interest whatever: he drifts about, entertained by Bohemians or upper-class people he despises, and has an unsatisfactory affair with a marchesa. He is not fully aware why he abandons his wife and children, but will obviously never return to them, and all we can feel is a kind of lukewarm irritation at his egoism, his irresponsibility, and his rootlessness.

There are the usual Lawrentian themes. Married people who are two in one "stick together like jujube lozenges." Marriage is *egoisme à deux*, and while love ought to be "a process of the incomprehensible soul," we have failed to realize that "the completion of the process of love is the arrival at a state of simple, pure possession, for man and woman." Instead, "we prefer abysses and maudlin self-abandon and self-sacrifice, the degeneration into a sort of slime and merge" (AR, 177).

There is the same contempt for ordinary life and "the horrible stinking human castle of life" (AR, 242). There is the same impulse to break woman's "implacable will," and the same dread of giving in sex. When Aaron has had sexual intercourse with the marchesa, he feels she has given him a scorpion. Meanwhile, the philosophy uttered in the book seems stale, tired, and hopeless.

The last chapter is revealing, though it takes us nowhere. Again, the novel is narcissistic, since Aaron is a part of Lawrence, but so is Lilly, the intellectual philosopher. Aaron's rod, his flute, which has been his creative instrument in prompting his existential quest, has been smashed in an anarchist explosion in the last chapter but one. In the next, "Words," Aaron has a dream. This is about an underworld country in which there are men about to eat a naked man stuffed with meat like a sausage. There are children, each with a wreath of flowers on its head. The men are tin miners, and there are greyish women crouching about, their wives.

What is most interesting is that Aaron sees himself as "definitely two people." There is great anxiety in the dream, about the direction a boat is going, conveying the two Aarons over a Mexican lake. By the side of the road is Astarte, with eggs in her lap.

It seems a dream about Lawrence's own psychic problems: the miner-figures, whose intention to eat the meat-filled man, may represent the ghostly ("industrial") father whom Lawrence fears always will castrate him. "The man's skin stuffed tight with prepared meat, as the skin of a Bologna sausage" is obviously a penis, and so the dream is about being castrated or annihilated, presumably because of his passion. The children are perhaps his (Aaron's) children whom he has denied (and Frieda's children whom Lawrence has denied, and his own children he has decided not to have—hence "there they all lay, in their flower-crowns in the vast space of the rooms").

One (invisible) Aaron seems anxious about where the other is going. Earlier in the book Aaron ruminates on himself as "maskless and invisible" like *The Invisible Man*. So, where is the schizoid self going? That the eggs are in Astarte's lap is ominous.

Aaron turns to Lilly, of whom he has once thought as a "wonderful chap" (which is what Ursula thinks of Birkin). But "Lilly *knew*." "He knew, and his soul was against the whole world" (AR, 301).

In the novel Lilly is even more shadowy than Aaron, but as Aaron reflects on Lilly, we see we have the author reflecting on himself, and Lilly is a vehicle for Lawrence's propaganda. What is it Aaron wants? Lilly delineates his own impetus: "'I should like to try a quite new life-mode... I would very much like to try life in another continent... I begin to feel caged.'" (AR, 303) But he hates a seeker. Is he looking for a new religion? Or love? "Is it the love urge?'" (AR, 306) "'And now you know it's all my eye!' Aaron looked at Lilly, unwilling to admit it. Lilly began to laugh" (AR, 306). The man who goes wooshing away on a love urge is likely to recoil, so that it becomes a horror, in the anarchist, the criminal, the murderer. What then?

"You *are* yourself and so *be* yourself. Stick to it and abide by it. Passion or no passion, ecstasy or no ecstasy, urge or no urge, there's no goal outside you, where you can consummate like an eagle flying into the sun, or a moth into a candle." (AR, 308)

Lilly's injunction picks up the dream:

There is only one thing, your very own self.... There inside you lies your own very self, like a germinating egg, your precious Easter egg of your own soul.... You've got an innermost, integral unique self, and since it's the only thing you have got and ever will have, don't go trying to lose it.... Your own singleness is your destiny. Your destiny comes from within, from your own self-form ... you develop the one and only phoenix of your own destiny. (AR, 308)

One might say this is an existentialist emphasis (see also, "there is only one law. I am I," *Fantasia of the Unconscious*). One might link it with what psychotherapists tell us they seek to draw out in their patients, a sense of their own uniqueness and form, what they feel they ought to be, their true self. But what about love?

"If your soul's urge urges you to love, then love.... If you've got to go in for love and passion, go in for them. But they aren't the goal. They're a mere means: a life-means, if you will. *The only goal is the fulfilling of your own soul's active desire and suggestion.*" (AR, 309; my italics)

He goes on to speak of "your developing consciousness ... the very self, the quick: its own innate Holy Ghost." Aaron is doubtful. There are two life-urges, Lilly suggests, love and power; now he finds we've got to accept the very thing we've hated—the *power-urge*. "It is a great life motive. It was the great dark power-urge which kept Egypt so intensely living for so many centuries. It is a vast dark strength in us now" (AR, 310). It is not, apparently, in Nietzsche's sense: not mental power, will-power or wisdom—but "dark living, fructifying power."

Where love is concerned, Lilly goes on, the great desire is not happiness. In the love-urge

"Now, in the urge to power, it is the reverse. The woman must submit, but deeply, deeply submit. Not to any foolish fixed authority, not to any foolish and arbitrary will. But to something deep, deeper. To the soul in its dark motion of power and pride.... A deep, unfathomable free submission." (AR, 311)

Lilly believes that,

"every man must fulfill his own soul, every woman must be herself, herself only, not some man's instrument, or some embodied theory.... But the mode of our being is such that we can only live and have our being whilst we are implicit in one of the great dynamic modes. *We must either love, or rule* ... women must submit to the positive power-soul in man, for their being." (AR, 312)

There is a serious and fatal flaw in Lawrence's existential concern for being. In its self-enclosed homosexual narcissism *it lacks intentionality*, and is sexist in its impulse to exert power over woman. The end is characteristic:

> Aaron looked up into Lilly's face. It was dark and remote-seeming. It was like a Byzantine eikon at the moment.
> "And who shall I submit to?" he said.
> "Your soul will tell you," replied the other. (AR, 312)

We are moving towards the fascistic mutuality between Cipriano and Ramòn in *The Plumed Serpent*, toward that strange homosexuality in Lawrence that is a form of self-worship, but there is a price to be paid for this self-enclosure. The world is lost, and there is no future. Aaron's dream spoke of the future, but the children wear wreathes, the eggs are on the lap of Astarte, and the boat lacks direction. In whatever circles Aaron moves with his flute, and whatever he thinks, we find only that limited concept of self-realization that Lawrence expresses through Lilly. Lawrence said, in the foreword to *Woman in Love*, "Nothing that comes from the deep, passional self is bad, or can be bad." But suppose we find there a prompting, according to which the fulfillment of one's destiny is no more than the satisfaction of basic urges towards power over woman? There perhaps we may recall:

> The real way of living is to answer to one's wants. Not "I want to light up with my intelligence as many things as possible" but "For the living of my full lame—I want that liberty, I want that woman, I want that pound of peaches." (Huxley, *Letters*, 1932, P. 95)

That is exactly what Aaron pursues, and it is exactly what Lilly is advising. He learns nothings, Aaron, except that it is all very boring.
What about civilization?

> Heaven bless us, we who want to save civilisation. We had better make up our minds what of it we want to save. The kernel may be all well and good. But there is precious little kernel, to a lot of woolly stuffing and poisonous rind. (AR, 160)

In *Aaron's Rod* Lawrence shows himself essentially philistine in many respects, and exposes the limitations of his fulfillment philosophy. Even Aaron's music is no attempt to serve anything, no service to civilized *meaning*. He plays to amuse himself, sometimes to amuse the drawing room, sometimes to help along his seduction of the Marchesa.

Aaron has a horror of responsibility. Of course, in marriage, he found that love was a battle in which each party strove for the mastery of the other's soul. His abandonment of his family, and his curious return, followed by a more painful breach, is seen by Lawrence as a step in the direction of mastery. "So far, man had yielded the mastery of women. Now he was fighting for it back again. And too late, for the woman would never yield" (AR, 135). What he wants is "perfected singleness," but this appears, throughout the novel as pure selfishness.

The most appalling episode is Aaron's affair with the Marchesa—not because it is adulterous or immoral, but because Lawrence endorses it as an act of self-fulfillment, and because in endorsing it he commends the underlying hate in Aaron's adultery:

> Manfredi knew that Aaron had done what he himself could never do, for this woman. And yet the woman was his own woman, not Aaron's. And so, he was displaced. Aaron, sitting there, glowed with a sort of triumph. He had performed a little miracle, and he felt himself a little wonder-worker, to whom reverence was due. . . . Aaron's face glimmered with a little triumph. . . . And Aaron said in his heart, what a goodly woman, what a woman to taste and enjoy. Ah, what a woman to enjoy. And was it not his privilege? (AR, 268–69)

By contrast, "the Italian's face looked old, rather monkey-like, and of a deep, almost stone-bare bitterness." We have the same discriminatory note as in the descriptions of the wife in *The Captain's Doll* and March in *The Fox*.

> His manhood, or rather his maleness, rose powerfully in him, in a sort of mastery. He felt his own power, he felt suddenly his own virile title to strength and reward . . . the husband sat there, like a soapstone Chinese monkey, greyish-green. So, it would have to be another time. (AR, 269).

Who can doubt on which side Lawrence has his thumb on the scales?

> Aaron's black rod of power, blossoming again with red Florentine lilies and fierce thorns. He moved about in the splendour of his own male lightning, invested in the thunder of the male passion-power. He had got it back, the male godliness, the male godhead. (AR, 270)

Thus, the wretched Aaron, who at home has been having sex on the side with the pub landlord to spite his unfortunate wife, is now a god, so to speak—which, as we know, sanctions him to do anything. The "black rod of power" is the idolized phallos again. He is "potent Jove" (AR, 270). Indeed, Aaron is now the *phoenix*: "The phoenix had risen in fire again, out of the ashes" (AR, 270). However, she is "against him," and is "throwing cold water over his phoenix. . . . He felt she was not his woman. Through him went the feeling, "This is not my woman"'" (AR, 273). He tries not to hate her, but he feels "she had given him a scorpion" though it is by no means made clear why he feels this.

He remembers Lilly, who has said "one must possess oneself, and be alone in possession of oneself." Aaron quite prides himself for not hating the Marchesa. Our life, he reflects, is only a fragment of the shell of life. It is as if he persuades himself that some other force is in charge of his actions. He has a little torment about infidelity, but "When a man is married he is not in love. A husband is not a lover. Lilly told me that: and I know its true now . . . all women want lovers" (AR, 278). He tries for a bit not to go back to the marchesa, but there is another soirée at which he plays the flute with the husband. "Everything was Al. . . . Still they were quite a little family, and it seemed quite nice." (AR, 280) But now "naked desire' is getting hold of him again" and "also pleased him," and not before long we are back at the "magic feeling of phallic immortality." (AR, 285)

Only now he reflects ruefully that in playing god he has become god and victim. "His remote soul stood up tall and knew itself apart." Yet it was beautiful: "The mystery of their love-contact. . . . He was aware of the strength and beauty and godlikeness that his breast was then to her—the magic" (AR, 285). But, "at the bottom of his soul he disliked her," and all the while he is remote and apart. There is no personal tenderness, no meeting, and no *interest*. We, the readers, simply do not care what Aaron does with the Marchesa, or vice versa. We are glad when the bomb goes off.

Aaron is a selfish bore, and Lawrence can't see it, but from Lilly we have some illumination:

> "The ideal of love, the ideal that it is better to give than receive, the ideal of liberty, the ideal of the brotherhood of man, the ideal of the sanctity of human life, the ideal of what we call goodness, charity, benevolence, public spiritness, the ideal of sacrifice for a cause, the ideal of unity and unanimity—all the lot—all the whole beehive of ideals—has all got the modern bee-disease, and gone putrid, stinking. And when the ideal is dead and putrid, the logical sequence is only stink." (AR, 293)

What is the alternative? Egoistical nihilism? Lilly's alternative is Lawrence's "an alternative for no one but myself."

Indeed, I believe Lawrence's only alternative, since "the old ideals are as dead as nails," was that which Max Stirner pronounced egoistical nihilism: "Get the value out of thyself," "I do not allow myself to be disturbed in my self-enjoyment." At any rate, it is something very like this position that one finds if one simply believes in the kind of "possession of oneself" that is expounded in *Aaron's Rod*.

The ultimate failure is a philosophical failure: a failure to find a relationship with the world for man, that calls him to life-tasks, to service and responsibility, and a responsibility to thought and civilization. Lawrence too much spurns intelligence and cultural achievement in man in favor of a Grossian iconoclasm.

And then, because the pursuit of self-fulfillment inevitably led, as in *Lady Chatterley*, to a fearful self-absorption in love (*egoisme à deux*), there emerges two dangerous political impulses. One is to respond to the unconscious fear of woman by seeking mastery (or abandoning woman or annihilating her). The other is to escape the problems of love by narcissistic forms of homosexuality. (Note in this book the strange and intense relationship between Aaron and Lilly and the excitement over the nude male statues in Florence [AR, 224]).

In this mode there is a cherishing of a kind of submissiveness, too: "the committal of the life-issue of inferior beings to the responsibility of a superior being" (AR, 294). But who is to choose the superior being? (Is there not a danger that we shall have the wool pulled over our eyes like Kate?) There is much discussion of slavery in this book, and we may well feel that Lawrence's distrust of democracy went with a deep feeling that people at large were so dangerous that they ought to be put under control for their own safety. Women, of course, must be brought (freely, of course) to submission, because they are a danger to men.

Aaron's "freedom" thus turns out to be a doom ("there's a doom for me"), and we cannot but help feel this is true of Lawrence himself. His solutions expressed in the upshot of this novel full for short of those suggested by existentialist psychotherapy—as by Frankl and May—that is, respect for the mystery of being and responsibility to our own knowing, to civilization, and to love and mutuality between the sexes. This, in turn, requires a new and more adequate view of woman, and this I believe Lawrence did not achieve.

# 6

## Demented Fantasies of Power—
## *Kangaroo* and *The Plumed Serpent*

"The novels come unwatched from one's pen." In writing *Kangaroo* in six weeks, Lawrence incidentally revealed a good deal of himself. Somers and Harriet are so clearly Lawrence and Frieda that there is no need to assemble evidence: he is so evidently dramatising himself. A significant figure appears: Who can it be? "a smallish man, pale-faced, with a dark beard." Both Richard Somers and Harriet have "that quite self-possession which is almost unnatural nowadays." The Australian workmen think him a comical-looking bloke, but they are silenced:

> They wiped their grin off their faces. Because the little bloke looked at them quite straight, so observant, and so indifferent. (K, 1)

He is a writer:

> As a poet, he felt himself entitled to all kinds of emotions and sensations which an ordinary man would have repudiated. (K, 8–9)

When the Calcotts look at the Somers, they see something special in the man: "he had a touch of something, the magic of the old world that she had never seen, the old culture, the old glamour" (K, 14). Later, Victoria sees even more:

> She seemed to see the wonder in him. And she had none of the European woman's desire to make a conquest of him, none of that feminine rapacity which is so hateful in the old world. She seemed like an old Greek girl just bringing an offering to the altar of the mystic Bacchus. The offering of herself. (K, 30)

Harriet has something special, too. She is a lady, a queen: "something quick and sure and, as it were, beyond the ordinary day about her, that exercised a spell over him." There was "a sort of magic about her." A discussion follows about what makes a gentleman, and what superiority means.

Somers's thoughts are recorded by Lawrence and often, as usual, they are Lawrence's thoughts. We especially know this when a character thinks about something of intense importance to Lawrence, and Lawrence completely gives his game away by making Kangaroo know Somers's poetry—which turns out to be *Lawrence*'s poetry. The poem Kangaroo quotes on page 124, "Your hands are fire-branded flames—*Noli me tangere*," is a version of the poem *Noli me tangere*! All the admiring references to the special magic of Somers, not least when a woman looks at him, are admiring references to himself!

In *Kangaroo*, all the other characters emerge from this narcissism, and are merely vehicles for the expression of the Lawrentian propaganda. Throughout Lawrence adheres to the secret belief that he was a god, with special powers. This fantasy urges him towards a "benevolent tyranny," as discussed in the novel. Education is no good except, of course, there is that overall didactic impulse: "I should like to teach people what it truly is to be a *man* and a woman." (K, 121) As we have seen, Lawrence offers to show us man and woman finding "independence," but in truth he doesn't really want anything of the kind. He wants man and woman put under very strict control.

And here we come to the complex symbolism of Kangaroo. Kangaroo himself is a projection of the impulse to put oneself under a dictator who will act for the Phantom Woman; he is a split-off from Lawrence's psyche who becomes an experiment in politics. There are difficulties, because Harriet (= Frieda) seems to suggest a new equality and mutual respect between man and woman.

Yet what about this blood-brotherhood yearning: "All his life he had cherished an ideal friendship" (K, 114), but in his self-debate he feels perhaps he didn't want it. Yet he wanted the joy of lordship, the joy of obedience: "the man is like a god, I love him." There is nothing like believing one is a god, splitting a bit off, and adoring that like a god, too.

Lawrence's admiration for authoritarian leadership, which he betrays in this book, is clearly, in light of D. W. Winnicott's analysis, a manifestation of his unconscious fear of woman:

> One can consider the psychology of the dictator, who is at the opposite pole to anything that the word democracy can mean. *One of the roots of the need to be a dictator can be a compulsion to deal with this fear of woman by encompassing her and acting for her.* The dictator's curious habit of demanding not only absolute obedience and absolute dependence but also "love" can be derived from this source. (Winnicott 1965, 165)

Moreover, Winnicott goes on, "the tendency of groups of people to accept or even seek *actual* domination is derived from a fear of domination by *fantasy woman*."

> This fear leads them to seek, and even welcome, domination by a known human being, especially one who has taken on himself the burden of personifying and therefore limiting the magical qualities of the all-powerful woman of fantasy, to whom is owed the great debt. The dictator can be over-human, and must eventually die; but the woman figure of primitive, unconscious fantasy has no limits to her existence or power. (Winnicott 1965, 165)

This symbolism will be discussed over Kangaroo. With what do we associate a kangaroo? She has a pouch in which her young are born—yet they are not in the womb. The kangaroo is thus an ideal symbol for a dictator who takes upon himself the qualities of the phantom woman.

Lawrence writes of Kangaroo

> His presence was so warm. You felt you were cuddled cosily, like a child at the breast, in the soft glow of his heart, and that your feet were nestling on his ample, beautiful "tummy." (K, 128)

Kangaroo's belly is "not so very fat"; "Neither is he flat there, like you and me" (K, 126). Kangaroo is a kind of woman, but he is against woman being spoiled by "the ants, who have tortured you with their cold energy and their conscious formic-acid that stings like fire." (K, 132). This is the "formic acid" of "social man." The answer is to seek the Ithyphallic God and to submit to him:

> a re-entry into us of the great God, who enters us from below, not from above.... Enters us from the lower self, the dark self, the phallic self, if you like (K, 147)

This is Somers, of course, uttering Lawrencese.

The phallic self (the "phallic me") is not love. Love (apparently) works from the head:

> Now it is the time for the Spirit to leave us again; it is time for the Son of Man to depart, and leave us dark, in front of the unspoken God; *who is just beyond the dark threshold of the lower self, my lower self*, whom I fear while he is my glory. (K, 148; my italics)

The relationship between Somers and Kangaroo also has that homosexual element that we find throughout Lawrence's work. *Kangaroo* reveals that homosexuality with Lawrence is related to the theme of *power*—the power that is invested in "the leader," who is a version of the phantom woman, or who acts for her.

> "You see," said Somers, trying hard to be fair, "what you call my demon is what I identify myself with. It's the best me, and I stick to it. I think love, all this love of ours, is a devilish thing now: a slow poison. Really, I know the dark god at the lower threshold—even if I have to repeat it like a phrase. And in the sacred dark men meet and touch, and it is a great communion. But it isn't this love ... love seems to me somehow trivial ... I know another God." (K, 149–50)

This seems to echo quite clearly the strange moral inclinations of the schizoid individual as diagnosed by Fairbairn: because of my fear of love I will give myself up to the joys of hatred.

> He wanted so much to get out of this lit-up cloy of humanity, and the exhaust of
> love, and the fretfulness of desire . . . why not break the bond and be single, take a
> fierce stoop and a swing back? (K, 151)

This is clearly a *fascistic* impulse: "Better anything on earth than the millions
of human ants. . . . Destruction is part of creation." (K, 164).

However, Lawrence also gives us clues in *Kangaroo* to the root of his
problems in the unconcious. These clues come in a sudden reference to
Somers's *mother* when we have not heard anything previously about his
mother and her importance in his life. Obviously, it is *Lawrence*'s mother in
question.

These thoughts come at a most important moment: when Somers is
becoming involved in Kangaroo's political movement, which is exclusively
male, and he does not tell Harriet. There is also a discussion of Somers's
political role. He is a writer, and he puts out new shoots in his writing, but
he'd like to have a go at politics. Here is a chance if he wanted to be a leader
of men (K, 100). We see this impulse often in Lawrence. He feels he has some
god-like power at least to awaken women ("She seemed to see the wonder in
him . . ."; Victoria looking at Somers—she was "bringing an offering to the
altar of the mystic Bacchus, the offering of herself" [K, 30]). But does he have
any capacity to exert this power over man? He speaks at one moment of how
the world needs a leader to unify it. The telling reflection come on page 101ff.
after Jack Calcott's declaration, "we're not going to let the women in."
Somers is drawn toward the "impersonal business of male activity," and
reflects on his fascination with Calcott's politics and Harriet's exclusion from
it:

> A part of himself that he was not going to share with her. It seemed to her
> unnecessary, and a breach of faith on his part, wounding her. If their marriage was
> a real thing, then anything very serious was her matter as much as his, surely. (K,
> 102)

Somers believes, like Lawrence, marriage to be at the heart of his life: what,
then, do we say about the exclusion of certain fundamental allegiances even
from the partner's knowledge? He insists "the pure male activity should be
womanless, *beyond woman*." (K, 103).

Somers knows *from his dreams* what she was feeling, and here we might say
that Lawrence does a psychoanalytical examination of his own dreams:

> his dreams of a woman, a woman he loved, something like Harriet, something like
> his mother, and yet unlike either, a woman sullen and obstinate against him,
> repudiating him. Bitter the woman was grieved beyond words, grieved until her face
> was swollen and puffy and almost mad or imbecile, because she loved him so much,
> and now she must see him betray her love. (K, 103)

We have noted Lawrence's distress, expressed through Paul Morel, at the thought of the mother's meaningless life. Here the internalized imago of this unfulfilled mother blackmails him by threatening hell because of his "betrayal" and damning him from there:

> That was how the dream woman put it: he had betrayed her great love, and she must go down desolate into an everlasting hell, denied, and denying him absolutely in return, a sullen, awful soul. The face reminded him of Harriet, and of his mother, and of his sister, and of girls he had known when he was younger—strange glimpses of all of them, each glimpse excluding the last. And at the same time in the terrible face some of the look of that bloated face of a mad woman which hung over Jane Eyre in the night in Mr Rochester's house. (K, 103)

The reference to *Jane Eyre* is revealing, for we will recall that Jane's sexual fulfillment, her marriage to Mr. Rochester, is frustrated by the mad, dark woman locked up in his house—a symbol herself of the internalized "bad mother." Somers is full of pity for the dream woman, and lays his hand on her arm saying:

> "But I love you. Don't you *believe* in me? Don't you *believe* in me." But the woman, she seemed almost old now—only shed a few bitter tears, bitter as vitriol, from her distorted face, and bitterly, hideously turned away, dragging her arm from the touch of his fingers; turned, as it seemed to the dream Somers, away to the sullen and dreary, everlasting hell of repudiation. (K, 103)

The dream fills him with horror. The way Lawrence writes of the dream woman makes it clear to anyone who knows *Sons and Lovers* that this is Lawrence writing about his own mother. The distorted face is the face of the depressed mother, which he tried to change when the sibling died. The references to bitterness and vitriol evoke tones of the death of Mrs. Morel, and the way he cries to her about whether she believes in him is surely the way a son cries to a mother?

The reference in the earlier passage, to other girls, is also illuminating. Lawrence saw every woman in relation to this "bad mother" image, needing redemption.

> The women in his life he had loved down to the quick of life and death: his mother and Harriet. And the woman of the dream was so awfully his mother, risen from the dead, and at the same time Harriet, as it were, departing from this life, that he stared at the night-paleness beyond the window-curtains in horror. (K, 103–4)

The protagonist feels the threat of a failure of confirmation: " 'They neither of them believed in me,' he said himself. . . . (K, 104) From his own private life, he found his dreams were like devils." This is virtually a confession from the author and he sees that the problem is the way the weaknesses in the psychic tissue threaten to overcome him:

> When he was asleep and off his guard, then his own weaknesses, especially his old weaknesses that he had overcome in his full, day-wakening self, rose up again maliciously to take some picturesque form and overcome his sleeping self. He always considered dreams as a kind of revenge which old weaknesses took on the victorious healthy consciousness, like past diseases come back for a phantom triumph. (K, 104)

Somers persuades himself that this only happens because in fact the triumph is won—the dreams are only the last kick of defeated weaknesses.

The dreams and their power to act on Somers reveals that the consciousness is neither healthy nor victorious; the danger is *not* gone. But then comes an astonishing indication:

> But surely his mother was not hostile in death! And if she were a little bit hostile at this forsaking, it was not permanent, it was only the remains of weakness, an unbelief which haunted the soul in life. (K, 109)

Somers must have the approval of both the dead mother and Harriet before he can move into activity: this, again, is revealing about Lawrence: "he could never take the move into activity unless Harriet and his dead mother believed in him" (K, 104). His dead mother and Harriet (we could say his dead mother and Frieda) confirm him in his *special nature*: "They both believed in him terribly, in personal being. In the individual man he was, and the *son of man*" (K, 104; my italics).

There is the strange note that Lawrence has about his specialness: "son of man." The man who "could go beyond them" (the dead mother and Harriet) "*with his back to them*," with an activity that excluded them—in this man they did not find it so easy to believe.

In *Kangaroo* there emerge desperate impulses in the attempt to solve the problems of the psyche that the revelations of the dream reveal. One concerns adultery; another, murder. Somers is attracted to Victoria and receives from her a kind of unspoken invitation. He can only see his disinclination for adultery as "puritanical"—which is no doubt how Frieda described it. "She looked at him with her dark eyes dilated into a glow, a glow of offering" (K, 156). It was, "Not love—just weapon-like desire" (K, 156).

We have seen that the most exciting sex for Lawrence is the "weapon-thrust" and "naked desire." If one is an Ithyphallic God, what objection can there be?

> The god Bacchus. Iacchos! Iacchos! Bacchanals with weapon hands. She had the sacred glow in her eyes.... Jack would not begrudge the god [that is the husband wouldn't mind a bit of adultery]. He decided almost involuntarily. *Perhaps it was fear*. (K, 156; my italics)

Somers feels he is a coward.

> He wondered if it was a sort of cowardice. Honour? No need as far as Jack was

concerned, apparently? And Harriet? She was too honest a female. She would know that the dishonour, *as far as she felt it*, lay in the desire, not in the act. For her, too, honour did not consist in a pledged word kept according to pledge, but in a genuine feeling faithfully followed. *He had not to reckon with honour here.* (K, 157; my italics)

The influence here is clearly Frieda's, with her Grossian immoralism. (This interpretation, written before I had read *Mr Noon*, is disturbingly confirmed by that novel.) Honor does not reside in your pledge to your marriage: the principle is to be faithful to genuine feeling, and if the dark ithyphallic impulse says it wants adultery, then it is honorable to obey. Harriet won't feel it much ("as far as she felt it") so scruple is easily disposed of.

The depths to which Lawrence was corrupted are made more clear in the next paragraph:

Why not follow the flame, the moment sacred to Bacchus? ... *He did not know why not. Perhaps only old moral habit* or fear, as Jack said, of committing himself. ... But his heart of hearts was stubbornly puritanical. And his innermost soul was dark and sullen, black with a sort of scorn. These moments bred in the heart and born in the eye: he had enough of them. (K, 157)

The passage clearly indicates Lawrence's moral predicament, his confusion. If one believes in the dark god below the threshold, and throws off the "old morality" under the Grossian persuasion by what does one decide in a moral dilemma? If one has "a sort of human bomb" in one, "a devil inside him," may one not, in one's acts, be simply serving evil and destructiveness?

In the subsequent chapter, "Volcanic Evidence," Lawrence writes the most corrupt propaganda for giving oneself up to the joys of evil and declaring "Evil be though my good!" As we have seen, Lawrence was deeply troubled by his own emotional cataclysms, not least his murderous impulses toward Frieda.

Somers ponders:

if I *am* finally a sort of human bomb, black inside, and primed: I hope the hour and the place will come for my going off: for my exploding with the maximum amount of havoc. *Some* men have to be bombs, to explode and make breaches in the walls that shut life in. Blind, havoc-working bombs too. Then so be it (K, 183)

The novel goes on in this vein: the mass of mankind is soulless, most people are dead (K, 299). Men in the streets are like lice or ants listening to their doom (K, 316).

At one point, Lawrence approaches an existential position and writes a superb rejection of scientific reductionism in its approach to human beings (the beginning of chapter 16, "A Row in Town"). This degenerates into drivel, about whales, reptiles, Caesar, and Napoleon. Lawrence even seems at one point to believe in theories of a collective consciousness:

The masses are always, strictly, non-mental. Their consciousness is preponderantly vertebral . . . like whales that burst up through the ice that suffocates them, so they will burst up through the fixed consciousness. (K, 338)

There are two elements that emerge as positives from *Kangaroo*, and both are negative, belonging to that fascistic inversion of morality.

One is the insistence that a man is most admired by a woman for his murderousness. Murder is far more exciting than sexual love.

The other element is nihilistic: a triumphant sense that nothing has any meaning.

The first view is represented by Jack, who kills some men in the political riots. Later, he boasts about it to Somers. Somers, as we have seen, has dismissed such concepts as honor. He has no sense, apparently, that if a murderer confesses to him, he ought at least contemplate the requirements of justice. But I believe Lawrence himself, by this time, has become corrupt.

As luck would have it, Somers comes upon an article in the *Sydney Daily Telegraph* on earthquakes.

he had read this almost thrilling bit of journalism with satisfaction. If the mother earth herself is so unstable, and upsets the apple cart without caring a straw, why what can a man say to himself if he *does* happen to have a devil in his belly! (K, 187)

That's all right then! To have a dynamic of hate within oneself, prompting one's immoralism and one's paranoid-schizoid misanthropy and loathing for society, is virtually a principle of the universe! Mother Earth demonstrates it to be so. What a corrupt argument!

In the subsequent chapter we have a diatribe on the subject of marriage. It is all clearly about Lawrence and Frieda: "he was to be lord and master, and she the humble slave. . . . Him, a lord and master! . . . And he was not even master of himself, with his ungovernable furies and his uncritical intimacies with people." The clue to solving the problem is not to find any mutual sense of freedom, in the recognition of the autonomy of the other being, in each, or in moving out toward life-tasks. It is the old fascistic remedy:

Richard . . . must open the doors of his soul and let in a dark Lord and Master for himself, the dark god he had sensed outside the door. Let him once truly submit to the dark majesty, break open his doors to this fearful god who is master, and enters us from below, the lower doors; let himself once admit a Master, the unspeakable god: and the rest would happen. (K, 196)

Lawrence-Somers is not in the least troubled by the sexual satisfaction Jack has had in homicide:

"Tell you what, boy," he said in a hoarse whisper, "I settled *three* on em—three!" There was an indescribable joy in his tones, like a man telling of the good time he has had with a strange mistress—"Gawr, but I was lucky. I got one of them iron bars from the windows, and I stirred the brains of a couple of them with it, and I broke the neck of a third...." "Cripes, there's *nothing* bucks you up sometimes like killing a man—*nothing*. You feel a perfect *angel* after it." (K, 358)

Richard feels a "torn" feeling in his abdomen.

"Having a woman's something, isn't it? But it's a fleabite, nothing compared to killing your man when your blood comes up."
  "...I can go to Victoria, now, and be as gentle—" He jerked his head in the direction of Victoria's room. "And you bet she'll like me."
  His eyes glowed with a sort of exultation.
  "Killing's natural to a man, you know," he said. "*It is just as natural as lying with a woman. Don't you think?*" (K, 359; my italics)

Richard "did not answer." Lawrence is strangely fascinated with the effect of murder on sexual relationships, and this may be related to his perversions.
  Despite the emphasis on the "dark unexplained blood-tenderness that is deeper than love flowing from the unknowable God," Richard Somers makes no progress toward existential meaning. The political dynamic, inevitably, ends in chaos, blood, and death. Somers's ultimate reflections seem to be a deepened version of Paul Morel's nihilistic feelings at the end of *Sons and Lovers*. Even life itself becomes a horror:

He saw something clutch in a pool. Crouching, he saw a horror—a dark-grey, brown-striped octopus thing with two smallish, white beaks or eyes, living in a cranny of a rock in a pool. It stirred the denser, viscous pool of itself and unfurled a long dark arm through the water. (K, 373)

Somers goes home, but home is "four walls" that make a "blanket I wrap around in, in timelessness and nowhere, to go to sleep." Harriet? "Another bird like himself."

If only she wouldn't speak, talk, feel. The weary habit of talking and having feelings. When a man has no soul he has no feelings to talk about. He wants to be still. And "meaning" is the most meaningless of illusions. An outworn garment. (K, 373)

We cannot doubt that Lawrence is writing about himself. In a sense Somers is a character, grieving because Kangaroo is dying, together with all his hopes of a new political future, but *Kangaroo* is also a clearly propagandist book for Lawrence's philosophy based on the dark gods. What has happened, so that Somers–Lawrence is now a man without a soul, who can find no meaning in existence, and find only that meaning is the most meaningless thing of all?

Harriet and he? It was time they both agreed that nothing has any meaning. Meaning is a dead letter when man has no soul. And speech is like a volley of dead leaves and dust, stifling the air. Human beings should learn to make weird, wordless cries, like the animals, and cast off the clutter of words. (K, 373–74)

As in *Women in Love*, the mere routine of life seems mere "tic-tac" "tic-tac! tic-tac! The clock. Home to ten. Just for clockwork's sale."

Only in this pause that one finds the meaninglessness of meanings—like the old husks that spread dust. (K, 374)

Now, "What was the good of caring": "One could float and deliciously melt down, to nothingness" (K, 375) This is surely as close as ever Lawrence came to nihilism?

Through Somers in *Kangaroo* Lawrence seems to abandon all such civilized efforts to seek meaning and value. Although Richard declares, "I won't give up the flag of our real civilised consciousness. I'll give up the ideals. But not the aware, self-responsible, deep consciousness that we've gained" (K, 390), he seems, at least in the mood above, to fail to find any way to meaning in love, or in his relationship with the world. At the end of chapter 17, we have a passage somewhat parallel to the passage at the end of *The Rainbow*, where Ursula encounters the dark forces represented by the wild horses. Somers feels for the kangaroo in the zoo: "a dark, animal tenderness, and another sort of consciousness, deeper than human." (K, 381) And now the moon rises. As always, the moon is deeply significant in Lawrence: "Rocking with cold, radium-burning passion, swinging and flinging itself with venomous desire." (K, 382) Some wild ponies came to him, as to Ursula, and he has a passionate sense of at-one-ness. But with what? Here, I believe we penetrate to the center of Lawrence's unconscious mythology. We have seen before his theme of "You are the call and I am the answer," and the sense that some voice or force calls him from the darkness. We have seen the yearning for some inhuman or state beyond the human. Here, I believe we have Somers-Lawrence yearning still to be united with the Dead Mother, for whom he is willing to sacrifice the world, love of woman, and all reality:

> Richard rocking with the radium-urgent passion of the night: the huge, desirous swing, the call clamour, the low kiss of retreat. The call, call! And the answerer. Where was his answerer? There was no living answerer. He knew that when he had spoken a word to the night-half-hidden ponies with their fluffy legs. No animate answer this time. The radium-rocking, wave-knocking night his call and his answer both. This God without feet or knees or face. This sluicing, knocking, urging night, heaving like a woman with unspeakable desire, but no woman, no thighs, or breast, no body. The moon, the concave mother-of-pearl of night, the great radium-swinging, and his little self. The call and the answer, without intermediary. Non-human gods, non-human human being. (K, 382)

This makes it clear that Lawrence was caught in a death circle. He wanted to escape from being human, into a state of nonhuman human being, into being a kind of god, but because there is no *living* answerer, the yearning is to merge with the dead mother, represented by the sea and the moon. And the "radium-burning" element, with its "mystic virtue if vivid decomposition" is a disintegration and dissolution into death.

## The Plumed Serpent

The first four chapters of *The Plumed Serpent* are superb—Kate Lesley's response to Mexico and especially to the bullfight, and even toward the end there is a splendid episode about a foal that is vivid and tender. There are many lovely passages, such as Kate's trip up the lake in a boat, and other descriptions of the Mexican countryside. But the rest of *The Plumed Serpent* is repugnant and false, and plunges further into the schizoid moral inversion of "Evil, be thou my good."

Lawrence draws us very sensitively and imaginatively into the experience of his characters, and we feel very close to Kate throughout the novel. Indeed, her experience is the subject of the book, and Lawrence conveys throughout that he has a good deal to teach us, as we shall see, about the relationship between our being—especially woman's being—and the realities of our world. Toward the end, we are brought to reflect upon, and to experience imaginatively, Kate becoming a little child, submitting herself to her Mexican husband Cipriano, and finding, instead of the sexual satisfaction ("the beak-like friction of Aphrodite of the foam") sought by western women, an experience "so deep and hot and flowing" that "she could not know him," while entering into "a mindless communion of the blood." (PS, 440) In this she experiences a particular form of submission, in which she gives up her western consciousness and her self ("I feel as if my soul were coming undone")—and we read of the "marginless death of her individual self." This is something more than lapsing into vaginal orgasm; it is a total surrender of the being to man's *power*, which Lawrence attempts to celebrate as superior to mere orgasm.

The man she submits to is a general in the Mexican army and has joined forces with one Don Ramón to bring back the ancient Aztec gods to Mexico to replace Christianity. Lawrence's argument for this is expressed toward the end of the book: "Let them find themselves again and their own universe and their own gods. *Let them substantiate their own mysteries*" (PS, 443; my italics). The novel is devoted to contemplating imaginatively the possibility of restoring gods that are more vital and capable of being present in the here and now than the Christian Christ or God.

In both the sexual story of the novel, and in this delineation of a possible restoration of new gods, chapter 23 is crucial, "Huitzilopochtli's Night." Cipriano, Kate's husband, enthroned and robed as Huitzilopochtli, executes some Mexicans who have tried to assassinate Ramón, who has made himself into the other god, Quetzalcoatl. The prisoners are brought in:

> ash-grey, (they) gazed with black glittering eyes, making not a sound. A guard stood behind each of them. Cipriano gave a sign, and quick as lightning the guards had got the throats of the two victims in a grey cloth, and with a sharp jerk had broken their necks, lifting them back in one movement. The grey clothes they tied hard and tight round the throats, laying the twitching bodies on the floor. (PS, 394)

Cipriano proclaims an incantation: "the grey dog belongs to the ash of the world. The Lords of Life are the Masters of Death. Dead are the grey dogs." (PS, 394) There is then a ritual discussion in front of four other prisoners, and the guards pronounce that they shall die. They are offered leaves. One of these is "the leaf of Malintzi"—and they are trying to persuade Kate to become Malintzi, who is Queen to Huitzilopochtli. The prisoners are bound, and Cipriano, taking a thin, bright dagger, stabs three of them to the heart. The bleeding bodies are quickly removed. The one man who had the leaf of Malintzi is pardoned. There is then a great deal of gloating mumbo-jumbo, in which the blood of the slain is displayed on Cipriano's hands, and then sprinkled in the fire. There is a ritual of expiation and in a prayer it is said that the slain shall "be made anew." In an exchange between the two men become gods, it is said that Cipriano's hand will always be red "till green-robed Malintzi brings her water-blow." It is all this murderous horror that makes Kate adore Cipriano and give her being up to him.

The novel begins with a superb portrayal of a Mexican bull-fight, seen through Kate's eyes. She is appalled by the cruelty, as the bulls plunge their horns into the bellies of the startled horses, and churn about in the insides of their bodies, so that their bowels fall out and there is a great stink. We feel, as she does, that all this is a revolting way for men to show their manhood, to prove themselves. As for the spectators, "They might just as well sit and enjoy someone else's diarrhoea" (PS, 24). The mob of Mexicans are degenerate; there can be little doubt about anyone's civilized response.

What is Kate's response to the sickening and cruel murders perpetrated by her husband Cipriano with all the accompanying mumbo-jumbo and fascistic ceremony? She is just a little shocked, of course.

> The executions shocked and depressed her. She knew that Ramón and Cipriano did deliberately what they did: they believed in their deeds, they acted with all their conscience. As men, probably they were right. (PS, 401)

Who says they were "probably right"? Both Kate and her creator Lawrence had access to several thousand years of human justice, and we may note that the prisoners had no fair trial, and were being denounced and executed by two *pronunciamentos*, who had dreamed up their own religious revival and its politicization. There were sinister aspects of the ceremony in which the prisoners were killed. No women were allowed to be present, for example, while the prisoners' fate was discussed in front of them (one prisoner protests that he does not want to die). The whole episode is disgusting and repugnant, by any standards, and the destructions are done without pity. They are, essentially, fascistic.

Kate does see that Cipriano is "driving the male significance to its utmost, and beyond, with a sort of demonism." "It seemed to her all terrible *will*, the exertion of pure, awful will ... And deep in her soul came a revulsion against this manifestation of pure will." But—

It was fascinating also. There was something dark and lustrous and fascinating to her in Cipriano, and in Ramón. The black, relentless power, even passion of the will in men! The strange, sombre, lustrous beauty of it! She knew herself under the spell! (PS, 401–2)

The spell is surely one that Lawrence would like to exert on woman. Does it redeem murder if it is "lustrously" done? We are on dangerous ground.

As we have seen, Cipriano declares in the ritual that his hands will remain bloody until Malintzi comes in her green gown. Now, he thinks that he needs her to complete himself ("You are the call and I am the answer"):

To him she was but the answer to his call, the sheath for his blade, the cloud to his lightning, the earth to his rain, the fuel to his fire.
  Alone, she was nothing. Only as the pure female corresponding to his pure male, did she signify. (PS, 403)

And then, significantly, "without her to give him the power, *he too would not achieve his own manhood and meaning.*" What else? ... The Star!

Don Ramón Morning Star was something that sprang between him and her and hung shining, the strange third thing that was both of them and neither of them, between his night and her day. (PS, 403)

"Ah, yes, it was wonderful," and so Lawrence goes on, and with it goes the characteristic rejection of the rest of humanity and of the responsible self:

It meant the death of her individual self. It meant abandoning so much, even her very own foundations. For she had believed truly that every man and every woman alike was founded on the individual.
  Now, must she admit that the individual was an illusion and a falsification? There was no such animal. Except in the mechanical world. In the world of machines, the individual machine is effectual. The individual, like the perfect being, does not and cannot exist in the vivid world. We are all fragments. And at the best, halves. The only thing is the Morning Star. (PS, 405)

Apparently Kate accepts that she must be a subdued woman, to complete the *manhood* of this *pronunciamento*, who, as she declares at one point, is pulling the wool over the eyes of the Mexicans and herself. In the name of the "Morning Star," whatever that may be, we are to relinquish the toils of consciousness ("the poisonous snakes of mental consciousness," [RS, 181]) and submit utterly to a ruthless impersonal exterminator of those who oppose his "godhead"? We are urged to take Lawrence's manhood, but he is recommending a very special elevated state under this name:

Many a man has his own spark of divinity, and has it quenched, blown out by the winds of force or ground out of him by machines.
  And when the spirit and the blood in man begin to go asunder, bringing the great death, most stars die out.

Only the man of a great star, a great divinity, can bring the opposites together again, in a new union. (PS, 435)

Richard Aldington surely demonstrates acute insights into Lawrence's problems in his "Introduction":

His American general, who is a projection of himself, sets about recalling those long-banished gods . . . he became so caught up in his own vivid incantations that he began to plume himself on being a "natural aristocrat" and even a new avatar of the snake-bird god. (PS, "Introduction," 8)

Actually, it is Kate who thinks of herself as a "natural aristocrat" ("intrinsic superiority of the hereditary aristocrat" [PS, 433]). Lawrence in his identification with the two pronunciamentos seems to think of himself as a god again, and here even as one who has the right and will to slaughter his enemies. What we have to realize is that the woman whose sensitive intimacy we enter into imaginatively has this intimacy with a mass-executor, and admires him for his murderousness.

It is startling, if one studies the whole of Lawrence, to find this underlying murderous fantasy, in all its religiose fanaticism. There is a touch of it even in *The Lost Girl*, as we have seen ("these were the true gods . . . who dipped their lips in blood," [LG, 344]). It is understandable in light of Winnicott's analysis of the underlying dynamics of fascism:

One of the roots of the need to be a dictator can be a compulsion to deal with this fear of woman by encompassing her and acting for her. The dictator's curious habit of demanding not only absolute obedience and absolute dependence but also "love" can be derived from this source.

Moreover, the tendency of groups of people to accept or even seek actual domination is derived from a fear of domination by fantasy woman. This fear leads them to seek, and even welcome, domination by a known human being, especially one who has taken upon himself the burden of personifying and therefore limiting the magical qualities of the all-powerful woman of fantasy, to whom is owed the great debt. (Winnicott 1965, 165)

The novel is the more sinister because Kate is such an attractive woman for much of the time. She has a good deal of Lawrence in her, and a good deal of Frieda. She is both admired and subjected to a critical note, vis-à-vis her Americanness: "like most modern people, she had a will-to-happiness." There is a note of contempt for "ordinary" people; the degenerate mob of Mexico are mongrels, while " 'I've had enough of *canaille*, of any sort,' she said." At the same time, Mexico is "oppressive and gruesome"; at night "grisliness and evil come forth" and the Aztec things in the background have "no hope in them." We suppose we are setting out on a novel in which Lawrence's intelligence and sanity is going to portray a characteristic civilization and show us a sensitive individual seeking her authenticity in it. The novel shows great wit at times (cf. Mrs. Norris: "she was an odd number: and, all alone, she could give the even numbers a bad time"), and even at its worst moments, the scene is "realized" superbly, as with the description of the church in chapter 3 and the evocations of the atmosphere of the lake.

But we find that Kate is yet another Lawrentian character who is flying, from a sense of death, nihilism, and fate:

> It ought to have been all gay, *allegro, allegretto*, in that sparkle of bright air and old roof surfaces. But no! There was the dark undertone, the black, serpent-like fatality all the time.
> ... she had heard the *consummatum est* of her own spirit. It was finished, in a kind of death agony. (PS, 56)

There are further comparisons of Kate with Christ:

> ... the glamour had gone from station to station of the cross, and the last illumination was the tomb. (K, 56)

She is forty now:

> Now the bright page was turned, and the dark page lay before her. How could one write on a page so profoundly black? (PS, 57)

We may detect, I believe, that Lawrence himself was writing *The Plumed Serpent* in some desperation about his own health and future, and that he put a great deal of himself into Kate. Out of this comes Kate's fascination with the old gods. There is a press account of their reappearance, in reality: "a different light from the common light seemed to gleam out of the words even of this newspaper paragraph" (PS, 64). She remembers the plumed serpent, "hideous in the fanged, feathered, writhing stone of the National Museum."

> But Quetzalcoatl was, she vaguely remembered; a sort of fair-faced bearded god; the wind, the breath of life, the eyes that see and are unseen, like the stars by day. (PS, 64)

The thoughts are given as Kate's, but they are clearly Lawrence's—Lawrence depressed by his own mortality, who wants to be reborn into a new life suitable for a superior being. He wants to break out of it, through her:

> Her Irish spirit was weary to death of definite meanings, and a god of one fixed purport. Gods should be iridescent, like the rainbow in the storm.... Ye must be born again. Even the gods must be born again. We must be born again. (PS, 65).

Christianity has only life in the next world to offer. A new kind of god must be sought who offers new life:

The powerful, degenerate thing called life, wrapping one or other of its tentacles round her. . . .

Ye must be born again. Out of the fight with the octopus of life, the dragon of degenerate or *incomplete existence*, one must win this soft bloom of being, that is damaged by a touch. (PS, 65; my italics)

The bearded fair-faced god bears a resemblance to the Birkin figure, the "man from Eternity" who is going to save the Ursula–Kate woman: none other than Lawrence himself. Thus, as Aldington sees, the whole of *The Plumed Serpent* is an act of narcissistic self-deification.

At first the Aztec things are objects of horror, the obsidian knife, the human sacrifices, but then Lawrence becomes fascinated with them. The tropical-scented flowers seem to smell of blood or sweat; there is a feeling of ponderous darkness, and a certain gleam of menace. But perhaps we were wrong to see evil as evil. Perhaps that is where the solution lies. Perhaps Evil could be our Good.

"the Aztec horrors! Well, perhaps they were not so horrible after all . . . like seeds, so full of magic, of the unexplored magic?" (PS, 68)

I think it's a bit overwhelming, says Kate; how good to be overwhelmed, declares Ramón. It is time for the gods to take "the bath of life" again.

There follows a passage of painful nonsense about mixed blood, and the white man's "dead white sea" consciousness as well as the way a certain racial consciousness is handed on to the child at the moment of coition:

all, everything depends on the moment of coition. At that moment many things can come to a crisis: all a man's hope, his honour, his faith, his trust, his belief in life and creation and God, all these things can come to a crisis in the moment of coition. And these things will be handed on in continuity to the child. (PS, 72)

Lawrence seems to become half-aware that his Mexican pronunciamientos are talking like D. H. Lawrence so he makes Kate say, "I believe it is true." Ramón goes on: "the only *conscious* people are half breeds, people of mixed blood, begotten in greed and selfish brutality" (PS, 72). For the Indian, "the moment of coition is his moment of supreme hopelessness, when he throws himself down the pit of despair." Another says, "we must make the miracle come. The miracle is superior even to the moment of coition."

Kate declares that she is the kind of woman who "*can* only love a man who is fighting to *change* the world, to make it freer, more alive"—presumably like Frieda—"*a man who is fighting for something beyond the ordinary life.*"

To Cipriano, to whom she had told her story of marriage with an Irish leader, she appears as the (mother) Madonna:

The wonder, the mystery, the magic that used to flood over him as a boy and a youth, when he kneeled before the babyish figure of the Santa Maria de la Soledad, flooded him again. He was in the presence of the goddess, white-handed, mysterious, gleaming with a moon-like power and the intense potency of grief. (PS, 78)

In the background is "a certain male ferocity."

Will, as elsewhere in Lawrence, is a "Bad Thing." Ramón demands: "what else is there in the world, besides human will, human appetite? because ideas and ideals are only instruments of human will and appetite" (PS, 81). He looks for something else: "My own manhood!"

"What does that mean?" she cried, jeering.
"If you looked, and found your own womanhood, you would know."
"But I *have* my own womanhood!" she cried.
"And then—when you find your own manhood—your womanhood," he went on, smiling faintly at her—"then you know it is not your own, to do what you like with. You don't have it of your own free will. It comes from—from the middle—from the God. Beyond me, at the middle, is the God. And the God gives me my manhood, then leaves it to me." (PS, 81)

It looks like an existential emphasis, urging us to seek our own authentic being, recognizing it does not belong to us but to some pulse in the universe. But how does this work out? The flow of Kate's life and broken; she knew she could not restart it in Europe (a statement actually that applies to Lawrence):

White men had had a soul, and lost it. The pivot of fire had been quenched in them, and their lives had started to spin in the reversed direction, widdershins. That reversed look which is in the eyes of so many white people, the look of mullity, and life wheeling in the reversed direction. Widdershins.
But the dark-faced natives, with their strange soft flame of life wheeling upon a dark void: were they centreless and widdershins, too...? The strange, soft flame of courage in the black Mexican eyes. But still it was not knit to a centre, that centre which is the soul of a man in a man. (PS, 85)

Lawrence cannot bear "white" consciousness, white humanity, because he cannot accept his common humanity with them, and yearns to find his new world in the primitives Mexicans, but they have no center to their eyes—and it has been no use giving them Jesus Christ as a center. "Against the soft, dark flow of the Indian the white man at last collapses; with his God and his energy he collapses" What shall we give them? "Quetzalcoatl . . . his huge fangs white and pure today as in the lost centuries when his makers were alive. *He has not died*" (PS, 86-87).

Jesus has died one might say; Quetzalcoatl lives, with his big teeth, and so hate is to be substituted for love as the means to give a center to the primitive men of Mexico, where new birth is to be had. Kate becomes the Madame to Cipriano in this. "She was the mystery, and he the adorer, under the semi-ecstatic spell of the mystery" (PS, 89). Kate is rowed across the lake, with a great deal of mystical accompaniment, to the territory where the Gods are to be reborn and given to the people. The water, for what it's worth, is spermlike. Chapter 5 is a marvelous evocation of this lake, but we must be alert to where the boat is taking us:

> She felt she could cry aloud, for the unknow Gods to put the magic back into her life, and to save her from the dry-rot of the world's sterility. (PS, 112)

We could say that Kate has Lawrence's subjective problem, but we can see that he cannot believe in any western magic. Europe is all politics or jazzing or slushy mysticism or sordid spiritualism. "And the magic had gone" (PS, 112). The younger generation are more and more "devoid of wonder." Kate wants to "shut doors of iron against the mechanical world." Also in the background is the Otto Gross cult of the primitive:

> at the same time, with her blood flowing softly sunwise, to let the sunwise sympathy of unknown people steal across to her, and add its motion to her, the motion of the stress of life, with the big sun and the stars like a tree holding out leaves. (PS, 113)

The solution is to yearn for a higher form of existence, as Kate does:

> So in her soul she cried aloud to the greater mystery, the higher power that hovered in the interstices of the hot air, rich and potent . . . addressing the silent life-breath which hung unrevealed. . . .
> She felt the fulness descended into her once more, the peace and the power. (PS, 116)

She goes into ecstasies over giving two boatmen an orange each, and exclaims: "There is something rich and alive in these people . . . they are like children, helplesss. . . . And then they're like demons" (PS, 118).

She feels in touch with the Great Breath, and feels the heart of the earth beating. She is not caught up in the world's great cog-wheels any more. She has gone native, and worships *power*.

But at the moment she found a house with the Mexican Juana, I found myself asking—*Where does her money come from*? For this woman to seek the Great Breath, some machines must be running somewhere—just as the machines were running to provide the royalties that paid for Lawrence to chase the Mexican gods.

How can one discuss seriously the incantations, the rituals, the fascist salutes, the hymns and prayers to Quetzalcoatl? Lawrence even at times seems doubtful of what he is doing ("How dare he take such nonsense seriously?" says Don Ramón's wife.) It is all directed against "the poisonous snakes of mental consciousness" (PS, 181) and to the worship of the "dark aura of power." And often mysogynist: "The itching, prurient, *knowing*, imaginative eye, I am cursed with it, the curse of Eve. The curse of Eve is upon me, and my eyes are like hooks, my knowledge is like a fish-hook through my gills, pulling me in spasmodic desire." (PS, 196–7)

But Kate, following a "fate like doom," comes to feel a "young virgin again." The men, she realizes, want to take her will away. Then Cipriano asks Kate to marry her. He doesn't and won't woo her. He treats her with that primitive disdain Lawrence admires. She is to become the wife of the god. The men's *manhood* is now a *demon* in them (PS, 204–5); it is howling, it wants to crush the world like an egg. It is all false solution. Meanwhile manhood seems to be achieved by rituals that seem somewhere between a boy scout rally and an evangelist meeting, with those odd homosexual notes, as when Cipriano and Ramón hold hands

> Only in the heart of the cosmos man can look for strength. And if he can keep his soul in touch with the heart of the world, then from the heart of the world new blood will beat in strength and stillness in him, fulfilling his manhood. (PS, 207)

There is more mumbo-jumbo about manhood and womanhood, the Morning Star and the Dawn Star, and the Son of the Star: "The son of the Star is coming back to the Sons of Men, with big bright strides." (PS, 213) And there is a touch of the New Sex

> "Do not kiss with the mouths of yesterday ... and let your navel know nothing of yesterday, and go into your women with a new body, enter the new body in her." (PS, 213)

Put oil on your hands etc and "on the secret places of your body"; you are not yet men and women. And at that moment the rains come.

Ramón is especially hard on Carlotta's concern for her sons, "You don't love the boys, you are only putting your love-will over them"—and so Carlotta is cast out, also in the name of manhood. Power is all.

The world, one might say even, is being remodelled to fit the unconscious needs of D. H. Lawrence.

> "I said to myself: I am a new man."
> "...my mother went even before me, to her still white bed in the moon...."
> "I am as a man who is a new man, with new limbs and life, and the light of the Morning Star in his eyes." (PS, 241)

The novel becomes a kind of black day dream. Kate alternates between being herself as a realized character, and an agent of the daydream. The book alternates between true art and false-solution propaganda, in a quite uncanny way. Lawrence has his thumb prodigiously in the scales.

The opening of chapter 16, "Cipriano and Kate," for instance, is superbly beautiful and evocative as a description of the Mexican scene:

> It pleased her to see the men running along the planks with the dark-green melons, and piling them in a mound on the rough sand, melons dark green like creatures with

pale bellies. To see the tomatoes all poured out into a shallow place in the lake, bobbing about while the women washed them, a bobbing scarlet upon the water. (PS, 242)

There is an "unutterable weight" that sinks on Kate's spirits in Mexico, even in the liveliest scenes, as it sank on Lawrence's, and so to go over to the moral inversions of the new cult seems very seductive. The Hymns of Quatzalcoatl seem to her "the only escape from a world gone ghastly." So she is half-persuaded, when Cipriano urges her "why should you not be the woman in the Quatzalcoatl pantheon? If you will, the goddess!" He asks her to marry him: "A strange inscrutable flame of desire seemed to be burning on Cipriano's face" (PS, 248).

Lawrence contests the "will" of the western individual, and especially the will of the western woman, yet what could be more willful (as he sometimes sees) than the way Don Ramón and Don Cipriano seek to revive the dreadful Aztec gods and impose them on the people of Mexico? Lawrence proclaims they are not an idea like socialism, but the gods—in the way they are conjured up—are rather worse than an idea. They are a lapse into barbarism.

There is something worse, under the impulse of that inverted moral dynamic, Evil be thou my good. We can follow this as Kate reflects upon the horror in Mexico: "the black eyes of he people really make my heart contract, and my flesh shrink. There's a bit of horror in it. And I don't want horror in my soul" (PS, 249). A black cloud seems to come over Cipriano.

"Why not? he said at last.
"Horror is real. Why not a bit of horror, as you say, among all the rest?" (PS, 249)

A bit of horror is good, he says, get used to it.

"A bit of horror is like the sesame seed in the nougat, it gives the sharp wild flavour. It is good to have it there." (PS, 249)

"Yet, surely, surely he was only putting his will over her." Who is pulling the wool over whose eyes? Lawrence seems here strangely divided, perhaps since Lawrence wants to believe that since "everything that lives is holy," the evil he recognizes in himself is really good. Kate reflects: "Surely it would not be *herself* who could marry him. *It would be some curious female within her, whom she did not know and did not own*" (PS, 249; my italics).

Thus, Kate, like Lawrence, begins to contemplate in fantasy a nonhuman world.

She seemed to see the great sprouting and urging of the cosmos, moving into weird life. And men only like green-fly clustering on the tender tips, *an aberration there*. (PS, 356; my italics)

There is the same fascination with a Holy War. "Ramón smiled. Already he saw in Cipriano's eye the gleam of a Holy War." (PS, 260)—and Ramón is clearly the transmutation of Lawrence's own worst ambitions to save the world, from a sense of being superior.

> "I would like," he said, smiling, "to be one of the Initiates of the Earth. One of the Initiators . . . the First Men of every people, forming a Natural Aristocracy of the world." (PS, 260)

The fascination is clearly Lawrence's and it is Lawrence speaking, of Thor and Wotan, Igdrasil, Tuatha De Danaan, Ashtaroth, Mithras, Brahma, and Astarte. By any account it is all mystical mumbo-jumbo, and shows no close acquaintance with the various forms of quest among various civilizations for meaning. The figures are merely wheeled out for the sounds of their exotic names as much as anything. Lawrence expands again his Pantisocratic ambitions: Rananim—"Let it be a union of the unconsciousness," yet as Kate sees it is all really a kind of Salvation Army.

She, on her part, has a complementary view rooted in a sense of superiority: "I like the world, the sky and the earth and the greater mystery beyond. But people—yes, they are all monkeys to me." (PS, 263).

Kate needs a man. "But between herself and humanity there was the bond of subtle, helpless antagonism."

> underneath it all was the unconquerable dislike, almost *disgust* of people. More than hate, it was disgust . . . she longed to fling them down the great the final oubliette. (PS, 264)

As Lawrence ruefully admits, "there is no great and final *oubliette*: or at least, it is never final, until one has flung *oneself* down" (PS, 264).

This disgust is clearly a schizoid fear of close contact leading to annihilation: "close contacts, or long contacts, were short and long revulsions of violent disgust." It is out of this schizoid disgust, hate, and need for "distance" that Lawrence devises his religio-sexual theory in *The Plumed Serpent*. Ramon reflect:

> Mere *personal* contact, mere human contact filled him, too, with disgust. . . .
> He had to meet them on another plane . . . intangible, remote, and without *intimacy* . . . . The quick of a man must turn to God alone: in some way or other. (PS, 265)

This explains Lawrence's fantasy yearning to be a *god* above those *human* contacts that brought the threat of disgusting "merging." It also explains the homosexuality:

> With Cipriano he was most sure. Cipriano and he, even when they embraced each

other with passion, when they met after an absence, embraced in the recognition of each other's eternal and abiding loneliness: like the Morning Star.
    But women would not have this. They wanted intimacy—and intimacy means disgust. (PS, 265)

The attempt to meet in love is now impossible, virtually blasphemous:

> Men and Women should know that they cannot, absolutely, meet on earth. In the closest kiss, the dearest touch, there is the small gulf which is none the less complete because it is so narrow, no *nearly* non-existent. They must bow and submit in reverence, to the gulf. Even though I eat the body and drink the blood of Christ, Christ is Christ and I am I, and the gulf is impassable. Though a woman be dearer to man this his own life, yet he is he and she is she, and the gulf can never close up. Any attempt to close it is a violation, and the crime against the Holy Ghost. (PS, 265)

Instead of looking to love, with its "horrible merging," the quest for confirmation of being is sought from some cosmic source that he calls the Morning Star.
    The universe, Ramón tells Kate, is a "nest of dragons" so we are back with the need for a bit of horror, and once more we return to the awfulness of woman. Ramón is a man who "yearns for the sensual fulfillment" of his soul, but he cannot feel he can meet a woman "where your two souls coincide in their deepest desire."

> "If I marry a Spanish woman or a dark Mexican, she will give herself up to me to be ravished. If I marry a woman of the Anglo-Saxon stock or any blonde northern stock, she will want to ravish me, with the will of all the ancient white demons. Those that want to be ravished are parasites on the soul, and one has revulsions. Those that want to ravish a man are vampires." (PS, 287)

We are back at the schizoid problem of the (emptying) dangers of love. The earth is "a place of shame"; he must "keep himself within the middle place . . . my Morning Star"—*to become a god is the only solution.*
    But, as it turns out, to become a fascist is the only solution. Ramón drives a knife into a man's throat and triumphs:

> His brow was like a boy's, very pure and primitive, and the eyes underneath had a certain primitive gleaming look of virginity. As men must have been, in the first awful days, with that strange beauty that goes with pristine rudimentariness. (PS, 310)

It is not of course that I object to Ramón's killings since he was faced with a situation in which it was kill or be killed. What is so deplorable is the spell that the killings and the blood cast on Lawrence, and the way he makes Kate enjoy the blood-lust. Now she finds the same power in Cipriano:

> She could *see* the black fume of power which he emitted, the dark, heavy, vibration of his blood, which cast a spell over her. (PS, 329)

She is entranced by the "heavy power of the *will* that lay unemerged in his blood," while he almost becomes a kind of cosmic phallus:

> She could see again the skies go dark, and the phallic mystery rearing itself like a whirling dark cloud, to the zenith . . . the old supreme phallic mystery . . . his body of blood could rise up that pillar of cloud . . . like a rearing serpent or a rising tree, till it swept the zenith, and all the earth below was dark and prone, and consummated. (PS, 324)

This is the mystery of the primaeval world, "that has indeed gone by, but has not passed away. Never shall pass away."

> It was the ancient phallic mystery, the ancient god-devil of the male Pan. . . . He had the old gift of demon power. (PS, 325)

This demon with his cosmic erection has a great value in the Lawrentian scheme:

> As he sat in silence, casting the old, twilit Pan-power over her, she felt herself submitting, succumbing. He was once more the old dominant male, shadowy, intangible, looming suddenly tall, and covering the sky, making a darkness that was himself and nothing but himself. *And she was swooned prone beneath, perfect in her proneness.* (PS 325; my italics)

At last, here is an instrument to deal with the threatening phantom woman of the unconscious: a Demon King! And so the dangers of "horrible merging" are overcome: "He would never woo: she saw this." When the power of blood rose in him, he would sweep her away like a whirlwind.

> Ah! and what a mystery of prone submission, on her part, this huge creation would imply! Submission absolute, like the earth under the sky!
> Ah! what a marriage! How terrible! and how complete! (PS, 325)

It is all sickening nonsense, and it is a great relief later for Kate to say "I am afraid I am just a woman" (PS, 340). But we are in for a great deal of mumbo-jumbo before then, about the Master, the everlasting Pan—the Big Ithyphallos.

It is impossible to read *The Plumed Serpent* without feeling again that Lawrence must have had delusions almost of a psychopathological kind. From time to time, it is true that Kate registers a doubt ("mistrusted him" [PS, 327] but immediately the prose sweeps on "himself like a wind of glory"). Lawrence does not treat Ramón's ambitions with irony, even when he says: "We *must* change back to the vision of the living cosmos: We *must*. The old Pan is in us . . . I am Quatzalcoatl himself, if you like" (PS, 230) because Ramón and Cipriano *are* identities of Lawrence, as Aldington sees. "Cipriano the master of fire. The living Huitzilopochtli he had called himself. The living firemaster. The god in the flame: the Salamander" (PS, 334).

This woman has to be sacrificed: "She was condemned to go through these strange ordeals like a flame," while on page 352 we are back with "the Sons of God" among the daughters of men: "among the low dark shrubs of the crouching woman stood a forest of erect, upthrusting men, powerful and tense with inexplicable passion" (PS, 355). The men are giving a fascist-type salute.

Now there is a strange process whose symbolism needs to be taken into account. This may be called *getting rid of mother*.

There is a strange enigmatic moment in the mumbo-jumbo rituals, Ramón offers the liquids of his body to the altar fire.

> "A man shall take the wine of his spirit and the blood of his heart, the oil of his belly and the seed of his loins and offer them first to the Morning Star," said Ramón. . . .
> Four men came to him. Then the first one pressed a small glass bowl to Ramón's brow, and in the bowl was white liquid like bright water. The next touched a bowl to the breast, and the red shook in the bowl. At the navel a man touched a bowl with yellow fluid, and at the loins a bowl with something dark. They held them all to the light. (PS, 356)

The fluids are all mixed, and he flings them into the fire. All this ritualistic nonsense, obviously based on the communion, is embarrassing, but so obviously belongs to a schizoid obsession with inner contents. (The episode also seems to have a strangely masturbatory element, which I do not discuss because I cannot find insights to explain it.)

Whatever meaning there may be in this, what happens next is that Ramón's wife, the mother figure, interrupts and proclaims the rituals blasphemous— and *is killed off in the process.*

> "Ramón, he's murdered me, and lost his own soul," said Carlotta. "He has murdered me and lost his own soul. He is a murderer." (RS, 361)

Cipriano denies this dying woman her sacraments, a profoundly cruel and inhuman act. At the end of it "Kate sat by the window, and laughed a little." This is, we surely feel, as demented as Lawrence can get.

We must detect beneath the surface a deep hatred of the mother (Lawrence's mother) who is felt to have denied Ramón-Lawrence a birthright of some kind:

> "You are glad because you never poured the wine of your body into the mixing bowl! Yet in your day you have drunk the wine of his body and been soothed with his oil. . . . You are glad you kept back the wine of your body and the secret oil of your soul? That you only gave the water of your charity? I tell you the water charity, the hissing water of the spirit, is better at last in the mouth and in the breast and the belly; it puts out the fire. You would have put out the fire, Dona Carlotta—But you cannot. You shall not. . . . You born widow, you weeping mother, you impeccable wife, you just woman. You stole the very sunshine out of the sky and the sap out of the earth. Because back again, what did you pour? Only the water of dead dilution into the mixing-bowl of life, you thief. Oh die!—die!—die!. . . Do nothing but utterly die." (PS, 362–63)

Cipriano utters this appalling curse with (of course) glittering eyes. Kate laughs, and her reason is interesting:

> The primeval woman inside her laughed to herself, for she had known all the time about the two thieves on the Cross with Jesus; the bullying, marauding thief of the male in his own rights, and the much more subtle, cold, sly, charitable thief of the woman in *her* own rights, forever chanting her beggar's whine about the love of God and the God of pity. (PS, 363)

Even at such a moment, Lawrence lets his spleen go against woman, dementedly. Kate is made to accept the obsequiousness of the doctor, and priest, as "monsters of love":

> She could hardly be called a thief, and a sneak-thief of the world's virility, when these men came forcing their obsequiousness upon her, whining to her to take it and relieve them of the responsibility of their own manhood. No, if women are thieves, it is only because men want to be thieved from. (PS, 363)

The drums begin again, and we glimpse in the light of Winnicott's insights the sexual themes under the politics of dictatorship:

> Perhaps after all, life would conquer again, and men would be men, so that women could be women. Till men are men indeed, women have no hope to be women. (PS, 365)

Once Carlotta is dying, Kate goes out over the lake with Cipriano, to "the deeps where Cipriano could lay her." He feels

> the mysterious flower of her woman's femaleness slowly opening to him, as a sea-anemone opens deep under the sea, with infinite soft fleshliness. The hardness of self-will was gone, and the soft anemone of her deeps blossomed for him of itself, for down under the tides. (PS, 367)

This is presumably because with the dying of Carlotta there has been another conquest over dangerous woman, while Kate's will has been broken by becoming increasingly involved in the atrocities. Cipriano chants "My hand is to hold a gun.... Our gods hate a kneeling man.... They shout *Ho! Erect!*" (PS, 377).

One might think that the above paragraph, with its beautiful image of the anemone, referred to a woman learning to yield in orgasm. Far from it. At the end, Kate declares:

> Without Cipriano to touch me and *limit me* and *submerge my will*, I shall become a horrible, elderly female. I ought to *want* to be limited.... *I will make my submission.* (PS, 457; my italics)

This submission is to a sinister male potency, murderous and cruel ("so soft-

tongued, of the soft, wet, hot blood"—almost the last phrase of the book),
but Kate must forfeit sexual fulfillment. Her strange seething feminine will
subsides in her and is swept away "leaving her soft and powerfully potent."
To achieve her potency, it seems, woman must forfeit sexual fulfillment.

Lawrence spares us the details, but the important thing appears to be related
to his cult of "indifference," of not really giving in love

> Cipriano would not. By a dark and powerful instinct he drew away from her as soon
> as this desire rose again in her, for the white ecstasy of frictional satisfaction, the
> throes of Aphrodite of the foam. She could see that to him, it was repulsive. He just
> removed himself, dark and unchangeable, away from her. (PS, 439)

We must say, I believe, that this is a rationalization of Lawrence's fear and
horror of woman's orgasm. Mellors speaks of the "beak-like clitoris":

> So different from the beak-like friction of Aphrodite of the foam, the friction which
> flares out in circles of phosphorescent ecstasy, to the last wild spasm which utters the
> involuntary cry, like a death-cry, the final love-cry. (PS, 439)

This was removed from her. Was this necessary because Lawrence was afraid
of woman's orgasm as a kind of death? She has to forfeit it.

> When, in their love, it came back on her, the seething electric female ecstasy, which
> knows such spasms of delirium, *he recoiled from her*. (PS, 439)

She comes to feel it "was really nauseous to her." Instead, she has a "soft,
heavy, hot flow, when she was like a fountain gushing noiseless, and with
urgent softness from the volcanic deeps." It is "curiously beyond her
knowing": "So deep and hot and flowing as if it were subterranean." Some
argue that Lawrence meant that she is now experiencing vaginal as opposed
to clitoral orgasm, having learnt this distinction from Freud. But Lawrence's
is really a different message. If the man is suitably dominating and powerful
and avoids any impulse in the woman to seek her satisfaction, she will lapse
out in an experience that approximates more to a fit of petit mal than anything
that could be called an orgasm. It is really more like a kind of death. Cipriano
won't have "intimacy": "there was no need for emotions," and there must
be "a mindless communion of the blood."

But, did "sexual correspondence" matter so very much to her? She has
found a territory beyond it—presumably of primitive superstition and murder.
This is preferred to her previous attempts to "voluptuously fill the belly of her
own ego"—rather the "hot, phallic passion," the submission and the "soft,
wet, hot, blood" to murderous power.

Before the end collapses into this propaganda of sex religion, we have a brief
glimpse of the old, true Lawrence in an episode over a new-born foal. The
message seems quite different from the fate-laden gloom of the novel:

The ink-black ass-foal did not understand standing up. It rocked on its four loose legs, and wondered. Then it hobbled a few steps, to smell at some green growing maize. It smelled and smelled and smelled, as if all the dark aeons were stirring awake in its nostrils.

Then it turned, and looked with its bushy-velvet face straight at Kate, and put out a pink tongue at her. She laughed aloud. It stood wondering, dazed. Then it put out its tongue again. She laughed at it. It gave an awkward little skip, which surprised its own self very much. Then it ventured forward again, and all unexpectedly even to itself, exploded into another little skip.

"Already it dances!" cried Kate, "and it came into the world only last night." (PS, 432–33)

The peon in charge of it looks at her:

The black foal, the mother, the drinking, the new life, the mystery of the shadowy battlefield of creation, and the adoration of the full-breasted, glorious woman beyond him: all this seemed in the primitive black eyes of the man. . . .

"It is sex," she said to herself.

"How wonderful sex can be, when men keep it powerful and sacred, and it fills the world. Like sunshine through and through one." (PS, 453)

There are different forms of the sacred. Lawrence's making sacred of sex in this book is in the service of a dark and evil reversal of values, and the conquest of woman out of fear, her annihilation, really, and the denial of her being. The lovely moment with the foal, and Kate's delight in it, are a final momentary recapturing of her true self ("But I'm not going to submit")— which, however, she is not going to be able to sustain in the face of the author's fascistic determinations to have her and her creativity put down.

\*          \*          \*

What about Lawrence's capacity to be a religious author, as Leavis sees him? What about Lawrence's definition of "manhood"?

In light of Lawrence's religious fanaticism, it seems to represent something quite different—a submission to the god, becoming an avatar. There is a revealing exchange between Kate and Ramón at the beginning of chapter 4, "To Stay or Not to Stay." Kate says "I rather hate this search-for-God business, and religiosity." It is one of those exchanges Lawrence often held with himself through his characters, and is here self-critical:

"I know!" he said, with a laugh. "I've suffered from would-be cocksure religion myself."

"And you can't *really* 'find God!'" she said. "It's a sort of sentimentalism, and creeping back into old, hollow shells."

"No!" he said slowly. "I can't *find* God, in the old sense. But I am nauseated with humanity, and the human will; even with my own will. I have realized that *my will*, however intelligent I am, is only another nuisance on the face of the earth, once I start exerting it. And other people's *wills* are even worse."

"Oh! isn't human life horrible!" she cried, "every human being exerting his will all the time. (PS, 80)

There's nothing but death ahead, says Ramón, unless I find something else. Before many more chapters are out, we find Ramón willfully enough, trying to spread a new religion based on the old gods. Kate, however, agrees here:

> "Oh, people are repulsive!" she cried. "My own will becomes even more repulsive at last," he said . . . "I must either abdicate, or die of disgust—self-disgust, at that." (PS, 81)

Ramón looks for something else.

> "And what do you find?"
> "My own manhood."
> "What does that mean?" she cried, jeering.
> "If you looked, and found your own womanhood, you would know."
> "But I *have* my own womanhood!" she cried.
> "And then—when you find your own manhood—your womanhood," he went on, smiling faintly at her—"then you know it is not your own, to do as you like with. You don't have it of your own will. It comes from—from the middle—from the God. Beyond me, at the middle, is the God. And the God gives me my manhood, then leaves me to it. I have nothing but my manhood. The god gives it me, and leaves me to do further." (PS, 81)

Kate won't hear any more. But Lawrence doesn't mean one must ask from one's deepest centers what is most authentic to one's mystery, admitting that one does not belong to one's self. Lawrence *literally* means *giving oneself over to the god*—not the Christian God (it was no good offering *Him* to the Mexican), but the revived Aztec god. By chapter 13 Cipriano and Ramón are discussing "manhood" in quite a different dimension

> "My manhood is like a devil inside me," said Cipriano.
> "It's very true," said Ramón. "That's because the old oyster has him shut up, like a black pearl. You must let him walk out." (PS, 209)

Later,

> "My manhood is like a demon howling inside me," said Ramón to himself. . . .
> And he admitted the justice of the howling, his manhood being pent up, humiliated, goaded with insult inside him. (PS, 205)

He is filled with rage, like the devil. Between them they discuss destroying the world (how often do Lawrence characters contemplate destroying the world!): "'Ramón,' says Cipriano, 'wouldn't it be good to be a serpent and be big enough to wrap one's folds round the globe of the world and crush it like that egg?'" (PS, 204).

It is true that they end this conversation by admitting the folly of such nihilism. Yet, "There would be *one* good moment at least." One cannot but sense the fascistic element in this, and behind it (this time from Kate) there is a political philosophy that has behind it a strong schizoid element: "*'Give me the mystery and let the world live again for me!'* Kate cried. . . . *'And deliver me from man's automatism'*" (PS, 114).

She had realized, for the first time, with finality and fatality,

> what was the illusion she laboured under. She had thought that each individual had a complete self, a complete soul, an accomplished I. And now she realized as plainly as if she had turned into a new being, that this was not so. Men and women had incomplete selves, made up of bits assembled together loosely and somewhat haphazard. Man was not created ready-made. Men today were half-made, and women were half-made. (PS, 115)

They are like insects, "a world of half-made creatures," eating food and degrading the one mystery left to them, sex. "Half-made creatures . . . acting in terrible swarms, like locusts . . . with a collective insect-like will" (PS, 115). Lawrence speaks of "the morbid fanaticism of the non-integrate," but that telling phrase could apply to him, with telling force.

Manhood thus becomes a submission impelled by hate, hatred of humanity, and will to some dark "other" (god-) force, in the abnegation of consciousness, to the phallos:

> And these like the gush of a soundless fountain, he thrust up and reached down in the invisible dark, convulsed with passion. Till the black waves began to wash over his consciousness, over his mind, waves of darkness broke over his memory over his being, like an incoming tide. (PS, 205)

As with the priests in *The Woman Who Rode Away*, Lawrence was fascinated by the possibility of lapsing out in this way, into the collective "greater, dark mind" that is "undisturbed by thoughts." This kind of manhood seems to me not at all a new touch with the springs of being, but a process of the abandonment of intelligence in dangerous fanaticism, with an intense and often morally inverted nihilism behind it. It is a submission to the blood, in the spirit of Otto Gross's egoistical nihilism—a submission to hate—believing that to give oneself to this hate is to become a god, a pure inhumanity.

# 7

## Submission to the Ithyphallic—
## The Chatterley Novels

Inevitably, from his private mythology of the Sleeping Princess to be awakened by the mystic DHL, Lawrence came to write a novel about sexual love, concentrating on it as a central theme. In fact he wrote three versions of his Lady Chatterley novel.

Lawrence originally called one of them *Tenderness*, and the general opinion has been that he sought in these novels to vindicate "touch" between man and woman. Can we, in the end, take their "upshot" for us, about what it is to be man and woman?

Lawrence clearly set out to *teach* us by these novels, but I believe we must bear two facts in mind. There were two kinds of manifestation of which he was terribly afraid. One was his tendency to *murderous rages* (a problem Frieda admits in her preface to *Lady Chatterley's Lover*). Second, according to Frieda, Lawrence had been impotent since 1926. The *First Lady Chatterley* was finished in 1927.

So, Clifford and Connie Chatterley, in the first version, embody Lawrence's most terrible predicaments, *neither of which he could amend*. Clifford is castrated by the war. Connie is frustrated by her husband's impotence. In both, the consequent murderous impulses tend to break out, and we find in him the form of a subtle tyranny over her, while in her, her "dark forces" terrify her, and she dreams of a mad mare (an archetypal symbol of the shadow). (Frieda herself, of course, was also capable of murderous assault, as when she attacked Lawrence from behind to smash a plate on his head.)

Parkin and Mellors, I shall argue, are the Ithyphallic self: the god-man. Connie is made to reflect that Parkin is "unique": "He was just a common man—No! No! He is unique." (FLC, 79) But in what sense is he "unique"? What she sees is a white body, and feels "naked desire" for it, and this seems mundane enough. We have tension between the unconscious myth and the reality of sexuality.

It is difficult to reject Clifford's remarks (in *The First Lady Chatterley*) about how Connie goes to Parkin "just for the breeding season." She wants a child by him, but she cannot live with him. Culturally, he "is another race" (FLC, 82). Yet "surely he was immortal!" He has the immortality of the body,

but how? Clifford is right when he says, "He's just so much human meat."
Is there "life-mystery" in him? We may believe there is life-mystery in all
human beings, but this is not Lawrence's view. It was Frieda who said
"nothing goes on in many people's insides, nothing at all" and (of Lawrence):
"It exasperated him to see how boring most people's lives are and how little
they make of them, and he tried with all his might, from all angles, to make
them see and change" (FLC, 11).

In the first *Lady Chatterley* there is nothing about Parkin to make him into
anything other than a stud. Lawrence depicts his feet as clean and white, but
I bet they weren't; he lives the life of a gypsy, and while Lawrence omits
physical details, I feel sure that because of the differences of life-style, Lady
Chatterley would have been repelled by the lack of hygiene and delicacy, never
mind the bloaters.

She had refinement and culture:

> She would always want to read Swinburne again sometime; she would always want
> to play a bit of Mozart to herself . . . she couldn't do any of these things in a game-
> keeper's cottage. Or if she could it would somehow be false and wrong. (FLC,
> 80–81)

All civilized modes of consciousness are split off from her affair with Parkin,
and this applies to sex. *Parkin does not court her.* Again, we have the kind
of man who offers depersonalized sex, yet it is *because* of this depersonalization that Connie suffers a volcano or earthquake in her sexual experience.

As we have seen, Lawrence detested love and was afraid of it, and he
caricatures it in Clifford. But there is something worse than Lawrence's
rejection of love—Parkin is in a rage, at vengeful odds with the world, and
he *takes Connie with contempt.* Yet *she likes that:* "She liked him because he
was at war with everybody." (FLC, 44) He talks to her contemptuously, and
he is hostile and a bully. He bullies her he will go to Canada if she goes to
France. Yet, as a member of the lower orders, he feels small, and a mere
"fucker" whom she can't respect. Her sister sees it all (more realistically) as
a mere "intrigue."

So what kind of relationship is this? I daresay some titled ladies have always
had sex with their footmen and grooms.[1] Lawrence is trying to teach us not
only how to make our lives less boring, but about our deepest existential needs,
in relation to civilization. He is trying to teach us

> The great facts of life, and the great danger, was this starting flux of the whole being,
> body and soul and mind, in a new flux that would change one away from the old
> self as a landscape is transfigured by earthquake and lava floods, or by spring and
> the coming of summer. (FLC, 78)

It is simply nonsense that in Parkin, Connie Chatterley has anything by way
of love relationship that can include "body and soul and mind." Nor is it true

that a split-off adventure like hers, a merely carnal relationship with a "common man" could satisfy the existential needs of "soul and mind" in such a woman. There is too little in the Chatterley novels about love—about, shall we say, the kind of experience we have explored in the relationship between Tom and Lydia Brangwen, that is, about love *sub specie aeternitatis*, that love that embodies a transcendent meaning in existence. He settles for what Viktor Frankl called "a thoroughly decadent sensualism."

How did Lawrence arrive at his falsity? Here we have to invoke his myth directed against the hostility of the unburied mother. We catch a brief glimpse of her again when Parkin is in bed at night with Connie for the first time: "his old dislike of the hard unloving woman he had known in his mother also fighting against his intense desire of a mature, lonely man for a woman to believe in his body" (FLC, 120). The echo of the passage in *Kangaroo* is clear.

We cannot however read the Chatterley novels merely as fairy tales. We are invited to read them as offering teaching as to how we should be men and women. When we do, Lawrence's attitude to his characters, and the attitudes he portrays in them, and especially his treatment of procreation, seem seriously false. The latter is surely a central question, where sexual love is concerned. Connie is angry at Clifford:

> "I won't," she said to herself. "I won't take Parkin's child and hand it over to Clifford! It shall *not* be a Chatterley and a baronet and a gentleman and another cold horror. If I've warmed my hands at the fire of life I won't spit in the fire. And Parkin is the fire of my life, and he warmed me all the length of my body and through my soul . . . . And I'll tell him his penis is more beautiful to me, and better, than all the bodies of all the people in Tavershall and Wragby." (FLC, 157)

It is extremely unlikely that a woman would ever think like that: "Parkin's child," "hand it over to Clifford." The stream of consciousness here lacks all credibility. Again, Lawrence's thumb is crippingly in the scales. The sense of her possible pregnancy—which in the circumstances would be a disaster—is simply not given the depth and gravity one expects from Lawrence. If we think of his best dealings with children, as in the poem *Baby Asleep After Pain* or little Anna in the cowshed, what was it that happened to him, to make the bringing of a new child into the world such a matter of superficial chatter in the mind of Lady Chatterley—and the swapping about of this child such an empty token in Connie's *vengeance*?

The reference to the penis above is indicative: this belongs to the myth of the idolized phallus. Here we must talk of the split-off of part-objects. In what sense can a man's penis be said to be "more beautiful than all the bodies of the people in Tevershall and Wragby"? It is significant that in these stories the human beings involved are often reduced, as in dreams, to component parts. Indeed, as the title of the second version indicates, the man becomes "John Thomas," a mere penis, and the woman "Lady Jane."

Parkin's penis flies about the first novel like a magic wand. Clifford's penis is merely "a tool for his own ego." (FLC, 157) Parkin declares "I'm not ashamed of what I've got atween my legs." (FLC, 156) I believe we may dwell on the particular solemnity with which all this happens, and I believe this particular solemnity in Lawrence, which many have noticed, is a form of fetishism that must be related to the way in which his mother made Lawrence into an idolized phallus—a self-image that he projects into Parkin–Mellors. The reference to fetishism here is very indicative because it indicates by phenomenological analysis a significant component of *perversion*. I must use this word with some care,but I will try to use it interpretively for there is no doubt that there are in Lawrence's works elements of what can only be called perversion.

Fetishism, as Robert Stoller points out, is the model for all perversions.

> One who cannot bear another's totality will fragment—split and dehumanise—that object in keeping with past traumas and escapes; he may then isolate a neutral fragment—aspect—of that person and displace his potential sexual response from the whole person to the part that more safely represents that person (fetishization). . . .
> The hostility (potential destruction of the object) floating around in the latent fantasies that energize the perversion must be neutralised and positively, pleasurably, erotically infused. (Stoller 1976, 132)

And here we must take in one of Stoller's most important emphases: "At the core of the perverse act is the desire to harm others." Perversion he sees as *the erotic form of hatred*, a fantasy that may be acted out or may not, but it is *primarily motivated by hostility*:

> By "hostility" I mean a state in which one wishes to harm an object: that differentiates it from "aggression," which often implies only forcefulness. The hostility in perversion takes form in a fantasy of revenge hidden in the actions that make up the perversion and serves to convert childhood trauma into adult triumph. To create the greatest excitement, the perversion must also portray itself as an act of risk-taking. (Stoller 1976, 9)

This paragraph alone explains a good deal about Lawrence: the continual rage against "them" and society; the risks taken with the authorities and the aggressive element in this, as in his sexually assertive paintings, poems and novels; his assault on his women friends like Lady Ottoline; his fascination with sexual acts performed in semi-public places; his fascination with Gross and "polymorphous perversion"—all of which belong to the impulse to redeem the childhood trauma. There is more *hostility* in Lawrence's fantasies than we have realized.

In this novel, rage and hostility, the desire for vengeance, and perversion are inextricably linked. One never has far to go before someone has a revulsion from the civilized world:

Connie felt herself seized with one of the violent revulsions she had sometimes from the civilised world, the world that man has made, and that everyone has to live in. (FLC, 154)

With this revulsion goes a revolt:

She was frightened with an old Mosaic fear, afraid of the horrible power of society and its commandments which she had broken. She felt she was dynamically an enemy of society, and she was terrified. She had all her life had a secret fear of people and of the ponderous crushing apparatus of the law. (FLC, 155)

When Connie is pondering her sexual experience, we can see again how we are watching the enactment of Lawrence's familiar myth of *Awakening the Sleeping Beauty*:

She wanted that, to sink back into the half-dreamy warmth of the unawakened life. She felt she had been wakened too wide and too long. She wanted to sleep again, the warm sleep of life, with a man who would go powerfully through the passion of life without waking her, yet always there in her life as if they were sailing in one boat. (FLC, 154)

"Waking" here means something different from "sexual awakening": it means being awakened too much into awareness and intellectuality—such as Clifford offers.

She saw the peasants, the fishermen, the wood-men, and saw they were gradually being wakened into the nervous misery of the civilised life. They were coming under the influence of the towns. Their life was passing away. (FLC, 154)

This is a continual theme of Lawrence's. He wants to rediscover the intuitive life of being, such as he believed he could see in peasants, and in peasant-like men such as grooms and game-keepers. In some way, men and women must be awakened in this mode. Note that the peasants become wakened by "the nervous misery of the civilised life" so that their life passes away. This is a manifestation of "the horrible power of society." With this horrible power are associated its commandments, which Connie has broken.

She dreamed at night that she had been arrested and had to stand up before a Judge, to be tried as a criminal. She could not make out quite what her crime was. But it was something shameful. (FLC, 154)

It is difficult not to use the term superego here, the internalization, in the form of a strict and punitive mentor, of society's bans. Here perhaps we may refer to a second dream in *Kangaroo*:

He was standing in the living-room at Coo-ee, bending forward doing some little thing by the couch, perhaps folding the newspaper, making the room tidy at the last moment before going to bed, when suddenly a violent darkness came over him, and he heard a man's voice speaking mockingly behind him, with a laugh. It was as if he saw the man's face too—a stranger, a rough sort of Australian. And he realised, with horror: "Now they have put a sack over my head, and fastened my arms, and I am in the dark, and they are going to steal my little brown handbag from the bedroom which contains all the money we have." (K, 157–58)

It seems to me a dream of such intense menace from the superego amounts to a castration dream ("my little brown handbag"). Something in the psyche, associated with a *male* assault, threatens to take all the meaning out of his life, just as the hostile mother seems to threaten Somers–Lawrence from the grave.

We may relate Clifford to Gerald in *Women in Love* and Skrebensky in *The Rainbow*. All represent what we may call "false male doing": intense, willed activity that has no core of spontaneous being or that is how they are taken to appear. They are also impotent: Skrebensky "cannot satisfy" Ursula; Gerald wants to kill Ursula when she tells him "you cannot love"; Clifford, of course, cannot love at all. These are males made impotent not so much by the hostile mother imago, but by their association with some mechanical process that seems to drive all the meaning out of existence:

The terrible bondage of this tick-tack of time . . . tick-tack, tick-tack . . . Gerald could not save her from it. He, his body, his motion, his life—it was the same thing, a horrible mechanical twitching forward over the face of the hours. What were his kisses, his embraces. She could hear the tick, tack. (WL, 523)

There has been, of course, the "slaughter-machine of human devilishness" (*Kangaroo*)—the war, but that isn't the origin of it. We meet the same mood again in *Kangaroo*:

Harriet? Another bird like himself. If only she wouldn't speak, talk, feel. The weary habit of talking and having feelings. When a man has no soul he has no feelings to talk about. He wants to be still. And "meaning" is the most meaningless of illusions. An outworn garment. (K, 373)

It is disturbing to have this mood displayed at the end of the novel:

Harriet and he? It was time they both agreed that nothing has any meaning. Meaning a dead letter when a man has no soul. And speech is like a volley of dead leaves and dust, stifling the air.
    . . . When a man loses his soul he knows what a small, weary bit of clock-work it was. Who dares to be soulless finds the new dimensions of life.
    Home to tea. The clicking of the clock. Tic-tac! Tic-tac! The clock. Home to tea. Just for clockwork's sake. (K, 379)

"No home, no tea," he muses.

Insouciant soullessness. Eternal indifference . . . it is only in this pause that one finds the meaninglessness of meanings—like old husks which speak dust. (K, 374)

As we have seen, it is the phantom woman, the hostile dead mother, who threatens with this meaningless. The parental sex that Lawrence was aware of as a child is meaningless, too.

There are two problems. One is the need to perform the resurrection of the mother, by bringing woman to life. The other problem is the male problem, where everything is explicit, willed, mechanical, and where one has been "awakened too deep and too wide"—because "being," the soul at the core, is missing, and all is held together by explicitness and will. With this impingement has been given a *false morality*, the punitive super-ego morality that not only imposes "commandments" but is also crippling. It castrates and makes impotent.

Thus, Lawrence, already impotent if Frieda is correct, sits writing fantasies of *revenge* against this original traumatic falsification—what his parents did to him—which seems like the work of "the civilised world," the "vast mob that is civilised society," and Christian religion, with its belief in "immortality" and its preoccupation with crucifixion and death.

The falseness of the (perverted) solution, however, is in its *dehumanization*, in the impulse to cut off the libidinal from the wholeness of the civilized being, mind and soul. Of course, these *can't* be included, because everything that seems to have gone to the making of the "civilized" self seems false.

> She knew perfectly well, as a woman does know when she is not befogged and falsified, that a passionate man remains pure as long as his passion remains unmixed and uncontaminated by his ego. (FLC, 149)

The uncontaminated passion is to be found in the mere meeting of penis and vagina, John Thomas and Lady Jane, in "warm-hearted fucking." And this is to be exerted in a spirit of *vengeance* against "Wragby Hall," against "Tevershall," against the "mobs" of civilization, against the people of the world who are dead and might as well be done away with. In the Chatterley books this rage, hate, and impulse to vengeance is disguised. It is subjected to the neutralization of perversion.

\*     \*     \*

Lawrence was fascinated by perversion, and in *The First Lady Chatterley* seems to believe that everyone must have one: "She knew that every woman, and hence every man had private sexual secrets which no-one had any right to betray." (FLC, 155). Parkin is reputed to have carried out perverted practices—or at least his wife is putting this about. She knows that Parkin shrinks from "the mass of people," a "shrinking which lay beneath his violent aggressiveness" (FLC, 155), but this does not seem to her to make his "private intimacies" doubtful. It is the public who will be covering him "with obscenity as if with excrement."

Through Connie, Lawrence is inclined to defend Parkin against the wife's report of the "vile things … immoral things" he did to her when they were married. These are "too shameful to mention" according to Mrs. Bolton, and to Clifford, "a curious, almost mediaeval assortment of sexual extravagance and minor perversities." (FLC, 152). But perversions, far from being "wrong," were an important *moral* activity in Gross's political eroticism, not least in their defiance of society's mores.

What has not been widely recognized is the essential pervertedness of Lawrence's fetishism:

> And she knew, as every woman knows, that the penis is the column of blood, the living fountain of fullness in life. From the strange rising and surging of the blood all life rises into being. (FLC, 156)

The message becomes intensely religious. "Fullness in life" is to be sought simply by the penis, without all the shared things of the intelligence and spirit.

> Whatever else it is, it is the river of the only god we can be sure of, the blood. "There is a fountain filled with blood," said the hymn. And it is eternally true. And every man is such a fountain. (FLC, 156)

It is all profoundly embarrassing but significant. Lawrence associates with the penis as fountain the Christian symbolism of blood, sinners in his mythology must be plunged beneath the flood of the penis:

> It is not the dead, spilled blood which will wash away all sin, but the living rush of the ever new blood ever renewed. (FLC, 156)

"The cross, as the symbol of the murdered phallus, is an evil symbol and carries evil wherever it goes." This is the strange conclusion at the end of this passage. But here the question of models arises. Is it enough to look at the penis for wisdom? Lawrence's penis (the god-like Ithyphallus) is cosmic:

> with the mysery of the phallus goes all the beauty of the world, and beauty is more than knowledge … it is the penis which connects us sensually with the planets. But for the penis we should never know the loveliness of Sirius or the categorical difference between a pomegranate and india-rubber ball. (FLC, 156)

There is eternal conflict between intellect and penis:

> Man need not sacrifice the intellect to the penis, nor the penis to the intellect. But there is an eternal hostility between to two, and life is forever torn across by the conflict between them. Yet a man has a holy ghost inside him which partakes of both … . Where are we when the penis is the mere tool and toy of the mind? (FLC, 156)

If we leave the mythology and come to earth, what has this lofty, religiose

nonsense to do with an aristocratic woman giving herself in naked desire to
a gamekeeper who snarls at her "'Cause yer think yer can take it or leave it
as yer like!' She could feel the mockery, the scepticism, the jeering in the
fellow's voice" (FLC, 96). In reality *The First Lady Chatterley* is full of
rage—propaganda rage against the mob, fear and hatred of civilization, of
hostility to Clifford's will, and the "commandments" of society, of
Christianity, and so on. Parkin is intensely hostile to his world, which he fears.
Unknown to Connie, he is a communist devoted to bringing down people in
the classes above him. He treats Connie with disdain and indifference; he has
appalling conflict with his wife, whom he has seemingly sodomized, and has
a bloody fight over her. Connie flies into a rage with him, and they struggle
with one another over the question of mastery.

Their coupling is without courtship, without foreplay, and is done in rough
circumstances where he prepares, crudely, to take her, and where there can
be little mutual enjoyment other than "fucking." And this is all called
"tenderness"!

Woman is reduced to lust for the penis. Self-respect, dignity, civilized
interests, all are shown to belong to "the ego" and the hated aspects of a
civilization pronounced dead, and that to which a woman's fulfillment cannot
but be directed, the creation of a child, is only barely allowed to impinge. She
takes no steps to prevent conception, she thinks superficially about how a child
might appear, and thinks only casually about its future, its family life, its
security, its emotional health, its fulfillment. The result is that woman is
reduced to that "animal," while she is also shown to be attracted by disdain,
contempt, harsh indifferent treatment, insalubriousness, cruelty, murderousness ("We'll shoot the buggers"), irresponsibility about children, and sexual
perversions.

Lawrence manages to persuade us that this is (as the blurb says) a "beautiful
rather pastoral tale." Yet apart from two or three idyllic moments in the
wood, the tale is of crippled impotence, sordid marital fights, conflict and
bodily harm, and mutual contempt between the partners in their struggle for
mastery. Implicitly it vindicates infidelity and deceit (as when Connie tries to
get Duncan Forbes to pose as the father of her child) and deep irresponsibility
to procreation and the future. In the end even the "phallic" love goes dead
and the pregnant Connie sees normal responses to her motherhood as
"baboon grimaces." Parkin preaches to us the politics of warm-heartedness
("What it needs is warmth of heart between you," [FLC, 172]). Yet in the end
a "deadly stream of hate came out of the gamekeeper" and Connie realizes
"the man always had some grudge against her" (FLC, 197–98). He
confesses, "I'm afraid of thee," and all ends in a further of welter of
contempt.

On the one hand what is urged upon us is a reckless sensuality. "I'd give
my life to stroke her and feel her open out to me" (FLC, 239)—a remark,
incidentally, that no man, certainly no working man, would make to a
companion, a comparative stranger, of a different class, as Parkin does.

On the other hand is the desperate fear Connie has at the end that the conception of the child is a "death-in-life." This is her punishment for following the "thing a woman calls her freedom, it's a devil's instinct." On her child she feels only "I'm afraid I may love it." (FLC, 212).

There seem to me three things about the book that are wrong and bad. One is the continual stream of propagandist hostility directed against Clifford to provide endorsement for Connie's adventure. This is repugnant, not least because it displays such animus, as he is taken as representative of a whole cold, will-impelled, overmental addiction to industry, and a dead state of civilized superficiality and spirituality.

Second, there is the endorsement of Connie's libidinal urges, without any questioning of her procreative irresponsibility. She could have used contraception, and would certainly have known about it. There is irony in this conversation and for once we touch truth:

> "You're up and I'm down . . . I don't want you. I don't want nothing of yours."
> She went pale. This was an obstinacy and an imperviousness as bad as anything she met in Clifford.
> "But—why did you make love to me then? she stammered.
> "You wanted it," he said crudely.
> "And didn't you? she cried.
> He turned and looked at her. "Ay! I love it . . . ."
> "Don't you care about your child?" she asked in angry amazmnt.
> "Me? No!"
> "But you're unnatural!"
> "It'll be thy childt. Tha'lt ha'e it." (FLC, 181)

These conversations in conflict between Connie and Parkin are the best things in the book. They are real and for once the protagonists come to life, live on their own. He turns out, as here, to be "like any other man"—and he, like Lawrence, wants to be "the master" after all. On this point they are irreconcilable.

When she sees Parkin suddenly in the street, he seems

> ridiculous, rather small, rather stiff, with his ragged moustache sticking out and his wary movement. A ridiculous little male, on his guard and wary in his own self-importance! *When the sex glamour is in abeyance, particlly every modern woman sees her man in this light, the light of her contemptuous superiority.* (FLC, 216–17; my italics)

This is a very revealing sentence for it reveals Lawrence's own contempt for woman who seeks her own freedom and self-fulfillment, but it becomes worse as he goes on:

> It is the sex warmth alone that makes men and women possible to one another. Reduce them to simple individuality, to the assertive personal egoism of the modern individual, and each sees in the other *the enemy.* (FLC, 217)

This reveals that to Lawrence the ithyphallic, the penis-worship, the mystical sexual idyll was a defense mechanism. To arouse a woman and to seduce her, to enter her and subject her to lapsing out and the rest is a form of triumph over a dangerous enemy. Again, we may suspect the ultimate unconscious urge is to destroy the object. Lawrence declares,

> At the same time she had her ridicule of him in her heart. (FLC, 247)

because

> The woman, *feeling for some reason triumphant in our day*, man having yielded most of the weapons into her hands, looks on her masculine partner with ridicule. While the man, knowing her has given up his advantage to the woman and *not having strength to get it back*, looks on her with intense resentment. (FLC, 247; my italics)

Thirdly, in *The First Lady Chatterley* there is a sense of an implacable enmity between the sexes, despite the idolized sexual encounters.

In the end Connie feels only nausea and dread.

> A hidden obscenity was creeping out of everything, and with it a terrible, cold fear in her belly. How was it possible? Was the child inside her turning to a corpse? The thought filled her with unspeakable fear. Was she already a grave yard in her body? Why did she feel this cold, dread fear in her inside. (FLC, 247)

Lawrence tells, us "it comes out of the semi-insane Clifford . . . the sulphur smell of the pits": "A grey, mildewy horror that would be the end of the world."

> The mildew of corruption and immorality. There was a strange immorality in Clifford . . . his own selfish egoism . . . Clifford had always hated sex. (FLC, 247)

We may say, I believe, that it is Connie, in her failure to involve her whole authentic being and body in her procreative sex, who has brought herself to this sense of death. She has that one outburst, that she was *afraid she would love the child*—a strange (schizoid) response if there ever was one (though Lawrence seems not to see this). What of this "tender, rosy thing that was between them"—the baby—suppose it died? "She felt it had suffered a death tonight. She had betrayed it, and it had died" (FLC, 248). She has tried not to realize the child had existed, but now there had been a "Holy thing, a living, flowing, intangible contact between her and the man." The "baboon world" had broken it. They are all now pinky grey baboons, and she falls into another froth of hatred of mankind. The terms in which she cries out are revealing:

> "Don't let me betray anything. Oh don't let me betray it. . . . I don't want to betray. Oh, don't let me betray! Don't let me betray! For the child's sake, I mustn't betray. I must bring it into life, not into death in life." (FLC, 249)

We may recall the hostile mother in Somers's dream in *Kangaroo*:

> That is how the dream woman put it: he had betrayed her great love, and she must
> go down desolate into an everlasting hell, denied and denying him absolutely in
> return. (K, 103)

We have to say, I believe, that in *The First Lady Chatterley* the Sleeping
Beauty fantasy has failed. The unconscious impulse was once more to give the
mother, whose life had been undermined by the failure of sexual fulfillment,
a fully phallic lover—to bring her a working man of ithyphallic proportions.

The hostile mother imago is too threatening for him to be able to deal with
the female aspect, the male dynamic is too mechanically assembled (too, "tic
tac") to have any meaning. (See my remarks above, on the possibility that
Lawrence retained the puzzlement of a frightened child, who had witnessed the
primal scene, p. 226).

\*          \*          \*

In *John Thomas and Lady Jane* there is still a great deal of hate abroad:
the colliers are hostile, Clifford has the virus of hate, Connie hates Clifford.
(She actually thinks—in revolting cruelty—"what are *you* doing here, hugging
your half-a-life and thinking it matters? Can't you see you're half-dead, and
you'd be much better wholly dead? You miserable thing!" [JT, 42].) Clifford
hates the miners, Connie hates "society," Parkin hates the gentry, and the
mass of humanity is repulsive, baboons, and doomed into the bargain: "the
working out of the new, unconscious, cold, reptilian sort of hate that was
rising between the colliers . . . and the educated, owning class" (JT, 112).
Lawrence was a sick man, and his view of the world is sick: "it seems there
is an evil spirit in my body." Out of this came the poignant yearning. "We'll
begin another life somewhere in the sun" and "my soul yearns for a new body
of man" (JT, 71).

Besides the tuberculosis was its psychic concomitant. This is hinted at in the
interesting letter from Dr. Edmund R. Clarke quoted by Harry T. Moore.
Almost all tubercular patients, he says, are individuals whose early life was one
"which did not provide the individual with the necessary amount of love,
affection and security." (Moore, 470) The individual develops an intense need
for the satisfaction that comes of accomplishment, recognition, and
achievement. They display an intense striving toward their goal in life. If the
individual comes to feel that the goal can never be achieved, he gives up in
despair, and shortly afterwards is found to have tuberculosis. He then
"undergoes a process of social isolation" (Moore, 1955, 470–71).

The roots of Lawrence's problems were also in the traumata he had
experienced as an infant: his schizoid problem, and the schizoid individual
makes those strange moral inversions we have followed. Love is repulsive—
mere egotism, in whatever form:

You have to have the malady in some form or another: either the fearsome, clawing tyranny of "love" and "goodness," which is the horrible clawing attempt to get some victim into the clutches of your own egoistic love, your own egoistic virtue, your own egoistic way of salvation; or you have the less high-minded, more ignoble but perhaps not so deadly clutch-clutch-clutch after money and success. The disease grows as a cancer grows. (JT, 106)

In this context Lawrence believes he has something to teach us about sex. It is true that he discriminates against mere "illicit" sex: "She disliked so intently any sort of conscious sexuality. It was so ugly and egoistic" (JT, 104). But how does "she" (Connie) go on?

A nasty, mechanical sort of self-seeking was the normal sex desire. Not spontaneous at all, but automatic in its cunning will to get the better of the other one, and to extend its own ego. (JT, 104)

Note, this is the *normal* sex desire. We enter upon a study of male and female sex. Connie knows, however, what Parkin wants—power:

Was what most men wanted: just to get the better of a woman, in the sexual intercourse; the self seeking, automatic civilised man trying to extend his ego over a woman, and have a sense of self-aggrandizement by possessing her .... The thing that people call free sex, and living your own life, and all that, is just egoism gone rampant. (JT, 105)

Women, apparently, have "true, sensitive flow of sex ... *with one another*" (my italics): "But with men, *almost invariably*, the whole thing was reversed" (JT, 105). Women wanted men to "parade a love animal called a man," like parading themselves in the skins of dead animals, in furs. "It was horrible. It was most horrible in rather elderly women ... they were the hyaenas" (JT, 105). All this is "semi-insane horrors of unscrupulous acquisitiveness ... mine! mine! me! me! got him! ... It was the horror of our insane civilisation."

Most men and most women lead insane sexual lives, which are really ego-trips, insane forms of acquisitiveness. Because of this, society is doomed:

Our civilisation has one horrible cancer, one fatal disease, the disease of acquisitiveness. It is the same disease in the mass as in the individual. The people who count as normal are perhaps even more diseased than those who are neurotic. (JT, 105–6)

We know what Lawrence wanted done to the neurotics: "a real neurotic is half a devil, but a cured neurotic is a perfect devil." He would prefer all neurotics to die (Moore 1955, 356).

Love is only acquisitive egoism:

This is called love. "She is terribly in love with him," the cant phrase means really: "She is mad to get him under her will." (JT, 106)

Thus, men and women are naturally enemies, and love is a mere disguise of the attempt to swell one's ego by swallowing another.

This is one manifestation of paranoia; another is a feeling of the hostility of the whole world. Our capacity to be in touch with being through sex takes place in a world in which we are surrounded by enemies: "the myriad hosts of the clutching and self important"

But when you come to life itself, you must come as the flower does, naked and defenceless and infinitely in touch. (JT, 115)

This is supposed to be what the Chatterley novels are about.

With quietness, with an abandon of self-assertion and a fullness of the *deep, true self* one can approach a human being, and know the delicate best of life, the touch. The touch of the feet on the earth, the touch of the fingers on the tree, on a creature, the touch of hands and breasts, the touch of the whole body to body; and the interpenetration of passionate love: it is life itself, and in the touch, we are alive. (JT, 114; my italics)

Attending to this intention, it is interesting to note the response of Parkin after he has begun his affair with Connie. As we know from all Lawrence's work, the initial onset of a love affair is always followed in him by the onset of a sense of doom and death: the moon-mother appears, like as not, to bring a doom-laden sense of guilt and betrayal. Lawrence attributes this to "society" and the natural inimical attitudes of "the world":

A curious dread possessed him, a sense of defencelessness. Out there, beyond, were all those white lights, and the indefineable quick malevolence that lay beyond them. (JT, 122)

Perhaps the white lights are little moons that look like the eyes of the mother. As we have seen, in the first version, Parkin has had the same trouble with his hard unloving mother as Somers and Lawrence. What Lawrence cannot see is that this dread-filled response is psychopathological and unusual: "By taking the woman, and going forth naked to her, he had exposed himself to he knew not what fear, and doom" (JT, 122). It is true that we all, in giving ourselves to intimacy in nakedness, experience the fear of dependence and vulnerability, but in Lawrence there is something worse. His lovers fear the possibility of their partners wounding them by withdrawing their love: we may follow this in Lawrence's honeymoon poems. But, of course, in Lawrence, there are deeper dreads than this:

> It was not fear of woman, nor fear of love. It was a dread amounting almost to horror, but of something indefinite. (JT, 122)

As I would put it, it was not fear of *the* woman, but of *woman*, essentially of the Phantom Woman who lurks in the unconscious and in the woman's matrix.

Lawrence wants to get away into a natural world into a kind of Garden of Eden, among the bluebells and pheasants, where "touch" could be enjoyed without any of this dread and horror. He wanted an Eden in which his lovers could touch without bringing into the garden their psyches, their parental history, their identification with mother and father, their role in the world, their beliefs and sense of meaning, responsibility to their own creativity, their family potentialities, their life-tasks. All these are the *humiliating* "complication of the human world." He must somehow detach "touch" from all reality.

This explains the unreality of much of the sex, and the consciousness of it. I do not mean only the gestures. It seems to me odd, for instance, for a man to want to suddenly whip his hand under the skirts of a woman as he leaves her at the gate after having her twice (JT, 129). "I could die for the touch of a woman like thee." At times Lawrence writes as though he did not know what sexual satisfaction was.

But the reflections are often unrealistic to a sickly extent, as are Connie's meditations on possible pregnancy. One cannot believe that a woman in her predicament would think like this:

> She felt sure she would have a child, a baby with soft live limbs, and a little life of its own, ensheathed in her own life. . . .
> A baby! The thought thrilled through her like the thrill of coition. What if it had *his* tight, reddish-brown eyes, with the passionate potency, the flames shut down in them! She hoped it might have; for the sake of some woman in the future. Passion like that was a gift indeed . . . she wanted her son to be elegant too. (JT, 139)

It is unconvincing and difficult to understand until we realize that what has happened is the magical awakening of the Mother ("It was as if passion had swept into her like a new breath, and changed her from her dead wintriness") and that the *son* she is thinking of is no other than D. H. Lawrence himself in yet another appearance.

Behind the impulse to reawaken the mother, then, is the need to give himself rebirth, and so to revenge himself on the childhood trauma, to throw it off. Thus, the idyll is really based on hate of a kind, and this generates the perverted element, and leads to the celebration of power and mastery.

It is startling to note that the first time Connie has an orgasm she is taken in rage. She meets Parkin unexpectedly:

> "You wasn't sliving past and not meanin' to see me, was you?" he said, putting his arm around her, determined.

"Not now!" she said, trying to push him away.
"But you *said*," he replied, rather angrily.
And his arms tightened instinctively, against his will. (JT, 132–33)

His body "presses strangely upon her" she gives up—"Her will seemed to leave her, and she was limp." He carries her to a heap of dead boughts, and she stands by "mute and helpness, without volition."

Then he took her and laid her down, wasting no time, *breaking her underclothing in his urgency.* And her will seemed to have left her entirely. (JT, 133; my italics)

She is virtually raped. Ah, but: "And then, something awoke in her. Strange thrilling sensation, that she had never known before woke up where he was within her, in wild thrills like wild bells" (JT, 133). He takes her twice: more bells, an ecstasy, an orgasm. She adored him. "'We came off together, that time,' he said." He has shown her who is master, he has shown "the god glisten." He is the Son of God (like Cipriano) who can master a woman, and bring her totally to submission.

The impulse to dominate is clear: "breaking her underwear in his urgency," "her instinct was to fight him. He held her so hard." And yet the woman does not appreciate her fulfillment: she may have "come off" with him, but *she does not even know it*: "'Did we?' she said" (JT, 134). But when she knows she is so grateful: "'I'm awfully grateful to you,' she said hesitatingly." (JT, 134).

Now, of course, she is like a volcano, and we have the passage from the first version about lava, etc. She is in a state of "incandescent *submissiveness*" (my italics). One moment she is flaming with desire, a volcano: the next in "infinite tenderness": "Like the soft ocean full of acquiescent passivity." But, of course, since men and women are natural enemies, "he became the enemy, the one who was trying to deprive her of her freedom, in the arms of his greedy, obtuse man's love." So, she revolts like the Bacchae, like an Amazon, "madly calling on Iacchos, the bright phallus that had no independent personality behind it" (JT, 135–36). The phallus is her own. As the inevitable complications of being human begin to threaten (fear of dependence), Lawrence briskly detaches the penis from the man, and opts for the idolized phallic object.

There follows the piece about the baby quoted above, and this baby is of the silky, adorable, Iaachos Parkin. Mrs. Bolton, however, when thinking of the possibility of the gamekeeper being her ladyship's lover thinks:

he was just a snarling nasty brute.
    Still, you never knew! When women did fall, they sometimes liked to fall as low as they could. Refined ladies would fall in love with niggers, so her ladyship might enjoy demeaning herself with that foul-mouthed fellow, who would bully her the moment he got a chance. But there, she'd had her own way so long, she might be asking to be bullied.

Parkin yearns outside the house and is seen in the dawn by Mrs. Bolton. Dismally he reflects, "A man must not *depend* on a woman." And again, we may reflect, there is no such thing as "touch" cut off from all the world, when people enter into a relationship, they bring all their needs for dependence to it.

Over the possible creation of a child, and its emotional health, its life potential, Lawrence sees nothing wrong with the *morally* stupid attitude of his irresponsible Connie.

> a charming cradle of rose-wood . . . somehow looked so cosy . . . How many babies had lain in it . . . . Well, and perhaps her own baby . . . she *felt* she would have a child by Parkin. (JT, 147 and 150)

When she is quizzed by her husband, she speaks "with that queer, unseizable simplicity that made her seem so innocent and remote from certain actualities. And she wanted to go to Parkin to give herself into his arms again." (JT, 154). She doesn't want to be bound. In her Grossian "freedom" she has become the model for the staple trollop in the modern novel, hopelessly adrift:

> She recognised, emotionally, that the idea of eternal love, or life-long love even, and the idea of marriage, had a disastrous effect upon the will. The idea of permanency stimulates the possessive instinct, the possessive instinct rouses the egoistical will to self-assertion, and there is a vicious circle. Let there be permanency if it happens so. But let there be no convention of permanency, especially in emotional or passional relationships. (JT, 154)

The pastoral element in these novels belongs to a daydream that carries along with it this Grossian propaganda. The obligatory bluebells and primroses, after a time, become a tic, and can be seen as a trick to hide the essential unreality. For instance, there is the unreal scene in which the lovers strip off naked in the rain. I do not believe that a working man like Parkin would do this, nor would he partake of the flower-sticking play. More important, this flower play and nakedness is associated with *rage and is done in vengeance*:

> "If they knowed we was like this," he said, "they'd want to kill us. If they knowed you had forget-me-knots in your maidenhair, they'd want to kill us." (JT, 260–61)

Why? "The world is the same all over . . . you can't get away." We may recall Helen Thomas's account of herself and Edward stripping naked and rolling in the bluebells. Indeed, those lovely passages in *How It Was* are an antidote to Lawrence because there is no *paranoia*. Why should these lovers of Lawrence's always feel that the world was hostile to their eroticism?

But then, the element that the pastoral "innocence" is meant to disguise or garland has a perverted element:

He glanced at the ground, tipped her over in a grassy place, and there in the middle of the path, in the pouring rain, went into her, in a sharp, short embrace, *keen as a dagger thrust*, that was over in a minute. (JT, 285; my italics)

I do not say that lovers do not, in lusty moments, take one another suddenly on the stairs or even in a path in the wood, but there is, as the act is described, the undeniable element of brusque, dominating hostility, with the under-current of unconscious murder, "keen as a dagger thrust." It is this essential sadism—the *hostility*—that the flower-pastoral writing is intended to disguise. Why idolize a sexual act that is "over in a minute" in such uncomfortable circumstances? Of course, the act is followed by such pretty talk and play: "'Charming!' she cried 'Charming!'" (JT, 259) The scene is acutely embarrassing, not because lovers don't behave quite like that (the Thomases did, and it is *not* embarrassing), but it is false, because it is hiding something—the essential *vengeance* behind the sexuality: "again she felt a certain fear, as of the wild men of the woods whom she remembered in old German drawings." (JT, 259)

Behind the pastoral garlands ("forget-me-nots, campions, bugle, bryony, primroses, golden-brown oak sprays") is the sadistic, hostile, and murderous lover, whom, Lawrence is arguing, the woman adores. His religiose adoration of the phallus has convinced readers and critics that Lawrence's depiction of sexuality is somehow "sacred." Critics have spoken of "love" as the subject of the Chatterley novels, but it is quite clear that Lawrence wants to *avoid* love. The discussions of love are few and far between

"But you love me?" she asked.
He frowned a little.
"It looks like it," he said. "But who knows?"
"And don't you care whether I love you or not?"
His eyes came back to hers, with that swift, searching look.
    "Nay!" he said with a faint smile; "What's the good of carin'?" (JT, 184)

Love is so dangerous to Lawrence that one must never ask about it, or even, really, discuss it.

"Do you know what love means? Tell me you do!" she said wistfully.
... "Tha can tell me! Tha knows doesn't thee? What dost ax for?" (JT, 241)

That she can "feel" him is enough so love is made safe by making it a matter only of touch and body: "I liked your body." The guide of the universe is in our own bodies so any considerations of other modes of being are beside the point: "You'll like me won't you—you won't just want me?" (JT, 185). But she has no answer to his question. "He got into bed and went straight into her. 'What is there more? What is there more than fucking?'" (JT, 236). There is nothing more than lust: this is the message of the book. Yet this message is disguised by the idolization of the phallus, split off from whole being (it may be added that, significantly, there is no idolization of the "cunt").

The sexual acts, glamorized, often full of rage, and detached from whole being, are done and described explicitly and fetischistically, in the attempt to overcome wounds. What thus becomes something that borders on perversion is offered in hte spirit of *vengeance*, to secure *triumph* over the wounds.

Parkin is a wonded phallus, and she is a healing power.

> While she would lie still and submissive in the circle of his enclosing arm, he was at peace, and his wounds were closed. But the moment she broke away, he would wake, and memory *would open like a wound*. (JT, 237; my italics)

We have seen many moments in Lawrence where peace is sought from an indefinite menace that seems to threaten from the wounds of memory.

She thinks of his "erect, sightless, overweening phallus." (I am perplexed by that "sightless"—it is at times as if Lawrence felt that the phallus had a life by itself, and so should see and speak.)

> Somehow she realised that it was the soul of his phallus, the overweening blind male soul in him, that had been wounded through his mother and his step-father from the beginning of his days, and whose wound gaped with the pain and hatred of sex. (JT, 237)

This could be a description of *Lawrence* himself, and so we can see that in this novel he is trying to overcome those (psychic) wounds that have always made him afraid of sex and of love, hostile to women, and impotent.

We have seen that Lawrence compares the wounded phallus with Christ on the Cross. The idolized phallus that Parkin displays is a symbol of Lawrence's own soul, but because of the complications, in some way this phallus must be redeemed in sexual passion itself.

Such is the fetishism in Lawrence's ithyphallic novel that sex must be detached from procreativity: "Sir Clifford can have the child, but we've got this." The needs of the whole being are cut down to the "whole body," now the whole body is cut down to the penis—the "part object," the organ, and activity.

But this part object is now divinized: "Between the two hesitating, baffled creatures, himself and her, she had seen the third creature" (JT, 238). This penis is "utterly unhesitating":

> It was like some primitive, grotesque god . . . alert with its own weird life, *apart from both their personalities*. (JT, 238; my italics)

As Leslie H. Farber says of sexology, it is as if the *organs themselves* will speak. This is a characteristic tendency in the modern consciousness. Speaking of the ideal scientist in sexology, Farber says

It would have to be an article of faith for him that the visible, palpable reactions of the organs themselves, regardless of whatever human or inhuman context they might occur in, would speak a clear, unambiguous truth to all who cared to heed. (Farber 1966, 66)

Lawrence's penis is a very special one: it is the focus of yet another form of schizoid superiority. "In most men it was dead." And, of course, in most men the penis is not pure, but an instrument of the ego:

To most men, the penis was merely a member, at the disposal of their personality. Most men merely used their penis as they used their fingers, for some personal purpose of their own. But in a *true man*, the penis has a life of its own, and is the second man within the man. It is prior to the personality. (JT, 238; my italics)

If the penis is prior to the personality—assuming us to be *true men*—how do we distinguish between lust and love?

We could agree that we need, in our living, to respect the mystery of the penis in ourselves, in a symbolic sense: "the personality must yield before the priority and the mysterious root-knowledge of the penis"—or, rather, the phallus.

For the phallus, in the old sense, has roots, the deepest roots of all, in the soul and the greater consciousness of man, and it is through the phallic roots that inspiration enters the soul. (JT, 238)

If we attend to the penis, and give it priority, we shall find that it has roots in the consciousness and the soul. I am a little lost here, because it seems a strange route. If the phallus has roots in the soul and the "greater consciousness of man," why not give soul and consciousness priority? And if this penis has this blind life of its own, does it draw the soul and the greater consciousness of man after it or not?

It is unlikely that a woman should think like that. A woman may love a man's penis and talk of it as "him," but she doesn't suppose that this is the way to his soul and consciousness, though these may be in complex with his libidinal life. If he is grieving, or even if he suddenly begins to think about something else while he is making love to her, his penis may lost its potency.

She knew now what he meant when he said: "I don't know what you mean by *only*!" To him, there could never be "only fucking." Because his phallus rose in its own weird godhead. (JT, 238)

Surely, with Parkin, with bits of bloater sticking to his whiskers, going into her at once, we feel he is quite clearly "only fucking." He shares with her only the minimal of other interests, not even love: "fucking went to the phallic roots of his soul." Well, it might to D. H. Lawrence, but we are surely lost in an idolization of this very special penis: "His phallus was not the vulgar organ, the penis. And with the life or death of his phallus, he would live or die." (JT, 238). From this clue, I believe we can see the origins of this idolization, for this penis—Parkin-Lawrence's—is the magic instrument of the revival of the mother, and the instrument—a magic wand—to overcome the infant trauma, and restore meaning to his world when the Phantom Woman threatened to blight it. This magical ithyphallus is supreme. Failure to aspire to this god-head is the failure of all other man: "Men like Clifford, and a vast number of modern men," (Again—how did Lawrence know?)

> lived in a petty triumph over the penis. They have a nasty penis, with which they play about like dirty little boys. But when it comes to the act, in spite of all the gush about love, it is merely fucking, the functional orgasm, the momentary sensational thrill, the cheap and hasty excitation of a moment. (JT, 238)

Next Connie is "enclosed within the phallic body":

> Tonight she realized. The root of the fear ("fear of life, fear of society, fear of what would happen") had been fear of the phallus. This is the root-fear of all mankind. Hence the frenzied efforts of mankind to despise the phallus and to nullify it. (JT, 239)

Now she is in touch with the bright phallic god-head: its folds were pure gentleness and safety.

> There was something that danger could not touch: one thing and one only: the perfect sleeping circle of the male and female body. (JT, 239)

She arouses him, and is "melted." "The warm-blooded are the sons and daughters of God" (JT, 244) Connie's sister declares that "other men have minds, and creative power, and power to command or control. And then the penis is *not* the most sacred part of the man." But Connie stubbornly declares, "I know the penis is the most godly part of a man."

> I *know* it is the penis which connects us with the stars and the sea and everything. It is the penis which touches the planets, and makes us feel their special light. I *know* it was the penis which really put the evening stars into my inside self. (JT, 312)

The sister replies, "the penis is like the grass that withereth, and the place thereof shall know it no more"—a splendid parting shot, and very much to the point, for the penis cannot create the meanings to set against death, and is itself liable to withering, that is, to place the whole basis of meaning in one's life on "naked desire" is to build on sand. Only if the phallic is at one with the whole complex of love can a sense of enduring have significance. To invoke Frankl again, if one fails to find love *sub specie aeternitatis*, and only finds "the penis," one is left only with a "decadent sensuality" that solves nothing, as the hold on meaning dies at every orgasm.

What about marriage? Anyone, you might say, can carry on a love affair in which there is no problem of coming to terms with reality. Connie wants an "intrinsic" marriage, in which they enter into their "sacred mutual destiny," including, no doubt, certain minor sexual perversions as well as his "starry" penis. The point is, of course, as we have seen all through Lawrence's work, if the couple live together, their lives will become like Mummy's and Daddy's, and so ugly and meaningless. Connie declares

> I believe in marriage but I don't believe in living together. . . . What ruins marriage is that the man and woman always live together, on top of one another. If they lived apart in separate houses, they'd be able to go on liking one another. (JT, 262)

It is like a child's solution to the problems of relationship. It would be nice if she could buy O.P. a nice little farm and come to visit him—another childish solution:

> "No!" he said. "No!' I don't. The minute you marry a woman, she's spoilt for you. She becomes a part of the whole my-eye bossing business as makes a man's balls go deader than sheep's kidneys."
> "And the woman hates it just as much," she said. (JT, 263)

"If only there weren't so many beastly people in the world"—another child's solution (JT, 264). (The trouble is, of course, that when Connie and Parkin talk, they are having a pseudo-Socratic dialogue in which Lawrence is agreeing with himself.)

This novel ends on a perverted note, again revealing the fascination with perversion, vengeance, and risk. He and she are having coition in the little hollow of a wood. Comes a keeper: "a big-faced, middle-aged man, striding round the brambles . . . . 'Now then!' said the burly keeper, in ugly challenge." The keeper is troubled: "Then he looked again, fascinated . . . . A queer sight, as she clung to him, covering his nakedness. The keeper was fascinated. He wanted to see her" (JT, 375). No, says Parkin, there's no chance of being in peace anywhere, for long. There's folks everywhere. They walk off, in a romantic mood, with the author in a romantic mood, too, talking of Byron. Parkin is to come to her, if she can't bear it: maybe they have a future. The little voyeuristic touch of the big fat keeper "wanting to see her," is significant, as is the title: *John Thomas and Lady Jane,* for the whole novel is a perverted act of making explicit.

One ends *John Thomas and Lady Jane* in rather less of a state of exasperation, because of the unreality (not the least of the attempt to turn a working-class man into a god).

Only the scenes at the end bring Parkin into reality, not least the comic scenes at the working class tea-table at Bob's. Connie herself is even seen with a little irony, and in these realistic scenes there is one very revealing word: "unscrupulous." When Bob's family reveal their anxiety over the hard work

Parkin is doing, Connie suggests bribery, and obviously has no sense of the codes of conduct of the working class community. But the word illuminates much in Lady Chatterley—Connie is unscrupulous, and in this again we have a glimpse of Frieda. She, as we have seen, with her aristocratic sense of being "special," was immoral and unscrupulous. In Connie, too, we have a touch of Frieda's amoral sensuality that we have seen in *Mr Noon*. At times, when Connie seeks to be "taken" without love or courtship, in a "take me if you want me" spirit, (JT, 333), she lacks *scruples*. One small example of this is when she tells Parkin she doesn't mind if he has other women (JT, 336), so long as he doesn't "betray" what is between them.

Of course, Connie's unscrupulousness especially extends to the child within her. The conversation in which she tells Parkin of her pregnancy is lame. It simly lacks the rhythm of a portentous moment.

> "I want to tell you," she whispered. "I think I'm going to have a child." He looked at her sharply.
> "Have yer told Sir Clifford?" he asked.
> "No! Not yet! I don't want to tell him yet."
> "An' what when yer have to?" (JT, 330)

Lawrence is thinking about his plot, and is failing to imagine what the man's real reaction would be. It trails off into a thin exchange about a bellyful of poison.

Later, however, the pregnancy does come into imaginative focus:

> Her flesh had taken that delicate softness and slightly animal, milky bloom that sometimes comes in the first months of pregnancy: a softness which is no longer fired ·by desire, a milkiness that is already touched with maternity. (JT, 345)

Connie at last gropes around for an authentic solution; rather than live in this false situation, she would go off and be a waitress in a tea shop.

> I am in a false situation, I feel false all the time, and I can't bring a child into the world like that. (JT, 368)

The reader at last feels a great satisfaction, that we have in this heroine a glimmering of responsibility and a sense of reality—of the very reality of wholeness Lawrence tells us we must have. If she is authentic, and lives with the child's father, then it will "have *some* freshness in its soul" (JT, 368). "I feel I am living here on false pretences." At last, the sense of human reality and need breaks through.

We also have a discussion of love.

> "I don't want you to promise to be faithful to me. If you *do* want another woman, then have her, never mind. But love me with your heart, won't you?"

"Ah! Be still! Be still!—Shall you love me with *your* heart?"
"You know I shall," she said.
"And lots besides," he said, smiling.
"No! No! with the heart that loves you. I shall only love you—other things will be different—not such a warm heart." (JT, 337)

Behind this, again, we can detect the compromise over Frieda's infidelities, and a Grossian indifference to the inevitable duplicity and failure of relationship with reality that made Lawrence's comments an *Anna Karenina* so lacking in critical perception. The Lady Chatterley books were written out of the predicament of being impotent and having to accept his wife's finding her satisfactions elsewhere, as she did. This gives an added poignancy to "You won't love anybody with the same heart you love me with, will you? I don't mind if you have them with another heart." This takes us onto another point: Parkin says (JT, 367), "I really don't know what love means." When Connie reflects over Byron's heart, "the sense of the greatness of human mistakes made her cry," there is great tenderness over "the child that lay unseen," and the way he takes her at the end, despite the perverted voyeuristic element Lawrence must introduce, is gentle and poignant: 'I must touch you, or I shall die!" (JT, 374). The Chatterley novels are full of deprivation and their disturbing effect has to do with that—the feeling of being menaced, the wretchedness of both woman and man, the sense of dread, of not knowing what love is. Lawrence attempts the magical solutions of the wand of the idolized phallus.

But suddenly, toward the end, we sense a different solution: human beings accepting the "greatness of human mistakes," and the sense that what is needed is for human beings to accept their needs and responsibilities—needs that are wide, and especially require the choice of that which is true to them and to others and in sexuality, to the child who is the future.

No doubt the life of Connie and Oliver after the end of *John Thomas* will be tormented and full of woe. At least Parkin has given up his stand in "mastery" in resistance to Connie's money. But her cry, "Will you come and live with me . . . " is at the end a recognition of what is true to both them, not idyllic, but real, and an act of love, not mere "naked desire."

*        *        *

## Lady Chatterley's Lover

In the last version Connie Chatterley is seriously compromised for us in one sense because of her easy affair with the successful Michaelis early in the book.[2] While in the first book she is a trollop in some respects, and irresponsible in both, she has at least our sympathy for the anguish of her predicament of living in the destroyed marriage. I do not accept Lawrence's view that *loss of consortium* (as the courts call it) must inevitably ruin a woman's health, as if no one could live without regular sexual intercourse, but if we allow that she was in a miserable state of being both married and not married, we can accept that she had urgent reasons, being a healthy young woman with an instinctual urge to breed, for her lapse. In the first two books, it is a lapse. In second version she gains our sympathy in taking Mellors on, with a sense of the inevitability of fate.

Connie Chatterley, in the third version, is less stupid but also less innocent. The version itself develops a hard-bitten quality: Lawrence attempts to demonstrate the difference between his holy and grave view of sexual authenticity by giving us mental conversations about sex between "modern" people. Then he inserts Tommy Dukes into the company, who talks explicit Lawrencese: *he* knows that knowledge comes out or your belly and penis as well as out of your mind. *He* wants "a chirpy penis and the courage to say 'Shit!' in front of a lady"—and by this caricature of himself, Lawrence reveals a coarse and offensive element.

In the middle of one of these destructive conversations, Connie suddenly says, "There are nice women in the world." The others are embarrassed by her sheer naivety and sincerity. But what about us? For she has given herself in a somewhat superficial way to Michaelis, *and it has meant very little to her.*

She has given herself to the ("rat-like") successful playwright *because he was a bounder*:

> the unscrupulousness of Michaelis had a certain fascination for her. He went whole lengths where Clifford only crept a few timid paces. In his way he had conquered the world. (LC, 29)

She is also seduced by him because under the worldly success is a needy infant, crying out for affection. In no way, of course, is he the answer to the profound existential restlessness Connie experiences, a restlessness that arises from her being *out of touch*. Here, Lawrence was registering an important aspect of human experience. Our relationship with the whole world (Mother Earth) is in complex with our personal relationships, from the time of our infant life with the mother onward. Connie Chatterley experiences a *void* at the heart of her existence, in place of *touch* (JT, 19). She develops a deep fear of the *nothingness* in her life (JT, 52). She is thus very much in the predicament of the Mother in Lawrence's mythology, needing the awakening that is to make reality beautiful and meaningful again.

Michaelis can do nothing for this, yet she loves him. Of course, a woman in her predicament might easily make such a mistake, but what is important is the author's attitude to the lapse. Here, again I believe, Lawrence shows himself compromised by Frieda, her infidelities, and her rationalizations. He says, "Perhaps the human soul needs excursions, *and must not be denied them*. But the point of an excursion is that you come home again" (LC, 46).

This is said by Lawrence. It emerges out of a "stream of consciousness" in Connie who is listening to Clifford on their marriage:

"You and I are married, no matter what happens to us. We have the habit of each other. And habit, to my thinking, is more vital than any occasional excitement. The long, slow, enduring thing . . . that's what we live by . . . not the occasional spasm of any sort."

Connie sat and listened in a sort of wonder, and a sort of fear. She did not know if he was right or not. There was Michaelis, whom she loved; so she said to herself. But her love was somehow only an excursion from her marriage with Clifford; the long, slow habit of intimacy formed through years of suffering and patience. (LC, 46)

Clifford's superficial discussion of how she might have a child by someone else is actually a deep insult to her authenticity.

What is surprising is Lawrence's failure to again see anything *intrinsically* wrong with "excursions." Connie does not know if her husband is right or not. To Michaelis she says, "I don't think it's wrong, do you?" after their first sexual act. Under Gross's influence Lawrence is concerned throughout that all normal conventions of what is right or not should be swept aside. And about excursions, he urges that human nature "should not be denied them," having learned as much from Gross, and from his need to countenance Frieda's infidelities.

Connie is attracted to Michaelis because he is a bounder, has in his way "conquered the world," and goes "further" than Clifford, that is, when an "excursion" represents a woman going in for a liaison that must lead her into duplicity, lying, and other forms of falsification. Might not what seems to be "generosity" then look very much like moral unscrupulousness? And here we have, I believe, to link Connie with Frieda, who was unscrupulous in this respect, as we know (for example) from her attempt to have an affair with Middleton Murry while Lawrence was still alive.

While he gestures toward amoralism over personal relationships, there emerges by contrast in Lawrence a very stern moral discrimination between good sex and bad sex. There is some consideration of orgasm in the second version, and much more in the third *Lady Chatterley*. In the third version the question of the nature of orgasm in the woman becomes a central moral theme and the whole direction of the book in terms of authenticity is that of the quest for a certain kind of orgasm. Orgasm becomes the focal test of the qualities of a person in the search for that impulse, "We've got to live." It is important to note the implications about how the particular kind of female orgasm is achieved. It is not achieved by mutual tenderness or by subtle caress in foreplay; it is not a manifestation of togetherness or mutual sincerity, nor is it a product of masculine potency; it does not belong to what the psychotherapists call mature genitality at all. In Lawrence it is achieved by the woman's total submission to "mastery" often to a somewhat brutal and even hostile sexual aggression, done without love, in uncomfortable and hasty encounters, sometimes in a risky place. It is brought about essentially by adoration of the phallic self, and it is of cosmic and mythological proportions. It belongs to fairy tale.

The stern morality attached to it, however, extends to an interpretation of society and history. It seems to emerge out of Lawrence's ponderings of Frieda's early life. Connie Chatterley, in the third version, is more clearly Frieda. Connie and her sister, like the Richthoften sisters, have had "enlightened" affairs with students in their youth. Lawrence sneers at their modern freedom:

> They lived freely among the students, they argued with the men over philosophical sociological and artistic matters, they were just as good as the men themselves: only better, since they were women. (LC, 6)

It is interesting to note that despite his explicit concern to find woman gaining her independence, Lawrence often displays a contemptuous antipathy to women's independence (Hilary Simpson traces this in *D. H. Lawrence and Feminism*). He is ironic about the girls' sexual freedom (it sounds like German girls' freedom rather than English girls of prewar time):

> The young men with whom they talked so passionately and sang so lustily and camped under the trees in such freedom wanted, of course, the love connection. The girls were doubtful, but then the thing was so much talked about, it was supposed to be so important. And the men were so humble and craving. Why couldn't a girl be queenly, and give the gift of herself? (LC, 7)

The discussions were important: the sex was a bit of an anti-climax. The great thing was the achievement of "an absolute, a perfect, a pure and noble freedom." Sex was a sordid connection compared with the beautiful pure freedom of a woman. Out of the conflict between the ideal free woman and the doggy men who insisted on sex, came the *self-asserting orgasm*:

> A woman could take a man without really giving herself away. Certainly she could take him without giving herself into his power. Rather she could use this sex thing to have power over him. For she only had to hold herself back in sexual intercourse, and let him finish and expend himself without herself coming to the crisis: and then she could prolong the connexion and achieve her orgasm and her crisis while he was merely the tool. (LC, 8)

Sex thus became "a spasm of self-assertion."

Connie has learned to exert power over the men students by letting them come, and then using them for her clitoral satisfaction. Next she does the same with Michaelis.

Clifford (JT, 13) doesn't bother much about his "satisfaction." It is difficult to know why Lawrence puts this in inverted commas or what he means. I suppose there are people to whom sex matters and others to whom it is less important, but it seems difficult to conceive of a man who wasn't concerned with his sexual satisfaction.

Michaelis, however, turns against Connie's power trick: "Connie found it impossible to come to her crisis before he had really finished his." (LC, 56)

What does that *really* mean? And what are the implications of that "impossible—the onus seems to be left to her":

> She had to go on after he had finished, in the wild tumult and heaving of her loins, while he heroically kept himself up, and present in her, with all his will and self-offering, till she had brought about her own crisis, with weird little cries. (LC, 56)

What are the implications of *heroically*? Detumescence is surely totally involuntary, and immediate? Michaelis turns, in hostility, against Connie on the matter: "You couldn't go off at the same time as a man, could you? You'd have to bring yourself on? You'd have to run the show!" (LC, 56) This is a deep shock to her, because she knows that "that passive sort of giving himself was so obviously his only real mode of intercourse." He complains, "and I have to hang on with my teeth till you bring yourself off by your own exertions."

"All the darned women are like that," he complains, "either they don't go off at all as if they were dead in there . . . I never had a woman yet who went off just at the same moment as I did" (JF, 57).

She replies, "But you want me to have my satisfaction too, don't you?" and he tells her he's "darned if hanging on waiting for a woman to go off is much of a game for a man."

This kills something in her.

For Lawrence, it seems to indicate a whole world in which this "lesser" (or *sinful*) sex goes with power and ego-exertion, and with the mechanical world, where will and the machine go together inimical to whole being. Michaelis has only himself to blame (that is clear from his comparison remark about women—he doesn't say, "Why didn't we enjoy that, my love?"). But Connie only has herself to blame, too, for (as Lawrence sees) she had "never positively wanted him."

Yet, of course, the problem remains as implied by that phrase, "that passive sort of giving himself was so obviously his only real mode of intercourse," but Lawrence is wrong about "so obviously." If only it were as simple as Lawrence makes out.[3] Here, certainly, there can easily be false solutions, for how, in the third Lady Chatterley version, is Connie brought to the "good" kind of orgasm? Actually, by the same medicine as in the second version: *by power*. The essential episode on page 138 is virtually unaltered from the version in *John Thomas and Lady Jane*. How does one bring a woman to orgasm, from the state of ego-willed orgasm as described earlier? The answer is *by force*.

It is completely convincing that Connie Chatterley, after all her distress, should almost fall into the sexual act with Mellors while looking at the chicks in spring; it is appropriate that she should feel as she does about Mrs. Flint's baby. Lawrence's descriptions of her feelings are superb and reveal his uncanny capacity to identify with woman.

But now, at a moment when she is in retreat a little from her new affair, she meets Mellors on the way home. She is late. "'Giving me the slip, like?' he said, with a faint ironic smile." (LC, 137) He steps up to her and puts his arms around her. "She felt the front of his body terribly near her, and alive. 'Oh, not now, not now,' she cried, trying to push him away." (LC, 137)

Her "old instinct" is to fight for her freedom, but she doesn't. "She saw his eyes, tense and brilliant, fierce, not loving." (my italics)

This is the kind of man Lawrence really respected, who is capable of detachment, domination, unloving, and brusque. "Her will had left her .... She was giving way. She was giving up."

> She had to lie down there under the boughs of the tree, like an animal . . . he broke the band of her underclothes, for she did help him, only lay inert. (LC, 138)

Mellors enters her at once and comes at once:

> She felt his naked flesh as he came into her. For a moment he was still inside her, turgid there and quivering. Then as he began to move, in the sudden helpless orgasm, there awoke in her new thrills. (LC, 138)

It is virtually a rape, and yet Connie has *her* first orgasm. It is the first idolized one, all bells and ripples, molten inside. We have then one of those (turgid) passages of orgasm in Lawrence, as Mellors takes her again: "the unspeakable motion that was not really motion, but pure deepening whirlpools of sensation, etc." (LC, 139) And they lay and knew nothing, not even of each other, both lost.

> "We came off together that time," he said. She did not answer. "It's good when it's like that. Most folks live their lives through and they never know it." (LC, 139)

And a little later, incredibly: "Have you come off like that with other women?" (LC, 140). It is all utterly false, and the starkness of the propaganda becomes increasingly evident, as the presentation becomes increasingly religious. She feels her passion and yet resists it, "for it was the loss of herself to herself," but because he has dominated her in that Cipriano way, "She adored him till her knees were weak as she walked." (LC, 140) She fears it because "if she adored him too much, then she would lose herself, become effaced." (LC, 141) She responds, like a Bacchante, while Mellors is but the *phallic self*: "He was but a temple-servant, the bearer and keeper of the bright phallos, her own." (LC, 141) He should be "torn to pieces now the service was performed," but she knows now who is master:

She felt the force of the Bacchae in her limbs and her body, the woman gleaming and rapid, beating down the meal: but while she felt this, her heart was heavy. She did not want it . . . the adoration was her treasure. It was so fathomless.

No, no, she would give up her hard bright female power. (LC, 141)

All this belongs to Lawrence's mythology rather than sexual truth. It has to do with the struggle for power. The Mother Woman must be given the Resurrection of the Body, the Phallic Self must bring about a reexperience of symbiosis, but that symbiosis had become protracted and menacing, like the woman exerting her will (ego) through the clitoris, menacing the man. To avoid these dangers, approach her *without love*, crush her will, show (schizoid) indifference, be "provident" and rape her, then in the ultimate submission of her will to man become nothing more than a phallos, the man will achieve mastery. For a moment she may contemplate being a Bacchante and tearing the phallos to pieces, but then she will relent and realize that is not what she wants. She will relinquish her woman's will and sing the voiceless song of adoration, in submission.

It might be a good recipe for achieving mastery over Woman in the Sleeping Beauty myth of Lawrence's unconscious. As a recipe for behavior in any earthly marriage between man and woman, this "upshot" is *disastrous*.

The episodes also, of course, belong to the mythology: Connie, entranced by Mellors washing himself in the wood, is Mrs. Lawrence washing her husband's back. Lawrence wants her to like it so a symbolic link is made between that revealed body and the flowers of spring that always surround Connie's progress towards resurrection.

And the keeper, his thin, white body, like a lonely pistil of an invisible flower . . . now something roused. . . . "Pale beyond porch and portal" . . . the thing to do was to pass the porches and the portals. (LC, 89)

After some more descriptions of the flowers, Lawrence quotes Swinburne's rejection of Christ: "the world has grown grey with thy breath."

But it was the breath of Persephone, this time; *she was out of hell on a cold morning.* (LC, 87–88)

Connie, then, is the mother in hell, the *keeper* is the keeper of the *gates of hell*. He is out of the world, and the world is blighted by the "bad" mother. (The underlying myth is not that of Persephone but Orpheus and Eurydice.)

She wanted to forget, to forget the world, and all the dreadful, carrion-bodied people. "Ye must be born again! I believe in the resurrection of the body. Except a grain of wheat fall in the earth and die, it shall by no means bring forth. When the crocus comes forth I too will emerge and see the sun." (LC, 81)

To Lawrence, at the level of his deep unconscious, the world is hell, and only in the woodland idyll glade is there the possibility of the god-managed rebirth of the mother. (Parkin, who is a variant of Birkin, the other self, becomes Mellors, whose name is an anagram of Morel and so a more direct reference to the autobiographical life.)

What Lawrence knew was that in the (hell) world, from which the dead bad mother was not exorcised, there was malignancy. Throughout Lawrence, this seems directed at sexual fulfillment, and against being. (As a social theory this fails, because we do not all have menacing mothers.)

He knew by experience what it meant.

> It was not woman's fault, nor even love's fault, nor the fault of sex. The fault lay there, out there, in those evil electric lights and the diabolical rattling of engines. There, in the world of the mechanical greedy, greedy mechanism and mechanized greed, sparkling with lights and gushing hot metal and roaring with traffic, there lay the vast evil thing, ready to destroy whatever did not conform. Soon it would destroy the wood, and the bluebells would spring no more. All vulnerable things must perish under the rolling and running of iron. (LC, 123)

As Graham Martin says in an open university study book on *The Rainbow*, Lawrence does not make it clear why the machine world should menace sex. What is this vast "evil thing"? Even though it is the basis of the "Scrutiny" educational-literary movement, the full subjective basis of it is elusive—the only thing that is clear is that it is deeply subjective and related to a bad experience of the mother. It menaces even the garden of Eden. "Society" is "a malevolent, partly insane beast" (LC, 124). No wonder Mellors, with such paranoia, has some strange tendencies in fear of love: "He hated mouth kisses," for instance, and has other tendencies to shrink from tenderness.

As one goes on reading *Lady Chatterley's Lover*, it becomes clear that there are a number of interests or impulses in Lawrence pulling in different directions. There is the true novelist who is looking at "the struggling battered thing any human soul is" (LC, 104). There is the man of sympathy who sees that there are positive processes even in the most unpropitious of relationships as when Mrs. Bolton makes Clifford more "effective" (a theme that runs contrapuntal to Lawrence's pondering of what Frieda did to him—there is, as Martin Green argues, a good deal of Lawrence in Clifford, a Lawrence who had not been infused by Frieda's sensual sunniness). Then there is the propagandist who emerges from the man who, like Connie, has a horror of civilization: "A kind of terror filled her sometimes, a terror of the incipient insanity of the whole civilised species." (LC, 114).

As I have said, the original seduction of Connie Chatterley is moving and convincing. Some of the scenes of sexual meeting seem to me perfect, as a significant novelist's work, but then there is a note of overinsistence that leads me back to the propaganda element. There is the emphasis on the woman's *submission*: "It was gone, the resistance was gone, and she began to melt in a marvellous peace." And then there is the latent murderousness: "So strange and terrible. It might come with the thrust of a sword in her softly-opened body, and that would be death. . . . But it came with a strange slow thrust of peace." (LC, 181)

The fear of murder here picks up both the need to awaken the Sleeping Beauty and resurrect the mother, together with the dread of symbiosis.

> The heavier the billows of her rolled away to some shore, uncovering her, and closer and closer plunged the palpable unknown, and further and further rolled the waves of herself away from herself, leaving her, till suddenly, in a soft, shuddering convulsion, the quick of all her plasm was touched, she knew herself touched, the consummation was upon her, and she was gone. She was gone, she was not, and *she was born: a woman.* (LC, 181; my italics)

Lawrence (in some dread) has brought the dead mother at last to full womanhood. The man she flinched from ("that strange, hostile, slightly repulsive thing . . . a man") is now recognized in his potency. What beauty!

> How was it possible, this beauty here, where she had previously only been repelled? . . . the strange weight of the balls between his legs! . . . that could be soft and heavy in one's hand. (LC, 182)

As I have pointed out before, although there is some development in this occasion in that Mellors caresses her genitals, such a touch as is suggested here would be most unwelcome immediately after orgasm. But we are not really in the realm of real sexuality at all: here they make love three times, in great force, with hardly a pause. Yet only a few pages further on Mellors declares. "That pneumonia took a lot out of me." The sexual descriptions belong to a theoretical assertion. This is "creative" sex rather than procreative. Mellors brusquely says: "'Now anybody can 'ave any child i' th' world,' . . . as he sat down fastening his leggings" (LC, 184). And it is done, in a spirit of Otto Gross, as an act of vengeance against Clifford. In the very next chapter Lawrence makes a serious artistic mistake, when he jeers at Clifford in his wheelchair:

> O last of all ships, through the hyacinthian shallows! O pinnace on the last wild waters, sailing in the last voyage of our civilisation! . . . O Captain, my Captain, our splendid trip is done! Not yet though! (LC, 192)

What does Lawrence mean, by "Not yet" and "the last voyage"? He means, surely, Clifford's death? And when we realize this we realize that the jeers are in a sense directed by Lawrence at himself for his is the impotent man who can only fantasize what has just gone on: "it was the Sons of God with the daughters of men." How, then, do we take Mellors's unpleasant insolence:

The keeper's face flickered with a little grimace, and with his hand he softly brushed her breast upwards, from underneath. She looked at him, frightened. (LC, 193)

Again, we have to say: murder. These jeers and gestures are in the tradition of Gross's unconscious impulse to murder woman.

Again the novelist exerts himself. The scene when Connie kisses her lover's hand surreptitiously as he pushes Clifford's chair is superb. So, too, in this version is the development of Connie's awareness that she hates Clifford and can no longer live with him. Once the reader realizes that she is now preparing to commit herself to Mellors, he feels that he must now regard this pair as virtually married, and one retreats, in a way—acknowledging that they must make their own fate, must make their bed and lie on it.

The novelist, too, realizes that when the woman comes to stay all night with her lover she is taking the wife's role so it is inevitable that she wants to discuss Mellors's previous wife and his earlier relationship with women. Though we know this will be emotionally disastrous, we know that in life we do behave in such ways with the inevitable consequences. The scene also enables Lawrence to put forward some of his own philosophy of personal relationships in a positive sense: "for me it's the core of my life: if I have a right relation with a woman." This (LC, 213) is a marvelous conversation because, instead of the supreme confidence of the Phallic Son of God, we have a man who admits that he is afraid of a *relationship.*

"It takes a lot to make me trust anybody, inwardly. So perhaps I'm a fraud to. I mistrust. And tenderness is not to be mistaken."

She is able, as a woman is, to feel some sympathy for the "bad" women in his life: "And perhaps the women *really* wanted to be there and love you properly, only perhaps they couldn't." He is willing to admit the possibility of his own impotence in the matter: "I know it. Do you think you know what a broken-backed snake that's been trodden on I was myself" (LC, 214). There are other times, however, when it seems clear that Mellors would not ever have talked as he does in the book. For instance, he says of Bertha Coutts, she had a "sort of bloom on her: a *sort of sensual bloom* that you'd see sometimes on a woman, or on a trolly" (LC, 209). The italicized phrase is too Lawrentian for a man like him, but then, of course, Mellors becomes Lawrence in this scene.

Once again, the account of problems in sexual experience is puzzling in its idiosyncracy. There is a discussion (which I think Frieda never comments on) on women "keeping the man inside them" and seeking their satisfaction with the clitoris "like a beak tearing at me" (LC, 210). (There are more varieties on page 212, all of which I have never known or heard about, and about which I have never read in any case-history.) One such accounts, are has to say, are has a perplexed feeling that nothing in one's own experience accords with his, and he seems strangely ignorant about sex (as when the character in *Mr Noon* talks of three sexual acts in fifteen minutes. See above, p. 243).

The associated moral blame of people who cannot "love properly" emerges inevitably from the Schwabing kind of sexual revolutionism. Since pleasure is the source of all values, and health is to be restored to society by immoral sensualism, not to be fully erotic is to be antilife, and morally bad. The creed is expanded (ridiculously) by Mellors. Connie accuses him of believing in nothing.

> "Yes, I do believe in something. I believe in being warm-hearted. I believe especially in being warm-hearted in love, in fucking with a warm heart. I believe if men could fuck with warm hearts, and the women take it warm-heartedly, *everything would come all right*. It's all this cold-hearted fucking that is death and idiocy." (LC, 125; my italics)

In one way it is patronizing for Lawrence is writing a kind of health-sex program for the working man. Even so, it is crass, and it becomes more crass when, after taking her, he says, "A woman's a lovely thing when 'er's deep ter fuck, and cunt's good" (LC, 221). Strangely, on the same page, this coarse propagandist, who is going to put the world right by "good cunt," becomes Lawrence, for she becomes Frieda:

> She lay naked and faintly golden like a Gloire de Dijon rose on the bed.

See *Gloire de Dijon*, (CP, 217),

> her swung breasts
> Sway like full-blown yellow Gloire de Dijon roses...

There is more of the novelist in chapter 14, and we take it from the start that Connie enjoys an intimacy with Mellors in the Garden of Eden that is far greater than her intimacy with Clifford despite his talk about something eternal in marriage. Then we lapse again. Mellors's address to his "tense phallos" is embarrassing because we feel we are intruding on a privacy, while Lawrence is also trying to make a phallic point about the "other life" of the loins: "Tha ma'es nowt o' me, John Thomas. Art boss? of me? Eh well, tha're more cocky than me, an' tha says less." (LC, 219) Lawrence cannot stop being religiose and at the same time blasphemous:

> "lift up your heads o' ye gates, that the king of glory may come in. Ay, th'cheek on thee! Cunt, that's what tha're after." (LC, 219)

(Actually, there is a typographical error here: it should be "O ye gates" not "o' ye gates!") But then, when she holds his detumescent penis—again a gesture that one might suppose would be most unwelcome at such a moment—he is religiose again. "Blest be the tie that binds our hearts in kindred love" (LC, 219), which echoes, of course, "the bonds of love are ill to loose" from *Sons and Lovers*. She replies "Even when he's soft and little I feel my heart simply tied to him" (LC, 220) while he,

> "He's got his root in my soul, has that gentleman! An' sometimes I don' know what to do wi' him. Ay, he's got a will of his own, an' it's hard to suit him. *Yet I wouldn't have him killed.*" (LC, 220; my italics)

It this exchange we have at least the recognition that the sensual life, the phallus, has a rooted connection with the heart and with the soul. This is a development from the earlier versions. The last phrase emerges from the undercurrent of Lawrence's castration anxiety.

They make love, as far as I can make out, four times in this chapter—just possible, I suppose, for a young man, but doubtful with a man of thirty-seven who has been damaged by pneumonia. However, even it this idyll, they do at least declare to one another: "I want soon to come and live with you altogether," she said as she left him. And she notices he has some books and is a reader!

In chapter 15, we revert to the bad Lawrence: the root of sanity is in the balls, and most people are becoming insane. He prophesies the extinction of humanity and she cries, "How nice!"

> ta-tah! to the human species! . . . the serpent swallows itself and leaves a void, considerably messed up, but not hopeless.

But what of their child?

> "It seems to me a wrong and better thing to do, to bring a child into this world." (LC, 121)

She tells him she is fairly certain that she is pregnant: "for me it seems a ghastly treachery to the unborn creature." She protests "there's another truth," but it is a critical issue at a critical moment. If all one can feel for humanity is loathing, and if the future is so doomed that one ought not to bring a child into the world, what happens to the sexual revolution?

> Bit by bit, let's drop the whole industrial life and go back. (LC, 228)

The answer is flight about wearing red trousers, combined with antics with flowers in the pubic hair, and frolics in the rain. Even so there are moments of cosmic despair even if one went to the moon:

> The moon wouldn't be far enough, because even there you could look back and see the earth, beastly, unsavoury, among all the stars, made foul by men. (LC, 230)

The men are all labor-insects, with all their manhood taken away. Who is to save us? Connie's antics have seem evidently to be those of Frieda, Otto Gross's sometime mistress, running into the rain with her "pointed keen animal breasts" and her "twinkling" buttocks, At least she is not taken by a "dagger thrust" as in version two. But, "suddenly he tipped her up and fell with her on the path ... and short and sharp, her took her, short and sharp and finished, like an animal" (LC, 231). The tenderness here is marred by the contempt Mellors expresses in his vernacular: "his finger-tips touched the two secret openings of her body, time after time, with a soft little touch of fire. "An' if tha shits an' if tha pisses, I'm glad" (LC, 232).

The somewhat insolent gloating, doing to a lady something Lawrence feels is daring and dominating, is given its rationalization as a political program:

> He laid his hand close and firm over her secret places. . . .
> "... An' if I only lived ten minutes, an' studied thy arse an' got to know it, I should reckon I'd live *one life, see ter! Industrial system or not!*" (LC, 233; my italics)

The latter, in its context, must be one of the most banal and ludicrous phrases in literature. (But the intention here becomes clear if we note Lawrence's attitude to using obscenities to Lady Ottoline.)

At least we are spared here the insistence of Parkin on "mastery." Mellors simply says "I'm not keen on being kept by you," and he lets her decide. At least in this version there is a measure of mutuality, and it bears the marks of Lawrence having worked things out with Frieda in his own marriage.

Soon, however, comes the worst scene in Lady Chatterley and the whole of Lawrence: the scene of enthusiastic sodomy. The relationship between Hilda and Connie is based on the relationship between Else and Frieda. Connie might well have said that Mellors "understands tenderness," but would she betray their private talk about Lady Jane and John Thomas (LC, 251)? The quarrel between Mellors and Hilda is not convincing, their argument over "continuity" is absurd, nor would Mellors used the word "cunt" to her. It is at one with Lawrence's failure to recognize the intense force of such words that he fails to make her respond explosively, and when he says "women like you needs proper grafting," there seems little cause for him to be so insolent and insulting to Hilda.

It is also unlikely that Connie would say at once, "kiss me" as soon as Hilda leaves, but, of course, Lawrence is here caught up in his need to rationalize perversion. His prose takes on that special kind of sickly persuasiveness we know from pornography. Of Mellors, he says, "his anger gave him a particular handsomeness." And Connie becomes the passive victim: "He jerked his head." The anger sits firm on his brows. It is almost as if in perverted play he is going to say, as in a pornographic story, "I must teach you a lesson."

The description is now also a *locus classicus*:

> It was a night of sensual passion, in which she was *a little startled* and *almost unwilling*: yet *pierced* again with *piercing* thrills of sensuality, different, *sharper*, more terrible than thrills of tenderness. (LC, 258; my italics)

The Penguin blurb says of the novel "It is never pornographic," but here, as attention to the prose shows, it is pornographic. It is full of perverted logic. She is more excited because it is cruel, and she is frightened:

> Though a little frightened, she let him have his way, and the reckless, shameless sensuality shook her to her foundations, stripped her to her very last, and *made a different woman of her*. (LC, 258; my italics)

Here is the clue to this ultimate effort to resurrect the mother, yet this is not done by love:

> It was not really love. It was not voluptuousness. It was sensuality sharp and searing as fine, burning the soul to tinder. (LC, 258)

It was, to be short, *hate* and unconscious murder:

> Burning out the shames, the deepest, oldest shames, in the most secret places . . . she really thought she was dying: yet a poignant, marvellous death.

We learn later that Mellors was given to subjecting his wife to anal intercourse, in the Italian manner, from Clifford's letters. And the earlier references to the secret places makes it all clear enough.

It is likely that any couple might experiment with sodomy, but the experiment could only be justified if it were mutual. The repulsive thing about Lawrence's enthusiastic account is that it is done in hostility and hate. Mellors's hostility to Hilda is inflicted on Connie.

But it isn't she who is offended! In a proper Otto Gross spirit, it is the *shame* that dies: "Shame which is fear: . . . which can only be chased away by the sensual fire." (LC, 258) This does not seem to square with findings in psychotherapy. If individuals are disturbed by a sense of shame within their inner life, it may be that a long process is ahead of their learning to overcome the crippling shame that inhibits their sexual lives. Perversions, which have as their unconscious goal the exorcism of phantoms, are likely to prove false solutions. To Lawrence they are "life":

> at last it was roused up and routed by the phallic hunt of the man, and she came to the very heart of the jungle of herself. She felt, now she had come to the real bedrock of her nature, and was essentially shameless. She was her sensual self, naked and unashamed. She felt a triumph, almost a vainglory. So! That was how it was! That was life! (LC, 258)

This *phallic hunting* is elevated *above* normal sexuality. Sodomy (which implicitly denies the womanness of woman) is "life"; this is the *real bed-rock of our natures* so "touch" at bed-rock is a not-love, burning, hate-sensuality, with its implicit murderousness.

> And what a reckless devil the man was. . . . The phallos alone could explore it. And how he had pressed in on her!
> And how, in fear, she had hated it. But how she had really wanted it! (LC, 259)

But then Lawrence makes it even worse;

> What liars poets and everybody were! They made one think one wanted sentiment. When what one supremely wanted was this piercing, consuming, rather awful sensuality. To find a man who dared to do it, without shame or sin or final misgiving. (LC, 259)

Mellors is superior to Clifford and Michaelis because he dares to sodomize a woman. He isn't ashamed. He is a *man*.

> Ah, God, how rare a thing a man is! They are all dogs that trot and sniff and copulate. To have found a man who is not afraid and not ashamed. (LC, 259)

Her nightdress is nearly slit in two. And now—having shared this experience of his unconscious hostility, she says, "We can't possibly *not* live together now, can we?" It is the freedom to sodomize that sets the seal on the marriage! This is the meaning of life. One lives for it: "Don't you think one lives for times likes last night?" It is strange that the novels entitled *Tenderness* should end up thus. "'I loved last night,' says Connie: "You'll keep the tenderness for me?"

Far from being a dissipation of shame, such celebration of perversion is a mark of compulsive fascination with shame itself. As in *The Rainbow*, it is clear that the excitement comes from the shamefulness. It is the unconscious elements of mother-murder, or exorcism of the dead mother, in the act that Lawrence is celebrating.

From this triumph of the phallic self, Lawrence returns to sneering at ordinary people—ordinary people presumably who do not enjoy such delights. *They* are the sinners! He sneers at their bodies

> Great puddingy things in black pudding-cloth, or lean wooden sticks in black funeral stuff . . . . The awful millposts of most females . . . . Awful, the millions of meaningless legs prancing around. (LC, 265)

Paris—false sensuality: all of it! The house-party in Venice, people plastering their stomachs against one another— "against some so-called man", the Lido-heaps of repulsive bare flesh.

But then, a dim thought about reality: she is pregnant, and reflects about Mellors, "*After all, he was the father of her child.*" After all!

Though in the end *Lady Chatterley's Lover* is better because it is more realistic than the earlier version, one feels that the novelist is losing his grip. There are many moments when we feel it couldn't be like that. Clifford, for instance, would have put two and two together much earlier. Connie actually confesses to him that she has been prancing about naked in the rain, not at the hut—but he divines nothing. The paranoia loses conviction: "People are always horrid": the child is the future, and so unwanted. Mellors "can't be your male concubine," yet "living is moving and moving on." In a way, it is all pathetic anticlimax. He is different from other men, because he has "the courage of his tenderness."

The most revealing moment comes as he is actually performing his last act of coition in the book (LC, 292). It is absolutely characteristic, but a pathetic contradiction in terms. Lawrence is urging us to be phallic, and the test is whether we "lapse out." Even as he reaches orgasm, Mellors is sloganizing and thinking politically, in an angry, hostile way. (Surely, if a man were to be thinking so actively like this at such a time he'd lose his potency?)

> He realized as he went into her that this was the thing he had to do, to come into tender touch. . . .
> "I stand for the touch of bodily awareness between human begins" he said to himself. . . .
> It is a battle against the money, and the machine, and the insentient ideal monkeyishness of the world. (LC, 292)

Even in what one might call the less enraptured acts of love, what man, at such a moment, would concoct slogans in his mind about 'the insensient monkeyishness of the world'? If Lawrence writes this fable, to indicate to us that we may find "being" in the mutual ecstasy of orgasm, that we may find a "pristine realisation of the infinite" in being-to-being, as we become aware of our partner's orgasm shared with us, surely this mental egoism is a poor culmination? For Mellors goes on, "Thank God I've got a woman!"—not "Thank God for Connie!" The following does not save it:

> "And as his seed sprang into her, his soul sprang towards her, too, in the creative act that is more than creative" (LC, 292)

—for his, is surely, the "mentality" that Lawrence warns us against? Is this what he means by "cunt-awareness" (LC, 290)? Is it this that makes people less "monkeyish"? Today, this message has led to a tide of explicit sex-language that threatens to swamp consciousness. This nonsense is the legacy of Otto Gross, and it makes a travesty of the Lawrence position here, because Mellors' "tenderness" is so full of hate ("it is a *battle* against the money, and the machine . . .", LC, 292; my italics).

Mellors' tenderness is after mixed with an impulse, such as we find in *The Fox* and elsewhere, to exterminate those who stand in one's way. Of Bertha he says, "I'd have her shot like a stoat, if I'd but been allowed . . . I ought to be allowed" (LC, 293). He wishes the Berthas and Cliffords all dead: "the tenderest thing you could do for them, perhaps, would be to give them death" (LC, 293).

We have seen how Lawrence felt that neurotics should be killed. What about perverts? Clifford, apparently, is to be condemned as a pervert. He has fallen under the spell of Mrs. Bolton and has in his anguish taken consolation of her body:

> He would put his hand in her bosom and feel her breasts, and kiss them in exultation, *the exultation of perversity*, of being a child when he was a man. (LC, 305)

This is "an intimacy of perversity" that "looked almost like a religious exaltation." "This *perverted* child-man" (my italics) is now "wallowing in private emotion." This is surely a case of the pot calling the kettle black! And what of the shame that was hunted out by the man's phallus?

> What I live for is for you and me to live together. I'm frightened really. *I feel the devil in the air, and he'll try to get us.* Or not the devil, Mammon: which I think, after all, is only the mass-will of people, wanting money and hating life. Anyhow, *I feel great grasping while hands in the air, wanting to get hold of the throat of anybody* who tries to live, to live beyond money, and *squeeze the life out.* There's a bad time coming. There's nothing lies in the future but death and destruction, for these industrial masses. (LC, 315; my italics).

We can easily list the horrors of our time, but who would accept, as Leavis did, following Lawrence, that we can only despair? Throughout disaster and war, men and women managed to keep their little flames alive: and have we not advanced, in insights, not least in areas where Lawrence has helped us? Lawrence makes Mellors' position too obsessively self-defensive.

> So I believe in the little flame between us. For me now, its the only thing in the world. . . . There's the baby, but that's a side-issue. It's my Pentecost, the forked flame between me and you. (LC, 316)

We end having made little or no progress, except the minimal commitment to some kind of life together, but the *menace* projected onto the world remains—the white hands, the white lights, the glittering machine—that actually seeks to strangle, and especially strangle one's sexual life.

Insofar as the "white hands" are other than tuberculosis and impotence, they can surely only be interpreted as parental ghosts—the impinging mother, the father who was rejected by her, the combined parents in their denial of body-life and sexuality—the mother now in death threatening to return if she is "betrayed." Her ghost is never *laid*. That is the terrible conclusion of these novels.

*       *       *

We have to come to the effect of Lawrence's worst book in its final upshot. There is a sense of poignant human "broken backedness," but when we ask what the effect on us is, on "society," on attitudes to sex, and on consciousness, can we really be happy about it?

If it is "the flow and recoil of our sympathy that really determines our lives," may not some of the enthusiam about hidden hate in *Lady Chatterley's Lover* encourage us to take out on woman the fears we have failed to acknowledge in ourselves?

The sodomy in Lawrence is the best index of the way in which he managed to disarm literary criticism, even in the face of his propaganda for hostility and perversion. There have been various discussions of the sodomy in *Lady Chatterley's Lover*. Frank Kermode sees it in apocalypic terms, as a death and transfiguration, an experience speaking for us all. The phallus for him is the Holy Ghost. But, Donald Gutiérrez, in a Canadian journal *Sphinx*, points out that sodomy is associated mainly, in our minds, with male homosexuality. As I would put it, there is thus in this a symbolic denial of feminity. As I have tried to show, throughout Lawrence, for him the sexual act is full of profound and deathly dangers because there lurks in it the phantom woman of unlimited destructive power. Yet he needs to find himself reborn, through touch with "being," in that dark realm so it must in some way be *exorcised*, and woman put under control. The secret places of her body must, as it were, be flushed out, while sodomy also provides the additional bonus of denying her femininity.

Gutiérrez's most telling point, however, is that the act is done in anger. Mellors is angry, not with Connie but with Connie's sister, Hilda. ("Outwardly angry, but not with her, so Connie felt" Gutiérrez, 267) But, as Gutiérrez sees, her response is also significant. As with all the episodes in which woman is humiliated, she likes it. "His anger gave him a peculiar handsomeness, on inwardness and glisten that thrilled her and made her limbs go molten." The episode belongs to the phenomena of domination we have looked at throughout. Mellors jerks his head swiftly, and they go up to the night of sensual passion.

She is "pierced," the sensuality is "sharper, more terrible than the thrills of tenderness," and Mellors is "reckless," Connie has to be "a passive, consenting thing, like a slave, a physical slave." (Gutiérrez, 116) The sensuality is "sharp and searing as a fire," and (as Gutiérrez says) the passage conveys the pain of unexpect anal possession. "One . . . had to be strong to bear him. . . . And how he had pressed in on her."

It is, also, a question of mastery. Far from being an act of symbolic renascence, it looks rather like the "selfish brutality of a stud." It cannot but be for all Lawrence's impulses to redeem are seen by our civilization as an act belonging to the lowest tier of enslavement and captivity.

Connie "thought she was dying" during the act, yet Connie made to admire Mellors for daring to do it. Gutiérrez says,

This scene reveals Lawrence's sexist values: the masculine agent must be the complete doer or possessor, while the woman must be the sex acted upon, the acceptor, who achieves her sense of worth from how much she can endure. (Gutiérrez, 118)

Although Connie thinks of it as a "poignant, marvellous death," she is, thinks Gutiérrez, "negatively degraded" by the act. Gutiérrez, however, rejects the view that the impulse in Lawrence's novel to turn out "the deepest oldest shames, in the most secret places" may be used to ridicule the idea that the novel affirms love and tenderness: he says that "Tenderness is the dominant sertiment in *Lady Chatterley's Love*". However, I believe it marks a serious failure in Lawrence's portrayal of sexual love—not because it happens, as it might happen between any pair of lovers experimenting enthusiastically with each other's bodies—but because it is done in hate, toward mastery, and because Lawrence, because of his strange unconscious mythology, offers this as the path to a new mode of existence. He could only regard normal sex with horror, and must guard against it with hate-sex, in a Grossian way.

# Conclusions

The original impulse in Lawrence as an artist was to pursue the question of the meaning of life. How this question is bound up with woman, love, sex, and marriage is clear from that great tragic novel *Sons and Lovers*. At the end, we see the hero struggling with nihilism, and one saving grace is that the dead mother is "in him." She is "in me," Paul Morel reflects, and so his life is in a sense devoted to the continuity of the being of the mother he loved.

But with her within him, too, is the traumatic experience he had of her handling in infancy (about which we can only guess), the fact that she is dead, her jealousy of other women in her (ghostly) possessiveness, and the unsatisfactory nature of her own sexual life. The nonfulfillment of the parent's sexual life is crucial, in Lawrence's experience, since it means that within him he felt he had the ghost of a bitterly unfulfilled mother who, in consequence, feels that life is meaningless and so threatens his life with meaninglessness. In complex with this I believe are other traumatic experiences: his own attempts to relieve her depression when she was mourning the death of his brother Ernest and perhaps also the effect of her confusion of himself with the much-loved dead sibling, and her idolization of him as a phallus during his infancy.

I have examined in detail the consequences in his work. Lawrence saw every woman as a threat, and needing to be awakened to sexual fulfillment, so that meaning could be given to her life. This can only be achieved by the Ithyphallic magic of the idolized Phallic Self the Mother created in him. This meant that he tended to see all human beings in all situations in terms of their sexual potentialities, and he wanted to save the world by fostering these potentialities.

The pressure of these intrapsychic myths, however, gave a certain narcissistic quality to his work at times because until he has solved the problem of resurrection he cannot establish the link in perception between the self and the world, with Mother Earth, though he is appreciative of its beauty. A characteristic solution in his later work is the lonely protagonist—often a woman who is lonely and alienated in a remote and beautiful part of the earth. From the bafflement recorded in his major novels written out of his marriage, Lawrence takes recourse more and more to *flight*, and this is a flight from being human ("Oh for a non-human race of man!").

He also becomes increasingly obsessed with the need for power over woman and over a dangerous world. Where the man is concerned, he must be remote, indifferent, noncommittal, enigmatic, and disinclined to be very close emotionally. He has god-like powers, or is a god, capable of effecting resurrection in this life rather than (like the Christ of Christianity) in the next. In the background is a deep fear of love (with its dangers of "horrible merging"): the awakening God must safeguard himself against the dangers of implosion. His aim is to be master in order to perform his task of resurrecting the Sleeping Beauty.

Woman must submit absolutely to this God: it must be "the *Sons of God* with the *daughters of man.*" Despite his avowed concern with woman becoming herself, what Lawrence is most antipathetic to is any impulse in woman to assert herself in ways that seem (to him) properly belong to the male. In one of the versions of *Lady Chatterley*, he makes the man have a phobia of women's pubic hair, perhaps because it looks like a man's beard, (as in the surrealist painting by Magritte—reference to this phobia is deleted from the last Chatterley novel), and there seems to be behind his work a dread of female sensuality, except in a passive mode. The search for satisfaction by the woman using her "beak-like clitoris" after the man's orgasm is also something that Lawrence sees as threatening—a dangerous assertion of self-will. Her true orgasm is a total submission to being overcome by domination. Behind this, in turn, I believe we may detect a castration anxiety. Perhaps Mellors, who is afraid of being caught with his head in his shirt, embodies an unconscious fear in Lawrence of castration? And, of course, we have castration fears in Somers's dreams. The urge for mastery and power seems certainly a form of ritual guarantee against the danger in woman.

Woman must be prepared to have some menace hunted out of her by the phallos as by sodomy. If she tries to seduce a man in a male way (as in the story *Monkey Nuts*), he seeks to exult in a triumph over her, and the word "triumph" as we shall see is important. At the same time there is an undercurrent of resentment at woman's creativity and of motherhood—this being subjected especially to powerful denial. There is also the strong undercurrent of murder to which reference has been made: woman is ecstatically murdered in the culmination of her quest to escape from corrupt civilization into a new state of being (in *The Woman Who Rode Away*). Lawrence expresses satisfaction in murdering a woman to get her out of the way of the fulfillment of a relationship (*The Fox*). Women often admire the murderer, as in *Kangaroo* and *The Plumed Serpent*. (We need to note here that if *Sons and Lovers* is true autobiographically then Lawrence himself performed matricide, albeit in mercy.)

These are only some of the tormented problems to do with sex and gender that arise in the works. While the false solutions are blatant in the late works, they are there in the early works, too. There are many contradictions in the whole complex position, and as Hilary Simpson (1982) points out, the position changes significantly from *The Study of Thomas Hardy* to *Fantasia of the Unconscious*, from being glad of woman's liberation and fulfillment, to becoming hostile, wanting to put woman under intense control. Lawrence turned from the power of love to a belief in male power of a Nietzschean kind, celebrated later in *The Plumed Serpent* in uncomfortably fascistic terms (while Frieda was making approving notes on *Mein Kampf*). Lawrence cannot be exonerated from modes of thought that could lead to a fascistic position, as in his often quoted remarks about a leader in his *History*.

What went wrong? I suspect that Lawrence found increasingly that despite his belief he was shedding his sicknesses in books, he wasn't winning against his psychic troubles. He became more and more afraid of and hostile to woman. Some say that he became impotent, and possibly his fear of the phantom woman lay behind that. He was more schizoid than many realize and in many ways he was very paranoid. I believe we have all picked up this paranoia. In a sense Lawrence's paranoia had a justification: the Great War may be seen as a gigantic demonstration of the ultimate failure of the male way of dealing with the world, and it was the first wholly industrialized war in which millions were literally sacrificed to the machine. This itself inflicted wounds on consciousness from which we have not yet recovered. At the same time women went out to work the machines and to become masculinized. As Hilary Simpson argues, sexual roles were changing and were becoming confused, and to many men this was a source of fear, as it still is.

But it was not true, as Lawrence sees it, with powerful endorsement from Leavis, that machines and industry were the cause of the catastrophe and the primary menace to civilization. This hostility to the machine was a projection from Lawrence's psychic make-up into his politics, taking in through Frieda, psychopathological German revolutionary sexual theories of an anarchistic, nihilistic kind. Whatever a mechanistic civilization and the predominance of ideas of "functional man" may have done to being, the simple equation Lawrence asserts will not do. It is rather a projection of Lawrence's feelings about male modes of dealing with reality, possibly with its origins in his mother's handling of him as an infant, and his experience of his mother's sexual life with her miner husband, and its bearing on his own life. There is, too, as we have seen, a feeling that the pit life made his father's life meaningless as well ("tic tac"). But, alas, in its increasing propagandist dynamic, it becomes misanthropist and an excuse for the "schizoid superiority" we have detected throughout Lawrence's work.

All this is not a diagnosis of a "sick" individual, though it would seem that Lawrence's tuberculosis was more important in his psychic life than many are prepared to see. It does suggest, however, that he suffered from a deep sense of not having begun to be his true self, at the very heart of his existence, and so he makes his characters continue to yearn for "something else."

This gives a special significance to his "phoenix" symbol, and his identification with Christ. Lawrence wanted to be reborn psychically speaking, and his own mythology is of being reborn. In order to achieve this rebirth, he needed to awaken woman to the condition of being able to give rebirth to him. He speaks (in *The Man Who Died*) of how "rare woman" waits for the "reborn man," and elsewhere of how a man is born first of his mother and later of his own woman: "I think a man is born twice: first his mother bears him, then he has to be reborn from the woman he loves" (Moore 1955, 176). In woman lay the clue to the capacity to *begin to be*, through the resurrection of the internalized mother, to reflect him further.

By contrast with this great mythological purpose in *his* sexuality, all other couples were inadequate, all other marriages were failures, all "ordinary coupling" repulsive. Woman had to wait for the very special and magic Ithyphallic god-self to awaken them, and he comes in many guises, even as a horse (St. Mawr being St. Lawrence). The trouble is, however, that we do not have magic penises, and if we are to be men and women, we need to come to terms with our mere humanity.

In no circumstances do men and women in Lawrence's novels find fulfilled sexual mutality, in freedom, giving respect to one another's being, from which they experience a joy that flows out into the world, in terms of their devotion to family life, their life-tasks, and spiritual meanings; toward a sense of new consciousness of the potentialities of existence enriched by love, and an outgoing toward the world. A great deal of Lawrence's later work is mean in intention, even vengeful, full of dread and hostility as we have seen, enclosed in an obsessive narcissism that becomes increasingly dismissive of the real world.

The most significant false solution coming from the "upshot" of Lawrence's late works has contributed to the perplexities of the modern consciousness at large: the obsession with idealized sexuality in a narcissistic way, when the clue lies in the opposite direction—the outgoing relationship between a love relationship and the world. It is strange that even as one enters into literary criticism of the work of Lawrence, one of the century's most important writers, one cannot at the same time avoid discussions of the most intimate sexual problems. This is characteristic of our age, which has so attached a sense of identity and meaning to sexual meeting: yet it places a profound strain upon us all because of the difficulty of finding any reliable source of truth about sexuality by which to judge the pressure upon us of a new and very moralistic faith, in which to be good is to have "good sex." This is in one sense a culmination of the erroneous Freudian model, in which sexual instinct was primary.

Fortunately, there are some useful books, not least in the realm of psychotherapy, which help us here. Rollo May's *Love and Will* is one of the most important; Viktor Frankl helps us to reach beyond the current fixation on sex as an existential therapist. It is important to penetrate beyond the present enlightened attitude to sexual realism, since this itself can be a defense against an approach to the real problems. Enlightened explicitness about sex is now a feature of our literary pages, and a great deal of it represents what can only be called "moral stupidity." Lawrence cannot altogether be absolved from responsibility for this. This becomes clear when any erotic book is mentioned, and his name is inevitably brought up. For instance, when *The Times* reviewed John Cleland's *Memoirs of a Woman of Pleasure*, brought out in paperback in the Worlds Classics for some unaccountable reason, the reviewer, Basil Boothroyd said:

> In spilling over, properly enough, into further erotic literature of the period, Mr. Sabor (who wrote the Introduction) maintains a scholarly and uninflamed detachment likely to elude some readers later receiving Fanny's unbuttoned confidences, which leave Lady Chatterley and her lover at the bedpost. (16 March 1985)

The headline is "Lady Chatterley Left at the Bedpost." This note is common, that each new venture outstrips the last, and in it we may even hear Connie Chatterley herself—"here was a man who dared to do it." One cannot escape the conclusion that Lawrence inflicted a certain coarseness on the modern consciousness as a consequence of his false solutions and his essential perversions.

The reality of human sexual problems is acutely difficult to discuss. We have seen how, according to Frieda, Lawrence was impotent in the last four years of his life, but in many places his novels record an emotional impotence, in which, time after time, his lovers find a surging chaos of hate and alienation rising even from the heart of their fulfillment.

We do have one clue, which is to Lawrence's sexual competence, and his anxiety about it. This comes from Compton MacKenzie, in *My Life and Times, Octave Five, 1918–1933*, pages 167–68. Significantly, it is associated with a discussion of homosexuality.

> What worried him particularly was his inability to attain consummation simultaneously with his wife, which according to him was still imperfect in spite of all they had gone through. I insisted that such a happy coincidence was always rare, but he became more and more depressed about what *he* insisted was the only evidence of a perfect union.
> "I believe that the nearest I've ever come to perfect love was with a young coal-miner when I was about sixteen," he declared.

As Paul Delaney suggests, when he quotes this, it was rather Alan Chambers, Jessie's brother, to whom Lawrence was so attracted, the model for George Sexton in *The White Peacock*.

There is a great deal, of course, about "coming off together" in the last *Lady Chatterley's Lover*, and in those books we have the sad spectacle of an impotent man whose efforts in his own love relationship and marriage have failed, offering an idealized, even idolized, sexuality, with multiple acts achieving orgasms of cosmic proportions. In the end Lawrence denounced the woman's search for a clitoral orgasm, by the "foaming," "beak-like" clitoris, demanding from her a total submission, in which she must lapse out into a state of total dissolution, something like a fit of petit mal, as one commentator put it, but more like a death of the self.

It seems likely that the obsession with orgasm in contemporary attitudes to sexual experience is itself a kind of displacement. I do not say it is not important to people to feel a sense of shared ecstasy in sex, or that mutual orgasm is not rapturous, but anxiety about this function in sexuality is itself a manifestation of false solution. In light of Frankl's comments, it becomes a focus of an attempt to demonstrate something, which is bound to be frustrated because of its obsessional nature. This may be related to the wider problems of love (*sub specie aeternitatis*) and meaning.

While Lawrence is scathing about the pursuit of happiness, his emphasis on the need for sexual fulfillment in "touch" does not take us far enough away from the belief that the aim of our existence is to satisfy the "wants" of "desire." Here perhaps it will help to invoke Viktor Frankl for an existentialist emphasis:

> if this normal reaching out for meaning and being is discarded and replaced by the will to pleasure or the "pursuit of happiness," happiness falters and collapses, in other words, happiness must ensure as a side-effect of meaning-fulfillment. And that is why it cannot be "pursued," because the more attention we pay to happiness, the more we make pleasure the target of our intentions, by way of what I call hyper-intention, to he same extent we become victims of hyper-reflection. That is to say the more attention we pay to happiness or pleasure, the more we block its attainment, and lose sight of the primary reason for our endeavours, happiness vanishes, because we are intending it, and pursuing it. (Frankl 1969, 401)

Frankl relates this to clinical work in the sexual neuroses. "Whenever a male patient is trying deliberately to manifest his potency, or a female patient to demonstrate her ability to experience orgasm, the very attempt is doomed to fail." This last sentence may be applied to Lawrence's obsessional pre-occupation with sexual fulfillment, as a closed circuit, throughout his work.

Our fulfillment—the existential psychotherapists argue—rather demands attention to the "demand quality" that life offers in the service of our life tasks. If men and women grope toward tasks and out-goings beyond themselves, being-in-the-world, their fulfillment, not least in sexual meeting, may follow.

The connections between the kind of obsession to which Frankl refers and will and anxiety are well indicated by Leslie H. Farber in *The Ways of the Will* in a chapter entitled, "I'm sorry dear," which is about the American obsession with mutual orgasm. He discusses there the problem of "the failure of our bodies to meet these imperatives." Farber tries to introduce some realism into the age of sexual enlightenment: sex, he says, is both utterly important and utterly trivial.

Sex may be a hallowing and renewing experience, but more often it will be distracting, coercive, playful, frivolous, discouraging, dutiful, and even boring. On the one hand, it tempts man to omnipotence, while on the other it roughly reminds him of his mortality. (Farber 1966, 54)

He discusses the idolized orgasm in a Kinsey film of masturbation. The person has become separated from the body (and he declares that Lawrence was one who would have understood this). However, as we have seen, his characters are constantly yearning for something beyond human sexuality, dehumanised into Phallic divinity. The physical function has been separated from the uniqueness of being that alone gives any meaning to love, which is the meeting of unique beings. The perfect orgasm, Farber suggests is the orgasm achieved on one's own:

No other consummation offers such certainty and, moreover, avoids the messiness that attends most human affairs. (Farber 1966, 69)

Farber's essay, actually, is about the destructiveness of the idealizing will. If we are to accept the "messiness" of personal relationships, we need to accept that in illness, in grief, in distress, and even at times without apparent cause, our sexual life will fail. In any case it is only human at best.

To Lawrence, as to Leavis, sexual failure (as in Gerald and Skrebensky) seemed an indication of a moral failure. In this we have the new Puritanism that Rollo May discusses so well. We can detect this puritanism in Lawrence's remarks to Compton MacKenzie. He must find evidence of a happy union, and the burden was put on mutual orgasm. This demand lies behind the Lady Chatterley books, and as I pointed out in *The Quest for Love*, the implication is a terribly false one there that our sexual problems can be solved by enthusiastic sensuality, or "warm-hearted fucking." The truth is that—as Compton MacKenzie says—happy mutuality is a matter of luck, sometimes it happens, many factors contribute to it, and the strange fact is that the greater ecstasies are experienced only to be forgotten, since they merge into a sense of harmony that spreads out into the world. It is only with those who are anxious for other and deeper reasons that the obsession with simultaneous orgasm becomes a point of fixed anxiety in the protracted discussion of clitoral, vaginal and "lapsed out" orgasm.

It is Lawrence, alas, who obliges us to embark upon such obsessive discussion, even in a literary critical work. Moreover, in estimating the "upshot" of his work, we have to defend ourselves against what can only be called perversions. If one accepts with Leavis that Lawrence offers normative sexuality and definitions of marriage, then anal sex is normative and a part of marriage. But this is nonsense, because it is associated in Lawrence's stories, as we have seen, with domination, and a good deal of cruelty in this respect. It could be that Frieda achieved orgasm more easily through masochistic responses to a lover's brusqueness or cruelty, or even by anal sexuality; but it is a doubtful and dangerous message to offer propaganda for such solutions—not least because of the disguised hostility we have examined, and the revengeful symbolism involved.

The same is true of Lawrence's advocacy of transcendant orgasm. As Farber suggests, the perfect orgasm belongs to oneself: it is narcissistic. It is possible that when Lawrence declared that he experienced the most perfect sex with a young man of sixteen, this may not have been homosexual intercourse, but masturbation. There is much in Lawrence about masturbation as, for instance, in *The White Peacock*. In *The Trespasser* the descriptions of torrid intensity between the man and the woman are so vague and wordy that it is difficult to suppose what is going on, but we know from Helen Corke that there was no "full" sexual relationship between her and her lover, on which the story is based, so this love story, too, may be about masturbation.

We may also go beyond this and say, because of the intense narcissistic element in so much of Lawrence, not least in his homosexual scenes, that he was happier seeking an ideal sexual union when this did not involve a being different from himself, and that his idolization of orgasm represented an idolization of the masculine self, in defiance of the female, or in revenge against her; and so is an idolization of solipsism. We may associate this with the persuasions of Gross's kind of sexual revolutionism, with its elements of egoistical nihilism. Certainly, Gross seemed significantly not concerned with the reality and welfare of women.

There is one important aspect of Lawrence's excited feelings of a homosexual kind. As Paul Delaney points out, what seems to appeal to him is being held and soothed by a stronger, older man; it is being massaged by George that makes the narrator in *The White Peacock* declare that he experienced with George a love more perfect than any love "I have known before or since." This was perhaps a yearning for a form of "handling" that did not have the dangers of the mother's "Impingement." Certainly it often has an element of defense against woman. Delaney says that Lawrence tried to form a "sacred" union with William Henry at Zennor, which was a connection with "ritual powers," of druidism, or human sacrifice, "that could repel the power of the moon" (Delaney, 1975, p.311). He relates this to the famous scene in which Birkin throws stones at the moon ("Moony," in *Women in Love*, chapter 19).

The homosexuality can be seen as being symbolically directed against woman, against the moon, against the blighting influence of the dead mother. In this, since he is projecting inner feelings over the world, the moon, and the other, it is (as in the poem *Eloi*, etc.) an attempt to destroy something in himself, the black, corrupt part that menaces his life and its meaning. In *The Plumed Serpent*, the ritualistic figures, aspects of Lawrence himself, combine to put the woman, Kate, into subjection, accompanied by strange masturbatory rituals; while elsewhere the ritualistic element is used to actually destroy the woman (as in *The Woman Who Rode Away*). The associations between homosexuality and murder are made clear elsewhere, as in *Kangaroo*.

Birkin's yearning toward Gerald, in whose face he sees a remembrance of his loved mother's face, belongs to the same dynamic. In Gerald Lawrence was wrestling with all the elements of unconscious murder he knew to lurk behind his experience of sex.

I do not know how far the attempts I have made her to unravel Lawrence's preoccupations may help us understand his work, but I believe that if we do develop some kind of phenomenological understanding of his symbolism, we may resist his "sexual" message, and perhaps see that its contribution to modern thinking is, in general, somewhat disastrous. Beginning from an existentialist concern for being, and meaning in existence, it gives over, as his work progresses, to a complex of false solutions in his impulse to teach us how to be men and women, and ends in orgies of hate.

Only at times does there come relief, from descriptions of the beauty of the world, or when some woman laughs at him, and relieves the tension ("He needs to be laughed at," said Katherine Mansfield). What has certainly been neglected in Lawrence criticism is the pressure of hate in his work, his deepening misanthropy and despair.

It is clear at times from his tone in his writing that strange disturbed needs lay behind Lawrence's oral aggressiveness—its direction and its tone. We must take this mischief-dealing element in Lawrence into account. Most revealing are the letters written at the time of completing *Lady Chatterley's Lover*. There are several references at about this time to "the change of life," and this seems to be associated in Lawrence's mind with trying to solve problems that had been inflicted upon one by "society" and one's times. To E. H. Brewster he says,

> You and I are at the *age dangereuse* for men: when the whole rhythm of the psyche changes: when one no longer has an easy flow outwards: and when one rebels at a good may things.... One resents bitterly a certain swindle about modern life, and especially a sex swindle. But it is nobody's individual fault: fault of the age: our own fault as well. (Moore, letters, 1962, 967)

One of the paintings Lawrence painted at this period was "A Holy Family," which is reproduced in the *Letters*. It shows an oldish woman, clearly Mrs. Morel; a man, bearded like Lawrence; and a woman with big bare breasts. The man has a nimbus: in the background there is a phallic symbol. Of another painting, the "Unholy Family," he says, "the bambino—with a nimbus—is just watching anxiously to see the young man give the semi-nude woman *un gros baiser. Molto moderno!*" (Moore, 1962, 945).

In these discussions of his paintings and in the paintings themselves, one can see Lawrence imposing his own mythology on the myth of Christ, and clearly identifying with Christ. (The Honorable Dorothy Brett paints him with a halo.) The "swindle" is perhaps that the mother's crippling influence cannot be overcome. In the letter to Brewster it seems clear that Lawrence was suffering some sexual inhibition that he associated with a climacteric. He attributes this to "modern life": "One is swindled out of one's proper sex life, a great deal" so he attributes his impotence to "society."

He sought to overcome these sexual shadows by his painting and by writing *Lady Chatterley*. For example, in a letter to Brett, he writes:

> I challenge you to a pictorial contest. I'm just finishing a nice big canvas, Eve dodging back into Paradise, between Adam and the Angel at the gate, who are having a fight about it—and leaving the world in flames in the far corner behind her. Great fun and of course *capolavore* [a major work].

He goes on, after describing this "masterpiece":

> I should like to do a middle picture, inside Paradise, just as she bolts in. God Almighty astonished and indifferent, and the new young God, who is just having a chat with the Serpent, pleasantly amused, then the third picture, Adam and Eve under the tree of knowledge, God Almighty disappearing in a dudgeon, and the animals skipping. (Moore, 1962, 969)

In his descriptions of the pictures, actual and proposed, there is a clear element of anarchism: the intention is clearly to thumb his nose at the Father, to invert Christian morality, and to assert the primacy of "naked desire." Eve (the mother) is to be brought back into Paradise. In this we see again the impulse to make the mother's life rich and good so that, as in the Holy Family picture, she could preside benignly over the son's sexuality instead of wrecking it, and threatening meaning.

We need to go back to Lawrence's reference to his own "perversity" that "borders on the insane." I believe we have to reconsider radically the whole Lawrentian impulse to explore sexuality as explicitly as he did, and see behind his "hygienic" impulse to redeem from the language of sex an element of perversion, the underlying impulses in which are by no means all positive and healthy; they are full of vengeance and hate.

There are two underlying elements in sexual perversion that are relevant here from Robert Stoller's book *Perversion: The Erotic Form of Hatred*. One is the wounded preoccupation with childhood bans that have come to inhibit the adult's sexuality. The other is the *element of risk*:

> when excited one moves between the sense of danger and the expectation of escape from danger into sensual gratification. Risk was taken and surmounted. (Stoller, 1976, 101)

There is also an element of (oedipal) revenge. All these may be found in Lawrence. For example, when Paul and Clara find their sexual life becoming cold, they not only take to mechanical forms, which (though not described) smack of perversion, but deliberately seek out public places to make love;

> They would be very near, almost dangerously near to the river, so that the black

water ran now far from his face, and it gave a little thrill; or they loved sometimes in a little hollow below the fence of the path where people were passing occasionally, on the edge of the tarn, and they heard footsteps coming, almost felt the vibration of the tread, and they heard what the passers-by said—strange little things that were never intended to be heard. And afterwards each of them was rather ashamed. (SL, 388)

*Risk* and *shame* often seem necessary elements in Lawrence's sexual excitement. Here, "Gradually they began to introduce novelties, to get back some of the feeling of satisfaction."

From the *Letters* we may see that his impulse to outrage was often revengeful and directed in hate at society:

Outwardly, I know I'm in a bad temper, and let it go at that. I stick to what I told you, and put a phallus, a lingam you call it, in each one of my paintings somewhere. *And I paint no picture that won't shock people's castrated social spirituality.* (Moore, 1962, 967)

And a few days later he declares:

I wish I could paint a picture that would just *kill* every cowardly and ill-minded person that looked at it. My word, what a slaughter! (Moore, 1962, 969)

Of course, in these letters he declared that his motives are pure: "I do this out of a positive belief, that the phallus is a great sacred image: it represents a deep, deep life which has been denied in us, and is still denied." And "I've done my novel—I like it—but it's so improper, according to the poor conventional fools, that it'll never be printed. And I will *not* cut it. Even my pictures, which seem to be absolutely innocent, I feel people *can't even look at them.* They glance, and look quickly away" (Moore, 1962, 969)

In these remarks we find that disturbing sense of "superiority"—a hatred of "the ordinary," combined with an extraordinary capacity not to see that his motives are in part very impure; *people's shocked reaction is what he requires* and that this is so is plain from the rest of the letters. An underlying motive is to *blame woman.*

(*deep life which has been denied*).... Women deny it horribly, with a *grinning travesty of sex.* (Moore, 1962, 967; my italics)

The "lingam" must, therefore, be thrust in women's faces to teach them: Lady Ottoline must be taught to use the basic words; Mrs. Morel must be painted as part of a Holy Family in which she approves of sexual sensuality. The curative motive is clear, but the perverted need is manifest, too.

The phenomenological interpretations of psychoanalysis have gained insight into two aspects of perversion. One is that perversions are "closer to the psychoses than the neuroses," that is, they need to be understood in the light of the phenomenology of madness. The second is that they are themselves often a desperate expression of the need for meaning.

Because for the individual it is a life-or-death question of freeing his own sexual life from the dread and inhibition introduced into it by the parents, there is a compulsiveness about perversion, and it is accompanied by an urgent need to create a certain kind of atmosphere in which it can be felt not only to be tolerable, but actually liberating. Masud Khan (1974, 22) says that, "The capacity to create the emotional climate in which another person volunteers to participate is one of the few real talents of the pervert." We can see Lawrence at work in this mode when he writes to Lady Ottoline Morrell:

> If a man has been able to say to you when you were young and in love: an' if tha shits, an' if tha pisses, I'm glad, I shouldna want a woman who couldn't shit nor piss—surely it would have been a liberation to you, and it would have helped to keep your heart warm. (Moore, 1962, 1111)

He adopts the language of his father, as does Paul when making love to Clara, and we can see that he wants to bring libidinal sensuality to the "lady" because he admires her as he admired his mother, but he also wants to inflict a certain coarseness on her, while (of course) making his motives seem pure by his talk of sex and consciousness. (Yet he really despises her: "Ottoline wrote very sweetly—very sweetly—but still coughing a *little* over *Lady C.*" he writes two days later.)

Because of this need to create a certain atmosphere, Lawrence becomes increasingly contemptuous of the authorities, of those who are upset by his "tender phallic" book, and of friends who do not support him. He also becomes increasingly obsessed with *Lady Chatterley*. In his later letters he seldom mentions any other prose works, and writes more and more of ways of distributing Lady C., how much money he is making out of it, and so forth. There is a sense in which his perverted need to thrust that book into the world damaged him seriously as an artist, and this is the inevitable consequence of his "impulse" psychology of pursuing one's *wants*, and being a "good animal."

Of course, there are many statements of his urge to purify consciousness and the language of sex:

> I believe in the living extending consciousness of man. I believe the consciousness of men has now to embrace the emotions and passions of sex, and the deep effects of human physical contact. This is the glimmering edge of our awareness and our field of understanding, in the endless business of knowing ourselves. (Moore, 1962, 1099)

And of course, the sanest and most insightful work by Lawrence is marvelous:

> Sex isn't something you've got to play with; sex is *you*.
> It's the flow of your life, it's your moving self, and you are due

To be true to the nature of it, its reserve, it sensitive pride . . .
And don't, with the nasty, prying mind, drag it out from its deeps . . . (CP, 464)

He offers a somewhat confused message, however, in the poem "Bawdy Can
Be Sane" (CP, 845), saying that "a little bawdy is necessary in every life" and
"a little whoring is necessary in every life / To keep it sane and wholesome",
while "Even sodomy can be sane and wholesome / granted there is an
exchange of genuine feeling"—but warned about getting "any of them on the
brain". Yet a glance over his work suggests that if anyone had these things on
the brain, it must be Lawrence himself, while his contribution to our time must
surely be a vast preoccupation with sexual explicitness (a reviewer, for
instance, will refer to a passage in a modern drama as a "Lady Chatterley
routine"). It is true that he said, in a letter to Lady Otteline, "God forbid that
I should be taken as urging loose sexual activity. There is a brief time for sex,
and a long time when sex is out of place . . . there should be a large and quiet
space in the consciousness where it lives quiescent' (Moore, 1962, 1111). But
this is surely not true of his influence on today's culture, neither is it true of
his own work, in which, as the Letters show is obsessed with sex, and a defiant
and angry gesture towardst the world.

Lawrence has come to be accepted as "the High Priest of love": what has
not been fully appreciated is that aspect of him that is exposed by Robert
Stoller's comment on the fundamental nature of perversion: "The hostility in
perversion takes form in a fantasy of revenge hidden in the actions that make
up the perversion and serves to convert childhood trauma to adult triumph"
(Stoller, 1976, 4).

For Lawrence became obsessively intemperate in pursuing what must now
appear to be Grossian persuasions of the value of polymorphous perversion:
of opposition to his sexual explicitness he declared:

The censor-moron does not really hate anything but the living and growing human
consciousness. . . . To arrest or circumscribe the vital consciousness is to produce
morons, and nothing but a moron would wish to do it. (Moore 1962, 1099)

Not all those who were made uncomfortable by *Lady Chatterley* were morons:
Lady Ottoline, Juliette Huxley, and Koteliansky, for example, all raised
objections. It is possible that they saw the problems examined by Erwin
Straus: the instrusion of the voyeur menaces the secrecy of creative sexuality;
overexplicitness can damage the surrender to creative fate that love itself is.
In the explicit obsession with sexuality, there is an element of the attempt to
control something dangerous.

It is this desire to exert control over dangerous woman and dangerous sex
that may well have lain at the core of Lawrence's concern to bring the tacit
and inexpressible in sex to explicitness and consciousness. His vindication of
sodomy belongs to a perverted need to seek to "exorcise" something menacing

from within the body of woman, as an act of hostility and revenge idolized. I believe the use of sex language belongs to the same syndrome, and the attitude to Lady Ottoline seems to reveal this impulse.

It is undeniable that there are disturbing moments of coarseness and hate in Lawrence:

> Well, I painted a charming picture of a man pissing—I'm sure it's the one Maria will choose: called "Dandelions" for short. Now I'm doing a small thing in oil, called "The Rape of the Sabine Women" or A Study in Arses. (Huxley 1932, 1052)

There was an impulse in Lawrence to make a malevolent phallic gesture, whose effect would be to turn people to stone:

> How glad I am to have lost certain of my "friends" through *John Thomas*—like the Israelites who fell dead when the Magic Serpent was erected. May they all fall dead! Pfui! (Huxley 1932, 1075)

We get the impression of a man who was becoming more and more sick (with consumption), and feeling hatred and envy for the healthy. It is very sad, but we may also associate this with the feeling occasionally expressed that his sexuality was spoiled by some parallel force. Devotees like Henry T. Moore and Leavis are always emphasizing Lawrence's love of his country or his friends, yet the truth is he caused great suffering to those close to him, like Lady Ottoline and E.T., and was imply contemptuous or thick-skinned when they were shocked at his abuse of trust.

And as for the English, so often we hear this note in Lawrence:

> Curse the blasted, jelly-boned swines, the slimy, the belly-wriggling invertebrates, the miserable sodding rotters, the flaming sods, the snivelling, dribbling, dithering palsied pulse-less lot that make up England today. They've got white of eggs in their veins, and their spunk is that watery it's a marvel they can breed. They *are* nothing but frogspawn—the gibbons! God how I hate them! God curse them, fuckers. God blast them, wish-wash. Exterminate them, slime. (Moore 1962, 134)

This was long before "society" had reacted adversely to his erotic work, even before *Sons and Lovers* was published.

Notice that here, as later, he reproves England for its sexual impotence; later he often upbraids England for being "ball-less." He wanted to do something to England, his mother-and-father-land, to give it sexual fulfillment. But he also wanted to annihilate England because it stood for the inhibiting ghosts of his parents who, internalized, threatened to spoil his life. This hatred of England would never allow him to settle there, and so he came to offer flight as a positive.

It also became a general misanthropy, as in *Lady Chatterley*, with its contemptuous references to "carrion-bodied" workers. And "I have decided

that the human scene is a mistake" (Moore 1962, 1170). In *Mountain Lion*
Lawrence spoke of his willingness to lose a million or so of humans, rather
than this one animal. In a late letter he declares.

> The world is lovely if one avoids man—so why not avoid him! Why not! Why not!
> I am tired of humanity. (Moore, 1962, 1199)

The impulse made Lawrence love the nonhuman world, as his mother and
Mirian loved it: "The cistus flowers are out among the rocks, pink and white,
and yellow sea-poppies by the sea." (from the same letter). Because of this
impulse to find solace in the phenomenological record of experience in the
MYSTIC NOW, Lawrence was a great artist, but there is a sense in which
he never found a place for man in the world—and instead of seeking this
he became diverted into the obsession with sexual explicitness that became
such a dead end, and has done such serious harm to the contemporary
consciousness.

# Notes

## Introduction

1. The note by Perdita, her daughter by Cecil Gray, at the end of H.D.'s *Bid Me to Live* is poignant, and a disturbing indication of the suffering caused by the sexual vagaries of some of those in the set to which Lawrence belonged.

2. Green, *The von Richthofen Sisters*, 1974, 40–41. Frieda's attitude to Gross seems ambivalent. In Robert Lucas's *Life* she is said not to have known about Gross's drug addiction, but Johanna in *Mr Noon* says of the character representing Gross, "He simply lives on drugs."

3. On Stirner, see the present author in *Education, Nihilism and Survival* (London, Longman, Darton and Todd, 1977).

4. Green quotes a letter from Jung in which he blames his lapse with a patient, Sabina Spielrein, on his former patient Otto Gross, with whom he had transference and counter-transference problems. Under the influence of Gross, he preached polygamy at her and praised her independent spirit in having an affair with him. Green, p.43: for more information see *A Secret Symmetry, Sabina Spielrein*, by Aldo Carotenuto, Pantheon, 1982, pp.174 and 176. The event had a seriously damaging effect on the psychoanalytic movement. If Gross could influence Jung for the worst, he could surely, if only indirectly, have influenced Lawrence?

5. The tone of condemnation obscures the absurdity of Leavis's comparison, for Anna is a character in a novel while Frieda was a living person. But Leavis goes on, "There are delicacies in the way of offering to push further our divinations from what evidence concerning Frieda we have, but we can see that what Tolstoy makes present to us in Anna is certainly something finer." (*Anna Karenina and Other Essays*, p.22).

Finer than what? Was the novel character Anna finer than Frieda, a living person? How can we possibly make such a comparison? Or does Leavis mean that the biographical presentation of Frieda does not compare with the story of Anna? Is he really trying to compare as *persons* two people, one of whom is a work of the imagination? From that we could, I believe, go on to find a profound philosophical weakness in Leavis, and a weakness in his whole position to do with woman, marriage, and sexuality, for what the problem requires is not so much the judgment of persons but philosophies of being.

6. Luhan, *Lorenzo in Taos*, 88.

7. Merrild, *A Poet and Two Painters: A Memoir of D. H. Lawrence*, 173.

8. Moore, *Collected Letters*, 565.

9. Nehls, *D. H. Lawrence: A Composite Biography*, 503.

10. Mansfield, *Letters to John Middleton Murry*, 1913–22, 620–21.

11. See the dire feelings experienced by Lawrence in *Song of a Man Who Is Not Loved*, when rejection is experienced. In *Sons and Lovers* and at times in *Women in Love*, a dreadful blankness overtakes the protagonist's perception consequent upon the loss of a loved face. The poem *Roses on the Breakfast Table* is a beautiful celebration of *being seen*, by contrast, giving a sense of security and meaning.

12. See Besdine, "The Jocasta Complex, Mothering and Genius," Part II, *The Psychoanalytic Review*, Vol. 55, no. 4, Winter 1968–69, 574.

## Chapter 1. Difficulties over Woman in *The White Peacock* and *Sons and Lovers*

1. The paintings I gather were those seen by Lawrence reproduced in magazines, not paintings

in Nottingham Art Gallery, or other local galleries. Carl Baron points out that one painting, *Idyll*, by Greiffenhagen, showing a swarthy "Pagan" embracing a half-reluctant girl in a field of poppies, had a strong influence on George Neville and Lawrence, both of them amateur painters. (See Mason, 1982.)

2. We have to make a considerable effort to recall the strong inhibitions against physical sexual love at the time. For instance, the relationship between the lovers in *The Trespasser* is nonsexual, and on this see Corke, *In Our Infancy*, 62–63.

3. See Harry T. Moore in *The Intelligent Heart*, 130ff. Lawrence at Croydon seemed to be involved with four women, and there seems a division between those he really loved and those who "gave him sex."

4. Leavis cannot understand why Lawrence uses the vernacular, but surely it is to bring the warm sensual intimacy of the father to the mother? I find it often very successful in *Lady Chatterley's Lover*, even when Mellors addresses his penis. It is embarrassingly awful however when he sloganizes in the Lawrentian way about saving the world by "fucking" in that vernacular language. The origins of the use of the vernacular in Lawrence are, I believe, in *Adam Bede*, where Adam lapses into it (as George Eliot says) when talking to his mother.

## Chapter 2. True and False Solutions in the Short Stories

1. Cf. in *The Virgin and the Gypsy*, "it was a black cock that crew for Yvette." See above p.     . The phallus often sneers at woman in disdain.

2. *The Fox* was written in December 1918. The honeymoon was in 1912, and the poems (*Look!*) sent off in 1919.

3. "Look! he has come through!—D. H. Lawrence, Woman and Individuation," Rosemary Gordon, *Journal of Analytic Psychology*, Vol. 23, no. 3, July 1978, 259.

4. Cf. for example *The Reef*, Edith Wharton.

5. It was Lawrence's mother, who had "natural aristocracy" while Frieda was a baroness.

6. It is, of course, a fundamental element of pornography that the woman is victim. As Robert Stoller puts it, no victim, no pornography (Stoller, *Perversion*, 65). He also says, "The essential dynamic in pornography is hostility" (88).

## Chapter 3. *The Rainbow*—once *The Wedding Ring*

1. In the spring of 1914 Lawrence was convinced that in *The Rainbow* he had resolved his conflicts with Frieda. "You will find her and me in the novel, I think, and the work is of both of us." (Moore, *Collected Letters*, 272; Delaney, 1979, 5). The novel was to have been about "love triumphant."

2. A parallel is his continual expectation of a new and blissful relationship with new friends, or in new places—only to be followed a few days later by disillusion.

3. It is significant that Lawrence was already striking this note of the denial of woman's satisfaction in 1916.

## Chapter 5. Authenticity and Inauthenticity: *Mr Noon*, *The Lost Girl*, and *Aaron's Rod*

1. *Mr Noon*, by D. H. Lawrence, in the *Works of D. H. Lawrence*, Cambridge Edition, CUP, 1984.

2. For the biographical events behind this infidelity, see *Letters* i 489; David Garnett, *The Golden Echo*, 297; and Paul Delaney, *D. H. Lawrence's Nightmare*, 395. According to Delaney, Frieda had at least three casual affairs in the first year they were together and made sure Lawrence knew about them. See Moore, *Collected Letters*, 122; Spender, *D. H. Lawrence: Novelist, Poet, Prophet*, 39; Nehls, *D. H. Lawrence, a Composite Biography*, 179.

3. Mason, "Wounded Surgeons," *Cambridge Quarterly*, Vol. XI, no. 1, 1982, 189.

4. It was maddening of Lawrence to call Weekley Everard and Otto Gross Eberhard. Presumably it was a joke about these previous lovers, whom he hated, being ever-hard, but it is most confusing—and, of course, a gift for the Lawrence industry.

## Chapter 7.   Submission to the Ithyphallic— The Chatterley Novels

1. "A caufe of Divorce was argued in *Doctor's Commons*, promoted by Sir F— C— against his Lady, aged 50, for being found in bed with her Poftillion" in *Gentleman's Magazine*, June 1734, 329.

2. Michaelis is said to be a picture of Dikran Kauyoumdjian, whose pen name was Michael Arlen, a friend of Philip Heseltine. See Delaney, *D. H. Lawrence's Nightmare*, 171.

3. The following essays may be found to cast light on this question: "Is the Vaginal Orgasm a Myth?" by A. Ellis and "A Contribution to the Orgasm Problem in Women" by Helena Wright, M.B., in *Sex, Society and the Individual*, ed. A. P. Pillay and A. Ellis, Bombay, International Journal of Sexology Press, 1953.

# Bibliography

Arnold, Armin. *The Symbolic Meaning: the Uncollected Versions of Studies in Classic American Literature*. New York: Viking, 1964.

Asquith, Lady Cynthia. *Diaries, 1915–1918*. Edited by E. M. Horsley. New York: Knopf, 1969.

Alpers, Antony. *Katherine Mansfield: A Biography*. New York: Knopf, 1953.

Balint, Michael. *Primary Love and Psychoanalytical Technique*. London: Tavistock, 1952.

Barrie, Sir James. *Sentimental Tommy*. London: Cassell, 1896.

———. *Tommy and Grizel*. London: Cassell, 1990.

Beede Howe, Marguerite. *The Art of the Self in D. H. Lawrence*. Athens: Ohio University Press, 1977.

Besdine, Matthew. "The Jocasta Complex, Mothering and Genius," Part II. *Psychoanalytic Review*, vol. 55, no. 4, Winter, 1968–69, 574.

Bierber, I. *Homosexuality*. New York: Basic Books, 1962.

Boulton, James T., ed. *Lawrence in Love: Letters to Louie Burrows*. Nottingham: University of Nottingham, 1968.

Brett, D. *Lawrence and Brett: A Friendship*. Santa Fe, Calif.: Gunstone Press, 1974.

Carswell, Catherine. *The Savage Pilgrimage: A Narrative of D. H. Lawrence*. London: Chatto and Windus, 1932.

Cassirer, Ernst. *An Essay on Man*. New Haven, Conn.: Yale University, 1944.

Chaloner, Len. *Feeling and Perception in Young Children*. London: Tavistock, 1963.

Corke, Helen. *In Our Infancy, An Autobiography, 1882–1912*. Cambridge: CUP, 1975.

Cowan, James C. "Lawrence's Phoenix, An Introduction." *D. H. Lawrence Review* no. 5, 187–199.

Darroch, Sandra Jobson. *Ottoline: The Life of Lady Ottoline Morrell*. New York: Conrad, McCann and Geoghegan, 1975.

Delaney, Paul, *D. H. Lawrence's Nightmare*. Hassocks: Harvester Press, 1979.

Delevenay, Emile. *D. H. Lawrence: L'Homme et la genese de son oeuvre*. Paris: Librarie C. Klincksieck, 1969.

———. *D. H. Lawrence: the Man and His Work. The Formative Years, 1885–1919*. Carbondale: South Illinois University Press, 1972.

Draper, R. P., ed. *D. H. Lawrence: The Critical Heritage*. London: Routledge, 1970.

Eliot, T. S. *Four Quartets*. London: Faber and Faber, 1944.

"E. T." (Jessie Chambers) *D. H. Lawrence: A Memoir*. London: Jonathan Cape, 1935.

Fairbairn, W. R. D. *Psychoanalytical Studies of the Personality*. London: Tavistock, 1952.

Faber, Leslie H. *The Ways of the Will*. London: Constable, 1966.

Forster, E.M. *Where Angels Fear to Tread*. London: Arnold, 1905.

Frankl, Victor. *The Doctor and the Soul*. London: Souvenir Press, 1965.

———. "Reductionism and Nihilism." In *Beyond Reductionism*, edited by A. Koestler and R. Smithies. London: Hutchinson, 1969.

Freud, Sigmund. *The Interpretation of Dreams*. London: Hogarth, 1953.

Garnett, David. *The Flowers of the Forest*. London: Chatto, 1955.

Gawthorne-Hardy, R. *Ottoline at Garsington: Memoirs of Lady Ottoline Morrell, 1913–1918.* London: Faber, 1974.

Gomme, A. H., ed. *D. H. Lawrence: A Critical Study of the Major Works and Other Writings.* Brighton: Harvester, 1978.

Gordon, Rosemary. "D. H. Lawrence: Women and Individuation." *Journal of Analytic Psychology*, Vol. 23, no. 3, July 1978, 258–273.

Green, Martin. *The von Richthofen Sisters.* London: Weidenfeld, 1974.

Guntrip, Harry. *Personality Structure and Human Interaction.* London: Hogarth, 1961.

———. *Schizoid Phenomena, Object Relations and the Self.* London: Hogarth, 1968.

Gutiérrez, Donald. "The Impossible Notation, The Sodomy Scene in *Lady Chatterley's Lover*." *The Sphinx*, Vol. IV, no. 14, No. ii, 109–125. (c/o English Department, University of Regina, Regina, Sask., Canada.)

Hahn, Emily. *Lorenzo: D. H. Lawrence and the Women Who Loved Him.* Philadelphia: Lippincott, 1975.

Hignett, Sean. *Brett: From Bloomsbury to Mexico.* London: Hodder and Stoughton, 1985.

Holbrook, David. *The Masks of Hate.* Oxford: Pergamon, 1972.

———. *The Novel and Authenticity.* London: Vision Press, 1987.

Huxley, Aldous, ed. *The Letters of D. H. Lawrence.* London: Heinemann, 1932.

James, William. *The Varieties of Religious Experience.* London: Longmans, 1913.

Khan, Masud R. *The Privacy of the Self.* London: Hogarth, 1974.

Kleinhard, David. "D. H. Lawrence and Ontological Insecurity." *Periodical of the Modern Languages Association* 89 (1974): 155.

Klingopulos, G. D. Review of *D. H. Lawrence—Novelist*, by F. R. Leavis, *Universities Quarterly*, Vol 10, No 2, February 1956, 189.

Koestler, A., and R. Smithies. *Beyond Reductionism, the Alpbach Seminar.* London: Hutchinson, 1969.

Lacy, G. M. *An Analytical Calendar of the Letters of D. H. Lawrence.* Ann Arbor, University Microfilms, 1971.

Laing, R. D. *The Divided Self.* London: Tavistock, 1960.

Lawrence, D. H. *Etruscan Places* (1932). London: Penguin Books, 1950.

———. *Selected Essays.* London: Penguin Books, 1950.

———. *Sex, Literature and Censorship*, edited by H.T. Moore. New York: Viking Press, 1959.

———. *Fantasia of the Unconscious* and *Psychoanalysis and the Unconscious.* London: Heinemann, 1961.

———. *Studies in Classic American Literature.* New York: Viking, 1961.

———. (ed. A. A. H. Inglis) *A Selection from Phoenix.* Harmondsworth, Peregrine, 1971.

Lawrence, Frieda. *Not I but the Wind.* New York: Viking, 1934.

Leavis, F. R. *D. H. Lawrence, Novelist.* London: Chatto, 1955.

———. *Anna Karenina and Other Essays.* London: Chatto, 1967.

———. "Justifying One's Valuation of Blake." *The Human World* no. 7. May, 1972, 42–64.

———. *The Living Principle: Thought Words and Creativity.* London: Chatto, 1975.

———. *Thought, Words and Creativity, Art and Thought in Lawrence.* London: Chatto, 1976.

Luhan, Mabel Dodge. *Lorenzo in Taos.* New York: Knopf, 1932.

MacKenzie, Compton. *My Life and Times, Octave Five, 1918–1923.* London: Chatto, 1966.

Mansfield, Katherine. *Letters to John Middleton Murry, 1913–22.* London: Constable, 1951.

Maslow, Abraham. *Towards a Psychology of Being.* New York: Von Nostrand, 1968.

———. ed. *New Knowledge in Human Values.* New York: Von Nostrand, 1959.

Mason, H. A. "The Wounded Surgeons." *Cambridge Quarterly*, Vol. II, no. 1, 1982, 189.

May, Rollo, Ernest Angel and Henri F. Ellenberger. *Existence—A New Dimension in Psychiatry.* New York: Basic Books, 1958.

May, Rollo. *Love and Will*. New York: Norton, 1969.

Merrild, Knud. *A Poet and Two Painters, A Memoir of D. H. Lawrence*. New York: Viking, 1939.

Middleton Murry, John. *The Autobiography of John Middleton Murry: Between Two Worlds*. London: Cape, 1938.

———. *Reminiscences of D. H. Lawrence*. London: Cape, 1933.

Millet, Kate. *Sexual Politics*. New York: Doubleday, 1969.

Milner, Marion. *In the Hands of the Living God*. London: Hogarth, 1969.

Moore, Harry T. *D. H. Lawrence's Letters to Bertrand Russell*. New York: Gothrun Book Mart, 1948.

———. *The Intelligent Heart: The Story of D. H. Lawrence*. New York: Farrar, Straus and Young, 1955.

———. *The Collected Letters of D. H. Lawrence*. London: Viking, 1962.

———. *The Priest of Love: A Life of D. H. Lawrence*. New York: Farrar, Straus and Giroux, 1974.

Moore, Leslie. *Katherine Mansfield: The Memoirs of L. M.* London: Virago, 1971.

Nehls, E., ed. *D. H. Lawrence: A Composite Biography*. Madison: University of Wisconsin Press, 1957–59.

Nietzsche, Frederick. *The Birth of Tragedy*. New York: Doubleday, 1956.

Poole, Roger. "The Affirmation Is of Life." *Universities Quarterly*, Vol. 29, no. 1, Winter 1979, 60.

Roberts, Warren and Harry T. Moore. *Phoenix Two: Unpublished and Other Prose Works by D. H. Lawrence*. London: Heinemann, 1968.

Russell, Bertrand. *The Autobiography of Bertrand Russell*, 1872–1914 and 1914–1944. London: Allen and Unwin, 1967 and 1969.

Simpson, Hilary. *D. H. Lawrence and Feminism*. Beckenham: Croom Helm, 1982.

Socarides, C. W. *The Overt Homosexual*. New York: Grune and Stratton, 1968.

Spender, Stephen, ed. *D. H. Lawrence: Novelist, Poet, Prophet*. London: Weidenfeld and Nicolson, 1973.

Stern, Karl. *The Flight from Woman*. London: Unwin, 1970.

Stoller, Robert J. *Perversion: The Erotic Form of Hatred*. Brighton: Harvester, 1976.

Straus, Erwin. *Phenomenological Psychology*. London: Tavistock, 1966.

Strickland, Geoffrey. "The First Lady Chatterley's Lover". *Encounter*, January 1971, Vol. XXXVI, no. 1. Reprinted in Gomme, A. H., ed., *D. H. Lawrence, A Critical Study of the Major Works and Other Writings*. Hassocks: Harvester, 1978.

Tedlock, E. W. *Frieda Lawrence: The Memoirs and Correspondence*. New York: Knopf, 1964.

Thomas, Helen. *As It Was*. London: Heinemann, 1931.

Thompson, D., and F. R. Leavis. *Culture and Environment*. London: Chatto, 1935.

Ulanov, Anne. *The Feminine*. Chicago: Northwestern, 1971.

———. *Receiving Woman*. Philadelphia: Westminister Press, 1981.

Ulanov, Anne, and Barry Ulanov. *Religion and the Unconscious in Jungian Psychology and in Christian Theology*. Philadelphia: Westminister Press, 1971.

Winnicott, D. W. *The Child, the Family and the Outside World*. London: Penguin, 1964.

———. *The Maturational Processes and the Facilitating Environment*. London: Hogarth, 1965.

———. *Playing and Reality*. London: Tavistock, 1971.

———. *Therapeutic Consultations in Child Psychiatry.*, London: Hogarth, 1971.

Zytaruk, G., ed. *The Quest for Rananim: D. H. Lawrence's Letters to S. S. Koteliansky*. London: Constable, 1972.

# Index